Also by Sherwood Smith

The Rise of the Alliance
A SWORD NAMED TRUTH

Inda
INDA
THE FOX
KING'S SHIELD
TREASON'S SHORE

BANNER OF THE DAMNED

* * *

Dobrenica
CORONETS & STEEL
BLOOD SPIRITS
REVENANT EVE

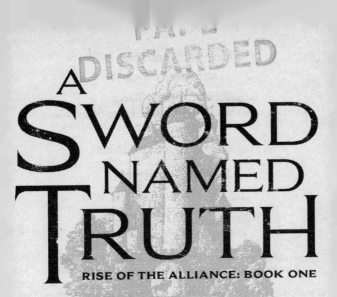

A SWORD NAMED TRUTH

RISE OF THE ALLIANCE: BOOK ONE

SHERWOOD SMITH

DAW BOOKS, INC.

DONALD A. WOLLHEIM, FOUNDER

1745 Broadway, New York, NY 10019

ELIZABETH R. WOLLHEIM

SHEILA E. GILBERT

PUBLISHERS

www.dawbooks.com

Author's Note: *A Sword Named Truth* takes place at roughly the
same time as *A Stranger to Command*.

First Mass Market Printing, June 2020
1 2 3 4 5 6 7 8 9

DAW TRADEMARK REGISTERED
U.S. PAT. AND TM. OFF. AND FOREIGN COUNTRIES
—MARCA REGISTRADA
HECHO EN U.S.A.

PRINTED IN THE U.S.A.

A SWORD NAMED TRUTH

Norsunder

THERE are, at present, two records that the world believes lost.

I know where they are. I've sat in the dusty chamber where they lie, my only company spiders spinning cobwebs into spectral lace over the years I was in and out reading both.

One of those records is *The Emras Defense*, a deposition with a later—secret—addition, written by Emras, the mage who wrote on advanced ward magic. The first version, without the addition, was surrendered to the Sartoran mage guild, and buried so deeply in the archives that it requires several levels of inquisition to be permitted to see it. Only a heavily redacted version is studied by senior mage students at present.

The other record predates Emras's confession by four hundred years, written by the man who went down in history as Fox, captain of the ship named *Death,* who sailed under the Banner of the Damned. He did not sign his history, which delves into everyone's thoughts but his, as his purpose was to record how Inda Algara-Vayir changed the world they both lived in.

I am taking him as my model in writing the history of

the disparate group later called the Young Allies. I, too, have a purpose beyond autobiography.

This will be unsigned, which permits me the freedom of anonymity.

At least, so is my intention in setting out. As I get farther in, everything might change, except the actual events: the consequences remain to be seen.

Since the war that nearly destroyed Ancient Sartor more than 4700 years ago, Norsunder—the ancient, evil enemy—had, until recently, dwindled from admonitory parable to vulgar epithet.

While assembling my facts for this writing, I was entertained by the various definitions of Norsunder by those who have never ventured to that retreat beyond the limits of the temporal. Most of them described Norsunder as a vast army with a single motivation, an oversimplification that borders on outright lie.

This much *is* true: Those in command of Norsunder withdrew from the temporal after the Fall of Ancient Sartor nearly wiped out magic as well as humanity from the world. So much was lost, including magical abilities that had become innate. With the dwindling of magic, these abilities vanished forever—or so humans thought.

But recently it's become evident that these abilities were only dormant, as magic slowly manifested in the world again before Norsunder was aware or ready, this being the disadvantage of existing outside of time.

Norsunder's center is commanded by two individuals who seldom venture out of their citadel, aided by four others who call themselves the Host of Lords, implying they are part of the inner circle. The struggle for power among these four will be addressed in time; before that, all you need to know is that they assigned much of the grunt work in the temporal world to an Ancient Sartoran who had fought successfully against them until he was captured and turned.

He has operated under a variety of names over the succeeding centuries. Currently he goes by Detlev. Under

Detlev—and straining against that short chain of command—is his nephew Siamis, who had been twelve years old when he was seized and used as the bait to entrap Detlev, in those terrible days at the very end of the Fall.

Bringing us to the year 4735.

When a new voice was heard in the mental realm for the first time in over four thousand years, it meant that one of the skills thought lost forever, Dena Yeresbeth—"Unity of the Three," cohering body, mind, and spirit in ways impossible to humans after the Fall—was emerging again. For his first assignment Siamis was sent to track down the child and secure the source of that voice.

Now on the threshold of manhood, Siamis used that opportunity to demonstrate his skills in magic and command by binding entire populations under an enchantment, to cover Norsunder's attempt to create rifts between Norsunder's timeless vantage and the temporal world in order to bring across the armies waiting there.

Siamis was so intent on proving himself by building this web of enchantment that locating and snapping up a ten-year-old shopkeeper's daughter named Liere became a secondary consideration, until she managed to elude capture. Aided by fifteen-year-old newly crowned king Senrid Montredaun-An and a growing host of allies, Liere brought down Siamis's enchantment as rapidly as he had created it.

That was the year previous to the beginning of this history.

In spite of what ballads, speeches, and poems about the Girl Who Saved The World, and new Golden Ages, will tell you, neat, discrete endings to stories don't happen in real life.

Of all the subjects of this chronicle, most of whom were young rulers brought too early to thrones, probably the one most distrusting of the ephemera of Golden Ages and happy endings was Senrid Montredaun-An.

It seems appropriate to begin with him.

PART ONE
The Alliance is Born

Chapter One

Early Rothdi* (Sixthmonth), 4737 AF
Marloven Hess

MARLOVEN Hess, a kingdom traditionally not given to taking any interest in its neighbors except as prospects for conquering, was still unsettled after the civil war that had removed their hated regent—who had been secretly supported by Norsunder. The Marlovens, never easy to rule even for a powerful and experienced king, found themselves with a fifteen-year-old boy trying to hold onto his throne.

Senrid had first become aware of Norsundrian game plans and stirrings of old powers during the bad days when he and Liere had been on the run from Siamis.

But right now? Norsunder was not his problem.

All his focus was on a boy several years older, who faced him across the stone court in the infamous Marloven military training academy.

At best, it would hurt. A lot. At worst, Senrid would be dead. No, that wouldn't be the worst, Senrid was thinking, because then he'd be gone. Unless he became a ghost, but

---

* All month names and festival days in headers given in Sartoran

if ghosts actually existed, he'd never seen any. If dying by violence caused haunts, by rights Marloven Hess should be wall-to-wall revenants, and Senrid had never even seen his father's—

Ten years of habit shut away *that* thought. He flexed his hands once, resisting the impulse to wipe them down his trousers, and faced the tall, dark-haired, angry boy who towered over him. Boy? Jarend Ndarga, the leader of the seniors of the academy, had four years and two hands of height over Senrid.

"Fight me," said Senrid.

He knew he hadn't a hope of winning, but since he was an underage king in a land where fighting has always decided everything, and all his future commanders were gathered in this one place staring at him like he was a squashed bug, what did he have to lose?

"Of course I can't fight you," Ndarga said bitterly. "I touch your precious kingly head and you'll have me at the flogging post so fast there won't be time to whistle up a crowd to scoff."

"That," Senrid said, "was my uncle. This is me. When I said anything goes, I meant it. Do you see a uniform tunic?" He lifted his hands and spun around, as if Ndarga hadn't been aware of his plain white shirt tucked into his black trousers. Senrid hoped no one noticed the tremble in his fingers.

"No," Ndarga said slowly.

"Then take off your coat. We're two people, and we're going to scrap."

"Rules?" Ndarga said in a goading voice.

Senrid exulted, in spite of his hammering heartbeat. *I've got him.*

He didn't pause to reflect on how. Who cared? He might not last until the next watch change, but at least he'd go out fighting, a fitting finish to the shortest reign in Marloven history . . . "Anything goes," Senrid said recklessly.

The low whistles and whispered comments from the perimeter were testament not only to how many had gathered on the walls and at the windows, but to what they thought.

"Oh, for certain," Ndarga sneered. "If I kill you, nothing happens to me?"

"Something is certain to happen, but it won't be by my command," Senrid retorted, and breathed out when he heard a ripple of laughter from the spectators. "Seeing as I'd be dead," he added, in case there were some a little short on logic.

Senrid dared not look around to see the reactions. With an effort he kept his gaze steadily on Ndarga's dark eyes.

"Kill him," a senior called from a safe vantage behind.

And as Senrid had hoped, Ndarga's upper lip curled in disgust. From that same direction behind came a fast, whispered exchange from the crowd:

"Swank!"

"I didn't see *you* walking out there when he called his challenge."

"And have the guard land on me for my pains?"

"He's not here as king."

"He's always king," someone else said.

"What's the matter, afraid of an untrained scrub?"

"We all know he's had training."

"But not with *us*."

Senrid listened without shifting his gaze from Ndarga, who was also listening as he took off the coat that only academy seniors wore, and handed it to a friend to hold. Now they were both committed. They could hear it in the whispers.

Senrid was not the only one who felt that the world had gone smash in the last few years. He didn't need his still-uncontrolled Dena Yeresbeth to know that Ndarga was furiously angry at the situation and at the world. Senrid might not have been traditionally trained at the academy with his future leaders, but the academy's commander had risked his life by personally training him in secret throughout Senrid's boyhood.

They began to circle, each watching the other for tiny signs—the twitch of an eyelid, attitude of shoulder, how a foot was placed.

While they circled, inside the castle, Hibern Askan, a Marloven-born mage student, arrived in the transfer chamber.

She stared at the patterned tiles on the floor, different for every transfer Destination. Her joints throbbed in slowly diminishing pangs, protesting being wrenched in and out of the world from a continent away.

She let out her breath, and as she headed for the stairs, she began to consider what to say to Senrid. This was not her usual time for their magical studies, and she knew he liked sticking to a schedule.

She ran up the stairs two at a time, not surprised to find Senrid's study empty.

She was far more unsettled to find the hallway empty, too. Usually there were guards moving on their regular patrols at every landing.

What now? Something violent, of course. Her heart banged at her ribs. It was strange. A few years ago, their respective guardians had expected Hibern and Senrid to someday marry. They were both Marlovens, and close to the same age, but in every other respect they could not have been more different. As she walked more slowly downstairs, she reflected on the thrill of excitement she'd experienced on discovering the world outside of Marloven Hess.

World? Worlds! The fact that there were seven worlds circling the sun Erhal, and that on three of them humans lived, made her long to read about them. But Senrid—one of the smartest people she knew—was totally indifferent.

Her passion was magic, a passion so strong it had lost her her home. Senrid's passion was his kingdom.

But, she thought grimly as she heard the low mutter of voices echoing along the stone hallway at the ground floor, in many ways she still thought like a Marloven. Maybe just as well. She'd discovered that the world outside her homeland's borders still distrusted her for being one.

A turn of a corner revealed guards talking in a cluster, mostly-blond hair glinting in the beating torchlight.

At the sound of her step, the four guards whipped around, two half-drawing swords. Then they separated and hustled away, presumably to resume patrols they never should have abandoned.

Something was definitely wrong. Hibern reached the landing, and said to the runner stationed there, "I'm looking for Senrid-Harvaldar."

The runner, who was probably twenty-five, looked about ten as he said stiffly, "Went to the academy."

"At this time of night?"

She didn't expect any answer, but the runner seemed to need to talk, as if to pass his tension on to someone else. "They say he went to the senior court."

The words were fraught with extra meaning. Hibern ran downstairs. Three steps in the direction of the academy, and she faltered in the middle of an empty, echoing stone hall. She wouldn't be permitted to set foot in the academy. No girls were, except at the barns, a holdover rule from the regent. Women do not carry weapons. It was said that the regent had killed his own wife . . .

Never *mind* that. Think! Hibern paused before the mighty iron-reinforced door that led in one direction to the tower stairs, and in the other to the ancient tunnel that debouched into the academy, now an inky darkness dimly lit by a distant torch.

The barns—and Fenis. Hibern and Fenis Senelac had played as children. Was Fenis still training horses at the academy barns? She would be if she could, Hibern knew.

Hibern ran, her proud new mage robe flapping at her knees. She encountered no academy boys. They had to be gathered as close as they dared to the senior court, wherever that was. She pounded down torchlit stone corridors between the unembellished sandstone buildings that had trained Marloven commanders for centuries. The sinkhole of the kingdom, that's what the academy was known as outside Marloven Hess. And there had been times, she'd discovered, that it had been known that way inside the kingdom, usually before some great ruction.

She reached the barns, where girls were busy bedding down horses for the night, and asked after Fenis until she was pointed in the proper direction.

She spotted a familiar dark, curly head. Fenis looked exactly like her brothers from the back, but when she turned, Hibern recognized her, though she was dressed much like the younger academy boys in her loose tunic-shirt and long riding trousers.

Fenis stared, brow furrowed. Hibern paused, waiting. She could imagine Fenis thinking: tall, black hair, black

eyes, riding clothes, but what's that sky blue robe over
them? Mage blue, hadn't she heard something about her
old playmate doing magic studies?

Fenis exclaimed, "Hibern! I thought you were . . ."

"Disinherited and driven from home?" Hibern asked in
a hard enough voice to hide how it still hurt, all these
months later. "Yes, I was. I'm now a mage student."

Fenis made a quick slapping motion in the air, as if to
strike the words away. "Magic," she said, and grimaced.
"Almost as nasty a subject as the regent."

Hibern knew that any magic but the everyday spells that
everyone used without thinking, such as the Waste Spell, or
those concerning bridges, roads, and water purity, was a
matter of distrust to her fellow Marlovens. And she was not
about to explain the difference between the dark magic that
Marloven mages had been using for several centuries, and
light, which was now her study. "Senrid? They said in the
castle that he's here. What's going on?"

Fenis scowled. "They won't let us girls anywhere near."
She gave Hibern a grim smile. "But if you really do know
magic, maybe you could make us invisible so we can climb to
that rooftop there? We could see everything." She pointed
toward a glow from many torches.

Hibern didn't bother saying that invisibility was impossible. What she needed was an illusion that would deflect
attention from them, and that was easily done—and as easily penetrated if anyone were actually looking for them,
illusions being mere tricks of the willing eye.

Illusions were the first thing mage students learned. A
word, a gesture, and Hibern said, "Lead on."

Fenis led the way to a fence. Hibern kirtled up her mage
robe, and followed Fenis onto the fence, then on a hard, fast
scramble onto the slanted roof until they reached the ridgepole.

Hibern clung grimly, hating heights, as she glanced below into a walled square around the perimeter of which a
huge crowd of younger boys crouched. Torches had not
only been jammed into the sconces at the edges of roofs,
but into cracks along the walls. Boy guards stood guard on
the wall, but their attention was bent solely on the tall senior and the shorter, blond figure in the gold-lit square.

Both boys were shockingly blood-splattered, as was the ground. In that ruddy light, the blood looked black.

"Why doesn't Senrid stop it?" Hibern whispered.

"Don't you see? They're in shirtsleeves. It means the rules are laid aside. Even for a harvaldar." She used the formal Marloven word for 'king.'

Hibern wanted to scream out her sudden upsurge of fury. Senrid, the smartest person her age she knew, was doing the *stupidest thing possible*. He risked his life down there in a useless fistfight when he could command the entire army to stop these obnoxious academy boys. He was a powerful enough mage to cast spells to hide the sun from the entire kingdom—and there he was, letting some brute beat the snot out of him.

She clenched her fists, wanting to drop a stone spell over them both.

In the court, Senrid tried to keep his focus on the blood-smeared face before him, though distracted by the drip from his own nose—did the drips coincide with the throbs?—and the horrible flutter in his muscles that he knew meant he was tiring . . .

Senrid saw the intake of breath, the tightening of muscles a heartbeat before Ndarga swung.

He was fast. Senrid had begun his block, but Ndarga's fist caught the side of his head. He shut his eyes against the pain-flash and used the recoil to torque his block, step, and kick low.

Ndarga shifted. Not quite fast enough. Senrid's boot heel clipped his knee, and he staggered.

That was the last blow Senrid landed for the next thousand years. He had one advantage, but it was untrustworthy at best: he could hear others' thoughts, if he concentrated. Dena Yeresbeth was a new idea, discovered when he and Liere had been on the run the year before. Ndarga's intent reached Senrid's mind less than a heartbeat before his body acted, giving Senrid very little time to react as he tried to avoid the worst blows.

His strategy, which had seemed like such a good idea before he started, was to use his being smaller and lighter to stay ahead of Ndarga until the older boy wore out. Senrid understood within the first half dozen desperate exchanges how wrong he was to base his strategy on his limited experience of real contact fighting.

Commander Keriam, who had trained Senrid, was in excellent condition—for a man in his fifties. The time it took to cause a man of fifty years to get out of breath was far shorter than that required to tire a nineteen-year-old who had been training hard for the past nine years.

Further—Senrid spared a moment to take in the watchers—his strategy looked like cowardice from the outside.

Think. Keriam had trained them all. Senrid saw familiar patterns in Ndarga's moves. Another thousand years was going to pass, and it was only going to get worse unless he did something . . .

What am I doing wrong? He was using the patterns to evade—

Oh. So think against the pattern.

He reversed. Jumped in instead of to the side, dealt Ndarga a stinging slap over the ear, then followed with a fist to the gut. It was like hitting wood. He danced back, wringing his throbbing fingers. Ndarga took a harsh breath. So the blow did have an effect.

It wasn't much of one, but it was enough to anger Ndarga, who returned with a wicked flurry of feints and strikes.

That was another thing that Senrid's training with Keriam had not taught him. They'd always halted when they began to puff, as Keriam discussed Senrid's errors. There was no halt for discussion now. Senrid crowed for breath, the edge of his vision smeary on one side, glittering on the other. Focus! Break the pattern.

Another half a dozen blows and he fell to his knees once, causing a shout to go up. Some laughter. He rolled, used the anger sparked by that derisive laughter to launch himself straight into Ndarga for a head-butt to the gut.

Ndarga smacked him away. Tears stung Senrid's eyes, his nose throbbing, but he'd heard that grunt. Patterns! Ndarga was taller, and used to hitting high, from the gut up. Senrid feinted high, then came in with kicks. One connected solidly with Ndarga's forward knee, causing him to nearly topple as he brought a fist up under Senrid's jaw.

Senrid threw himself to the side, deflecting most of the force of the blow. Still felt like his neck had broken. Sick, dizzy, desperately thirsty, he knew he was going to lose. The question was how badly.

Listen! He could make one more try. Go out fighting . . .

Senrid sensed that Ndarga's thoughts were nearly as inchoate as his own, but by now Senrid had the patterns. He sidestepped—barely—two blows whizzing close to his ears. Could've crushed bricks. Then Ndarga followed through with what was intended to be the final series: a lunge, uppercut, two side blows.

Senrid put all he had into avoiding the uppercut, but instead of retreating, he whirled into Ndarga, fists together, straight into the point below the breastbone. Being shorter, he had the advantage of thrusting upward. *Thud.* Ndarga's eyes widened, and his breath whistled.

Senrid was aware of a roar. Inside his head or out?

Then Ndarga's hands hit either side of his head and Senrid's vision flashed into scattered lights. He found himself on the ground, arms and legs twitching, the side of his face gritting in dirt. Dust got in his mouth. He groaned, trying to spit it out. Then fingers gripped his shirt collar and yanked him up.

The roar in his ears resolved into voices, then into words as his bleary vision took in Ndarga looming over him. Ndarga was on one knee, swaying. Senrid squinted up at him, waiting for the last blow.

But it didn't come. "Shit," Ndarga muttered, and flung him away.

Senrid landed with a splat, nose first. Pain shot through him. He had just enough strength to flop over and gaze up at the sky, which revolved gently. One by one round brownish blobs appeared. Then a familiar voice . . . "Satisfied?"

Keriam stepped into the court, looking neither right nor left. The boys, out of long habit of obedience, stilled.

"Ndarga. Satisfied?"

Jarend Ndarga was mopping his bleeding nose and looking around as if he'd find his wits among the blood splatters on the stones. "Yes," he said.

Whispers from the walls, but no one moved. The rules

held, barely. The boys stilled, a breath away from chaos as Keriam bent over Senrid, and repeated, "Satisfied?" Because that was the rule in these personal scraps.

Senrid struggled to speak. "Yes."

It came out sounding like "Wheh," but Keriam straightened up, and turned his toughest glare around the waiting faces. Then in a field command voice, "Fight's over, both satisfied. Anyone out of place by the time the watch change rings—and I'm sending a runner to the bell right now—wins a breeze from my own hand." He pulled a polished length of ash from his belt and whacked it against his leg.

The rumble and dust of many feet running followed. Clear chain of command, Senrid thought. Keriam ruled the academy. Could he take the kingdom? Yes. No. They'd kill him. *They might kill me.*

He couldn't find a reason to care, as hands took hold of various portions of his body. Now, he knew from experience, was going to be the worst of it. He couldn't speak, but he could sort sensations and interpret their meanings.

Senrid knew who he was. The thing he'd figured out by the time he was eight was that he wasn't the same person to everyone. To Uncle Tdanerend, he was the stupid little boy whose inconvenient birth kept Tdanerend from kingship. As long as Senrid was small, and acted stupid, nothing fatal happened to him.

Now he was going to find out if he was Senrid-the-dead-king, Senrid-the-former-king, or . . .

He was carried, not hauled. He was put on something soft, not flung down into stone and darkness. Without having to make the effort to listen for unspoken thoughts, he knew from the way he was handled that he was still—at this moment—Senrid-Harvaldar.

Chapter Two

KERIAM followed the runners carrying Senrid, and watched as they laid him gently on his bed.

"Fetch the healer," Keriam said to one, and "Strip him, and clean up the blood," he said to two others.

Keriam had scarcely breathed during the endless agony of that fight. He could have told Senrid all the reasons why it was a bad idea, but Senrid had launched straight out there, driven by a desperation that Keriam understood.

The former regent had so distorted his brother's attempt at re-instituting rule of law that Marloven Hess had been thrown back to the worst days of the old Olavair kings, under most of whom rule by whim had been the norm. Jarls had been petty kings in those days, unanswerable to anyone. The regent, in buying favorites, had been eroding all his brother's hard-won attempts at establishing a justice system that extended to everyone. So here was Senrid, trying to prove that he was fit to rule, young as he was, in the only way that Marlovens would understand: by the oldest tradition.

It had taken all Keriam's control not to interfere.

The runners were quick and efficient, Senrid mercifully

unconscious. When they were done, Keriam carefully checked
Senrid over.

Long experience with battered bodies convinced him that
his first assessment was correct: Ndarga had retained enough
self-control not to do permanent damage, though he had
used all his years of hard training to make this thrashing as
painful as possible. As Senrid stirred, muttering something
through puffing lips, the garrison healer arrived, breathless
from running.

Downstairs, Hibern arrived from the seniors' private court
in the academy. She sent a runner up to Senrid, hoping he
was in better shape than he'd looked, then prowled the
lower hall, trying to figure out what to do if she was denied.
She was on her fifteenth lap (she'd first said she'd give herself ten, then twenty) when the runner reappeared and said,
"King will see you."

She ran upstairs to the royal residence on the third floor.
Instead of the plain stone walls of the lower floor, here were
fine frescoes in shades of gray, depicting running horses
and swooping raptors.

When she entered Senrid's bedchamber, she recognized
Commander Keriam, the grizzled man in charge of the
Marloven military academy. He stood beside the bed, looking tired and exasperated, but Hibern thought she saw
something worse in the tightness of his forehead and the
deep lines on either side of his mouth. An echo of horror,
not quite gone?

A healer in uniform was holding a cup to Senrid's lips.
The air in Senrid's bedroom filled with a sharp, distinctive
aroma that made her feel slightly heady—green kinthus.
Magic could bind bones and teeth so they could heal, but it
didn't do anything for pain. The fact that Senrid drank
green kinthus, which could be dangerous if drunk in large
quantities, instead of the much milder listerblossom, meant
that the pain was bad. As if you couldn't tell by the distortion of swellings and bruises all over the parts of him visible
above the sheet.

"This stuff will make me go off my head," Senrid muttered as the healer lowered him to the pillow. Senrid's dic-

tion was usually crisp, and his speech a headlong reflection of his thoughts, but now his words were slurry and nasal, even plummy. As one would expect from someone whose nose was being held in place by a magic spell.

"You were already off your head," Keriam retorted from the other side of the bed. "What made you do something that stupid, Senrid?" Keriam sat down on the bedside stool that the healer had just vacated. "You couldn't possibly win a real fight, for the same reason he had to win."

"I know." Senrid touched his jaw, and winced. "But they had to. See me try. And see me. Stick to my word."

"Assuming," Keriam said cordially, "you survived."

"Thought he would stick to academy rules. And not kill me."

"So you did have a strategy. Even if it was poorly thought out."

One of Senrid's eyes was puffing up fast, but his other narrowed. Soon the kinthus would have him mentally floating, then he'd drop into sleep. Hibern watched Senrid struggle to hold onto his wits. "The yelling. Did it change?"

Hibern wondered if he'd already lost the battle, but Keriam's grizzled brows lifted. *He* clearly made sense of those words. His gaze went distant, then he said, "I'd say it was even. At best. When you began, probably more for Jarend Ndarga, but you must remember he's been the academy leader for two years."

"End?" Senrid asked, carefully touching his jaw. "Ow."

"By the end, they were mostly yelling for you," Keriam admitted. Then he scowled. "By academy rules—with the four-year handicap on his side—you won by two points. It was that last blow you got in before he let you go. But you are not to consider that a real win. On the field, nobody lets you go because you're too pitiful an object to kill," Keriam said bluntly. "You *know* that. Senrid, don't do that again."

"Shouldn't have to," Senrid said. "See? Took on toughest senior. Nothing happened to him. See?" He winced. "It worked. Didn't it? Did it?" He looked up at Keriam, his one functioning eyebrow puckering anxiously.

"For now." Keriam sighed and then got to his feet. "Hibern is here. Said it was an emergency." He started toward the door. "Don't talk long," he warned Hibern, and left with the healer.

Senrid squinted at Hibern. "Isn't our day. Or time."

"I know. Clair of the Mearsieans asked me to come," Hibern began.

Senrid leaned on an elbow, wincing. "Emergency," he muttered. "Keriam said emergency. My cousin?"

"I'm not here about your cousin. Far as I know, Ndand is perfectly safe."

Senrid blinked at Hibern through his one functioning eye. "What's happened?"

"Today—yesterday, I guess it would be, here, the Chwahir invaded Mearsies Heili."

"Invaded? Wait. Wait. Wait." Senrid clutched his hands to his face. The pain was beginning to recede, to be replaced by the soft cottony blanket of kinthus, which made him feel like his brains were leaking out of his ears. But at least he could talk without his jaw sending lightning through his head at every word. "I don't get it. Chwahirsland is huge."

"Yes."

"It lies at the other end of the continent. *This* continent."

"Yes."

"Mearsies Heili is a small blot, lying across the ocean to the west. Opposite direction of Chwahirsland."

"Yes."

"Why would the Chwahir go all the way there? And no one else noticed an invading force sailing up the strait? Oh, but it would have launched when the rest of the world was under Siamis's enchantment . . ."

Hibern sighed. So the pain relief of the kinthus had temporarily restored Senrid's habit of muttering, his thoughts zipping with frenetic speed. If she waited, he usually returned to the subject, and sometimes managed to answer his own questions.

". . . so people wouldn't have noticed if the warships had galloped up to their doors. But Siamis's enchantment has been over for how many months? How long does it take to reach past the Nob, way up north, then it's all open sea . . . no. The Delfin Islanders would have known. They always know everything in those waters." He looked up at Hibern. "How many warships?"

"Three," she said.

"That's not an invasion. Even for something as small as Mearsies Heili, which is mostly farm. Oh. Right. Didn't the Chwahir already have an outpost of some kind there? But that's real small, too, isn't it? Not much larger than a castle and half a day's ride of bad farmland, under permanent magic-made shadow."

"Yes, and yes."

Senrid peered one-eyed at the huge map of the world up on the wall on the other side of his bedroom. But that wouldn't show much. Mearsies Heili was too insignificant in both size and influence.

Its capital was no larger than a market town in Marloven Hess, but it was distinctive because it had been raised into the sky, surrounded by magical vapor so it looked like a city in the clouds, dominated by a towering palace made of white stone.

"It wasn't an invasion," Senrid stated, this time firmly.

Hibern let out her breath. "That's what *I* said. *They* said that the Chwahir and the Mearsieans are enemies going back for generations. And there is that outpost."

"So what does this have to do with me?" Senrid asked, and added sarcastically, "Don't try to tell me Clair wants my military advice."

"Not in the least," Hibern retorted calmly. "She needs your help to break into the citadel of the King of the Chwahir."

"What?"

Now she had his complete attention.

Hibern took a deep breath, surprised to find it shuddering against her ribs. It felt as if she hadn't breathed for the past . . . how long had it been? "It's even stranger than you think. And I can tell you everything, because I was there."

Chapter Three

Same day, earlier
Roth Drael

AT dawn that day, while Hibern had been tossing and moaning in the grip of yet another nightmare, her tutor-mage Erai-Yanya, woken by the noise from across the hall, had decided she might as well get up.

She moved into the oddly shaped remains of a chamber, used to the broken walls and half roof overhead—weather-warded by considerable magic—and touched the glow-globes to light. And there she saw a newly arrived letter on the polished wood tray that she had ensorcelled as her transfer Destination for letters. Her heart wrung as Hibern coughed a low, rib-sucking sob into the bedding.

As she had countless times, Erai-Yanya considered getting doors fitted into those arches. Then she forgot doors, archways, and nightmares when she picked up her letter and read it.

And read it again.

She dropped the paper and stared at the window. The sun was still somewhere behind the thick forest to the east, which meant it was still night in Mearsies Heili, on another continent south and west. How to handle this request from her old mage school comrade-in-sneaking, Murial of Mearsies Heili?

Erai-Yanya was still thinking about it as she trod out in the early morning air to fetch some wild grapes from the garden, and had made no decision by her return.

As she set about making breakfast, at the other end of the hall, Hibern woke at last, and knew from the stinging along her eyelids and the panging of her head that she'd had another nightmare about the home that was no longer home.

Hibern rubbed her eyes, consciously breathing against the hurt in her throat as she listened to the little sounds of breakfast being readied—the click of crockery plates and cups on the table—and smelled the scent of fresh bread, which arrived each day by magic transfer, wafting enticingly to her room.

Hibern grimaced down at her hands when she remembered that this was her day to endure the long transfer to the magic school in Bereth Ferian, the northernmost city in the world. That was the last thing she wanted to do, with this headache, but no one would be interested in her whining.

Marlovens learned early that most people had a limited budget of pity. In the last year, Hibern had found that true outside their border, as well; people might have more conventional expressions than Marlovens did, accompanied by a dip of the head and rueful smiles, but they wanted you to pretend their words did away with the pain and get on with it. Marlovens, in her experience, didn't waste the breath.

She stepped through her cleaning frame, which zapped away the dried tear tracks from her face as well as the normal grime, dressed, and went out to face the day.

Erai-Yanya never paid attention to her appearance, but she seemed even more distracted than usual, her brown hair looking like she'd just woken, the shapeless dress she'd been wearing for a week rumpled. She was surrounded by a moat of open books and scrolls. Hibern suspected that some kind of magical emergency having to do with wards had to be happening somewhere in the world.

"Another nightmare?" Erai-Yanya said, her glance sympathetic.

Hibern opened her hands. And because she knew that

all that could be said had been said, "Today is my day to go north. Any messages?"

Erai-Yanya knew that the rational person would have felt only relief to escape Hibern's dreadful home, but emotions were not always rational. She also knew that she, a recluse from a long line of positive hermits, was never going to understand whatever it was that bound families together for good or ill. She had sent her son off to be trained by an excellent mage, and was proud of him having that place, but she wondered if she would have chosen differently if she'd had a daughter.

But those kinds of what-ifs were useless. She said, "I do have a letter for you to carry, as Clair of the Mearsieans apparently did not take her notecase when she went visiting up there. Murial sent this to be handed off to her niece." A quick smile as she pushed a sealed note toward Hibern.

Wondering why Murial didn't send the note to the scribe desk up north, Hibern shrugged. She didn't understand the ways of royalty outside of Marloven Hess, even the royalty of so small a polity as Mearsies Heili. Or maybe 'royalty' was the wrong idea here. Murial, Erai-Yanya had said once, was a regent at a remove, being a fellow hermit-mage living alone somewhere in the wild woods of that country's western border. She watched over the pastoral little kingdom from a distance, avoiding people as much as she could. Her niece, Clair, led the kingdom day to day.

Midway through breakfast Erai-Yanya startled Hibern by clapping a book shut with a soft, "Ha!" She tucked the book under her arm, and trod to the Destination-book to leaf through it for some tile pattern. She muttered the transfer spell and vanished, the air in the room stirring strongly enough to flutter the abandoned pages.

Hibern sat back and breathed. At least breakfast had vanquished the nightmare headache. She picked up her magic study books, and braced for the magic transfer to the north to Bereth Ferian.

She endured the usual joint-wrench, and staggered in the new space, breathing cooler air that smelled of aromatic trees. She sank onto one of the low benches surrounding the tiles until the transfer magic effects had worn off, then left the Destination chamber.

Since she had the note to deliver, she bypassed the hall leading to the magic school and entered the grand marble-floored hall leading inside the palace, where Erai-Yanya's son Arthur studied magic separately.

'Arthur.' It always snagged at her, that foreign-sounding name. She knew it was a nickname given him by some world-gate crossing friends. She was going to have to find out that story someday, she thought as she passed the gorgeous decorative motifs and statuary, gifts from various northern governments over the generations.

Arthur's kingship was fiction in a way that Hibern found difficult to understand, coming as she did from Marloven Hess, where kingship had historically been the center of violent struggles for power. For command. Arthur's title was traditional, a courtesy.

When Siamis had spread his enchantment over a good part of the world a year or so ago ('or so' was the only way to consider a period in which time seemed ephemeral, and people had walked about as if in a dream world, obedient to whatever command Siamis gave them, without remembering any of it), the elderly mage Evend, King in Bereth Ferian, sacrificed his life to destroy Norsunder's rift magic. Everyone accepted Evend's title passing to Arthur even though he was no older than Hibern was. A title with no responsibility, as far as Hibern could discover, except presiding at official gatherings.

The sound of girls' laughter broke Hibern's dour mood. Odd, how a duty visit would turn interesting as soon as she heard someone having fun.

"But once you find people, you have to race them to home base," one of the Mearsiean girls was earnestly explaining as Hibern entered an enormous drawing room lit down one side through tall arched windows by slanting shafts of light.

Arthur stood over by the opposite wall, absently running ink-stained fingers through his short blond hair. His habitually vague expression altered when he saw her, and he beckoned for her to enter. She joined him in a few quick steps.

"Erai-Yanya said the Mearsieans were still here. Why?" Hibern whispered. The noisy Mearsieans seemed out of place in this quiet, archival atmosphere.

"For her," Arthur said, pointing to scrawny Liere, the girl the world had begun calling Sartora. She sat in the circle of girls, her raggedly cut, lank, almost colorless pale hair framing an earnest face dominated by huge light brown eyes. "I asked them if they'd stay. She seems, I don't know, happier, with them around." He sent a puzzled look Liere's way.

Hibern's gaze shifted to Liere, then to the other girls. Young people played games in Marloven Hess. Of course. But the games tended to be competitive, often related to military training. Hibern had hated them from early childhood.

This game the Mearsieans played was messy and complicated—the rules seemed to be changing constantly—but Liere clearly found it funny when a freckled, red-haired Mearsiean girl waddled across the far side of the huge drawing room, waggling her elbows and quacking like a duck. Another girl slithered over the beautifully woven rug, graceful even when pretending to be a snake. In the background, the rest of the Mearsieans made barnyard noises, as Liere shook with silent laughter.

"I won!" the freckled girl shouted, her bristly red braids flapping, arms and legs pumping as she danced around. "I'm It! I'm It!"

Liere watched, lips parted as if she were about to laugh out loud but didn't dare. She looked unchanged since Hibern had met her the previous year, right down to the same worn old tough-woven tunic and riding trousers.

Hibern glanced past her and found Clair, who stood out as the only one with pure white hair.

Clair was short for thirteen or fourteen, ordinary-looking enough except for that white hair. It wasn't the cobwebby, floating hair of the morvende, nor did she have their fish-pale skin or their talons, but her ancestors had to number among the underground people.

Erai-Yanya had told Hibern about Clair's upbringing, how her dejected mother drank wine and took sleepweed until she died. Clair had been educated by her aunt Murial, who started her on magic studies when she was small. "Don't be fooled by her young age. She probably knows more magic than you do," Erai-Yanya had finished.

When Hibern first met the Mearsiean girls, she'd thought one of the other girls the Mearsiean queen, as she was loud and tended to swank about. But when Clair spoke, the way the others instantly deferred made it clear that her gang of runaways and castoffs regarded her as their chief.

Clair must have felt Hibern's gaze, because she turned around and then smiled. "Greetings! Hibern, isn't it? I'm sorry. I didn't see you come in."

"Hibern?" Liere whirled around as if someone had poked her.

"Hi, Sartora," Hibern said.

"Please call me Liere," Liere whispered.

"My pardon, Liere," Hibern said, thinking that mighty mind powers or not, Liere was very odd.

Hibern could not understand why Liere would reject an honor that most would be proud of any more than she could understand why the girl wore ragged old clothes and bare feet, when surely she could ask for anything she wanted in that massive, wealthy palace.

Liere's light brown eyes looked golden in that light. "You're Marloven, aren't you? It's just that I hope everything is all right with Senrid."

"I see him each week for magic studies. Want me to pass on a message?"

Liere's thin fingers twisted together. "Yes. No! It's just that he was my first friend. But I understand. He's a king, so he must be extra busy. Much too busy to visit. It's just that he once said . . . no, forget that."

Her skinny shoulders hitched up near her ears. Hibern suspected Liere had no idea how to get out of that hopeless tangle, so she turned to Clair. "I have a message for you."

Clair took the note and broke the seal. Then she looked up, her hazel eyes wide. "The Chwahir have invaded," she said. Her voice changed, dropping a note or two, as if she had to convince someone. "We have to go *home*. Right now."

"Invaded?" CJ asked, skinny arms wide, her long, straight black hair swinging. She was Clair's best friend. Clair had made her a princess, though she'd been born on another world and brought through a world-gate. "Like, war junk and everything?"

Clair held up the paper. "Three ships of warriors, plus those from the Shadowland outpost, under the direction of the King of the Chwahir."

Hibern made a mental wager that Murial had sent the note begging Clair and these girls to stay here, out of trouble, queen or no queen.

CJ scowled. "I call this completely unfair!" And when everyone turned her way, she pointed at Liere. "Here's the world saved from the villain Siamis by Sartora. We deserve a golden age of peace, like in all the songs! But thanks to the Chwahir, as usual, we get rotten luck instead."

'Luck'? But no one asked what that was as Clair's mouth pressed into a thin, pale line. "The note says the main attack is magic, on our capital. Aunt Murial is there, trying to fight against it. She said we should stay here in safety—"

I was right, Hibern thought.

"—but I have to go home," Clair stated.

"To a magic attack?" Hibern asked, and then it hit her, why Erai-Yanya hadn't told her where she was going. "I think Erai-Yanya went to help." Hibern studied Clair's tense face, knowing the other girl was going to go regardless.

Hibern bit her lip, instinct at war with duty. Erai-Yanya expected her to go to the mage school for her long day of study. But she was learning to become a mage because she wanted to help people, and right now, Clair needed help. She'd let Clair's reaction decide. "Shall I go with you?"

Clair let out a soft breath, her eyebrows lifting in a revealing expression of relief. "I know we'll need any help we can get." She waved the paper. "Aunt Murial can protect the country, if we try to protect the cloud top so she won't have to. Does that sound right?"

Hibern thought, cloud top? She said with more assurance than she felt, "I'll be glad to help any way I can."

Clair turned to her friends, who stood in a tight circle, waiting. "Transfer to the Junky, count five between each, okay?"

Her friends reached inside shirts and dresses for the medallions they wore, then began winking out in transfer magic, each disappearance sending a wild current of air whooshing around.

While they did that, Clair described her home transfer Destination tiles to Hibern. Then, in turn, they vanished.

Mearsies Heili, cloud city above Mount Marcus

Erai-Yanya, satisfied that her single student was safely removed from danger, transferred to the Destination in Mearsies Heili and, once she recovered, gazed upward in astonishment.

Her home was in Roth Drael, once a center for Ancient Sartoran magic until blasted in the Fall of Ancient Sartor. It was a ruin, no complete building standing. The fragments left behind indicated the city had been built out of a strange white stone that looked like a blend of ice and metal. She had discovered on her first visit to Sartor that there was a single tower in the heart of its capital, made of the same material. She was reverently told by her guide that this tower was the oldest edifice in Sartor.

Now she was standing in front of an *entire building* built of the same material.

Murial appeared, looking mostly unchanged from their student days, except for strands of silver in her dark hair. "Erai-Yanya," she called, hurrying across the terrace. "You're here."

"I came as soon as I found my mother's old border protection spells." Erai-Yanya brandished her book. "Where're the invaders? Have you contacted the school for help?"

"The Chwahir have already landed." Murial's voice was tense.

That meant ships, warriors, borders breeched. It was now a military matter. Mages took an oath not to meddle in such, not that magic was much use in warfare anyway.

Murial went on, "They entered the Shadowland outpost during the night, but emerged on the mountain road a while ago. They can only be marching on this city."

"Shadowland?" Erai-Yanya looked around. A fountain splashed behind her, and beyond that, a pretty little town seemed quiet, no movement except the stirrings of a breeze in what she suspected were brightly colored flower boxes in windows, though this early before sunrise the world appeared a thousand shades of gray and blue.

Murial pointed down at her feet. "The Chwahir outpost below the city. It's held by Prince Kwenz, brother to Wan-Edhe, the King of the Chwahir."

Erai-Yanya glanced down at her dusty sandals, remembering that the Chwahir king never used his name, only his title—'Wan-Edhe' in Chwahir meaning *The* King, as if there never had been and never would be another. Then she blinked past that, remembering that only this palace was actually located on the mountaintop. The adjacent village extended outward on a magically maintained cloud. Unimaginable magic had raised it in the far past, though for what purpose no one now knew. Mearsies Heili had no importance whatever, either magically or politically.

She scowled down at her sandals, struggling to make sense of the situation. This palace, made of material that only existed elsewhere as ruins—the tiny capital held up by magic equally impossible to mages now—Chwahirsland so very vast, located on the other side of the continent across the sea. Instinct insisted she was missing something important.

"The Chwahir must have set sail during the Siamis enchantment," Erai-Yanya said slowly, considering what she'd learned about the Chwahir from Gwasan, the runaway Chwahir princess she and Murial had been close to during their years at the northern mage school. Until Gwasan was hunted down and killed by assassins sent by the head of her own family, this very same king.

"Murial, what could Wan-Edhe possibly want *here*? If we know, maybe we can form some kind of plan to thwart him, or at least get the right kind of help."

Murial rubbed her forehead in slow circles. "The Shadowland army has tried a couple of times to take our east provinces. They could feed all Chwahirsland if our people were forced to labor for them, growing crops to ship back to their homeland. You know Chwahirsland is ruined. But I don't think Wan-Edhe is after farmland. Why come halfway around the world for that? I think he's after the palace."

Erai-Yanya turned her gaze upward, toward the asymmetrical towers shimmering in the pale predawn light. Knowing that distracting herself from an impossible situation wasn't going to improve it, she still spoke. "When we were girls, you said you lived in a marble palace. And every time I leave here I *remember* it as marble."

Murial stared at her old friend, fighting impatience, because she'd had this conversation before. At least twice, if not more. And Erai-Yanya never remembered it. "We were *told* it was marble. By the time I found out it wasn't, I'd learned not to talk about it." She sighed. "Erai-Yanya, it was here when the first Mearsiean refugees reached this shore, seven hundred years ago. It could be it . . . wasn't here, before that. There are rooms up there that come and go. We never thought much about it, having grown up with it, and furthermore, every visitor, including you, goes away and forgets about it. But right now, *here is what's important*, Wan-Edhe doesn't seem to forget. When he overran this kingdom a few years ago, he was not able to get past the second floor."

"Your wards?"

"No." Murial's thin fingers pressed against her temples, her eyes closed. "I don't know that much magic! Something so old I have no record of it, and so powerful I can't perceive what type of spells, only that they exist."

"Is it possible to extend something off that spell?"

"That's what I was thinking right before you came. But it'll take two of us."

Both found a semblance of relief in talking about what they knew was possible. In cryptic conversation honed over the years, they discussed the intricacies of magic as they hurried inside and upstairs to the library, where Murial began hunting through old tomes.

From long habit, Erai-Yanya reached for the end of her sash and tied a knot, whispering to herself as she did it. She was going to remember this old palace and its mystery, and research it as soon as she got home.

The tall glass windows in the hall outside the library were open to the air, through which came the high sound of young voices. Murial paused in the act of thumbing through an ancient text.

She said with annoyance, "Your Hibern doesn't seem

capable of passing on a message," as they hurried out of the
library to the window.

They looked down on the tops of three heads: Clair's
white, Hibern's dark, with CJ's shiny blue-black locks between them.

Erai-Yanya retorted, "That niece of yours doesn't seem
capable of following orders either. Just like someone else I
remember."

Murial sighed. "She got my sense of duty, and my
younger sister's impulses for poking her nose into trouble,
always with the best intent. Let's get back to work before
they come inside."

She was right about Clair's sense of duty, and where Clair
went, the girls had to go. On the floor below the mages, CJ
complained with a graphic list of which muscles and bones
hurt worst after that long transfer, and Clair winced and
swung her arms.

Hibern breathed away the nausea and ache as she gazed
in witless amazement at the palace. The three started up
the shallow, wide terrace stairs. When they got inside, Hibern walked to a wall to examine it. She knew this strange
material, not quite stone. It was more like ice without the
cold—ice and stone mixed with a hint of metal, only with a
pearlescent sheen. It was the very same material as the broken building she lived in with Erai-Yanya.

"Oh, no!" Clair cried, and uttered a soft, breathy laugh.
"Now I know we're in trouble."

In ran a tall boy, saying breathlessly, "Thought I heard
CJ crabbing. I just got here from below. Did you know the
Chwahir are marching up the old road right now?" He
jerked his thumb toward the window.

In answer, Clair held out her aunt's note, and he bent
over it. He was so tall that at first Hibern took him to be
older than he was, until she noticed the still-round cheeks
over a square jawline, and the gangling proportions of a
teen. Though he had brown hair, his face so resembled
Clair's he had to be related.

"It's Clair's cousin," CJ whispered to Hibern, as they

mounted the stairs. "He doesn't actually live here. He's always on the Wander."

The Wander wasn't a tradition in Marloven Hess, for whatever reason, but along the rest of the vast Sartoran continent, and even on other continents, underage people often traveled the world, working their way along in ships or caravans. Most trade cities and harbors had Wander Houses, where young travelers could bunk. A lot of businesses offered food or goods in trade for the sort of enthusiastic but unskilled labor expected of the young.

CJ went on, "Puddlenose seems to have this . . . this weird kind of sixth sense, where he'll be somewhere traveling around, then he suddenly gets this idea that he has to come home, and it always means trouble."

Puddlenose? Hibern repeated to herself, then shrugged it off, attributing the unfortunate name to CJ's penchant for creating nicknames—whether the recipient liked it or not.

". . . had to come by transfer, and I hoped you'd be here," Puddlenose was saying. "I think Wan-Edhe has ordered up every sword in the Shadowland, and they are on their way up the mountain." He pointed at the floor.

The air stirred, bringing an eye-watering whiff through the open windows. It smelled like rusty metal placed too near a fire.

"Dark magic," Clair breathed, then glanced up as the two mages came running down the stairs. "Oh! Aunt Murial—?"

"I sent that message to keep you *safe*—" Murial started, before both Murial and Erai-Yanya stilled, gripping the bannister, as greenish light flared outside the windows. Everyone felt the hairs on the backs of their arms lift.

Then the building shivered all around them.

As one, they moved upstairs to broad windows. Hibern glimpsed another terrace made of the same iridescent material as the walls around her. Beyond this terrace a formation of men gathered. They wore uniforms that looked black in the aggregate, but the strong sunlight revealed some grayish with age, and others' dye tended toward rust or green.

The biggest group surrounded a tall, stooped old man in a night-black robe, with unkempt white hair and beard. He and a slug-pale man stood beyond the terrace on a grassy sward between the palace and the town, the houses mostly whitewashed with colorful tile roofs.

"The Chwahir king," Murial breathed. "Here himself. All right, we're going to have to take a stand inside this palace." To the girls—"*Don't* go anywhere. Watch him. Let us know when he moves. Erai-Yanya, we might be able to get Clair and your student to help us chain a deflection ward . . ."

The two mages dashed back up to the library, talking fast, as Hibern and the Mearsieans hung out the window, too terrified to take their eyes away.

The building trembled again, a significantly stronger rattle.

"Is he doing that?" Clair asked.

No one answered.

"Look." Puddlenose pointed at the Chwahir warriors below.

The ranks shifted, pale Chwahir faces looking around fearfully. Hibern's stomach tightened when she saw their eyes. There was no color, no white, even, visible. Their eyes were all black, as if their eye sockets were empty.

That had to be illusion, she reassured herself, as Clair said, "I think . . ."

Another tremor rumbled through the building, and the warriors below reacted with wild looks and raised hands as if they felt it as well. Hibern's knees locked, and her insides swooped in an odd way that she had not felt since her older brother had pushed her in a tree swing, before their father's spells had made Stefan crazy.

Clair's face had blanched nearly as pale as her hair. "I think we're sinking," she whispered.

At the same moment, inside the library, Erai-Yanya set down her useless book, saying, "Murial? Is this normal?"

"No." It was said on an outward breath.

They rushed back to the windows in time to see another weird flash of magic, more powerful than the earlier flicker: beyond the edge of the terrace the air shimmered with thundercloud green.

Hibern's teeth buzzed as she tried to blink away a blurring shadow in the air. But it did not blink away. The shadow coalesced into a writhing line extending from the sky to the ground, and as they watched in horror, it began to widen into a lightless fissure.

The Chwahir below began to edge away from that pulsating darkness, their voices rising in fear.

"That's a Norsunder rift," Clair cried, leading them back upstairs.

"It can't be," Erai-Yanya said sharply. "Norsunder cannot make rifts anymore. Evend *died* binding that magic."

CJ gasped in horror as a slim young man with short, black, curly hair emerged from that darkness. He stepped onto the grass a pace away from the King of the Chwahir. "That's Kessler!" she hissed, hands pressed to her mouth.

"Who?" Hibern asked.

"Villain." CJ's blue gaze was stark with terror. "Descendant of Wan-Edhe, got away. But they got him in Eleven-Land. And now they've opened up one of those rifts!"

Eleven-Land was a euphemism for Norsunder, Hibern remembered as she shook her head in disbelief.

Murial breathed, "It's illusion. We're to think it's a magical rift."

"*They* are to think it's a magical rift," Erai-Yanya muttered.

Prince Kessler Sonscarna spoke in a soft voice, barely above a whisper, yet it carried distinctly on the air. "Come along, uncle. You made a bargain with Norsunder, and I was sent to collect you."

"Kill him!" The old man waved at the big guards surrounding him, his protuberant eyes wild with rage.

The guards shifted, some with hands to their swords. The renegade Chwahir prince smiled, and the guards looked at one another as they pulled their weapons. But no one dared to take the first step.

The king's face mottled with fury as he raised his hands. Dry old lips muttered behind the yellow-stained mustache, and light glowed around his fingers, but Kessler ignored the magic as well as the guards closing in.

Prince Kessler reached with his left hand and gripped the skinny arm of the King of the Chwahir, who stared aghast. No one had touched him for over fifty years—his formidable personal protections were gone.

"Right hand," Erai-Yanya muttered. "See that?" Something in Kessler's palm glinted in the pale light, too quick to catch.

The prince's teeth showed in a brief laugh as he performed a circle gesture, his fingers wide. A scintillating magical fog curled outward to swallow the slug-pale dungeon master and Wan-Edhe's personal guard and commanders; they appeared to be drawn into the rift, but the experienced mages saw the truth past the illusion: they dissolved into enchantment, not transfer.

And were gone. Prince Kessler and his prisoners vanished less than a heartbeat before the massive transfer spell closed with a snap like a blow to the chest. The stench of burning metal torched the air. Nothing made sense, except one fact that the two elder mages clung to: no one would be able to make a transfer in that spot without burning to ash, maybe for years.

And the danger was not yet over.

The ground jolted again, rumbling through the city. The quake caused Mearsieans hiding inside the houses to creep outside, looking around fearfully.

The grinding rumble seemed to come from everywhere at once, but the towering spires above did not creak or grind. It was more like a deep, uneven hum, punctuated by a shivery tinkle, like a silver hammer tapping on glass.

A man called out orders in Chwahir, a phrase picked up by others. Puddlenose said, "The company captain just ordered the mainlanders back to their ships. Ah, did you do that?" He turned to his aunt. "If not, who did?"

The floor jolted underfoot again, sharper, causing the ground to roll. "No," Murial said. "The city beyond the terrace is sinking. It's not the prince's spell. This is something else entirely."

"The entire city?" CJ said, her voice high. "I thought you didn't have earthquakes here!"

Puddlenose pointed out the window, beyond the Chwahir, who were stampeding away in barely controlled order. "Look. People are coming out, now that the Chwahir commanders are gone and the rest are on the run."

Another quake caused a loose tile here and there to clatter down from roofs. People began to cluster in shrill groups, asking questions no one answered, while others ran around without apparent purpose. A few started toward the palace.

Erai-Yanya said, "If the cloud top is sinking, we need to get out."

Hibern said quickly, "Will you need help transferring people?" At last, something she could do!

Murial turned to them. "Everybody in the city wears a transfer token. It's always been that way, at least since the Chwahir chased our ancestors to these shores to carry on the old war, and established themselves in the Shadowland under us." She pressed her hands against her eyes, then brought them down. "We have to warn people to get out. We don't know how bad it's going to be."

Erai-Yanya turned to Clair and Hibern. "You two do that." She drew Murial back into the library.

Clair grabbed Puddlenose by the arm. "I want you to go warn the Chwahir in the Shadowland that the city is coming down on top of them."

Puddlenose and CJ exclaimed at the same time, "What?"

"You speak Chwahir, Puddlenose. I think the Shadowland people should be warned if the city is really coming down," Clair said. "They are directly underneath. It will crush them."

"Oh, sure, I guess you should warn the ordinary people. They can't help being Chwahir. But not Jilo," CJ said.

"Jilo?" Hibern asked.

CJ scowled fiercely. "Kwenz's heir, our age, and a complete and total villain! If you ask me, he deserves what he'll get."

"He's a person."

"A villain!" CJ shrilled.

"The villains are those who told them what to do. Who kept them living in the Shadowland, and made them act that way. That includes Jilo, who has to do what he's told," Clair said. "You *know* that. You *know* what would happen to him if he didn't obey Wan-Edhe. Puddlenose, go."

Puddlenose made a comical grimace. "Do my best." He vanished.

"You watch. Jilo will be busy plotting something nasty,

with Kwenz the Fumbler gloating around right behind him," CJ said. "And if Puddlenose warns him, he'll get a knife in his ribs as thanks."

"Jilo never *killed* any of us," Clair said over her shoulder as she ran toward the stairs. "CJ, we can't do an evil thing just because they did."

"It's not evil, it just makes sense," CJ muttered not quite under her breath as Clair led the way downstairs, followed by Hibern.

"Who is Puddlenose?" Erai-Yanya asked, distracted as the building shook around them, loose books falling from their shelves. "Why do you call him that?"

Murial's tense face tightened into hatred. "That horrible name is from Wan-Edhe. I told you he suborned my brother after he killed Gwasan."

Erai-Yanya remembered something about Murial's brother going to the Chwahir. Willingly, Erai-Yanya thought, but kept it to herself. She had never liked Murial's brother, or her whiny, sullen youngest sister, Clair's mother.

Murial looked around wildly as the building trembled again. The weird tinkling seeming to come out of the air around them. "Puddlenose is my middle sister Malenda's. We don't know his real name. Malenda was killed before we even knew about the boy. Wan-Edhe apparently uses derisive words instead of names, and—" She slapped her hands together. "Never *mind* that," she said as another tremor ran through the building. "I'm babbling." She gripped her head with her fingers as if to hold her skull together.

"When did you sleep last, Murial?"

The hands came down, revealing ravaged eyes. "I don't know."

"Breathe." Erai-Yanya said with a calm she didn't feel. "Think. You know what Gwasan would tell us if she were here. If you can't do anything about this building shaking, whatever the cause, then we must act where we can."

"Here?"

"Chwahirsland."

Murial's eyes widened. "What?"

"Think about it, Murial. Wan-Edhe, who has ruled over eighty years, which should be an impossibility, is now completely out of reach. He probably transferred straight to his flagship this morning when they docked. Nothing in his history indicates he would risk himself away from his citadel for a four-month ocean journey, or however long it takes to get from the other side of the Sartoran continent to here. So whatever his intent, well, is there a chance we could discover something back in his citadel, if we act now? No one knows that he's gone, except that young Prince Kessler."

"Who could be taking the throne in Chwahirsland right now."

"Perhaps. But he said he was sent, and that was definitely Norsunder magic taking Wan-Edhe away. So we transfer to Chwahirsland, where we're bound to find Wan-Edhe's things awaiting his return." And on Murial's doubtful look, "Come on. You're the one who did Queen Lammog's Back Door with Gwasan."

Murial nodded slowly. Like Erai-Yanya, she was never able to recollect without sharp regret their wild days as fearless mage students: Murial of Mearsies Heili, Erai-Yanya of Roth Drael, and Gwasan of Chwahirsland. They both knew that the mastery project called Queen Lammog's Back Door was, like so many mastery projects having to do with penetrating or comprehending dark magic, theoretical.

The time had come to see if it worked.

Murial drew in a deep breath. "For Gwasan," she said in a hard voice. "Whatever is going on with this quake is beyond us. The girls can be trusted to get the city evacuated. Let's go to Chwahirsland."

Long ago, the last great Chwahir queen had foreseen the troubles that had isolated Chwahirsland for the centuries to come. As Lammog Sonscarna was also a powerful mage, she had fashioned a magical trapdoor in the fortress central to Chwahirsland's capital, Narad. She had given the key to this backdoor to the Sartoran mage guild to be kept as a secret.

In a sense it was still largely a secret, though the trapdoor gradually had become an intricate magical puzzle for the rare magic journeymage interested in Chwahir history to solve before they could advance to mastery. Murial's friendship with Gwasan had prompted her to take that as her mastery project.

The result was right there in that library. She sprang to fetch the little hand-bound book, and looked down at her girlish handwriting as she repossessed the details.

Then, holding the book out so they both could read it, the two pronounced the transfer words together.

They appeared in another library, the transfer magic worse than either had ever experienced. It took a long time to recover, perhaps the longer because of the atmosphere, a lour of dark magic mixed with stale fug, weightier than the massive stone blocks around them.

Erai-Yanya choked, putting the crook of her elbow over her nose. The stuffy, oppressive air reeked of acrid male sweat.

Murial whispered, "Do you feel them? This place is *coated* with tracers and traps and wards."

"The whole thing is a trap," Erai-Yanya stated, glancing down at the central table. Light distorted, as if the table were farther away than it was. "But look at those books."

Two magic books lay open on the table, as if recently consulted. Erai-Yanya took a cautious step closer. Murial reached toward one book, fingers spread to sense traps on the table itself. She felt nothing, which made sense as it was a work table, but she wouldn't put it past that horrible old man to make and remove traps every time he worked on one of his destructive projects.

She pulled a pen from her sleeve, where she always kept one in reach, and extended it to the book, which was written in Chwahir. The pen wavered as it neared the book, its nib glowing greenish in warning. She snatched it back and squinted down at the books, taking care not to let any part of her clothing brush against the table.

She'd had to learn the rudiments of the Chwahir language to do her project; some of it came back, enough for her to say, "These appear to be written in two different languages."

Erai-Yanya ventured in a circle around the table. Her magical senses wavered, expanded and contracted in a slow, sluggish manner that made her skin crawl and her stomach lurch.

Murial glanced up with her lips crimped as if she were going to be sick. "This is beyond us. Much beyond."

Erai-Yanya nodded. "Let's get out of here. I can't even breathe anymore. I don't think the air in here has changed for a century."

Chapter Four

ON the mountaintop, another quake jolted the ground, severe enough to make people clutch at one another or hold out their arms for balance. Windows rattled in the houses.

"Spread the word," Clair yelled, her light voice barely audible above the grinding of stone. "The city is coming down. Everyone must leave!"

Hibern stopped on the terrace and gazed upward at the spires overhead. The palace was even more amazing when seen from this vantage, the mystery material nacreous in the spring light. Hibern was afraid that if those impossibly tall spires toppled, the entire town would be crushed.

If the Mearsieans hadn't caused the quake, and the Chwahir hadn't, then who? Who was watching them, and to what purpose? The back of her neck prickled with warning.

She shook off the dread and looked around. The last of the Chwahir were disappearing in one direction, while the Mearsieans dashed back to their houses, yelling at family, friends, and neighbors. Many ran back inside to grab belongings, but here and there people paused, touching bracelets or necklaces, and vanished.

"I'll go tell the staff," CJ offered, hopping anxiously from one bare foot to the other.

"Do. Then go to the Junky." Clair named the girls' underground hideout. "Meet you there."

As CJ ran off, Clair turned to Hibern, her face almost as pale as her hair. "Did you see where my aunt went?"

"No. But Erai-Yanya seems to be with her."

"They must have gone to the cave. Trying magical protections."

"Cave?"

Clair pointed at their feet. "Below us. In the mountain. Above what we call the magic lake. There are beings in the water. One of the girls is actually from there, wearing human form."

Hibern stared at Clair in astonishment, wondering if this 'cave' was the Toaran Selenseh Redian, one of the mysterious caves full of what looked like, but were not, crystals that shed their own light. Some of the strongest indigenous magic pooled in those caves. As far as she knew there was only one on each continent.

This little kingdom, so small and isolated, tucked up in the right-hand corner of Toar, seemed to be full of mysteries. And the rest of the world appeared to be completely unaware. But then, the indigenous beings, whose magic was far more powerful than anything humans had achieved, had so far demonstrated no interest whatever in human conflicts, governments, or affairs. Except when they were angered by human excess.

Or so Hibern had been taught.

Clair said urgently, "We'd better get people safely away."

"I'll help," Hibern said as they raced together across the terrace, past the fountain, and into the first street of houses.

The rest of the day was spent covering the city street by street, sometimes dodging falling flowerpots on window sills, or decorative bric-a-brac along eaves. The quakes were frequent, but never strong enough to knock the girls down as they ran along, flushing people from their homes.

Some were witless with fright, and needed someone telling them to move. Twice they caught thieves lurking on the

verge of looting. One look at Clair sent both running off
into the gathering darkness.

When the girls reached the last street, they looked back,
shocked to see that the palace and its terrace lay far above
their heads, broken pavement sliding slowly down raw-
looking gouges in the side of the mountain. The palace still
stood undamaged, glowing faintly as if the strange material
absorbed the emerging starlight. As quakes shook and rumbled, the spires rang glassily above.

Finally Hibern and Clair seemed to be the last ones left.
The streets had emptied, and doors stood gaping open in
houses, no one inside.

Another quake jolted through, cracking windows. The
girls' stomachs dropped as their hands reached wide in instinctive balance.

"The ground is starting to slant," Hibern said shakily,
arms out wide.

Clair shouted, "I need to check that the girls got safely to
the Junky!" She clutched a medallion on a necklace, and
held out her free hand.

Hibern closed her fingers around that small, square hand,
hoping whatever transfer magic lay on that medallion was
strong enough for two.

One last vicious transfer-jolt, and they fell heavily to the
floor. Hibern blinked away the vertigo, to discover herself
lying in the center of a brightly woven rug in what appeared
to be a cave carved out of soil, with tree rootlets working
in and out of the rounded ceiling overhead.

The light from glowglobes fell on furnishings set against
the equally rough, curved walls. On these walls pictures
had been affixed, obviously drawn by the girls themselves.
At either end of the round room tunnels led off, one upward, one downward.

Hibern sat up, her head panging, and saw most of Clair's
gang surrounding a figure lying on the smoothed dirt floor
near the downward-leading tunnel. This was a lanky teenage boy with limp black hair and the pasty complexion of
the Chwahir. He stirred, groaned, then subsided. A lump
distorted the side of his head.

"Ugh!" CJ exclaimed as Hibern approached.

"I found Jilo lying on the floor in Kwenz's magic chamber," Puddlenose said. "The other Chwahir had abandoned him. Or maybe they didn't know he was there. I think a bookcase fell on him during one of the quakes. There were books all over the floor, and smashed wood."

"You shoulda . . ." CJ glanced at Clair, halted, and crossed her arms, scowling. "Well, what are we going to do with him?"

Clair shut her eyes. "I don't know."

Puddlenose said cheerily, "Until you do, I'll tie him up and stash him somewhere. Got a handy closet down here?"

"Use my room," offered a tall, soft-spoken girl.

Clair sighed. "I'll think about Jilo later. If only I knew where my—"

Transfer magic buffeted them, forcing them back. Murial, then Erai-Yanya, appeared in the middle of the multi-colored rag rug. Hibern, Clair, and her friends stilled as the greenish-gray complexions of the women mottled. Erai-Yanya swallowed convulsively, and Murial leaned down, hands on her knees as her breath shuddered.

"Aunt Murial!" Clair said, voice high with relief. "Where have you been all this time? Were you in the cave?"

The woman leaned against the archway decorated with clumsily drawn patterns of leaves and four-fold flowers, echoing the time-blurred carvings Hibern had noticed in the archways of that amazing palace on the mountain.

"No," Murial said hoarsely, wiped her shaking hand over her eyes. She cleared her throat, and began again. "Erai-Yanya and I were in Chwahirsland. Then transferred back to the palace before coming here. I would swear we were in Chwahirsland scarcely a turn of the finger glass, but night has fallen."

"Chwahirsland?" Clair repeated, her face blanched nearly as pale as her hair. "Why?"

"We thought to discover something of use, even if only a map indicating Wan-Edhe's plans. But all the books are written in the language of dark magic, and worse, the wards are lethal, far more layered than either of us have experience with."

Clair let her breath out in a long sigh. "Puddlenose told us a long time ago that you need magical protections to survive walking those halls."

Everybody looked at each other, then at Jilo, who was in the process of being dragged away by Puddlenose.

Clair pointed to Jilo's loose hands bumping over the ground before they vanished downward around the corner. She said slowly, "Jilo wears an onyx ring. That must be his protection."

Murial said, "Queen Lammog's spell only gains us access. I'm not the least surprised that moving about requires protection. Just standing there was as much as I could bear."

"I'm going back to Bereth Ferian to report everything we saw to the northern mages," Erai-Yanya said. *And to search the records for explanation of that palace on a cloud.* "As soon as I can stand another long transfer."

Murial was still thumbing her eyes, then dropped her hands. "And I had better see to replacing the border protections that Wan-Edhe destroyed."

They all knew that 'protections' in light magic were really not much better than tracers, warning spells when dark magic has been done. But warning was better than ignorance.

One of Clair's friends brought the two women cups of listerblossom steep.

They drank, exchanged looks, braced themselves in a way that ignited a visceral reaction in the others familiar with magic transfer, then with soft pops of air, they vanished.

Hibern said to Clair, "I don't know how much help this would be, but Senrid knows dark magic."

Senrid's name usually brought either blank looks, or grimaces of distrust.

To Hibern's surprise, Clair's demeanor brightened. "Senrid! Of course! He was a great help against Siamis. Sartora told us how he helped keep her out of Siamis's clutches."

CJ crossed her arms, scowling. "I still don't trust him," she muttered, and while Hibern knew it was a rational response, she couldn't prevent a pulse of resentment.

Clair turned to Hibern. "You know Senrid, don't you? Aren't you from his country? Should we ask him for help?"

Nothing was going as expected, but that didn't mean Hibern couldn't think ahead. Senrid expressed as much contempt for light magic workers as they did for him; he wouldn't be taught by any of them. Though Hibern wouldn't be a full mage for years, he'd asked her to tutor him. "You'll teach me what I need to know without all the blabber about high-mindedness and oh-we-are-so-pure," he'd said, his expression caustic.

And Hibern remembered that the Mearsieans had sheltered his younger cousin, refusing to send her back even after Senrid defeated his uncle.

Hibern blinked, and turned to Clair. "First. About Senrid's cousin Ndand . . ."

". . . and so that's it," Hibern finished relating to Senrid.

Senrid had listened in silence, his fingers pressed against his eyes, one of which was now completely closed. "I guess I could help. Clair isn't so bad. I talked to her a little up north, when we were running from Siamis. She was a whole lot less annoying than the rest of those magic school mages." He looked up, his puffy, bruised face making his expression difficult to read. "But she never sent my cousin home."

"That's next." Hibern flicked her fingers open, showing Senrid an open palm. "I asked about that, last thing. Your cousin Ndand isn't even in Mearsies Heili. She left. Went somewhere else, to study music."

Senrid struggled painfully up on one elbow. "Where? I can—"

Hibern said, "Ndand made Clair promise not to tell . . . anyone where she was going."

"Nobody besides me would ask," Senrid retorted, collapsing back again. In spite of the nasal plumminess of his voice, he still retained enough wit for that. "Tell who?"

"You," Hibern said, hating the conversation. But she and Senrid had always promised the truth to one another. Both had dealt with far too many lies. She hastened on. "Clair wanted you to know this, though. You aren't the problem. It's Ndand's father, your uncle. She's afraid he'll reappear from Norsunder. That you can't hold the kingdom against him. I'm sorry, Senrid."

He said with an attempt at briskness that didn't fool either of them, "At least I know Ndand's still alive. All right. As soon as I sleep off this kinthus. Right now I don't think

I could walk across a room, much less smash my way past dark magic wards. But I'll go to Chwahirsland. You if anyone would know why."

Hibern grimaced. Her own father had been an associate of this wretched King of the Chwahir, through whom he'd obtained the experimental mind control spells that the former regent had asked for. *If* Senrid could get into a citadel that no one had broached for at least a century, Hibern made a mental note to ask the details of Queen Lammog's Back Door, and make certain Senrid knew them.

"Come back tomorrow," Senrid said. "It might already be too late, but . . ." He made a weary movement, flicking his fingers.

"Tomorrow," Hibern repeated, and left.

Outside Senrid's room, she drew in a deep breath. Her head panged. Three long transfers in one very long day, and two more ahead. But she'd promised. This was to be her future, if she wanted to be a mage. She had to get used to it.

Anyway, she was just as glad to get away from the hurt that Senrid had tried to hide about his cousin.

Clair had given Hibern her medallion-necklace, bespelled to transfer one directly back to the girls' underground hideout.

When she recovered, Hibern blinked away the tiny stars at the edge of her vision, a warning that she'd been using too much transfer magic. One more, she thought. One more. "Senrid is going to go with me tomorrow." She held out the necklace.

"We got Jilo's ring," Clair said, taking the medallion back from Hibern, then pointing to where a glinting black circle lay on top of a small bookcase.

"I'll return tomorrow, then," Hibern said.

And transferred back to Roth Drael, where she found Erai-Yanya had arrived ahead of her. The senior mage was in the midst of slicing bread and cheese.

"There you are," Erai-Yanya said cheerfully, using the knife handle to brush back an unruly lock of brown hair from her tumbling bun. "I knew those girls wouldn't stay up north in safety. Clair is just like her aunt. Murial was always dashing off home when we were mage students, mostly to rescue her appalling siblings."

Hibern suspected the cheerful talk was meant to distract her from thinking about Marloven Hess. Every mention of home or family hurt, and she suspected would always hurt.

Erai-Yanya pushed a plate of sliced fruit and fresh bread toward Hibern, saying, "For now Wan-Edhe is gone, though if Norsunder has him, he will no doubt be sent back at the worst time."

She glanced at the day glass on its pedestal in the corner, and the hour or two of sands left to trickle through before dawn, and added prosaically, "But not today. So. While you were on your errand, I did my duty and reported to Oalthoreh at the northern school. She said she would pass my report to the Sartoran mages." Erai-Yanya gestured southward with her bread, and then glanced down at her sash, and the knot still tied in it. "You were there when I tied this, right? So much was going on I forgot why I tied it. Can you remember what it was I was supposed to do?"

Hibern gazed in surprise. She knew about Erai-Yanya's habit of tying a knot somewhere to help her remember something she needed to do. But she'd always remembered the knots. "Was it about Wan-Edhe?"

"It must have been," Erai-Yanya said, in a dissatisfied tone. She untied it and smoothed the worn fabric. "So that's that."

"Not quite," Hibern said, and told her what she, Clair, and Senrid had decided, ending, "And so, whatever Senrid learns, he said he'd share. Like everyone keeps saying, our ignorance is the enemy's first weapon. And I have no idea why, because Mearsies Heili is so small, with no strategic importance whatsoever, but Clair said that this wasn't the first time Wan-Edhe moved against them."

'Strategic importance.' Erai-Yanya knew that Hibern wasn't thinking magically, but militarily. She drank some fresh berry juice to hide her grimace. Hibern could not help her upbringing any more than Gwasan had, all those years before.

Gwasan had had the habit of making similar remarks, until she learned better. During their student days, she,

Murial, and Gwasan had covered for one another when they'd felt the necessity to steal away in spite of the strict rules. Murial had invariably returned home to deal with whatever disasters her siblings were causing their father, who had had four children over a number of years, all by different mothers.

Gwasan's private excursions had always stayed private, until she left the school for the last time, an assassin from home right behind her.

Erai-Yanya's private expeditions had been ventures into magical experiments that she knew she was ready for, but that the school's strict ladder of permissions forbade.

All three had had what they considered vital reasons for breaking the rules. In retrospect, out of all of them, her own were probably the most dangerous and least well-thought-out, which had proved to Erai-Yanya that the rules were there for a reason.

So when she had taken on this Marloven student, who would have been summarily rejected by both schools because of her birth kingdom, Erai-Yanya had made a vow to avoid setting rules in favor of talking out situations, especially as Hibern had been used to struggling against a nearly impossible situation on her own.

As a result, Hibern talked to her. Erai-Yanya prided herself on that. But there were times when she was not as forthcoming in return. This was one of those times; she knew how Hibern would react if she pointed out how adamant both mage schools would be about preventing Senrid of Marloven Hess from gaining access to what probably was the best collection of concentrated evil intent in the world. So she just said, "Senrid wants to explore in the Chwahir capital?"

Hibern nicked her chin toward her collarbones, fighting impatience. Erai-Yanya wasn't forbidding her, but her long silence, followed by the question in the carefully neutral tone of adults, meant distrust.

It was a justified distrust, Hibern had to admit. If you didn't know Senrid. He'd been raised to think violence the first tool of kings, and when Hibern first met him, they had been enemies. But he had slowly, painfully, begun to change.

"He's in no shape to be raiding Wan-Edhe's library for evil magic, if that's what you're thinking," Hibern said.

"Even if he wanted such. He doesn't. He's seen the cost. Lived it. He really does think in terms of defense, knowing what your enemy is capable of. And the enemy he fears is not his neighbors but Norsunder."

Erai-Yanya exerted herself to sound approving. "That is an excellent idea, actually. So excellent that, rather than train you in Queen Lammog's Back Door, which is complicated and dangerous, partaking of dark magic, I'll go with you. Also because we still cannot explain why Murial and I were gone no more than the turn of the finger glass, but returned several hours later. So I'm going to prepare a time candle."

Hibern exclaimed, "Oh, what a good idea."

Erai-Yanya shook her head. "Everything this day has been disturbing. Some mysterious connection between the Chwahir and Norsunder? Some kind of artifact that swallows a group of people? I have deep misgivings about powerful ancient relics suddenly turning up, when we've gone centuries without 'em."

Busy, determined, the two turned their minds to all these problems, and once again the mystery of the white palace sank below the surface of their thoughts, and faded out of memory.

The day following, Hibern again endured the long transfer to Marloven Hess, though she had misgivings about Senrid's ability to sit up, much less sustain a magic transfer. However, a promise was a promise.

But when she was conducted to his study, there he sat, squinting down at some papers with his one good eye, an empty cup beside his hand. His other eye was swollen shut. His hands looked as raw and bruised and swollen as his face. Hibern smelled listerblossom in the air.

"Are we still doing this?" he asked, his voice plummy.

"Erai-Yanya is already in the Chwahir capital, with Clair."

"You have transfer tokens? I can't make any right now."

She frowned. "Senrid, are you able to transfer? You look—"

"I know what I look like. Let's go."

Transfer magic is always jolting. The farther one goes,

the stronger the wrench, though no more time elapses; the distance is felt in the transfer reaction. When you add magical spells forcing past wards, it doubles the intensity.

Hibern and Senrid both emerged staggering. Hibern shut her eyes and gulped for breath, aware of a sour tinge to the air, the smell of a tightly closed room with heaps of old laundry and unwashed bedding, and under that the metallic nastiness of layers of dark magic.

She felt the last tremors of transfer reaction fade rapidly, and turned her head to discover Senrid leaning against the wall, fingers splayed against it, both eyes shut. The little portion of his face that had not been bruised looked distinctly greenish in the pale light of a glowglobe.

She tried to find words to ask if he was all right—words that would not get her nose snapped off—but then his good eye opened, and he said, "Where?"

They turned, to meet the twin shocked gazes of Clair and Erai-Yanya taking in Senrid's battered condition, the thin flame of Erai-Yanya's time candle reflecting in their eyes. But Erai-Yanya was by nature an observer, and seldom spoke before those she didn't trust—and Clair knew how much Senrid hated being weak.

So she only pointed to the inner room, the thick, moldy lour curling its vapors in her throat if she tried to speak.

Senrid walked slowly into what had to be a magic chamber, his hands held out, fingers spread as he used every sense to detect lethal wards. This was certainly a place to expect lethal wards.

And there were. Erai-Yanya had brought an old quill to test for further wards and traps. A long table dominated the room, which was otherwise bare stone age-darkened with mold in the grouting. Around three sides, bookshelves extended nearly to the ceiling, and it was to these Erai-Yanya moved first, testing with her feather, as Senrid drifted toward the table, looking down at the books lying there, some open. It was clear that Wan-Edhe had expected to return.

Senrid began muttering, and the greenish flash of magic strengthened the metallic singe in the air, then all four sensed a chain of wards breaking. A chain. So much magic potential bound for such little purpose.

Senrid rapped the table lightly with his fingertips, and when nothing happened, Erai-Yanya set her little hour candle down in its wooden holder. The flame burned steadily, sometimes flashing greenish, and once, a disturbing blue.

Erai-Yanya thought sourly that that bruised-looking bluish flame was Wan-Edhe's effect on the world in living metaphor. Clair wondered if there was anything in this terrible place that could help them ward against Wan-Edhe when he came back (because she didn't believe for a moment he was gone forever—of course Norsunder would send him back) and Senrid faced the realization that this situation was far beyond his knowledge. He should be studying harder, but when would he find the time?

Erai-Yanya cautiously extended her quill toward the books on the shelves, then lowered her arm and glanced Senrid's way. "Can you remove any wards on these?"

Senrid took a step toward the bookshelves, one hand out, then shook his head. "Only the ones I know. But it'll take time. Every book is separately warded. And there are traps beneath 'em. On top of 'em. And . . ." He raised his head, squinting up at the top shelves. "I think there are even more up there."

Clair pointed at the table. "These must be the books he was using before he invaded Mearsies Heili. What are they?"

"That's what I want to find out." Senrid moved back to the table. "That one seems to be written in Chwahir, I guess, as I've never seen the alphabet. This one here is . . . dark magic. I recognize some of the words . . ."

He looked back at the one written in Chwahir, switching his gaze between the two books. "This one is his experiment book, or one of his experiment books," he said slowly, with an air of uncertainty as he touched the book.

Erai-Yanya eyed him, as questions bloomed in her mind. "You know Chwahir after all?"

"No. But these words are all in Sartoran, the version used for dark magic. And I can see the same number of letters in sentences here and here. Patterns, you might say. So I'm assuming he's chained experiments onto these spells. Experiments."

"What type of experiments?"

Senrid flashed a quick look her way. It was easy to see

that she didn't trust him as far as she could throw a mountain.

Hibern and Clair saw him hesitate, though his distorted face gave even less clue to his thoughts than usual. Then he shrugged, and bent over the dark magic book.

The others waited, Clair trying not to breathe too deeply in the poisonous lour, until they understood that he was done talking. Hibern and Clair both suspected the reason, and Clair cast a speculative look Erai-Yanya's way.

The mage sensed the Marloven boy shutting her out, and turned to examine the shelves, to hide her disgust. She had spent a night digging out all her notes from her days of study with Gwasan and Murial, before Wan-Edhe killed Gwasan. She knew she only had a partial list of spells to remove traps and wards, but she began to try those, as behind her, Senrid leafed through the experiment book.

Erai-Yanya successfully removed three wards before she nearly killed herself in a trap. She sensed the building of magic as internal heat, then Senrid snapped, "Don't!"

Erai-Yanya had already abandoned the spell a heartbeat before he spoke, but she said gravely, "Thank you," as an oblique truce.

He heard it as typical lighter condescension, suspecting she'd made a judgment about evil Marlovens before he'd even turned up. Or else why was she even here? It was Hibern who'd asked him to come.

Hibern glanced between them, understanding that nothing was going to be learned. Meanwhile, her head throbbed. "This air is making me sick," she said.

At the same time, Erai-Yanya pointed to the time candle. "It's nearly gone. I think we'd better go." She rubbed her temples, forgetting the quill in her hand, which jabbed her in the ear. Her breath hissed out.

Senrid had been studying the experiment book. He backed away, and approached Clair. "Didn't Puddlenose talk about a boy our age who was Wan-Edhe's current target?"

"Jilo is sort of an heir, but mostly like a hostage," Clair said. "Wan-Edhe would never have a real heir. He wants to live forever."

Senrid snorted in contempt, then muttered, "If you trust the hostage, then tell him to take a look at that page right there, all set up for renewal. I think . . . I'm not sure . . . I think it's the sort of mind control spells my uncle was messing around with. The patterns are familiar—I'm almost certain my uncle got that magic from Wan-Edhe, or his brother."

He stopped then, aware of Erai-Yanya and Hibern looking his way.

"Wan-Edhe and your uncle were allies?" Erai-Yanya asked, eyes stark.

"No," Senrid said shortly.

Clair said peaceably, "Prince Kwenz and Senrid's uncle traded magic books. But that's all I know."

Hibern put in, "Makes no sense to have an alliance, as Marloven Hess and Chwahirsland lie at opposite ends of the continent."

Senrid had gone back to studying the two books, then carefully fingered his good eye, blinking several times.

"I think we are done here," Erai-Yanya said, and waited until Senrid was safely gone before transferring home.

When they recovered, all four got quite a shock: the time candle had been set for half an hour . . . but the entire day had vanished.

Chapter Five

Mearsies Heili, the Junky

NOW I must introduce one who will become an important member of the Young Allies, though no one, he least of all, would have thought of a Chwahir being anyone's ally. Being accepted as anyone's ally.

Another quake rolled through Mearsies Heili.

Jilo, son of Quartermaster Dzan, had been chosen by old Prince Kwenz Sonscarna of the Chwahir for his meticulous bookkeeping and excellent handwriting. Perhaps the old man had seen something of himself in the boy, or perhaps he merely chose him out of idleness, but he'd been training Jilo in magic as well as in running the outpost. He'd even enjoyed sitting up in his magic library, talking about the fundamentals of magic with Jilo, who couldn't get enough of magic studies.

Now, Jilo sat against the dirt wall of the Mearsieans' underground hideout, hands tied behind his back and ankles bound, his head throbbing and his heart beating in his ears as the cave bedchamber around him rumbled. Rocks ground in the walls and dirt ceiling above his head, and tree roots creaked and shivered.

But again, no dirt sifted down from the smooth ceiling, and no roots broke through the walls decorated with pictures. The rumble subsided, as had the many before it. The Mearsieans might be weak and sentimental, their light magic as strong as candle wax, but their spells seemed to be holding this cave chamber together.

Jilo had been trying to puzzle out what had happened, but thought seemed to come slower than ever, a jumble of confusing memories that seemed to have no connection. He tried unsuccessfully to ease his aching arms, then gave up with a sigh.

The world seemed to be nothing but contradiction. Prince Kwenz and his brother Wan-Edhe had both lectured Jilo about how the waxers were stupid, weak, and sentimental, and deserving of being conquered. The Chwahir rulers despised as sentimental and weak those who practiced light magic. The term 'waxer' had started out as slang for the lowest of the low—usually women—who followed nighttime military parades, scraping up the wax drippings from torches, to be used again, dirty as it was.

Worst of all waxers were these Mearsiean brats, entirely ignorant about military discipline or training, and yet they ran around free. They'd even managed to make this underground hideout, which Jilo envied, and wanted almost as much as he'd wanted to be left alone to his studies and sketches.

And here he was.

But a prisoner.

"They are stupid," Wan-Edhe had said repeatedly.

Jilo knew the Mearsieans weren't stupid. The weakness was debatable. Or maybe that was his excuse for his own failures against them. And he *had* failed. He was still alive only because he'd always done what he was told. Another truism of life among the Chwahir was that heirs weren't exempt from extreme disciplinary measures should they disobey orders, or make mistakes.

Especially heirs, for Wan-Edhe had no true heirs, having systematically killed off his entire family save only Kwenz, his brother, and Prince Kessler, who had escaped at a young age—though not young enough to keep a hold on sanity, from all accounts. Wan-Edhe fully intended to live forever. He'd held Chwahirsland in his ever-tighter grip for more than eighty years.

Though Kwenz was the elder, he'd always deferred to Wan-Edhe, which was probably the single reason he was still alive. If he was still alive. The last thing Jilo remembered was Prince Kwenz being sent to do some kind of magic in support of his brother's latest attack against the Mearsieans, though the frail old man could barely move, these days. Jilo had used the chance to nip into the forbidden magic chambers for some unsupervised study, but then there was this loud, grinding noise, the castle stones shifting, and his stool had tipped over, pitching him backward.

Then he woke tied up in this chamber, where he'd been ever since. Except when Puddlenose brought meals, untied him, and lounged in the doorway, sword in hand, until he finished eating. Then it was back to handkerchiefs around wrists and ankles and another stretch of bone-aching tedium. At least he'd been able to feel that lump on the back of his head, and that it was going down.

Jilo tried to ease his stiff neck, stilling as a small quake shivered the cave around him. He sat with his back against the cave wall, his head uncomfortably bent forward to avoid bumping the tender spot on his head against the smooth dirt wall.

He sat between a clothes trunk decorated with painted flowers and a shelf containing ornaments. The Mearsieans didn't even seem to have a prison, at least not in this cave hideout, for they'd stuck him in a bedroom.

He didn't know how long he'd been a prisoner, not that it mattered. Jilo didn't want to think of what disciplinary measures Wan-Edhe would deem suitable for a Chwahir who had let himself get captured. He knew only that if he survived, the punishment would last a long time.

Maybe Clair was trying a hostage exchange. Jilo could have told her it was futile, that Wan-Edhe would sooner see him dead.

Let the Mearsieans find out the hard way. His report to Wan-Edhe would have to begin with scoffing about the ruffle-edged cover on the bed over there, and the awkwardly drawn sketches of animals and people affixed to the dirt walls. Waxer sentiment was also evident in the fact the girl the room belonged to had set the single candle high on a shelf so it wouldn't worry at Jilo's magically altered eyes.

Clair's cousin Puddlenose was another contradiction. Jilo couldn't understand anyone who'd keep a ridiculous name because (he said) it was so much fun to see officious clerks writing it out. Puddlenose seemed to regard that shameful, humiliating name as a badge of triumph.

The kind of mind finding triumph in that was as incomprehensible as the Mearsiean perceptions of the Chwahir. Jilo could not reconcile them. His head hurt inside as well as outside when he tried. How could the Mearsieans laugh at Wan-Edhe's given name, Shnit, one passed down by many Chwahir kings? In Chwahirsland it was now dreaded so much that no one whispered it out loud, as if he had spells that spied if anyone said his name, the way Norsunder was supposed to have. *Everyone* referred to Shnit Sonscarna as Wan-Edhe, *The* King.

While Jilo stewed as their prisoner, in the tunnel directly above him, Clair, CJ, and Puddlenose debated what to do with him.

CJ was in full rant mode. A short, skinny figure even for twelve, she stamped barefooted in a circle around the cousins, who sat on the brightly colored woven rug that covered the smooth cave floor. Nothing about CJ's moods was ever subtle.

". . . and so, I think it's a big mistake to let Jilo go free."

Another quake rumbled through, as if in emphasis to her words. Instinctively they all looked up, though all they could see was the dirt ceiling overhead, marbled by tree roots.

"That one was different," Clair said. "I'd better check."

"Again," CJ sighed.

Clair heard the sighed word a heartbeat before the transfer took her. She could understand CJ's puzzlement. Clair wasn't sure why she had to keep checking. There was nothing she could do, and for such a monumentally dramatic event, there actually wasn't much to see: the white palace seemed undamaged, as far as she could tell, and all one could see of the city was a lot of white fog extending eastward from Mount Marcus. A fog that was lower every time she looked at it.

With Clair gone, CJ scowled down at Puddlenose, who lounged in the middle of the brightly colored patchwork rug on the smooth dirt floor. "You shouldn't have brought Jilo here," she said, fists on her hips.

He only shrugged. As usual. He rarely took anything seriously—not with a wild past like his. He didn't even have a real name, or at least if he did, it had long ago been forgotten, along with his real parents. Puddlenose had heard nothing but insults from Wan-Edhe from his earliest memories, the one used most—for a sniveling, frightened little boy—having been Puddlenose.

After CJ had stamped around the edge of the rug three times, she pointed to the floor, below which their prisoner sat. "I just wish Jilo wasn't *here*. For one thing, I'm scared Clair is going to just let him go."

"What else should she do? Execute him?"

"That would make us just like the Chwahir," CJ retorted. "I think, oh, we should find some spell and turn him into a petunia for a hundred years. Let someone else worry about what to do with him."

At Puddlenose's skeptical look, she relented. "Ten years, maybe. Look, you know as well as I do that Jilo is nothing better than a villain- in-training."

Puddlenose shrugged. "Don't know anything of the kind."

CJ scoffed. "He's a friend?"

Puddlenose shrugged again. "Don't know what to call it, except maybe a truce. Once or twice. When Wan-Edhe had us both under death threats."

CJ scowled down at the rug.

"It was either truce or—" Puddlenose drew a finger across his neck. "And we talked. Sort of. And he looked the other way when I escaped. I don't claim to know much of what he thinks, but I do know he hates Norsunder as much as we do."

CJ jerked her skinny shoulders up and down. "So he hates the eleveners! That just makes sense. But what about us? If we let him go, what's to stop him from coming after us just like Wan-Edhe has sixty billion times?"

"Ben doesn't think Jilo will," Puddlenose said, glancing around the room for the boy who could shape-change into birds or animals. "Ben's the one who listened to Kwenz and Jilo most."

CJ's scowl eased for about a heartbeat. She liked and trusted the boy who had spied on the Chwahir for Clair, but Ben wasn't present in either boy or beast shape.

CJ crossed her arms. "What you want to bet Ben's not coming anywhere near the hideout until we get rid of Jilo, any more than the girls are coming out of their rooms?"

Her goading tone caused nothing more than another shrug. Puddlenose was used to CJ's moods. He thought of them as personal thunderstorms, loud and messy for a time, then soon gone.

"Jilo is our responsibility."

The two turned at the sound of Clair's voice. She walked down the tunnel and plopped on the rug beside her cousin. "As far as I can tell, the cloud city seems to have settled along the east side of the mountain and a ways beyond."

Puddlenose said, "Who wants to bet your plateau was what got lifted into the air in the first place?"

"I think it is too obvious for betting," Clair said in her careful way. "As far as I can tell, many of the buildings lost their windows, and probably glass things inside, and the streets are a jumble of brick and cobblestone. But everything else is still there."

"The white palace?"

"Not even a window broken," Clair said, and returned inexorably to the issue at hand. "Anyway, I think it's time to let Jilo go. I don't see what else we can do."

CJ smacked her hands over her face. "Let him *go*?"

Clair said, "But we don't have to tell him everything—"

"We shouldn't tell him *anything*," CJ burst out, and around they went again.

Clair knew the argument was going in circles, but that was often the only way to achieve consensus. She could see she wasn't going to get it this time.

Everyone knew the final decision was hers, so when she got to her feet, CJ and Puddlenose both fell silent.

Clair said, "I can't do a wrong thing just because I think Jilo might."

She took a step in the direction of the tunnel leading to the lower levels, then paused, arms lifting wide as another strong quake rolled through.

"Wow," CJ exclaimed. "It's been, what, three years? Four? Since I escaped from Earth, and I know you said that magic is supposed to take away the dangerous quakes, but those things still scare me."

"I don't see why the people of Earth don't control quakes with magic," Puddlenose said as they tramped down the tunnel, which curved around, with rooms leading off to the left and right; as they passed, a couple of Clair's gang peered out, saw where they were going, and vanished again behind their tapestry doors.

CJ grimaced. "Reason five thousand four hundred and thirty-two why I hate remembering living on Earth: no magic."

"I find that so hard to believe." Puddlenose shook his head. "No magic. Huh."

"But plenty of smog." CJ snorted.

They reached the flower-and-vine tapestry door to the room Jilo was kept in. CJ and Puddlenose stood aside so that Clair could remove the ward spell protecting the doorway. It vanished with a flash of glittery light, then the tapestry that served in place of a door was batted aside.

Jilo lifted his head and squinted their way as Puddlenose entered, his tanned, square face—usually good-humored, even in a scrap—rueful. At his shoulder was Clair, square-faced like her cousin, but there the resemblance ended. Most noticeable was that weird white hair.

Last came CJ, shorter even than Clair, scrawny and glowering. CJ was, and looked, ready for verbal battle. Jilo hated her more than all the rest of Clair's irritating, obnoxious gang of girls.

"A lot has happened," Clair said abruptly. "I'll start with what everyone knows: your king is gone."

As always, as soon as the enemy was nearby, Jilo found it difficult to think, even difficult to see. It was like thoughts were reduced to one or two fireflies bumbling around in fog. The more he tried to follow them, the worse they winked in and out of existence.

"What?" Jilo couldn't help it. He saw the contempt in

CJ's face, emphasized by the scornful crimp in her black brows, but it was no stronger than the contempt surging through him. Why couldn't he think? He really was as stupid as Wan-Edhe constantly claimed.

Clair looked doubtfully down at their prisoner, who stared back, his magically altered eyes squinting, which was a mercy. At least when he squinted they didn't have to see that unnatural blackness, as if he were an empty shell containing only darkness. She didn't like to think that about anyone, but it was hard to tell your mind not to notice what your eyes saw.

Puddlenose said, "Clair asked me to go to the Shadowland under white flag to look for you or Kwenz. And tell your people to evacuate. Kwenz was dead, someone said. Dropped down clutching his heart when the quakes started. I found you lying in Kwenz's book room. So I brought you here."

"As what?" Jilo found his voice. "Wan-Edhe wouldn't trade for my life."

"Wan-Edhe," Clair repeated, "is gone."

"And so is the Shadowland," CJ said in a gloating voice from behind Clair's shoulder.

"Gone?" Jilo repeated, wincing as a pang shot through his forehead. He tried to recapture the sense that he'd been here before, that the conversation had come full circle.

"Squashed flat." CJ clapped her hands, grinning smugly. "The cloud city came down on top of it. All your people skedaddled."

He became aware of the quick patter of footsteps, and opened his eyes to discover a thin, shaggy-haired brown boy more or less CJ's age. Ben was dressed in a rumpled gray lace-up tunic and old, baggy gray kneepants, his feet bare. Ben didn't like to admit to strangers that he could shape-change. He was not about to tell Jilo that he'd been wearing the form of an eagle; that he'd seen Jilo fall, and if Puddlenose hadn't found him, Ben would have seen to it that he'd be found.

"Kessler came for Wan-Edhe. Straight out of Eleven-Land," Puddlenose said.

Eleven-Land, Jilo knew, was the waxer euphemism for Norsunder. He still didn't know why they called it that, and on impulse said, "Why?"

Three faces looked at him as if he'd sprouted wings. "Why what?"

"You say 'eleven' for Norsunder. I've heard you."

Clair's face reddened, and she looked away. Definitely a euphemism, then.

Puddlenose said, "Insult."

Clair glanced at him, then said earnestly, "My aunt says that Norsunder used the number themselves, at first, as a kind of nasty hit against the Ancient Sartoran Twelve Blessed Things. They were going to destroy them one by one. But they never got past eleven for some reason or other, maybe the Fall of Ancient Sartor."

"Or maybe our side lost count," Puddlenose said cheerfully. "At least, if anyone knows what those Twelve Blessed Things are, they do seem to be pretty much . . ." He drew his finger across his throat and made a squelching noise.

Clair finished, "So 'eleven' became the word to say if you didn't like to speak of Norsunder. It's bad manners in some places."

Jilo had asked because he wanted to know if they would answer. Having no interest in Norsunder, old theories of magic, blessed things, or bad words, his thoughts went straight to Prince Kessler, who was the only person Jilo found more terrifying than Wan-Edhe. Warning tightened his neck. Kwenz dead, and Wan-Edhe now in Norsunder? Wan-Edhe had always claimed autonomy from Norsunder, hiding in his fortress protected by decades of carefully interlocked, deadly wards.

But though he was a powerful mage in his own right, eventually you had to pay. Norsunder never forgot bargains.

"Does that mean Norsunder is taking over Chwahirsland?" Jilo asked, though why he asked the Mearsieans, he wasn't sure. But his thoughts seemed to come from farther away than ever, now more like little wormy things groping around in the dark, and less like flies.

"Not yet," Clair said. "But this is what we know," she said, gesturing for Puddlenose to loosen the bonds around Jilo's wrists. "Right now, the Land of the Chwahir has no one on the throne."

Jilo's head felt like it did when someone clapped him

over the ears, only this was worse, like an invisible vise was squashing his brain.

Jilo's hands were now free.

Puddlenose tossed the binding onto the bed, and stood back against the curved door frame, his arms folded, the old enemy. Though once or twice, just for survival, they'd had almost what could have been called a truce. Never acknowledged by either afterward.

Jilo hesitated, then with a mental shrug reached to untie his ankles. The Mearsieans didn't stop him.

"There's no place for you here," Clair said. "I think most of Kwenz's warriors left the Shadowland, under the command of someone from Chwahirsland. They crowded onto the ships the invaders brought from Chwahirsland, and sailed away on this morning's tide."

Jilo felt the last knot give, and he kicked free of the silk. He looked up. "Wan-Edhe will come back if he can."

CJ crossed her arms, her scowl now a glare. "We know. But if we smell that grunge-bearded old geez, we'll be ready." She flexed her bare toes and made a kicking motion.

Clair said, "In the meantime, let me point out again that there's no one on the throne in Chwahirsland."

"Prince Kessler has to be there," Jilo said.

Clair said, "As of yesterday, no one is. Some friends went to scout, but they only stayed a short time, because there are so many wards and traps. In spite of this." Clair held out a small black circle, and Jilo felt at the base of his little finger.

He hadn't even noticed his ring was gone. Jilo blinked at her as he slid the ring back into place. Though he was taller than the Mearsiean girls, roughly the same age as Puddlenose, Clair and her noisy, irritating gang had always managed to combine and defeat him when he'd tried to find and take this hideout, a perfect retreat where Wan-Edhe would never have found him.

His private conviction was that Clair's gang was more like a Chwahir *twi*—a group of eight, the fundamental unit of Chwahir life—than the false twi, spies all, that Wan-Edhe had formed around Jilo. Now all gone, leaving him to be found by an enemy.

Jilo retrieved enough thought-flies to realize he'd been staring.

His heart thumped as he stood uncertainly, waiting for their laughter if he tried to make a break for the door. What then, the knife? That was a favorite ploy among the Chwahir, to let prisoners think they'd escaped just long enough to make it really hurt when they were brought down again. And again. And again, until they gave up.

So he stared at his enemies, and the enemies stared at his strange black eyes with no hint of white, his lips chapped from too much biting, his greasy black hair hanging lank and unkempt on his brow.

Clair took a step back, holding her hand out toward the doorway.

Jilo took one step. Then another. A third. He heard CJ mutter to Clair, "It seems so weird to let a villain just go."

A villain. She meant him. Jilo snorted. A meaningless term, 'villain'—at least, when applied to someone like Jilo, who had always done what he'd been told, and tried to survive. Villains were Norsundrians, the ones with power, the ones who tried to take whole worlds, who consumed souls. Or they were Clair's gang, so galling with their fast talk and incomprehensible private jokes and smug superiority about their underground hideout.

Five, six, eight steps . . . Twenty. Jilo passed CJ, who held her nose, her fierce blue eyes a scowl above the pinching fingers. Much as he despised her, her obvious hatred was oddly steadying. He didn't trust anything else about this situation, but he could trust her hatred to be real.

Clair said, "Before you go, I'd like to ask you a question."

Jilo shrugged. Here was the expected ploy, the slammed door, the real end. "See me stopping you?"

"Are you coming back here with an army?" Clair asked.

Jilo snorted a humorless laugh. "If I understand you, the Shadowland is now crushed under your city. Kwenz is dead, everyone else gone."

Unless she meant . . . She couldn't mean . . . They all expected him to transfer halfway around the world, walk in and take the throne of Chwahirsland itself.

The magnitude of the idea defeated him at first, and he stared at the floor, trying to think, and found that—as always—when he needed clear thought, it would not come.

He looked up. Clair stood before him, waiting.

He remembered her question.

A few facts squirmed their way to consciousness. He said, "It never made any sense to come months' journey by ship just to take this tiny country."

"No," Clair said.

"But that never stopped King Beardo the Stink in Human Form," CJ put in.

"Prince Kwenz said that that was Wan-Edhe's preoccupation with the old enmity between the Chwahir and Tser Mearsies," Jilo said. "I think. If he had any other purpose, he never shared it."

The Mearsieans stood in silence while he grasped that the old goal had gone with Wan-Edhe. He didn't have to do *anything* that Wan-Edhe had ordered.

He was free.

So he said, "No. I would not."

Clair nodded. "Then I have something to tell you. In Wan-Edhe's magic chambers, Senrid, one of the people who went there yesterday, said there is a book on the big table, open to a page you ought to see, first thing."

Jilo found no point in saying anything more. He gathered his concentration enough to make a short transfer spell, to the usual Destination point at the base of Mount Marcus, at the edge of the Shadowland.

The transfer worked, leaving him with the usual vertigo. He blinked, breathing deeply, his eyes tearing up from the strong sunlight. He raised a hand to shade them as best he could, and squinted around.

Instead of the long stretch of darkness to the east, shrouded by the dense vapor-bounded city above, he perceived the sloping line of the mountain, visible in the bright sunlight. Terraced down the east side, the tile rooftops clearly visible from where he stood, was the Mearsiean capital, roads a jumble of brick and tile. It would take a year to clean that up, he thought.

More important, it had completely buried the Shadowland fortress and its outlying buildings. The Shadowland really was gone. A faint pall of dust still scintillated high in the air, and another tiny quake rolled through.

Jilo stared at the aprons of rockfall that had cascaded down the rest of the mountain, smothering scrubby brush. This was all that was left of Kwenz's castle. All Kwenz's belongings. All Jilo's, not that he'd owned much beside the clothes he stood up in. Chwahir prentices were always dependent on their masters. Now all of it was gone.

Where were Kwenz's servants? Though Wan-Edhe would have had no compunctions about squashing them under a mountainside—in fact, he would have enjoyed the prospect— Jilo suspected that the waxers would have a moral objection to crushing enemies who hadn't been on the attack. Oh, yes, Puddlenose had said something about scuttling in all directions.

Now Jilo understood what that meant: the Mearsieans had gone through the Shadowland chasing people out while the cloud was descending.

Jilo squinted up the mountain, the daylight painful on his magically altered eyes. Tears leaked down his cheeks, but he ignored them as he studied the few spires of Clair's castle that were visible from this vantage, glinting in a sky murderously bright.

Wan-Edhe's harsh voice echoed in his ears, *You have a single goal. One goal! To take that white castle. And you can't even do that.*

And Prince Kwenz's snivelly reply, *You don't understand how much magic is on that castle.* To which Wan-Edhe would snarl, *Of course I do. Which is why I want it!*

Jilo turned away, hating the place all over again. Looking at that glaring whiteness in sunlight was like knives stabbing his eyeballs. He'd have to find the spell to restore his eyes to normal, or he'd go blind.

But first, he had to contemplate the idea that he was free.

He belonged nowhere.

He could do anything. Well, except he had only one skill, magic. According to Wan-Edhe he was incompetent at that, because the white castle on the mountain remained unconquered, in spite of all Prince Kwenz's labors and Jilo's mad studying of wards and how to break them.

He turned around slowly. Southward, grassy hills stretched away into the meadows of No One's Land, buffer between the Shadow and Wesset North, the Mearsiean province. To the west, the green line of the vast woodland that occupied the entire center of the kingdom, somewhere in the center of which lay Clair's underground hideout. To the north, the mountain, bulking above him, and right there on his eastern side, the Mearsiean capital with its jumble of colorful tile roofs dotted the mountainside, connected by broken streets. He couldn't see much beyond that.

Jilo thought of the Land of the Chwahir, vast, desolate, its huge army waiting for its master to return from his latest gambit against his old enemies.

Now no one was there.

He gathered his strength, and concentrated, and made the transfer spell to take him halfway around the world.

Chapter Six

Narad, capital of Chwahirsland

THE transfer room in Wan-Edhe's great fortress was
empty.

Jilo steadied himself on the wall.

Transfer magic was always wrenching, but for some reason, transferring to Narad hurt so very much worse.

When the black spots faded from his vision, he opened
the heavy, iron-reinforced oaken door and took a cautious
peek down the torchlit stone corridor. As always the light
worried at his eyes, sending stabbing pains through his
head, but that was part of life in Narad Fortress. In the
Shadowland castle, Kwenz had kept the torches high, above
his soldiers' lines of sight. Wan-Edhe would never have
made any such accommodation. Flickering light did not
bother *his* eyes, and as long as he was comfortable, anything else was pandering to weakness.

If Norsunder had held the city, Jilo knew he would have
transferred straight into a trap. Perhaps Norsunder was going to permit Wan-Edhe to return if he performed whatever it was they had required of him. A quick look around
disclosed that nothing had changed. The fortress, the city,

the kingdom waited, without the tiniest deviation from standing orders, for Wan-Edhe to return.

Jilo had nowhere else to go. Nothing to do. If Wan-Edhe or Norsunder appeared, he would be dead anyway. So why not see how far he got?

So. The first thing Jilo needed to do was find the spell to restore his eyes to normal. He left the heavy door open and proceeded with care.

Jilo did not know how Clair and her allies had managed to gain entry, but it couldn't have been through the regular transfer room. The way from there to Wan-Edhe's private chambers was so laden with traps that the air felt thick, and smelled of burnt metal. Jilo used one of the secret passages.

How silent the fortress was! It had been afternoon in Mearsies Heili, so it had to be hours short of dawn in Narad, Chwahirsland's capital city.

The weight of stone seemed to press on Jilo's bones. Strange. Jilo had felt no such weight when he was the Mearsieans' prisoner, and yet he'd been underground.

He smelled dust, and mildew, and stone, and steel, and stale sweat: the smells of power, and of fear, familiar as his own hands.

The stone wall of a secret passage slid silently open on judiciously greased pintles. At the top of the narrow stairs, he slid another door open, into an empty corridor leading to rows of uninhabited rooms.

This was the private Sonscarna family wing, where the magical wards had always been thickest, as Wan-Edhe did not trust his own guards in his private quarters. The fortress guard clustered below, company upon company, guarding night and day against an attack that no one had dared to mount since Wan-Edhe had caught his last grandson in a plot, and had him and his twi, and their families' twia, all put to death before the entire city.

Jilo entered the magic chambers. The glowglobes cast blue-white light at the edge of Jilo's tolerance, making that lump at the back of his head throb. The shelves of books seemed untouched, oldest on top, some snow-gray with piled dust. Old records, those. And old lists of proclamations and laws.

On the great work table, just as Clair had said, lay one

of Wan-Edhe's private workbooks. There was the tiny, crabbed handwriting, a combination spellbook and diary, which surprised Jilo. Maybe it shouldn't. The only person Wan-Edhe really trusted besides his dungeon master was himself. Of course he would write a journal about himself. Puddlenose had said once that Wan-Edhe found himself the most interesting, as well as the most important, person in the world. *He is*, Jilo remembered saying. Stupidly. *No, he spends a lot of time and power making you think he is,* Puddlenose had said. And then escaped, yet again, helped by some mysterious mage Puddlenose called Rosey.

Jilo had never been able to escape, much less discover who Rosey was and why he aided Puddlenose. Because he was stupid.

A quill lay at an angle across one page, and all the wards had been lifted from the book. Jilo lifted the quill, and nothing happened. He bent to decipher the writing, which was a mix of dark magic language and Chwahir.

The date was three years previous. Someone had been paging through the book.

Kwenz does not want the loyalty spell on that fool he's training. He will know if I perform it, so I will give the fool this instead. And, after he's proven to be worthless, he will be replaced with someone of my choosing.

'The fool.' Wan-Edhe had never granted anyone the dignity of their name. He'd always issued a label for others, usually diminishing, mostly insulting. Like Puddlenose. Jilo was *the fool*.

Jilo blinked against eyestrain, a headache already throbbing through his skull as he labored to recover his previous thought. Fool? Names? Oh yes. The book. Eyes. Below that bit pointed out by the quill was a notation, the name of a spell. Jilo looked at the book lying next to the great one. It was an older one, slim, its binding cracked. Jilo followed the cryptic notation—categories of numbers—until he found a match to the notation.

He read the antidote to the spell three times, and then—slowly—performed it. The faint snap made him dizzy and skin-prickly, followed rapidly by a rush of sensation so strong that he stumbled backward into Wan-Edhe's big wingchair, which smelled rank with old grime, sweat, and mildew. He breathed through his mouth, his heartbeat loud in his ears. Sensation streamed through his mind, the mental fireflies so plenteous and bright that he became more giddy, not less. He blinked rapidly, then looked around, dazed. The dull stone, begrimed by centuries, glinted with thousands of subtle shades.

Was he dying?

No. Death could not be this amazing breadth of subtle coloration, the speed of thoughts, the heightened detail of sound: his own breathing, wind soughing against stone, and, beyond the window slits, the rhythmic clatter of marching sentries in one of the stone courtyards far below. Even the variety of odors in the stale air.

The meaning of the note seeped through the sensory brilliance.

He had been enchanted. These things he was seeing, feeling, thinking? This was normal thought and sensation! This was the way he'd been when he was little, when Kwenz had taken Jilo from the lowly Quartermaster Dzan and made him his apprentice.

Wan-Edhe had befogged his mind and his movements, quite deliberately. A fogged mind would never lead a coup. Would never originate one.

Anger burned corrosively through Jilo.

He stood up, and again almost overbalanced. Had his strength increased? He tried jumping around, then slammed his hand on the table. Ow. No, no extra strength. The change was more subtle; he felt easier in his body, a readiness to move. Before, it had taken more thought, more concentration just to walk around without colliding into unexpected doorways, corners, furniture, as his depth perception had been untrustworthy.

Before, he couldn't have even had that thought about depth perception.

Jilo laid aside the book of mind-altering spells for later study, and searched for the spells that altered the physical self. Though he could perceive color, he could also perceive a sense of glare, of visual distortion: the Shadow spell enhancing darkness vision.

His stomach growled, reminding him of the Mearsieans, with their astonishing variety of foods.

No one knew what Wan-Edhe ate because he never ate with anyone, but Kwenz, in recent years, had only taken gruel. Old man's food. Jilo had had a choice: either eat gruel with Kwenz, or go to the mess with the soldiers. Their food wasn't much better, all the ingredients boiled together except for the bread. That was life in the military. Anything else was decadent weakness.

Prisoners got what the soldiers didn't, or wouldn't, eat, days old and cold. Once a day. If that. He wasn't hungry enough to face mess hall food, so he bent over the books again and got to work.

The light of day grayed the narrow slit window out in the hall when at last he found the spell to restore his eyes to normal. He performed it, and pain lanced through his head. When he dared to open his eyes again, the chamber had shadowed to gloom. He swayed, dizzy, then clapped, and the glowglobes brightened.

Color had both intensified and become more subtle in its gradations. Light didn't hurt. He thought of the Shadowland warriors on board ship, and how painful their vision must be out on the water, with little shadow to protect them. He'd have to remove the spell, but he needed strength first.

He walked to the window, and looked down.

There in the great courtyard, the first drill of the day had commenced. Jilo watched the wheeling soldiery marching, turning, raising swords, slashing, all in unison.

It was like a body moving when the head was gone.

He turned around. There lay the great book, it and the antidote to that spell an unexpected gift from Clair of Mearsies Heili, the old enemy. It was an inexplicable gift. She could have kept it from him. Jilo remembered the fogginess of his mind, and shook his head. He never would have found the book, much less the spell: he would have blundered into one of the wards or traps he could feel all around him.

Experience dictated wariness. He'd endured lengthy sessions with Wan-Edhe lecturing about how no one gave gifts without expectation. Life was a struggle for power. Offense, defense.

Jilo looked around, sensing thick skeins of dark magic.

A few minor protection wards were gone, but a dense miasma of enchantment still bound the old stone. Wan-Edhe had never trusted anyone; his favorite experiments were control of mind and will. And his favorite victims had been his own family, and then Puddlenose's family, first his uncle. Wan-Edhe had loved the exquisite cruelty inherent in the idea of sending Clair's own cousin against her.

The first thing to do was to find the wards and traps, and then maybe to turn them all against Wan-Edhe. That, too, would take strength. But then, there was no one else to do it. And Jilo had spent ten long, and very hard, years being tutored in one area of dark magic: wards. The idea of turning all that learning against Wan-Edhe instead of that blinding white castle burned through Jilo in such intense joy it made him giddy. Or maybe that was hunger.

As Jilo walked to the door, his stomach growled more insistently. His last meal had been the braised fish and rice with chopped greens that Puddlenose had brought him . . . when? It didn't matter.

He stood there thinking. No one would dare to walk into the throne room at the other end of the wing and sit down. Jilo knew his fellow Chwahir. Wan-Edhe had picked his subordinates for their steadfast, unquestioning obedience, and horrific punishments awaited anyone who erred. Wan-Edhe was also reputed to have spent magic in fashioning spy-windows all over the castle, so he could be watching at any time.

But one thing Jilo had learned in his secret reading of Chwahir history: if enough time went by, and things got really bad, there would be mass uprisings. Unless someone stepped in, right now, and took command. Not just of this room, or the fortress.

Right now.

Someone like . . .

Someone . . .

Why not? He loved magic studies, and puzzles, and here was a wealth of both. He had nowhere to go, and nothing to lose. Nothing but his life, and that had been in danger for so long that it was a given.

He walked out of Wan-Edhe's library, his shoes scuffing on the stones. In the heavy, stale, burnt-metal air, the silence reminded Jilo of snakes moving, or of the whisper of bound spirits.

He looked around, but the idea refused to settle into his mind; instead, questions flickered through, leaves on a cold wind, whirling with increasing speed.

He stopped at the great double doors. It took both hands and all his strength to throw back the huge cast-iron bolt. Usually the guard did that in the morning.

Jilo gripped the door, and swung it open. He let it crash into the wall, a dull, flat sound.

Three runners sat silently on their bench, waiting to be summoned. All three looked up in mute question, not quite surprise. The miasma of heavy magic was too dense for that.

"Wan-Edhe is gone," Jilo said, watching them recoil reflexively. "And Prince Kwenz. The Shadowland over on the Toaran continent is no more as well."

Shock stripped all personality from the three faces. The first reaction, when the shock began to diffuse, was fear.

"For now, carry on as before." And then he knew instinctively what his second command ought to be. "Tonight, double rations for all, including ale."

The only reward they'd felt reasonably sure of was food. Promotion had been rare, and arbitrary; much more frequent had been punishment.

Food. Jilo's stomach growled, and he remembered his own hunger, and he thought of what waited down in the kitchens. Food the only reward, and that was stuff that a bunch of barefoot girls in Mearsies Heili—enemies all— would turn their noses up at.

What pitiful lives we have, Jilo thought, continuing past the runners down the stairs to the great halls. He would change that.

He heard whispers, one fierce, another voice edged with nerve-grating anxiety: "What does he mean, Wan-Edhe is gone? Wan-Edhe will never be gone. He said so himself."

And the answer, "It's a loyalty test. Didn't he just say 'carry on as before'?"

"When Wan-Edhe comes back, he'll want to see everything as he left it."

When Wan-Edhe comes back.

Jilo walked away, aware of the tightened gut, the tremble in his limbs, the fear gripping the back of his neck, aware that he believed in Wad-Edhe's return as strongly as they did.

Norsunder couldn't stop Wan-Edhe. Nothing could.

Mearsies Heili, the Junky

We are coming at last to the birth of the alliance, which was the result of no grand council or far-seeing strategy on the part of the wise and powerful.

Quite the opposite.

As soon as Jilo left the girls' hideout, the rest of Clair's gang began to appear from their bedrooms, until all seven girls joined Clair and CJ. They were a disparate group, ages roughly from eleven to fifteen, from all kinds of backgrounds. All were either outcasts or runaways, adopted by Clair.

Puddlenose and the small, scrawny shape-changer named Ben slipped out of the last room in the tunnel—the lair of Puddlenose and his various traveling companions, and a catch-all for storage—to join them.

"Is he really gone?" one of the girls called.

"Yes! Time to decootie-ize this place!" CJ yelled. She waved her arms as though dispersing a terrible stench, and began stamping around the rug.

Three girls passed out plates and spoons, as the day's cook came around with a pot of oatmeal.

"Jilo did have spells on him to ward initiative." Clair sat cross-legged in the middle of the rug. She dug her spoon into the oatmeal. "Just as I always thought. Senrid found the evidence in Wan-Edhe's personal spellbook, left on a table awaiting his return."

"Urk." CJ stopped stamping, and flopped down to eat. "If there is anything worse than Chwahir, it's Marlovens. I still think it was as big a mistake to bring him in on it as it was to let Jilo know. If Jilo really is as smart as Ben says—"

"He's smart," Ben said, with conviction, as he took a bowl. "I've spent more time spying on him than any of you have. I think Jilo's plenty smart. It's Wan-Edhe's spells that made him go stupid. It was always worst when we were around, or Wan-Edhe was around, or certain words were said. Like Wan-Edhe did it on purpose."

"Of course he did," Clair said.

Puddlenose had already downed his first bowl. As he got up to help himself to more, he said, "I can tell you this, after all my time as Wan-Edhe's prisoner: he was afraid of Jilo. That is, afraid that when Jilo got old enough and learned enough magic he'd depose Kwenz, take over the Shadowland, then come after the homeland. After all, pretty much all the rulers in Chwahirsland over the past couple centuries got their thrones the quick way, rather than waiting for the previous throne-warmer to croak of old age."

CJ glared his way. "I just hope Jilo doesn't pop up on the horizon with a million ships full of Chwahir military loaded with swords and stuff."

Clair shook her head. "I don't think he's going to. I can't say why, I just don't believe he will."

"He wanted to take our Junky," one of the girls put in, pointing dramatically to the braided rug. "How can you forget him and his group of groanboils riding around just to try to catch us sneaking in or out?"

Puddlenose shrugged. "True. But I bet that's because Kwenz wouldn't let him have a hideout like ours in the Shadowland. And pinching a hideout is not conquering. Besides, who could blame him for wanting a place to get away from Kwenz, especially when Wan-Edhe turned up?"

"I still hate him," CJ said.

Clair got up to dunk her empty bowl in the water barrel with its purification spell. As she clacked the bowl back onto the stack, she said, "Aunt Murial is busy trying to replace the old protections, and I think I ought to learn how. The Chwahir might be gone, but there are worse villains."

CJ groaned. "It's not *fair*. I thought we were supposed to have a happy ending, after Siamis got defeated. We deserve a happy ending. We earned it. Yeah, don't say it, villains aren't fair."

"That's why they're villains," a redhead said, raising a forefinger.

Clair smiled as the girls laughed, then turned serious.

"Before I go study magic, maybe we should make a patrol through the forest, as we always have. Aunt Murial said we couldn't trust that all the Chwahir went away. She was going to talk to the regional governors about watching for any bands of Chwahir looking for trouble. We can help out by patrolling the woods."

"I'll take to the air," Ben offered. He was wondering what he would do without any Shadowland to spy on.

CJ scowled. "I wish there was some kind of spell that would take an invading army and turn them into a field of petunias." She kicked at the colorful mural that the girls had painted. "But no matter how much magic we learn, it doesn't really stop villains. We need an Idea to Save the World." The capitals conveyed themselves through extra sarcasm and an eye-roll.

The girls jumped up, some glad to be getting outside, especially after their long stay up north.

Puddlenose offered to help, and as the gang started up the tunnel toward the cave exit, he said, "If you see any Chwahir, give a yell. They probably know their king is gone. No one in control. They'll be looking for sport." He made a gesture, drawing his forefinger across his throat.

"Our rules haven't changed," Clair said. "Pairs or threes!"

"Follow anyone we find, then use our transfer medals," Irenne recited, rolling her eyes and flipping back her long light brown ponytail. "Puddlenose, it's *not* like we haven't been doing this for *simply ages*."

Puddlenose patted the air. "I know. I know. What we don't know is if Wan-Edhe's experimental loyalty spells and all the rest of his weird magic and crazy proclamations will still keep 'em afraid to try anything. When those spells do break, the Chwahir are going to be really, really angry."

A short time later, Clair tramped along next to CJ, looking up and down the gentle hillocks and rocky glades, before saying, "While you think up your idea, I'd better find my aunt."

"But the idea is so obvious," CJ said, throwing her arms wide. Birds rose out of a nearby shrub, squawking. "We lived it, there at the end. None of us kids could defeat Siamis by ourselves. But when we worked in a big group, we were great. We worked it all out, some searching, others decoys, you remember!"

Clair said doubtfully, "The nine of us have always worked together."

"I don't mean just our gang. I mean, like a . . . a pact, with other kids. Who could help." CJ smacked the front of her black woolen vest, then said, "There's the stream."

Clair ran beside CJ down a grassy hill. They plunged into the green shadows of a shaded path, and CJ went on. "By others I mean the kid rulers, the new generation, like those old mages called us. Sartora's generation. Yeah, we don't have mind powers like she does." On the words 'mind powers,' CJ whizzed her hands around her head as if she were shooing flies. "But we still are smart. Look how many villains have tried to wipe us out."

"Look how close we've come to being wiped out," Clair said, then shook her head, her blue-white hair a silky curtain around her arms. "No, no, I agree. And I know you're not saying we should go looking for trouble."

CJ whirled so that her green skirt flared and fell back to ankle length as she walked backward. She knew the forest well, and if strangers had been lurking around, the local birds would have been sending up the alarm. "The way I see it is, Eleven-Land is grown-ups who all want power. Siamis is a grown-up, or so close you may as well call him one." She made a sour face. "I don't know if he's younger or older than Disgusting Rel the Disgusting Hero, but anyway. From what everybody said, Siamis was able to pull off his enchantment because grown-up rulers found him so handsome, and so well spoken, and good at everything he did," she warbled in a syrupy coo. "No kid is going to fall for *Oooo, yer so haaaaaaandsome, Siamis!*"

Clair squashed the impulse to remind CJ that they'd met plenty of kids who would have wanted to *be* Siamis, and that she not only trusted but relied on adults, beginning with Aunt Murial. And Janil the Steward, queen of the kitchen, who had seen that Clair ate, bathed, and dressed when she was small, while her mother was drinking or dosing under the effects of sleepweed. And the city's guild leaders, and the oldest of the provincial governors. She was a queen because they let her be one, she thought privately. It was not a new thought.

But she understood CJ, who had come from a home in which the adults were abusive and untrustworthy, and further, she understood what CJ was trying to do. Their group of friends looked out for one another, and so CJ wanted to form a larger group to do the same.

Like . . . an alliance.

"Maybe an alliance is a good idea. I remember Senrid of Marloven Hess saying that he didn't think Siamis was really defeated. He said it was a retreat, that Siamis is coming back."

"Senrid *would* say that," CJ scoffed. "Being a Marloven. He probably *hopes* Siamis comes back, so they'll have an excuse for a lot of battles and military junk. But Siamis skunked so fast he left behind that Ancient Sartoran sword of his, remember? What else can that mean except he's too scared to come back? But. We need an alliance to be ready for the next villain. Because one thing you know about Norsunder is, they have to have a crop of 'em, ready to come boiling out to try their next evil plan."

Clair was nodding slowly. She hoped Senrid was wrong in saying that Siamis's retreat wasn't even a defeat in any real sense, just an abandonment of a plan when it ceased to be successful. She didn't want to tell CJ that she'd been having occasional nightmares about the pleasant, smiling young man who so easily put the world under a web of enchantment. Not horrible nightmares, which somehow made it worse: he always seemed so friendly and kindly. She found that more sinister than evil old Wan-Edhe, who never pretended to be anything but mean, and who had labored for years to create his web of spells over his own people. Siamis had bound people in enchantment in moments.

CJ paced in a circle, one fist pounding the palm of the other hand. "It has to be a kid alliance, ones who aren't villains or power-mad. Friends only! Code names, so anyone nosing in won't know what we mean. And we'll have code words, too, ones that the grown-ups would never pay attention to. And if someone gets into trouble, we all promise to go and help out."

"I'd be glad to send out messages to see who else might like the idea. Whom were you thinking of inviting?" Clair asked.

"Our friends. Ones we know and trust."

"Of course," Clair said. "Beginning with . . . ?"

"Arthur and Sartora up in Bereth Ferian. That is, Arthur would join. He's like us, though he's been learning magic forever, and Sartora might, if she's not too busy being famous."

Clair made a face. "Sartora asked us to call her by her real name."

"Liere, Sartora, it's all the same," CJ said, whirling her hands upward. "We should ask her, too. Of course! I'm just saying she might be too busy being important."

"Is that fair?"

"It's true. They made her a queen up there, after all, and she's got those weird mind powers, and she knows how to use that even weirder dyr thingie from the days of Ancient Sartor, that thing that broke Siamis's enchantment."

"I'm not certain that thing is trustworthy," Clair observed as they turned onto the forest road.

"I agree," CJ said fervently. "After all, if Siamis wanted it, it has to be evil, in spite of all that hoola-loola about how it was made of this mysterious stuff that no longer exists, and it has Great Powers, and all the rest of it. If Detlev used to use one of those things back in the old days, and everybody up north seems to agree that he did, it definitely has to be evil, right?"

Clair said doubtfully, "Maybe not evil, not in ancient days. But old. Really, really old, and no one understands how to use them, or what they're for."

"Except Ancient Sartoran villains," CJ stated.

"And Lilith the Guardian," Clair countered. "Sartora said she's real, not just a story from ancient days."

"Real or not, she never seems to be around when she's needed." CJ sighed.

"Well, I'm just glad Arthur's mother took that dyr away. She'd know where to stash it so it can't do any more damage if anyone does. So, who else in this alliance?"

"The Queen of Sartor, of course," CJ said quickly. "They say she's fifteen. And. You know. Sartor. If the Queen of Sartor joins, then others will follow."

"No argument from me," Clair said, and, relentlessly, "Who else?"

CJ heaved a long-suffering sigh. She knew where this was going. So she sidestepped. "Hibern. Your aunt said that she's really advanced in light magic studies, and that Arthur's mom would only take a really smart student."

"Good. But what about Senrid? He helped Hibern when she asked. And for that matter, he was the one who suggested that plan when Siamis was defeated."

CJ made a face. "Isn't Hibern enough? We don't need any more Marlovens."

Clair said, "Senrid knows more magic than anyone our age. Even Hibern, I think, though it's dark magic. But he's learning ours really fast. And you did make your peace with him."

CJ sighed, rolling her eyes.

"Or is this alliance just supposed to be 'people CJ likes'?" Clair asked.

"That's not fair." CJ scowled.

"You don't look dangerous with that whipped cream mustache still on your upper lip from breakfast." Clair tipped her head to the side.

CJ had to laugh, a big guffaw, startling more birds from the trees.

"You still don't trust Senrid?" Clair asked.

"No."

"I do. I think. Oh, I know that he started out badly. Very." Clair frowned down at her hands, remembering their first meeting with Senrid the previous summer, when he'd snatched one of them for execution, on the regent's orders. "But I think he's changed. The Senrid we dealt with before Siamis came wouldn't have bothered looking for that spell on Jilo, much less warning me to pass it on if I thought it a good idea."

"Maybe. He's still a know-it-all and a bigmouth."

"You mean, as fast as you with a nasty crack?"

CJ's grin was quick and rueful. "Well, maybe it's better to have him on our side than against." As they turned toward home, she added under her breath, "Maybe."

Chapter Seven

Three days later
Valley of Delfina, home of Tsauderei

BEFORE I get to how the alliance began to spread, I need to sketch an overview of the mage relationships of that period.

Before Sartor was enchanted the century previous, the magic world acknowledged two leaders. First was Lilith the Guardian, who had fought during the Fall of Ancient Sartor. Since then—like the Norsundrians she had dedicated her life to opposing—she had recourse to refuge beyond time.

Her appearances had been less rare than those of Detlev, but rare enough that many believed she was mere myth. One of her purposes was to seek promising youth and put them in the way of training, though often her next appearance would be decades later, sometimes a century or more after they died.

Next was the Sartoran mage guild led by Chief Veltos Jhaer, oldest guild in the world. Ninety-seven years ago, when Norsunder Base attacked Sartor, the kingdom was frozen in time.

With Sartor inaccessible to the rest of the world, the gap in magic leadership was eventually filled by Evend of Bereth Ferian. He'd nearly gone to the Sartoran mage school, but then the war between Sartor and Norsunder Base broke out. So Evend's family kept him in the north to study magic, and eventually he became the King in Bereth Ferian (a title that meant little more than presiding over treaty meetings concerning the ancient wards against the Venn) and head of the newly expanded northern school of magic.

Tsauderei, ten years younger, was one of Evend's first students. Tsauderei was so gifted that Evend broke many of the traditions of magic teaching, maintaining that education had to evolve as did everything else. His style of teaching, individual lessons tailored to the interests and abilities of the student, had worked well for the northern school.

Once handsome, vigorous, and strong, Tsauderei at over eighty was still commandingly tall, though gaunt under the robe that had been male fashion in his young days. Every year, as soon as the snows of winter began to melt, Tsauderei had dared to explore as close to Sartor's enchanted border as was safe, which enabled him to discover that the enchantment was gradually receding. This discovery he kept to himself in hopes that Norsunder would overlook it.

His determination strengthened one spring fifteen years ago, when his journey disclosed two living persons in century-old clothes: a palace guard, her wound still fresh, protecting an infant who turned out to be the youngest of the royal children. This baby was the last living member of the ancient Landis family, who had ruled Sartor for a couple millennia.

This girl, nicknamed Atan (for her name was surely warded), had been raised by Tsauderei and taught magic and history according to the northern school's teachings, until the enchantment broke at last, and Atan was joyfully reunited with the Sartorans, who crowned her queen and surrounded her with guardians—and guards.

But once the enchantment was broken, bringing Sartor back into the flow of time, Sartor was striving to reclaim its ancient authority. Its mage school objected strongly to any deviation in their centuries-old tradition of moving students through classes in cohorts, overseen by Sartor's mage guild.

To their objection, Evend had pointed out that they were now a century behind. And so the northern school stayed separate from the Sartoran.

That was one cause of tension. Tsauderei's refusal to put himself under the authority of the outdated Sartoran mage guild was another. He prized his independence and all the knowledge he had learned after decades of watching over enchanted Sartor in his effort to break the enchantment.

And so, after Atan was restored to Sartor, Mage Guild Chief Veltos and the rest of the Sartoran mage guild— though professing gratitude and friendship—effectively shut Tsauderei out.

Roth Drael

Erai-Yanya woke up to a friendly note from Tsauderei that from anyone else would be a summons.

Erai-Yanya grimaced. It had to be politics, and she hated politics. She had chosen early to live and work alone largely to avoid mage politics. Further, she knew Tsauderei loathed politics as well, but as the oldest of the senior mages, almost anything he did had political repercussions in the mage world. He had also been her tutor during the time she studied with Gwasan and Murial.

These days, Tsauderei seldom left his cottage on the border between Sartor and Sarendan. His colleagues, new and old, were accustomed to going to him.

As soon as Hibern transferred to Bereth Ferian for her deferred day studying with the northern mage school, Erai-Yanya braced for the long shift from winter to summer. She found herself standing on the grass outside the small one-room cottage with its broad front window. She blinked away the transfer haze, gazing down into the deep blue of the lake at the bottom of the valley, then turned toward the door and walked in.

She glanced around at the three walls filled with books and scrolls as she waited for the transfer-throb in her joints to subside. Why was the sight of books so reassuring? Mages intent on destruction surely had libraries, too . . .

Tsauderei waited until his former student regained her focus and said, "You went to Chwahirsland again?" He leaned forward.

How did he even know? Of course he'd know.

Men had worn beards when Tsauderei was young. His was long, white, and the diamond he wore in one ear glittered against the ordered locks of his long snowy hair. His gaze was reassuringly direct, the many lines in his face emphasizing his ironic view of the world.

"Yes, a useless journey," she said. "More interesting on our return than for anything we discovered."

"Please tell me what happened, even if it was disappointing."

"First you need to know that Hibern and the Mearsiean girls, without consulting Murial, decided that Senrid of Marloven Hess ought to go along, as he could probably read the books."

"Senrid Montredaun-An. Taking an interest in something outside of that benighted kingdom? I might have to meet that boy some day," Tsauderei said, his interest sharpening exponentially as Erai-Yanya reported the rest of the visit.

At the end, she said, "The time candle had burned down and we all felt ill, so I insisted we leave." She let out a breath. "And now we come to the disturbing discovery, that a full day had passed while we were gone, though I had watched that candle. Which I had cut and bespelled myself, binding it to half an hour." She held two fingers apart, indicating the length of the candle.

Tsauderei looked grim. Several possible reasons for the time anomaly occurred to him, all of them dire, but he didn't know enough about dark magic to determine which was right. "That, too, will have to be sorted out, if Wan-Edhe is really gone. Which I don't believe. It's too easy. Right now, I need your advice."

"On what? You know I have nothing to do with so-called world affairs, except magical, and your knowledge outstrips mine there."

"Except in other-world studies," he observed. "But

that's a conversation for another day. This is as political as you can get, as is everything having to do with Sartor. But I still think you're the best advisor. Erai-Yanya, I have yet to see Atan. They keep her so busy she can't even visit me. But she writes to me via magic transfer." He leaned out to tap a golden notecase. "She wants a study partner, and asked me to find one."

"She asked you, not the chief mage?"

"Precisely." Tsauderei uttered a soft, sardonic laugh. "Now, if I ask Oalthoreh up at the northern school, she'll send Atan the same sort of student that the Sartoran mages would give her: scrupulous, obedient, careful, and who will think it his or her duty to report every word they exchange. I was hoping you might have a suggestion of a smart, dedicated mage student who'll permit Atan that one hour of freedom from being Queen of Sartor."

At first Erai-Yanya turned her mind dutifully to the northern magic school's seniors, but as she sifted them mentally, the sense of Tsauderei's words sank in, and she laughed at the obvious. "I believe I can help with that. Hibern would be perfect."

"I thought she might."

Two weeks later
Marloven Hess to Sartor

Remembering how bad Senrid had looked the day they went to Chwahirsland, the next week Hibern dutifully put in her skipped day of northern study instead of going to Marloven Hess for her weekly magic session with Senrid.

The week after that, she transferred to Marloven Hess, having dressed carefully, her best polished cotton robe under her blue mage robe, her hair brushed and braided. But she did not transfer directly to the capital.

She appeared on a low, forested hill from which she could look down at her family's castle, and her old tower room. Now empty. Each time she did this, she promised herself it would be the last, but after a few weeks she couldn't resist another visit, for all kinds of reasons that she knew were weak.

No one moved in the narrow windows, built for archers to shoot through and not be shot. The clear air over the tower indicated that her secret structure, which had taken two years to make, was gone as if it had never happened.

As if *she* had never happened. Except that she could feel the wards against her entry if she began the transfer spell to her old Destination.

No one looked out, and if her father detected her presence, no one was sent to invite her in. Her imagined triumphant conversation with her parents about being invited to be study partner to no less a person than the Queen of Sartor faded like morning mist.

She turned away, knowing it was stupid to keep returning, because it always hurt. "That will be the last time," she resolved. "Absolutely the last."

And she transferred the short distance to Choreid Dhelerei, where she was expected.

Senrid's face had resumed its normal shape, and his skin looked less like someone had thrown a set of paints at him. As she took her seat, she found the resumption of everyday schedule calming, and once again she tidied the pain away.

Ordinarily they argued about magic and history as much past their hour as Senrid had time for, but today, as the castle bells clanged the watch change, echoed from farther away by the city bells, Hibern closed her book. "We're done."

Senrid eyed her. "And you're all dressed up."

"I am." Hibern shook out her robe as she rose. "Oh yes. I forgot to mention when we went to Chwahirsland, but I made a promise to pass this along: the Mearsieans want to start some kind of alliance."

Both knew it wouldn't be military. "This is to prepare for Siamis's return?" Senrid asked.

"That, and to be an alliance between underage enemies of Norsunder, especially rulers and magic students, against whoever else comes along."

Senrid sighed, remembering CJ's annoying rants about how all adults were stupid. Maybe on that weird world she

came from they were. He wouldn't have survived if he
hadn't had Commander Keriam in his life, but on the other
hand, that older generation of lighter mages? Before the
defeat of Siamis, those old lighters up at Bereth Ferian had
looked at him as if he'd kill them as they stood when they
found out he was a Marloven.

"Like who?" he asked cautiously.

"Like you." Hibern held up three fingers. "You inherited a throne, you know magic, and you're an enemy of
Norsunder."

He could see that kind of alliance being useful, if it
really was an alliance. "What am I expected to do? If it's
to waste time at lighter celebrations, listening to forty-verse
snores about Golden Ages and Lo, How Great We Be, I'm
not doing it."

"Nothing was said about celebrations," Hibern said.
"The idea is kind of like what we just did for Clair in Chwahirsland."

Senrid snorted. He'd really gone to find out how far
Wan-Edhe had gotten in developing the mind control spells.
Looking for some kind of evil plan for taking over Mearsies
Heili (as if Wan-Edhe would be idiot enough to write such
a thing in a magic book) had been secondary.

But he'd looked, and as a result, had stumbled on that
ugly little spell designed for Jilo. Which he duly passed
along to Clair once that stiff-necked mage of Hibern's was
not listening.

Hibern went on. "If someone in the alliance asks for the
kind of help we can provide, we give it."

"That I can do." But Senrid wondered how any of them
could possibly help him. Assuming they would want to.

To say that out loud might sound like whining. He'd been
up studying far too long the previous night, but had still
risen before dawn to practice with bow and knife. As a consequence, his mind was tired, making it more difficult to
control his nascent Dena Yeresbeth. So he heard thoughts:
Hibern's regret, and from farther away images of Hibern's
crazy brother Stefan.

Physical distance didn't seem to matter to Dena Yeresbeth. Stefan himself was at Hibern's family castle, glowering at phantasms that may or may not be there. What

snagged Senrid's focus, however, was the strength of Hibern's regret, shame, and bitterness.

Senrid closed off Stefan and listened to the whisper of minds in relative proximity. Jarend Ndarga? Yes, surrounded by other minds, some scoffing, others angry, some laughing. A few afraid. *Nothing good ever comes of tangling with kings, my dad says . . .* And someone else, *Yes. You wait. He's a young scrub, so he might smile and pretend there's no repercussion, but next season, next year, if he thinks he can get away with it . . .*

Senrid knew he shouldn't listen to Ndarga, but he couldn't resist. Just the surface. Ndarga had been so surprised and angry over his own hurts, believing he shouldn't have had any after fighting a scrub of fifteen. He had spent days (Keriam told Senrid grimly) watching for retribution after that fight.

That's who he was to the senior academy boys: a scrub. So much for his ancient lineage . . . Senrid laughed at himself, and then made another reach with his Dena Yeresbeth. It was a long reach, very long, and yet it was so easy: Liere. There she was, far away, struggling with Ancient Sartoran verbs . . .

Senrid shut the mental door. He shouldn't do that. It was wrong. Liere hadn't come to see him because she hadn't. If she'd wanted to, she would have. There was no point in guessing at reasons.

Senrid didn't realize he'd spoken Liere's name out loud until he opened his eyes to find Hibern paused at the door. "Senrid, this is none of my concern, but when I was in Bereth Ferian last, Sartora asked when you were going to visit. It didn't take mind powers to see she was disappointed."

"'Sartora,'" he repeated. "Liere hates that stupid name. Or she did. Anyway, she's got to be surrounded by an army of mages. Heralds. Arthur. All busy stuffing her head with lighter magic and . . ."

The word 'hyperbole' died.

Hibern said, ". . . and?"

Senrid sighed. "She could visit any time she wants."

Hibern said, "I think she misses you. She did say that you were her first friend." She found Senrid's wide gaze disconcerting. "Senrid, I don't know her, but everybody says she came from a family of shopkeepers who don't travel. If that's true, then she would probably never think to invite herself to visit a king. Even one who'd said he was a friend. She's probably been told how little words of friendship mean from nobles, much less anyone who considers themselves above that rank."

"Oh," Senrid said. "Never thought of that." He grimaced, his ears reddening.

"Study those wards!" Hibern said as the last of the castle bell-clangs died in the distance.

Now that she was about to transfer to Eidervaen, ancient capital of Sartor, anxiety tensed Hibern. It was a different sort of anxiety from the sick grief and betrayal of being rejected by her family. For several days she had happily tackled her studies, bolstered by the knowledge that the new Queen of Sartor wanted a study partner, and who had been suggested? Not some favored student at either magic school, but Hibern.

Doubt formed into question about why she'd been chosen. Or maybe she was merely the latest in a very long line already interviewed and sent away again.

All she knew about the new queen was that she was more or less Hibern's age, and a formidable mage student. Nobody seemed to know much else about her, except that she had been raised by Tsauderei, hidden away in a mountain cottage until she and a band of war orphans had made their way into the disintegrating enchantment that had held Sartor beyond the reach of the rest of the world—beyond *time*—and by so doing, broke the last of it so that Sartor could rejoin the world.

After nearly two weeks of wondering, Hibern was about to meet her now.

She clutched the transfer token she'd been given. Magic wrenched her out of Senrid's dusty castle and thrust her into a cool space smelling of an herb a little like cinnamon mixed with lemon, with undertones of beeswax, and faintest of all, a vague scent that reminded her a little of mildew.

As Hibern gasped from the effects of the transfer magic, she looked around the Sartoran Destination chamber. Three walls were plain blue-white marble. The fourth divided into three long panels, a gilt sun placed high above the middle one, with rays slanting down through all three panels. Dragons wound in a sinuous curve up the outer panels, their open mouths reaching up toward the sun.

It was Sartor which, history insisted, brought through the world-gate the notion of dividing the day into twenty-four hours, eight sets of three. Everything in threes. Even the Marlovens had threes, though those were military in nature.

At the exact moment Hibern recovered her breath and could move, a door opened in the middle panel, and a teen-age page conducted Hibern out of the Destination chamber. Behind her, someone else appeared by transfer, causing a flurry of air that brought a faint whiff of some unfamiliar place.

The girl leading Hibern wore a gown of soft green under a paneled robe of dark blue edged with white. There was a stylized star worked in white thread along the edges of the white border, the symbol for the Sartoran mage guild. It was small and subtle enough that Hibern only recognized it when the girl was two paces away.

The girl said, "I bid you welcome," as she guided Hibern to a cushioned couch. Conventional greeting, Hibern said to herself. Polite, for the widest circle. The next circle in would have been acknowledged with a polite question about well-being.

Hibern made the conventional response, "I thank you for the welcome," then the girl offered her a tiny cup of fresh steep—the best Sartoran steep, the aroma like summer grass clearing the last of the transfer malaise from Hibern's head. Hibern accepted the cup. It was not too hot or too cold, and tasted fresh and slightly astringent, slightly tart.

A skinny boy appeared, wearing livery edged in lavender, and once again Hibern completed the conventional outer-circle exchange of greetings, after which she said in her best Sartoran, "I am here for my interview with the queen."

The attendant took the empty cup and made a polite gesture to follow.

The hall was also marble, with round windows high above, framed by stylized running vines. They let in summer light indirectly, keeping the air cool.

Hibern breathed in the complicated scents—more elusive spice, a trace of nut oil (furniture polish?)—as they passed a sideboard with no straight lines, and complicated knotwork inlays in various types of colorwood. Then a tapestry depicting some historical occasion, a treaty from the looks of the figures, the long robes and tiny ruffs and rosebud "mouse ear" headdresses the fashion nine centuries previous. To the Sartorans, a nine-hundred-year-old fashion was probably next thing to modern, Hibern thought, turning slightly to take in the last of the silvery blues and golds of the colors.

A broad landing was next, a carved door full of knotted vines in threes, and Hibern found herself inside an interview chamber with an amazing vaulted ceiling. She tried not to gawk, catching a glimpse of a night-blue sky and stars painted on it: so they were in mage territory.

The attendant bent to whisper to the young man at the desk, then gave Hibern a nod and retreated noiselessly as for the third time Hibern was given the conventional greeting, to which she responded politely.

A girl of about twelve appeared through a door at the back of the office, carefully bearing a silver tray, which she set down noiselessly next to the young man. Hibern couldn't help but compare these gliding, quiet runners with those in Senrid's castle, with their clattering boot heels and unmodulated voices and weapons at their belts.

The young man then indicated one of the several empty chairs, all upholstered in pale blue, and said, "If you will have a seat?"

Hibern did, looking askance at the empty chairs. Maybe Erai-Yanya had been wrong, and there was a line of interviewees before her. Or—her heart sank—maybe this wait was some kind of insult because Hibern didn't belong to either mage school, but was taught by Erai-Yanya, the hermit-mage of Roth Drael.

Erai-Yanya had said when Hibern first came to her as a student, "These bare feet of mine? Yes, I find it comfortable to go like this. But there's a reason why I've always gone before various kings and queens with my hair tumbling down, my toes bare, even in winter, and wearing an old gown I carefully preserve for these interviews: it is a reminder that I stand apart from their social and political hierarchies, and I will not be 'managed.'"

Hibern wondered if it was a mistake to come in her best robe. Maybe she should have routed out an old horse blanket.

The orderly quiet of the hall was broken by a quick ticketty-tick sound, followed by the abrupt emergence of Hibern's first sight of one of the southern morvende, the cave-dwelling people. Like the morvende of the northern continent, this boy was pale-skinned, with drifting blue-white cobwebby-hair. He wore a knee-length, sleeveless tunic woven out of a gold-dyed fabric that rippled like gauze. His lower legs and his feet were bare, the talons on his toes ticking on the marble as he walked.

"Greetings and welcome! Prosperity and well-being! You must be the one Erai-Yanya sent to Atan," he exclaimed.

Hibern blinked. How many of Sartor's strictly defined social circles had the morvende blurred with his unexpectedly informal greeting?

"I thank you for your greetings and felicitations," Hibern said, groping for the right words. "But who is Atan? Do you mean the Queen of Sartor?"

"It is short for Atanrael. It is her heart-name. Who would go by 'Yustnesveas Landis the Fifth' if she did not have to?" He flicked his long, thin fingers through the air, the talons at the ends painted a cheery orange. So were his toe talons.

"As for me, you must call me Hin," he said. "For Hinder. You'll meet my cousin Sinder around here somewhere, but she is never 'Sin' to anyone but me. Not to confuse you. Just to help you sort us out," he went on in the same cheerful tone, thereby doing away with all the careful formality on which Hibern had been coached. "Atan is presiding over the high council interviewing the Colendi ambassador. If you can call a formal assembly in Star Chamber a mere interview. I suspect the idea was to intimidate Colend into agreement." He grinned. "We have a saying, 'A juggling snake has no time to bite.'"

How does a snake juggle? Hibern said, "There are

problems with Colend?" Aside from the gossip about their king being mad, the Colendi were renowned for using politeness as a weapon.

Hin's fingers lifted to the side of his face and twiddled, as if he played a flute.

"Oh," Hibern breathed. "The Music Festival?"

Hin's smile vanished. "That interview was to last a glass." The orange talons flashed as Hinder mimed turning over a small sandglass. "It's been an entire hour."

Chapter Eight

Elsewhere in Eidervaen's royal palace

THE time has come to introduce Atan, saddled with the name Yustnesveas, queen at fifteen of the oldest country in the world. Therefore her influence would always be disproportional. She knew it. She hated it.

She also hated crying.

When she was small and impatient with chores, in her haste once she'd accidentally splashed boiling water on her hand and wrist. She'd refused to give in to tears while her hand was wrapped with soothing keem leaves, because nowhere in the records she'd been given to study did any queen of Sartor cry.

Tsauderei, her guardian and tutor, had said, "Atan, you keep forgetting that those records you're reading are what people want you to remember about the individuals, not necessarily what they were truly like. Go right ahead and howl, if it helps."

But Atan hadn't. Queens were supposed to have self-control. Their decisions affected a lot of people, so giving in to passion was the next thing to evil.

Even so, there were three occasions when she did cry.

She'd felt the sting of tears when she first walked into the Tower of Knowledge, known for centuries and centuries as Sartor's mind. But she'd been too hurried and frightened to let the tears fall, for she had to break the cruel enchantment that had been bound to the Landis family (who Norsunder thought had all been safely killed), while Norsundrian warriors were chasing her people into the square below.

The second time she cried happened a few days after Sartor was freed from the enchantment, during her first Restday-dawn walk through the Purrad, the twelve-fold labyrinth in its secluded garden at the oldest part of the royal palace—the place sometimes called Sartor's soul.

She had not expected the ancient silver-barked trees, lit by slanting shafts through time-worn stone traceries, to be so beautiful when seen from all sides as she walked the Purrad's interlocking circles; she had not expected the rush of sorrow and wonder when she imagined her own parents having stepped on these same smoothed pebbles so carefully placed and tended.

The third time she cried was when she walked into her parents' bedroom, and saw the little signs of haste: her mother's nightgown tossed on the rumpled bed, her father's desk scattered with papers and books.

However, she had not cried when she first walked into Star Chamber, Sartor's oldest chamber of governing, known as Sartor's heart. High under the complicated vaultings of the ceiling, windows let in the light at different times and seasons, golden shafts in winter, cleverly multiplied through crystal, and in summer, coolly diffused to silver. At night, or on a gloomy winter's day, floating lights glimmered above in ever-changing patterns, like stars.

It was winter's golden light that she had first seen: so clear, striking the marble and diffusing, so the vast room seemed infinite as sunrise.

The tree-shaped throne where she sat now, an elaborate combination of carved golden marble, real gold, mirror, and magic so that she could be seen from all sides, stood in the center of the room, around which the floor circled in wide, shallow marble tiers on which courtiers could move in the ancient complexities known as Circles.

Right now she was bored, irritated, and increasingly angry as the beautifully modulated, carefully cadenced adult voices murmured in the first circle tier below her throne. The high council was gathered there, where only the duchas and the mage guild head could stand in more formal gatherings.

There stood Chief Veltos, head of Sartor's mage guild, tall, thin, and grim-faced as she glared at the Colendi ambassador. The first time Atan met Chief Veltos, she had insisted on taking Atan to this very room. As they stood beneath the vaulted ceilings in this chamber freighted with history, the chief mage had said in a low, bitter voice, "Everyone knows that our army lost the war with Norsunder, but your father, as commander, is dead, past blame or care." She paused, her tone flattening. "*I* lost the magic battle, for it was my strategy that Detlev of Norsunder ripped apart so easily, before binding us under enchantment. Our first job must be new, and better, protections. Because we must expect Detlev to attack again."

Atan had been too overwhelmed for tears.

Her next visit to this chamber had been her coronation on New Year's Firstday 4735—for the Sartorans, a jump of ninety-seven years—that she only recollected as great noise and color as the remnants of Sartor's Three Circles gathered to see her take her father's place. After fifteen years of secluded life she had been too terrified to raise her head beyond the formidable array of staring faces.

Most recently, Midsummer's celebration felt hollow without the ancient tradition of the Music Festival, which now took place in Colend. As it had for the last ninety years.

She'd been unprepared for the anguish and sorrow in every adult who'd gathered to make the Progress through the Twelve Stations, when for the first time in centuries, it would not signal the start of the Sartoran Music Festival.

Centuries, everyone had repeated, their voices ringing with the weight of moral outrage.

So here they were in the summer of the year 4737, and all Sartor wanted the Music Festival back.

The Colendi ambassador's lovely singsong echoed through the chamber now, mellifluous and rehearsed. ". . . And our king is the first to acknowledge Sartor's respect for tradition, but his majesty bade me speak for our own traditions, beginning with honoring the treaties we have made with the Alliance of Guilds. For, if you will permit me to offer a reminder, it is not merely the hostelries and bakeries and eateries and houses of entertainment in Colend, but those along the road leading to us, who have invested much in expectation of the yearly gathering."

The elderly Duchas of Chandos, who stood first within the first circle opposite Chief Veltos, lifted his hand. "I hear no objections being offered to Colend establishing its own music festival in complement, but it seems reasonable to us to expect that the Sartoran Music Festival would continue to be held in Sartor, as it has for centuries."

"What greater way for Sartor to rejoin the world?" stated a baras, her chin elevated, eyes darting glances from side to side. She was in the high council, though as baras she was only third circle, because her daughter was deemed one of Atan's Rescuers.

The dapper guild chief bowed to the duchas, light shimmering along the tiny mois stones embroidered on his formal tunic as he said to the ambassador, "Our Sartoran guilds will suffer greatly if denied the yearly gathering. And we are already sorely burdened due to the war which, for us, was recently lost."

The Colendi ambassador turned to each, his hands and expression apologetic, but Atan suspected that he was not really sorry. His voice was too smooth, the corners of his mouth easy, as he went on in the musical Colendi version of Sartoran, "My king respects Sartor's place in history. Were we not once a part of the Sartoran empire? Did not my own ancestors travel here every summer, claiming their summer sojourn the pinnacle of their year?"

He paused to bow in Atan's direction. "My king commanded me to beg her majesty's forbearance, and assure her that no one understands better than he the difficulties besetting a new monarch, especially in this troubled time."

Though he bowed to her, Atan could see how his attention stayed with the high council as he opened his hands in a graceful gesture, fingers pointed starward, slightly opened. If she stuck her tongue out at him, she suspected he wouldn't even notice.

Chief Veltos would.

"I am enjoined to request a hiatus of five years," the ambassador oiled on, "that our own treaties may be renegotiated, and his majesty also hopes that in that time Sartor will have fully recovered its rightful place in the world."

The bells rang then. Atan wondered if he had chosen his time.

The high council had not risen. They didn't even look at one another, much less at Atan. That meant they'd already agreed to force the interview to last until they got what they wanted.

Atan stirred impatiently. Chief Veltos, at least, should remember that Erai-Yanya's student was coming. No, she was probably already here. But it was Chief Veltos who had said so reasonably, "We will honor you all our lives, your majesty, for yours was the hand freeing the kingdom from the enchantment. However, now that we of the guild are no longer enchanted, we can free you of the necessity for continuing those studies . . ."

And they still had not invited Tsauderei to visit, much less found time in the schedule for her to visit him—the mage who had saved her life when he found Atan as a baby, lying in the border mountains with the wounded guard who had run with her. It was Tsauderei who had tutored Atan as well as guarding her for fifteen years.

Atan meant to be good. She meant to wait for the signal that the interview was over, but she could not contain the surge of resentment at this evidence that they intended to talk through her impending interview as if it did not matter. As if *she* did not matter, as if she were part of the decoration of this ancient room. Perhaps not as important as those decorations, as she wasn't centuries old.

She knew that that was self-pity, but the prospect of a study partner was important to her. And they kept reminding her of her duty as queen.

So . . . maybe it was time to act like a queen.

She put her hands together in the old gesture of peace. It caught the attention of the ambassador, as she had hoped.

She then opened her hands and held them out, palm up, the signal that he could withdraw.

She saw at once from the little smile the ambassador gave her as he raised himself from his bow that he had won some kind of contest. Yes, there it was, in the faces of the council, the little narrowing of eyes and thinning of lips that indicated she had done wrong. They all rose as the ambassador touched his fingertips to the air above her palms and bowed, retreated the full twelve steps backward, then bowed again at the door before it boomed shut behind him.

"Five years," the Duchas of Chandos began in a querulous voice.

"'His majesty,'" the Duchas of Mondereas repeated contemptuously. He was one of the few leaders who had survived the war previous to Detlev's enchantment. "Just because we were away a century can he possibly think we are not aware that his king is mad?"

"Who really makes the decisions in Colend?" a duchas asked. She was young, and very new to both her title and her place on the council, as her elders had all been killed in the failed defense of Sartor before the enchantment.

A babble of voices broke out.

Chief Veltos had turned away from Atan as if she really were an invisible part of the throne. But now she placed her hands together and bowed to Atan, saying, "We would not keep you from your interview, your majesty. We will take counsel among one another and wait upon you at your convenience."

In other words, they would tell her what to do.

Atan made her first-circle bow. The high council bowed, heads low until she left the chamber.

She knew she shouldn't complain. She had not been raised as a royal heir, in spite of all of Tsauderei's efforts. Neither he nor Gehlei, the bodyguard who had run with Atan, could train a Sartoran queen the way monarchs had been trained for centuries. She had a lot to learn, and she knew that the high council worked tirelessly to bring Sartor back into a world that had gone on for nearly a century while Sartor was frozen beyond time.

As Atan walked back, she glanced along the corridors, mentally ticking off all the people who watched over her.

First was Chief Veltos, who headed the Sartoran mage guild as well as the high council that governed the kingdom while Atan learned statecraft.

There was the council-appointed herald-steward, who taught her the traditions and protocol of that statecraft.

There was the wardrobe mistress, who chose exactly the right clothing for every occasion and saw to it that everything was fresh, the embroidery perfect, the panels creased.

There was a personal maid whose job it was to brush out Atan's hank of brown hair, trying to coax highlights into it, and dressing it up with pearls and tiny gems worked into butterflies and blossoms. There was a maid whose job it was to expertly twitch away any evidence of a tiny hangnail on her cuticles, to keep her nails buffed and trimmed.

Then there were the scribes, heralds, and pages who inexorably swept her from one event to another all through her day.

There was somehow in her carefully orchestrated schedule scarce time or place for friends.

Hibern's mood had turned uneasy when the morvende boy reappeared. "I found her! They had her closeted with the Colendi ambassador." He said that as he opened a door, and fluttered those distracting orange talons in invitation for Hibern to go through.

Hibern gained a vague impression of a beautiful room, full of light and color, but her attention went straight to the girl her own age who rustled in from another door, her smile tentative until she saw Hinder's orange talons. She laughed, a quick, soft sound. "Orange, Hin?"

"Sin considered purple, then decided your overseers would be even more aghast at orange." He walked out, shutting the door behind him.

The two girls were left alone.

Both Hibern and Atan were used to being the tallest of anyone their age. Their gazes met at eye level, each appraising, and a little shy. Each wanting to like, and to be liked. The two girls took one another in: Hibern a thin girl plainly dressed in cream linen with blue over it; Atan a big girl wearing an elaborate costume consisting of a stiff brocaded under-gown in green, made high to the neck, the lace edging goffered, an over-robe of pure white silk embroidered with stylized patterns of wheat, and over that, a brocade stole of gold, with interlocked patterns connected by stars picked out in gems and tiny pearls. Her brown hair was bound into a coronet made of three braids, threaded through with gold.

"Welcome," Atan said—just one word, no ritual greetings, but the tone made it sound real. "Before we begin I must apologize for keeping you waiting."

Hibern belatedly remembered her bow, and performed it, feeling intensely awkward, as Marlovens did not bow.

"Come within, please, and do make yourself comfortable," Atan said, indicating an oval-backed chair, as she sat in its twin.

Hibern had been warned that most outland rulers would keep visitors standing. In Sartor's history, she'd read, people once had had to kneel before royalty. In Marloven Hess, the throne was on a dais, so the jarls in the back could see the king and the king could see them. As Senrid said, "Kings up on daises were also great for target practice when the jarls wanted a new king."

Hibern sat on the edge of her chair, hands flat on her knees. So far Atan was not using the formalities she had been told to expect. So she must rely on her own eyes and ears.

"I may address you as Hibern?" Atan asked.

"Yes, your majesty."

"And you learn magic from Erai-Yanya?"

"Yes, your majesty."

"Have you studied at all at the northern mage school in Bereth Ferian?"

"I go there once a month. My tutor wishes me to study certain things with the students, your majesty." When Atan seemed to be waiting for more, Hibern said, "Erai-Yanya goes there to visit her son, as well as to lecture to senior students on advanced magic. Arthur was made heir to King Evend. Before Evend died—"

Atan's hand came up. "I'm familiar with the tragic history. That is, I've heard about Evend dying and taking the Norsunder rift with him, which ended the Siamis enchantment last year. So you learn from these northerners, and yet, if I'm not misled, you're from the south?"

"Marloven Hess, your majesty," Hibern stated.

Atan's eyes widened. Hibern was distracted by the color of Atan's eyes, a rare dark blue. One couldn't call such protuberant eyes pretty, but they were distinctive, a familiar feature of her exalted lineage. Anywhere else in the world, she'd be called plain—as would Hibern herself.

"How is it that a Marloven came to study light magic? From everything I've heard, they have been . . ." Atan made a gesture. "Not allies. Your family differed, or have I been given false information?"

"Yes, and no, your majesty." A gesture invited Hibern to elaborate. She forced herself to say, "You're not wrong." She'd known this subject would come sooner or later. May as well get it over with. "My father practices dark magic. Traditional in Marloven Hess. He was responsible for spell renewal, wards, and protections. But the regent wanted more, things like loyalty spells. My father, well, the short answer is, he tried his best to find such—did some experiments for the King of the Chwahir in return for certain spells—and used the household for the experiments. My brother most of all."

Atan grimaced. "What happened to your brother?"

"He went mad, your majesty. Even worse, the regent was impatient, as Senrid was learning magic fast, and beginning to question his uncle's decisions. The loyalty and obedience spells were intended for Senrid. The regent tried some of those on his own daughter, as he didn't quite dare to try them on Senrid until he knew they'd work."

"May I inquire after the result? You did say yes and no."

"The 'yes' part of my answer is that one of my aunts is connected to the local governor, your majesty. She was always giving me books about history. I told her I wanted to learn magic, to fix poor Stefan, and to save the rest of us—well . . ." Despite her best efforts, Hibern could feel her throat tightening. "The short answer is, I began to study light magic. In secret. To counter my father's spells."

Atan leaned forward. "Who taught you?"

"Lilith the Guardian."

Atan sat bolt upright. "You've *met* her?" The mysterious mage Lilith the Guardian appeared in the world perhaps once a century, guarding the world from Norsunder. Though she certainly didn't guard Sartor a century ago, Atan thought to herself.

"Yes. She found me. I don't know how. Gave me my first light magic books, and introduced me to history outside our own. Pointed out the green star, so bright in the sky, and said that it was Songre Silde, a world circling our sun. And that the tiny dull one is Aldau-Rayad, destroyed in the Fall. She told me that we have a sister world—"

"Geth-deles!" Atan exclaimed. "Circling opposite us, so we never see Geth-deles in our skies. Do you find that amazing, too?"

Hibern's tone lightened as she said, "When I first heard about Geth-deles being a twin world opposite ours, I thought that Lilith meant a world exactly like ours, and that there was a Hibern on it, but she moved backward to me, maybe using this hand instead of this." She held up one palm, then the next.

Atan rocked back on her chair, her fabulous silks rustling and crushing as she clapped in delight. "Oh, that's wonderful! So Lilith taught you magic?"

"Well, she gave me my first magic books. Our visits were brief. She warned me they would be. She couldn't always come." Hibern paused to take a deep breath. "She cautioned me about studying secretly, what it might mean if I got caught. By my family. I didn't care. I wanted to fix Stefan, and I knew I was *right*..."

Another pause, as she gazed into memory, evoking the pain of the past year. "The regent's rewards to my father turned to threats. The king was getting harder for him to control. He also offered one further reward: to marry me to the king when we came of age. My family has never married into the royal family, but they've served loyally for generations. My family would gain thereby."

"So you would have been married off to an enchanted king."

"Yes, your majesty."

"Go on, please, Hibern."

"I was eleven then. I wanted more study time. I turned

an accidental fall into a fake permanent injury. Got a reputation as poor mad lame Hibern. Ah, being physically strong is important in my country. Crippled limbs from war wounds give one prestige, but falling down the stairs makes one despised. I studied in secret, countering my father's spells when I could."

Another deep breath.

"Lilith the Guardian came one last time, to say that Norsunder was rising again, and she could no longer come as she had too many places to watch that might be under imminent attack. She introduced me to Erai-Yanya, to see if we might fit together as tutor and student, then Sartor came back, and Siamis appeared. You know the rest better than I."

Atan leaned forward, her gaze intent. "I know the history of the Siamis enchantment, though I spent that year enchanted into a dream sleep, like most of the rest of the kingdom. The world. Go on, please."

Hibern went on in her most neutral voice, "Your Sartoran mage guild had sent mages north, so they didn't fall into the enchantment. When they came back, they put out the call for aid. Erai-Yanya said it would be good practice to come here to Sartor, to help your guild close those rifts through which Norsunder could move armies as fast as the Norsundrian mages made them."

Hibern dropped her gaze, remembering the Sartoran Mage Chief Veltos exclaiming, *A Marloven? Have we come to such a pass?* Even worse, when Erai-Yanya fell into a dark magic trap, Hibern was the first one questioned, as if she'd been responsible. And even after Tsauderei managed to break Erai-Yanya out, the Sartoran mages still insisted that Hibern be assigned to help the elementary students. She was never let anywhere near the Tower of Knowledge.

But none of that was Atan's fault, Hibern knew.

While Hibern thought, unaware that her pause had stretched almost to a silence, Atan watched Hibern's tightly clasped hands and her lowered gaze, before Hibern said, "I could only help with elementary spells. When Siamis was defeated and the rift magic destroyed, I returned home."

By then the memories crowding her mind were so strong she was unaware of the pain in her face, and her white-knuckled grip on her hands. She shut her eyes against the betraying sting of tears. "When I got home, I . . . my father had discovered my study. What I had been doing. To counter his wards."

The image of her father's face replaced Atan's, his eyes wide with fury, his mouth twisted with disgust as he screamed at her.

A vile traitor in my own home? 'Help Stefan'—what do you think I've been doing this past year? What you have done has worsened everything. I could have reversed those spells by now.

Sick dismay chilled Atan as Hibern's gaze blanked and her voice lowered to a whisper of pain. "He told me to go. So I left."

Still gripped by memory, Hibern felt the echo of her father's finger poking into her forehead, then his open hand as he slapped her away.

Get out of this house. Hibern remembered lying on the floor dizzily, looking up at the vein ticking in his forehead. Then turning to her mother as she cried, *But I wanted to fix things. That's what light magic does.*

Hibern's throat ached as she remembered her mother's furious face, her low, angry whisper, *Then you could have done it another way besides sneaking behind our backs.*

Abruptly Hibern recollected time and place. And shut her eyes, mortified. She strove for a normal voice. "So I live with Erai-Yanya now. And Senrid—our king—asked me to tutor him in light magic. Your majesty," Hibern belatedly remembered.

"Call me Atan," was the answer, with a quick gesture, as Atan looked away, disturbed by the pain her question had caused. "You may drop the 'your majesty' if it's not part of your habit of courtly speech. It certainly wasn't part of my own upbringing."

"I don't have any courtly speech training, your majesty," Hibern said. "Other than being coached to always append 'your majesty' to a response asked for by, well, you."

Atan cast an uneasy look at her hands. "Does your king require such honorifics?"

"We don't have any honorifics such as 'your grace' or

'your majesty.' Titles are part of the holder's name. King Senrid is Senrid-Harvaldar in our tongue."

Atan gave her a sober glance. "I asked Tsauderei for a study partner my age, who wasn't from an exalted family that would expect favors, and who wasn't considered a part of either of the magic schools . . . well, because. Do you have any questions for me?"

"What was it like?" Hibern asked. "Coming back into the world after a century, I mean?"

"I didn't, really. I mean, I did, but as a baby. I was born a century ago. My mother's last act was to send me away, carried by one of her bodyguards. Gehlei fought her way out of the city, and even though she was wounded so badly she lost an arm, she made it with me almost to the eastern border when the enchantment caught us. We were discovered by Tsauderei, lying there on the mountainside. I was a crying baby, and Gehlei's wound was still fresh. He took us back to his valley, which is a very old mage retreat that Norsunder cannot get into. There, I grew up during the last fifteen years of the enchantment. As I was just a baby when it happened, I don't remember anything of the war, or the time before. But I spend all day every day with those who do."

Atan's smile was pensive. "It was so happy, at first. Then . . . then they started learning what it meant for them, that their yesterday had happened close to a century ago in the rest of the world. We had ninety-seven-year-old stores in the cupboards, and all our old ties with the world had been broken. The treasury was completely empty, because of the war my father lost. Trade monies had vanished, treaties no longer had meaning. Reclamation is near impossible from those long dead. People who had relatives outside the country . . . don't. A lot of them had already lost their families in the war."

Like yours? Hibern thought, but didn't say it. She'd been bitter about being driven out of her home, troubled as it was, but at least her family was alive. Atan was never going to get her family back.

A distant bell bonged, and Atan sighed. "The steward will send someone to fetch me soon. My duties leave me this one hour a week, and I mean to keep up with my magic studies. I don't want to lose what I worked so hard to gain. I study better if I have someone to do it with. Will you come back?"

"Yes," Hibern said. That would mean several transfers in a day, but from Marloven Hess to Sartor was considerably less than from Roth Drael to Sartor. And she did have to get used to it.

"Thank you," Atan said. "I so look forward to it!"

"So do I," Hibern said, but before she could add anything else, there was an insistent tap on the door.

Atan said, "Enter."

As the door opened, Hibern got to her feet, bowed self-consciously, and slipped past the entering servant, who gave her a stern glance before greeting the young queen in formal language.

Hibern walked slowly back to the Destination, her mind filled with that conversation, so unexpected in every way. Despite all the coaching about protocol, and her knowledge of Atan's prestigious background, it struck Hibern that Atan was a lot like herself.

In a thoughtful mood, she shifted back to Roth Drael.

Erai-Yanya looked up at the flash and air-stirring of transfer magic. She took in Hibern's closed expression and turned back to the letter she was writing to her son.

Hibern went to her room, where she stood, head bowed. Except for that wakening of those horrible feelings of rejection, she thought it had gone well. Enough of that shudder inside remained for her to breathe in and out, reminding herself that she had the life she wanted, and further, the Queen of Sartor had accepted her, despite her background and mistakes, to be her study partner.

She went out to find Erai-Yanya sealing a finished letter.

"Hungry?" Erai-Yanya asked, indicating a covered dish from which steam still trickled. "How did it go?"

"Oh, Atan is great. Her majesty. She wants me to call her Atan." Hibern sat down. "The best moment was finding out we both like history. And the study of worlds. The formal language from the servants was what I expected, public circle, polite and correct, but the moment I met the morvende boy Hin, everything went different."

"How?"

Hibern told her, then added baldly, "I told her the truth about myself. Because that was a promise I made to myself. The queen—Atan—did me the courtesy of listening. And kept herself from saying anything about Marlovens."

Erai-Yanya ran a quill through her fingers. "Pause, Hibern. Do not invest her words with insult that was not there. So begins misunderstanding. I feel fairly certain that the impression she has of Marlovens is that when they are not at war, they practice civility. Sartorans practice courtesy. And the Colendi practice politesse. You do perceive the difference?"

Hibern flushed. "I take it back. When I was done, I guess I hoped it was me she would find interesting, not a Marloven oddity."

"I expect it was both." Erai-Yanya chuckled. "Orange talons! The morvende are doing it to annoy the Sartoran first circle, and maybe even the high council, I should imagine."

"Why?" Hibern's emotions swooped.

Erai-Yanya pursed her lips, still running the feather through her fingers. "Is it not clear? Atan's had a strange upbringing, as she told you herself. What she didn't tell you is that she's next thing to a prisoner." As Hibern gasped, Erai-Yanya stuck the quill into her untidy bun. "Oh, it's not like your kingdom, iron bars, torture chambers—"

Hibern was going to interject that Marlovens, for the most part, despised torture, but kept silent.

"—kings and jarls murdering one another right and left. Everyone in Sartor seems to be doing their duty as they see it, but they have Atan nearly strangled in protocol and obligation, the more so because they're all certain that Detlev of Norsunder, or Siamis, whoever gains the ascendance over the other, is going to come back."

Senrid believes it, too, Hibern thought, but decided against saying it, after that crack about Marlovens. She knew Erai-Yanya didn't intend to be mean, but she was so ignorant about Marloven Hess. And she had no interest in learning about a primarily military kingdom with a problematical past.

Erai-Yanya continued, "The thing to understand is that the young queen's morvende friends are trying to loosen those constraints as best they can, since they have the freedom to do it."

"I've never heard of morvende being in royal palaces like that."

"They usually aren't. Even when they come sunside, they have nothing to do with sunsider governments, and they pay no attention to political boundaries. But in Sartor, it's always been different. And those two, Hinder and Sinder, were part of the Shendoral Rescuers, the youths who helped the queen break the century-long enchantment. They have a special status."

"But the queen—Atan—"

"Call her Atan. She really needs to be Atan to someone, without expectation in return, even if it's only for an hour a week."

"Well, that's easy enough."

"Hibern." Erai-Yanya leaned forward, her expression sardonic. "Nothing is ever easy in Sartor."

THE alliance, so far, numbered thus: the Mearsieans, whom nobody had ever heard of and nobody would pay attention to if they had; Senrid, whose kingdom everyone had heard of and distrusted; and Hibern, a lowly mage student unclaimed by either school, who had lost her home.

All of them approached the idea of recruitment in significantly varying ways. The single shared conviction was that any alliance must form some kind of defense against Norsunder.

However, 'Norsunder' was no more a unified entity than their alliance.

The same day that Hibern visited Sartor, a week's ride south of Sartor's border, everyone in the vast fortress called Norsunder Base stilled as greenish lightning flashed in windows. The vast granite construct resonated with an abyssal boom more felt than heard.

The burnt-metal smell to the air, gone in an instant, warned the mage Dejain that a mass transfer had been attempted, and had failed. Those who had attempted it had vanished into whatever-it-was between physical locations.

She met the eyes of Lesca, the fortress steward, and sighed. "Why *do* they keep trying to transfer in groups? They know the rifts are gone."

Lesca grimaced. "Because everyone's plots need to have happened yesterday, of course." Her eyes crinkled with amusement, as she sat back comfortably on her chair, a large, curvy woman with a taste for the delicate embroideries and fragile silks of Colend. "I guess I won't be needing to find space for this latest bunch."

"I had better go see what's happened," Dejain said, though she'd just arrived at Lesca's request. "They'll be wanting the mages."

"Do that," Lesca said. "Then come back and tell me everything."

Dejain left the steward's chamber and turned the corner toward Norsunder Base's command center, where she was waved past the sentries. She started down the hall to the room at the other end of the soot-blackened, torchlit hall.

She had expected to be the first arrival, as Lesca's suite was two short halls from the command center in the enormous fortress. But she didn't expect the only two voices in the command center to be speaking in the lilting Ancient Sartoran that Dejain had expended much effort to attempt learning.

Siamis and his uncle Detlev, alone? She glanced back. As expected, the sentries faced outward. All she saw were their backs. She didn't quite understand all that talk about mind-shields, but she knew from personal experience that Detlev really was able to invade someone's thoughts, and so she closed her eyes, and imagined a brick wall encircling her head. When she had that image, she tried to listen from within it, the way one would listen to a conversation from the other side of a fence.

". . . and you were wrong by at least a century." That was Siamis, the handsome young nephew, grown up under the aegis of Norsunder. Everyone knew that Siamis had been taken hostage as a boy of twelve, over four thousand years ago, forcing Detlev to go into Norsunder-Beyond to try to rescue him. What no record revealed was what Ilerian, the most terrifying of the Host of Lords, had done to Detlev to turn him against Sartor.

Siamis's voice was tenor, expressive—a singer's voice, though Dejain had never heard him sing.

"Yes," Detlev said. His voice was just a voice, never very expressive. In her mercifully brief encounters with him, Dejain had never heard him angry, which made some of the things he did far more unnerving. "Which means we have to find it first."

"You must," Siamis retorted.

"I must," Detlev agreed.

What was 'it'? Dejain did not understand the tone. Was that anger or laughter?

Siamis went on in that same tone, "And so. My plan. The spells need alteration, not the strategy."

"Evend may be gone, but Tsauderei is very much alive, Oalthoreh in Bereth Ferian has sent her journeymages through the world to create tracers specifically to reveal your presence, and Sartor has been adapting to a century of change with commendable speed. Today is probably evidence of that."

"My very dear uncle," Siamis drawled. "When you point out the obvious—"

"—it means you have overlooked something obvious. The new orders must supersede the old."

"Are we back to the brats, then? I've seen to it that Liere Fer Eider is afraid of her own shadow. I cannot improve on what you did to Senrid Montredaun-An. Between the two of them, they are sufficiently intimidated into hiding behind childhood. It has even become a fad."

Detlev's voice quieted. Dejain held her breath. "See that it spreads. I need time to investigate the Geth claims. And you must make readiness here your first concern."

"I thought that was *your* first concern." Siamis's retort betrayed nothing but good humor. "Or is my freedom to act conditional after all?"

"I condition for nothing. The Host might see a different view from the Garden of the Twelve—"

Clattering echoed up the stairway opposite Lesca's suite: armed warriors on the way. Dejain must not be seen lurking outside the command center.

Keeping her steps noiseless, she scurried toward the sentries, and just before the new arrivals reached the corner and the sentries she whirled, so she would be seen walking toward command.

Before she stepped over the threshold, she glanced back at the group of warriors. That arrogant young Henerek strode at the front, recognizable instantly by his size and his thick, sandy hair. He was followed by lesser talents and ambitions.

Dejain passed inside the chamber, darting a quick glance at Siamis and Detlev for any sign of awareness of having been spied upon. Detlev stood directly below the big world map on the far wall. He was an ordinary-looking man above medium height, brown hair worn collar length in a military cut, tunic and trousers of so plain a design he would go unnoticed in most kingdoms of the south, and probably in the north as well. His expression revealed nothing.

Beyond him, his nephew Siamis lounged against a table, slim and graceful, his head bent, so all Dejain could see was his fair hair, gilt in the glowglobes' light.

Detlev turned Henerek's way. "I take it you were the fool who just obliterated four well-trained captains by attempting a group transfer. Or was that your intent?"

"They were *my* captains. For the challenge," Henerek retorted, then added sullenly, "There's never been any problem with transferring from Five. I distinctly recollect bringing two others along the last time I transferred."

"That," said Detlev, "was previous to Sartor's mages' recent gift. Or someone's. You did not get the general order: single transfers only, no more than four in a day, then test with a stone first?"

Henerek looked down, then up, his fingers twitching absently at his sword hilt. Or was that a sign of intent?

Siamis bestowed on them his gentle smile. "Henerek seems to feel that he's the exception to general orders. Or we wouldn't be gathered today." He made a lazy wave toward the window, through which Dejain glimpsed the long line of warriors moving into the broad plain where the wargames were held. She remembered that today's wargame was different from the usual: a challenge for command of Norsunder Base—Henerek against Siamis.

Detlev did not acknowledge the interruption. He said to Henerek, "If you were taking the field against Ralanor Veleth today, and four of your captains dropped with arrows in them, would you request a postponement from Szinzar, until such time as you could arrange for replacements?"

The scrape of a foot and a half-suppressed chuckle from the watching circle caused Henerek to glance back, a flush of anger on his heavy-jawed countenance. The avid audience fell silent.

"Regard your failed transfer as a . . . shall we call it a tactical error? Your challenge will go forward as planned."

Siamis sighed, sounding weary and bored.

For the time it took for Dejain's heart to beat three times, no one moved.

Dejain held her breath, aware of the shifts in stance, the brush of hands over hilts, among the watchers. Henerek had gone still, almost rigid. Nobody needed mysterious mind powers to see how much he loathed the two Ancient Sartorans. Though Dejain had never seen Detlev wearing a weapon, and Henerek positively bristled with steel.

Finally Henerek muttered, "I'll see you on the field." He stalked out.

With quick glances in Detlev's direction, the rest of the military clattered after him, leaving Dejain wondering whom they would have helped if Henerek had assaulted Detlev.

She wondered whose aid, if any, Siamis would come to.

With the warriors gone, Dejain saw the two mages who had come in behind the warriors.

Detlev lifted his head. "Dejain. Attend to the transfer problem, please."

Dejain said, "I just came from the steward, who sent for me."

Detlev replied, "Give Lesca anything she wants, of course. Then investigate the transfer problem, and fix it." He vanished abruptly, as usual, not even going to the Destination in order to transfer.

Siamis's gaze lifted from the window. "This should be fun," he said. Gone was the affect of boredom that had so goaded Henerek. His expression was thoughtful as he walked out. Unlike Henerek's, his step was noiseless, but

Dejain thought that he was just as dull and simple as Henerek, really. All men were simple, she thought sourly as she faced the two mages still left in the room.

The mages were both men, one old and unfamiliar, and Pengris, young and ambitious. "What happened, exactly?" she asked him. "Were either of you in the Destination chamber?"

Pengris said, "I was. Henerek summoned me to sweep the Destination for traps or wards, which I did. I found nothing amiss. The transfers nearly made it. I saw four silhouettes, then that flash of light. When I could see again, there was no one on the tiles. They were gone."

"Silhouettes," Dejain repeated, her skin crawling. "I've never heard of a transfer failing . . . like that."

"Neither have I," the elder said uneasily. "Who could have warded our Destination?" He turned to the young one. "They were coming from Five, am I correct?"

The Norsunder base on the world the lighters had once called Aldau-Rayad before it was destroyed in the Fall had as much protective magic over its transfer Destination as this one. Because Aldau-Rayad was the fifth world from Erhal, the sun, it was known among them as Five.

Dejain and the gray-haired man turned to Pengris, a weedy, sparse-haired fellow. Dejain had pegged him for the type who often studied magic because they hated people.

He sighed, a loose strand of reddish hair lifting, his eyes shifting in a way that reminded Dejain of a rat caught in a trap.

He was young, but experienced in subterfuge, misdirection, and imaginative nastiness. Right now he was caught square: the Destination at Five was his responsibility.

"The problem is not at this end," Dejain said. Pengris licked his lips, and Dejain knew he was trying to slither out. Transfers hurt, everyone knew it. World transfers hurt far worse. Younger bodies sustained the effects better.

He sighed again, resigned and irritated. "I'll shift to Five to investigate."

"Wait at least two hours. Then use a token," Dejain warned. An already-spelled transfer token had the best chance of escaping any general wards, though they hurt substantially more than established Destination chambers.

He walked out, already nervous as he exited.

How Detlev managed to transfer so easily without Destinations, Dejain wondered, not for the first time. He was so very much older than she was, some would say impossibly old. But then Ilerian, the strangest of the Host of Lords, who seldom emerged from the Garden of the Twelve at the center of Norsunder, was said to be far older. And neither of them looked a day over thirty. Her shoulder blades prickled with a crawly sensation.

Detlev was just a man. They are all the same in essence, she reminded herself as she turned over her hands, so small and youthful-looking.

She'd begun to use dark magic to halt her aging when she turned twenty-two, and so she knew she appeared as she had then, a dainty, blonde figure. Even before that spell had been broken once, nearly killing her, she'd begun to feel the subtle pull of age. It was inescapable, and the best way to keep that pull from becoming direr was to live very carefully. Sometimes she felt ancient, and certainly far more aware than those around her, but Detlev and Siamis managed to make her regain all the awkwardness and uncertainty of youth, without any of its strength.

Still, they obviously had their limits: for all their vaunted powers, they hadn't perceived her listening outside of command.

She smiled as she rejoined Lesca and reported what she'd seen and heard.

Though Lesca was no older than forty, she was far from stupid. To double-check, Dejain finished, "I heard the words, but the context completely escapes me as much as my presence escaped them. Though I'm fairly certain that Siamis is fretting under Detlev's control."

"That's been the case for a year," Lesca drawled.

"But that about 'it.' What can they mean?"

"Something they're looking for," Lesca said, amused.

"The dyra? The lighters got the one, and destroyed the other."

"Why does it have to be a thing? How about a person, an idea? A specific place that gives them military advantage? All I know is, it's more plotting." Lesca yawned. "Present company excepted, I find mages unspeakably tedious, even more than I find politics. Everybody wants something they don't have. Except me. I sometimes wonder if I'm the smartest person in this place, because I am wise enough not to have ambition." Lesca lifted a lazy hand to encompass her comfortable rooms.

"Detlev and Siamis are not like the rest of us," Dejain stated.

"And here's me wondering if Siamis leans right." Lesca tipped her head.

Dejain understood the current idiom, at least among Norsunder's warriors: 'right' meant right hand, sword hand, preference for men. 'Left,' shield hand, ring hand in some cultures, preference for females. Both-handed for interest beyond gender limitation.

"Someone insisted they saw him in one of the more exclusive houses up north somewhere, under a guise. As one would expect with a very young man. I wonder if Detlev is made of wood, and I don't mean that in any interesting way." Lesca chuckled, running her hand through her silky hair, which was now colored a rich chestnut. "This I do know. Neither of them shows the least interest in any of the hirelings I take such trouble to recruit." She shrugged, tipping her head in the direction of the rec wing, across the great courtyard, where Lesca had installed pleasure house workers for those who earned the privilege.

Dejain knew that discipline had been better since Lesca brought them in. Before then, warriors at Norsunder Base, which was considered a way station, were on their own during their liberty watch. No sexual outlets beyond what they could find among one another usually meant more fights, and horrific punishments. The former commander had felt that that made for better fighters. Siamis—young as he was—had told Lesca that fighting was better if there was an immediate reward for exertion, like her present arrangement.

Lesca lifted her upper lip. "Do you think he goes off-world to seek perversions, as they whisper about Efael?"

Dejain grimaced at the name of the youngest of the Host of Lords. In so many ways he was the worst of them. At least the nastiest, and his sister the second worst. If rumor was true, the least objectionable sexual play those two indulged in was with one another. "You would think there would be whispers if he did."

"If Henerek wins, and his face isn't distorted, I'll crook my finger, and he'll be here as fast as he can." Lesca shrugged indolently, and turned her head toward the far wall, which was smooth, painted white. "But if Siamis wins, and I crook my finger, he'll look at me with that air of question. I loathe that. I hope Henerek wins, though Siamis is so much prettier."

Lesca picked up the wand that Dejain had ensorcelled, and pointed it at the wall, whispering. An image replaced the wall, the vantage from the topmost tower of the fortress, with an unimpeded view of the cracked plain beyond, on which no blade of grass had grown for centuries. In ragged lines, the contending forces were drawing together according to each commander's placement.

Dejain had put together the spells: Lesca had only to visit a spot somewhere in the fortress once, look at the view she wished to see, touch the wand, and speak the simple charm Dejain had set up. Thereafter she could sit in her comfortable chamber and watch from that vantage. Dejain had thought at most Lesca would limit herself to three or four views, maybe half a dozen, as the spells pulled a great deal of magic potential.

"How many views have you set?" Dejain asked.

"I've lost count," Lesca said cheerfully.

Dejain suppressed an exclamation. She'd carefully explained how much magic was used for each, but Lesca seemed to have as little regard for magic as Dejain had for sex. No wonder the Destination was becoming more unstable. It probably wasn't Sartor at fault, or Five.

But she did not know for certain. She glanced up, to find Lesca regarding her with that narrow, observant gaze. "Speaking of petrified wood," Lesca said. "Have you considered that those two knew you were listening to them? You know their reputation."

"I think most of that is hyperbole." Dejain settled back on her cushion. "Oh, I know they can speak from mind to mind. And listen. But you will probably have experienced the latter: there's a pang like a needle stuck behind your eyes, and your own words echo inside your head, and that didn't occur while I was eavesdropping just now. As for the talking from mind to mind, surely it must take even more effort than normal listening must."

"At least, outside of the Garden of the Twelve." Lesca's profile was avid as she watched Henerek riding to the front of his force. Though the foot and mounted warriors all carried wooden swords, Henerek brandished naked steel, evidence that he was willing to fight Siamis to the death for command of Norsunder Base. "Ah. There's Henerek, sword a-swing. The show is about to begin. Why is it that the boys can finish a fight with the other sword still a-swing, but the women just want a hot bath?"

Dejain didn't bother making the obvious observation that there were exceptions to everything, even among warriors, whose minds she found dull or repellent.

Dejain glanced to the other side, easily spotting Siamis by his white shirt and blond head. He scorned uniforms, and as the weather, for once, was clement, there he was, without his famous sword. She did not understand why he'd left it in Bereth Ferian after his defeat there. Another game, no doubt. Like his uncle, he seemed to prefer carrying no weapon, a different sort of arrogance.

Dejain listened with the least part of her attention as Lesca began a dispassionate catalogue of various captains' physical attributes and drawbacks. Once, very long ago, Dejain had cared about such things, but that had been in her young days, before she found her way to dark magic. She remembered standing silently as a servant as the baras's daughter and her friend held just such conversations, but of course no servant's opinion would be sought.

Dejain uttered agreements during the pauses, to hide her disinterest. At least the divan was comfortable for her sensitive joints. She cooperatively turned her gaze to the window, but her attention was inward rather than on the two lines racing together as she mentally reviewed varieties of transfer traps, tracers, and wards. She would have to delve into research, once the witnesses' reports had been heard . . .

"Yes indeed," Dejain said again, when she became aware of an expectant pause from Lesca. When you haven't been listening, agreement is almost always safest.

Lesca shot her an inquisitive glance. "But coming back

to Henerek. He's willing enough, even delightfully brusque, but I sense he's not seeing *me*. I pride myself on my not-inconsiderable skills, but whose face is he seeing over mine? One wishes to be noticed for one's efforts."

"Most certainly," Dejain said tranquilly, thinking that though Lesca's favorite subject was herself, at least she didn't prate of love.

Lesca sighed.

Men were useful only as toys. For companionship of the mind, Lesca preferred women—but they had to share at least a sense of humor, if not Lesca's interests.

Smart women in command positions were rare at Norsunder Base: Vatiora was dead (and good riddance, as she'd been crazy); Yeres was infinitely worse, but at least she rarely appeared and then only for moments; the new spy, Elzhier, was a smart-mouthed teen and kept constantly in the field; Nath, a female captain with brains, was down there behind Henerek right now, which just left Dejain. Mages were generally unsatisfactory as company, male or female. Their minds were always in magical fogs.

Below, the trumpet blared, the signal to begin.

The neat lines of marching and mounted warriors began to waver, and met. Lesca leaned forward to watch, wishing she could pick out details better. Henerek smashed and clubbed at the center of his line, two big men at either side. Whatever clever strategy he'd come up with had had to be abandoned when he lost his best captains, so he'd fallen back on the old charge, strongest at the midpoint, the intent to cut the opposing line and roll them up separately.

Siamis rode directly behind his main two lines, one making a shield wall and the other armed with cudgels. He looked so easy in the saddle with those graceful straight limbs unencumbered by any weapons. He could have commanded by mental communication. He'd forestalled complaints about advantages by using signal flags, same as Henerek—not that the latter signaled, with his captains gone.

Siamis turned his head, then spoke to one of his outriders. A whirl and dip of the flag, and chosen squads in the reinforcement line formed up into wedges. They muscled up behind their mates in the first two lines, who were still struggling to resist the chaotic charge.

The two lines stirred as squad captains shouted orders. Henerek's chargers, clearly taking this movement for surrender, lost all form as they pressed together, all struggling to be first through the openings, presenting a solid target for the wedges.

Smash! They hit Henerek's straggled line and shattered it and all semblance of order, as everyone began fighting. Those who surrendered fell to their knees.

Henerek stilled, head twisting back and forth, and then Siamis turned his head, beckoned, and pointed.

A familiar short, slim, black-haired figure, also instantly recognizable, launched through the melee like an arrow from a bow. Dejain's heart jolted with fear when she recognized Kessler Sonscarna, the renegade Chwahir prince she'd once worked with on his mad plan to replace the world's most powerful rulers with people of his own training. Dejain had never believed he would succeed, and had betrayed Kessler to save her own skin. As was expected in Norsunder. But Kessler was . . . mad.

He fought his way through Henerek's big guards as if they were straw targets, hitting them with unnerving speed in nerve clusters that caused limbs to freeze in breath-hitching pain. Then he found Henerek.

Lesca was leaning forward, elbows on knees. "Look at him," she said appreciatively. "He's smart, he's fast, and he's brutal. I think he's broken Henerek's arm! This will make him a captain at last, one would think. Why isn't he a captain?"

"Because he's insane," Dejain said.

"But that's so often an attribute." Lesca uttered a deep chuckle as, below on the field, Kessler threw away Henerek's cudgel and attacked with his bare hands. "I heard that Efael himself sent him to bottle up that disgusting old crock in Chwahirsland, but he doesn't seem to be grateful for the privilege, does he?"

"That's because Kessler would have preferred to gut the old crock and watch him die at his feet," Dejain said.

Below, Henerek circled around Kessler, who waited in stillness, only his head moving. Henerek's left arm dangled, but he gripped a sword in his right.

At last Henerek struck. He lasted about four blows, then

measured his length in the dust. "Do you think Henerek's dead? No, he's moving." Lesca shook her head. "You worked with him once. What kind of lover does Kessler like?"

"Never saw him with anyone," Dejain said. "I think Kessler's too insane for anything normal like sex."

"They say he never lies."

Dejain understood. The more she warned Lesca away from Kessler, the more interest Lesca would take, especially since Henerek was on his way to the lazaretto, probably for some weeks' stay. "He's a Chwahir," she said.

Lesca grimaced. "I forgot that. He doesn't move like them, or act like them. They're so . . . so furtive," she finished in disgust. "No wonder I've never seen him at the recreation wing."

Dejain didn't bother explaining that she knew little about his life other than that Kessler had escaped Wan-Edhe at age ten, and thus half of his life had been spent away from Land of the Chwahir. The thinking half.

Lesca made a noise of disappointment. "See there! It looks like Siamis is reorganizing them into drill groups. Now he'll work them until they can barely crawl after their commander back to their bunks." She rose. "What a disappointment. I may as well see about the cornmeal shipments, as soon as I know you mages have fixed the transfer. At least we should be able to get non-living things through."

Chapter Ten

Bath Rennet (Midsummer), 4737 AF
Bereth Ferian

IN Bereth Ferian's Hall of Light, the music swelled to a
glorious climax, four melodic lines braided by women's
voices, men's voices, children's, and the soloist as dancers
leaped back and forth, their streamers rippling in the air,
symbolizing the propagation of world-healing spells.

Every beautiful chord, every repetition of words such as
'glory' and 'peace' needled Liere Fer Eider's spirit.

She squirmed in the great chair that was so much like a
throne. She wanted to love the beautiful music and the brilliant dancing, because it was all for her. But she couldn't
enjoy it because it *was* for her. That is, it wasn't really for
her, it was for Sartora. Someone she wasn't.

The performance closed in a many-voiced *Hail Sartora,
who saved the world!* that made Liere prickle painfully all
over as if someone had stuck pins in her.

She forced herself to smile, though her teeth felt cold.

She then forced herself to turn in all directions in the
way taught her by Arthur, but she looked over the people's
heads so she couldn't see their faces, and she shut her mind

in tight so she wouldn't hear the thoughts people sprayed all over so freely.

She spoke the words of thanks that Arthur had helped her put together, and tried not to listen to how spindly and high her own voice sounded. ". . . and so I invite you to partake of refreshments in the Hall of Amber." She rushed the final words together, embarrassment making her skin crawl as she whispered *please-don't-bow please-don't-bow*.

A rustle and sigh as all the visiting Venn merchants made a profound, deliberate bow.

It was so sickening, so horribly false, and it wasn't her fault, it wasn't. If she could choose she never would be clumsy, stupid Liere Fer Eider, so boring the Mearsieans had been glad to go home and leave her behind.

Liere forced herself to smile. She got up and extended her hand toward the Hall of Amber, breathing freely once they turned toward the archway leading to the next room. As soon as the guests spied the food and drink, she sensed their attention shifting. A few lingered, apparently wanting to talk to her, but she'd gotten good at evading that.

The visiting Venn were quite tall. She found the tallest, slipped behind him, and waited while Arthur kindly drew attention by pointing out what people could already see: "Here's our attempt at Venn berry drink. Let us know how it tastes? And there are baked cabbage rolls that we are told are a Venn delicacy . . ."

Liere backed up. A quick step behind a substantial man with a complication of lemon-colored braids, a pause behind a carved column, and she was almost free. She tiptoed to the door, the back of her neck tight until she escaped into the empty hallway beyond.

On the other side of the room, Arthur watched her go, and sighed. She'd told him once that he was an "almost," that he might "make his unity," which had something to do with Dena Yeresbeth. If hearing others' thoughts turned one into a nail-biting, anxious mess like Liere, he didn't want this Dena Yeresbeth. In fact, if he detected any mysterious signs of such an ability in himself, he would do anything he could to avoid it.

"We have offended Sartora?"

Arthur turned around quickly, to find the Venn emissary standing there. The man was old, his face lined, his pale hair silvery white instead of the mostly-yellows Arthur saw in the rest.

"Not at all," Arthur said, and because he'd found the emissary easy to talk to, in spite of the Venn reputation for truculence, he added, "She's not comfortable in crowds."

The man inclined his head, the light running along the thin gold band around his brow, not quite a coronet. Arthur had seen that some wore them, some didn't, but he didn't know what they meant. He knew so little about the Venn, who historically never came out of their kingdom except to make war, centuries ago.

"Tell me about this child who can save a world, yet not endure a little conversation. Unless you are being diplomatic, and it is not crowds but Venn to whom she objects?"

"She doesn't know anything about the Venn," Arthur said quickly. "She came from a town where reading, especially for girls, was discouraged, as they were meant to keep shop. She told me she really liked your crown prince, whom she met after she broke Siamis's spell over your country."

The emissary's brows went up, and he smiled. "He is well-beloved, our Prince Kerendal. I shall take your words as truth, then, though it still does not explain why someone who did what she has done will not remain with us long enough to be thanked."

"She doesn't . . ." Arthur began, then halted. Maybe he was saying too much. He had already failed Liere, he felt, though he didn't know how to fix it. All along he'd wondered why she wanted the Mearsieans to stay, some of whom he found tiresome with their endless private jokes that they clearly thought so hilarious.

It wasn't until they'd left that he'd seen in Liere's dejection her hope to be invited back with them.

The sad thing was, though they might be silly or annoying, none of them were snobs. Arthur was very practiced at identifying snobs, after having served as a page and then as King Evend's chosen heir. The Mearsieans didn't think they were better than anyone else. They were a closed group. It didn't seem to have occurred to them that anyone new might want in. Especially Sartora, the Girl Who Saved the World.

The Venn emissary lifted his head. The Venn had divided into groups the way people tend to do in big crowds, a couple of them venturing apart to talk in a stiffly polite way with the magic students on duty.

"It would appear natural," the emissary said as they paced the perimeter of the Hall, "that someone who had done what she did could enjoy the accolades she earned."

"But that's it, she doesn't," Arthur said.

"Why not? She cannot think she failed."

"She was convinced by a friend that Siamis wasn't defeated. That he retreated, and will come again."

The Venn lifted his gnarled hand, his embroidered sleeve dropping back to reveal a diamond of Venn knot-work tattooed on his forearm above his wrist. "Norsunder always returns." Arthur had heard of Venn body art, but had never seen it; then the sleeve dropped back, hiding the mark. "We know that, and perhaps the knowing requires us to celebrate every defeat the more. Surely we would not wish to think, 'why bother?' Sartora does not have wise friends, if she has such an attitude at so young an age."

"It's not that at all," Arthur said. "Her friend is a Marloven."

"Ah-h-h."

The word was exhaled on a different note. Arthur remembered there was some ancient connection between the horrible, warlike Marlovens and the Venn. He had never wanted to meet any of them, though he'd come to rather like Senrid, puzzling as he was.

The emissary stared down at Arthur, an earnest young mage student without a fragment of the experience that had made wily old Evend such a splendid diplomat as well as mage. The emissary reflected that in olden times, before the magical construct called the Arrow had bound Venn magic, the Venn would have overrun this entire region in three days. In truth, they could do it now without magical aid.

But the old queen had spoken: *We will heed the treaty, and thereby we turn dishonor to honor. Norsunder will be back soon enough, and when they come, our former foe shall release the Arrow and welcome us as allies. In the meantime, let us continue to trade.* "So in fact her young Marloven friend feels that if Norsunder does return, Sartora will be looked to for defense, perhaps single-handed?"

"That's it." Arthur gave a sigh of obvious relief. "Oh, and you should hear the stories about her father—" He caught himself. That was gossip, and he knew better.

The emissary's gaze sharpened with interest.

Arthur chewed his lower lip. King Evend had always said that the personal would win over the theoretical in almost any discussion. Arthur hadn't always understood it, as he hadn't understood a lot of what Evend had said while ruminating during or after their lessons in history and magic, but he was discovering how many of Evend's observations about human behavior were true.

"Might that explain," the emissary ventured in a mild voice, while watching Arthur closely, "why Sartora was not restored to the bosom of her family, but lives here among you, young as she is?"

A vivid memory hit Arthur: Liere's sour-faced father who all three times Arthur saw him had been criticizing Liere in a bitter, scolding voice. The first time made sense. No parent would want to see their child looking the way Liere had, her hair hacked off with a knife during her run, wearing the clothes she'd taken from her brother, worn and patched and outgrown.

But the second time, Arthur had heard Liere's father whispering to Liere as he held her skinny arm in a tight grip, "Who do you think you are, mentioning people of rank by their private names, as if you were one of them? We thought you'd grown out of putting on airs to be interesting." And the third time, "Nothing good *ever* comes of girls getting above their place."

That was the one that made Liere go silent for a whole week. Until he met Lesim Fer Eider, Arthur had sometimes wished he had a father. Lesim Fer Eider had interrupted his daughter's every utterance with some criticism, and the morning after his arrival, they'd found him scolding his shrinking daughter for "idling around palaces belonging to her betters," and had issued an order demanding that she "return home to prepare for her future as a shopkeeper's wife," upon which old, sour Head Mage Oalthoreh had retorted, "I never speak against the wishes of families, unless that family is using the bond to propagate ignorance and prejudice. The child has declared her desire to remain here to learn. She may remain here until we have nothing more to teach her."

Having no answer he would vouchsafe to a mage, who might turn him into a tree stump, or worse—and no real value for his tiresome daughter—Lesim Fer Eider had used the transfer token the mages gave him to take himself away, leaving a general sense of relief when he was gone.

Arthur looked up. They'd walked halfway around the room without him being aware. He glanced the emissary's way, to encounter an expression of polite inquiry. He couldn't stop his neck from burning as he said, "Sartora stayed to begin the study of magic."

"A worthy aspiration," the emissary said smoothly as he lifted his head.

One of the castle pages entered, leading a familiar boy, white shirtsleeves rolled to his elbows, black trousers and riding boots, his yellow hair squared with military precision just above his collar in back, the unruly waves combed back from his forehead, unlike Arthur's messy hair flopping on his own forehead.

"Senrid," Arthur exclaimed in blank surprise.

Heads turned, and Arthur had time to wonder whether it was the name or the person that caught the interest of his Venn guests, before Senrid's quick step closed the distance between them. His searching gaze was just as Arthur remembered, the only difference being the faint marks of healing bruises on his face. Arthur's stomach tightened. He'd heard plenty about those Marlovens.

The emissary studied Senrid with interest, and though Arthur knew it would sound stupid, there was no etiquette for the sudden and unannounced arrival of kings: "How should I introduce you?"

"Senrid Montredaun-An," Senrid said with his quick, wry smile. "Came to see Liere."

That took care of introductions, but not the quandary. What was Arthur's duty? There were invited guests, and here was a king.

"I can wait," Senrid said quickly, and Arthur remembered that Senrid, too, could hear thoughts. His neck burned again.

The emissary said suavely, "Perhaps we might resume

our conversation when you have more leisure, your high-ness?"

Arthur knew what that meant: the man was going to interrogate him later. But that was all right. He'd have time to talk it over with his tutors, or his mother, by letter, and he'd know exactly what to say. He and the emissary exchanged courteous bows, and Arthur turned in relief to Senrid. "She's not in here."

Senrid's brows twitched upward. "Tactical retreat, eh?"

"Yes," Arthur said, though he had no idea what the 'tactical' part of retreat meant. He thought in dismay of all the places she could be in the enormous palace . . . but he knew where she had probably gone. "Come with me."

Chapter Eleven

IN spite of the thick walls and the magic spells aiding the hot air vents, a wintry current snaked along the marble floor, making Liere shiver. Winters had never been this cold in Imar, nor was it dark from midafternoon to midmorning, the sun, when it appeared, riding low and weak far to the south, the light even at noon a soft bluish shade.

She avoided looking up at the long clerestory windows and ran until she couldn't hear the hubbub from the Celebration Wing. When she reached the huge vestibule with its fine carvings centered around acorns, of all things, she slowed. That way lay the mage school wing, and over this way the living quarters where she had rooms. She still didn't think of that grand suite as hers, and she didn't want to go there now. She was afraid to disturb anything, to make work for the servants, and found the silence unsettling, after growing up in a tiny house with a large, noisy family. And though she loved the fine furnishings and bright rugs with their complicated patterns, she couldn't live among them.

Maybe she should go and stand there, even if she scarcely dared sit. Anything was better than the irresistible urge to see *It*, to make sure *It* was still there. She knew she shouldn't, though she couldn't say why. It was just wrong.

But she had to. Just a peek. Because Senrid had said before he left that Siamis hadn't surrendered that ancient sword named Truth, he'd left it as a warning.

Liere took a step and another across the elaborate mosaic depicting a winged dragon surrounded by flames, or petals, or both. She hunched her shoulders, refusing to look up at the great dome overhead with its many long windows that should be showing sunlight. They were nearly dark, though the ceremony had begun at noon.

She reached the richly gleaming double doors higher than the eaves of her father's shop back in Imar. She ran her fingers along the gold carvings, a riot of flames that Arthur had said represented the Gate between Worlds, whence the dragons had come millennia ago, and through which they'd vanished again, leaving behind the inspiration for strange pieces of art and music and stranger tales about their sojourn in Sartorias-deles.

She yanked her hands down guiltily and scurried inside the antechamber before the old throne room.

Arthur had told her that this beautiful building had once been a royal palace, from which kings and queens had ruled over a federation of territories bound together to defend themselves against the ancestors of those very Venn who were eating pastries over in the Hall of Light on the opposite side of the palace, as they talked about trading foodstuffs—hard to grow in the storm-battered Land of the Venn—for their wonderful stoves, beautifully soft yeath fur gathered from the bushes where the animals scraped it off each spring, and wool.

Father was right. Revealing that she'd been born with the ability to hear people's thoughts and remembering everything she'd been told seemed to make her so awful, or boring, or *something*, that no one wanted to be around her. Like the Mearsiean girls. She had spent weeks with them, had done everything they suggested, had laughed at all their jokes, but when Clair got that letter, did they think about asking Liere to join them?

No.

All those girls had been adopted by Clair. They were Liere's age. Senrid had said . . . She sighed. No use in remembering what Senrid had said. She had to stop having imaginary conversations with him.

She tapped the carving in the discreet side door, then held her breath and stepped through. The door looked solid, but Arthur had taught her that this was illusion. Glowglobes much plainer than the pretty ones outside in the silent halls revealed a narrow stone passage. She ran down the stairs to what had once been a treasure room, and before that a dungeon. At the end of the hall, there was an iron-reinforced door, with a magic spell bound into it for extra protection.

Arthur had showed her how to get past the spell, after which she used both hands to lift the heavy latch and ease the door open wide enough to slip inside.

The room beyond was even colder. She clapped on the glowglobe, and let out a breath of relief. *It* was still there, lying alone on a carved stone table. She tiptoed up, knowing she was being silly. That sword would not jump up and slash around the room at the sound of footsteps. But still. She kept her hands laced behind her as she stared at the thing made four thousand years ago.

She tried to imagine Siamis her own age, being given this sword, in a world that shared the same seas and lands and sky, but in all other ways completely different. She tried to imagine having to grow up in Norsunder while thousands of years passed. Her father scolded her, and despised her, but at least he wasn't a Norsundrian villain.

She heard an echo of Senrid's wry voice. *Nobody throws away a four-thousand-year-old sword. He's going to come back for it.*

"Liere?"

Liere knew that voice so well that she thought at first it was inside her head, another memory vivid as life. But the quick step that followed caused her to whirl around, joy and surprise sparking into light inside her. "Senrid!"

Senrid and Arthur stood side by side in the treasure room door, two blond boys of roughly the same age, but to her eye they were utterly unalike: Arthur slightly taller, but slightly stooped, skinny in his formal robe, and Senrid short and slender, his shoulders and hands tension points, his body poised to move. Just as he had when she first met him, he wore a perfectly tailored white shirt with loose sleeves, and black riding trousers with a dull gold stripe down the side, disappearing into high blackweave riding boots.

His reaction to her obvious joy was too quick to catch before he shuttered it away, but she recognized that wry grin of self-mockery.

"I hoped you wouldn't be here," Arthur said. Then he grimaced, knowing he sounded petty, but he was worried.

And he'd forgotten that both the others could hear his thoughts. Liere turned to Senrid as if had been a day or two since they'd last seen one another, instead of months. "Tell him. What you said. Siamis didn't surrender that sword."

"Definitely not." Senrid shrugged, a jerky movement. "Arthur, have your mages checked it over? There's only one reason to leave it behind. Because it's loaded with magical traps."

"They checked it first thing," Arthur said in a defensive tone.

Senrid opened a hand, palm down. "Second reason, maybe he left it here so his uncle couldn't have it." At Arthur's surprised look, Senrid said, "They were squabbling when I was a prisoner in Norsunder. I mean, I only heard it—sort of—once, but everybody in the Norsunder Base gossiped about some kind of trouble between Siamis and Detlev. And you should remember at the end, there, before Evend ended the rifts, your mages were all willing to back Liere in ending Siamis's enchantment. But Detlev didn't back Siamis. Though we don't know why."

The mention of Evend caused a quick contraction of grief in Arthur's face. He was obviously remembering, too. Arthur said, "Oalthoreh and the senior mages think that Detlev abandoned Siamis."

"Or it was a test," Senrid said. *Or a feint.* He didn't want to reveal how much he'd been worrying at that question, knowing it was futile. He simply didn't know enough.

Senrid shrugged tightly. "So I think the sword got left so Detlev can't have it, it being some kind of family heirloom. It even has a name," he added, for Marlovens did not name weapons, considering them extensions of their hands, instruments of will and skill. But Senrid knew that in other lands, weapons had names because warriors felt a kinship with the implement that was expected to defend their lives.

"Emeth," Liere said in a low voice, her gaze fixed not on the sword, but beyond it, into memory. "Ancient Sartoran word for 'truth.' Siamis said once when he attacked me by mind, wasn't it funny that he had a weapon named 'truth' when there isn't any truth. That truth is whatever the strong say it is."

Both boys stared at her. Arthur had never heard her speak a word about the harrowing days when she had been on the run from Siamis and Norsunder, being the only person who could use the dyr, an Ancient Sartoran artifact, to rip apart Siamis's enchantment like a broom clearing moth webbing.

Senrid remembered the chase, remembered the day Siamis had attacked Liere mind to mind, but she had refused then to tell him what was said.

When the pause became a silence, Arthur cleared his throat. "Well, *I* believe he's wrong. Just because he doesn't want to believe there isn't any truth doesn't make it so."

Senrid shrugged, quick and sharp. "What matters here is why he left that sword behind."

Liere stirred, her huge light-brown eyes golden in the shafting light. "I think . . . I think he left it on purpose. As a sort of warning."

Senrid's brows shot upward. "You mean, like throwing down a war banner? Yeah, that I can see."

But Liere gave her head a little shake. "Not that. Not *just* that. Norsunder makes threats all the time, don't they? Everything they do is a threat of war, or attack, or bad things. I think there's something else." She looked up at the boys. "Though maybe you're right about him not wanting Detlev to have it."

"Sounds kind of petty," Arthur said doubtfully. "But maybe they are that petty."

Senrid turned his palm upward. "Not so petty if there's magic on it that even your mages can't find, or there's some power struggle going on in Norsunder, and the sword is part of it."

Senrid knew his speculation was getting wilder with every word, but he pursued it anyway, because he wanted to hear what Arthur, who had the ear of all the senior lighter mages, would say.

But Arthur merely shook his head, and Liere's gaze narrowed. "Senrid, what's that on your face?" She peered at the nearly faded bruises.

He jerked one shoulder impatiently. "Walked into a door." And, "I didn't hear from you. Thought you'd . . ." He flicked a hand up, taking in the palace.

Liere's joy altered to dismay, and Senrid knew instantly that he'd managed to talk himself into misjudging her. ". . . be too busy learning," he amended the sarcasm, striving for neutrality.

"And I thought *you* were too busy. But here you are. You remembered!"

"Remembered?" he repeated.

"You promised. I could visit your country. If things settled down. Have they settled down?"

Senrid was about to say that she could have come to visit any time she wanted, but recollected what Hibern had said. It matched with Liere's anxious twisting of her fingers, her wistful expression. He should have known that she would never ask for something expensive like a transfer token.

The bards could warble about Sartora, the Girl Who Saved the World, but she saw herself as a shopkeeper's brat. She'd been scolded her entire life into believing herself clumsy, stupid, and unimportant. He knew it better than anybody, but he'd managed to let himself believe she'd swallowed all the twaddle about 'the great Sartora.'

Furious with himself, he said, "Things are . . . things. No use in boring on about home."

Liere said quickly, "I've been learning." Her thumbnail dug at the cuticles on her forefinger in the worried gesture he remembered from the desperate days they were on the run together. "You know how ignorant I am. So I'm going to read everything in the archive. I started with the first shelves, which turned out to be the oldest ones, copies of Sartoran taerans. Do you know that word? It means their old scrolls, and they are ever so difficult. But sometimes there are these events, and Arthur says it's polite and proper to attend . . ."

Senrid was gazing at her, unsettled by how quickly she detected his emotions. He'd forgotten how quick she was, and he wasn't used to anyone seeing past the bland face he'd used as his shield ever since he could remember.

". . . though Arthur said to pretend that Sartora is a role, and I'm on a giant stage, but it doesn't work. When people go to a play, they know that the players wear roles. People who come here expect Sartora to be a real person. Not me," she said in a breathless rush.

Senrid exclaimed, "This is why I don't see any jewels? Royal robes? Isn't that your brother's old tunic? I can't believe there isn't any cloth in the entire north to sew up a new shirt or pair of trousers, at least."

Liere's thin cheeks reddened. "They've given me so many beautiful things! Enough for a family of ten. But I don't really feel comfortable in all that stuff." She looked helplessly at Arthur. "Everyone here is so generous and kind . . ."

So no one teased her? Senrid would fix that. "And it makes you feel even more like a fake. Oh-h-h-h, wo-o-o-o-oe is me!" He grinned when he won a small laugh at that.

He'd meant to make this a short visit. But as he listened to her sudden laugh, he thought about how much he'd missed it, and he had to face the truth: he really didn't want her in Marloven Hess. It was too easy to imagine her looking around in horror, or saying something about warmongers.

Who was being stupid now? He said recklessly, "Come on, let's cure your gloom with some broiling weather."

Liere's lips parted. "What? You mean—"

"Unless you don't want to risk poisoning your purity by setting foot in my evil kingdom, why not come along and watch the academy gymkhana?"

Her joy flared, a flash of sunlight in the realm of the spirit. "I'd love that!"

Liere remembered where she was, and her obligations, and turned to Arthur, who was staring at her like she'd grown an extra arm. "Um, ought I to be back at a certain time? Or—" Liere spread her stiff, nervous fingers.

Arthur gave them a determined grin. "That's the good part about being a symbolic queen. Come and go as you

like. Long as you aren't forgetting an appointment to meet
with any powerful sorcerers or guild chiefs that you might
have made?"

"Just breakfast with Siamis and three other Norsundrian commanders," Senrid put in, his face straight. "I can
transfer her back in time for those."

Liere had been shaking her head somberly, but now she
looked up, startled, then laughed.

It was the first real laugh Arthur had heard from her, so
different from those self-conscious, sycophantic giggles
she'd expressed at the Mearsean girls' antics.

". . . it'll be hot, and dusty, and you're going to see more
horses then you've probably ever seen. Or smelled—"

"Could I ride one? I so miss riding."

Arthur stared at Liere, his lips parting to say, *You never
told us that.* But Senrid forestalled him. "After the exer-
cises, I'll introduce you to the girls at the stable. How's
that?"

Liere whispered, "Don't tell them who I am. Then nobody will pay any attention."

Senrid knew that 'no one paying attention' was impossible for anyone in his position. He was a walking target, at
least for talk, maybe for assassination. But he could use his
position to keep people at arm's length until she felt more
comfortable. If comfort was possible in the Evil Marloven
Hess.

"Oh, let's go," she said, sensing his mounting doubts.

They soon transferred away, leaving Arthur wondering
what was he going to say to the Sartoran mage guild when
they sent their next emissary. *She hates being here, and
would rather go watch Marlovens play war and ride horses*
didn't sound very diplomatic, even if it was the truth.

The transfer made Liere feel as if she'd been turned inside
out, then stuffed back right side in again by an impatient
hand, like a pair of socks readied for the washtub.

She found herself in a room with a row of tall windows
open to the air. She looked out as she drew in a long, unsteady breath to settle her insides. The windows looked out
over some kind of square filled with color, and noise, and a
whole lot of shades of brown, gray, and yellow. Gradually

the noise resolved into what seemed to be a thousand versions of Senrid, all speaking quick, sibilant Marloven, with horses in a long string at one wall.

Among all the blond heads were ones with dark hair, and red hair; tall boys, short, even a few girls, all dressed pretty much alike; clear consonant-sharp voices in the hot air. They sounded like Senrid because they spoke with his accent, and they kind of moved like him, except none so fast, or with three stiffened fingers, the way Senrid tended to gesture when he was tense.

Because he was definitely tense. She saw it the moment she turned around. She remembered all his sarcastic remarks about Evil Marlovens, and knew instinctively that he was waiting for her to judge. But what was there to judge? When she'd broken Siamis's worldwide spell, she'd had to do it kingdom by kingdom. A light-being called Hreealdar had taken her on that journey, which had lasted several weeks, during which she'd seen people from across the world. All kinds of people. From places famed down the ages to ones no one had ever heard of. But the people in all those places had all shared so many of the same emotions: puzzlement, fear, anger, relief, when the spell restored their minds to them.

To her, Marlovens looked like people.

"Arthur resents your muscling into a title up there in Bereth Ferian?" he asked, startling her out of her reverie.

"Oh, not at all." Liere glanced at him in surprise. "Not at *all*. He is still a kind of king, too, as Evend's heir, and anyway those titles are what they call a courtesy." She squirmed, hating that sense of being a fraud, even if her 'title' didn't actually mean anything.

"What does a courtesy title entail?" Senrid asked, coming to stand beside her at the window.

"Arthur told me that a king or queen in Bereth Ferian can't make laws, or give commands. It's a presiding thing, over the federation, and also over the archive, and all the old magical protections. Did you know the library is the biggest one in all the north half of the world?"

"Not much competition, from what I remember of our run," Senrid said.

"Arthur says that humans are outnumbered by all the

other types of beings in the north. It's here in the south where there are more humans," Liere said, looking slowly around the room with interest. "Anyway, I'm not a *real* queen, but Arthur said if the federation ever comes to argument, and I'm presiding, they might think I'll do some kind of mind spell, and I shouldn't tell them I can't. I still don't get that, whether he was joking or not. Like when he said that what he really wants to be is King of the Libraries. I like this room," she exclaimed, taking in the fine desk, the cabinet by it, and the colorful map on the wall behind the desk.

"It's my study." Senrid jabbed the three fingers toward the door. "Come on. I'll give you a tour."

She followed him into a hall formed out of light brown stone, not the expected gray of granite. The sandy color seemed warm, though maybe that warmth was the strong summer light brightening everything, so welcome after the horrible dark and pervasive cold of the far north. Someone had carved reliefs of dashing horses and flying raptors into the plastered walls, in colors of silver and white and gray.

She paused to look more closely, almost touched, then yanked down her hand—her father's scolding voice was never far from memory. She found Senrid looking at her with that peculiar question, his mouth awry, and she said, "These carving things on the walls are pretty."

"The ancestor who put those up was actually from Colend," he said, but dropped the subject when she wrinkled her nose. Mad King Carlael of Colend was not a great memory for her, however brief their contact.

"This way."

They ran downstairs and out to the parade court, then climbed into the stone stands where Marlovens had been sitting for centuries. She could see the dips in the stone worn by shoes down the many years, the benches smoothed by weather.

Senrid gave Liere a quick description of the academy, which turned out to be a school where the Marlovens trained their future army officers. Senrid had mentioned so little about this part of his life during their travels together, though they had talked about everything else, that she had this odd sense that he was revealing something private.

No, that's silly, she thought as he laughed, and gestured, and interspersed the running stream of talk with waves or calls. It wasn't as if you could hide an entire kingdom in a trunk.

She was distracted by a tall older boy with curly dark hair whom Senrid kept glancing at, and when Senrid's head was turned, stared at Senrid. "Who is that?"

In the mental realm, Senrid's reaction was like a flash of lightning, instant, painfully intense, then gone. "Jarend Ndarga," he said, and then, his reluctance obvious, "I had some trouble with him recently. Just local stuff."

Liere nodded, suspecting that asking further would be nosy, especially as she wouldn't know what 'local stuff' meant.

A lot of little boys her younger sister's age ran out to do something or other with loose horses. After them came the excellent, sometimes frightening dash and skill of the gym-khana riders. Oh, how she would love to ride that well! Not doing those tricks, like shooting arrows at a post while galloping—she couldn't see ever needing such a skill—but how easy they looked on the backs of horses, like horse and rider had been born together.

After a last amazing set of stunts involving boys leaping from the back of one horse to another, Senrid kept his promise and brought Liere to a teenage girl with black curly hair and dark eyes. "Here's Fenis Senelac. She can give you your first lesson in riding," he said, and to Fenis, in the Marloven language, "Send someone with her when it's over, will you?"

He flicked up a hand. "We'll eat when you're done," he said to Liere in Sartoran, and vanished into the crowd.

Fenis Senelac's straight brow lifted, and she said, "What do you know about riding?"

A mage had performed for Liere the Universal Language spell. It was not perfect, she'd been told; mages were always adding to it, but some languages were more up to date than others, especially with idioms. But Liere had discovered that if she listened on the mental realm as well as with her ears, she could understand idiom as well as intent. What she had trouble with was pronunciation.

"A little," Liere said carefully, trying to emulate Senrid's accent. "I rode a pony once, for many days, but there were two of us, and we never galloped. Then I rode . . ." She clipped her lips.

"Rode?" Fenis asked, amazed that the king would bring this grubby scrub here, who spoke with such an odd accent. It was a first, for though she had the light coloring one saw a lot of in Marloven Hess, she was obviously no Marloven. Fenis's interest increased sharply when the girl's cheeks mottled red, and she mumbled to the dusty ground, ". . . something like a horse."

Fenis stared. Though the king was closer than a stone about whatever had happened during the Siamis time, gossip from the little neighboring kingdom of Vasande Leror, where several Marlovens had relatives, had brought word of their own king's heroism. You had to call it that, though everyone knew how much Senrid-Harvaldar hated such words.

The thing was, he hadn't been alone when chased by Siamis and half of Norsunder. He'd been with some little girl who turned out to have amazing powers of some kind, enough to vanquish a Norsundrian sorcerer, even if a young one.

Fenis looked at that untidy head, the old clothes, and wondered if she was seeing the same 'little girl.' Part of the rumor put this girl on the back of a horse made out of light.

"Well, we have ordinary horses here," she said. "So let's put you up on a nice, well-mannered mare, and see what you know."

She held out a hand, indicating the barn, and led the way. At first Liere wondered if Fenis was related to the mysterious Jarend Ndarga, but no, her features were completely different, her skin browner. All they really shared was the curly black hair, she decided when she saw Jarend Ndarga walk by.

The tall boy looked so threatening. Was there trouble for Senrid? Liere skimmed his thoughts, catching an angry, confused jumble of a lot of images and words she didn't know, then the horrible jolt of memory: a bloody fist smashing into Senrid's face.

Her stomach lurched. That's what she got for listening. That memory would never go away.

She drew in a slow breath, and discovered Fenis gazing at her, brows raised. Liere's face burned. "They were so good," she said, feeling stupid and awkward. "Leaping from horse to horse like that."

"The girls do that when they're ten," Fenis said with a snort. "But in the bad days, before Senrid-Harvaldar, they never got any credit."

"Is Senrid going to change that?" Liere asked, not knowing how much was revealed in her easy use of Senrid's name with no formal 'harvaldar' attached.

"He says he will, but slowly. Marlovens don't like change. Unless they make it themselves. Jarend Ndarga, who seems to have caught your eye, hates it more than most." Fenis stopped at a stall, and paused, one hand on a halter. "You'll get an earful if you stay around here, how much the men and boys all hate change. How much they all want the good old days back. Only, of course, better." She snorted a laugh. "So. If you're going to learn to ride, you need to learn how we get the horse ready. Here, don't be nervous. You'll make the horse nervous."

Liere had been staring up at the animal in fascinated terror. This was not a fat, placid old pony like her first mount, nor was it like the strange beings in horse form whom she had met up north. Once she'd been this close to a Norsundrian horse, its mind warped with terror and anger. All she'd had to do was touch that mind and urge the animal to run.

But she couldn't do that now. So she put out a tentative hand, laying it on the horse's bony flat head above its nose, and as Fenis said, "Good, good, they like scritchies, calm and steady . . ." Liere sorted through the strange mental landscape, her instinct to hide from danger prompting her to send the thought: *Don't see me, I am invisible.*

The horse promptly began panicking. Fenis broke off her praise with a startled, "Hai, what's wrong?" She gripped the halter of the wild-eyed, plunging horse.

Senrid's thought came from somewhere near, straight into Liere's head: *Don't do that!*

Liere jumped.

In answer to her unspoken question, Senrid's thought blared, too strong and uncontrolled: *It smells you, and hears you, but doesn't see you—you are a threat!*

Liere jerked down her hand and scrambled behind Fenis as she calmed the horse, then sent a wary glance at Liere. "Shall we try that again?"

Liere blinked back tears of shame. "Just tell me what to do," she said.

Narad, capital of Chwahirsland
Roughly the same time—very roughly

Jilo was so exhausted that he wondered if Wan-Edhe's poisonous enchantment had seeped into his brain and bones again, until it occurred to him that he ought to lie down and sleep. There was no way of knowing how long had passed in this airless, windowless space unless he remembered to go into the hall to see if sunlight came through or not. And he seldom remembered to do that. Time measures, whether candles, sandglasses, or mechanical clocks, never functioned well in Narad's fortress's inner chambers, probably because of the layers of magic.

As he walked to the old room (cell, really, except that it was above ground) where he'd stayed when he and Kwenz were forced to visit, he wondered if he would wake up to discover Siamis there. Or Detlev. Or some other even more terrifying Norsundrian, except if anyone would return from Norsunder to take control of Chwahirsland, wouldn't it be Wan-Edhe?

Or Prince Kessler.

Maybe Jilo should lay warning tracers over the already-thick layer, just to be safe.

When he'd finished that, he fell directly into slumber. He didn't stay asleep, waking often, usually in a sweat, though the room was chill. When he rose at last, the narrow arrow slit he had for a window showed gray light. He frowned, trying to think past the panging in his temples. Was it daylight when he'd gone to sleep?

What about breakfast? He'd had to beg meals from Wan-Edhe, and half the time he was denied on the pretense of some wrongdoing or failure or disappointment. Jilo felt under the mattress. He'd sometimes brought rolls from the Shadowland and stashed them in case; two were there, but they had hardened to rocks.

It didn't matter. He wasn't even hungry.

As always, he had to find out what he could, to protect himself. Being taken by surprise was never, ever, a good thing in Chwahirsland. Wan-Edhe still had not returned. No one was giving him orders.

No one was stopping him from learning. Or removing wards and traps.

He really ought to get something to eat, though the thought of cold food was unappetizing, and anyway there was so much to do before anyone showed up with orders or threats . . .

Chapter Twelve

Dyavath Yan (New Year's Week), 4738 AF

... JILO finished checking for wards and traps in Wan-Edhe's library and magic chamber. He knew that next it was time to be systematic about finding out what was on those shelves in the magic chamber. The first book he touched sparked. Blue flame singed his fingers as the book vanished ... somewhere. He stuck his throbbing fingers into his armpit, and studied the shelf in dismay. If only the air weren't so thick! It was as if he never could get a deep enough breath.

All right, clearly he hadn't removed all the worst wards. Maybe he'd only found the obvious ones. That was dismaying, after all his effort.

He still wasn't sure how much time had passed, but no one disturbed him. Everyone in the castle seemed to be sticking to the schedule as if they expected Wan-Edhe to reappear at any moment. Maybe it was time to see to something else, like removing the spell that rendered the former Shadowland army's eyes a solid black, making sunlight acutely painful. Though he didn't feel any better than he had before he slept, a promise was a promise.

He forced himself to breathe deeply as he picked up Wan-Edhe's book of spells. Balancing that on one hand, he fixed in mind an image of the fleet captain who had brought the Chwahir to the Shadowland. It was dangerous to use a person as a Destination, but it was either that or nothing.

He transferred, and fell with a splat, the reaction nausea worsened by the movement of a ship.

A sentry bent over him and pulled him to his feet, his tight grip loosening when Sentry-Captain Mossler recognized Jilo. "You were sent by Wan-Edhe?" the man asked Jilo fearfully.

"No. The Shadowland Chwahir no longer need the shadow vision." And Jilo began the spell.

It was almost worse than the transfer. From the beginning of the spell, he felt that internal burning of strong magic. Two days ago he would not have been able to hold it. Now he could—barely. But it worked.

"Augh!" Mossler clapped his hands over his eyes.

"You'll soon get accustomed," Jilo whispered.

"But Wan-Edhe," the sentry-captain said, still in that fearful voice. "Is Wan-Edhe still gone? Commander Henjit went with him, and there have been no orders. We're doubled up here with the homelanders." He gestured down the deck, where Shadowland Chwahir rubbed their eyes, or stood with their hands covering their faces. From the looks of things, they had been sleeping on deck.

"I have orders from the throne," Jilo said, having planned that much, and watched the easing in Mossler's sunburned face. "You are to bring them back to the homeland."

Jilo had just enough strength to transfer back to the Destination in Wan-Edhe's chambers, where he fell to his hands and knees, the book thumping onto the grimy floor. He waited until the black spots had swum away from his vision, then sat back, his breath coming in shuddering gasps.

He had to do something about the Shadowland warriors before he forgot. What was it?

He went to the door, and beckoned the waiting runner. "Tell the Quartermaster Commander that the Shadowland Chwahir are to be dispersed, by twi, to reinforce any strongholds shorthanded. They will arrive . . ." When? Already he had lost grip on time. "Soon."

The runner bowed and withdrew.

All right, back to the traps. Jilo turned too quickly. Dizzy, he stumbled down the hall, and fell headlong through the magic chamber door. He knee-crawled to the first bookcase. Before, he'd tested shelf by shelf, but now he was going to have to proceed book by book. He extended a forefinger, not quite touching the first book, waiting to see if he sensed the faint magical burr that probably meant a trap.

And traps he found, as if they'd grown overnight. The process was long and laborious, too dangerous to be boring—lethally tedious. He nearly fumbled into a couple of especially nasty traps, after which he forced himself to take a break.

Both times he slept right there on the floor.

When he remembered meals, he ate methodically, permitting his mind to range over his life so far. With that damping spell gone, he was able to remember more. Even think about it. What he came back to most was the fact that Clair of Mearsies Heili, long regarded as his chief enemy, had helped him.

Time wore on.

He was peripherally aware of the guard going about its daily routine, and surprised when no one came to ask orders. But of course they wouldn't. Wan-Edhe had trained his guards to never interrupt him. Not that they wanted to. If he didn't like what they said, it could be their last words.

"They probably go about their day and hope they never see me," he said to the dead air.

He'd taken to talking out loud. The sound of his voice seemed to break the heavy stillness, as oppressive as the stone. If for only a moment.

But as time labored on, he found it more difficult to think, to rest, to get anything done. It was as if that terrible spell had seeped out of the stonework, taking over his mind again, an invisible and smothering fungus. It wasn't until he sat down to pick up the quill that he caught sight of his own hands.

They looked like someone else's hands. The nails were longish, the beds ridged in a curious way, grayish in color.

He dropped his hands to the table, steadying himself by feeling the grain of the wood, and looked at the shelves he'd managed to complete: one and a half bookshelves. Then he looked at the enormous volume of books awaiting him in the rest of the room, and admitted defeat.

He gathered his strength, shut his eyes, and transferred to the old Destination square outside of what had been the Shadowland. Transfer reaction knocked him tumbling. He blinked stupidly. The square was covered with snow and ice. Snow and ice?

He peered upward at a low, gray sky. The air was so cold that it hurt to breathe. Wasn't it . . . warm when he left? When did he leave, anyway? Two days ago? Three? Trying to remember made the headache worse.

So he stood up, brushing snow off with numbing fingers. The area seemed wild, as if the Shadowland had never existed. He couldn't comprehend that, so he braced himself, and transferred to the mountaintop.

Clair's magic did not ward him. If anything, this transfer was far easier. It was only a relatively short distance, but still, it barely hurt, compared to the agonizing transfer from Chwahirsland.

He looked around. The city was different, now that it didn't stretch over a cloud. It lay across the top of the mountain, cut into a gentle slope and connected by switch-back streets, the buildings either whitewashed or painted with colorful shutters, now mostly closed, and roofed with patterned tile. The Destination square was still in the terrace before the palace, whose blinding, glaring white no longer tortured his eyes. He stared at towers that looked like they were made of ice.

He tipped his head back, running his gaze up the asymmetrical series of towers. He hated the idea of trying to enter. Wan-Edhe had (briefly) managed to get inside a couple times, but that after endless magic, and not for long, and never past the ground floor.

He dreaded walking into some kind of waxer trap, but if he did, well, life would probably be no odder than it was already. So. He trudged the short distance to the palace, his breathing labored. He halted near the archway, his attention caught by the intertwined carvings, age-softened, of four-petal blossoms of a sort he did not recognize. The walls appeared to be luminous, though he didn't trust his vision when it came to this building.

A step.

Another step.

He was inside! He was actually inside, and no magic, or guards, or anything had stopped him!

He made it about ten steps before he encountered one of the Mearsiean servants, an older man.

"May I—oh, aren't you . . ."

"Jilo." His voice was hoarse. He stood poised to run, to fight, though he really hadn't the strength for that.

"Come this way."

Jilo followed, too weary to question, though a mild surprise bloomed in him when they walked not into the throne room but down a side hall. The enticing smells of warm food of some kind (he didn't even know what it was, just that it smelled so good the sides of his mouth watered) met him before he walked into a warm, bright kitchen.

There CJ sat on a high stool, a bowl of whipped cream next to a silver pot of hot chocolate. A book lay on the table.

She scowled in astonished recognition, poised to fling the hot chocolate at him since she didn't have a weapon. Why hadn't she been warned? Where was Ben, their trusty spy on the Chwahir? Except that there was no more Shadowland to spy on, and Ben had traveled off somewhere with Puddlenose.

Meanwhile, Jilo just stood there, swaying on his feet. To CJ, he looked terrible. Her alarm forgotten, she said tentatively, "Jilo? You look like a week-old corpse!"

A spurt of laughter bloomed in Jilo's throat, but it didn't come out. He could only manage a dusty huff of breath.

CJ raised a finger. "No, I don't know what a week-old corpse looks like, but if I did, it would look healthier than you. Have you been in the clink?"

"Clink?"

She waved her hands. "Dungeon. Jail. Where you skunks used to try to stick us when Kwenz was trying to take over."

"No, I've been busy." That much talk seemed to make

him breathless. He gulped in air, and tried again. "Where is Clair? I have a question."

CJ bit down on a retort, so long a habit. She'd promised Clair: assuming they ever saw him again, Jilo had to move first in resuming the old conflict. And saying he had a question wasn't a gesture of war in any possible way. "Clair's tobogganing with the girls, and I'm keeping an eye on things here, just in case." Another glance at that drawn face. "Maybe you're an 'in case'?" Her thin black brows lifted in puzzlement as Jilo swayed on his feet. "Are you going to croak right on our floor?" She dashed across the room, picked up a cup, returned, and poured out a brown stream of chocolate. "Drink that."

Jilo was beyond questioning. He sipped. The flavor was completely new, and so delicious he gasped. More, the warmth, the fluidity seemed to send silver fire all through his veins, chasing out the dust. He drank it off, then reeled, dizzy.

"Whoa! I think you better sit down. I've never seen anybody get snockered on hot chocolate before!" Small, insistent hands pushed Jilo onto a chair, where he collapsed like a bag of old laundry.

When he had blinked the world straight again, there was Clair, wearing a bulky coat. Snow glistened in her white hair. Next to her, CJ stood, a small, adamant figure wearing the familiar white shirt, black vest, and long green skirt. Jilo had hated the sight of that outfit, and that girl, for too long to count. While Clair had been his chief enemy, CJ had been a personal enemy. But now he couldn't seem to find . . . any thoughts at all.

Clair whispered, "I have never seen anyone actually gray before."

"Is it a sign of good health in a Chwahir?"

"Does he act healthy?"

"Noooo." CJ's quick footsteps departed, returning with the tread of Janil, the Steward, a stout, cheery woman who bustled about, and soon set before Jilo a plate of brightly colored, delicious foods that he couldn't name—but the flavors were indescribable. With it he drank down four glasses of clear, sweet water.

Warmth chased the silver in his veins, and reached his

head, clearing it. He felt strange, like someone had replaced his head with a dandelion puff. Other than the wobbly sensation, the feeling wasn't bad. "How long has it been? I can't seem to remember if it's been four days, or five?"

CJ's fierce blue eyes rounded. Clair said carefully, "I don't quite know if it's been four or five days from what, but you left here eight months ago."

"Eight—"

"Months," Clair said. "It's New Year's Week. Jilo, Senrid said there was really heavy magic in that chamber."

"Senrid? Who's that?"

"Better ask *what* is that," CJ said darkly, and when Clair began to protest, CJ raised her hands. "No, no, I couldn't resist the crack. Boneribs is . . . Boneribs. Uh, Senrid," she corrected quickly.

Jilo was too exhausted to listen to CJ, who was always making up names for people.

Clair wasn't listening, either. She gazed past CJ and Jilo both, wrestling mentally with a new idea.

Court historians like to point to ceremonial treaty signings, battles, and royal marriages as turning points in history, but it is the archivist in possession of insights into such moments as this who recognizes the individual decisions that change the world.

So it was now, as Clair drew Jilo into the nascent alliance.

She gave a tiny nod of decision. "Senrid lives in Marloven Hess, on your continent, but at the end closer to us. He knows dark magic, and he's the one who found that terrible spell on you, in Wan-Edhe's experiment book."

Clair waited. Jilo waited. Then he understood she was waiting for permission to introduce him to someone, something he was utterly unprepared for.

"Ah, yes," he said, feeling stupid.

Clair nodded. This had to be how an alliance really started, not with everybody making promises, but by doing the right thing, an item at a time. At least, she was pretty sure this was the right thing. She had to test the idea herself before trying it on CJ, who she knew would not like the idea of allying with a former enemy.

So she said to CJ, "I'll take him to Senrid." And then,

as a hint, "Maybe our alliance is going to need a name?" She went to get a transfer token for Jilo, as she was afraid he couldn't hold a transfer spell on his own.

Marloven Hess

Hibern pulled her coat tighter around her, as the distant rhythm of a drum rumbled through the winter windows, followed by the rise and fall of voices in long-familiar martial melody. It was the end of New Year's Week and the Marloven Convocation.

The sound of Marloven singing threw her back to memories of home. She'd managed to stay away from that spot overlooking Askan Castle since the last visit. Erai-Yanya was right, thinking of home hurt a little less, but the difference seemed akin to a hard stab with a knife compared to a lot of little cuts. The cuts were questions: Would her mother ever contact her again, or her aunt? Had Father succeeded in removing his spells from Stefan?

When she was honest with herself, she knew why she kept at these study sessions with Senrid, when she could have found someone else for Senrid to study with. Like Arthur. But she wanted word to get out, to her family. If she worked hard, might they be proud of her, ask her to come back, say all was . . .

Was what? She still didn't believe she had anything to be forgiven for.

And yet she knew if her mother required her to beg forgiveness, she would do it, if it meant she would have her family back.

And she *knew* what Senrid would say: "Lighter sentiment and weakness."

She let out a sharp sigh, then entered Senrid's study. He looked up, his slight frown altering to a wry grin. Mind-reading? No, she suspected that it wasn't her thoughts but her expression that had given her away. "That mind-shield thing is hard to maintain," she said.

Senrid jerked a shoulder up. "If you're going to tangle with Norsunder, you lighters are going to have to make the mind-shield into a habit. Siamis made a strategic retreat. Detlev didn't even retreat. They both are Ancient Sartorans, and they know how to listen in on thoughts and dreams from a day's journey away. A continent away."

Hibern's neck prickled with warning. "You're still saying 'lighter' in that tone, as if you're still dedicated to dark magic. If so, why am I here tutoring you in light?"

"Because light magic has its strengths," Senrid retorted. "Dark magic is only useful for brute force. People using either for long enough to build customs around them have managed to make some stupid ones. Dark for mindless destruction, and light for mindless hypocrisy."

"Mindless!" Hibern exclaimed in the same tone of genial sarcasm. "How did I miss the fact that I think exactly like every one of those Sartoran or northern mages, not to mention every hair-colorist or bridge-mender? Oh wait. None of us can think."

"I didn't say they were alike," Senrid shot right back. "I said—"

"You said we're mindless."

Senrid grinned. "Okay," he said. "I take that back."

Hibern sighed, still finding it strange when Senrid used the slang he'd picked up from the Mearsiean girls while they were all in Bereth Ferian. "Lilith the Guardian said to me once that we—humans—are still changing. We lost our civilization in the Fall four thousand years ago. We're still trying to catch up to the place where we lost ourselves."

"A grim thought," Senrid said. "That we need to catch up to the time when we nearly managed to destroy the world." His expression tuned sardonic. "Strange, the idea of her living back then."

"What I think stranger is the idea of being . . . somewhere . . . beyond time, and only coming back every now and then over the centuries, when you're needed," she said. "How could you bear that, knowing that everyone you met would be dead by your next return? How would you even know you're needed? I read about a conversation with Lilith the Guardian in a record written a couple centuries ago, in which she said we can't make the same mistakes our ancestors did, and that what you call lighter hypocrisy is a kind of standard to aim for. If it makes life a little better when we try, the failures don't matter so much."

"There's the moral superiority drumbeat banging my ear," Senrid said, but his tone was no longer as derisive. He jumped up and moved restlessly to peer out his window, then turned. "Everything is about getting power. Keeping it. People can talk themselves into thinking they're worthy, but they want power, same as anyone else."

Hibern wondered what that was about, and then remembered the day. Senrid would have given his speech before the jarls on New Year's Firstday, outlining new laws, new policies. When Marlovens squabbled, they didn't argue about who had the moral high ground. Instead, out came the knives. And he was waiting for the first sounds of steel being drawn.

Senrid reached for the books stacked neatly on his desk as Hibern took the hint and brought her own study materials out of her satchel.

Time passed as they studied together, looking at ways to layer building wards. When Senrid asked a question she didn't know the answer to, he waited for her to look through all the notes she'd written in her classes at that mage school up north.

At one point she halted, and her gaze slowly went diffuse.

Senrid was tempted to try to read those thoughts, but he pictured Liere's questioning face. Her disappointment. They'd had enough talk about that. He could hear her pointing out that just because somebody knew how to kill someone five different ways with only their hands didn't mean they should do it.

It was one thing when Hibern was so intent on a subject her mental images and emotions splashed out, like her grief and betrayal and pain for a long time after that idiot mage Askan had kicked his daughter out of his house, as if she were to blame for all the regent's rot. It was another to deliberately invade. He knew how much *he'd* hate it, and she certainly intended no threat to him.

A runner appeared. "Visitors," she said. "Just transferred to the Destination. Said they are here to see you, Senrid-Harvaldar."

"Then we're done." Hibern got to her feet and pointed to the book she'd brought. "Study that, King Mindless Destruction." She hefted her satchel and transferred.

Clair and Jilo found themselves on a hilltop Destination.

A cold wind whipped at them. Jilo shivered in spite of the bulky coat Clair had fetched from Puddlenose's room, and Clair turtled her head deeper into her own coat.

A scarf-muffled guard beside the Destination turned their way. "Go ahead," he shouted against the wind.

Former enemies, Clair and Jilo began trudging down a pathway toward the high walls of a fortress city, barely visible in whirls of snow. They could not have looked more like opposites: she short, sturdy, hair the same white as the snow; Jilo gaunt and gangling, his lank hair blue-black. But their thoughts were not all that dissimilar at that moment, Clair worried about Jilo, who looked so ill, and Jilo worried about pretty much everything.

Clair tried to reassure Jilo with a description of Senrid, but she was wondering if he had the strength to toil through the wind-driven snow all the way to Senrid's castle. Then horseback riders thundered toward them, and reined to a halt.

"The king sent us," said one of the riders.

The two were each pulled up behind a rider, and they galloped the rest of the way, through the massive gates, and up to the castle.

Clair wondered if she'd made a deadly mistake as she eyed the sentries on the walls. Everything looked threatening. Senrid had once said that she was welcome to visit. Maybe he hadn't meant that as a real invitation, but as a kind of dare.

Jilo wondered if this was going to be a deadly mistake. He'd heard of Marloven Hess. Who hadn't? There had been glancing references to some sort of encounter between the Marlovens and the Chwahir in the past, though he'd never found out what happened.

Then he was distracted by the wintry sunlight changing the color of the stone to an almost gold, and by the fine weave of the sentries' uniforms. The histories insisted the

Chwahir used to be the finest weavers of sailcloth and related fabrics in the south. If that wasn't all lies, why was everything so shoddy now?

He remembered he was living where a king once had, and might again. In spite of his headache (which was actually rapidly diminishing), Jilo looked around the way he thought a king might. He felt sorry for anybody who would try to attack this city. The walls were high and thick, and the guards walking along them looked alert. The street leading to the royal castle bent to the left, which would make it tougher for attack than a straight street—he'd read that once—and easier for defenders to pick invaders off.

If you listened to Wan-Edhe, the danger wasn't always from the outside. Nobody had tried to attack Chwahirsland for centuries. All Wan-Edhe's magical protections, laws, and rules, were for a single purpose: preserving his own life against conspiracies among his own people. No, two purposes, the second being the gathering of power.

They dismounted in a huge stable yard. It was much larger than any in Chwahirsland, but Chwahir were foot warriors, and the Marlovens were reputed to be mostly mounted.

A waiting runner beckoned for them to follow.

The castle's inside looked luxurious to Jilo, according oddly with what he expected of another military kingdom. The stone wasn't the slate-colored stone he was accustomed to, but something more the color of sand, and the upper reaches inside had plastered walls, with bas-reliefs of swooping, stylized, powerful figures. Jilo longed to stop and take them in, but he'd learned when young to hide his interest in art.

Yet those dashing equine figures, the sweep of raptor wings, stayed with him, kindling the burn of resentment in his middle. All his life he'd heard that art was for the weak, and here were these Marlovens, who got the rep but still got to have art.

But he could have art now. Jilo tested the idea as he and Clair were led into a huge room with actual windows. Maybe the Chwahir wouldn't revolt if they found out there was art in the royal fortress.

Or maybe they would.

Nice rugs, a fine table. These Marlovens had it soft. Clair glanced toward a desk where a short blond boy sat before three neatly aligned stacks of papers.

Jilo turned to stare at their host, who stared back, thinking that their timing could hardly have been worse.

Oh, wait, yes it could. They could have showed up yesterday.

The others saw no sign of Senrid's bitterness as he got to his feet in a quick move. He was shorter than Jilo by quite a bit.

"This is Senrid," Clair said.

"Senrid," Jilo repeated. He looked around, rubbing his temple. "You are a mage student? Mage?"

"Senrid is the king," Clair said. "He's like us. Under-aged ruler." And to Senrid, "Jilo has taken over Chwahirsland."

A voiceless laugh escaped Jilo. "I think."

"*Chwahirsland?*" Senrid's eyes had widened. "You led a revolt?"

"No."

"Wan-Edhe didn't kill off all his relatives?"

"Yes. No. I told you before, Kessler Sonscarna is still alive. Or somewhere. In Norsunder." Then she remembered that Senrid had been beaten bloody at the time. She decided against mentioning that.

Senrid whistled. "So how did you get the throne?"

Jilo spread his hands. "Walked in."

Senrid stared up at the tall, slope-shouldered, shambling boy with the pasty-pale skin and unkempt black hair who mumbled at his shoes. He was barely holding onto his own throne, and this fellow strolls in and just . . . takes over one of the biggest, nastiest kingdoms on the continent?

At what cost?

Senrid hadn't met many Chwahir, but he was willing to bet anything that Jilo hadn't slept since he'd 'walked in' and sat on that faraway throne.

Clair said, "Senrid, you know I'm ignorant about how dark magic works. That spell you found helped Jilo."

"I didn't really find it," Senrid said, his gaze on Jilo, "as in a search. The book was left open by someone who probably expected to come back to it. All I did was read a few spells, since the language they were written in was the old-fashioned Sartoran everyone uses for dark magic."

Clair flicked a look Jilo's way, and he bobbed awkwardly in assent, then winced as if his head hurt.

Clair went on, "There's something else. It's really creepy. Jilo thinks he was gone a few days. But it was eight months ago."

Senrid's astonishment wiped away all the other reactions. Jilo was fingering his nails, which were an unhealthy shade, even for someone so leached of normal skin tones.

Senrid said, "How many times did you sleep?"

"I don't know. Two or three . . . I don't remember."

"Did you go to sleep at night and wake up in the morning?"

Jilo flushed. "I know it sounds stupid, but I really don't remember."

"How many times did you eat?"

"In Chwahirsland? Um, I didn't. Yes, once. When I first got there. Then I got to work. Then a couple more times. I remember that. But it's been a few . . ." Jilo reddened to the ears as he said on a questioning note, "Hours?"

"Weeks? Months?" Senrid drew in a breath as his nerves tingled cold. "Jilo, unless you're dreaming right now, it sounds like your king managed to distort time's flow."

"What?" Jilo said.

"You can do that?" Clair asked, her green eyes wide.

"It's difficult magic. Probably the most difficult there is," Senrid said. "Think of it this way. It's like creating a piece of Norsunder all of your own. Because that's what Norsunder is. That is, not the Norsunder Base down south below Sartor, but what they call Norsunder-Beyond. It's a place beyond time and temporal constraints."

Jilo said, "I can believe that Wan-Edhe was busy creating a Norsunder of his own. He's been resisting time as hard as he could."

"But that kind of magic needs tremendous power," Senrid said. "So what are you here for?"

Clair said, "Senrid, you're the one who said we should

know what dark magic can do, so we can defend ourselves. And this is our chance to see if our alliance will actually work."

"Right." Senrid had completely forgotten the alliance. He said to Jilo, "It looks to me like you need sleep, and in a place outside that magic chamber. Eight months." He shook his head. "Clair and I were there a sand—" He pointed to a small sandglass. "And I felt like I was swimming in mud. Especially my head. How did you endure that? You must be made of iron."

Jilo's ears burned the more. He was so used to insults, derision, and humiliation, that he tried to understand Senrid's words within the context of mockery, then gave up.

"Sleep," he heard himself say. "Oh yes."

Senrid gave him a sardonic grin. "That, I can give you." He touched a stack of reports, on top of which lay a smooth, heavy paper different from the rest, a very expensive, fine paper made from silk and rice. "If I was my uncle, I'd be seeing conspiracies, especially this week. First this letter from someone claiming to be a Renselaeus, and in the name of our supposed mutual ancestors, wanting to send his son to the academy. And the day after I receive that, here's someone I've never met who walked in and took a throne . . ."

He looked up, but saw only polite disinterest in Clair's face, and non-comprehension and exhaustion in Jilo's. It was clear that neither of these two knew anything about the Renselaeus family, whose descendants in the former principality of Vasande Leror had spearheaded the treaty forced on Marloven Hess by its neighbors a couple generations ago. They not only didn't know, they clearly didn't care.

Conspiracy there might be, ten conspiracies, but these two were obviously not part of any of them.

Senrid promised Clair a report, turned Jilo over to a runner to be put in a guest chamber, and dipped his pen, wondering if life would ever be normal again . . . and if it did, if 'normal' would seem unusual.

Chapter Thirteen

*Y*OU *must be made of iron.*

Was that sarcasm? Maybe it was just an insult, like Wan-Edhe used to use, when he'd strike him across the face and snarl, "Get that into your rock-thick skull."

Jilo woke up ravenous and light-headed, but he knew what time it was: morning. He knew that he'd slept all through the night. And he remembered that conversation the day before, with the king of the Marlovens. A boy his age.

There was a cleaning frame in the room, and also a vent that brought in warm air. He'd been raised to scoff at these things as waxer weakness, so how did that fit the ferocious reputation of the Marlovens?

He made a wager that the food would be as good as the Mearsieans', and, after stepping through the cleaning frame, poked his head out of the room. There was the tower stairway, right where he'd remembered it. Senrid had said something about his being not far from the dining room. Dining? Did the Marloven warriors dine instead of mess?

When he reached the lower level, he found a pair of guards. The older one said, "You're the guest, aren't you? If you go down that hall there, you'll find a runner. But if you don't see one, just follow your nose."

Guest. He was a guest. Jilo tried to get his mind around the word. He knew what it meant in language, but not in behavior. Chwahir in his experience didn't have guests. They weren't guests. He had no idea what was expected of him.

A runner appeared, a boy his own age. He carried a basket. "If you want breakfast, just duck through that arch there, and you'll find the dining room." The runner passed by on his errand.

Jilo stepped inside, and discovered a room with a table, chairs, and a sideboard laden with dishes, some covered so the food inside would stay warm.

He carefully lifted each lid to sniff the treasure inside. Then he went back and just as carefully picked up one item each from inside those dishes, though one or two burned his fingers.

His first bite into a hot rye biscuit, the crunch of the crust, the softness inside, the delicious sharpness of the rye blending with a trace of sweetness in the bread . . . the explosion of tastes in the potatoes and cabbage topped with crumbled cheese . . . the way the astringent coffee spread over his tongue . . .

Though he savored every bite, his emotions swooped from pleasure to shame. Why shouldn't the Chwahir eat this way every day? Or did they, and he didn't know it? But how could they, when the laws required half of every crop to go to the army, and so much of it was storehoused, then cooked together in a mass . . .

He was so very ignorant. Surely someone was going to walk into the fortress at Narad and have him shot for his temerity. Maybe someone had already taken the throne, and was waiting for him to come straight back to execution.

While Jilo struggled mentally, Senrid rammed his way through his expected tasks so he could leave for the day, if Jilo wanted him to look at that chamber again. Though he wondered—if he left, would he come back to find an assassin waiting? Or a delegation of jarls to demand that he abdicate in favor of one of them? They were probably still arguing over that, elsewhere in his castle. If they weren't plotting an overthrow.

Senrid climbed up to the tower room where Commander Keriam's office was located. One nice thing about being king: when he was tired and full of anxious questions, he didn't have to wait to talk to someone.

Keriam's office was crowded with tall, strong third-year seniors, several flushed, one or two white-faced with anger. Great. More trouble among the academy boys. Jarend Ndarga wasn't among them. Bad or good? Both, probably.

When they saw Senrid, most of them snapped their fists to their chests, one or two belatedly. Senrid made sure he met each of those boys' eyes, and yes, there was anger and resentment. He didn't have to listen on the mental plane. If he did, it would feel like a hammer on his head. Or his heart.

He forced himself to do and say nothing. He was not his uncle.

He had said that a lot to himself over the past year.

"Dismissed." Keriam turned a thumb outward at the boys.

Senrid prowled the perimeter of the room as the seniors clattered out.

Keriam looked tired. "Want a report now?"

"Trouble with the exhibition?"

"Trouble because they're listening to those . . . to the jarls."

Senrid flat-handed the subject aside. "Unless it's academy business, or a direct threat, I don't want to know what they say."

Keriam understood the tremendous conflict Senrid had gone through to speak those words. No spies, he'd said after he took the throne. But that had been in the euphoria of winning. No spies, no punishments for speaking their minds, he'd said after the Siamis enchantment was over, and people got their will back, because it had been what Senrid's father Indevan-Harvaldar had said. Although after he'd said it all those years ago, he got a knife in the back. From his own brother.

Indevan was gone, but not forgotten: two days ago, Senrid faced his jarls on the first day of Convocation and told them that he was upholding Indevan's Law, which meant they no longer had the right to execute citizens without royal dispensation. The jarls listened in silence at the time, but now it seemed every corner was filled with angry liege-men talking in knots.

But Senrid had said, *No spying*.

"I understand," Commander Keriam said. "This problem is going to carry to the academy, Senrid, so be prepared."

"I don't care what they say about me, as long as they obey regs."

"I know. The problem really lies in how they handle being disagreed with. You might say the biggest problem is not with you, though they're getting plenty of that at home, but with one another. How do we handle disagreement among peers, if not by duel? Except for your father's too-short reign, it's been generations since we could disagree without it being a matter of steel. Jarls have been ruling like little kings off and on since the Olavairs, encroaching on the throne a little more with each weak king. Your uncle was the weakest in two centuries." Keriam lifted his gnarled hands in a vague circle. "Those seniors? Nothing is going to rein them in short of assembling for punishment. I know you wanted to stop that, but they all expect it, and if we don't, we'll lose them."

Senrid kicked the wall lightly with the toe of his riding boot. "How can watching someone get caned into bloody pulp be 'expected'?" Senrid waved his hand. "I know, I know, we can argue it later. We're all mad, and bad, and dangerous, especially to ourselves. Speaking of that, I'm expecting to have to leave for a glass or two."

Senrid laid a transfer token down on Keriam's desk as he explained briefly about Jilo. Keriam (of course) had heard about the surprise guest. Marloven kings seldom had guests. Tdanerend, as regent, certainly hadn't. But last summer Senrid had brought a famous one, the Little Girl. She'd come a few times since. Everyone had gotten used to the Little Girl who had rid the world of Siamis through some kind of magic. It seemed fitting that she would visit their king.

Keriam liked the Little Girl not because she was famous, but because with her, for the first time, Senrid could be a boy. He'd never had a chance to roust about like other boys, but with the Little Girl, he built big cities out of books and a jumble of items as they argued back and forth and laughed, or they rode, or they just chattered, even if their chatter was in a different language. It was their laughter. Keriam couldn't remember ever hearing Senrid laugh like that, before the Little Girl came.

Senrid finished up, ". . . so if I don't show up within a glass of the exhibition practice, which I very much wanted to see, hold this token and say my name."

Keriam had considered canceling the exhibition and sending the new seniors home, like recalcitrant little boys. But it was so good to see Senrid acting like a normal boy, wanting to see the exhibition. "That will be after the mid-afternoon bell," Keriam said, making the decision. He'd slam the lid on the seniors' strut some other way.

"Then I'd better go soon."

"Why go at all?" Keriam said, and regretted it. Senrid had probably just told him, somewhere in all that gabble about Chwahirsland and Mearsies Heili that he hadn't really listened to.

Senrid stilled, his lips parted, his gray-blue eyes startled. Then his gaze went diffuse, and Keriam suspected that the question had struck Senrid differently than he'd intended.

He was right.

Senrid stared at Keriam, thinking that he wanted the real reason.

So what was the real reason? Senrid knew the real reason. It was both simple, and impossible, to say out loud: I'm going because Clair of the Mearsieans asked me to.

It would sound so sickening, maybe even sentimental. But there was no sentiment about Clair. She was offering to trust him, by coming to him in this alliance he'd agreed to so carelessly months ago, figuring it was more lighter hypocrisy that would be forgotten as fast as the self-righteous speeches about great Us battling nasty Them. (He did agree about Norsunder's being nasty.)

"Jilo seems to have no one. Can you believe that? No one, except that bunch of Mearsiean girls. And they're his enemies, at least former enemies. At least I have you." Senrid's words tumbled quickly. "Here's the irony. I have you, because I know you're the only one who wouldn't conveniently lose the token if I vanish into whatever awaits in that chamber. And it makes me afraid. Yet, here's more irony, you'd be a better king than I am."

"You will be a great king," Keriam said, careful not to show how profoundly Senrid's quick words moved him. "Besides, I've got the wrong name. We both know who of those fools arguing about their inherited rights, as if those haven't changed at least once a century, would try to take this castle if he thought the others wouldn't fight him."

Senrid snapped his fingers. "Then I'd better get to work. While my name still means something besides a catch-all for cursing."

He whirled around before Keriam could answer, and shot through the door as if trying to outrace time.

Senrid found Jilo in the formal dining room, which had been used exactly once so far in Senrid's short reign, the first time Liere came to visit. After they sat uncomfortably across from each other for a tense meal, they had both admitted that they'd rather eat in Senrid's study, or in the kitchens. By her third visit, that was now habit.

But the servants had put this new visitor there. Jilo lurked at a window overlooking the southern part of the city. He was even more unprepossessing in daylight than he'd looked at night, but at least his unpleasantly pasty complexion appeared somewhat more natural, and less like the gray of a corpse.

Jilo glanced up sideways through his lank, unkempt black hair, his manner furtive. Senrid reminded himself that this shambling, slope-shouldered fellow had endured eight months of the poisonous atmosphere of that magic chamber in Narad fortress.

Senrid said, "I've made some magical preparations, in case you still want my help. I'm sure you don't want to get caught again in that time . . ." Senrid didn't even have a word for it. "Smear. And I can't afford to vanish that long. I don't plan on returning in half a year, or longer, to everyone fighting, their only point of agreement that they should execute me."

Jilo shrugged, like execution squads were part of everyday life. Yes, from what Senrid had heard about the Chwahir, especially in the last century, they probably were.

Jilo's shoulders didn't come down out of the shrug, but stayed tense under his ears as he mumbled to the tops of his shoes, "Ah, what is it . . . that you want to do?"

"Find out if there is a time-binding spell. And how it's bound. If we can." Senrid sighed. "This is way, way beyond anything I know. But I think it's the first thing to do."

Jilo ducked his head in agreement, Senrid stuck out his hand, and Jilo understood that he was to make the transfer. He swallowed. "Brace yourself."

Jilo stretched out the hand wearing the onyx ring and clamped his fingers around the other boy's wrist. He muttered the spell, and magic hammered them against a wall, then scraped their components off and flung them into ice to reconstitute. Or that's what it felt like.

They found themselves in Wan-Edhe's magic chamber.

Senrid drew a shaky breath, then nearly choked. He'd forgotten that thin, yet pervasive stench of stale sweat tinged with a musty, animal smell of old, unwashed clothing. There was nothing in the room but the huge central table, made of wood so old it seemed petrified, a chair, and shelves and shelves of books. The stink had permeated the stone, if such a thing was possible. Either that or no one had cleaned the room in decades.

Jilo rubbed trembling fingers across his eyes, then said, "This small book is experimental spells. The large one is Wan-Edhe's log."

Senrid had figured that out on his short visit before, but he didn't point it out to Jilo. It was a way to establish a starting place.

"Here's where I can help, I think," Senrid said. "I learned this ward because of my uncle, who had a habit of protecting all his secrets with traps. It's laborious, but you can find the traps faster than careful feel by fingers."

"I've already searched for traps," Jilo said.

"You really think you got them all?" Senrid countered.

Jilo didn't have to think about it. "No."

Senrid explained his tracer spell. It had to be cast for specific objects as well as specific spells. If there was a hidden fire trap on whatever you touched, you'd see a red flare. A stone spell would make a blue flare. And so on.

Jilo's forehead eased. "So these kinds of tracers do exist.

Neither Wan-Edhe nor Prince Kwenz would have let me near any such magic. Though I tried to find it."

"I'll start on this half. You over there."

Jilo ducked his head again.

Senrid worked fast, the spell having become habit during the bad old days before his uncle turned to Norsunder. His mind was free to run with questions. This was an enormous library; there must be at least a thousand books on the nearest wall alone. Some of the ones on the highest shelf looked crumbled. They were most likely records of various types. But somewhere lay the solution to the lethal atmosphere here.

Or maybe not. How long had it been in making? The size of the task ahead of Jilo pressed down on Senrid, making it hard to breathe. No, he could breathe. It was more that he had to think about breathing, that he was aware of all the potential pain his body could be in if he moved wrong. His joints seemed ill-fitted, his skin tender in a way he couldn't describe.

It was a relief when he found himself sucked away and deposited in Keriam's room, where he collapsed onto the floor, head on his knees as his ears roared.

When he looked up, the air in the familiar office smelled sweeter than spring, light as noon, though the sun was weak behind streaky clouds, and low in the sky.

"What a life." He enjoyed the miracle of easy breathing. "Next time I whine about things here, remind me of Chwahirsland."

Keriam did not comment on how very little Senrid whined. "Did you complete your task?"

Senrid made a flat gesture with his hand. "Not even close. But we got a start. The rest is up to Jilo. I think he knows what to do. Better than I. He knows the territory." Then his mood changed. "Let's go watch those seniors, and I can pretend I don't see their fathers glaring at me because I won't let them kill their civilians whenever they get a blister or a bellyache. Hah!"

Chapter Fourteen

JILO was startled when he noticed that Senrid was gone.
A brief pulse of gratitude made him look around to
make sure. Jilo wanted to thank Senrid not only for the
spell, but for illuminating a hitherto shadowy path of magical logic. He knew what to do, now. It felt so . . . so
steadying—was that the right word?—to know what to do.

He straightened up, aware of a sense of malaise sapping
at his vitality. After carefully pulling out the last book he
had tested, so he could find his place again, he sighted the
door, and walked out. It was like walking through . . . fog.
No, fog didn't resist you, cold and wet as it might feel.

He noticed the farther he got from the magic chambers,
the more easily he moved; one floor down, and he encountered servants. The two he saw looked at him fearfully, one
jumping as if prodded.

"Any orders?"

"A meal," Jilo said. "Bring it here."

"A meal?" the young one asked, eyes wide. "Here?"

"Is there a standing order against meals brought here?"
The stink of fear was almost as bad as the magical malaise.
"Until Wan-Edhe returns," Jilo forced the hated words out,
"I will have meals here."

The young one bowed, hands out to his sides and open, as Wan-Edhe had required, showing no weapon. With his head bowed like that, Jilo could see the roundness of his face beneath the pallor and haggardness that marked everyone in the castle. He didn't look all that much older than Jilo himself. Was he worrying about what was going to happen?

Jilo hesitated, then ventured a new idea. "I will be making an inspection, to be ready for Wan-Edhe's return."

Was that relief? Yes. Routine was steadying, and the order clear. And readying the castle for inspection would keep everyone busy.

The meal arrived, and the boiled grain with cabbage and dried fish was as tasteless as the Shadowland food Jilo had eaten all his life. However, it did what it was supposed to do. Or maybe it was the thinner air downstairs. When he returned to the magic chambers, he did not immediately take up the task of checking for traps on the books, but explored the other chambers. There was little to find.

Then he remembered the anteroom off the throne, the one Wan-Edhe had always kept locked to anyone but himself and his dungeon master. Jilo went downstairs to discover the throne room empty and cold. Kwenz must have removed most of the spells on the anteroom door while executing a fetch order from his brother, for there was only a stone spell on the latch, easy to remove.

The room beyond had a table, in the center of which sat a plain wooden frame with what looked like black slate inside it. At the left and right of this framed slate were polished scry stones, each with flickers of movement inside. All different.

Jilo bent over the nearest, trying to see what was going on. He brushed his fingers over the top of the stone to remove a thin layer of dust, and found himself staring at the inside of one of the guard command centers. This time he kept his fingers on the scry stone and heard voices.

". . . I tell you, just fit them in."

"But we are already overcrowded."

"Not down the coast. They're all undermanned."

"Under leaky roofs, without beds or supplies. What are

they going to do with two thousand extra mouths to feed
and bodies to house?"

The Shadowland Chwahir were already *here!* 'Already'?
He'd lost eight months upstairs.

"Do you really want to ask for clarification of orders?"

The youngest said, "If he's truly gone, I will."

They all looked around on the word 'he.'

Then the oldest said, "I'll wager a neckin he's watching
you right now."

Jilo said, "Neckin?"

In the command room, all three jumped as if they'd
been stabbed. Jilo almost found it funny, except the yellow-
ish fear in their faces was not at all funny.

The three straightened up. One said, "May we request
clarification of orders?"

Jilo remembered the relief in the runner's face. "Carry
out as specified. But you are to send orders across the land.
Everyone ready for inspection. That includes a list of necessary repairs."

Hands snapped out, palms bare, fingers stiff. "It shall be
done." Though already the three commanders were worrying about what 'necessary' might mean, and what would
happen if they interpreted the word incorrectly.

Jilo touched the scry stone, and a different room appeared. Another touch, a different room. Of course Wan-
Edhe would have spent months, maybe years, setting up
this elaborate spy system. As for 'neckin,' it obviously was
slang.

Jilo stretched out his hand to return to the first room.
He could listen to what they said about their orders . . .

No. If he did that once, he'd do it again. And again. And
he'd never stop. The words flowed through his head, feeling
like an argument. Against whom? There was a sense in his
chest, like . . . like a beating was nigh. Like Wan-Edhe was
watching. Like . . . threat. He couldn't characterize it beyond that.

So he ran out of the room, pausing only to restore the
stone spell. No one should be in that chamber, that much
seemed sensible.

As he returned upstairs, he thought about slang, and

how he'd known pretty much all the Shadowland slang, but
that didn't mean the warriors here shared the same slang,
though they shared a language.

Comfort. The slang he knew had to do with sneaking
ways to get better food, better everything. Ways around
the rules. And of course the shorthand for various punishments.

We Chwahir have to sneak to get comfort, he thought
grimly.

He left the thought behind. He used one of the secret
passageways to reach the magic chamber, and got to work.

Senrid had discovered that even when he was deeply asleep,
some part of his mind was awake and aware enough to
sense subtle changes.

Something broke into his dreams. When he was small,
one of his survival habits had been to remain lying still, his
breathing even, when his uncle stole into his room to see if
he slept or was conspiring, and later, to attempt magical
spells that Senrid had managed to spy out and so had already warded; the only reason he was still here was because
the regent had been a terrible mage, and hadn't taken the
time to study to become a better one.

Senrid lay still except for one hand. His heartbeat
crowded his throat as his fingers wormed under his pillow
to close on the hilt of the throwing knife he always slept
with.

His door opened a crack wider, the hinges noiseless.
Whoever opened it slipped inside equally noiselessly, except he couldn't completely hide the soft sough of breathing.

Senrid sat up, spotted the man-shaped shadow barely
visible against the pale wall, and hurled the dagger all in
one motion.

"Shit."

The voice cracked. An adolescent voice. This was no
sinister Norsundrian spy mage, and anyway a Norsundrian
would set off tracers.

Senrid snapped his fingers, lighting the glowglobes, and

stared as Jarend Ndarga grimaced, yanked the dagger out of his bicep, then sank onto Senrid's trunk. "Your aim stinks," he said with a fair attempt at a steady voice.

"Didn't aim for the heart. Shoulder," Senrid said, with no attempt at hiding his shaky voice.

"Then your aim still stinks." Ndarga grimaced. "Why don't you have bodyguards?"

"Not going to live like my uncle, always expecting assassins," Senrid said.

"I'm not an assassin," Ndarga retorted in somewhat breathy outrage, his hand clapped tightly over his arm. "If I wanted a fight, it would be—"

"I know, I know, according to the rules," Senrid said, his heart still hammering as he rolled out of bed and reached for his clothes. "Here." He pulled a winter scarf from his bureau and tossed it to Ndarga, who wrapped it around his dripping arm as Senrid yanked on yesterday's trousers and shirt. "So why are you snaking into my bedroom in the middle of the night?"

The look of acute pain that Ndarga shot at Senrid came from something other than a dagger puncture, nasty as that was. Ndarga's surface emotions were like a hammer inside Senrid's skull—regret, anger, anxiety—causing Senrid to wince, and tighten his mental shield.

It took him a few breaths to resist the almost overwhelming temptation to delve behind those surface emotions, but he controlled it. He wasn't good enough not to risk being detected, and he knew how very angry, justifiably angry, that would make Ndarga.

So he said, "Come on. My study is right down the hall."

A short time later, Ndarga hunched on a guest mat, a heavy mug in his hands containing a healthy dose of the sometimes double- or even triple-distilled liquor called bristic, made from rye, with a blend of almond and pepper.

He sipped, blinked rapidly, and some of the blue shade vanished from his lips. Senrid loathed the taste of bristic almost as much as he hated the blurring effect of alcohol, but he knew it could help blunt pain. Listerblossom or green kinthus would be better, but he'd have to send for those, and he sensed Ndarga wanted to keep this interview private.

Ndarga let out a long, ragged sigh, glanced distractedly

at the crimson- splashed scarf he'd knotted around his arm, then looked up. "Nothing happened."

Senrid knew exactly what that meant. All these months had passed, with Ndarga neither penalized nor singled out in any way; he was now beginning his two-year stint serving in the city guard with the rest of last year's senior class.

Senrid said, "Won't. Like I said."

"You took away capital rights from the jarls."

"Not completely. Decisions to execute anyone have to be reviewed," Senrid said. "It's not new. The Senrid-Harvaldar I'm named for introduced it when my family got back to the throne five centuries ago. My father reintroduced it under the new regs." When Ndarga raised his hand to speak, Senrid said, "Yes, I know I'm not my father. Underage. Never went through the academy, and you know why."

Ndarga looked away. Then he said, "If I tell you something, will it be a capital case?"

Senrid sighed. "How can I know that before I know what it is?"

"Still. It's about *my* father," Ndarga said. "I'm not going to rat if it will get him put up against the wall."

There again was the impulse to sift through Jarend Ndarga's thoughts, but doing so was like trying to swim in a weed-choked lake, while being screamed at and burned and frozen by the person's emotions. And, of course, Liere would say it was wrong.

Senrid said, "I won't promise anything I don't know about first."

Ndarga let out his breath, trying to think clearly in spite of the throbbing pain. One thing he was sure of. If the king had agreed immediately, he wouldn't have believed it.

Neither understood the other, and so they sat there like that, at an impasse, until Senrid said, "You came in here. I didn't yelp for the guard. So speak your piece, or let me get back to sleep. And you better get that wrapped properly in any case."

Ndarga spoke reluctantly, as if each word was yanked out of him the way he'd pulled the dagger from his arm. "My father. And the Jarl of Waldevan. Others if he can get them. I think Torac will also ride, as he owes my father for our help against the Gorse Gang—horse raiders—on the border two years ago. First thaw, they're moving to take the coast back." He raised a hand. "They know they won't be able to keep it, that there are international treaties that separated off the Rualese. But if you have to defend that treaty, which only benefits outsiders, then they mean to force you back to the old ways, before you can raise the rest of the kingdom."

"Which old ways would those be? The ones under my uncle, with executions and floggings any time he didn't like someone's expression? Or my grandfather, who got us into two wars, which resulted in that same treaty being made by every other kingdom ganging up against us?" Senrid retorted cordially, and as Ndarga just shook his head miserably, Senrid sighed. "Forget that. I know what it is. They want to be petty kings again. But it isn't going to happen while I'm alive."

Ndarga got to his feet. "If you win. Exile him, or all of us, if you think that's fair. Whole family. You'll probably want to give Methden to someone new, and I get that, how it works. I hope it goes to the Senelacs. But don't execute him."

Senrid grinned. "The Senelacs probably wouldn't take it. Jan and Fenis both are ridiculously proud of that stupid old saying that Senelacs are great captains and terrible governors."

Ndarga ignored this attempt to ease the atmosphere, his hand clutched tightly to his arm. "You still haven't said. Look, Senrid-Harvaldar, I don't want my father against the wall. Because I ratted him out."

Senrid clawed his hair out of his eyes, his mind wheeling uselessly without being able to light anywhere sure. Lying had come easy when he lived under his uncle's tyranny, and without guilt. Lying fast and well was a survival tool.

The urge to lie shaped his lips, but he forced himself to meet Ndarga's angry, wary gaze. "I promise you I'm not going to ride down to Methden waving a war banner and order him shot in his own courtyard, on the strength of 'he might.' I'll wait for action. If he breaks capital law, not talks about it, but actually breaks it, then, no promises. How's that?"

A flick of the fingers. "I can take that."

"You know," Senrid couldn't help adding, "If I end up having to send your father and all his captains into exile, they might make it in Toth, or Telyerhas, but in Perideth, Marlovens are shot on sight."

"We have relations in Toth," Ndarga said in a gritty voice.

"Right then. Cut along." Senrid lifted his hand.

Ndarga cut. Senrid ran back to his room to clean the gore off his dagger, and replace it under the pillow. Then he jumped through his cleaning frame and pulled on socks, boots, and a tunic. As he did, he rapidly made and discarded plans. His first instinct was to race up to Keriam's tower.

Then he caught himself up short. He had to start acting like a king, instead of running to Keriam, or he may as well hand over the throne.

Senrid ran back to his study and snapped the glowglobes to light.

Chapter Fifteen

SENRID scowled at his desk. He needed more Scouts.

But recruiting the elite group, once known as royal runners before his family regained the throne, and King's Scouts afterward, was a slow process at best. They had to be trustworthy, vigilant, impartial, smart, and they had to go unnoticed. They had to listen, and be loyal to Marloven Hess. So far, most of his recruits were women and girls, who he knew would go unnoticed by even the most suspicious jarls.

He had to be careful about their selection and their deployment. Never far from his awareness was the sinister fact that all his uncle's Scouts (who had been expert spies as well as assassins) had vanished without a trace. Senrid still had no idea what had happened to them. In Marloven Hess, that usually meant they'd been scragged.

It was possible that some had scuttled for the border as soon as the regent was deposed. But all had vanished. Keriam said that argued for concerted action. Senrid found the idea unsettling that someone had the skill to get the drop on them all, as his uncle had recruited his Scouts for their sneakiness as well as their viciousness.

He'd think about Scouts later.

Senrid whirled around and studied the big map on the

wall behind his desk, twin to the one in his bedroom. He'd made that map himself, with as much detail as possible. His uncle had thought it a harmless task, not knowing that Senrid had undertaken it to get his own kingdom's landscape thoroughly into his head.

If Jarend Ndarga was right, the Jarl of Methden was going to invade Enneh Rual. Senrid eyed long, thin Enneh Rual. It was a country that existed only as a result of a treaty, but it would be foolish to overlook the sea-trained hardiness of the folk there, whose ancestors were partly Marloven, and partly Iascan, the fisher folk who'd lived there before Senrid's ancestors rode a-conquering out of the north.

Senrid had been listening to the seniors talking about command class ever since he was little, and he'd begun testing all his reading against what he heard. When he looked at the map, the strategy seemed obvious. He could even name a couple of battles in which it had been used. If Waldevan took Tarual Harbor, which dominated the bay, and Methden supported him from the southern end, that would secure both population centers, and the rest of Enneh Rual would fall easily.

But Senrid had learned from Keriam that 'obvious' was not inevitable, or even exactly the same thing to every commander. Senrid considered what he knew of Jarend Ndarga's father. The jarl was tough, hardened from years of riding the southern border in the ongoing effort to curtail the constant horse-raiding going back and forth, but actual battle experience? Senrid was fairly certain that David Ndarga had been an academy scrub, consigned to the horse pickets, when Senrid's grandfather last led the Marlovens against the neighboring countries. He could always ask Fenis Senelac, who seemed to know the history of every battle, as a result of having two older brothers in the academy.

Senrid scowled at the map, then darted for the library, warded and locked, where what remained of the royal records were kept. Marloven rulers who took their thrones by violence had a habit of eradicating all their predecessors' records. Senrid's uncle had been no different, trying to remove Senrid's father from everything but memory, but he'd not succeeded as well as he thought.

Older records were harder to find. The year before, Senrid had made a foray into his ancestral home, deep in the tangled, dark-magic-distorted forest of Darchelde. His ancestors' castle was a ruin, blasted by unimaginable magic, but careful exploration had disclosed an enormous archive filled with books. Most had been destroyed by four centuries of wind and weather. But not all.

Senrid had set teams of young scribes to work sorting them and recopying the most fragile. The reward was the filling of some of the holes left by long-dead usurpers. Senrid sought some of those now, to read up on how his ancestors had commanded past battles, skirmishes, and routs, successful and not.

He was still at it when Keriam found him lying on the floor in a welter of maps. Senrid looked up, startled to discover wintry light blue in the windows, and Keriam standing at the door, ready for their morning briefing.

"Keriam, Methden is going to war. I have to stop it." And before Keriam could respond, Senrid scrambled to his feet, sending papers flying. "Hibern is due soon. Have the runner tell her we had to leave. She'll understand. I'll meet you in your tower. There's somebody I've got to talk to first."

He bolted out the door and raced down to the academy.

He knew where he was likely to find Retren Forthan, one of his few friends among the academy boys. Forthan was that rarity, a boy from a laborer family. He'd been scooped up during one of the regent's mass conscriptions for building a super army with which to reclaim the Marloven empire of old. Forthan had been assigned with the other laborers' boys to the foot, but he'd proved to be so skillful that he'd been put forward by his infantry captain to be considered for command training at the academy.

Senrid's uncle had been ambivalent, knowing that his cronies among the jarls would not like this precedent, for places in the academy were much prized. Keriam had been insistent. And now Forthan was about to embark on his second year as a senior.

The academy was mostly empty during the winter, but a few boys stayed on. Forthan was inevitably one. Senrid knew he'd find him up early, drilling contact fighting in the same seniors' forecourt where Senrid had gotten his teeth loosened by Ndarga last year.

He hopped up and down, cursing himself for running out without a jacket, then forgot the cold when Forthan appeared, wrestling his clothing straight before saluting, fist to chest.

"I've got a situation," Senrid said in a quick, low voice. "Come on. Let's go where we won't be overheard."

Forthan followed without question, matching Senrid's quick step until they reached the archery yard, empty except for pools of icy slush here and there on the ground. Senrid whirled to face the older boy. "You've probably been reading the same histories I have, right? Of course you have. But you've been getting lectures in the military thinking behind all the glory, and that's what I need, that knowledge. Keriam agrees we need to know our own history better than just singing the same old stupid songs."

Forthan muttered with uncharacteristic ambivalence, "That's so." And to get off the subject of reading, "My father said once that nobody seemed to know any songs but the ones that made their family look good."

Senrid laughed. "True!" He kicked at the slush with the toe of his boot. "But I'm talking about reading. I mean, you can read and read and read. I have. I know. Reading makes you able to quote the significant facts of every battle, but it doesn't make you a commander. I know that. I knew that."

He looked sideways. Forthan could barely make out his expression in the weak light, but he could see the self-mockery in Senrid's tight shoulders, his sharp gestures.

Senrid went on. "Not many have heard this, but it was a near thing with Siamis, there at the end, up in Bereth Ferian. And it was all my fault. Mine was the decoy plan, because those mages up there didn't take anyone our age seriously. Well, they were right not to take *me* seriously."

Forthan gestured with a flat hand, as though pushing something away.

"It's true," Senrid said. "I should have known that Siamis would be ahead of me." He kicked the slush again. "Nobody knows this, either. When I was a prisoner. In Norsunder. Detlev looked right at me, and said that I wasn't worth his time yet. That's why I've done the no-growth spell."

Forthan stared somewhat helplessly. Like most Marlovens, he knew nothing about magic other than the little spells people were raised with, and trusted it less. He did understand that Senrid had done some kind of spell that kept him from aging. He said slowly, "Some people think that you did that spell because you wanted a chance to play, now that the regent is gone. You want a boyhood you didn't get."

"Let 'em," Senrid said carelessly.

"But others think you are running some kind of ruse, only not against us, but against outsiders."

"I suppose that's going to happen. Especially if I . . ." *Win*, Senrid thought. But he couldn't say it. Instead, "The rumor I want going to those outsiders is that first one, at least until Detlev is defeated. He and Siamis read minds like we read books. Forthan, Siamis was a step ahead of me all the time. One step? Ten steps. I fell right into his trap. If it hadn't been for the lighter mages coming to Liere's call, I'd probably be right back in that cell. So let any Norsunder spies hear that Senrid wants to play with the little brats."

Forthan remained silent, feeling very much out of his depth at this careless reference to personal encounters with Norsunder's most sinister villains.

Senrid kicked again at the slush. "I don't want to look like I'm worth Detlev's notice, but I still need to make the jarls see that my father's rules are back. Where was I? History. Reading history." He began to pace back and forth. "Look, Forthan, I've got no *harskiald* whom everyone will follow." Senrid used the Marloven word for supreme army commander, who in wartime was second only to the king. "We both know that we've had no upper rank commanders when we need them often enough that we've got jokes about it: 'the empty tower', and 'waiting for an elgar.'"

"Elgar" was a centuries-old slang term for the heroic commander who won every duel as well as every battle.

"All because of our Marloven would-be kings taking out the opposition's strongest leaders before they strike at the king they want to replace. Or, in my uncle's case, purging the academy of all its smartest seniors, because he'd watched as a scrub as a handful of the smart ones helped my oldest uncle when he tried to take the crown from my grandfather."

Forthan made a vague gesture of agreement. He'd grown up hearing bad or unpopular commanders joked about as 'waiting for an elgar.' It was the next thing to saying they were cowards. Or stupid. And he'd heard some of the jarls' sons repeating gossip about the boy king and his empty tower.

Senrid said, "If I did have a great harskiald, and handed my problems off to him, then I'd probably end up with another regent. Don't want that! So *I* have to learn to command. I've read everything I can find, and I know the details of countless battles, but I can't find *why* they did things, that is, their thinking before they gave the commands that led to wins."

Forthan was still silent. If the king asked directly, he wouldn't lie. But he dreaded making the humiliating confession that he was illiterate, convinced it would end his academy days summarily.

"Our greatest hero, Inda-Harskialdna, left the least direct evidence. All we have of him are the two versions of the Fox record, neither of which agree with the other, and a lot of hearsay and bombast about people who came after, you know, 'hearkening back to the great days of.'"

Senrid threw up his hands, fingers stiff. "In some of the oldest, moldiest stuff, I've found hints that there's a third Fox record. One that has everything. Though I'm sure it's not in this kingdom. Too many have searched for it. Horseshit! There goes the bell. But you don't have to go, right?"

Because the academy was not in session, Forthan wasn't expected anywhere. He flicked his fingers in agreement, and Senrid went on, "Here's why I need you. You know I've been watching the academy games ever since I was little. And I got so I could predict who would lead wins, who wouldn't. What they'd do."

Forthan opened his hands in assent, relieved to find himself back on familiar ground. He and Senrid and Jan Senelac had sat on the seniors' roof many a summer evening, little Senrid avidly listening as the two older boys dissected the games, before the regent put a stop to it. "Academy games are different from a war with Siamis, is that what you're going to say?"

Senrid whirled around, then stabbed the air with three

fingers. "But it's the same, really. Isn't it? Siamis plays for keeps, but it's all a game to him, he even said so. And I see that, I do, because what we're talking about are patterns, predicted by the way somebody thinks. The choices they always make. Right? Right?"

Forthan tried to follow the quick voice, and turned up his palm again in silent assent.

"So how do you know how and when to give orders, when in the heat? Because *you* always win."

Forthan scowled into the middle distance, then said, "I don't always win. Well, I guess it's always if I know the ground. Or if I'm up against someone I've been up against before. If I know the ground, and I know them, I pretty much know what they'll do next."

Senrid's breath crowed. "So it's true! What they say about picking your ground. Right?"

Forthan shrugged, acutely uncomfortable at being pulled from familiar to dangerously unfamiliar territory. He wanted to help Senrid, whom he liked and admired, even though he found it difficult to follow Senrid's quick changes of mood and subject. "I know the ground. Here. At the academy," Forthan said stolidly.

Senrid gazed at him, suspecting that Forthan's meaning was metaphorical as well as specific. He grinned, socked Forthan companionably on the arm, and raced off.

He pounded up the stairs to Keriam's tower, and burst in as the man was just being served a cup of freshly ground coffee.

As soon as the orderly was gone, Senrid kicked the door shut, and out it all came, from Ndarga's sudden appearance to Senrid's talk with Retren Forthan, in a headlong cascade. Keriam listened, knowing when Senrid was like this there was no halting him.

". . . and so it must have taken them the better part of two months to put this together. I think I need to confront them on their own ground. Waldevan is a rat, I know that much from my uncle's day. No, rats fight. He's a . . . a beetle. He'll squeak and try to scuttle but if he's penned, he'll go belly up. That's his pattern of behavior! But the Jarl of Methden will go all out, don't you think? And from everything I've seen, it would be a mistake to hit him in his own territory. Like Forthan said, ground is important. Don't you think he'll fight?"

Keriam had gone through the academy with David-Jarl Ndarga of Methden. "Oh yes. He'll fight," Keriam said grimly.

"Then we have to catch him outside Methden, right? Outside his territory, but before he gets to the Rualan border and drags us into war. I have to get there first, so I can pick the ground. It'll be just like the academy, won't it?" Senrid's voice pleaded. "Patterns."

Keriam said, "I can't predict the outcome, Senrid. You've studied Headmaster Gand's command text, from long ago. Think of what the man said about himself. That could speak for me. I'm excellent at analyzing what has happened, but I've never been good at predicting what will happen. The best I can ever give you is a set of possibilities, culled from the records. That's why I teach, and don't command."

Senrid rapped his knuckles on the desk. "How does this sound? You send the order for West Army to split. Give me two wings of horse, no, better make it three, a full company, for Waldevan's got three wings of his own. Then send the rest to ride south for . . . here. Where Methden borders with the Rualans." He pointed to the plain map on the wall adjacent to Keriam's desk. "The West Army winter quarters are closest to Waldevan, which means I can threaten him first, soon's my company gets there. Should only take them a day, or three if the weather is bad. Then I'll transfer down here, and walk the ground, until the rest of West shows up. By then I'll have a plan. I'll pick the ground. I've already been studying the terrain maps, and I think I know where to look, because I know maps never give you a real feel for what's actually there."

Keriam said, "And if Waldevan fights? If he wins?"

"Then I'll probably be dead, and it's up to you," Senrid retorted with a toothy grin.

Keriam stared down into that face. The fair hair came from both Senrid's parents, but the eyes that gazed back at him so intently were Evan's eyes, the Indevan-Harvaldar everyone had loved.

Grim memory seized Keriam, beginning with the days when David Ndarga of Methden had been riding mates with Kendred, the king's oldest son, until Kendred's unsuccessful revolt against his father had caused him to disappear, after which David's loyalty had gone to Indevan. Who had been an excellent king until his younger brother, Tdanerend, (it was everywhere believed) stabbed him in the back.

Tdanerend, as regent for five-year-old Senrid, had ordered the entire city guard out in search for the assassin, and the regent had even put a deserter-turned-thief through a grisly execution, but the man had maintained to the end he wasn't anywhere near the royal castle that night. Everyone believed he'd been a scapegoat, but after Tdanerend had handed out savage floggings for rumor-mongering among castle guards saying so, the rumors went underground.

More than ten years later, Keriam still felt like a coward for not speaking up, and he knew many others did as well, but what could they have done? Accusing the regent would not have brought Indevan back, but it would have touched off civil war. Tdanerend had made concessions and promises to gain powerful support among ambitious jarls, or those who wanted to become jarls, enough to make the outcome uncertain. The only sure thing would have been a high body count.

David Ndarga, like the other jarls, had thereafter been forced to swear fealty to Tdanerend or die with the knowledge that his family would be replaced by Tdanerend's sycophants. And so Indevan's dreams of justice had died on that balcony with him.

Keriam shifted uncomfortably, and Senrid stilled, a rarity for him, and waited as Keriam considered the present. Waldevan, Keriam was sure, would back down. He was a weasel. Had always been one. But David Ndarga of Methden was a wolf: loyal to his old mates and to an image of Marloven Hess that had not existed for ten years; fiercely bitter toward everyone else.

"It might work," he said finally.

Chapter Sixteen

Bereth Ferian

"YOU *are?*" The journeymage named Sigini threw her head back, pale hair rippling, blue eyes wide in astonishment. "*You* are?" No, that wasn't astonishment. That was affront. The senior mage student looked at Hibern as if she'd spat on the beautiful marble floor.

Hibern stared back. Fhlerians were like that, everybody said. Fhlerians sounded arrogant because of those Venn-sharp consonants and the drawled vowels of their version of Sartoran. Because those strong enough to become citizen-warriors, with the right to vote for their own government, considered themselves better than anyone else. They were all that way, it was nothing personal.

Not true, Hibern decided as she met that unfriendly gaze. It didn't take mind powers to guess what this Fhlerian was thinking: *But you're a Marloven.*

Sigini opted for the veneer of politesse as she asked, "Why would the Queen of Sartor pick you for a study partner?" Her fellow mage students crowded around, some sharing her expression of personal insult as she added, "You are her own age. You cannot possibly be ahead of us."

"Not in general studies." Another girl hefted her mage notebook. "But she must be in non-human magical studies, as she's with Erai-Yanya of Roth Drael."

"Tsauderei probably arranged it," a tall boy interjected, his tone reasonable, but speaking as if Hibern weren't there in front of them. "She's probably a compromise, since either mage school wouldn't like the other being so honored."

Sigini, who looked about eighteen, rolled her eyes. "Of course. That explains the diplomatic side of it."

Hibern breathed out through her nose, trying to rid herself of the irritation Sigini obviously wanted her to feel. Not long ago, Erai-Yanya had told Hibern, "You're going to meet with jealousy, I expect. Remember, no one at either Sartor's or Bereth Ferian's school knows Atan, much less who might be best for her. They are all thinking, quite naturally, that they should have been picked. It's human nature, and if you're going to work with mages of both schools for the good of the world, you must learn how to deflect such slights, and forget them."

Hibern forced a smile at Sigini, who someday might save Hibern's life, or the other way around. "Speaking of diplomacy, I don't want to be late." She walked out of the lecture room.

A couple of Bereth Ferian's mage students walked with her. One of the younger girls said, "Do you transfer all the way to Sartor from Roth Drael? Isn't it brutal?"

"I do it in stages," Hibern responded, walking quicker. "Spend an hour in my home kingdom. Then on to Sartor." At the corner of the hall, she turned away from the archive, knowing that most of the students would be heading that way to get started on their new assignment.

The younger girl cast a quick look back at her seniors, then stayed with Hibern. She matched pace and asked, her voice low, "What's she like? The queen, I mean."

Hibern didn't want to say that she didn't really know. Even though she called the Queen of Sartor 'Atan,' the most personal conversation they'd had so far was at that first interview. Since then, their weekly meetings these past eight months had been strictly about magic.

But Hibern's earliest lessons had been to keep her own counsel, and though this red-haired mage student with all the freckles seemed friendly, Hibern didn't know any of the Bereth Ferian mage students well enough to predict how they would hear her words. So she said, "She works very hard. She's earnest, and quick. She knows more about the history of magic than anyone I've ever met."

"That would be Tsauderei's doing," the student said confidently. "We all hear about how he and Mage-King Evend used to argue about how to teach magic, how Tsauderei felt that history ought to come before basics, not after." She tossed her curls. "As for the queen, she sounds boring."

Hibern didn't find Atan boring. Well, maybe the mask was boring. But the day of her interview, Hibern had glimpsed somebody behind that mask.

The girl went on, "Though she could be a dragon come back and Sigini would have volunteered to tutor her, just for the prestige." The redhead laughed and ran off with a flick of a hand, her silvery-blue mage robe rippling.

It was not actually Hibern's time to go south, but the other students didn't know that. Hibern transferred back to Roth Drael, and shivered at the sudden shock of damp chill. Magic warded the heavy sleety rain slanting down, but not the cold of the late summer storm.

She ran down the short hall, by now so accustomed to the place she no longer noticed the startling jagged lines of the broken walls, some fixed with regular stone centuries ago, others protected by layers of warding spells. She'd learned on her first interview with Erai-Yanya that Roth Drael was one of the few untouched ruins left from the Fall of Ancient Sartor four thousand years ago. Mages had vowed to leave the ruin as a memorial, but an ancestor of Erai-Yanya's had withdrawn from the world to study ancient magic in it, and heeding the vow, managed to make a cozy home of the ruin, using magic to ward weather. Bright woven rugs, comfortably shabby rigged bookcases, and low, cushioned chairs made for ease of reading, with plenty of small tables that could double as desks.

Erai-Yanya sat in one of these old chairs, a lapboard stretched across the padded arms, her bare toes propped on a fender near a leaping fire in the fireplace. Two old-looking scrolls lay half-furled on the lapboard, with an empty mug, an inkwell, and a stack of paper on which the mage was busy writing.

She looked up. "How did it go?"

"Well enough." Overhead, the roar of rain ceased abruptly. Hibern lowered her voice. "We got assigned some reading about magical displacement spells and banks and treaties. The same reading you gave me last year."

"Did you tell them that?"

"I kept it to myself."

Erai-Yanya smiled. "Good. Anything else?"

"Yes. At the end of the lecture, someone asked something about wards. I confess I was only paying partial attention, as I'd already done that reading. But the tutor said something about Sartor, then she pointed at me and told them that I was the new queen's study partner, and perhaps I could better answer their question. They all stared at me."

"And?" Erai-Yanya asked.

"It went pretty much as you predicted. Even who."

"Sigini," Erai-Yanya said unerringly. "Did she, or anyone, ask what you study with Atan?"

"No. But that'll probably come," Hibern said.

"And what will you say?"

Hibern suppressed a sigh. "This is an old lesson. I'll be as brief as possible. Tell them as little as I can. Without claiming great secrecy."

Erai-Yanya dipped her head in a nod. "I beg your forgiveness for being repetitive, but when it comes to Atan, everyone wants to know everything. And one can never quite be sure what people are hearing in the most innocuous-seeming answers."

"What if I tell them that we studied wards? Won't that be innocuous enough?"

"For anyone else, maybe. But someone hears that, and passes it on, and it gets passed farther—because Sartor is always interesting—and before you know it, some diplomat appears before the Sartoran Star Chamber, and demands a treaty to prevent the magic war that rumor has it the queen is about to begin because she's expanding her border wards. Then someone at Twelve Towers, or the Sartoran mage guild, gets busy and traces the rumors back to you."

Hibern sat back. "Muck! I didn't think of that."

"Do," Erai-Yanya said earnestly. "You gained enormous prestige in being picked as Atan's study partner. But prestige . . . well, you don't need that lecture."

"Yes, we Marlovens have the opposite of prestige," Hibern said. "Old news!"

Erai-Yanya smiled, but she did not deny it. Hibern said, "The sun is out. I'm going to take a walk before I have to transfer again."

Erai-Yanya shook her head. "Better not. I noticed a migration earlier."

"Oh." A migration usually meant the Fens, animals of Helandrias, who had been cursed with speech, because of some well-meaning but misguided mage long ago. The animals were very definite about speech being a curse; the mages had discovered that the animals called humans the Snakes with Two Faces.

Hibern grimaced as she hung up her shawl. The Fens might or might not attack her. Better not to tempt them. "This two-faced snake will work, then."

Hibern discovered she still had a turn of the glass before she was due in Marloven Hess.

She walked to her own room, with the old tapestry covering the massive crack in the single wall, and a strong weather-ward making a window of the missing part of the roof. This room had probably been a conservatory once, with its broad windows on three sides, through which Hibern could watch the forest life. She'd decided to live in this room during the summer. During winter she retreated to a smaller, cozy room.

She sat down at her desk, virtuously pulled out her notes from the year before on the incredibly boring subject of banks and displacement wards, then sat back, thinking about what the redhead had said about the Queen of Sartor and Sigini the Fhlerian.

She could be a dragon come back . . . The expression had all the cadence of a popular saying. Dragons occasionally appeared in colloquialisms in the world, though no one had seen one for thousands of years. It was said that the Chwahir language was full of dragon references, but that was a secondhand report. Hibern knew no one who spoke it.

When it was time to go, she packed up her books and transferred to Marloven Hess.

Senrid's study was empty. Not only empty, but it looked like a windstorm had been loosed, for books lay haphazardly on the table, and papers had been scattered all over the floor, their edges curling. More books kept them flat, which dispelled her first impression, that someone had ransacked Senrid's study. He was always so tidy. Something had clearly happened, probably bad.

The door opened. A runner stuck his head in and eyed Hibern. "Blue robe. Are you the mage student?" he asked. On Hibern's open-handed gesture of assent, he continued, "I was to tell you that Senrid-Harvaldar and Commander Keriam were called away."

Hibern sighed with disgust. Why hadn't Senrid written her a note and saved her a wrenching transfer for nothing? She knew he had a golden notecase. That had been one of their first projects together. He'd even insisted it actually be gold, though that metal hadn't been used exclusively since centuries ago, back when only the wealthy and powerful could afford to have mages make them. Senrid had been skeptical about the fact that anyone could send a note or a small object if it fit inside the case, as long as the 'sigil,' the notecase's Destination, was known to the sender.

He'd asked for gold simply because it would stand out, as he had no other gold objects. But he still thought like their ancestors, who never trusted magical communications. If he had some emergency, he would go straight to his army of runners, who would carry messages without revealing them to anyone else.

She walked out of Senrid's study and paused on the landing, staring sightlessly at the curving lines of a running horse frescoed on the wall, a raptor wing-spread above its flying mane.

She now had an entire hour to explore Eidervaen, the capital of Sartor and the oldest city in the world. She hadn't been permitted to wander alone during the rift-fighting days, but surely nobody was stopping her now.

She walked back to Senrid's personal Destination,

transferred to Sartor, and after recovering, asked the chamber attendant, "Which way is outside?"

A formal gesture toward the opposite archway sent her down a hall with a shiny tiled floor into a vault-ceilinged intersection made of gray, peach, and silver marble.

She tipped her head back to study the tall windows high up on the wall, the strong afternoon light shafting in, lighting up slow-moving dust motes. As she slowed, she became aware of a quick, light sound, followed by the hasty whisper of slippers on marble.

She suppressed the urge to turn and look. There was no danger here. She picked another tile-floored, marble hall, hoping it would lead to the famous dragon door that she'd read about in her studies.

The pitter-patter neared. Hibern whirled, to find herself looking down in amazement at the strangest-looking child she'd ever seen. This girl would have been ordinary enough—brown of skin and hair—save for the wide, slightly protruding eyes with the droopy lower lid that marked her as some relation to the Landis family, and for the fact that she was dressed in some kind of ragged garment that was way too large for her.

"Are you a mage?" the child asked. She couldn't have been more than five.

Hibern said, "I'm a mage student," as she lifted her gaze to the servant, correct in livery, who halted a pace behind the child. This servant, a young woman, clasped her hands tightly, saying in a low, firm voice, "Come, joel, this is not appropriate."

"I am only asking," the child stated, owl-eyed.

'Joel,' Hibern had learned, was a familial honorific, which could also be used for small children. Hibern said, "I am a student of magic, joel." Nobody reacted, so she was not incorrect.

"Teach me a spell to become invisible?"

"Do you know your basics?" Hibern responded.

The child scowled, and the servant stepped up to her. "Come, joel, do you not see? It is necessary to learn your letters."

The child whirled away in a flutter of tatters and uncombed brown hair. "I *won't* do letters," she stated, then ran off without another word.

The servant sent Hibern a look that the latter took as regret and worry, then scurried after her charge.

That was odd. Not just the way the child was dressed, but how much she looked like Atan. And yet Atan had said her family was dead. But then the word 'family' could differ in meaning—to some it meant only parents, guardians, and siblings, and to others it could encompass an entire clan.

Hibern forgot the child when she reached a door, carved around with leaves and flowers but no dragons. She opened it and slipped outside, pulling her coat close about her. So far, no one had stopped her. No wards or alarms, though the Marloven was loose.

The sun was out, so it was comparatively balmy for a winter's day, sunlight shining weakly on a series of broad, shallow steps, worn by countless feet over the equally countless years. She looked down at the pale gray stone, then up, overwhelmed by the profligacy of grace in color, shape, and style: tower, archway, statue seduced the eye, demanding adulation. And the decorative motifs, as if to compete against the monuments of kings! Here was the famous stylized wheat pattern, there a Venn knot in reverse. Above, the sun with the sword rays, and facing it from that tower, the sun with the waving rays . . .

She had an hour. She forced her attention downward to the street, where people came and went, walking and riding in carriages, carts, and pony traps, and driving long wagons full of goods. Where to begin?

"Need transportation?"

The clatter of small hooves neared, and Hibern whirled around to discover a small pony trap pulling up, only the animals were a pair of silky-haired goats. As she stared in amazement, the nearer goat gave her a stern look, and uttered a soft "Mah-a-a-ah."

The boy driving the trap was no older than Hibern, a round fellow with rusty red hair tied back. He wore a thick yellow tunic with a green shoulder-cape and green cuffs, a yellow and gold wheel patch sewn on the shoulder. "Where to? Or are you just lost?" the boy asked, making the polite bow for third circle. "I can give directions. Things are slow today."

Hibern was intensely interested in talking to someone born a century before. "How much to ride around, and maybe get information on what I'm seeing? I have an hour."

The boy's business-smile widened to a grin. "I can get you around the Way in under an hour, if we don't stop, for a sixer. Ask any questions you like. You get your money back if you stump me."

The Way. Hibern knew that had to be the Grand Chandos Way, the street built on the foundations of what had once been the walls of the most ancient part of the city. And 'sixer,' she knew, was idiom for the six-sided brass coin, twelve of which made up one silver. Not to be confused with the six-sided silver coin, half of a gold-piece, that was called a 'six.' Erai-Yanya had counseled her to always carry a few coins in her pocket when transferring, and here she was, needing them for the first time.

Feeling worldly, she said, "I'd like that," and hopped into the trap.

A whistle, and the goats trotted neatly off, their prettily shod hooves clicking on the street paved in chevron brick pattern. "Do you get a lot of custom from the palace?" Hibern asked, to hear his accent again. It was different from Atan's, which was more like Hibern's own.

"Almost none. Those who come to the palace usually have palace business, and go away again either by their own wheelers or by magic. The good trade's at the guild Destinations." He flapped a hand behind them. "The senior wheelers get the best spots. But I like getting foreigners, because they're fun to talk to. As long as I can understand 'em."

As he spoke, he drove them under the enormous windowed archway that connected to a white stone tower. Hibern looked up at that smooth, glistening stone, like ice and yet not. Here was the same strange not-quite-stone of Erai-Yanya's ruin at Roth Drael. Some of the most awe-inspiring, and frightening, stories about Sartoran history involved this tower.

"Mages' Finger, that is, the Tower of Knowledge," her guide said. "Been here as long as the city. Some say longer.

Only mages go in. And the royal family. Behind it is first district's labyrinth."

"Is that just for the royal family, too?"

"Oh, no, they have their own on the other side of the palace. Many families have their own. Each district has a public one, maintained by citizens."

The west wing of the palace hid the tower from view. They were making a wide sweep to run alongside the northern branch of the Ilder River. On the other side of the river ranked in elegant rows the famous Parleas Terrace, the aristocratic houses. The boy called off a list of statues and towers, about half of them names she recognized from history.

At the end, he said, "Any questions?"

"I know that kings and queens put up monuments to their rule, here, in Colend, and in many other kingdoms."

"They start thinking about it right when they're crowned. So the stories go," her guide said cheerily. "Some don't last long enough to put one up, and some dithered until it was too late. If there wasn't one put up to honor them, they just become another name in the list."

"So I take it rulers don't remove former monarchs' efforts?"

"Not in Sartor." He sounded surprised that anyone would do such a thing.

"So is this because the Landis line is unbroken here? Or because Sartor hasn't been conquered, outside of a hundred years ago?"

"Oh, there have always been Landises, but I don't know what you'd call unbroken," the guide said. "No, they don't knock down anyone else's monument, but build in front? Around?" He laughed. "I wish you had longer than an hour. I could show you some peculiar ones." He glanced back at her. "They don't build monuments where you come from?"

"No." Royal legacies of any kind in Marloven Hess didn't often survive changes of kings, save the shields and swords on walls, commemorating battles.

He clicked to the goats, who veered expertly between a dashing high-sprung two-seater carriage, pulled by a pair of gray horses, and a slow covered wagon behind a team of oxen. "Things'll be slow today up in the palace for you scribes."

"Slow?" Hibern repeated, not correcting his misapprehension. Erai-Yanya had deliberately given her a robe of a sky blue, different than either the dark blue of the Sartoran mage guild or the silver blue of Bereth Ferian's mage school. Scribes also wore various shades of blue. Scribes and mages had been tied together as long as there was recorded history. And in those histories it was clear that people didn't always like mages.

"Oh, yes." The boy chuckled. "Rumor has it Rel the Traveler himself just arrived. He and the queen'll be talking up old times. He was there, you know, when the queen lifted the spell off us, and broke the hundred-year sleep. Now over yonder, we've King Jussar the Golden, which referred to his singing, not his hair, which was black, and . . ."

Hibern had never met Rel, but she'd heard plenty of gossip about him, mostly praise from those who knew him, except from CJ of the Mearsieans, who seemed to waver between a wary friendship and a scowling conviction that he was an overgrown blowhard. All Hibern knew about him was that he came from some small kingdom in the middle of the Sartoran continent, and that he was often on the Wander.

Hibern waited for the guide to draw a breath after his history of another sword-bearing monarch on a marble horse, and asked, "What did Rel the Traveler do?"

"He got the queen to safety, by way of a morvende geliath. He's friends with them," the guide said proudly. "Not many sunsiders get to say that. He was also there at the end, fending off Norsunder when they tried to kill the queen. Not that I saw it. I was still asleep on the other side of town. But I've met him, twice, when I carried a fare to the garrison while he was visiting. He's friends with what's left of the Royal Guard, being very good with the sword."

Hibern was done with the subject of Rel. To stem the flow of friendly chatter, she commented when he stopped for breath, "I really like the embroidery on your livery. Did you do it?"

"Yes," he said proudly. "My dad taught me. He was a sailor, before the war." His smile lessened. "He was out to sea when Nightland attacked." Hibern was caught by his use of 'Nightland.' She'd read it on old records, a euphemism like 'eleveners.' "So I was gone for a century, but he wasn't," he finished.

"That must be very difficult."

"I'm better off than most. At least I can hope he got a good long life, unlike mates whose families were killed by the Nightlanders. But you wanted a tour of the Way, not of my life." He went on with his recitation of famous sights that Hibern had read about, and some that had local meaning; the patterns of his speech indicated he'd worked hard to memorize it.

When he paused, she asked the history of the various five-story buildings. Presently they rounded through the expensive shop area east of the palace, and curved back along the winding middle branch of the river to their starting point.

She recognized the square as the melodic bell rang the four chords, echoed by other city bells. She was sorry to climb out of the cart. "Thank you," she said, digging for her coins.

"I'll take half," the boy said.

Hibern was startled. "But you answered all my questions. And I know they weren't very good questions. I think I need to spend a week just walking and looking."

The boy leaned on the edge of the cart, his mouth wry. "It's the questions you didn't ask: Where's the spot where King Connar XXIII died, and are the bloodstains still there? Where's the house where Alian Dei entertained the first Connar, before he married her? Where's the stone marking the place where they executed Efran Demitros?"

Hibern smiled ruefully as she handed over the coins. "My unasked questions are all about the white tower, and I know whom to put them to." She belatedly remembered her first-circle bow.

The boy returned her bow from his seat, and she hurried inside, to find the desk attendant peacefully reading his book. Hibern was considering whether to interrupt him and ask for a message to be sent, when Atan's laughing voice preceded her appearance with a very tall, dark-haired fellow with deep-set dark eyes. Though he was dressed plainly in the ubiquitous traveler's loose, belted linen tunic over riding trousers and boots, his size and breadth of shoulder drew the eye.

"Hibern," Atan exclaimed. "I apologize. We went to visit friends over at the guardhouse, and just got back."

Hibern had never heard that happy lilt in her voice before. Atan was usually so serious.

"I hope you didn't wait unduly long," Atan went on. Hibern was opening her mouth to say something diplomatic when Atan bent over the shoulder of the desk clerk, and exclaimed, "Oh, no, you were here an hour ago?"

"I came early because someone else canceled," Hibern said quickly. "And so I wanted to see the famed dragon door—which I didn't see—and the Grand Chandos Way, which I did."

Atan turned a wide-eyed glance up at the fellow. "Rel, did you hear that? Dragons?"

Hibern gazed in surprise. So this was the Rel whom CJ of Mearsies Heili spoke so disparagingly?

Atan turned a hand her way. "This is my study partner Hibern. Let's find Hin and Dorea—no, that's right, the scribes put Dorea on archive duty, did they not? She would love that. Wouldn't want to leave." She turned her gaze from Rel to Hibern as she said with a return of her old, careful, sober manner, "This is *my* hour. Perhaps we could visit Tsauderei. Is that all right with you?"

Hibern didn't need coaching to know that when a queen asks if something is all right with you, you say, "Yes, your majesty." Yet she'd heard a tone in that soft declaration, *this is* my *hour*, as if all the hours belonged to someone, or something, else, and she remembered what Erai-Yanya had said about Atan needing a taste of freedom.

Tsauderei was old enough to find little to surprise him and much to amuse him in the vagaries of human nature. He had expected the newly enchantment-free Sartoran mage guild to be jealous of their prerogatives, which extended to their new young queen. And so it had proved.

Few people in the world were granted immediate magical access to Tsauderei. Atan was one of them. When magic warned him of multiple transfers, with Atan's tracer among them, he waited, ready to drop a stone spell over them in case there was treachery afoot. But a quick glance at the little group recovering in the Destination outside his one-room cottage made it clear that she was with them willingly.

"Tsauderei, I'm so very glad to see you," Atan exclaimed as she led the way inside. "I apologize for not sending a message ahead, but I only have my hour."

"I'm entirely free," Tsauderei said, as Hibern looked around with intense interest at the living quarters of one of the world's most famous mages.

Tsauderei lived in a one-room cottage with a loft above. Three walls were entirely covered with books. The fourth was an enormous glassed-in window looking out over a steep valley above a deep blue lake.

The old mage turned the hourglass sitting on his side table and said, "That'll warn us. So, begin with introductions?"

"Here's Hibern. This is our magic study hour, actually. But she agreed. You've heard me talk about Hinder." The morvende boy flicked a hand in greeting, his talons today painted a distinctly virulent green. "And this is Rel, who helped us against Norsunder." She clasped her hands together. "I remember going through your books about dragon legends when I was ten or so. You used to tell me, when a subject comes up three times during separate circumstances, the wise mage pursues it?"

Tsauderei laughed. "And that subject is dragons?"

"Yes. Is there any truth about their once being in the world? And if not, why do legends about them persist?"

Tsauderei laid his gnarled hands in his lap. "I can answer that. Of course I've never seen one. No one has. But I have seen where they once lived." He paused, and saw four pairs of interested eyes. "As you can see, we are quite high up. Much higher are the mountains between your Sartor and Sarendan below us. Imagine an enormous plateau of heat-blackened stone. It's cold there all year round, with either snow or dry wind. Far in the distance, what looks like small hills are huge caverns, the walls black and glassy, as if melted by fires of unimaginable heat. The plateau is where dragons once perched, and the caverns, we believe, were where they sheltered their young. I spent a very cold summer studying those caverns when I was a journeymage. I wasn't the only one. Despite the thin air and the barrenness and the cold, there were many of us who went over that place looking for any hints of dragons' lives all those thousands of years ago. But all there is to be found are the faint remains of carvings in the rock, made by the humans who lived among the dragons and cared for them. Those carvings are yet to be deciphered, but the carved images make it clear that the dragons chose to be there."

Atan said, "So humans did live with them, even in such a terrible place! Is that the appeal of dragons, then? That they were immense?"

Tsauderei gave a crack of laughter. "Atan. I taught you better than that."

"I know there's seldom any 'simply,'" Atan hastened to say. "But the dragons have been gone so long we don't know anything about them, other than that they were large. And flew, and breathed fire. So I'm thinking that humans seemed to admire large creatures for being large as well as the dangerous predators for their ability to kill."

Rel looked down at his hands.

Tsauderei leaned back, eyeing him. "Your large friend appears to disagree," Tsauderei observed. "Is that due to your size, young man?"

Rel lifted a hand. "Has nothing to do with my size. If you've ever traveled by earning your way cross-country, you'll discover that the easiest job in any city is to work for the Wand Guild. Anyone can wave a magic stick over horse droppings in a street. But the bigger the beast, the bigger the pile, and you soon lose any admiration for size."

He stopped there, shrugging.

Hinder laughed, his cobwebby hair drifting. "I did not think of that. What a nasty job—surely that had to be during the days of slaves, for who else would wand dragon droppings? Not I!"

Tsauderei's smile was sardonic. "Then you'd be wrong. You're forgetting the chief appeal of dragons: their treasures."

"I thought dragon hoards were the false part of the legend," Atan exclaimed. "It makes no sense. What use would an enormous creature like a dragon have for cups of gold, bejeweled crowns, and the like?"

"Cups of gold are certainly the distortion of legend." Tsauderei chuckled. "Dragons breathed fire. They melted rock to make their caves, so what do you think their internal arrangement was like?" He studied the four bewildered faces before him, clapped his hands on his knees, and laughed again. "Their excreta came out as gemstones, my dears. Volcanic glass. Sometimes precious metals, depending, I guess, on what they'd been eating, which was mostly ores of various sorts from mountaintops, left from very old volcanos. Their caves were piled high with the stuff, until humans carted it off."

Atan said, "Why didn't I know that?" Then she winced. "Now I feel stupid. Dragon-stones, dragon-eyes, the rare and expensive gems—those were dragon droppings?"

"Yes." Tsauderei chuckled again. "There are few real dragon gems left, though there are numerous types of rock misnamed dragon-eye and the like, usually rocks with a thin layer of some other substance compressed in the middle."

"'Greed and beauty. Two human traits,'" Atan quoted as she moved to the little kitchen arrangement in the corner opposite the door.

Tsauderei delighted in how unconsciously she resumed old habits, but it was not an unmitigated pleasure. Atan had not changed at all since he'd seen her last, which meant she had not only performed the Child Spell, keeping her from maturing to her adult form, she was holding onto it. It would be too simple to assume she had done it to keep her court from negotiating a marriage. He suspected her reasons were more complex than that, connected to the emotions Atan seemed to be trying to hide.

He could have told her that emotional attachments were not avoided by doing the Child Spell, only the physical component of such attachments. Even in this short visit it was clear that she was developing feelings for Rel, and that Hibern, the age-mate whom he and Erai-Yanya had so carefully chosen for her, seemed oblivious.

As for Rel, there was no more heat in his gaze than there was in hers, but then, big as he was, his cheeks were still smooth. That sun for him was clearly still below the horizon, as it was for her.

Well, and if the sun came up, so what? The passions of the teen years were like thunderstorms, wild for a short time, soon gone. Rel seemed an excellent young man for Atan's first experiments into relationships, whenever she decided to step over that threshold. But he foresaw yet more conflict from the Sartoran first circle, who could not be prevented from talking about a future royal marriage.

He watched from under hooded eyes as she went about preparing hot steep. She knew all the spells. The firestick under the tiny grate had probably been made by her, one of a magic student's first projects, to repeat, over and over, the spell to capture the sun's heat.

Unaware of his scrutiny, Atan was trying to recapture the sense of being Tsauderei's student again. It was good to be here again, and with people she liked, and yet that sense of goodness was so conscious. She knew it would end soon, which hurt.

She glanced a fourth time at the sand trickling relentlessly through the glass, and scolded herself. She would never want to go back to the days when Sartor was enchanted, never, never, never. She was *happy* to be able to make steep with fresh leaf, because Sartoran leaf was growing again on the northern slopes, and she should celebrate that its trade all throughout the world would help fill an empty treasury.

"Hot steep in moments," she said with forced cheer, bringing the tray of cups to hand out.

The water boiled. Atan poured it through the new leaf, filling the cottage with a delicious summery smell. She sniffed it in, hoping the aroma would chase the resentment out of her heart.

Hinder held out a hand. "Steep I can get any time. Everybody says that people can fly in this valley."

"They can," Tsauderei said, pointing to the ledges and small plateaus around the steep slopes above the lake, on which could be seen, amid the trees, tile roofs. "It's the way the villagers get from ledge to ledge. By ancient magic, beyond anything we are capable of now."

"I want to try flying," Hinder said, bouncing gently up

and down so that his painted toe talons clicked on the clean-swept stone floor.

Tsauderei said, "Here's the magic word and sign." He demonstrated. "Perform them at the same moment, then spring up. You should figure it out fast enough—"

The door closed on the last word. The others watched Hinder through the great window. He did the magic while running, then flung himself over the side of the cliff, causing Hibern to suck in her breath, the backs of her knees gripping sickeningly, the way they did when she was confronted with heights.

The boy vanished, then he reappeared, hands outflung, the wind ripping through his snow-white hair and his tunic as he shot skyward, cartwheeled clumsily, began to fall, righted himself, then arrowed off to the west and vanished from view.

"Now we'll never get him back in time," Atan said, hating how she could not keep her heart from twisting anxiously as the sand spilled inexorably into the lower chamber in the glass, already much less above than below.

Tsauderei smiled. "I can send him along when he's finished flying." He then filled the remaining time with easy questions about Atan's and Hibern's studies and Rel's travels.

When the last sands ran out, they got up to leave. He noted the regret Atan tried to hide, and said merely, "Come again when you can." So she didn't want to talk about whatever was bothering her. He reminded himself that it was right and good for her to cleave to her Sartorans. She would always be his student, but they'd talked frankly about the fact that if the enchantment did break, and Sartor was freed, he would cease being her guardian.

"I will," Atan promised, hating the way her throat tightened. She refused to add, *If I can.*

She, Rel, and Hibern transferred to Sartor in time to hear the bells of the hour ringing melodiously.

The break from the customary hour of scholarship had caused Hibern to remember outside affairs—specifically Clair and the prospective alliance.

She turned to Atan. "Have you met any other rulers our age?"

"I haven't met any at all," Atan said. "I know there are several, many due to troubles with Norsunder, and others due to civil disturbances. Have you met them? Besides the king of your country?"

Bong-g-g-g!

Hibern said quickly, "Clair of Mearsies Heili. She mentioned some time back that she wishes to start some kind of alliance, among only people our age. Mutual help."

Rel said, "That sounds like Clair."

Atan gave him a glance of surprise. "You know her?"

"Pretty well. I travel a lot with her cousin. I haven't been back this year, but this doesn't surprise me at all."

Bong! As the last ring died away, the door opened to a silent waiting steward, bringing the invisible yoke of duty to tighten around Atan once more.

"Tell me about it next time," she said, walking backward, and to Rel, "Where will you be?"

Rel said, "I'm off to visit Mendaen and the others. Do you want me to carry any messages?"

Atan lingered in the doorway, and as they talked quickly about people Hibern had never heard of, she decided not to interrupt them. She transferred back to Roth Drael, her emotions in turmoil.

Tsauderei was wrong about her obliviousness. Hibern had immediately been aware of the difference in Atan's behavior, the way she glanced at Rel when he spoke, and the way he looked at her.

Hibern hadn't the experience to be certain about the bond that she perceived, but she could guess. She could also guess how much trouble there might be because of it. In spite of Atan's wish to be regarded as an ordinary person, she wasn't ordinary, would never be ordinary, because Atan was one of a kind: the last Landis of a very, very long line, Queen of Old Sartor.

Whereas Hibern knew she herself was one of many, and disinherited at that. But she had the freedom to pick any friends she wanted. There was no family to care, no council to disapprove. Atan was so special that every aspect of her life was inspected by her formidable household and council, and so it was only when she escaped to Tsauderei's that she could behave like an ordinary girl who liked a boy.

Since Atan hadn't said anything about it, Hibern kept these observations to herself when Erai-Yanya asked for her report. Hibern talked about dragons, and described the encounter with the odd little girl.

To her surprise, Erai-Yanya's brow lifted. "Ah, you've met Julian Dei, Atan's cousin."

"Julian Dei?" If there was any family as famous as the Landises—some might say infamous—that would be the Deis.

"Atan promised to adopt her, but she is a troubled child, some think from events before the war ever happened. She balks at any notion of education or even social polish. I'm told she didn't speak for months, she was so determined against any education."

"Is that why they called her 'joel' instead of 'princess'?"

"Yes. A nice compromise."

"How old is she?"

"No one knows. Records about her were destroyed, probably by her mother, who, it's rumored, had to sign a marriage treaty that cut her and her offspring from the line of succession. There was a scandal with one of the Deis before the war, but as all of the individuals concerned are now long dead, the details don't matter. Anyway, the child was hidden away with other refugee children."

She paused, noting the tension in Hibern's brow, and suspected it had nothing to do with Julian Dei. "If you are not writing down all your observations after these visits, you should start the habit. You don't have to show them to me. The idea is to chart your self-reflection as well as keep track of details while dealing with powerful people."

"That's just it," Hibern exclaimed. "Though she's Queen of Sartor, Atan doesn't seem to think she's powerful at all."

"She's still young. But that," Erai-Yanya stated, "will change."

PART TWO
The Alliance Grows

Chapter One

Arad (Secondmonth), 4738 AF
Marloven Hess

SENRID let Chwahirsland and the alliance slip to the
back of his mind. No outsider would be the least help if
Marloven Hess was in trouble. The Marlovens had never
had allies, but then Senrid was well aware that their worst
enemies were themselves.

Through all the violent upheavals of Marloven history
there was one constant: you obeyed orders, or you died.

Another constant was knowing which rules could be
bent, and how to bend them. A wing—three flights, or nine
ridings, or eighty-one warriors—of horse and foot taken to
a conflict without duly informing the king came under the
heading of treason. But any less was deemed enough to
defend against hill brigands, horse thieves, or the like.

Therefore, strictly legal were the two flights apiece of
horse and foot that the Jarls of Methden and Torac were
bringing to the border of Enneh Rual. (The third flight
followed at a distance to 'maintain the supply line.')

If they attacked the Rualese, that would be war in the
eyes of the world. Marlovens would see it differently. If the

attack was successful, fellow jarls would hail their success as a just recovery of ancestral lands—and many would no doubt soon be planning similar sorties.

If they lost, diplomatic legalities would be the least of their worries.

So the two jarls had reasoned before issuing orders to their followers.

David-Jarl Ndarga of Methden was aware of a divisive atmosphere among his ranks, signaled at the beginning of their ride from Methden Castle when someone way back in his double column whistled a few notes of a compelling melody, instantly recognizable: the Andahi Lament. No one *ever* sang that in battle. It was for memorials.

This was nothing less than an exquisitely insubordinate condemnation of the orders.

The jarl heard both flight captains riding down the column to deal with the individual, restoring superficial obedience, but the fact of the whistle disturbed the jarl. In his experience, the lower ranks only dared such insubordination when they had sympathizers.

Traveling from Methden's castle to the border in winter took a few days. The jarl used the daylight to enforce strict columns, the foot marching in rhythm, to reestablish one mind obedient to his will.

His captains, under his direct orders, were on the watch for disobedience, which would earn immediate and sharp punishment. There was none. Everyone knew what happened if they did not follow orders.

Likewise, nothing untoward happened when Torac and his two flights joined them two days from the border.

They camped early the day before they were to reach the hilly ridge that marked the border, their third wings joining them with the supplies. The jarls spent the last watch of light drilling in preparation for any resistance, not that Methden expected much. The Rualans had once been Marlovens when the rest of the subcontinent was ruled by Marloven Hess, but they had stolidly and stubbornly kept to their Iascan roots as much as they could, their customs inclined toward the sea.

The jarls set out early in the morning under a reasonably clear sky, and Methden, as leader, was reviewing flag signals with his fellow jarl and their captains when one of the outriders came galloping back.

"It's Senrid-Harvaldar," the outrider reported. "Sitting athwart the road with several wings of the West, from the banners, and more on either side of the bluffs above the road."

The words caused absolute silence from behind, save only the jingle of gear and the clop and whuff of fresh horses eager to move.

Torac muttered a curse, scowling at the outrider as if he were the cause of this unexpected wrinkle. Methden knew better than to expect anything but oaths and empty threats from Torac, who had been a follower since their academy days, of each prince in succession. No ideas could be expected from him, and sure enough, he looked back at Methden, blue eyes angry, but empty of intent. He, too, was waiting for orders.

"We'll flank 'em," Methden said. And when the outrider made a movement, his horse's ears twitching, "Or?"

"There's at least a riding tracking me."

That meant that this encounter was no happenstance. The boy Senrid had—somehow—got hold of their plan. Lookouts would be posted far to either side. There'd be no surprise flanking maneuver, and a charge would be impossible over such difficult terrain.

"Who leads?" Methden asked.

"Keriam is no commander," Torac said, and spat into the snow.

The outrider said flatly, "Senrid-Harvaldar."

Torac uttered a derisive laugh, and scorn was Methden's immediate reaction, followed by uneasiness. Senrid might be riding in command position, but who was really in command?

A short time later, Methden glared down the road at the fair-haired boy in the center of the mounted warriors, ranged behind the front three rows of foot warriors who stood ready and waiting, shields locked together. Sentiment had no place in ruling the Marlovens. Evan's boy had never been to the academy, the reason whispered being weakness.

Methden wished he had his own son at his side, but Jarend was doing his two years in the guard, and had received direct orders from this boy king to serve under Senelac in East Army, on the opposite border, for the rest of the winter.

Obey or die.

Senrid watched Methden's and Torac's force pull up. He'd picked the ground after hours of agonizing, and here they were. He gulped air, trying to still his thundering heart. He knew he shouldn't be listening on the mental realm, but he was. Not that anything was clear. He may as well have been standing in the middle of a shouting crowd, only this was worse because of the bombardment of emotion-drenched images, against which he had no defense when he lowered his mental shield.

"What orders?" the wing captain asked, breaking into his streaming thoughts.

Senrid listened, and sensed his intent to obey in spite of skepticism about whether or not a boy could lead. But so far, everything was right.

So far, everything was right. Senrid shivered, though his nerves were on fire. He'd only had to ride back and forth before Waldevan's gate three times, his force arrayed behind him, before the parley flag was sent out, at which time Senrid knew he'd subdued Waldevan without shedding a drop of blood.

Now, here were the other two errant jarls. If Methden wished to engage with the cavalry lined along the bluffs, his riders would be forced to ride uphill. And Methden was definitely in command. Torac kept looking his way.

What orders? Senrid said the obvious, to be clear. "If they kill first, then it's a capital matter. After which you're justified in fighting to finish."

He listened again on the mental realm, then shut out the hammer-blow of emotion. The visible signals were clear enough: tight mouths, gloved hands gripping weapons. The shift of horses, sensitive to their riders' emotions: ears alert, snorts and tossed heads.

Senrid could see the effect of his words on his own force. Waiting for Methden to kill first meant that someone here had to die. Senrid could see righteous anger kindling, and sensed the bloodthirsty determination to break bones and

dump Methden's and Torac's men out of saddles before letting one of those strutting cockerels get steel into a riding
mate's gut. Much less one's own.

Senrid's hands sweated inside their gloves. His toes
curled in his boots. He'd transferred back twice to talk out
the plan with Forthan, drawing out the terrain on the slate
floor in one of the lecture rooms at the academy, and moving rocks and coins around as they talked out endless com-
binations, but here he was, he didn't know the pattern, he
wasn't sure when to loose his people . . .

Methden's force stirred as if a breeze had gone through
them. Senrid sensed a corresponding tightening all around
him, and *knew*. "Now," he said, his voice cracking in a ridiculous squeak.

He cleared his throat to repeat, but the drum of hooves
smothered his shout, and then two masses met in a violent
meshing of individuals, voices howling in anger and anguish amid the clang and clatter of staves and swords.

Senrid gave up trying to make sense of the conflict, which
so far was not quite battle, but more heated than a wargame.
Each side was waiting for the other to deal a death blow,
while doing their very best to knock one another out of the
saddle, or whack each others' knees out from under them.

He had to hold his mount, which had been trained to
charge, but Senrid had no experience with lance, and very
little with sword. He could shoot to precision, but had forbidden arrows to his own side in this exercise. He was
equally skilled with knives, but did not want to kill his own
people. He'd defend himself, if attacked, but he found four
riders from West Army grimly ringing him in guard position, probably on Keriam's orders.

Liere had once said, *It's just like sorting through a crowd
of voices for those you know, only you're listening with
your mind instead of your ears.* Senrid shut his eyes and
listened.

There. He sensed more than saw the instinctive division
in Methden's ranks: there were many, maybe most, who
labored under sharp misgivings.

He clapped his legs against his mount's side. The mare
leaped forward; the ring of guards followed a heartbeat

after, the captain roaring something Senrid did not try to distinguish. It was enough. Cleaving clean through the Methden force, he led his own in an arrow formation—

His nerves flared painfully: intent. On him. A glance. Over there, a Torac man drawing bow. The honor guard that rode so tightly around Senrid made him an easier target in this crowd, Senrid saw in a heartbeat. Instinct was faster than thought. He snatched the shield hanging at the saddle, whipping it up.

Thunk! The arrow hitting the shield was surprisingly loud. Senrid recoiled, heels locking down hard in the stirrups so he wouldn't fall as his guards cried out, two going after the Torac man, the others motioning more around Senrid—

And the jarl's men fell back.

They fell back!

Senrid had already forgotten the Torac man as he sustained the mental bombardment of frustration, the barely-controlled urge to kill. His own force was the worst, the dangerous anger of self-justification, which the leaders were expressing with deliberately broken bones, filling the air with dust and the rumble of hooves, the thuds of blows, cracks, clangs of steel, and cries of pain and outrage.

Senrid shut them out, his thoughts racing: the jarl had lost before he began—act now or it will turn lethal—save honor—

Senrid kneed his horse once again, trusting in his ring of guards, and plunged into the middle of the melee. "Weapons down!" he shouted, hating how shrill he sounded. "Weapons down!"

As he hoped, the guard took up the shout, their bigger voices ringing outward through the entire body. To his captain, Senrid said, low-voiced, "Cut Methden out."

A nod, a gesture, and with a token resistance, the Methden personal guard fell back—again, nobody willing to kill outright, though from the looks of some, there were bad wounds and breaks.

Senrid found his throat dry as the dust hanging in the air. "Form an honor guard around the Jarl of Methden and we'll return to Choreid Dhelerei." Senrid addressed the tall captain of the foot warriors with the rust-red hair. "Captain Marec, you'll escort Methden's people home. At a sedate walk, your pace. Take as long as you like."

Captain Marec's lips twitched; these Methden turds were going to be eating their own belts before they reached their home castle. He cast a fast, expert glance over the wounded, the worst already dealt with. He recognized from his years of equally rough games during the bad times under the regent that no one was in immediate danger, and struck his fist against his chest, mentally formulating his orders. Methden and his fools could stand around in the cold contemplating their own stupidity while his own people saw to the animals and ate a good meal.

But first.

"What about Torac?" a cavalry captain asked, sending a glare in the jarl's direction, and Senrid, his nerves unsheathed, winced under the impact of the man's fury. It was echoed in many, and he caught a stray whisper, "Did you see that boy whip up that shield? He wasn't even looking . . ."

Senrid wanted justice. Justice, or revenge, or something. He wasn't certain now which man had tried to shoot him, any more than he knew if that had been on orders or impulse. All he'd sensed on the mental plane was the intent.

"Captain Sereth will escort the Jarl of Torac and his ridings back," he said, and saw a glance of understanding—of grim intent—pass between Marec and Sereth. They were going to take their time. Good. Torac and his followers wouldn't enjoy the trip, but it would give everyone a chance to cool off, to think.

It would give Senrid time to think.

A fierce whisper serried through both ranks. He heard words: "shield"—"betrayed"—"Scouts?"

Senrid tried to calm his drumming heartbeat. He'd survived. He'd live another day. Let them think that his Scouts had winnowed out the truth about Methden's plan. Senrid would not tell them that the Scouts were all outside the kingdom, because one thing for certain, the Rualans would not be sitting on their hands, and he knew he'd have to deal with beyond-the-border trouble over this mess.

Chapter Two

Sartor

ON the third day of Rel's stay in Eidervaen's huge, rambling royal palace, the elderly steward in charge of the visitors' wing came to Rel's room himself. The man made a first-circle bow, and then asked if everything was all right, if anything could be fetched. The briefness of Rel's responses ("Yes, thank you," and "No, thank you") seemed to inspire the steward to longer inquiries: could he order a meal, would Rel be traveling, could they arrange horses for carriage or riding, recommend posting houses?

Rel repeated, "No, thanks."

The steward put his hands together. "It is our privilege and pleasure to heed the queen's command that any and all of the Rescuers be housed in this wing, but at the same time, we owe duty to those illustrious guests who have traveled from afar to rediscover, and reconnect, with Sartor . . ."

The soft, pleasant voice went on about how vital communication and trade was, ending with eternal gratitude toward the Rescuers, especially Rel, who had selflessly risked his life though he owed no allegiance to Sartor.

'Rescuers.' This was a heroic name for the band of ref-

ugee children smuggled by an old mage out of the city when
Norsunder invaded. He'd taken them to the forest of Shendoral, where Atan met them in her journey to the capital
to break the enchantment. Some had helped her, others
had been less helpful, but all were hailed as heroes by the
Sartorans. That was all right. Rel had learned that it was
good to have heroes, sometimes.

Rel patiently waited the steward out, thanking the man
at each pause—assuming that that was what he wished to
hear. Finally the steward withdrew, and Rel glanced around
the room in puzzlement.

What was that all about? It wasn't as if he asked for
anything, ever. He scarcely left a trace in the room, for he
always made up his own bed wherever he stayed, and as for
his belongings, they remained neatly folded in his pack so
he could grab and go.

He shook his head as he headed out. Atan, he knew, was
scheduled tightly all day, but Rel had friends to visit. If it
wasn't for Atan's insistence, and for the fact that it was
difficult to catch Hinder anywhere else, he wouldn't stay in
the palace. He didn't like palaces, or at least, he wasn't
used to them. That odd conversation was one of the reasons he didn't like them.

Halfway to the garrison, he stopped short on the bridge
leading out of the elite first district, and gazed back at the
palace towers jutting above the jumble of city roofs.

Had he just been invited, in the nicest way possible, to
leave?

Thoroughly uncomfortable, he resumed his walk into
the southern half of the second district, which was shared
between the mages and the garrison in a silent struggle that
went back centuries.

At the old garrison, he found Mendaen, another of the
Rescuers, a tall, weedy fellow with clubbed black hair, who
was verging on adulthood.

Rel always exercised with the guard, which had been
severely diminished not only by the war, but also by edict
of the royal council.

As with his previous visit, Rel stood in the back of the
yard, knowing that his size drew the eye. Though Mendaen
was a couple years older than Rel, everyone assumed it was

the opposite. It was easier to go to the back, to avoid attention. From the back he could also see the interactions of the others as they worked through a warmup drill set more than a century ago, everyone's breath clouding the cold air.

Mendaen took his place next to Rel. As they swung their swords to loosen up muscles, and stamped to waken their feet and legs, Mendaen said, "I've applied for leave to go to Khanerenth's military school."

Rel hid a grimace, then spoke the truth. "Not a good idea."

Mendaen gave him a pained glance as he switched the hilt to his other hand. "But it was your idea. Leastways, I remembered you telling me you had a season there."

"And I should have had longer," Rel said ruefully.

"You're better than most of us," Mendaen said.

"Mainly because I'm bigger than most of you," Rel said. He sensed by the cants of heads, and the stiffness of arms, that many were listening. "I'm good enough to fight off a brigand or two. Which is my only aim. I'm not going for a life in the military."

"But you do get people trying to recruit you?"

Rel couldn't prevent the flash of memories: on his first journey being jumped by Kessler Sonscarna's recruitment gang, and waking up to Kessler's mad blue stare as he talked about killing off the decadent, useless world leaders who got crowns through inheritance, and replacing them with people promoted by merit—these meritorious new leaders trained and promoted by Kessler. Though Kessler had also hated Norsunder, Rel was secretly relieved that Kessler ended up there after he was defeated.

Rel had encountered him again when Kessler was sent by Norsunder to kill Atan before she could end the century-long enchantment. Rel still had nightmares about losing his fight with Kessler. The only thing that fight accomplished was winning Atan enough time to end the enchantment . . .

Rel shook away the memories, recollected the question that had prompted them, and said easily, "What do you expect, when you're my size?"

Mendaen sighed. "I'd love someone to recruit me."

Rel knew that Mendaen would hate being recruited by force, but kept his peace.

"Reaaaaaady!" the drill captain called from the front.

Mendaen and Rel began working through what Rel thought of as the standard set of block-and-lunge, feint-and-backswing moves that were common all across the continent, even Chwahirsland, which he'd been to a couple times, disguised as a flatfoot, the common infantry soldier.

The front rows wore livery, not uniforms. The back rows were a mix of guards-in-training, like Mendaen, and guild guards sent to exercise with the palace guards. The Royal Guard was all but gone, having been the first line of defense when Norsunder had invaded. None of the many dead had been replaced, because the mage guild had decided that they were useless, and that the only real protection was magic. So the bulk of defense spending went to the mages, who labored to find ways to thwart Norsunder's magic. Meanwhile, many of the former guard had gone to the guilds, which didn't bother trying to fight the council. They simply beefed up their private security—as evidenced by familiar Guard faces now wearing those guild colors.

When they broke up to work in pairs, everybody separated off into their own particular groups. Mendaen looked at Rel expectantly, and as they pulled on their practice pads, Mendaen said, "Tell me, why isn't it a good idea to go to Khanerenth?"

"I left because there was political trouble," Rel said. "Reaching into the school. Not a good time to be a foreigner."

"Oh," Mendaen said, disappointed. Then, "Well, seems to me we need more training, because as our captain says, what if Siamis comes back again, only this time at the head of an army? The mages all think magic is the answer, but it wasn't, was it?"

"What about the military school at Obrin, over the mountains? Isn't the trouble ended in Sarendan?" Rel asked.

"Everybody says Obrin is closed to outsiders."

"Century-old 'everybody says' or recent?" Rel asked, and Mendaen's lips parted, but he was forestalled by a bawled command to stop yawping and attack.

As the yard filled with fighting pairs and trios, gradually conversation returned. Rel listened, picking up a general dissatisfaction among the Royal Guard, even bitterness about the mage guild's regarding them as not worth the tax money to maintain.

At the end of drill Mendaen had to go off to duty in the armory, so Rel walked along what the Sartorans called the middle river, his coat pulled up tight to his chin, until he reached Blossom Street, where Hannla Thasis, another of the Rescuers, lived. Hannla's aunt ran a pleasure house.

Hannla greeted Rel with a happy smile. Hannla was the oldest of the Sartoran-born Rescuers, sixteen or seventeen, and genuinely popular. Rel had discovered on his previous visit that Hannla's aunt's pleasure house was the unofficial meeting place for all the Rescuers who weren't aristocrats. Rel was always assured of a free bed, especially as he offered to turn his hand to any task needing doing.

After he'd finished bringing up the last of the jugs of cowslip wine (the label dated a century ago), carried down stacks of washed and clean old jugs, rotated the barrels of ale, and helped sweep the stone floor, he went up to find a substantial meal waiting, and Hannla sat down to keep him company.

"How'd you find Mendaen?" she asked. "Is he going outside the borders, then?"

"I may have talked him out of that."

"Why?" Hannla's face was heart-shaped, her eyes wide, her hair a curly brown. The rest of her was as charmingly round . . . Rel's gaze caught, then he hitched it upward again, to find her grinning.

She'd always liked his thick, glossy dark hair, a little unkempt above his collar in back, his dark eyes deep set under equally dark brows, the strong bones of his face tapering to a truly heroic chin. The rest of him was both trim and powerful under the old travel-worn tunic and baggy riding trousers.

She put her cheek on her hand and said, "You ready for upstairs, then?"

Rel's reaction was a mix of curiosity and something else too subtle to define, but which he recognized as attraction, though it still hadn't warmed into the urgency his guardian had told him about when they'd discussed these matters. "Not yet," he said.

Hannla's eyelids flashed up. "Don't tell me. You, too, did the Child Spell? You?"

Rel chuckled, a low sound deep in his broad chest. "My guardian told me once I'll probably grow another half-finger before I have to do the beard spell. But yes, I found a mage to do the Child Spell on me."

"Why?" Hannla put both elbows on the table to support her chin.

Rel lifted a shoulder. "Promise I made to myself when I first set out, to find my father first. That was before I discovered the benefit of being a youth on the Wander. Most places, there's little prejudice against the young wandering. Whereas a man without a home or employment is often looked at with a suspicious eye."

"Of course," Hannla exclaimed. "That makes perfect sense. But . . ." She paused, considering how to express her doubt.

He flashed a brief grin. "No, it doesn't always work for me. Even though I'm not full age, just because I'm tall, I can't tell you how many stints in lockups I've done for vagrancy, though it's pretty much always in places where they seem to need free labor for road repair or construction. And in other places you can find yourself summarily recruited into someone's army."

Hannla's eyes widened. "You never told us any of that. All you said was that you weren't a duchas or a prince in disguise."

Rel had to laugh. "Nobody asked. Except Atan. Mendaen, too, though at that time, he didn't have much interest in anyplace beyond Sartor's border."

Hannla's expressive smile turned rueful. "Mendaen. I meant to talk to you about him, then got sidetracked by your pretty face." When Rel blushed to the ears, she rocked with silent laughter, which faded too soon. She said with an air of regret, "Atan's told you, right? That the mages now have total control of wherewithal, what little there is, for defense? That the Guard is reduced to patrolling the outer city and the southern border to watch for anyone riding out of Norsunder Base?"

"Yes. Result of losing so badly in the war, though I don't

see how the mages did any better, considering they didn't stop Norsunder's attack any more than the army did, and they, too, ended up enchanted for a century."

Hannla shrugged. "That, I can't tell you. Doubt Atan even hears the inner councils. But this I know. Everyone is looking around the next corner for that horrible Siamis to return, or his uncle, the villain Detlev. That's the worst of them, they hide in Nightland and don't die!"

Rel fervently agreed, thinking of his own brushes with Norsunder.

"But with Mendaen, there's the personal reason he wants to go outside the border for training."

"Personal?"

"Yes. Like a lot of others, he's trying to find out if his father had a family. You knew his father was a sailor, right?"

Rel began mopping up gravy with a piece of bread. "Mother in the queen's guard, killed defending the palace. Father was at sea when the enchantment happened. Right."

"Well, Atan's probably told you that the entire kingdom is still trying to fit itself back in the world. When all the poems and songs were over, what was left? As my aunt says, 'All the vexations of broken families, trade agreements, inheritances.' For Atan, it means the mages and diplomats and that sort of thing, but for Mendaen, it would cost far, far more money than he or his two orphaned cousins have, trying to trace relatives who were shut out a century ago."

Rel grimaced. "I never thought of that. And it has to be expensive, paying someone to sort through records. That's a lot of work."

"It's even more work if you have to trace a sailor on a ship, especially if the ship was attacked by pirates. The scribes at the archive told him he might have to apply at a lot of countries, or pay to have the scribes do it."

"Mendaen didn't tell me that," Rel said. "Maybe it's not for outsiders."

"He doesn't talk about it to anyone outside his family. He knows all his friends would give him money if they had any. He doesn't want them to feel obliged. I know because his younger cousin works at the pastry shop we deal with when patrons order fancy baking beyond our menu, and she talks a lot."

Hannla got up from the table, dashed off, then returned with a folded piece of paper. "So I'm asking you, and Mendaen will never know and feel embarrassed. But in case you happen to be anywhere where you might find something out," she said. "On that is written his father's name, the name of his last ship, and what he did on board. The year they think might have been the pirate attack, and the location."

Rel slid the paper into his tunic pocket. "It's easy to check for someone else while I do my own search."

"So you're still wandering the world to look for your father?"

"Yes."

"Did you have a wicked guardian?" Hannla asked, eyes wide.

"No." He didn't mind talking to Hannla, who was so ready with genuine sympathy. "Excellent guardian. Like a father in all ways except the one."

"Well, why won't this guardian tell you about your father?"

"Because he promised he wouldn't."

"Why?"

"I don't know. But think about it. Why would anyone keep that secret, especially if he'd gain nothing by it?"

Her brow puckered, then cleared. "To protect him, or to protect you."

"Right. Here are the clues I've gathered: My father does something dangerous. He's not from any royal family. Actually, there's some hint about a disgrace. Last and most important: he found me the best place he could before he left."

Hannla jumped up and kissed his cheek. "Of course your guardian was a good man. A wicked man would not raise a darling! Make sure when you're ready for upstairs that you come to us, mind. Half of 'em want to be your first, and do you think you like men or women? Both would be charmed." Hannla chuckled.

Rel didn't see her. He saw Atan, so earnest and studious and capable, and how her entire demeanor changed with her sudden laughter. He wasn't sure exactly what the hollow feeling behind his ribs meant—it wasn't the same as that mild warmth when Hannla leaned forward, or smiled at him.

Rel was fairly certain that his attractions were slanted toward women, but he was reluctant to talk about such things lest the talk somehow point at Atan. Hannla, he knew, was very observant. So he said, "Not sure," and Hannla sighed, then offered him another slice of cake.

"I don't need that, thanks, but maybe you can tell me the real meaning behind a conversation I had this morning." And he repeated the entire exchange with the steward.

When he finished, he could see by the way Hannla looked down at her hands that he'd actually guessed right. "What is it?" he asked. "Did I break some rule of etiquette? I know Atan wants me to stay."

"And that's the problem," Hannla said.

"Then all that about cherishing the heroic Rescuers is a lie after all?"

Hannla made a quick gesture. "No, it's true. But. You have to remember who Atan is. The high council has to be talking about whom she will marry."

Rel shifted in his seat, but the hollow feeling in his chest now felt more like a stone had taken up residence. A boulder. "I know that one day she'll be expected to make a dynastic marriage, and that those have nothing to do with personal choices. But that's a long way off, yet."

"Not for them." Hannla shook her head. "I'll wager you anything they're up there right now, worrying about when she'll lift the Child Spell. And watching all her relationships. Especially with foreigners."

"And so that's why all those questions this morning," he said, and with reluctance, "This is the fourth day of my stay as her guest. I'm going to guess that three days is their limit. I guess I'd better leave."

"Perhaps it's best. But come back next season. Really, if you turn up now and then, stay for two or three days only, then they won't fret so much," Hannla said earnestly.

"Thanks," he said, not wanting to load her with his bad mood.

He walked back toward the palace, determined to get control of his annoyance before he saw Atan again. Much as he might have liked to rant to Atan, he knew she already felt hemmed in, and it wasn't as if the high council was a bunch of Norsundrians in disguise. They meant well, and they had a wreck of a kingdom to deal with, along with a very young queen who hadn't been raised to her job.

The council was going to plan Atan's future, because that was what Sartoran first circle nobility did.

He waited patiently until he caught Atan between scheduled activities, said he had to get on the road before the weather changed, grabbed his pack, and walked out.

"You'll come back when you can?" she asked.

"I will," he promised.

That chest boulder resolved into the ache of loss as Rel walked away from the city a day later. He paced steadily northward, already planning his return.

In spite of his mental turmoil, habit ever since the days of Kessler Sonscarna's recruitment attempt kept him wary. As he climbed and descended the gently rising hills toward the border mountains, he always found a vantage from which to look ahead and back without being seen, and discovered among the various carts and coaches and travelers on horse and foot a single constant over three days: a lone figure, male in silhouette, matching his pace. It was quite likely that he was being followed.

He kept watch until he reached the last market town before the steep road to the pass that marked the border. The possible tail was still there, but too far back to be seen.

Rel looked around the widening road as he plodded through the slush. It was far too cold up this high for sleeping under the stars, so taking off cross-country was out. As he walked past the slant-roofed buildings edged with icicles, he reflected on how often he traveled this road, knowing which inns had beds long enough for him. He chose his favorite, a large place bustling with custom.

His tail had blended into the city traffic, as expected.

Rel wasn't worried about being attacked in Sartor. The roads were busy, the patrols intermittent but frequent enough. But Oneh Kaer on the other side was another question, for an old treaty required Sartor to patrol the three roads that branched from the border pass. But Sartor was not patrolling.

The traffic along the three roads, most of it north toward Mardgar and the biggest harbor on the Sartoran Sea, or northeast toward Colend, and a very few west toward the ancient aristocratic estates along the rough coast, abandoned after the war, tended to move in well-guarded caravans, which made the lone traveler vulnerable to attack.

Rel opened the door to a hostelry he'd used before and liked. He breathed in the warm complexity of human scents and spices. After a polite exchange with the boy at the counter, he paid down his money for a bed, adding a coin for the tuft-haired urchin who offered to take his knapsack upstairs. From the common room, the hubbub punctuated by the clatter of cutlery indicated the evening meal had begun, so Rel hung up his hat on one of the pegs inside the porch to avoid issues of etiquette involving whom he should doff to and whom he shouldn't. Sartorans could be prickly about customs that had changed up north.

He paused in the doorway to give the crowded room a quick scan. He recognized the old timers, each in his or her usual place, and moved his gaze past; all over the continent, regardless of kingdom, locals who met regularly seldom welcomed interlopers, and never liked it if someone presumed to take a seemingly empty chair, if that chair was in the middle of their invisible boundary of privacy.

"Welcome, tall stranger," one of the oldsters called, beckoning Rel to the table.

Rel hesitated only a heartbeat. Now everyone was looking his way. He saw no signs of hostility. Curiosity, yes. The empty chair the man indicated was not a place he would choose—he hated having his back to the door—but he shrugged away instinct. Whether he had actually been followed or not, it was highly unlikely he would be attacked in this mob.

So he took the chair, touching fingers to his heart as he swept his gaze around the circle. He spared a thought to the irony that the exact same gesture considered respectable for a stranger would be perceived as a dismissive insult between high-circle acquaintances.

"Haven't I seen you passing through here before?" the oldest, a tall, gaunt man, asked.

"Might have," Rel said.

"Tried to get work with the guard, have you?" a gray-haired old woman asked, as she worked swiftly at a piece of crewel. She chuckled, shaking her head. "We coulda told you nothing but moths in the guards' pay, is what we hear from Eidervaen."

The oldest man shook his head slowly.

"The mages are fools. It's an invitation for brigandage," a balding glazier said, making a spitting motion, as the innkeeper brought a plate of the day's meal.

The vegetables might be withered, but the rice was fluffy and the braised fish smelled of wine and garlic. Rel dug in as the glazier went on, "These hills yonder are full of brigands, ever since the soul-rotted magic lifted. Now everyone wants guarded caravans."

"Where can a fellow go to get work as a caravan guard?" Rel asked.

The old folks laughed. They'd clearly established Rel's intention the moment he walked in. "You go over to the Main Square Hostelry. *You'll* get snabbled up quick enough." He jerked a gnarled thumb over his shoulder back toward Sartor. "And if you like it, why, the Duchas of Oneh Kaer will be looking for hires soon's he declares himself king."

"He's going for a crown, is he?" Rel asked, when he saw expectancy in the faces.

A miller at the other end of the table said, "A lot of talk about loyalty and honor and that, but what it comes down to, and everybody know it, if the duchas makes himself a king he can keep the taxes. Then maybe we'll see the roads cleaned up at last."

Rel didn't pause in his eating. "Is that a fact, or rumor?"

"Everyone knows," the woman said comfortably. "As much as we know this: if Siamis comes marching back at the head of an army, Sartor won't even be able to protect Sartor, so they won't be looking out for anybody else. That's for certain."

The next month

After Hibern's visit to Tsauderei's house, Atan dutifully wrote down what she'd said about the alliance in her private

daybook, but in memory she returned most frequently to
Tsauderei, the dragon cliff, and to the freedom of talk when
she was away from the palace she was supposed to be reigning over.

The girls met the next week, Hibern thirsty for knowledge, reveling in the fact that Atan could summon any
mage book she willed, and Atan determined to learn twice
as much to make up for their escape the week previous.
They met three more times after that.

On the fourth visit, Hibern arrived to find everything
changed.

As soon as the door closed behind the young page who
always conducted Hibern to Atan's little study, Atan gestured for Hibern to come close, but instead of inviting her
to sit down, she reached behind her chair, pulled out two
very heavy coats, and silently handed one to Hibern.

Wondering—curious—excitement quickening her
heartbeat—Hibern complied, and when Atan pulled from
the capacious side pockets of her coat a scarf, a knit hat,
and gloves, Hibern checked hers and discovered that she
was similarly equipped.

The only sound was the soft rustle and hiss of cloth as
they wintered up, then Atan smiled, and held out on her
gloved palm a transfer token. Hibern looked from that to
Atan's eyes, which gazed back at her, straight dark brows
lifted in question.

Hibern opened her hand in assent, remembered that
nobody outside of Marloven Hess gestured a 'yes' in the
same way, and brought her chin down in a nod.

The magic shifted then released her with such a powerful buffet that she fell to her knees. An icy wind shrieked
overhead, and her eyes stung when she tried to open them.
She fumbled the scarf over her face, pulling it up tighter as
the wind tried to rip it away.

By then the transfer magic reaction was gone and she
steadied herself, still on her hands and knees, and lifted her
head. Atan was scarcely more than a shadow a few paces
away, also crouched on all fours.

"This way," Atan shouted.

She crawled farther into the gloom, Hibern following.
The icy stone ground had long been scoured smooth.

They rounded a stone outcropping and the wind lessened abruptly.

"I think we can stand now," Atan said. Her voice echoed.

Hibern got to her feet, shivering inside the bulky coat. Then she forgot the cold when Atan muttered something and glowglobes lit.

Hibern gazed up in amazement at the vaulted ceiling overhead. At first it was difficult to make out the proportions, due to the black stone curving most of the way overhead, shiny as glass.

"You know where we are?" Atan asked. "We're inside the dragon caves. *A* dragon cave. Is this not amazing?"

Both girls looked up, trying to imagine the huge space filled with a dragon. "This way," Atan said. "I think either humans or baby dragons might have lived here." She walked across the smooth stone floor, marbled with thinly branching patterns of minerals glinting coldly. She thought of unknown hands at work here, as she often did when encountering an old road, an ancient building, a crumbling wall with a weathered figure carved in: so many had left their work behind them, but unlike the monuments of Sartoran monarchs, seldom with their names.

The far side disclosed smaller oval chambers that had been scooped or scoured out. These were still sizable—twenty-five or thirty people could have sat comfortably in one—and just as cold, but at least the wind did not reach. They could talk in normal voices.

More glowglobes set around testified to previous visits as Atan said, "I've been sneaking here for bits of stolen time all this past month. Something Tsauderei said gave me the idea."

Hibern said, "To explore these caves? Look for the mysterious writing?" She peered around as she spoke, disappointed not to see any such carvings.

"To get away," Atan said, mittened hands extended. Her expression was difficult to see because of the shrouding scarf; nothing much was visible but those heavy-lidded gooseberry eyes. "Did you know that the mage council did not want me to have you, a Marloven, as a study partner?"

Hibern opened her mittened hands, not wanting to say that that was no surprise.

"After all our sessions, they convinced me it was my duty to tell them every single thing you and I studied. Everything we talked about. It's so funny. I've known Tsauderei all my life, and he's so very old, but the high council considers him too young and dangerously wild in his ideas, you being one of those ideas. The mages on the high council wanted me to study with one of their people. Maybe it's unfair to judge. I know they mean well, but I couldn't bear having every one of my words repeated, analyzed, discussed. They said it was for safety, that they should know what you were taking away from our sessions."

Atan's words chilled Hibern inside as effectively as any mountain wind. Hibern said, "Erai-Yanya warned me when she first began to train me that people would think a Marloven learning light magic was some kind of spy."

Atan sighed, watching her breath cloud, freeze, fall. "I don't believe the problem is your origins so much as your not being Sartoran, one chosen by them. There's a ledge here, where we can sit. And no one can overhear us."

"Do they really watch you so closely?"

"Everything," Atan responded, tipping her head back. "Everything I do. Everything I say. What books I read. Even how much I eat. It's all for my own good, so what answer can I make to that? I was so very ignorant about court affairs. Tsauderei did warn me that it might be like that. He got all the records he could, of course, but he didn't have access to first-circle privities." She made a quick gesture, with thumb and forefinger making a ring shape. "I was so ignorant that I was, and am, grateful to learn. I am! But . . ."

She hugged her arms around herself, and Hibern recognized that shoulder-hunched posture, those tight arms: Atan was holding anger in, the same way Hibern had after being disinherited. An echo of that sick hurt and futile rage pulsed through her, and she tried to breathe it out. Her breath froze and fell before vanishing.

"I *know* they mean well," Atan said again. "Sometimes I almost wish they were evil. No, I don't! That's wrong. It's just that everything I do and say seems to have endless possible dire consequences unless it's precisely what they tell me to do and say. What to think, even. They always sound so reasonable. But I was beginning to have dreams of shrinking so small that I could be locked in a ring box, and thrown down into a vault. So late nights, when they think I'm asleep, I sometimes experiment by myself. The first time I did, I had no nightmare, or not one of *those*."

She reached a stone ledge, turned around, and sat. "I've also been reading about places you and Rel described. Tell me more about this Clair, and her Mearsies Heili. Rel's told me a little, but I want your perspective."

The alliance! Hibern said, "Mearsies Heili is very small, located at the northeast corner of the Toaran continent."

"About which we know so little. Rel said that Mearsies Heili has no court, and no military, just five or six provinces, each with a governor who pretty much sees to things. One or two market towns to each province, one border is desert, and the middle of the kingdom is forestland. Clair's family is said to originate in the far north, a wooded area called the Shaer, where morvende and dawnsingers both used to live. Clair's family has only been on the throne three or four generations. That tells me so little. What is she like?"

"Clair has one cousin who is always on the Wander, and a group of friends, all sort of adopted by her. I believe they are all either orphans or runaways."

"Ah!"

"They used to patrol to watch for enemy Chwahir at an old outpost, but that's gone, and now they mostly seem to have fun. Except Clair, who studies magic."

"It sounds so . . . so free. So jolly," Atan said, then burst out enviously, "I'm told she even has her grandmother or great-grandmother back again—seemingly her age as she did the Child Spell—so she can be friend and companion, to share the throne."

"Yes," Hibern said slowly, recollecting the things Erai-Yanya had said about the mysterious Mearsieanne. *She might have escaped Norsunder after being imprisoned for all those years*, Erai-Yanya had said, *but she was forever scarred.*

Hibern wasn't going to repeat that. More diplomatically, she said, "Mearsieanne was the first of her family on the throne. She was a seamstress originally, but renamed herself Mearsieanne when she took the throne as a compromise in response to an impasse reached by the noble families of that day. When her son reached our age, she was taken by Norsunder, about the same time as the war here in Sartor. She was enchanted by Detlev in one of his evil experiments, and brought back into the world to be put in Everon. Another of his experiments. That failed, too."

Atan rubbed her mittened hands over her face. "I only know the gist, that the enchantment was the first one broken by that dyr thing that Liere used against Siamis."

"True enough," Hibern said slowly, remembering what Erai-Yanya had also said: *Two queens, even as girls, will eventually be a problem. I hope later than sooner. I'm glad Mearsieanne spends most of her time in Everon and Wnelder Vee at present.*

Hibern did not understand why the rediscovering of a missing relative should be a problem, queen or no, and to bring it up felt like gossip.

"I want to meet them," Atan said. "I want to meet them all." She got to her feet. "The mage guild thinks it a waste of my time for me to keep up my studies of magic, now that I have them." She spread her hands.

Hibern grimaced in sympathy.

Atan said in a rush, "Here's what I truly wanted when I asked for you: someone who'll show me the world that the council will not let me see. And, keeping your alliance idea in mind, we can begin with these Mearsieans."

Chapter Three

Spring, 4738 AF
Marloven Hess

SENRID had discovered that the jarls, seated on their
benches a few steps below his dais, couldn't see his butt
scootched to the edge of the throne so that his feet could be
pressed flat against the floor instead of stupidly dangling.

As the captains finished giving their well-practiced reports, Senrid watched the jarls watching him. There wasn't
much to be seen in their straight figures, but he was aware
of each flicked glance above his head at the enormous black
and gold screaming eagle banner that once had been the
Montredaun-An's house banner, and now belonged to the
kingdom, and at the impassive guards at their stations at either side of the dais, the only people bearing arms inside the
throne room. Senrid hoped these reminders bolstered the
aura of authority that he knew he so sadly lacked.

He held firm to his determination not to listen to surface
thoughts, a determination strengthened by his awareness of
his lack of skill. He dreaded discovery. They would, quite
rightly, consider it the worst sort of invasion.

Besides, there didn't seem to be any surprises waiting.

Everyone knew what was going to happen, but they'd all come as summoned, though they'd come a few months before, for Winter Convocation. But hearing capital cases concerning jarls was their right.

They listened as the captains of West Army reported, followed by both jarls' captains mumbling and stuttering through their reports, all of which established a clear line of command that pointed straight to David-Jarl Ndarga. Torac had owed the Ndarga family allegiance, which technically exonerated him. Senrid wished he could send Torac into exile. He thought the man just as much of a weasel as Waldevan. But he didn't dare.

At the end, Senrid stood, and delivered his carefully prepared speech. "You are foresworn, David-Jarl Ndarga of Methden. As you have broken your fealty to me, mine to you ends. You are now David Ndarga. Methden reverts to the crown, and Marloven Hess is closed to you. I shall detail a riding to accompany you to the border, which you shall not recross on pain of death."

After a silence that seemed to last forever, the former jarl said, "My son?"

Senrid let out the breath he discovered he'd been holding. He hoped his voice wouldn't squeak as he delivered the second part of his speech. "I shall appoint an interim captain for the remainder of the year, at which time the question of Methden will be revisited in time for Oath Day during New Year's Week. Jarend Ndarga, who had no part in oath-breaking, will continue to serve as is."

The former jarl's eyes closed for a heartbeat, his face full of pain. His fist came up, froze halfway to his chest, and then he laid his hand flat, the salute of the civilian, and his expression shuttered. The scrape of a foot, an audible indrawn breath, the shift of clothing among the jarls indicated their reactions, and how silent the room had been. Senrid wondered if he had not been alone in holding his breath.

The captain of the guard motioned his chosen escort into place around the former jarl, and out they walked.

Senrid rose, indicating that the convocation was over. He spoke the words inviting the remaining jarls to a meal, seeing in their faces that no one wanted to stay. Good, because if he didn't get out of that room by the count of ten he was going to puke.

When he knew he had himself under control, he walked into his study and dropped onto the floor next to Liere, who scrambled up, her book falling unheeded from her lap.

"You didn't do anything about that nasty Jarl of Torac?" Liere's thin shoulders were tight, hunched up under her ears. "He told a man to shoot you!"

"You listened." Senrid tapped his head.

Liere was small and thin, her single prominent feature a pair of large eyes so pale a brown they looked gold. So when she rolled her eyes, it was a very effective expression. "He was thinking it right *at* you!" Her chin came up. "And it scared him, how you raised the shield to stop the arrow. But Senrid—"

"I can't do anything without visual evidence or witnesses."

Liere's fingers gripped her elbows. "That other one, he thinks you had spies to find out his plot."

"That's better than the truth," Senrid muttered. If Jarend Ndarga hadn't ratted his father out, a whole lot of people would have died. Including the jarl. Because Senrid would have had to throw the entire army at them, or lose the kingdom. And Jarend had known it.

But he didn't want to load Liere down with those worries. "Methden is used to raids, which means a lot of spying back and forth." Senrid sighed. "There's a lot of trouble on the border, mostly horse thieving. Our horses bring a fortune in other lands, especially trained."

"I thought you had border guards," Liere said.

Senrid shrugged. "Well, South Army patrols all along there, but short of standing across the hills that make up the border, fingertip to fingertip, there's no way to guard all the gullies and trickles, especially on moonless nights, the favored raiding time. Then there's the problem with at least half the raiders having relatives on our side of the border, because Toth and Telyerhas both share ancestry with us. There are even some who make a good living being either Marloven or Toth as suits them."

Liere took a chance. "You didn't guard your thoughts, Senrid. I know you want to know who that jarl sent to shoot you."

He grimaced. "The mind-shield isn't quite habit yet. It needs to be, if Siamis comes back. That's what worries me much more than that horseapple Torac, whom even my uncle despised."

Liere couldn't prevent herself from casting a worried glance at the door. She sensed Senrid observing it, and did her best to pass her apprehension off as a question. "What happened with that emissary from Enneh Rual?"

"Oh. He was lurking in the hall when I came out." No need to mention how long Senrid'd had to hide until his stomach stopped twisting itself in knots. Liere had probably heard him, anyway. "As soon as he saw me he spoke his piece about how they didn't want our exiles, and threat, threat, threat, and I said that Ndarga was surely going south, and when he started in again, I told him he and his government were welcome to capture Ndarga and hold an execution if they really wanted one. He stomped away, and I hope he's on his way back home now, because I didn't offer him any meals."

Liere sat up, her gaze distant. "Yes. He's going."

"You could pick out his thoughts from everybody else's?"

"I can pick out anybody's if I know them," Liere said. "I mean, I don't know that man, but I met him, and so I can find his thoughts. He's so afraid of you Marlovens, and hates you so much. But he's going away." She heaved a sigh. "If you want to know how to listen, just send out a tendril," she said.

"Tendril," he repeated. "You say that, but thoughts aren't tendrils. They're loud and jumbled and . . ." Senrid paused, reaching for the words to describe the violent babble intensified with emotional color, sometimes with a physical overlay that he found even more unsettling—even painful—and gave up. "Loud," he finished.

Liere accepted the repeated word with a nod and shrug. She was used to failing to find words for Dena Yeresbeth, which nobody else in the world understood, and it wasn't as if she had great control, herself. Far, *far* from it.

She picked up her book, then said, "I don't see why you had to go through all that. You already knew what everyone was going to say. That Jarl of Methden, I mean, the man who used to be jarl, he's really, really angry."

"He would have been angry no matter what." Senrid sat on his desk and swung his leg back and forth, his heel hitting the wood, tap, tap, tap. "Yep. Every jarl there knew what the reports would say. But everybody heard chain of command, according to law. Methden's. Mine. Have to remember how important obeying orders is here . . ."

Liere nodded seriously, fighting the urge to gnaw her nails. She despised herself for being afraid of these Marlovens who had all these rules for raids, as if raiding were some kind of game.

But Senrid wouldn't let anything happen to her. He wasn't afraid. Why did she have to feel these stupid, useless emotions?

Senrid was still talking. ". . . Keriam thinks Torac won't try any plots on his own. At least, not now. I hope he's right. Here, let's get something to eat. I just discovered I'm hungry, and I'm sure you are, too."

He looked at the book in her hand, and though he couldn't hear her thoughts, there was a quickness in the way that she said, "I've nearly finished it," that served as a kind of signal.

It had become a kind of habit to limit her visits to the time it took for her to work her way through whatever books she brought.

Mearsies Heili

Spring rain roared on the ground overhead, a soothing muffled thud familiar to the Mearsiean girls. Ordinarily they saluted the first rains of spring with toasted bread and cheese, but the astonishing news that they were about to be visited by the Queen of Sartor had caused a flurry of excitement.

Now they stood around in the main chamber of their underground cave, staring at the mural that had hung on the back wall opposite the fireplace ever since they'd first made the hideout.

"I think it needs to come down."

"No it doesn't! It's funny!"

"It's mean," tall, quiet Seshe said.

The others looked her way.

"What?"

"What?"

"No!" Irenne crossed her arms in a flounce. "Mean would be if Fobo and PJ ever saw it."

"But we had such fun making it," blue-eyed Sherry, one of Clair's first friends, said wistfully.

This mural had been painted on sailcloth, the only type of canvas that was large enough and sturdy enough. The wrinkled, battered sailcloth was thick with paint, having been corrected and added to by various hands.

The girls stared at the mural, each seeing a different picture. CJ glowered, aware of her inner conflict between pride and the old, old feelings of not being good enough, left over from her terrible early childhood on Earth. Clair had discovered how to go through the world-gate without any idea how very dangerous it was, and offered CJ a better life. CJ had followed her through the world-gate without a backward glance, determined to leave the horrible memories behind, but she'd discovered that even when one is happy, memory can't be snipped and tossed away like toenails and split ends.

She'd come desperate to please Clair's other adopted and rescued friends, offering what she regarded as her only talent: drawing. It was her idea to satirize these ridiculous people who had made Clair's early reign miserable. She'd sketched it out and the girls had worked together to paint it, laughing and adding their own inventive touches. And it had cheered them all up during the awful days when Kwenz of the Shadowland had aided the grasping princess from Elchnudaebb in her efforts to annex Mearsies Heili.

So here was this mural depicting the snooty, ill-tempered princess the girls had nicknamed Fobo, wearing one of her typical court gowns loaded with lace and ribbons, festoons and flosses, bangles and spangles. Beside her sulked her son, Prince Jonnicake—he really was named Jonnicake— decked out in extra jewels, lace, ribbons, and whatnot, as if to hide his scrawny body and pimply face. Around them passers-by fainted at the sight, and above, birds and insects were falling out of the sky.

Seshe shook her head, her long river of ash-blonde hair rippling down her back. "It's mean," she said again, her voice apologetic.

Irenne sighed loudly. "*You* loved it as much as *any* of us did. I remember."

Seshe said, "It was funny when Fobo was acting so horrible. But now that we know that her brother has exiled her from Elchnudaebb's court, I just don't think it's funny anymore. I especially don't think PJ's part is funny. You know how much I felt sorry for him, how horrible it must have been, living with such an awful mother. She bullied him into doing the Child Spell, just so she wouldn't look old. I find that so cruel."

CJ stared in disbelief. To her, the Child Spell was the best thing in a world she loved passionately. "It's not like the Child Spell hurts anybody."

"But nobody should be forced, should they?"

Silence fell.

Seshe said, "Anyway, now that we know that PJ ran away, well, when I see the mural, I can't help but think that it's mean. People change."

CJ was thinking: not us. But she didn't say it, because it wasn't really true. Dhana wasn't actually human, and Falinneh, who had run away from the last remnants of a justly feared magic race, did her best to pretend she wasn't a shape changer—she wouldn't even say if she'd been born a boy or a girl, insisting she didn't remember. That might even be the case.

CJ knew she wasn't the only one with bad memories of her old life. She knew Diana had them as well. Same with some of the other girls. You could say they hadn't changed since they had formed the gang . . . Except, in a way, they had. You had to, if villains kept trying to do villainous things. The girls were good at patrols now, and some were even pretty good at defending themselves long enough to run away. And they were all very fast runners now.

Dark-haired Diana—the only one with weapons training—looked sober, as usual. She said, "Queen of Sartor won't know what it is. So it won't look mean to her."

Everybody listened, because Diana so seldom spoke.

Clair stood at the far end of the circle, her head a little

bent so that her waving locks of white hair curtained her face from view. The girls shifted their attention from Diana to Clair to see what she thought.

Clair rarely gave orders to the gang. She liked it when they found a way to agree. "Do we want the Queen of Sartor seeing the mural?" she asked.

Falinneh grinned. "Why not? I'd love to tell the story of Fobo and PJ versus us!"

CJ shifted from foot to foot, digging her toes into the bright rug. "We don't have to change things just to impress her, do we?"

Clair rubbed a knuckle against her lip. "I don't know how to answer that," she admitted. "I know I want her to see Mearsies Heili at its best. I also hope she'll join our alliance. I mean really join. I know Hibern said she would, but since we never heard another word, maybe that was some kind of courtly politeness."

"The alliance is dust anyway," Falinneh said, flapping her hands. "How many people have asked for our help in galoomphing villains? Not one!"

"Jilo came."

"But he didn't really want our help. He went straight to Boneribs in Marloven Hess," someone else put in.

Seshe pointed at the mural. "This picture doesn't really show us the way we are. That is, we're no longer defending Mearsies Heili against Fobo and PJ."

"It's our past, but it's a funny past," Falinneh protested.

Sherry's big blue eyes rounded, and she pointed to the far end of the mural. "But we've already folded over that corner where we'd painted in Jilo."

Everybody stared. They had woken up the morning after Jilo left and found it that way. Nobody had said anything, but they all suspected that Seshe had done it.

CJ glared resentfully at the mural. She hated change, but she didn't want to go back to the bad old days of the Shadowland. She had not minded seeing the Jilo part of the mural folded, even though she had been the one to paint him in, making him look extra stupid and gawky, with a gloppy pie about to fall on his head. But it was kind of nice not seeing those all-black eyes staring out at you, like empty pits. And now that Jilo had removed Wan-Edhe's horrible eye-spell that had characterized the Shadowland Chwahir, the picture was no longer even right. Jilo turned out to have ordinary light brown eyes, not much different from Sartora's color.

Clair said, "How many want the mural to stay?"

Three hands shot up. Irenne crossed her arms, and seeing that, another girl curled her lip and put her hand up.

Diana remembered the exhilaration of belonging to a group for the first time in a very hard life. She lifted her hand.

CJ hesitated. She would feel better if Clair put her hand up. Then she could raise hers as well, because the whole mural had been her idea and she had planned most of it. She sighed, thinking it was more honest to stick with her real feelings, but Clair forestalled her.

"That's a majority, so it's decided." She looked around. "I guess that's it. Maybe we should have an early night, because Hibern and the Queen of Sartor will be here at dawn. It's the only free time the queen has."

CJ grimaced at the rug. The underground hideout was already clean. The girls had swept it earlier that day. CJ couldn't scorn anyone for primping because she'd stood in her own room, looking at the pictures she'd made and trying to decide if she should keep them or make a new one, just to impress this unknown girl because she happened to have been born queen of the oldest country in the world. CJ could tell herself that she merely wanted the gang, and Mearsies Heili, to look their best, but really, showing off was showing off.

Clair said, "If we're done here, I'll go upstairs."

Upstairs was the white palace on the mountain. Clair had made only one request: that she be the first to meet the Queen of Sartor, show her whatever she wanted to see, and then bring her to the underground hideout to meet the girls. "Throwing an entire group at a newcomer might not be the best introduction," she'd said, and everybody agreed.

CJ said, "I'm coming with you."

Clair had layered transfer magic into the medallions all the girls wore. She and CJ each touched their medallions, said the transfer word, and felt themselves snatched out of the world and thrust into the white palace on the mountain.

They went to Clair's room, where CJ flopped on the bed, and Clair stood at the window, gazing out at the rain.

CJ sighed. "You wanted us to take down the mural, didn't you?"

Clair turned around. "I don't know." She made a face. "I have such mixed feelings. I like everything you girls make, and it was such fun when we made it. Also, if they were here, I suspect Puddlenose would have voted to keep it. Christoph, too," Clair named Puddlenose's most frequent traveling companion, a boy who'd come from Earth from a time centuries before CJ's time, nobody knew how or why. "Puddlenose always says he loves coming back and finding things just the same. I don't quite get what he means, because things change every single day, don't they? A tiny bit? Or we'd be like statues in a garden."

"I know exactly what he means," CJ said.

Clair turned around. "Do you?"

CJ sat up cross-legged, her green skirt spread around her. "No icky changes, but most of all, no icky surprises."

Clair walked to the window and back. "Maybe it's just as fake as courtly behavior to want this girl queen to see us at our best. I've been thinking I ought to wear my interview dress," she confessed.

"Why not? It's pretty. Everybody likes wearing something nice, as long as we don't have to every day. As for the rest . . ." CJ snorted loudly. "Falinneh's right. We already *are* our best. Mearsies Heili isn't the largest, or the richest, and it's not famous for anything, but it's still the best. Anybody who doesn't like it, even if she's queen of the universe, is a windbag."

Clair heard the utter conviction in CJ's voice, the loyalty. She smiled. "When you say it like that, I'm a windbag to be worrying about it."

"Never," CJ said, with equal conviction. "Okay. I feel a bit better. See ya." She made the sign and transferred back to the Junky, where she stood in her room, tried to see her artwork as the Queen of Sartor would . . . then laughed at herself and got ready for bed.

Chapter Four

Sartor

IN the heart of Sartor's royal palace, Atan was at that moment lying awake, staring through the east windows at the distant line of mountains, barely discernible as darkness began to lift over the capital city.

She still hadn't decided which room she wanted to be her private space: she couldn't bear to let anyone touch her parents' things in the old royal suite, flung aside so carelessly as war overtook them, though she knew that the Norsundrians had rifled through everything before casting the enchantment. Detlev himself had sat down at Father's desk and penned a threatening message that Atan had found ninety-seven years later, after breaking the enchantment he had cast over the kingdom—she still did not know why that enchantment had been cast. No one did.

Maybe it was that, and not her parents' memory, that kept her out of their rooms.

She had also bypassed the nursery where she'd been an infant for so short a time, next to the larger, airy nursery where her siblings had played together. She had offered the entire nursery to Julian, who had stood there, arms crossed, face sulky, and said, "This is for princesses. I hate it!"

Atan had chosen her mother's winter morning room for her bedroom through the dark months, because the curved bank of windows gave the best view of the dim northern sun in its arc, but now that spring was here, Atan found herself back again in the eastmost room in the royal wing, with its windows that only caught the morning sun. She'd looked in records, discovering that this room had been a bedroom before, as well as a study, a third-circle receiving room, and an antechamber when the big nursery had been a bridal suite.

Sometimes she liked to imagine those ancestors moving through these very rooms. What were they like? What did they talk about when they looked out this window? Which one put the beautiful marble carving of the heron in flight in that little wall alcove, made by a sculptor from Tser Mearsies up north . . .

Her meandering thoughts jolted to a halt when she remembered Mearsies Heili. That's why she'd woken so early! She was going to meet Rel's friends. Not that Atan had gleaned many details. Rel wasn't talkative about other people, or even things he'd done, only things he'd seen.

She bathed, still loving to watch the marble tub fill with steaming water. She plunged into it while the water was still churning from its transfer from the hot spring veining the city far below ground. When she was done, she stepped into the adjoining room where her staff waited to dry her, order her hair, and dress her in a morning outfit chosen for the interviews that awaited.

As she moved through the tightly scheduled day, she was thinking, what to wear to her secret visit? In the wonderful days when she lived hidden in the hermit's hut in Tsauderei's Delfina Valley, she'd had three old shirts, two sturdy sets of trousers, and a dress she'd made herself.

But you can't go back. Clothes were communication. You could pretend to be someone else, but people still looked at you and made judgments about what they saw.

Atan only knew that the Mearsiean girls had been on a surprising number of adventures, and that they lived in a tiny kingdom that the youths in the school for aristocrats up on Parleas Terrace called a *honas*, an outsider. *Selas* were kingdoms big enough for their names to be written inside their drawn borders. *Honas* were too small, their names written with arrows pointing to the correct tiny splotch on the world map; the words reflected the organization of social circles, words Atan (an outsider in just about all ways except birth) thoroughly loathed.

So, what to wear. She would be meeting a fellow queen, but one a couple years younger than she was. From a country that had no court. Atan didn't want to look pompous, but neither did she want to appear condescending.

She worried at the question off and on all day. Most of what she had to do was listen—she was told what she thought, not asked—which caused her to escape inside herself.

When it came time to get ready, she shed her elaborate court gown in favor of an undertunic of plain, cream-colored linen, slit up the sides, with loose trousers of the same fabric, and over it a robe of spring green embroidered with tiny blossoms in cherry and gold. She picked out her plainest gold tiara, knowing it was loaded with protections in case any Norsundrians might be lurking about. She felt . . . bumptious, wearing crowns. But this was a compromise with herself for not telling anyone in the high council or mage guild what she planned to do.

She was ready before Hibern appeared on the first ring of the hour. She wore her usual long tunic over riding trousers under her sky blue robe, and Atan was glad she'd chosen the clothes she wore, which were more or less the same style as Hibern's.

"How do you want me to introduce you?" Hibern asked.

"As Atan," she said, suppressing the urge to wipe her damp palms down her skirt. "They know who I am. But I don't want them seeing Yustnesveas Landis The Fifth of Sartor, I want them to see *me*."

Hibern had misgivings about that, but she said nothing as she handed Atan the transfer token she'd prepared.

The Destination for Mearsies Heili's capital had been set on the white stone terrace before the palace. Atan let the reaction die, and gazed up in astonishment.

The palace was definitely Ancient Sartoran in origin, or

at least in design: no attention paid to symmetry. The design was more graceful than that, the complication of soaring arches, towers, and spires angled for exposure to the sun's path at different times of the year.

The topmost spires glimmered against the clouds as Hibern recollected a fact she'd forgotten. "Clair said that they've tried to count all the rooms in the palace, and always come up with a different number."

Atan said, "I believe it. Our tower can make you dizzy, because time isn't always . . ." She reached, not finding the right word, and made a gesture with her hand, waggling it from side to side.

Hibern grinned. "I can't imagine what that's like."

"Remind me some day, and I'll ask the mages to schedule a tour." Atan turned her back to the palace, expecting to see the rest of the cloud top city, and gazed at the little village zigzagging down the mountainside, the steep rooftops catching reddish highlights from the early morning sun rising over the line of the ocean to the east. "This was the cloud city mentioned in the records? This really isn't a city, at least, the way I define city. Nor is it a cloud top, except perhaps in a figurative sense."

"City or village, it was definitely on a cloud. I was there when it began to come down. I believe it took two days to settle. Took them most of a year to rebuild chimneys, reset windows, and redo the roads in these switchbacks you see leading down the mountain. See how young the trees are at the corners? All that is new."

"Who brought down an entire town? For that matter, who put it up in the air in the first place?"

"No one knows on either account. I think that even includes the Chwahir who had come to invade, and that horrible Prince Kessler Sonscarna."

"*He* was there?" Atan turned sharply.

"Oh yes. But only for a moment. It was a very strange day, still a mystery. Erai-Yanya thinks it was some spell made centuries ago, that ended suddenly."

The palace's arched doors stood open onto a vestibule bare of ornamentation, the light falling so perfectly that the space itself was an ornament, filled with the pearly light of early morning. Beyond that, another doorway opened into a magnificent vaulted throne room, empty except for the morning light.

Atan paused. "This palace doesn't seem to be warded at all, at least against us." She walked right up to a wall, and extended a finger.

Now that she was close, she made a discovery: the material wasn't like marble, or even ice, at all. The silver component was much more present, causing that curious glisten. When she bent so close her eyes almost crossed, she perceived specks of all kinds of colors, just like the stone Tower of Knowledge was made from, except the Tower was more like bone, and this seemed . . . almost alive, somehow.

"We'd better go," Hibern said, and Atan backed away hastily. "This is actually a shortcut," Hibern said as they crossed this empty chamber, Atan hesitating long enough to take in the curved balconies above, and above those the arched windows.

"Where is Clair?"

"Probably in the kitchen, though she might be in her study upstairs. But we'll check the kitchen first."

"The kitchen?" Atan repeated. She'd never gone into her own kitchens, except on her first tour through the palace. The cook staff would be scandalized if she set foot there—not that she knew anyone there, or had any reason to go.

"The cook is also the steward, a woman named Janil. Erai-Yanya says she was like a mother to Clair, when her own mother died. Before that, too."

"Was her mother killed by treachery?"

"Erai-Yanya was told by Murial, the queen's sister, that it was a mixture of wine and sleep-herbs. She was reported to be dark in mood, and started early in the day with wine. Clair was about the age of your little cousin when it happened."

How awful, Atan thought, and below that stirred an unsettling thought: Who would stop kings and queens from doing stupid things? Maybe the high council was not such a curse. Unless they did the stupid things.

Several people bustled about the roomy, airy kitchen.

At first glance they all looked like servants. Atan's eye was drawn to the one white-haired figure among the ordinary variations of light and dark brown hair. A morvende? No, the white hair, though pure blue-white, was not the drifty cobweb hair of morvende; it fell in waves down below the girl's waist. The girl herself was ordinary, light brown skin, no talons at her fingers' ends, and she wore slippers, which morvende never did. She was dressed in a plain gown reminiscent of Colendi shopkeepers a generation or two ago, the only decoration a ribbon tied around the upper part of the slightly belled sleeves, a round neck, sashed waist, plain skirt.

"Hibern! And . . . how do you wish to be called?" Clair asked, forestalling Hibern's carefully thought-out introduction. "I've never met another queen before, outside of my own ancestor. Are we supposed to bow?"

A year ago, Atan would not have known how to answer that without getting tangled up in confusion. "Atan will do. We can skip bowing, if it's not your custom." When she saw the relief in Clair's serious, squarish face, she added, "I haven't met any other rulers either. Only emissaries, and two new ambassadors, for the old ones fled before the war."

"A century ago, is that correct?" Clair asked.

"True."

"Would you like to meet the other girls, or have the tour first? Um, we were putting together a nice breakfast, then I remembered that it's not morning for you. Are you hungry?"

Atan did not want to waste any of her hour on a meal. "Not really," she said. "Thank you."

"Would you rather have the tour, then? And meet the others?"

Atan heard in Clair's *the tour* that she'd made a plan. So she agreed. It was clear from the slightly self-conscious way that Clair conducted her through parts of the palace that indeed she'd thought it all out. Atan found it strange, to see such simple, relatively modern furniture inside the rooms whose lineaments were pure Ancient Sartor in a way that she'd only seen in archival drawings. But when they came to the library, and Atan saw from Clair's attitude that this was her favorite room, Atan thought, *we are a lot alike.*

She did not comment on how small the library was, relative to that at Sartor's palace, which had been added to and refined over thousands of years. Clair was proud of her library, and made reference to her studies of magic. Atan envied Clair her quiet life and the chance to study so much. So far, being queen here seemed to be largely symbolic, again like Atan's own position, but Clair appeared to be blessedly free of the demands of symbolic presiding. "Do you see glimpses of the past when you walk about?"

Atan had meant the age of the furnishings, but Clair answered matter-of-factly, "Only upstairs in the towers. There are rooms that we sometimes see, and sometimes don't. We can't always find them again when we go looking—but it's great fun for playing hide-and-seek."

Atan shivered, realizing Clair meant it literally. But . . . hide- and-seek?

The mages did not permit Atan to go alone into the Tower of Knowledge, lest she make an error and slip inexplicably into some fold in time, yet these girls played hide-and-seek in this building that seemed to be made of the same mysterious not-quite-stone. They had *time* to play hide-and-seek. "May I ask about your ancestral background?" Atan asked.

Clair shrugged, her smile fleeting. "I believe we were weavers, from somewhere way, way up north."

"The Shaer?"

"That's the place. Shaer Wood. Mearsieanne had a grandfather with white hair, but nobody else in the family did. The rest pretty much looked like my cousin Puddlenose."

"Puddlenose?"

"We don't know what name he was born with, only the insults Wan-Edhe called my cousin during the time he was a hostage in Chwahirsland," Clair explained as they walked out into a chilly spring wind, and stopped on the Destination.

From there they transferred down to the base of the mountain. For a short time Atan could do nothing but gaze in amazement at the bubbles rising slowly from the waterfall filling the rock-framed pool. The bubbles spun in the air, each flickering with what looked like facets, before thinning and vanishing.

Clair said, "We used to swim in it, though it made us feel drunk. We stopped when Dhana, who wasn't born human, told us we were thrashing through her people. See those wriggling lines, like facets in a gemstone? Those are the people. Dhana said our swimming doesn't harm them in the least, but we hated the idea of swimming through someone." She shrugged.

"The Selenseh Redian," Hibern exclaimed, having kept quiet all this time. But mention of one of the weirdest and most powerful and least understood magical phenomena in the world broke her determination to stay in the background. "Erai-Yanya said to me once that you have one here. Is that true?"

"Oh! The jewel cave. Yes. Right up there," Clair pointed up the craggy cliff above the waterfall. "The jewels have the same lines in them. You can go in, and ask questions, even, and sometimes they kind of put answers into your head . . . but again, it makes you feel drunk."

It *was* the Toaran Selenseh Redian! Atan stared upward, thrilled at the idea of its proximity. To live near one! Tsauderei had taken her via long, wrenching magic transfer to see one once, and Atan recollected the glowing gems inside, facets coruscating like sunlight sparkling on water, though no light source could be seen. The air had been warm, and breathing it somehow made her feel heady, as if the space was much larger than what she saw.

As far as the mages knew, there were only seven such caves in the world, and none—except, apparently, this one—located anywhere near human civilizations. And they could vanish abruptly, if they were disturbed. The archives maintained that Norsunder once expended tremendous effort to invade the caves and dig out the gems, which some believed were living beings, but in any case somehow gave access to tremendous magical power.

But the caves no longer were open to Norsundrians; it was said that dark mages who entered deep within never came out again. When the stones nearer the entrance were threatened, the caves would close somehow, and reappear somewhere nearby, always in mountains.

These Mearsieans don't understand what they have here, Atan thought as Clair said, "If you don't mind another transfer—it's short—it will give us time to visit the others. They wanted to show you our underground hide-out."

Atan heard the pride in her voice, and began to imagine a grand, abandoned morvende geliath, full of ancient carvings. In fact, it wouldn't be surprising, because Atan now was certain she understood the purpose behind that palace being built here: its presence had to be connected to the Selenseh Redian directly below it. Maybe even to that lake full of beings, so rare in the south, much more common in the north.

But all three together? As far as Atan knew, there was no such combination in all the *world*.

Did Clair—who had to have morvende ancestors—have an ancient morvende geliath nearby, that the Mearsieans called an underground hideout?

But when the short transfer jolt dissipated, Atan found herself in a cramped, stuffy room dug out of soil. The Mearsieans had made an effort to domesticate it with a clumsily made colored rug, rough wooden furnishings, and a lot of very badly drawn pictures affixed to barren dirt walls that at least had been smoothed by magic.

A host of girls appeared from two side tunnels, smiling with pride, and Atan was stunned at the thought that *this* was their home. Why didn't they live in that astonishingly beautiful palace on the mountain?

Clair stepped forward and introduced each of the girls to Atan. At first there seemed to be too many to count, all talking over each other, but CJ named them one by one, finishing, ". . . here's Gwen, another escapee from Earth, and over there is Falinneh. That's all nine of us."

Hibern had told Atan a little about Falinneh, whom she'd met shortly before Senrid became king. Falinneh was the most colorful as well as the dominant talker: a short, sturdy girl with bright, wiry red hair and thousands of freckles, who wore crimson satin knee pants and a shirt of green and yellow stripes under a blue vest edged with little crimson pompons. "Fal-IN-neh," Falinneh declared, wiggling her red eyebrows. "My name is Fal-IN-neh—everybody always leaves out the AL, and I get stuck with Flinna, which I hate!"

"Oh, don't talk to ME about 'Renna,'" a prissy girl in a very old-fashioned Colendi morning court gown declared, swanning about the room, her long light-brown ponytail swinging. "My name is EAR-ren-neh, please."

Odd, how Falinneh made Atan want to laugh, but Irenne was instantly irritating.

Falinneh said, "Now, about that alliance. We can also show you how to go about defeating villains. We've become such experts that I've decided to write a book, once I finish learning how to write." She hooked her fingers in the arm-holes of her vest and twiddled her fingers absurdly.

Atan said, "You have instructions? Besides assembling armies of mages and warriors?"

Falinneh waved a freckled hand. "Who needs all that nasty stuff if you can defeat 'em without? Not that wig-lifting or pie-beds will defeat them all," she added. "I suspect Siamis would only laugh if he put his foot through a sheet, or fell out of bed, and he didn't wear a wig, and I wouldn't have dared do anything to that horrible Kessler—"

"Kessler," Atan repeated. "The renegade Prince Kessler Sonscarna of the Chwahir? Hibern said he was here when your city came down."

The girls' smiles vanished at the repeat of the young man's name, and Atan remembered that the Mearsieans had also been mixed up in Rel's bad experiences with Prince Kessler.

"He was sent against us when we were trying to free Sartor from the enchantment," Atan said. "Rel the Traveler, the outlander who helped us, said he had encountered him before."

At the mention of Rel, CJ groaned. "Here we are again, back at the Great Hero. Rel, schmel."

"CJ, Rel's not a villain," Sherry exclaimed.

Atan stared. "Is this another Rel? I understand it's a common enough name on both coasts of the Elgar Strait in particular—"

CJ sighed, her thin black brows a scowl-line above vivid blue eyes. "Taller than a house? A face like a sour lemon, only sourer? Thinks he's the greatest thing ever?" CJ shifted her gaze to Clair, who studied her bare toes, and CJ flushed. "All right, I know that's not fair. It's just that I thought, just once, we could get through a single conversation without the Perfect Rel."

CJ was so busy watching Clair that she did not notice Atan's expression of extreme reserve.

"Rel the Traveler is a friend to Sartor," Atan said in her most polite voice. "He's *my* friend."

CJ sighed, struggling against the old, familiar, hot pit of jealousy. "He's everybody's friend, he's just so perfect," she said in a sprightly voice, trying to sound polite, but she could hear how false her own voice sounded.

And so could everyone else. "Is anybody hungry?" Sherry asked a little too brightly. "I made some berry muffins."

"Did you show Atan the Magic Lake?" Falinneh asked.

"Yes," Atan said.

She knew her answer was short. She felt the pause afterward as a silence, and saw that the others did, too.

This is a disaster, Hibern thought, and to fill the awkward silence, began blabbing about how difficult it was to find histories about parts of the world that didn't have humans. Clair aided this limping conversation.

Because both girls turned toward her, Atan fell back on the politeness with which she'd been raised, and agreed, but she was waiting for CJ to apologize for her crack against Rel.

CJ fumed, wanting to explain, to justify, but she didn't know how to get around Atan's statement, which sounded like an imperial declaration from the Queen of Sartor. So she grinned, and agreed heartily with everything Hibern and Clair said without listening to a word of it, and pretended nothing had happened, hoping everyone else would, too.

Clair had no idea how to resolve the tension she felt, so she kept on talking about magic until her mouth felt dry, and somehow it never seemed right to mention the alliance again.

The hour ended. Hibern and Atan vanished, after the latter thanked them formally for the tour. Just as formally Clair told her she was welcome, and even then, she couldn't bring herself to talk further about the alliance.

Well, Hibern had said Atan would join. There would be other times for figuring out what it all meant, she told herself as everybody went off to eat.

In Sartor, Hibern spotted the approach of the inevitable steward, and said quickly, "I don't think you saw the Mearsieans at their best."

A pause grew into an uncomfortable silence.

Atan frowned at her hands. "Thank you very much for the tour," she said a little too politely.

Sick with a sense of failure, Hibern took her leave, and Atan turned to the steward with an equally intense sense of relief.

As she changed into the proper set of formal robes for a third-circle reception, she struggled with her emotions. She recognized that, aside from the impulse to dislike that CJ for those remarks about Rel, her disappointment at finding the Mearsieans so ignorant was prompted by jealousy. They were such friends. The stories they all shared, even those stupid jokes they all laughed at. You could call them a family.

They didn't realize what they had in any sense, she thought as she stalked out of her bedroom, twitching her brocade over-robe into place. Further, they were self-satisfied in their ignorance, pigging it in a stuffy cavern rather than living in that airy, pretty marble palace, and doing the Child Spell to play, rather than as a defensive measure . . .

What *possible* use was an alliance with *them?*

The bad mood she had tried to scold herself out of was worse by the time she reached the antechamber where the duty page awaited her. She was in a thorough stew of righteous indignation when she glanced down at her golden notecase on the table, and as always, touched it. To her surprise, the cool brush of magic on her fingertip indicated a letter inside. Her mood lightened to anticipation.

All of her correspondence as Queen of Sartor was handled by the scribes. This was her own personal notecase, and few of those she regarded as friends had one. Rel didn't. So she never carried hers, but she'd trained herself to check it when entering the room, though it was usually empty.

Since the duty page was standing there looking expectantly at her, she tucked the notecase into the pocket of her under-gown, and went off to do her duty. It was a reception for the weights and measures branch of the scribe guild, which had finished touring all of Sartor to make certain that officially recognized scales had been calibrated to current international standards.

Atan was glad that some people liked such exactitude in their lives enough to go around seeing that people got honest measure, but she found their anecdotes excruciatingly boring. She saw no reason why she had to preside. The guild could just as easily celebrate on its own. But she had to be there because the high council put her there. It was they who ruled Sartor. She only provided a warm body with the right face to decorate Star Chamber, while they did the real work.

Nobody could really think she understood all the weights-and-measures scribes' arcane references, and she was aware that these people were talking at her, not to her.

But she smiled and made the appropriate formal gestures, and as soon as everyone had had their say, she invited them to partake of refreshments. In the general movement that ensued, she retrieved her letter. It was a note from Tsauderei.

My dear Atan:

Until you command me otherwise, I will claim my privilege as your old tutor to speak up when I feel that you are in error. Though I will admit that the fault is probably my own for having kept you sequestered during your childhood. The need for secrecy prevented you from learning simple, yet vitally important, rules of social engagement, one of the first being: do not neglect your friends until you find you have a need for their service.

I was very glad to meet your friend Rel, yet a month and more has passed, and you have not found another free hour to visit your first and oldest friends outside of my valley, Lilah and Peitar Selenna. I never visit Sarendan without either Peitar or Lilah asking for news of you.

Atan crushed the note into her pocket, her face burning with guilt.

Chapter Five

Two weeks later in the world
Hours later in Chwahirsland

THE alliance, still a vague idea to most, and a negative
one to Atan, might have died right then, but for two
people: Jilo, and Rel.

Jilo had learned to shift out of the magic chambers whenever he noticed his fingernails turning gray. He just had to
remember to check.

When he did remember next, a distant pang of shock
accompanied the thought, *whose hands are these?* The
nails were ragged, the beds gray. In the dull magical light
of the chamber, they looked like old man's hands.

He'd finished the trap removal on another shelf, but
none of the books there were the least use. Most were old
records. Of the magic books, all he found were magical
histories—lists of wards done and by whom—and plenty of
elementary spell books. Nothing about binding time.

What was he missing? He stood in the room trying to
think until he found himself struggling to remember why
he was standing there. The effort to penetrate the fog closing

around his skull like an ironmonger's vise reminded him of those days when he'd had that spell on him.

Go outside. Breathe. It was less a thought than an unconscious urge, insistent enough to penetrate his mental fog.

He walked out, down the hall, and down the stairs.

When he reached the side court, he blinked. The air wasn't cold, the light daytime under the ubiquitous cloud cover. His hands looked more like normal hands, though his nails were still a dull color. And he'd have to trim them. He wondered if that gray was happening more often, but then time didn't seem to mean anything anymore. He only knew that once he got outside the palace it seemed easier to breathe, and his stomach woke up. He felt real hunger. His thoughts were clearer, or at least he could remember them.

Since the air wasn't cold, he set out to walk into the city. The guards all knew who he was—that is, they took him for Wan-Edhe's mouthpiece—because they snapped rigid when they saw him, eyes straight forward, hands tight on their regulation weapons, or hanging down, open and empty.

When he reached the city, he slipped into a side street and no one paid him any attention. It had always been that way, but before, he'd been under that magical fog, so he hadn't noticed much. Now he could see the uniformity of buildings, all gray granite, the sounds of footsteps or the occasional clop of hooves echoing along the stone canyons. No one spoke unless it was for business, and no woman spoke at all.

For the first time he wondered if people really did obey Wan-Edhe's insane laws. Jilo grimaced at the cobblestoned street, worn almost smooth by ages of tramping boots. He struggled with anger and a sense of humiliation, not wanting to believe that the Chwahir had been reduced to the status of worms, blind to injustice, their entire lives spent in mindless toil as Wan-Edhe's evil perpetuated itself on the strength of invasively malevolent spells.

Jilo's stomach rumbled again. He gave in to impulse and picked a street at random. There were no street signs, but he could orient easily enough on the castle's highest tower, looming above. At the street's end he found what he expected, a way station, for restaurants and inns of the sort to be found in other kingdoms had also been forbidden. Everything in Chwahirsland existed to service the army.

Jilo had no shoulder flashes or armbands. He had never changed out of his probationer's uniform, which Wan-Edhe had required him to wear to remind him of his place.

He ducked his head and sniffed at himself, wondering if he stank as badly as Wan-Edhe. He imagined the stale whiff of old sweat and unwashed laundry trailing after him, after his long toils in Wan-Edhe's chambers, but he also remembered what the barracks had smelled like on a normal day in the Shadowland.

Nobody was going to say anything.

He walked into the way station, and as he expected, the cowled women behind the counter only glanced at his uniform, then away. He moved to the counter. The women waiting to serve rotated in a practiced circle as they ladled boiled oats, boiled beans, and vinegar-dressed spinach onto a plate, then a girl handed him a regulation shallow-bowled wooden spoon wrapped in a napkin.

He took them without meeting anyone's eyes, of course; he did not want to alarm them. In Chwahirsland, meeting the eyes of a superior was rarely a good thing. But as he turned away, he glanced to the side. That snub-nosed girl reminded him of one of Clair's gang, only he caught a glimpse of a ruddy dark braid inside the cowl. The Mearsiean's short hair was light brown, streaked by the sunlight, because in Mearsies Heili, people only wore hats in winter, or for formal occasions.

Jilo found a table at the back and sat down.

The place was nearly empty. He'd caught either the early or the late portion of a service shift, which, he knew, ran counterpoint to the military watches by which the entire kingdom was governed. No one spoke, of course, as Wan-Edhe had strictly forbidden public chatter on pain of a hundred lashes. And he'd enforced it by having his spies also turn in anyone who didn't report infringements.

That had been a sore point between the brothers, Jilo recollected as he dug into the tasteless oats, always getting the worst over with first. Kwenz kept reminding Wan-Edhe that he hadn't enough guards in the Shadowland to have most of them in the lazaretto recovering from punishments, and whom would he put in the field if there were an emergency? Wan-Edhe had always said, *Force them to take duty anyway, and let 'em bleed. It enforces the necessity— the wisdom—of obedience. Idle talk is what leads to conspiracy. There should be no time for idle talk, as well as no place.*

Jilo set his spoon down, aware for the first time of scents, of the food, other people, dust. The small noises of wooden spoons clattering against clay bowls, the hissing shift of a foot, but what was that tiny sound, almost like rain against a window?

He knew better than to look directly. It took a moment or two to figure out what to do. He dropped his spoon, and in the process of retrieving it, got a sideways look at the four people sitting at the table on the other side of the room. They were all in uniform, of course: a grizzled oldster wearing the brown armband of a stable troop, and two youngish men, one wearing the shoulder flash of a horse troop and the other that of a squad leader in the infantry. The youngest, a boy Jilo's age, wore an unmarked gray-black uniform similar to Jilo's own. A trainee.

At first Jilo thought the older man had something wrong with him, the way one shoulder twitched, then the other. It took a second look as Jilo got up to get a biscuit from the bread basket and walked back to notice what was going on: finger taps on the table or one's arm, twitches, touches to chest. All quick, furtive. He would not have noticed if he hadn't been staring. It seemed to be some kind of sign language.

Jilo became aware of his empty plate. He'd eaten his food without noticing. He rose to get another biscuit, and this time took a sideways glance at the women. They stood still, waiting to serve, except for the one who came out from the kitchen with another tureen of oats. Before she turned away, one of the others brushed her sleeve, and the tureen woman rippled her fingers, then wiggled her forefinger three times. She turned away, and vanished back inside the kitchen.

He walked out, and took a long tour of the city, pretending to look at shops, but using the occasional reflective surface to see behind him. Twice he caught forefingers turned his way, making a tiny circle, as someone else turned an empty palm up. Question, and answer? They wanted to know if he was a spy.

Jilo wondered why he hadn't heard about this—why the Court of Rule wasn't lined up with people waiting for punishment. The people must know who the spies are, Jilo thought, and question became conviction when he walked along an armory street at the same time an otherwise undistinguishable man wearing a lowly green suppliers armband appeared. Only because he was watching did Jilo perceive heads dropping minutely, as if a chill wind had blown down the street; gazes dropped streetward, quick as the eye. Hands hung at sides, except when executing business; all words spoken had to do with orders given and received.

They knew who the spies were, and they had a secret language.

Joy suffused him as he walked back to the palace. They had a secret language! He spared a sympathetic thought for the Shadowland Chwahir, now surely absorbed into the massive army structure. He hoped that someone was teaching them the secret language.

Jilo examined his emotions as he trod toward the castle. Pride, and a sense of isolation. He had to do his part, and unravel Wan-Edhe's web of spells. His determination renewed, he turned his mind to reviewing the search he'd made so far. Outside, he could think more clearly. In fact, he could remember his painstaking search among the books, one by one, first to remove wards and traps. He could remember the shelves, even in large part what was on the shelves; yes, he must catalogue everything that was there.

He paused in the forecourt, frowning down at the stones. Wait. Why was it that he could recollect so clearly the archives, the old lists of wards, the elementary spells, but other places were a blur? He'd been over every part of the archive at least three times.

Hidden language, hidden things. We Chwahir hide things. What if Wan-Edhe had hidden his chief treasures where nobody but he could see them, much less touch them?

Oh, yes.

Wherever he had slid past without paying attention, that was where he must begin to search.

Along the caravan route from Sartor to Mardgar Harbor

Rel stood in a circle with the other caravan guards. From the uneasy sideways glances and the uncertain stances, he suspected that most were even more inexperienced than he was.

A scruffy woman faced them. She appeared to be somewhere between fifty and sixty. She was short, reminding Rel of a gnarled old apple tree toughened by years of hard weather. She said, "Now that it's just us, here's the truth. Fact is, I been running caravans for forty year, twenty as leader. Been no problems to speak of until lately, after the border opened. Don't mistake me. I'm glad Sartor is in the world again, but." She turned her head and made a spitting motion. "Instead of picking right up with their side o' the treaties, they send us nothing. And so our woods is filled with brigands. Came across 'em twice, now, in only four trips."

Rel knew he should keep silent, but he couldn't bear to have his friends maligned. He didn't want to cause trouble with his new boss, so he raised his hand.

She paused, and nodded curtly. "Something to say, Shorty?"

Some of the others chuckled, apparently never tired of the joke.

"Only that I just came from the Royal Guard at Eidervaen. Have to remember that the war for them was recent. Aren't enough of 'em left alive to defend the kingdom, much less patrol."

"Nobody's forgot when the war was for them." The woman grunted. "But this is what I'm thinking. If they wouldn't hire the likes o' you, then they must indeed have moths in their purses."

The others chuckled louder, and a weedy fellow said, "It's true. I heard it over in Mandareos. They got no treasury. No hiring at all."

Rel didn't correct the misapprehension that he'd gone

into Sartor to look for a job, as the woman said, "Well, that's a big problem, and they have my sympathy that side o' the border, yes they truly do, but the fact is, these here woods north o' us are mostly full o' former border riders who got shorted their pay when the guilds up and decided they weren't going to pay Sartor the old taxes. So here we are, with a lot of 'em lookin' to turn brigand, because it's easier to carry on doin' what you've always been doin' than to look for new work."

She paused, and when nobody argued, she said, "Now the truth is, most of 'em aren't much better than us. So far it's been, make some noise, look tough, and they ride off, looking for easier pickings. But one of these days we're going to come across something better run, and I tell you honest, I know pretty much everything there is to know about tending the horses—I was first a farrier—but as for leading a real defense, well, if any of you has some real training, speak right up."

And all heads turned expectantly toward Rel.

He suppressed a sigh, wondering what would happen if he claimed that his only training was in maintaining Colendi orchid conservatories. But the problem was a real one, and he was the biggest and tallest there. He suspected he would always be the biggest and tallest. So he said, "I did get a bit of training here and there. Can't say I know how to command." He didn't mind mentioning Khanerenth, but he hated mentioning Everon, as he still had regrets about turning down a Knighthood. And he knew he'd sound like he was swanking.

"But you're the biggest," the weedy fellow said doubtfully.

Another fellow, a stout redhead, said, "Leader has to see everything at once. Knows what to do."

Rel gave a nod at the redhead. "All I know is something about defending myself against whoever comes at me with sword or knife."

The woman said, "If you're willing to do point, that is, you take the front position in any squad, and make a lot of noise, and wave that sword of yours around—that's a nice blade, youngster, inherit it?—well, seems to me, that's the next best thing."

Rel did not offer any explanation for the sword that Atan had given him, just shrugged, and everyone accepted that as assent.

The leader said, "Good. Then here's how we'll divide up the watches . . ."

The caravan left at midday, under gentle drifting snow that slowly turned to sleet, then slushy rain, making everyone but the oxen miserable.

By week's end, they had descended far enough down the weather-pitted, neglected road to feel the thaw of spring, which made for somewhat cheerier campfires, at least for the hired guards. One of the two merchants, a young woman, was unrelievedly anxious about her barrels of winter flush Sartoran leaf. It wasn't the best leaf, but even the last winter pickings would bring a tremendous price in a world that had been deprived of steeped Sartoran leaf for a century. The other merchant was more cheery, a plump old bookseller serene with the conviction that few bandits ever showed any interest in books.

Oxen were slow, but their pace guaranteed little jiggling or smashing of contents. Spring storms flooded the ancient wheel ruts in the roads, left bare after three generations of raided flagstones while Sartor was beyond reach. Consequently it was nearly a month after they left the border when the caravan entered the rolling hills that, the caravan leader said cheerfully, meant that they'd soon be at the west branch of the Margren River.

"That means we've left the woods behind, and surely the brigands," the redhead stated, and the others nodded, as if saying it would make it true.

Rel had been placed either at the front or the rear, where he'd be seen by lurking scouts. From either position he had an unimpeded view ahead or behind; he was fairly certain that the caravan had been watched on at least three occasions, and he was definitely certain that a lone horseman was following them in spite of their crawling pace. The only thing he couldn't be sure of was the horseman's target.

When he pointed out the follower to the caravan leader over their meal of pan bread and fried fish, she shrugged. "One shadow, I don't worry about."

Nobody else seemed concerned.

The next night they reached their first market town. After all those weeks of camping (for few of the tiniest southern villages had inns above their taverns, after a century of no travel), it was most welcome.

The next day, two of the caravan guards went missing, but the rest set out without them, made confident by the sight of traffic on the road, and the thought that the Mardgar Harbor was only three days away.

They'd just settled the oxen for the night, and a good fire was going under a kettle of trail soup, when Rel, who had picket duty, noticed all the horses' ears twitching in the same direction.

Rel turned. All he could make out was a hillock topped with an ancient, overgrown hedgerow, marking some long-abandoned boundary. He'd learned that abandoned houses made great hideouts if they were isolated enough.

Drawing his sword, he yelled, "Alert—"

The word was lost in the thunder of hooves. From over the hedge in one direction and around the hill in the other galloped a gang of brigands, swords and knives upraised.

Rel had little practice fighting upward, but he'd learned one trick. Sheathing his sword again, he dashed to the wagon and snatched up one of the poles, snapped it free of ties, and spun it humming as he dashed between the first two riders. He ducked one's slashing sword, knocked the man out of the saddle, and clopped the second rider across the back of the head on the backswing.

He had enough time for a brief spurt of triumph. Grinning, he launched into the thick of the skirmish. For a short burst he was too busy staying alive to be aware of anything beyond a wailing cry; the wagon leader shouting, "Jem, get back here!"; the leaf merchant's hysterical shouts of "Help! Help!"; and the wheezing breathing of the book merchant from under one of the wagons.

We're losing, Rel thought, anger burning through him hot and bright. He'd take as many of them with him into death as he could—

Then the sounds changed, and he stumbled, fighting for breath, aware of a furious increase in the noise of battle from the other side of the shifting, lowing oxen. Rel slung the stinging sweat out of his eyes and pushed himself forward.

Brigands lay dead or wounded, except for a knot still furiously fighting, these all on foot. Rel launched himself at the fight, tossing away the pole and pulling his sword. He got in a kick and warded a blow, then his burly attacker gave a shocked, eye-bulging, mouth-open stare. Foamy blood dripped out of his mouth as he began to topple. He jerked as a sword was pulled from his back.

The burly man dropped dead at Rel's feet. Beyond him, Rel glimpsed a pale Chwahir face flicking a look his way. Shock froze him.

He knew that face. It was Prince Kessler Sonscarna.

The short, slim renegade prince fought with unnerving speed and brutality; with one accord the remaining brigands turned and ran. Kessler chased after the five of them for a few steps, blood-smeared sword raised, then slowed. He stooped, wiping his blade on the jacket of a dead brigand.

Rel caught up, heart beating painfully. "It was you following us?" He might as well get the worst over.

Kessler was breathing hard, his quiet voice husky with spent effort. "No." He reached with his free hand into a pocket of his black tunic, and with an ironic gesture, held up a transfer token. "Had you tailed. He sent for me when you were attacked." He jerked his chin at the brigands.

Rel glanced back. Those left of the caravan were just beginning to pick themselves up, exclaiming questions no one listened to, and checking themselves, the animals, the wagons.

"That was fun," Kessler said, looking up at Rel with that well-remembered flat stare, out of light blue eyes shaped unsettlingly like Atan's, evidence of a long-ago treaty marriage between a Landis and a Sonscarna. "Haven't had a good fight for too long."

Fun, Rel thought, sick with disgust as he glanced down at the dead scattered about in a rough circle around Kessler.

Kessler said, "You had fun, too." His smile was brief. Knowing.

Rel had scarcely exchanged a hundred words with Kessler since their disaster of a first meeting. Since then, instead of words, there'd been a near execution and two sword fights, both of which Rel had lost. Rel's shoulder still ached in cold weather from where Kessler had stabbed him moments before Atan lifted the Sartor enchantment.

He was going to deny having fun, but the vehemence of the urge unsettled him, and he remembered that moment of triumph. He was not going to admit it to Kessler. There could be no possible good result.

"I'd think you can fight any time you want to, in Norsunder," Rel said.

"Not the same," Kessler said, with a slight shrug. "You were seen by my scout in Eidervaen. I had him follow you until I could get the time to interview you. This attack forced things."

Rel's heartbeat thudded in his ears. The first time he'd met Kessler was right after Rel had turned down the Knights' invitation to join them, during his very first journey. He'd just met up with Puddlenose and Christoph on Everon's border when the three of them were jumped by Kessler's recruitment gang, and transferred to a hidden compound that Kessler had set up in some desert, where he was training assassins to take down all the major rulers of the world.

Kessler really hated kings.

Oh yes, and he also hated ugly people.

Rel always reminded himself of that when encountering venal authorities who had inherited positions of power, in case he caught himself ever thinking Kessler's plan the least bit sane.

"You had me followed," Rel said, reaching for the immediate, and the personal. "Are you recruiting again? If so, my answer is still no." Rel forced a shrug. "Sorry you had to go to so much trouble to save me, if you're going to haul me off and finish the execution that got interrupted the last time I turned you down."

Kessler's mouth twitched, and he continued in the same tone as before, as if they sat together over a tankard of ale instead of standing over the fast-cooling body of an unknown man. "I still do not understand what you could object to in ridding the world of corrupt rulers, leaving the way for a system based on skill and brains."

"Because," Rel said, "your plan began with assassina-

tion." He didn't mention the wholesale slaughter of ugly
people; when he'd asked, during that first interview, "Who
decides who is ugly enough to die?" Kessler had replied
without a hint of doubt, "I do."

Kessler made that slight shrug again. "Do you think the
likes of Wan-Edhe of the Chwahir would relinquish their
thrones any other way?"

"Do what you want in Chwahirsland," Rel said. "But I
don't believe Clair of the Mearsieans is evil," Rel said, then
wished he hadn't brought her name up.

"When I investigated Clair of the Mearsieans, she appeared to be an ignorant brat, unable to rid herself of the
senile Kwenz, or even that fool from Elchnudaebb. I underestimated her, as I underestimated her friends' sense of
loyalty."

Rel didn't want to cause those girls to become targets
any more than they might already be. He said, "Norsunder
seems to be the place to recruit for assassination plans."

Kessler glanced sideways as the caravan leader began
limping toward them, then shifted from Sartoran to Mearsiean, spoken with a heavy Chwahir accent. "Worse cor-
ruption and stupidity there than in the world. Everyone
fighting one another for place. Siamis swanking around
thinking he can conquer the world by cleverness. Even his
uncle is giving up in disgust."

Good, Rel thought, but said nothing.

Kessler said, "The goal is the same, but the game has
changed. Your friend King Berthold of Everon might not
be corrupt, but his precious Knights are divided, one side
ruled by stupidity and privilege, the other half merely ob-
solete in strategy and tactics. You know that. You saw it. Is
that why you turned down their invitation to join the
Knights of Dei?"

Rel said nothing. Somewhere behind, the caravan leader
called, "Rel?"

Kessler glanced over his shoulder, then said, "Tell your
friend King Berthold that the danger is not from me, or
even from Detlev, right now. Ask him if he remembers Henerek."

"You want me to warn him?" Rel asked.

Kessler's teeth showed in what might have been meant

as a smile. "Do what you want. If Berthold is ready, Henerek won't succeed."

"Why are you telling me this?"

"Because I want Henerek to die trying." Kessler spun a
transfer token into the air, caught it, muttered the spell, and
vanished.

Sickened, Rel turned away. He remembered Henerek, a
fellow Knight candidate, a bully and a braggart. If Kessler
meant that Henerek had made his way to Norsunder, Rel
was not surprised. The only question was why he would go
to this trouble to give Rel the message to pass on. Rel would
have expected that pettiness from Kessler's followers. Kessler's grudges had been reserved for kings.

Then it hit him: if the world was watching Everon, Kessler could attack somewhere else and take his target by
surprise.

"Who's your friend?" the caravan leader asked, as she
closed the distance. "He coming back?"

"He's not my friend," Rel said.

She grunted. "Friend or not, we could use him, if he
does. He musta accounted for half these deaders. I'll give
him an entire journey's pay for the next two days. You tell
him that."

Suppressing the impulse to declare that he never wanted
to see Kessler again, Rel stared at her. The sense of unre-
ality was fast changing to urgency, and even dread. He had
to spread the word. He had to . . . "Last night, did anyone
say anything to you about the northern route, once we reach
Mardgar?"

The caravan leader squinted up at him. She looked old
in the flickering firelight. "I thought you was headin' east."

"Changed my mind," Rel said. "Going north first."

She grunted. "Just avoid Remalna, directly next Mardgar, but that's nothing new. Bad king there. Getting worse."
She pointed at the burly man lying so still on the ground.
"Help me lay out these deaders, so we can describe 'em
exact for the Road Guild, or the local magistrate, which-
ever we find first. Then we'll Disappear 'em, nice and decent. Though I always wonder why we treat 'em decent in
death when they didn't treat us decent in life."

Chapter Six

Winter, 4739 AF
Chwahirsland

J ILO shivered.

Was it really cold, or was it time to go out again? He leaned against a work table, looked around the dim room, and sniffed the stale air. What had Clair said when they were walking toward Senrid's city, talking about his castle up ahead? Something about how clerestory windows could let in light and air, but still leave a place defensible. Jilo looked, imagining windows. Oh, what a good idea.

He shivered again. Surely the air was cold, it wasn't just him. Either way, he had better get out again. He became aware of the familiar drag on bones, teeth, muscles. Breath. Thoughts.

One more search. He'd gotten adept at teasing out the traps and wards as he went over the empty hall finger-measure by finger-measure until he found a space midway down the gloomy, moldy stone hallway between the magic chambers and Wan-Edhe's quarters.

Jilo's heart lump-lumped in his chest. His head panged. He gripped the magic protection-layered token he'd hung around his neck in mimicry of Clair's medallions. He whispered the key words, then staggered back. When he peered into the weird space, he spied a book about as thick as his thumb, its size somewhat bigger than his hand. It seemed to be floating in a thick murk.

Cautiously he extended a finger, wary of yet another trap, though reason would say that having come this far he was safe. But you were never safe with Wan-Edhe—ever.

Closer . . . closer . . . he touched it gently, as if that would matter to magic. The book jolted from the murk and began to fall. He bent to catch it before it reached the stone, his head pounding from the sudden exertion.

It was definitely time to go out.

Clutching the book to him, he made his way down and down, the air colder with each turn in the stair, each door gone through. When he approached the last door, he slowed. From the other side of the iron-reinforced wood came the moan of high winds. The door guards stood inside, which meant winter.

Winter? Already?

But he needed to get out. He thrust the book inside his tunic and signed for the guards to open the door.

The icy wind nearly took him off his feet. He bent into it, each step a struggle, the cobblestones slippery under his feet. His socks squidged, and his toes itched and tingled. His body began trembling, but the headache actually diminished, though his nose and ears and lips were numbing painfully.

He wasn't going to make it to the street, not like this. He raised his head, and descried a sentry box, a gray silhouette barely visible against the outer wall. He fought his way there and stepped inside, surprising the watch gathered around a table. They exclaimed, words cut short as they recognized him.

"What's a neckin?" he asked.

The youngest froze, staring as if he'd been stabbed. The older ones shifted, gazes dropping or sidling.

Jilo said, "This is not for Wan-Edhe. It's for me. What is a neckin?"

The oldest said to the lintel of the door, "It's by way of being a trip to the wall. For two, you might say."

"Trip to the wall? I don't get it."

Jilo gazed in frustration as they tightened into rigidity. They were afraid. Somehow he'd ventured into punishment territory. But then with Wan-Edhe, everything was punishment territory. Whatever it meant, it seemed to have nothing to do with him, and so he said, "I need a place to sit." He pulled the book out of his tunic.

Nobody asked why he didn't find a place to sit in the vast fortress on the other side of the courtyard. Chwahir did not ask questions. Everyone except the two on duty faded through a narrow door on the other side of the sentry box, leading to the covered corridor to the guard station.

Jilo was left to himself. He sat down at the table on the side nearest the little stove, wherein burned a single firestick. He set the book before him, opened it, and stared in amazement.

The words were too uniform to be handwritten, which pointed to a magical cause. He had no idea what kind of spells produced words, other than the copy spells that book makers sometimes used, though it took as much magical exertion to make them as it did the exertions of a copyist. But magic didn't wear down pens or run out of ink.

This book, though, could not possibly be a copy, for its text was nothing more than a list: first a name, then the location of the person. No date.

Jilo scanned the names. Early on, nothing was familiar, except for Detlev of Ancient Sartor. Then there was Kwenz, farther down. Paging on, Jilo found more familiar names: Wan-Edhe's sons, nephews, then grandsons. Gradually the names became more familiar—and then his own name appeared, along with Clair's and CJ's. Paging back, Jilo discovered 'The Brat,' and wondered if that was Puddlenose.

Jilo flipped to the end, to find the pages blank. He paged back until he found text, and as he looked, words appeared at the end of a solid block of notations after Kessler's name: 'Norsunder Base.'

He stared, his nerves flashing hot and then very cold as he comprehended what he had in his hands. This book was a list of all Wan-Edhe's enemies, or people he wanted to track. And each time they transferred by magic to Destinations warded by Wan-Edhe over what must have been decades, their location appeared.

Jilo flipped back, scanning carefully. There was Siamis, mostly Norsunder Base, but many other places. That must have been when he enchanted the world.

Jilo turned back to Detlev's entry. His location was seldom mentioned, and nearly all of those were Norsunder Base. Not all the transfers linked up the way Siamis's did. So the book had some limitations. It never mentioned Norsunder-Beyond, only the Base. Even so? Wan-Edhe was going to want to retrieve it.

The sense of threat pressing down on Jilo intensified as he fumbled his way back inside the castle.

Colend

After six months of hard travel, which included visiting harbors along the Sartoran Sea in quest of Mendaen's father lost a century ago, Rel finally cut north into the vast Sartoran continent, which—if Halia, where Marloven Hess lay, was included—reached three quarters of the way around the southern hemisphere.

He rode down the single street bisecting the small market town of Wilderfeld in western Colend. Snow had been swept but ice lurked between the fitted stones in the frigid air.

Like in most places he'd been in Colend, the snow had been formed into neat white walls. Mounds were unsightly.

Rel hunched into his scarf as a cold blast of wind scoured straight off the frozen river alongside the town. Beneath his legs, he felt the horse bunch its muscles as he himself leaned into the wind.

The street abruptly widened into the town square, which was empty of people, snow blankets covering the plots that would be gardens in spring. He expelled a cloudy breath in relief when he found what he had been looking for: a rambling two-story building. Judging by the different patterns to the stones, the lighter growth of ivy up the walls, and the sizes of the windows, it had been added onto at least twice. The sign hanging from the awning over the long porch stated in the flowing Colendi script:

Wilderfeld Scribes and Messengers

Puddlenose of the Mearsieans had taught Rel many of his traveler's tricks when Rel began his wanders, such as to always seek out the scribe guild when reaching a new town. Young and friendly scribe students were usually willing to recommend places to go (and places to avoid) to someone their age. In fact, Puddlenose had scribe friends here in Wilderfeld, whom he had introduced to Rel the last time they traveled together. The Colendi scribes Thad and Karhin Keperi were always a valuable source of information, and Karhin in particular seemed to have correspondence friends in every city on the continent.

Rel clicked his tongue, though the horse needed no encouragement to lift its head and pick up the pace, as it smelled a stable. A short time later, Rel stamped his boots at the back door porch, and then walked inside to a rare sight: near emptiness.

The rest of the year the shop was crowded with custom, lines at each of the slanted desks where scribes wrote messages for people, couriers coming and going. Rel stepped inside the long main room, noted the duty scribes—mostly adults, none of the young ones familiar—then took the officially stamped greenweave wallet from his pack and handed it to the duty apprentice scribe who sat at the courier desk, writing in beautiful script.

"This is to go to Alsais," Rel said. "I'm heading northwest."

"You're the first in several days," she said, laying her pen carefully on its holder. "Where from?"

"Lisdan, in Melire," Rel said.

The scribe's thin face brightened. "Oh! My cousin Albet is at Lisdan. Did you see him?"

Rel shook his head. "Not on duty when I was through there, but everyone seemed cheerful. There was a smell of cinnamon buns in the shop that day." Puddlenose, who had initiated Rel into the mysteries of getting bonded as a courier (which basically meant being paid to travel where you were going anyway) had told Rel that scribes liked to hear bits of detail that most people would shrug off.

Sure enough, she thanked him, and when he said, "Is Thad or Karhin about?" she didn't apologetically tell him the siblings were off-duty, which was the Colendi way of brushing one off. She said, "I can send the duty page to see, if you wish?"

Rel thanked her, and waited as the scribe tapped a tiny bell. A short time later, he was ushered into a plain room, where Thad and Karhin both sat on cushions before a low table, finishing their midday meal. Tall, weedy, with bright red hair, they rose and put their hands together and then outward in the graceful Colendi greeting called 'the peace.'

Karhin was the first to smile with recognition. "Puddle-nose's friend, I believe? Rel?"

"Yes. The year before the Siamis enchantment you helped me become bonded as a courier for Colend, and I've been grateful ever since."

Colend was so important all across the Sartoran subcontinent that the Universal Language Spell was kept up to date on Colendi idiom more than any other language in the world, except Sartoran. But mere translation did not guard against cultural pitfalls, such as avoiding questions that might require a negative, and other Colendi peculiarities.

When they had gone through the politenesses of Colendi greetings, Thad and Karhin offering food and asking about his journey, and Rel thanking them and replying suitably, Rel brought out the first of his carefully planned requests, worded so that a Colendi could avoid a negative.

"There are two subjects on which I hoped to ask your advice. First . . ." He brought out Mendaen's information. As soon as he said, "Sartoran boy from the old days. Can you tell me where I'd go to begin my quest?" Karhin flicked her fingers outward like a flower opening, a gesture of pleasure, as she exclaimed, "Oh, please, would you honor me with this precious investigation?"

Rel said, "I did not want to burden you with it, only to ask advice—"

Thad grinned. "You must see, it's the very type of task some of our friends like the most. Old Sartor, you know!"

By 'Old Sartor,' Rel knew that they meant Sartor of a century previous, as opposed to Ancient Sartor.

Karhin added, "This is *exactly* the kind of project to gain a scribe student great credit." She bowed over her pressed palms. "Thank you for entrusting it to me."

Rel thanked her on Mendaen's behalf, then said, "There is a second thing. I've been thinking for weeks how to describe it, and maybe it is not possible. I hope you can advise me . . ."

He really had been thinking about it for weeks. The sense of urgency after that encounter with Kessler had driven him to race northward, but as the days slid by while he was first stuck on a boat riding out a series of storms, then at a border that was closed because of trouble, he'd had time to think about the alliance.

He shrugged off CJ's rants about adults. Her reasoning might be faulty, but he believed that the idea of underage rulers uniting to form their own circle of communication was exactly what Atan needed. Especially if he, or any of them, ended up with what might be crucial news like what Kessler had told him about Henerek and a possible invasion, information that they might not be able to get past governmental watchdogs to deliver.

Rel imagined trying to tell Atan's high council about Kessler's warning earlier in spring. It didn't take much imagination to predict the way he'd be ushered right back out again on a wave of polite skepticism. After all, he couldn't prove the truth of anything the renegade prince had said, and he knew what they would say about Kessler as a reliable informant.

Rel described the theory behind the alliance to Karhin and Thad. ". . . so my thought is, if I, or any of my friends, stumble on information that might be important to know, there ought to be a way for us to spread it without having to go before nobles, councils, and others who might see fit to block information before a young ruler gets it and can decide what to do. For example, you might remember a few years ago, Wan-Edhe of the Chwahir tried to invade Colend." Rel lifted his hand northward. "Using magic as well as marching his army over the middle pass. And when the mages united against him, he took a couple of hostages to cover his retreat."

Thad tapped his palms together in the peace, trying to hide his excitement at the idea of being a part of such an alliance.

Rel eyed him uncertainly. He'd learned that the Colendi peace gesture could mean many things, from *Hello and welcome* to *Don't mind my interruption* (or, more bluntly, *We know that*), to *Quiet down, mannerless lout.*

"Puddlenose has told us a little about that story," Thad said, hoping for more—though he could see in his sister's careful politeness that she was uneasy.

Rel eyed her. He rarely talked about his own part in that ugly business, which had happened right before Kessler's recruiting gang had come along. He suspected that the Keperis probably knew the general history, but not that he'd disguised himself as a Chwahir flatfoot in a desperate attempt to rescue the hostages, both of whom were friends.

Rel had to be careful, because it all began with Puddlenose's futile attempt to warn the Colendi king about the invading Chwahir. It had occurred right after Puddlenose made his final escape from Wan-Edhe, knowing that the army was on the march to invade Colend. Yet King Carlael had ignored him with royal and serene loftiness.

Rel knew that no Colendi liked outsiders referring to their king as mad.

Thad raised a hand. "Would your example perhaps relate to Puddlenose's idea of a scribe circle?"

Karhin said helpfully, "Some of whose members are young monarchs who might like to correspond on subjects of mutual interest."

Rel let out a long sigh of relief. "Then he's already talked to you! Ha, it figures. And here I've spent the past several weeks thinking about how to approach the idea."

Karhin said more seriously, "Puddlenose described it as a message relay, saying that he never can keep hold of a notecase. He told us on his last visit he's lost three, and had two stolen. He wanted a way to send us news from any scribe desk if he thought it might be important, and for us to send it on. We can always relay messages without charge, as practice, for us, but when you say 'the relay of information,' that suggests a different purpose."

Rel bent his head, peripherally aware of the rising wind

howling outside. "I'm seeing something entirely new. It might not be possible. It might not be useful." He hesitated to mention Atan.

Instead, he recounted his recent journey as a caravan guard, and Kessler's warning about Henerek's impending attack on Everon. "So you see," he finished, "I believe the threat is real. But I can't predict this attack with any certainty. Yet I feel I ought to warn anyone who'll listen, especially at high levels."

He'd come this far, why not tell it all?

"The new king of Erdrael Danara, who is no older than you—" He nodded at Thad. "Was one of those hostages during the abortive Chwahir invasion. He's become a friend, and that's where I'm headed next. I believe he'd welcome such an alliance. And I also plan to ask the princess and prince in Everon."

He couldn't tell if he was making sense or merely sounding pompous. But he had to try, because of Atan's frustration, her sense of being caged by her high council.

There was another quagmire, too. He wouldn't betray Atan's ambivalence about Colend, though on the surface the two kingdoms were firm allies. However, Atan had told him that Sartoran courtiers had begun removing the Colendi lace from their court clothes. Until he'd spent time with Atan, he had been completely oblivious to how galling it was to the Sartorans to have lost the yearly Music Festival to Colend, not only for the sake of music, but because that festival served as the center of cultural exchange for most of the continent, and even farther out.

Thad listened with abating interest. Instead of suggesting a relay crossing countries with news, Rel seemed to want letter writers. It would be a lot of extra work obtaining the expensive paper, and inks, appropriate to royalty, and composing in formal scribe mode for an idea that probably wouldn't last out the winter. Kings writing to kings, relaying through the scribe desk of a tiny outpost such as Wilderfeld? Unlikely! Kings were surrounded by senior scribes, with elite, magic-protected scribe circles.

As Thad's interest waned, Karhin's intensified. She was passionate about being a scribe, and had not only read twice as much scribe history as her brother, she enjoyed voluminous correspondence with scribe students all over, including two new ones, girls from Old Sartor who wanted to catch up with world news, and who'd passed along interesting tidbits of information about the friendship between their young queen and the mysterious Rel the Traveler.

"I'd be happy to relay letters, as part of my service time," Karhin said when Rel finished. "I'll register a sigil with the scribe mage at once, before you depart on your next journey. Please carry it to any of your contacts that you wish."

At last, a success! Even if a small one. Gratefully, Rel began to thank them, but was interrupted by the chimes ringing downstairs.

"Time for tutoring," Thad said apologetically.

Rel thanked them again, and went downstairs to catch a meal at the courier annex, leaving the brother and sister alone.

"You really think we can run a scribe circle for royalty?" Thad asked Karhin as they assembled their study tools. "King of Erdrael Danara—the Queen of Sartor—the royal children in Everon!"

"It's not just royalty," Karhin said. "Rel would be part. And other travelers like him, such as Puddlenose."

"He's cousin to a queen," Thad said.

"But he doesn't tell everyone. His friends are all over, every rank." She indicated them both. "Ah-ye! The question of royal correspondents aside," Karhin said practically, though inside she was thrilled at the idea of being central to so much royal correspondence, "from what Rel describes, it seems they want not just a circle, but a back door scribenet. Only instead of some senior scribe or noble at the center, *we* shall preside. Think what it would do for our future positions, once we're given permission to reveal it!"

"For you," Thad said, laughing. "You know I haven't any ambition. And this sounds like a lot of work of the sort I like least. Especially if it has to be written out in formal mode, for all those royal eyes."

"I'll handle that part," she promised.

Thad studied the signs of secret pleasure in the quirk of her eyes, the little smile, and comprehended that she truly relished this extra work, if he didn't quite perceive why.

Thad was a scribe because it was the family business. He didn't have the passion for the world of paper and words that Karhin had. He was far more interested in people. He only went along because of the prospect of interesting visitors coming by to leave messages.

As they started out of the room, pen cases tucked under their arms, he stretched out a hand to halt Karhin. "There's Puddlenose's request," he said at last.

Karhin's gaze shifted away. Thad recognized in her averted gaze the discomfort he felt: looming unspoken between them was Prince Shontande, heir to Colend, who Puddlenose thought might like being invited into the alliance because he was young.

Their stepmother, before she joined the family, had been a scribe at the royal palace. Of course she said nothing about the personal lives of the king and prince. That oath was drilled into scribes as they practiced their first letters.

But Thad and Karhin were both good at discerning the shapes of silences, and intensely interested in the young prince, who was so rarely seen. They'd gained an impression of a very lonely boy sequestered in his exquisite palace at Skya Lake for most of the year.

The question no one ever asked out loud, but everyone thought, was: is he also mad?

Karhin said, "There are no scribe students at Skya. I asked."

For her, that was clearly the end of it.

Thad lifted his hand. "Leave that part to me." This mystery was the sort of challenge he liked best.

Karhin duly registered the new sigil, gave it to Rel to pass along, and wrote to the contacts whose sigils he had furnished.

Spring, 4739 AF
Marloven Hess

Senrid seldom remembered to check his golden notecase.

He couldn't imagine writing letters to anyone. And it wasn't as if he didn't have plenty of things to do.

Now that winter was over, the castle staff was cleaning and airing out rooms. As the snows melted in Marloven Hess, they began to fall up north in Bereth Ferian, and Liere came as usual to visit Senrid. She was there when one of the stewards discovered underneath piles of old winter armor some trunks that Senrid's barely-remembered mother had brought from her own land. They turned out to be full of carved and painted toy houses.

Liere was so delighted that Senrid gave orders for the trunks to be brought to his study. The pieces now sat all over the floor, along with the plain wooden blocks that Senrid and his cousin had made castles with when very small.

Liere crouched over the beautifully carved toys, marveling over the detail, round Iascan houses (the doors never face west!), steep-roofed Telyer houses, farms and cottages and even one castle.

She moved them about in cozy patterns, built around squares and circles. She didn't want her town to look like South End, laid out in a strict grid. How did villages and towns and cities grow, anyway? When was a town a city? Well, that might be just a matter of names. The Mearsiean girls called their capital on its mountain a city, but Liere had discovered it was smaller than South End, which was a town.

She sat back, hugging her bony knees against her chest as she wondered how towns began, and if people first chose each other as neighbors before they began building.

If only she weren't so ignorant! She glared at the little town she'd built, wishing she were smart. It had been fun until her mind filled with all these questions. If she could make up answers for herself, it stayed fun, but she knew the real world surrounded her little play town, and in the real world people called her Sartora, as if she knew all the answers to their questions.

Senrid found her sitting there beside the play city, rocking back and forth on the floor, thumbs digging at her cuticles, her skinny arms wrapped tightly round her legs and her chin grinding on her kneecaps. "Liere?"

"Maybe reading every book on the shelves is the wrong way to go at it. Maybe I should start with something like a history of towns," she said. "How they grow."

Senrid sighed, knowing that her anxious mood had to be related to 'Sartora' again.

"I don't think there is such a book." He dropped cross-legged to the floor opposite her. "Except maybe in a general history. Or local histories of a specific place. Towns generally grow beside rivers, or at crossroads, I know that much. Then there are walled towns, like in my country. Here, let me turn this into a Marloven town. I'll show you how we defend them. Did you know that in the old days, the women and girls handled defense while the men roamed around on patrol?"

She watched his quick hands moving the pieces around. She had so little interest in defense that she let his words stream past. Instead, she watched his deft fingers below his wrists with the rope scars. He didn't wear knives strapped to his forearms when he played with her, so she could see the scars, and his strong forearms, below the sleeves he rolled to his elbows. It was interesting, how differently he saw things. He was defending the town, and he didn't even know the families she had imagined in the houses.

He looked up, and recognized her distant gaze. He let out his breath, and clapped his hands to his knees. "You don't want to hear about town defenses."

She blinked, and ground her chin harder on her knee. She knew Senrid would scoff about the Sartora worries. He already had. Not to be mean. It was just that he didn't seem to care what people expected of him, or thought about him. No, she knew that was not quite right. He did care, but he was able to do things. She didn't even know where to start.

How about with what she was most scared of, then. "I want to learn about *me* defenses. If Siamis comes back, and takes away the sword, everybody will want me to defend them, but he's sure to kill me with it first," she said.

"That, we can fix." Senrid grinned. "Why didn't we think of sword fighting lessons before? I need 'em, too. I'm terrible at it, because Keriam didn't dare teach me when my uncle forbade it. Too easy to catch us out, because it's noisy. Contact fighting is quieter."

Liere let out a slow breath. "But I don't have any strength."

"Same as anything, you start simple and build it up. Come on. Let's go get the practice blades for the pups, the ten-year-olds in the academy. They don't arrive until next week, so we have the place to ourselves."

Something new to learn! Liere followed him. Before long they stood in an empty room, wooden swords in hand. Senrid said, "I'll show you the basics. We won't even put on padding. If you take to it, I'll get you proper lessons."

Liere knew by the way he looked upward he was counting the things he needed to be doing, and she thought sadly that it was time to return to Bereth Ferian. Senrid was getting behind in his real duties, and she was terrified of becoming a burden.

Senrid was so busy, and yet he always made time for her. Guilt squeezed all the joy away, because she was sure if she listened on the mental plane, the first thoughts she'd hear would be people annoyed because Senrid was spending time with her that he should be spending on them.

"Liere?"

"I'm ready."

"Here's the stance . . ." When she got that, he demonstrated the four basic blocks for a foot warrior against another on foot.

She picked it up quickly, laughing with him as they slashed the wooden swords through the air. Already her hand stung a little, and her arms tingled.

Then it came time to try the first block. "I'll stab, and you block. Slow at first. Very slow. Then we'll try it a little faster."

Slow was fine. She knew what to do, but the first real strike sent a sting of pain from her hand to her shoulder.

She dropped the sword and wrung her hand.

"Maybe gloves, until you build up some calluses," Senrid said. "I'm sorry."

Liere shrugged. "I asked you to show me." As she stooped to pick up the wooden sword that was used by boys two years younger than she was, she knew she didn't want to learn to fight. She didn't believe that even with practice she'd be any good against a grown man unless she released the Child Spell and grew up.

With that came a memory that always tightened her
stomach with horror: she was nine, listening idly to her
mother in the mental realm when another woman said,
*She's plain as mud now, but you wait. She'll one day be a
beauty, and you'll make a fine marriage for her.*

Liere rubbed her hand up and down her skinny leg,
loathing the thought of people staring at her.

She jumped when Senrid tugged the sword from her fingers. "Maybe we should stop before you get blisters. They
hurt."

"It'll take forever to learn," she breathed.

He had become adept at keeping his mental shield in
place, but it didn't take Dena Yeresbeth to hear the fear in
her whisper.

"If you don't want to fight, then you learn to hide," he
said. "Siamis can't carve you up if he can't find you. So, let's
talk about hiding places. I know. Let's play hide-and-find.
My cousin Ndand and I used to play it a lot, when my uncle
thought we were with the tutors, before he started putting
spells on her."

That was a game she'd begun to be good at, thanks to
the Mearsiean girls. She grinned. "I'd love that!"

Everon

The alliance was spreading slowly, but not all its members
defined it the same way. Rel and Puddlenose were the first
to realize this, as in Ferdrian, Everon's capital, the people
gathered for a royal exhibition on the royal parade ground.

Trumpets played a sweet fall of notes.

"Wheel left!"

Rel leaned in the saddle, aware of the immediate response from his borrowed mount, aware of his old friends
Enthold and Seiran at his left and right, Seiran, his own
age, having been a Knight candidate when Rel found himself invited into the elite cadre of military protectors of
Everon. He caught her eye. She flashed him the briefest
grin, then faced forward, her ornamental lance couched at
the correct angle. Rel belatedly adjusted his.

Except for the lance, which he'd drilled with perhaps three times before he turned down the offer to join the Knights, everything else came back as if he'd drilled two weeks ago, and not two years.

It was a brilliant day in early spring, and Rel had enjoyed the journey once he discovered Puddlenose in Erdrael Danara. The two crossed the strait then rode to Everon together, straight to the royal palace in Ferdrian.

Rel knew that in Everon, he would get a hearing. Sure enough, the king listened seriously to Rel's warning, and Commander Roderic Dei invited Rel to participate in the exhibition.

It was good to feel the spring sun strengthening each day, good to be listened to, good to be with friends. And it was good to ride with the Knights again.

Exhilaration flooded through him as the trumpet raced up two chords, and the captain bawled, "Wheel right!"

As the command echoed from company to company, horses and riders wheeled with thrilling precision. Rel gloried in being part of a mighty whole moving as one. The fresh cheers from the sidelines made it clear that Ferdrian's citizenry found the sight just as impressive.

The brisk spring air flirted with ribboned horse manes and tails, and tossed the bright pennants on the pavilions lined along both sides of the grassy sward. This parade ground, generally reserved exclusively for the Knights of Dei, was today open to all, tables of tasty things having been provided by the royal kitchens and the two most popular inns.

The high mood carried Rel through the end of the exercise, and accompanied him to the king's pavilion, where he'd been invited to join the royal party and their guests.

As Rel stepped up onto the platform, ducking under the wind-tossed canvas awnings, he heard Prince Glenn say fiercely, "Let Norsunder come. In fact, I hope they do."

Like a pinched candle, Rel's good mood was snuffed out.

Glenn's sallow, sullen face eased when he saw Rel. He straightened up from his slouch and waved Rel to a seat beside Puddlenose. "Isn't that so, Rel? If Norsunder comes, we'll *thrash* them."

Rel lowered himself onto the cushioned bench next to Puddlenose, who had stretched out his legs and was studying his bare, sun-browned toes. Rel took the time to sort his words, shutting out distractions—the rising wind, the changing light promising rain, the fact that this bench was lower than that of the princess and prince—and finally said slowly, "One thing I learned here is that the Knights are all still new."

Glenn flushed. "It's not our fault we were enchanted—"

Puddlenose's gaze flickered, but he didn't stir, and Rel wondered if he was thinking back to those strange days when evil seemed to shadow them at every turn. Wan-Edhe—Kessler—Norsunder. Only in retrospect was it obvious how many of the things that had befallen them were linked. The only exception being Detlev's experiment with forcing Everon into the same weird enchantment Sartor had been in, placing them beyond space and time. No one knew why he did anything he did—what he had planned to do with enchanted Everon, had not the experiment failed when the magical dyr thing fell into the wrong hands.

Queen Mersedes Carinna leaned over to touch her son on the shoulder. "Glenn. This same observation was put to us by Roderic this very day. It is no cavil, merely observation. Experience will come. It is the way of things. I'd as lief it comes later."

Glenn sent an impatient scowl up past his shoulder at his mother on her throne next to the king, and then at grizzled Roderic Dei, commander of the Knights, who stood at the king's right, where he could signal the trumpeter.

Roderic said, "The queen speaks true."

Glenn's scowl altered to brooding puzzlement, then he swung back to Rel. "Just so you understand. We're not cowards."

"Opposite," Rel said. "I know Harn and Seiran, there in Company Ten. Can think of few braver. And everyone respects Lord Valenn." He pointed with his chin at tall, dark-haired Erhold Valenn of Valenn, who as a newly inherited duchas, was first in rank among the Knights, and usually won firsts in all the competitions. "But each of them will tell you themselves they have yet to face battle."

Glenn chewed his underlip, then glanced warily back at Rel. "And you have?"

"Not war. Brigands only. I hope to keep it that way as long as I can."

Glenn leaned forward, about to protest, but was stayed by his father leaning down to rest his hand on Glenn's shoulder. "No one doubts your courage, my boy," the wine-flushed king said genially. He nodded at the field, his craggy face looking younger as he grinned at someone among the riders lining up for the mock battle.

Glenn crossed his arms, his mouth going from sulky justification to tightly controlled disgust when a curly-haired knight grinned back at the king, the pure white feather on her helm indicating a captain.

Rel guessed that this merry captain was probably the king's newest lover, or the latest one in his favor. He never quarreled with the old ones, Rel had learned (hearing far more than he wanted to about the royals' complicated lives from his friends among the Knights). The king was privately known as 'the butterfly lover.' A light touch, a flutter, and he was gone.

Unlike the queen's lovers, who all seemed to stay in love with her, though none so devoted as Roderic Dei, captain of the Knights.

The queen lifted her hand to the captain, who saluted her respectfully back, hand to helm. Then the trumpet played the charge.

Not hiding his disgust at the secret signaling, Glenn sat back with a snort. "I hope they can beat Norsunder," he muttered under his breath. "If only they'd listen to Valenn! Mama would have done better to . . ."

He shut his mouth, but Puddlenose and Rel had both heard Glenn on this subject: the Knights were an elite group not many generations old, elite in name as well as prowess, their command granted to the Dei family. The Knights had been confined to well-born males who passed stringent tests, until Mersedes Carinna, wearing male guise, had applied, made her way into the Knights, and into the king's heart. As queen, her first proclamation had been to open the Knights to women. And now there were plenty of women among them.

Glenn respected his mother as a person, but he resented her influence. It was bad enough that princesses ranked over princes in all countries influenced by Sartor, just because a million years ago, apparently Ancient Sartor only had queens. He thought that some things should belong to men, like warfare, because they were stronger than women. He was sure the women weakened the Knights. After all, they were smaller, and never as strong as the Duchas of Valenn or even Uncle Roderic.

Princess Hatahra, a year younger than her brother, and perhaps even more unprepossessingly narrow-faced and sallow, turned a scowl her brother's way. Under cover of the adults discussing the complicated maneuver being executed on the grounds below them, she muttered, "Seiran is the second best archer. And the first best is Captain Alstha." She pointed at the white-feathered captain. Both women were common in birth.

Glenn crossed his arms. "Having royal favorites never is good for discipline," he muttered back.

Tahra glanced skyward, sighed, then said, "True. But Uncle Roderic is fair."

Whenever Princess Hatahra spoke, she was listened to: she was, all knew, the royal child who had broken herself free of Norsunder's evil spell all on her own. Her parents, the nobles, Roderic Dei—everybody in Everon respected her for that. They respected the fact that when the evil Siamis and Detlev ranged over the world searching for Liere, it was Princess Tahra they came to first. Even though she did not have Dena Yeresbeth, she was respected as if she did have special mind powers, and she was the one spoken of most often as the possible royal heir.

Tahra, aware of that respectful silence, sat back, and shut up.

She would never tell anyone the real reason she'd broken the spell was through happenstance, just because she hated to be touched. Strong emotion broke the illusion, that much she'd learned in her magic studies since. And illusions were like spider webs—if you broke one, the entire web of illusions tore. It had been the flimsiest of enchantments. Norsunder kept trying to find ways to control minds, she had learned, but all they could do was distract or fool people with these various experiments—Detlev's, Siamis's. All of them broken in the end. Worthless.

She smiled grimly.

Glenn said to Puddlenose, "I really wish you'd join the Knights, even if Rel won't. I've seen you in the practice field. I know you can handle that sword."

"Only if someone threatens to air my innards," Puddlenose said, patting his stomach. "And itch-feet don't make good knights."

"You'd have to change your name, of course," Glenn said louder, aware of the adults listening. "But you should anyway. Pick something honorable, and when you make your oath, you'll no longer be mistaken for a vagabond."

"I like my name." Puddlenose reached into the basket of fresh apricot tarts. "I'm the only one in the world who has it. What could be a finer distinction than that? Even kings can't claim such exclusivity!"

The Queen of Everon chuckled, glancing covertly at her son, whose behavior increasingly worried her. "There is no finer, ha ha!"

Queen Mersedes Carinna was probably the plainest woman there, except when she smiled or laughed, which she did often. That laugh, a gusting waterfall of sound, seemed to come up from her toes, curving her thin lips, turning her close-set eyes into crescents of mirth, and flushing her sallow skin that had been privately sneered at by Colendi visitors as surely inherited from some Chwahir ancestor.

King Berthold also laughed, though only because his wife did. He kept to himself his conviction that it was irresponsible for a prince to shrug off inherited duty, but Puddlenose had aided his children when he himself was under enchantment, and so Puddlenose would always have a welcome in Everon.

The laughter ended when Tahra muttered, "I hate war." She sent a wary, accusing glance Rel's way, as if he'd been encouraging her brother.

The adults were quiet again, considering her words for extra significance.

Puddlenose said, "We all do, Tahra. At least, anyone sane does. Me, when someone wants to throw a war, I do

my best to be two kingdoms away, snoring in bed. And if
the eleveners come galloping out of one of their black rifts,
I'd like to be a continent away."

Everybody laughed, of course. Rel laughed as well, but
as he glanced from Puddlenose to the queen, who slapped
her thigh and stamped one foot, repeating, "Snoring in
bed! Or doing something in bed!" Rel reflected that she
wasn't the only one whose entire identity seemed to be
bound up in laughter.

But Puddlenose could be serious. Rel had seen him so.
Once. Deathly serious, with the deliberate intent to kill. So
unfamiliar had been that familiar face that Rel would have
walked right past him, had he not recognized the ragged,
blood-stained prison clothes he'd been looking at for
weeks, and smelled the prison stench: the moment they'd
been freed from the prison in Kessler's assassin camp, Puddlenose had headed out, weak as he was, his purpose to kill
Prince Kessler's chief lieutenant, who'd renamed himself
Alsais, after the capital of Colend. Alsais's penchant for
petty cruelty had escalated to torture and murder among
the prisoners. Puddlenose could not have survived a fight.
He'd had barely enough strength to throw a knife. Which
he'd done.

They'd never spoken about that day since. Rel wondered
from time to time if Puddlenose remembered it.

Puddlenose's lazy gaze flicked his way, then back again,
his smile fading. "Rel?"

Puddlenose was also unsettlingly quick at times.

Rel said, "*Two* continents away."

Tahra lifted her chin. "Perhaps we should invite Sartora
here. She might know how to use that dyr thing to protect
kingdoms."

"Or she could teach you," the king began.

"Dyr!" The queen turned her head and spat. "Any such
magic smacks of Detlev. He made those things, everybody
says. Even if that thing served us once, I am certain it was
inadvertent. As far as I'm concerned, 'dyr' is another word
for 'damnation.'"

Glenn grimaced. "I wish Mother wouldn't spit," he said
beneath his breath.

Whether the king heard or not, he clapped his son on

the shoulder, and brushed his fingers over the top of Tahra's head, his touch brief and light. Even so, she stiffened.

The king gestured toward the field. "Come, my dears.
Enjoy the last of the exhibition! Tomorrow they begin hard
training." His smile turned Rel's and Puddlenose's way.
"Thanks to our friends, who brought us warning. When
Norsunder comes, we shall be waiting."

The next morning, Rel woke early out of habit, aware that
he'd heard something. As he pulled on clothes, he identified the sound: a closing door.

He moved to the window and looked through the colon-
naded archways into the secluded garden between the
guest wing and the residence of the old, rambling royal
palace. There was Puddlenose, ten steps from the huge gate
that would let him into the big formal garden at the front
of the palace.

Rel knew instantly that Puddlenose was heading quietly
for the road.

Even kings you've done a good turn for do not like
abrupt departures, and so Rel got up and dressed, sought
out the royal family, and made farewells for the both of
them in proper form.

Mid-morning, Rel caught up with Puddlenose on a bend
in the Royal Highway. Puddlenose gave Rel a lopsided
smile. There were a lot of things that Rel could have said,
but he confined himself to, "Glenn wouldn't let it go, eh?"

Puddlenose heaved a sigh. "Sometimes I think the enchantment is still on him." He kicked at some weeds tufting
along the roadside. "Christoph won't come here anymore.
Signed on for a cruise with Captain Heraford."

Rel gave a nod. He'd been wondering where Puddlenose's usual traveling companion had gone off to.

Puddlenose bent to pick up a pebble, and shied it along
the newly smoothed road, then he sniffed the air. "Ah. Beyond that hill ahead, isn't there a village with a good bak-
ery?"

Puddlenose's method for dealing with problematical people and situations was to walk away from them. They'd told
the royal children about the alliance, and they had passed
Kessler's warning to King Berthold. Both had witnessed

how Everon's court almost welcomed the prospect of a fight. Prince Glenn definitely did.

Maybe that was what you had to do to prepare for what was coming anyway.

But if you weren't a king, and you hated war, sometimes the only thing you could do was walk away.

Chapter Seven

Winter-spring, 4740 AF
Sartor

A S the previous year waned into winter, everyone in the alliance was busy.

When so much is happening, record keepers usually begin with Sartor, then spiral outward.

Directly after the festivities of New Year's Week, one of Sartor's mages tasked with monitoring their young queen for her own safety discovered Atan's hoard of transfer tokens, and promptly reported it to the head of the guild, who discussed it with her senior mages before reporting it to the high council. They then waited for her next magic study hour, and sure enough, she was gone, transfer residue left behind in the air for those trained to perceive it.

Naturally the outlander Hibern was blamed.

Atan, at her next session with the high council, was presented with a unanimous recommendation: "We, as your counselors, feel it is best that you limit your magic study hour with the outland student to once a month."

In other words, *we know you have been going outside our borders unguarded.*

Chief Veltos looked into that shocked young face, and added with an attempt at kindness, "But if you wish to study the specifics of Sartoran magic, I can find a volunteer among our students. Or I will take time aside from my own tasks to tutor you myself, your majesty."

Your majesty. What a horrid irony. There was nothing majestic about being controlled like an erring child. Atan flushed, and spoke without considering: "I thank you, but I believe I have too many state matters to learn."

"Ah, an astute observation," exclaimed the Duchas of Ryadas, with a deep curtsey.

"I shall see to it that you are provided with tutoring in Star Chamber procedure," the chief of the heralds said, bowing.

"But I do not wish to lay aside my magic studies," Atan said quickly. "And Hibern teaches me what the senior students in the north learn, which no one here knows."

All faces turned to Chief Veltos, who had to admit the truth of that. What Veltos didn't acknowledge publicly was that she meant to change that. She saw the stubborn jut of Atan's chin, and said in her most soothing tones that once a month with Hibern would permit her to continue her studies, but the rest of the month that hour would benefit the kingdom as well as the queen if it went to tutoring in state matters. Oh, that inescapable moral superiority!

Atan managed to accept that, though her throat hurt.

All winter, she and Hibern had faithfully restricted themselves to Bereth Ferian's history and magical practice, which Atan duly reported on to Chief Veltos, in hopes of proving that the monthly hour was not wasted.

Hibern had also spent the winter with a changed schedule. Erai-Yanya vanished on some quest that she was not yet ready to talk about. Hibern spent the winter alone in the strange, cracked building kept warm by magic bindings, except for two days a week when she transferred to Bereth Ferian for her northern school classes, after which she had study time with Arthur. There were also weekly visits with Senrid.

She tried not to be lonely, or to brood about what could

not be helped. Study, learning, mastery were the only solutions.

And yet, in spite of her resolve, Hibern was so glad one day early in spring when her next Atan study day arrived again after weeks of incessant rain, that she didn't even mind the prospect of the double transfer as she shifted to Marloven Hess.

She found Senrid's study empty. Hibern knew that he hated tardiness, so there had to be a reason. No, there had to be trouble. Magical or military? His academy had barely begun its season. Surely the trouble couldn't be there?

She walked to the bank of four tall windows, and looked out over the academy. Her eye was caught by a short, slight, white-shirted figure among the many moving around the sandy-stone corridors. There was something about the set of those shoulders that caught her attention, though the curly blond head was exactly like so many others.

She was about to turn away when Senrid's thought overwhelmed her own: *Hibern? I've trouble in the academy. I sent Liere home last night. Next week?*

The words hit her like a mental shout, strengthened by a whirlwind of emotion, most prominent being anger and remorse. Guilt. Fury, which came with an image of a tall, blond boy of about eighteen or so. Self-condemnation. Hibern recoiled, her head throbbing with protest, then as suddenly as it had come, Senrid's thought was gone.

So once again, Hibern was given an extra hour, and decided to use it to take another tour of Eidervaen.

Hibern's guide this time was a cart driver with bright red braids. She gave a practiced patter as the goat cart whisked along the patterned-stone streets of Eidervaen.

". . . and this is Peri's Corner." A quick look from the guide. "Are you interested in romance?"

"Not really," Hibern said. "But tell me anyway. I did ask for famous sites in Eidervaen, where important things happened."

The guide flicked a smile back at Hibern. "This isn't important in the world of kings and queens. But it's important to *us*." The girl indicated the five-story buildings bordering the square, one with carved tree-columns on the first story and gargoyles peering down from under the roof, another with two false spires, a third with patterned stone blocks and colored glass windows, the fourth the plainest, and the oldest. It was below this one that a small fountain had been built, around which scattered flowers lay, petals fluttering in the spring breeze.

"If you want to make a public declaration of courtship, you bring flowers here every day until either you're accepted or turned down."

Public declarations? What if you get turned down just as publicly? The whole idea made Hibern feel squirmy.

As the cheerful guide went on about the history of tree-columns and what they meant during different centuries, Hibern tried to concentrate, but she kept seeing those blossoms, wilted and fresh. Declaration. Challenge. The squirmy sense settled between her bellybutton and ribs. Someday, that might be her. No. She'd never make a private declaration in public.

The cart rolled past, and eventually turned back toward the palace.

"You look thoughtful," Atan said when Hibern entered her study as the last echoes of the bell died away.

"I need to learn how to make a mind-shield," Hibern said. "Earlier today I was thinking about Siamis, and Dena Yeresbeth, and what hearing others' thoughts really means. I want to talk to Sartora about mind-shields."

"Yes," Atan exclaimed. "Yes, include me, too." She ran restless fingers along the queensblossom embroidery edging her sleeve and said slowly, "Sartora isn't alone in having this talent, is that right? Your king is another one?" The fingers shifted to tapping. "Have you met Sartora?"

"As it happens, I see her occasionally. Sometimes when she visits Senrid. Sometimes when she's back in Bereth Ferian and I go to study with Arthur."

"She visits your king? I should like to meet them both," Atan said. "I had a bad experience in Bereth Ferian's school, when I was still living with Tsauderei. No one knew who I was, and . . ." She shook her head. "Maybe it was my upbringing, not knowing how to act around people my age in groups. Anyway, I've been reading about Marloven Hess. 'Marloven.' I tracked down the history of the word, and there is 'Venn' in it. Did you know the Venn took their name from Sartoran '*fen*,' meaning 'family,' or 'clan,' and turned it around to mean 'The People,' as if they were elite?"

Hibern laughed. "One of my first mage lessons, learning our history from the outside view. And so we Marlovens became proud of our 'Outcasts of the Venn,' until the word 'Venn' came to imply barbarians and murderers, and the connection with them was frowned upon."

"In Sartoran many words still include 'ven' or 'fen' or 'vaen,' which means 'of the people.' It's odd, how words migrate and then come to mean different things."

Hibern agreed, but she wondered about Atan's experience at the northern mage school. Her tone suggested something unpleasant. Would the two mage schools, both dedicated to the good of the world, ever really be united in more than lip service? She hated it when Senrid was right about the hypocrisies of those who swore to dedicate their magic studies to the good of the world.

Atan shrugged. "Enough of that. The senior mages are busy with some project behind closed doors, so I believe we can resume our escapes for an hour. Have you ever been to Sarendan? Lilah and Peitar were my first friends."

"No." Hibern knew a little of its history. Peitar was another young king, barely adult-aged, unexpectedly inheriting his throne after a terrible revolution. Another for Clair's alliance? She said, "I'd like to meet them."

"I think you'll like Lilah. I've never known anyone who makes friends so easily—when I first left Delfina Valley to release the enchantment over Sartor, Lilah traveled with me. So she's one of the Rescuers. Peitar is so smart he'd be intimidating if he wasn't as friendly as his sister," Atan said as she handed Hibern a token.

They transferred to Sarendan, which lay east of Sartor across the jagged border mountains. It took Hibern longer to recover, as this was her third of the day, but she struggled to hide the reaction, walking to the Destination chamber's window to look out. *I have to get used to this*, she thought, noting that the building she stood in was positioned along a hilly ridge, a jumble of city rooftops layering away at the extreme edges in both directions. Directly below the sheer cliffs under the window lay a lake, wind rippling patterns across the water that reflected the rapidly moving clouds overhead.

"Ready?" Atan asked, and Hibern remembered they only had their hour.

"Of course," Hibern said, though her head still panged.

A servant took them down a hallway. Waiting side by side in the cheerful room overlooking the long lake below were stocky Lilah, her slanted eyes slits of mirth under her short thatch of rusty red hair, and slender, dark-eyed Peitar, whose only resemblance to his sister was the tilt at the corners of his eyes, and the quick flash of laughter when he smiled.

"Atan!" Lilah exclaimed. "I'm so *glad* to see you again!"

"This is Hibern, Lilah, and Peitar—"

Lilah was bursting with her almost-surprise. "I've wanted for *ages* and *ages* to introduce Derek to you, but I know you're so busy in Sartor, and he's always so busy all over Sarendan, doing stuff for Peitar."

Derek? Hibern's curiosity sharpened when she recognized the name: he had to be Derek Diamagan, the leader of the bloody revolution against the former king. He was also the one who very nearly got himself and Peitar executed.

Atan, aware of time streaming away, said, "Hibern was just suggesting that we ought to learn mind-shields. I think it a great idea, if we're to be facing Ancient Sartorans from Norsunder again."

Peitar Selenna turned to Hibern. "You've met Sartora, right? Perhaps you've heard her mention whether such things as mind-shields can only be used by those who have her ability?"

"I haven't spoken to her long enough," Hibern admitted. "But I wondered about that."

Lilah clasped her hands. "A girl my age defeating nasty villains!" Her face clouded. "Or is she all noble and solemn, only talking in Ancient Sartoran? She can't be a snob, because Derek told me everyone says she came from a little town of shopkeepers somewhere up north."

Hibern thought of that tense little figure with the enormous, staring eyes. "She is definitely not a snob—"

The door banged open, and in strode a shaggy-haired

young man, his bony face high with color. He wore a dusty shirt, the laces swinging carelessly at the open neck, baggy old riding trousers covering long legs, and shabby forest mocs on his feet. He brought in the scents of dust, and sweat, and a tinge of horse.

Hibern blinked, disoriented by aromas from home.

Lilah sprang up. "Derek!" she exclaimed happily.

Derek Diamagan flashed a boyish grin at Lilah, then he and Peitar exchanged the open smiles of brotherhood, absent the heat of passion.

Lilah waved proudly at Derek as she said to Hibern, "Derek helped us defeat our horrible uncle, who used to be king."

Hibern nodded, noticing Peitar's wince that Lilah did not see.

As Lilah spoke, Derek was taking in the two newcomers: both tall girls, one with black hair and what seemed to be a scribe's or mage student's robe over ordinary travel clothes, the other in a fine linen gown embroidered in gold with flowers, her shining brown hair bound up in a complication of braids above a pair of distinctive, protuberant eyes.

Into the short silence, he said, "Peitar, I've an idea about how we might get those city urchins off the streets. So many of 'em orphans." He jerked a thumb over his shoulder. "Why didn't we think of this before? They can become an orphan brigade. Maybe we can even resurrect your old Sharadan Brothers name."

Lilah hopped from foot to foot. "Oh! I want to be one!"

Derek laughed. "You are one, Lilah. They all expect you to join them. I've got them drilling in the old coopers' yard down on the east side, near your old hideout."

"Drilling?" Peitar said.

Derek swung his way. "Sure. Learning to work together. To defend themselves and their families."

Peitar sighed. "I thought the goal was to get the sword *out* of everyone's hands. Make negotiation, not force, the way."

Derek held out his hands, palm up. "That's all very well for civilized folks. We're agreed on that, but we're also agreed that Norsunder won't be civilized if they come again." His voice was low, serious, coaxing, gentle. A curiously attractive combination of all, and Hibern watched Peitar's sensitive face change, his brow puckering.

Derek turned to Lilah. "This is why I thought of the Sharadan Brothers, champions of justice for all." He opened a hand toward Lilah, who grinned, drumming her heels against the legs of her chair as Derek took a quick turn around the room. "This isn't a military in the way you fear, Peitar. It's home defense. Readiness. You know we were our own worst enemies during the revolution, because we had no idea how to stand up to your uncle's trained army, or even the city guard."

Peitar said slowly, "Well, we do have a problem with orphans who don't seem to have a place, yet who don't trust us enough yet to come forward so I can help them find one."

"Exactly. I want to draw them out. Give them purpose!"

"Let's talk about it. But later. I don't want to be rude," Peitar said, turning toward the visitors. "This is Atan from Sartor, and here's Hibern from . . . where is it, exactly?"

General attention switched from Atan to Hibern so quickly that only Atan saw Derek's reaction to her name—the crimped upper lip of contempt, and narrow-eyed mistrust.

Mistrust?

Derek's expression smoothed when Hibern said, "I'm from Marloven Hess, but I live in Roth Drael, where I'm prenticed to the mage Erai-Yanya."

Derek leaned against a chair, and began asking Hibern about Roth Drael—where was it, how many people, she lived alone with the mage, really?—and from there, questions about the study of magic, who got chosen, if there were ability tests like some guilds gave potential prentices.

The talk shifted from magic to the history of magic. The Siamis enchantment. Travel. The hour sped by, the conversation so quick and full of laughter that Atan wondered if anyone else noticed that Derek controlled it, and that he was excluding her. He behaved as if she were not even in the room, talking so fast that no one else seemed aware.

A chill branched down her nerves as the idea formed: Derek had done it on purpose. He'd kept Lilah waiting, and

Hibern and Peitar talking, in order to cut Atan out of the conversation.

Surely she was misreading him—she felt like Tsauderei's hermit student again, whose early friendships were all people in books. This was the hero of the revolution, the admired Derek Diamagan, who could do no wrong in Lilah and Peitar's eyes. There was no reason for him to be rude.

But then Derek touched Lilah on the shoulder and said, "How about we go and talk to some of the orphans, see what they think of the idea?" and then to Hibern, "Do return again. I want to hear more about magic in the north." Atan felt certain her exclusion had been deliberate.

Had the others noticed? Hibern and Peitar were deep in discussion about the two magic schools. Obviously they'd noticed nothing amiss. Atan reflected wryly on what Tsauderei had once said about how people are sure to notice what impacts precious self, but not so quick to detect slights to others.

"We'd better go," Atan said, and took Hibern's transfer token from her hand.

Hibern broke off. "Already?"

But Atan didn't answer. She was whispering an alteration to the transfer spell on the transfer tokens.

"Come again when you can," Peitar said to them both, but now that she was leaving, he let his gaze linger on Atan.

Atan didn't see that gaze. She handed Hibern her token, and Hibern braced for the wrench of transfer to Eidervaen. But instead, she felt a mere jolt, no worse than missing a step. She blinked, disoriented, until she recognized the round cottage belonging to Tsauderei, and breathed in the colder, thinner air of the mountain heights.

Tsauderei was there in his chair, a lap desk loaded with books and papers. He looked up, bushy brows lifted.

Atan said, "I know this is rude and sudden, but it'll be short. I really, really need your advice." And she summarized the conversation, then said to Hibern, whose expression had rounded in surprise, "Did you notice that? How Derek completely ignored me?"

"No, he didn't," Hibern began, then halted. Thought back. "Well, we were talking about history, magic, and the north . . ." Her expression changed. "All the questions were directed to me." She blushed.

Atan said, "No, don't apologize, or feel badly. Peitar didn't notice, either, and he is usually the most sensitive and discerning of people. I think Derek Diamagan cut me out deliberately."

Tsauderei said, "Of course he did."

Hibern rocked back a step, and Atan let out her breath in a sigh. "Why? What have I done?"

"Nothing. It's what you haven't done, which is to earn your place. No, no." The mage raised his gnarled hands, and pointed his quill at Atan. "Save your breath. Who in the world knows better who you are, how you learned, and what you've done? What's more, Derek Diamagan knows, too. He's heard the story about the freeing of Sartor from Lilah, but in his eyes that doesn't alter the error you made in being born a Landis."

Hibern exclaimed, "But . . . weren't Lilah and Peitar related to a territorial prince? If that isn't royalty, it's the next thing to it!"

"It's nobility, but in any case, Derek makes an exception for them. And he argues with them, his first point usually being, *You nobles cannot begin to understand*," Tsauderei said. "Peitar depends on Derek to argue the position of the commoner."

"Derek speaks for all commoners, and yet he resents a king presuming to do the same?" Atan retorted.

Tsauderei chuckled.

Atan flushed. "I shouldn't have said that. I shouldn't return a hatred he obviously holds for me though I've done him no wrong, because then I'm lowering myself to his standard."

Tsauderei gave a gust of laughter, then wiped his eyes. "I'm glad you came to me first," he said, the laughter fading.

Atan let out her breath again, trying consciously to dismiss her anger. How much of politics came down to personal antipathies, really? "Don't worry. I'm not going to declare war against Sarendan. Even if I could get such a stupid thing past the high council and the three circles."

Tsauderei leaned forward, completely serious now. "Derek is Peitar's most trusted friend and advisor."

"I know that," Atan said, and winced at how petulant she sounded. She made an effort. "I've heard wonderful things about him ever since I first met Peitar and Lilah. And I know he's done a great deal of good—"

"Spare me," Tsauderei said, waving the quill to and fro. "You don't have time for dither. Your people are no doubt looking all over for you—"

"Oh, I'm aware," Atan said, irritated all over again. "To dress the doll for another function at which I will make empty gestures and count steps to and fro, and measure the depth of their bows."

Tsauderei said, "You can sulk later. Right now, you'd better let me finish, since you came here to hear what I have to say."

Atan flushed. "I'm sorry."

Tsauderei went on. "I suspect that you were right that Derek deliberately ignored you. And you're equally aware that you cannot say a word against Derek before Lilah or Peitar."

Atan said, "Of course not."

Tsauderei went on in a milder tone, "I know you won't say anything, and you won't do anything foolish, but this much I know about human nature: within ten years, maybe even sooner, I strongly suspect Derek Diamagan is going to lead another revolution. This time against his 'brother' and friend Peitar Selenna, and oh, it will be for the best of reasons, but it will kill Peitar. Whether or not they put a sword through him, he will never recover from the betrayal."

Atan shivered.

Tsauderei finished inexorably, "And if that does happen—I repeat, I truly hope I'm wrong—but *if* it does happen, then all the other nations will look to Sartor for clues on how to react. You're going to need to think through how you're going to respond."

This is why I stay away from politics, Hibern thought, and when Atan had taken a sober leave of them both, and vanished, she transferred back to Roth Drael.

After she recovered and sat tiredly down at her desk, she remembered the alliance, which she had completely forgotten to ask Peitar about.

Next time, she told herself, though she wondered if it was worth the effort. It didn't seem to be going anywhere.

But she'd promised Clair.

Four days later, Hibern woke up to tiny sounds. Not the sounds of the forest, but the clink of a spoon on ceramic, the rustle of papers, the thud of a trunk closing.

Erai-Yanya was back.

Hibern whirled out of bed and pulled on her robe. She padded barefoot through the archway into the study, and there was her tutor, hair falling down, dressed in an unfamiliar robe rumpled from long wear.

Hibern said, "You're so brown!"

"Hah!" Erai-Yanya exclaimed. "That's because I was on our sister-world, Geth-deles. Got back last night, after you went to bed."

Hibern stared in astonishment. Though the oldest history books seemed to indicate that shifting between the worlds circling the sun Erhal had been much more common before the Fall of Ancient Sartor, nowadays it took serious magic to transfer between them.

Erai-Yanya said, "It's much warmer there, or at least, where I spent most of my time. Norsunder seems to be stirring there, though what they could want in a world full of floating islands is impossible to guess. I trust it'll turn out to be rumors, but . . ." She shook her head. "Enough of that, until I learn more. I'll have to go back. I hope, I *hope,* for a short time, until we prove the worries are nothing. This I can tell you: it was dreadfully hot and humid." She spread her fingers and ran them through her hair, tangling it even more. "So! Tell me what you've done, and what you've learned . . ."

Chapter Eight

Bereth Ferian

EARLY summer on the Sartoran half of the world was
early winter in the north.

Liere listened to the crackle and crunch of her footsteps
on ice as she walked the whisper-silent avenue of birch that
bordered this wing of Bereth Ferian's marble palace. It was
so pretty, the way the bare white limbs stretched up, the
branches weaving together, blurred slightly by tiny round
nubs that would soon be buds. From a distance the marble
palace, seen through the branches, reminded Liere of her
grandmother's white silk lace work.

Arthur had told her that back in the bad old days, when
everyone leagued together to keep the Venn from overrun-
ning the entire north, the various kingdoms in the alliance
were in a silent sort of competition. Each was to contribute
to the building of a headquarters that eventually became
this enormous palace, one of the most beautiful in the world.

She could attest to that, after flashing from city to city
in those awful days when she had to break the Siamis enchantment by visiting leaders, one by one, to disenchant
them, and through them, their citizenry. This really was

one of the most beautiful palaces, all that luminous marble, the acorn carvings around the windows, the way the tapestries all seemed to form doors into another place, one of past majesty and magic. Even candle sconces were made of gold in the central public areas, and polished brass above, in orderly knotwork shapes that incorporated the unlikeliest elements—vines, blossoms, wheat, and more acorns—but for some reason they drew and kept the eye.

She wished she understood art. Stamping her feet to kill the sense of pins and needles in her toes, she wished she understood people better. Maybe Erai-Yanya was right, and she wasn't going to understand until she lifted the Child Spell and grew up. But the very thought of that made her want to run and hide in the deepest hole she could find.

No, she simply had to learn on her own.

She stamped up the avenue. It wasn't fun to crash the thin ice layer, or to make footprints anymore. She was getting cold in spite of her mittens and scarf and knitted hat pulled down to her eyebrows. Her nose hurt, her fingers hurt, and she tried not to worry about Senrid, from whom there had been silence ever since he'd sent her home in the middle of the night a few weeks before.

All she knew was, there had been trouble in that academy. He'd been white-lipped with anger that night, too upset and angry to remember his mind-shield. So she'd seen what he'd seen: a host of seniors at Senrid's academy fighting, with knives, in a courtyard.

She hadn't understood anything she saw, except that it looked like a war to her—and she'd felt Senrid's sharp fear that civil war would break out if these expertly trained seniors started killing each other.

She'd shut him out, let him give her a transfer token back to Bereth Ferian, and after that, silence.

She tried to understand, but couldn't, how somebody, *anybody* would want to be a king. She longed to run and hide every time they wanted her to preside as Queen in Bereth Ferian, and nobody expected her to pass the smallest law, much less prevent civil war.

"But they expect me to get rid of Siamis, if he comes back," she said to the air, and watched her breath cloud.

Saying his name out loud felt like uttering obscenities.

She waved her hand through the already-dispersed cloud of steam as if she could wave the words from having been spoken, and broke into a run to leave them behind.

She found Arthur in the small room they used for mealtimes during the winter. The warmth tingled not unpleasantly on her nose and toes and fingers as she shed the scarf, mittens, hat, and heavy coat.

Arthur sat hunched over an old tome, his feet wound around the legs of his stool, his shoulder blades poking at his shirt as he put his finger on the page and looked up. He had a blue ink-smear on his cheek where he'd scraped his pen when sticking it behind his ear, and brown ink smudged his fingers. She couldn't explain why she liked these smudges any more than she could explain the appeal of art, but they made her smile.

"Warm corn muffins and tartberry jam?" he asked.

Liere grabbed a muffin, tossing it from hand to hand when she discovered it was still hot. As she reached for a knife to cut it and smother both halves with jam, Arthur said, "Hibern made her visit at the school. She stopped by here to talk to you, but you were outside, so she asked me to ask you when you are going to Marloven Hess next."

"I don't know," Liere said. "You remember, I came back because of some kind of trouble. I don't know if it's over."

Arthur sat back. "That place sounds terrible. You really prefer it to here?"

Liere knew that when she wasn't listening in the mental realm, she was not a good judge of character, but the hurt in Arthur's expression was plain to see. "It's not Marloven Hess I go to," she reminded him. "I don't see much of it. It's Senrid. He's like my brothers, only better, because my real brothers thought I was stupid. Well, one did. And the nice one didn't live with us."

Arthur wondered if that was why he was failing with Liere. He'd never had any brothers or sisters to practice on.

"And there are a few Marlovens I like very much," she added, thinking of Fenis Senelac, under whose exacting tutelage Liere's sporadic riding lessons progressed slowly but surely.

But Marloven Hess, like Bereth Ferian, was a place to visit. It wasn't home. Home still brought images of South

End, yet Liere never wanted to go back. Maybe the word 'home' was at fault. It wasn't truly a thing word so much as a feeling word. She hated emotions. They were so *useless*. 'Home' was definitely an emotion word. She should never think it or use it.

Arthur perceived her tensing up, and understood with a kind of sick certainty that despite all his efforts, it was clear that Liere was never going to love Bereth Ferian. That's what his mother had said, and she was right.

He couldn't understand it, but he did understand that to pressure Liere with his own sense of failure or fault was unfair. So he pointed at the book. "This fellow is really funny. The translation is Sartoran. Do you want me to read some of it to you?"

"Who's the writer?"

"A long-ago southern king, writing to his descendants. It's called *Take Heed, My Heirs*, and I've been laughing all morning."

Liere had no interest whatsoever in old kings. "I need to practice Ancient Sartoran," she said. "I'm having such trouble understanding a book, and all it's about is farming."

"Ancient Sartoran, that reminds me. Hibern says that the Queen of Sartor seems to want to meet both you and Senrid."

Liere jerked her shoulders up to her ears. "I dunno when I'll go there next."

Arthur did not understand Liere at all, but she was one of his responsibilities. Hoping to ward off one of those awkward silences during which she'd sit there fighting some inward battle while chewing her cuticles bloody, he pretended she'd shown interest in his book, and translated a couple of the funnier incidents from the early years of Prince Valdon's life. His reward was a grin, then a chuckle, and pretty soon she was laughing, and begged him to read more.

Chwahirsland to Marloven Hess

Jilo blinked. He stared into the empty closet in horror. The air rippled slowly, the stone walls appearing to be a day's journey away, the floor a thousand paces below. He blinked and they closed in on top of him. Jilo struggled for breath, his heart squeezing in his chest.

The enemy-book in his hands seemed to pull him forward, forward, toward the abyss he could barely sense . . .

He lunged backward, and stared down at the object leached of dimension, of its essential bookness. He blinked at the rough-cut papers pressed between stiffened canvas, stitched on the outside by blackweave . . .

His head began floating off his shoulders. The tiniest dart of alarm brought his attention back long enough for him to glance at the stranger's hand lying on the square thing whose purpose he no longer recognized, gray nails . . .

Gray nails.

He knew that was important. He shut his eyes.

Breathed.

Each simple action required concentration, and appalling effort.

Frightened, he clutched convulsively at the token that thumped against his ribs at every move. Heat flashed through him, shocking him thoroughly awake long enough to clutch the book to him and stumble backward through the door. He shambled down the hall, though his limbs had come unhinged, and his feet had turned to blocks of stone.

When he got outside, he leaned against the rough wall, drenched in sweat as he labored to breathe. Waves of black rolled across his vision, punctured by pinpoints of light. Slowly the darting fireflies brightened, and gathered more brethren from the darkness. Did they form into twia? He should count, see if they darted in eights . . .

One, two, three, hold still . . . Gradually sense returned, and with it, awareness of thirst, weakness in knees and wrists. He had stayed much too long. Oh no. Had ten years passed?

He shoved the book inside his shirt, then walked up to a duty guard he knew. Thought he knew, only he looked so much older. "What is the date?"

The fellow looked at Jilo as if he'd spoken in Norsundrian, fear widening his eyes. "Date?" he repeated.

Jilo tried again. He knew these questions were important. No, it was the answers that were important. No, it was how the fellow didn't answer. "How old are you?" Jilo asked.

The guard said, his tone placating, "I joined at my twelfth year."

Jilo stared at the guard, horror curling inside him, and the guard stared back, his pupils wide and black. Like the Shadowland days, only this was fear. Jilo forced himself to move. He pushed on in search of water and food.

It was easiest to walk into the city, to the place he knew. Habit. That was important. Habit was as strong as . . .

As strong as? Twi. Groups. Loyalty. You stayed loyal to your twi, you survived. Every Chwahir grew up knowing that. Survived what, that was the question for a king to face. Survive an evil king who had no twi, who had killed everyone close to him?

The Mearsiean girls always won. They'd had a real twi, almost the right number, even. They did have the right number when Clair wasn't there, something that had always irritated Jilo, as if they somehow made game of the fundamental strength of Chwahir life. A bunch of silly waxers . . .

As he blew the steam off the soup, his thoughts shambled on. Waxers. Lighters. Where had he had that conversation? That boy king from, what was it? Somewhere far to the southwest. Senrid, that was it. Tutored in dark magic. Came to help, once. Said to find the source, *and I've found it.*

Jilo left the tasteless food after only two bites and sloped out to the street. He looked around, trying to remember why he was there. Passers-by distracted him, the way they watched one another . . . were they doing the hand-signs? Hands. Talk. Talk? Yes, he was going to Marloven Hess.

He recollected the Destination that Clair had taken him to, braced, and did the magic.

He found himself standing on the windswept tiles, the sun barely risen. He fell painfully to his knees, fighting for breath as black spots drifted across his vision.

Senrid had done his morning drill earlier, so he could take a fast horse out to ride the plains below his city. As the strengthening sun made its way each day a little farther along the distant eastern ridge of mountains, he liked to pause and watch the sky lighten, then the first rays of ruddy light outline the towers of Choreid Dhelerei, his city.

He sighed out his breath. It barely frosted. After a very cold, late spring, summer was coming at last.

The tug of obligation pulled him cityward. The mare, a young one newly released into the garrison stable, sensed his decision, and she tossed her head, sidling. She wanted to run some more, so why wasn't the two-leg giving her the signal?

He obediently tightened his thighs, and she bolted off the mark like an arrow from the bow. And that was what Jilo saw, as he stood there on the Destination below the city wall, horse and boy so well melded in the rhythm of the gallop that they looked from a distance like one of the northern centaurs he'd seen pictures of in some old book.

The round face turned Jilo's way, the horse veered, and clods of mud flew up behind the animal's hooves from the rich soil so different from the sandy clay found in Chwahirsland.

Senrid reined in with an ease that made Jilo's heart yearn for such unthinking skill. He'd always been so awkward on horseback.

"Is that you?" Senrid asked. "Jilo?"

"You said I could come back." Jilo looked around. "Wasn't it snowing last time?"

"So you've solved the time riddle?"

"Not the time riddle," Jilo said painstakingly, picking out each word.

Senrid could see the effort. At that moment, the inner perimeter riders approached, and Senrid motioned for one to surrender his horse.

Jilo grimaced. Here came the humiliation. He wondered how quickly that horse would boost him off at that thunder-and-turf pace.

Jilo scrambled up onto the saddle pad (barely any saddle, he noticed dismally), and clutched the reins desperately, braced for the inevitable fall. Senrid cast him a quick look, then his horse, which had begun to trot, unaccountably slowed to a walk. Jilo's, trained to follow, also slowed.

Senrid said, "Now we can talk. What've you found?"

"I think I've located a . . . I'm not getting the word. It's a locus of power? Where it draws . . ." Jilo breathed hard against the pressure in his throat. "Just thinking about it strangles me." His breath shuddered as he fingered the medallion at his neck. Cold tightened the muscles and nerves along his spine when he contemplated how very close he had come to . . . what? Would the servants who finally dared to come looking for him have found a desiccated body? How long before they would have come?

Or would they?

He was not aware of having fallen into reverie, but Senrid noticed the absent gaze, the squint of oncoming headache, the desperate clutch on the reins. The first thing Jilo obviously needed was a decent meal between his belt buckle and his spine, and then sleep.

They reached the castle and dismounted, and part of the reason for Jilo's oddly stiff, awkward style of riding became apparent. Jilo looked shiftily around, then stuck his hand into his heavy-weave tunic-shirt, and produced a thin book.

Jilo already whiffed of the distinctive burnt-metal stink of intense dark magic, a stench more psychic than physical. When the book appeared, Senrid reeled back a step. "Jilo, whatever wards you put on yourself are killing you."

"Oh." Jilo blinked rapidly, clutched at the medallion, muttered, and took a cautious breath.

The miasma of intense dark magic eased, but did not disappear.

"Come on," Senrid said, resisting the unnerving sense that he was being towed into deep and unfamiliar waters.

Jilo tucked the book under his arm, his head drooping, and he followed Senrid in silence. Along the way, Senrid hailed a runner and gave swift orders for a meal to be brought to the study. As soon as the door was shut, Jilo sank into the chair beside Senrid's desk, then held out the book.

Senrid stretched out his hand, then recoiled from the smell of stale sweat and mildew and dark magic emanating from the thing. "Go ahead." Jilo's voice husked with the effort he made just to speak. "I think I got all the wards and tracers off it. And the wards on me are gone. They were the only protection I had in the King's secret chamber." He tapped the medallion.

Senrid could feel layers of magic from a palm's breadth

away. "Are you sure?" Jilo didn't look sure of anything, even his own name. *Be specific.* "What type of spells are in that book?"

"No." Jilo dropped the book onto the desk, leaned back in the chair, and shut his eyes.

"No?" Senrid prompted, clamping down hard on impatience.

Jilo's throat knuckle bobbed in his skinny neck as he said, "Purpose. It tracks the movements of any enemy if they visit designated Destinations. A *lot* of them. And I've added Wan-Edhe's name."

Fire shot along Senrid's nerves. That thing would track enemies who moved about by magic?

He stared at the thin, grubby book, no longer seeing the oily smudges along the edge from frequent openings, or smelling the mildew and the rank odor from that terrible chamber in faraway Narad. Senrid reached convulsively, then stilled, eyeing Jilo, who sat there, eyes closed.

What was the danger? There was no danger.

Even if Jilo weren't obviously exhausted, Senrid suspected he could take him in three strikes. This was Senrid's citadel, he could command the guard, he could drop a stone spell over Jilo and set him aside to deal with some other year.

He could take the book, add Destinations within Marloven Hess, add names of troublemakers, and track every one of his enemies . . .

Once again he reached, his fingers halting a grassblade's width from touching. He sensed the layers of magic. Maybe Jilo had put protective wards over the thing as a trap. Senrid knew he would.

The door banged open, and in came the runner with a tray loaded with oatmeal drowned in milk, and rye buns, with a little bowl of blackberry jam to spread on them. Since Senrid ate what everyone else ate, from garrison to castle staff, it was easy to dish up extra for a sudden guest.

Hoping his voice sounded normal, he said to Jilo, "Eat up." And to the runner, "Some listerblossom steep. Make it strong."

Jilo's color was never going to appeal to anyone outside

of Chwahirsland, but as he worked his way through the food, the pale, pinkish sallow that replaced the mottled gray looked almost healthy.

Senrid possessed himself in patience, but never had a meal lasted so long. Through his mind flitted images, sustained by the alluring, the sweet image of knowing. At all times. Where his enemies were.

When the steep came, filling the air with the astringent summery scent of listerblossom, Jilo gulped it down hot. He blinked away tears from the scalding liquid, and sighed.

"So tell me how this book of yours works," Senrid prompted.

"Go ahead. Take a look," Jilo said.

"I don't want to touch it," Senrid replied, the instinct to grasp and keep it so strong that his voice must have changed, for Jilo looked up, one eye narrowed. Senrid cleared his throat. "There might be other wards on it. Against outsiders. Non-Chwahir. Anyway, I can't read your language."

Jilo's blinks made it clear that he had not thought this far ahead. Flipping the book open, he pointed. "As you can see. Wan-Edhe had a lot of enemies. This book is just the last year. Before he got snatched by Norsunder. There must be pages and pages stored somewhere. Or maybe he burned them. He writes in a name. It shows when and where they transferred by magic."

"It has to be transfers? Can it track them if they travel by horse or walking?"

"Magic transfers only. Specific Destinations."

"Let's get to who. Start with Detlev? He has to be in there."

"Yah." Jilo's ragged, grimy nail pointed to a line. "Few notes, as you can see. Spaces between entries, like holes. Because otherwise, why would it say 'Norsunder Base' four times in a row? He wouldn't be transferring around inside, would he?"

"How about if he transfers to Norsunder-Beyond and then back? Or off-world?" Senrid guessed.

Jilo blinked slowly. "I hadn't thought of that."

Senrid grimaced. "So you just write someone's name in? Or do you have to find the person and bespell them, the way you do if you put a tracer on them?"

Jilo bobbed his head. "There is a very complicated spell, requiring the person to step into a warded Destination. I don't know how he differentiated between people. I just know it works."

Senrid whistled. "My uncle wanted something like this book. Had me working on it from the time I was ten. Best I could do was lacing objects with tracers, then you had to get the person to take the object with them." He whistled again, more softly, as he extended his hand over the top of the book. "There's lethal magic on this thing."

Chill flashed through Senrid to pool in the pit of his stomach as he recollected some of the stuff he'd overheard when he was a prisoner of Siamis's bully-boys. They hadn't known he could understand their language. Most of it had been brag, threats, and lies, but once one of them said, *The Host of Lords sit in the Garden of the Twelve and watch anywhere they want, any time.*

Senrid had shrugged that off as scare-brag, but if the likes of the King of the Chwahir could construct this book, maybe it was real.

Yet even the Host of Lords can only watch one thing at a time.

Right?

Senrid shook off the dread, reached across his desk, and closed his fingers on one of his steel-nib pens.

He pushed pen and ink toward Jilo. "Try an experiment? Write a name in another language. Someone you know enough to make the spell work."

"Who?"

"How about Puddlenose of the Mearsieans?"

Jilo glanced up in surprise. "He's an enemy?"

"No. I just want to see how it works."

"He's already in here. I think he's this one, 'The Brat.'"

"Already in there?" Senrid remembered Puddlenose as a jokester, but there had been some brief, sharp moments hinting at some kind of past. "Someday I want to hear about that. Try Arthur of Bereth Ferian, then. Have you met him?"

"No."

"Try. His real name is Irtur Vithyavadnais, and he's the son of Erai-Yanya, if that helps." And Senrid described Arthur.

Senrid breathed out silently, considering the feeling that he'd dodged a falling rock as Jilo closed his eyes and whispered a long spell. Senrid heard Arthur's name mixed in, but when Jilo wrote the name down, nothing happened. He shut his eyes. "I don't know what I did wrong," he whispered. "I think maybe I need to do the spell again after he steps into one of the warded Destinations?"

All right. It had limitations. Still. Senrid wanted so badly to try it, his fingers twitched toward the pen.

He forced himself to sit back. "Okay. Go hole up. Sleep it out. No one will touch this thing," Senrid added. "Including me."

SENRID'S natural inclination was to turn to Commander Keriam, but not for anything having to do with magic.

His second thought was Hibern, but he suspected she would go straight to her tutor if she had any idea that something like this book existed. He couldn't imagine the lighter mages doing anything other than ganging up on Jilo to take away that book for his own good.

For the rest of the day Senrid's body moved about his various tasks, his mind on that book lying there on his desk, as he asked himself useless questions, such as *Where is Jarend Ndarga's exiled father right now?* And, *How could I locate any conspiracy if I don't know who is conspiring against me?*

He knew the cause of his ambivalence. This desire to possess that book was his uncle's thinking. Tdanerend had always been frantic about conspiracies. Toward the end, he had a full flight of guards on duty around his sleep chamber at night, plus his three handpicked private guards, men he bribed and flattered then changed if he thought that they, too, might be conspiring. Thirty thinking, breathing beings on the watch all night so one man could sleep, and even then, Tdanerend had often been wakened by a noise, and fearing attack from his guards, set up traps, because though he demanded loyalty he never believed he had it. How could he, when he had professed loyalty to his own brother up until he stabbed him in the back?

Senrid tried to shove the book out of his thoughts, but when he found himself thinking about *thinking* about it, he hopped up onto the fence to watch the choosing of colts after summer-long training, and let his mind ride down the what-if trail.

He saw himself taking the book away from Jilo. Learning Chwahir. It shouldn't take long. He was good with languages. And he could easily get proximity to all his targets, in order to bespell book and person, if that's what it took. Warding the city, each jarl's capital, the army garrison Destinations, to begin with.

And then what? Spend the entire day creeping back to check on their movements? Or would he carry the book around with him all the time, and constantly sneak peeks?

That was exactly what Tdanerend would have done. Senrid understood, now that he was king, the relentless desire to know, to brace for attack, to be ready for the knife in the dark. Anywhere he went, he was a moving target.

The colt selection ended. He ran to the quartermaster, who was waiting with reports related to the stables. He was supposed to know all that stuff, so he forced himself to listen and concentrate. When he finally retired, he was still so ambivalent he tossed and turned, finally falling into an uneasy sleep in which he dreamed that he and Liere were lost and Siamis was chasing them, but Senrid's feet had turned to rock and he couldn't run.

Sleep fled at sunup, leaving him groggy. A cold bath shocked him awake. He ran to the garrison side, where he found the sword master waiting. "You haven't tried the sword again for quite some time," the man said, indicating the rack of practice swords. "Or would you prefer our usual?"

Senrid was tired, his mind full of Jilo and his damned book. He eyed the swords, hating his slowness, his clumsiness: by now he'd had enough lessons to know that to be really good he was going to have to unlearn everything that had become habitual with knife fighting. He hated that.

"Knife," he said. "Some castle guards took against my learning the sword," he added when the sword master evinced a little surprise. "Thought it some kind of reflection on their ability to keep me alive."

It was true—in a sense. They'd been mostly joking, when some of the morning shift had come in while Senrid was finishing one of his lessons in basic sword moves, not long after Liere's last visit.

The sword master's brows went up. He opened his hand in assent, accepting Senrid's not-quite-lie, and Senrid sensed the man's opinion of the guard lessening.

Senrid picked up his practice weapons, throat tight with disgust and self-condemnation. Lying was so *easy*. That was another path down which his uncle had gone, only Tdanerend had also lied to himself. Senrid had lied to survive. He could not claim that this lie was even remotely about survival.

Usually Senrid enjoyed these lessons. He reveled in being skilled, and fast. He had to be fast, if he was to defend himself against a grown man, and he usually came out of these sessions less weary than exhilarated, muscles aching enough to free his mind for the day's tasks. But that smarmy lie stayed with him, souring every movement.

He was glad when the watch bell rang and he returned to the residence side, in a thoroughly vile mood.

And there sat Jilo in his study. Senrid nearly stumbled. He'd actually managed to forget all about Jilo during that practice session.

He strove to sound normal. "Breakfast should be along soon. I hope you liked yesterday's, since it'll be the same. Did you sleep well?"

"Your food is much better than ours." Jilo's face was a lot less gray. "Slept very well."

There wasn't any talk during the meal. Both were too hungry. But as soon as his plate was empty, Jilo thumbed his eyes. "Maybe I should stay away for a time. My head's clearer when I get distance."

"Distance from Wan-Edhe's magic chambers?" Senrid asked.

"From the castle. Maybe . . . maybe from the capital." Jilo's gaze strayed to the study windows.

Senrid exclaimed in surprise, "You could leave that long and not come back to find one of your commanders on the throne and an assassination team waiting for you?"

Jilo's gaze returned. "I worried about that. At first. But they know now that Wan-Edhe was taken by Norsunder." He looked down, his embarrassment clear. "They expect him back any day. After eighty years of Wan-Edhe, no one believes he's gone for good. Won't, until his dead body is seen. But I think, from my walks in the city, they only want to get on with their lives. They fear the castle. No one wants to go into it, and risk being his first target when he does return."

Senrid was on the verge of saying, *Why don't you just walk away?*

Jilo went on in his painstaking, monotone mumble. "I think . . . I think I need to find out what they expect from the castle, besides fear. Wouldn't that be what a king would do, find out? One who wasn't Wan-Edhe?"

Senrid said sardonically, "If they're like people anywhere, one person will say the king ought to lift taxes. The next one will say the king should improve roads. The third will say better patrols against brigands, the fourth will demand exports of Bermundi rugs."

Jilo nodded unsmiling on each point. "Yes, but eventually the demands will repeat. Won't they? Then won't I see how many want the roads, and how many are worried about brigands, and so forth?" He ran his fingers through his lank, unkempt hair. "Won't that give me an idea of what I should be doing?"

"If you have big numbers demanding this or that, isn't rebellion more likely?"

"Maybe." Jilo shifted on his chair. "The way I see it, their idea of the king is in his castle. Doing what kings do. So as long as I'm pretending to be a king, shouldn't I try to be the king they want, and do what they expect me to do?"

Senrid stared at him. It sounded so simple. Simple-minded, even. Tdanerend would have said so.

He could suggest Jilo just walk away, to which Jilo could retort the same to Senrid.

He could do it. If he got up from the table right now,

walked through the castle, saddled a horse, and rode for the border, nobody would stop him. Maybe (if they figured out what he was doing) they might even chase him, like the stories about his Uncle Kendred. Senrid still didn't know whether they'd chased Kendred to capture and kill him, or if they'd run him over the border. As always happened to displaced Marloven princes or kings, Kendred had been eradicated from the most accessible records, as if he'd never existed.

Senrid squirmed. He couldn't bear the idea of running. Of being anywhere else. This was where he belonged, the only place he felt like himself. Even if he died staying.

He thought of older writings, the few not destroyed, in which one of his ancestors had defined kingship as an idea shared by the many minds a king ruled. Or he would have to spend all his time forcing his own idea of kingship onto them.

They just want to get on with their lives. Senrid's gaze fell on the book, and he shifted uncomfortably as he recollected the headlong plans, images, and thoughts of the previous day. Sickness churned inside him at the awareness of how close, so very close, he had come to following his uncle's path. He knew exactly how it would begin, how you convinced yourself what you were doing was perfectly justified. Sensible. Self-protection. And the only thing that had stopped him was wondering how he could find enough time in the day to check the book.

"Everyone follows the law." He had to stick to it. He'd seen what happens when you don't . . . the seniors at the academy had been extraordinarily subdued ever since the senior revolt in spring, during which Ret Forthan, the best of the seniors, had broken the rules and used steel on the worst of the seniors. The entire academy had been humiliated by the sight of Forthan, the most popular boy, tied to a post and caned before the entire school, though *everyone* knew his action had been justified.

But that was the law.

The scars on Senrid's back crawled. How he hated remembering watching that, knowing exactly how Forthan felt. All these months later fury still burned in him, and beneath that a sense of failure, though he knew it was not his fault. That senior revolt was a direct result of his uncle's lies and playing of favorites among those boys' fathers.

Senrid forced his attention back, and pointed to the book. "Listen, Jilo, I don't know how your king managed to make that thing, but you'd better keep it tight."

"I will."

"I mean really tight. Don't tell anyone about it. I wish you hadn't told me. But if word of that gets out, you're going to have every mage, light or dark, hunting you down." He shook his head. "I don't even know how that king of yours drew enough magic to make that thing. The magic on it is stronger than most kingdom wards."

Jilo's eyes widened. "But I told you. Didn't I? The chamber. I did tell you. You said it was killing me. And you're right. I think I'd be dead if I hadn't made these wards." His fingers clutched the medallion on its dirty string hanging around his neck.

Senrid leaned forward. "We got to talking about the book, and got stuck there." *Or I did.* "What exactly did you find in that chamber?"

"The source of Wan-Edhe's power." Jilo's complexion blanched again, his cracked lips thinning. "He's using the life force of the palace inhabitants. That is, everyone's but his own."

Senrid's head rang as if struck by a bell clapper. "You're sure about that?"

"As sure as I can be. No one has a sense of time passing. And yet they're aging faster than time is passing outside. I asked a guard, one I recognized. Not much older than me when I first met him. He didn't know the date. Or how old he was, but he looks old. Too old. It's like time . . ." He groped. "Inside the castle, we forget time, but they age fast. I believe their lives are being sucked out of them."

Senrid had felt all day as if he were on a rough ride, but Jilo's words sent him tumbling over the metaphorical horse's head. "He what?" He'd already known that there was some kind of weird time distortion in that castle, but that happened naturally in some places around the world. "That king of yours is using *lives* to recreate a simulacrum of Norsunder-Beyond, right there in that fortress."

Jilo mumbled, "I don't know where to begin to fix it."

Senrid said slowly, "This is way beyond me, too. Way beyond."

"I guess I ought to go." Jilo sighed.

"Wait. Wait." Senrid rubbed his eyes, realized he was trying to rub an awareness into his head that wasn't going to come, and dropped his hands. "Is it okay with you if I bring in someone else? Not about your book. You better hide that thing, and pretend it doesn't exist."

"'Okay.' The Mearsieans say that," Jilo observed, oblivious to the advice about his book; hiding it was too instinctive. He blinked rapidly, then said, "Who?"

"Her name is Hibern. She knows more than I do about lighter wards, though I suspect she won't know what to do about yours. But maybe she knows the right archives to search in." When Jilo shrugged, Senrid dug around on his desk, and recovered his notecase.

He found a paper inside, scanned it—from some Colendi stranger about Clair's alliance—and tossed it to the desk to be dealt with some other time. He scribbled a note to Hibern and sent it.

"What is that thing?" Jilo asked, pointing to the case.

Senrid stared in surprise. "You mean to tell me, you've managed to discover a pocket Norsunder, and survived, but you've never seen a notecase for letter transfer?"

Jilo said, "Who would I write to?"

Senrid laughed.

Hibern listened in stomach-cramping shock, and remembered Erai-Yanya saying, *I know you prefer to solve things on your own. I'm that way myself, or I wouldn't be living alone in this ruin. But some problems are beyond you, and recognizing that is part of solving. If that happens, Tsauderei explicitly told me that you could contact him any time. Promise me you'll remember.* And Hibern had said, *I promise.*

She looked up. "I think I know what to do."

"Over to you," Senrid said.

Hibern gave Jilo a doubtful glance. He looked like he'd been sick for months. "Jilo, shall we go to someone who might be able to advise us?"

All he cared about was the possibility of help. "Yes."

She didn't think he had the strength to perform transfer magic, so she spelled the transfer token she always carried for an emergency, gave it to Jilo, then fixed on the Destination Erai-Yanya had taught her for reaching Tsauderei.

This Destination was located far from the valley where Tsauderei lived. It was a first line of magical defense. Their pending arrival alerted the old mage, who passed them through his secret wards, and permitted them direct access.

All they experienced was an extra-long and bumpy transfer, then they found themselves standing on a grassy patch outside of a round stone cottage.

Tsauderei opened the door. "Come in, come in," he began, then halted when his magical sense, honed over a lifetime, sustained a tidal wave of toxic dark magic.

The source was the pallid, slumping black-haired boy in his mid-teens, who stood next to Erai-Yanya's student Hibern. Tsauderei spoke swiftly, activating several protections, which caused a startled, uneasy glance from Hibern. The boy just stood there wanly, looking as if a strong breeze would topple him.

Hibern gazed at Tsauderei in question. "Erai-Yanya is gone. Out of contact. She said I should bring emergencies to you. I think this is one." She repeated Senrid's words.

Tsauderei's sense of immediate alarm diminished slightly, but by no means did he relax.

As for Jilo, he was still struggling against transfer reaction. Words jabbered over his head as he gazed at a tall, thin old geezer who at first reminded him unpleasantly of Wan-Edhe. As the transfer reaction slowly dissipated, he recognized that the only characteristics the two had in common were white hair uncut for decades, a tall, thin form, the corrugated face of age, and the old-fashioned robe, popular all over the southern continent a century ago, like beards.

But where Wan-Edhe, with his protuberant, mad stare, had been unkempt, often wearing the same robe for years, this Tsauderei dressed in fine velvet with embroidery at the cuffs and hem, and his beard was clean and braided. In one ear he wore a diamond drop that sparkled with deep lights within, probably magical. His eyes were alert, thick brows quirked at a sardonic angle.

Tsauderei thought rapidly. Chwahirsland and its problems were far beyond his reach, or understanding. The sense of dangerous magic permeating this Jilo so disturbed him he had no idea what to say, so he decided that nothing was safest. "Thank you, Hibern," he said when she finished. "You did the right thing. I'll take it from here."

Hibern stared. Just like that, she'd been dismissed. She wanted to protest. If she'd been talking to Erai-Yanya, she would have protested. But she didn't know Tsauderei well enough, and his reputation was daunting. So she said, "I'd like to learn what happens, and how."

"So you shall," Tsauderei promised, and thinking that it was best to get Jilo out there as soon as possible, leaned forward to touch the boy's scrawny arm in the worn black sleeve.

Transfer wrenched Jilo once again. When he came out of it, black spots swimming before his eyes, he tried to blink them away, and discovered that he was shivering. He seemed to be on another mountain plateau, and next to Tsauderei stood another man, this one huge and powerfully built, with a thick, curly black beard and long black hair.

Jilo's head ached. Though the black spots had faded, the mental fireflies were back, each thought flaring and flying wildly, making it nearly impossible to connect one to the next. He knew that Tsauderei was important. He was Wan-Edhe's enemy. His name was in The Book. That did not necessarily make him Jilo's ally.

Jilo tried to blink the blur from his vision as he took in his surroundings. He sat in the middle of a grassy space in front of a sturdy cottage, high on a cliff. In the hazy distance, meandering streams and canals of gleaming blue stitched farmland in rich shades of gold and green. This could not be any part of soil-poor, parched Chwahirsland, and yet the wind from the west brought familiar scents of old stone, dust, rusty metal, moss.

He was subliminally aware of Tsauderei speaking in a low, rapid voice to Curly Beard, who stepped close and bent down, elbows out, huge rough-palmed hands on his thighs. He peered into Jilo's face.

Jilo's limbs tingled unpleasantly as life returned. He glanced southward at the farmland as he struggled to get up. "Where is that?"

One of those strong hands took hold of his upper arm and lifted him to his feet. Though his body felt heavier than stone, and far more unwieldy, Curly Beard seemed to expend no effort, as if Jilo were as light as duck down.

"That, my boy, is Colend. To be precise, yonder land westward is the duchy of Altan, and there, eastward, lies Alarcansa, two of the greatest jewels in the Colendi crown. The targets of your ancestors, and your king, many times over. And to the north lies the Land of the Chwahir. We are perched on a cliff in the mountains between."

"Border," Jilo murmured, trying to blink away the blur.

"I think he's confused," Tsauderei said from the side, where he sat on a stone bench. "Perhaps you ought to show him."

Curly Beard chuckled, the sound resonating in that mighty chest like a rockfall. "We can call it the border, but it really isn't. Do you see the actual border?"

His hand had not loosened its grip on Jilo. He found himself swung around, so he faced north, and the ranks of mountains, like serrated knives rising up and up. "What do you see?"

"Mountains." Jilo tried to swallow, but his throat was too dry, and the lingering effect of transfer magic made him slightly dizzy.

"What do you see in those mountains? Look closely."

Jilo blinked harder. Gradually detail resolved: the barrenness of the stone, blurred by rare, twisted trees, black with age and . . .

He drew in an unsteady breath. "That's the border."

"Yes. Burdened with magic so strong that very little survives. You know what an Emras Defense is, right?"

A flare of resentment burned through Jilo. He'd sought help, not this interrogation, or this iron hand gripping him like he was about to be tossed off the cliff. "Of course I do. You learn of it in your first year. Strongest ward in dark magic. Spell fashioned some four centuries ago."

"Strongest because it finds the exact balance between light and dark, so *this* doesn't happen." Curly Beard's free hand swept northward. "But your king scorned that balance, and has spent decades layering more wards over wards. One of the virtues, if you can call it that, of your dark magic." And when Jilo didn't answer, he turned his head. "Tsauderei, your turn. Show him."

Tsauderei held up some kind of cloth. Jilo couldn't make out the details, as his vision was still blurry, but he suspected it didn't matter what it was, as Tsauderei said slowly, "This is a piece of my clothing, with a personal ward over it. As far as the border magic is concerned, this shawl is Tsauderei."

He laid it down, put a transfer token on it, and whispered over it. Then he glanced up. "I am now sending my substitute to your capital city."

The shawl vanished. Light flashed over the mountains to the north, followed by a thunderous *voom!* Hot, metallic air buffeted Jilo's face, stirring Tsauderei's long hair and beard.

Then, as Jilo gawked, fire rolled from mountaintop to mountaintop in both directions. The firestorm lasted no more than a heartbeat or two, but when it vanished, it left a thousand tiny fires as the twisted trees, scraggly bushes, and tough grasses burned to ash.

Jilo stared, appalled. "The entire border?" he said in his own language, knowing that they understood—that in fact their version of the Universal Language Spell was better than the dark magic equivalent.

"No," Curly Beard said, letting go of Jilo. "But only because Wan-Edhe was a single person, and hadn't the time to traverse your entire border laying that spell, and also run the kingdom. The wards are worse over the old roads, and lines of transfer to your capital. But as you can see, it's bad enough. If anyone had been on the road below that point, they would be dead. No matter who they were, which includes Chwahir patrollers."

Jilo finally managed to swallow. "That's terrible."

"Yet you've done nothing about it."

"I didn't know."

"How long have you been in Narad?"

The blur was getting worse. Jilo covered his face with his hands. "Time isn't the same," he mumbled through his fingers. "Why I asked for help." He sat down abruptly. The dizziness had also worsened.

Curly Beard hunkered down to peer into Jilo's face. "So

you went for help to another user of dark magic, a boy who also answers to no master. Who holds the throne of a large and powerful kingdom. If your two kingdoms weren't almost at opposite ends of the continent, I should think half the monarchs around you both would be quite alarmed."

Jilo stared at the harsh-boned face revolving gently before him. "I, I, I . . ." He shut his mouth and took a deep breath. Again, anger steadied him, enough for him to get the words out: "The first time. I asked Clair of the Mearsieans for help."

As soon as the words were out, he braced for the "Who?" but instead, Curly Beard put his fists on his hips as he exclaimed, "Ah! Clair? Indeed! I shall ask her. Go on."

"She took me to Senrid. He helped me. Twice. When I found Wan-Edhe's hidden chamber . . ." He swallowed again, an action that took concentration. "It's bleeding their lives out. To make that chamber. Slow time."

Curly Beard's heavy black brows shot upward, and he sat back. "Very well. Very well." He laid his hand on his chest. "This is no easy problem to solve. But there might be some ways to begin."

"Who are you?"

The big man laughed, white teeth flashing in the blue-black beard. "You may call me Rosey."

"Rosey," Jilo repeated, and glared at the man, hatred giving him enough strength to fling back his head. During those terrible days when he'd spied on the Mearsieans in order to find out where their underground hideout was, he'd heard references over and over to 'Rosey.' "You're the one who rescued the Mearsieans from Wan-Edhe."

"When I could. When I could. I've had to be very careful to avoid my real identity being discovered by your former king. He's gotten close enough as it is. Now." Jilo was so weary he was not surprised when Rosey shifted to perfect Chwahir, command mode, captain to flatfoot. The language, the mode, reached back into Jilo's earliest memories, and he found it oddly comforting as Rosey said, "You are going to march into that cottage, and lie down. You'll find an extra bed in the loft. It's clean. There's water in the pitcher. When you're slept out, we will talk. Go."

Jilo wobbled inside, clutching the book tightly against his stomach as he tipped his head back and gazed up the ladder to the loft. Those ten or twelve rungs seemed to stretch up forever. He forced each hand and foot to move, but it took all his strength, and finally he fell onto a low bed.

The moment he caught his breath, he took the book out of his shirt and checked the names, though he was fairly certain he'd memorized them all. Yes. Tsauderei was there, near the top. As he'd expected, there was no listing for 'Rosey.'

He ran his gaze down the other names. Detlev: nothing new.

Siamis: nothing new.

Prince Kessler: Norsunder Base, Norsunder Base, Onekhaer, Mardgar, Imar, Everon, Norsunder Base. He'd been moving around a lot since the last time Jilo had looked. And when had that been?

Even thinking about time made Jilo's mind swim unpleasantly. He blinked, and stared down at the book again. What did those spaces between the Norsunder Base entries mean? He remembered what Senrid had said about the named targets possibly going out of the world. Wan-Edhe would not care what they were doing somewhere so far away that he would not feel threatened.

So much of the book was useless. And yet. Jilo clutched it against him, fighting for concentration. Hide it? No. The medallion he wore with its wards might mask the magic, but if Jilo tried hiding the book in this cottage, Rosey was sure to sense its magic. Oh. Old habit: the hollowed tree where he had kept his drawing supplies, back in the days under Kwenz. Drawing was strictly forbidden, one of the many, many forbidden things. So he'd sneaked it.

That tree lay outside of the old Shadowland, so it ought still to be there.

With the last of his strength, Jilo transferred the book to the hidey-hole.

Then he fell back and dropped into sleep.

It had never occurred to Jilo how difficult for others it might be to fashion magical hidey-holes and transfer objects to them. He'd needed it, found a way to learn how to do it, and did it. Such was the pattern of his life.

Rosey—whose name was Mondros—and Tsauderei had watched Jilo slowly climb to the loft, his thin figure bowed as an old man's. As soon as he vanished up the ladder, they spoke in Ancient Sartoran, which had never been added into the Universal Language Spell.

"That horror did not seem feigned," Mondros said.

Tsauderei didn't really know Mondros that well. Mages were notoriously reclusive; you didn't dedicate your life to magic without being somewhat solitary. But he knew less about Mondros than any of the other powerful mages he had dealt with over the years.

He did not understand what drove Mondros to dedicate his life to fighting Wan-Edhe from a distance, as the man was not a Chwahir, but he respected Mondros for it. Everyone else seemed inclined to overlook Chwahirsland, and forget its ancient problems.

He sat down on the stone bench in Mondros's tiny garden. "My predecessor's records indicate two things: that Wan-Edhe of the Chwahir was not much older than this boy when he made his first kill. In defense, yes. And some records even seem to hint that when he started out, he meant well. By the Chwahir, I hasten to say."

"It's true, all of it." Mondros dropped down beside him. "And so, what? Do you want me to go up there and knife that boy in his sleep? How do you justify that?"

Tsauderei gave a snort of disgust. "Of course not. But I mislike this pattern."

"Jilo turning to Senrid Montredaun-An for help? What's the truth about him? His grandfather had a terrible reputation, and so did the oldest son, but the middle son was supposed to have been fairly benign. For a Marloven."

"I was an assistant mage at the border parley when the grandfather was forced by an alliance of all his neighbors to accept the treaty," Tsauderei said, looking back down the years, then shaking his head. "If the grandson is anything like him, we can expect nothing but trouble. But that's the future. Right now, I don't like the way these children are turning to one another, and not to us."

Mondros, he noted, did not ask him to define that 'us.' "You said Erai-Yanya's prentice brought Jilo to you," Mondros said.

"She did." Tsauderei sat back on the bench. "But not because of established procedure. This particular problem seemed beyond her reach. Let's consider what we just heard about your young Mearsiean, Clair. Why didn't she report this Jilo and his actions to you, who saved her from Wan-Edhe's vindictive pettiness? Why didn't she go to Murial, her own blood relation?"

Mondros pointed a thick finger. "Did *you* always turn to the elders? I know I didn't."

"In matters of great import, I did. As did Evend. And even Igkai, who I believe is the most reclusive of all of us. We followed established procedure. Not that we didn't make mistakes. Plenty of them. My point is, we find ourselves with a number of children in key positions. Many of them smart and well educated. And impatient of guidance."

Mondros sighed. "You see Detlev's hand here."

"Possibly," Tsauderei said. "A poke here, a threat there, an experiment over yonder, then fading back to watch a tragedy unfold. That's his usual style, the rare times he comes out of Norsunder."

"That we know of," Mondros said.

"True. So let's look at what we know of Detlev's latest exploits. We know Senrid was Detlev's prisoner during Siamis's enchantment, before the morvende sent Rel into Norsunder Base to rescue one of their friends, and discovered him there. Did whatever happened to Senrid there make him even less trusting of outsiders than Marlovens are reputed to be?"

Mondros's gaze had shifted sideways, and his hands tightened on his knees. But at Tsauderei's question, he sat back and loosened his grip. "You're right. If there is one thing Detlev's known for, it's rarity of visits, and something always happens, usually wide-reaching and devastating. But even Detlev could not have foreseen the emergence of this Dena Yeresbeth after four millennia. That desperate search before Siamis launched his enchantment in '36 indicates Norsunder had no more notion of its re-emergence than we did. I think it took them as much by surprise as it did us."

Tsauderei was silent a long time before he said, "Dena Yeresbeth." His tone made the words a curse. All his life, it seemed that he'd no sooner gain some understand of the world and how to keep it safe from Norsunder, than some new, larger, more sinister threat would appear. This one seemed the worst one yet because the only people who truly understood it were Lilith the Guardian, whose appearance was ephemeral at best—and the Norsundrian Host of Lords, with Detlev as their minion.

Mondros got to his feet. "Well, that's yet another problem for the future. Right now, I have this boy upstairs. The first thing to be determined is if I'll trust him enough to send him back with some carefully fashioned spells. Time bindings using lives! Wan-Edhe's depredations were even worse than I'd thought. If Jilo really does intend to loosen those deadly wards from within Narad, then we'll know how to proceed."

"Good," Tsauderei said, with feeling. "This one is all yours."

Chapter Ten

WHEN Senrid showed up in Bereth Ferian the day after Hibern took Jilo away, he made no reference to whatever had caused him to end Liere's previous visit so abruptly in the middle of the night. And she, remembering those vivid, horrifying images he didn't know he'd shared, was too afraid to ask.

"Hibern has relatives who knew my mother," he said to Liere as if they had parted the day before, and not a couple of months ago.

Though his voice sounded the same as ever, the quick flex of his hands, the pulse of horror he couldn't quite mask on the mental plane, made her middle tighten with dread. But all Senrid said was, "I guess since I've managed to stay alive so far, or maybe because they wanted to get rid of the stuff and reclaim their cellar, they sent me some art things that my mother had brought from her home country. I remember you liked the blocks. Want to help me sort through this art and see what to keep and what to stick in our cellar?"

"Shouldn't you ask somebody who knows about art?" Liere asked doubtfully.

"Nah." Senrid made that quick motion, his palm down, hand flat, as though shoving something away. "I don't care

what some blathering expert on art likes. I have to look at
the stuff, not them. So it makes more sense to go through
and find what I like. But you have a good eye, I noticed that
before. You'll be able to tell me why I like it. Or not, if you
don't want to."

"Oh, it sounds like fun, if you put it that way," she exclaimed.

"Good! And Hibern is bringing the Queen of Sartor to
our next tutoring session. They want to learn how to make
mind-shields, and asked if you'd teach them."

When Liere began to tense up, Senrid grinned. "Atan—
Hibern says she wants to be called that, instead of The
Great and Mighty Queen Yustnesveas Landis the 152nd of
Ancient Sartor, or whatever her number is. 'Yust-ness-vey-
ass!' No wonder she wants to be called Atan. Who wouldn't,
saddled with a load like that? Anyway, she's my age. And
was raised in a cave, or some such thing."

Liere's doubt turned to perplexity, and Senrid said
quickly, "Liere, think about it, would anyone really come to
Marloven Hess in a lot of pompous state, spouting speeches
and old poetry that nobody can understand, or whatever
these Sartorans and Colendi do when kings go calling?" He
made a face. "Hah. Come to think of it, I don't think any
kings or queens have ever made any kind of visit here, state
or not, unless they were wrangled into marrying one of my
ancestors. That would be princesses, since nobody ever
wanted any foreign princes snouting in."

Liere's tension eased slightly, and he said, "The cook
even ordered more of that cocoa to make hot chocolate,
just for you."

Liere brightened. "Oh, that is so kind!"

They transferred to Marloven Hess.

And for the rest of the day, as she adjusted to the heat
of summer, she hugged to herself the delight over knowing
that the cook had ordered hot chocolate. For her.

By the end of dinner, she had come full circle to wondering if another word for 'belonging' was 'expectation.' Was
she turning into one of those spoiled princesses everyone
hated, who expected special treatment? And she wasn't
even a real princess!

And of course, by then, late at night, as she sat in her

room trying to read in spite of eyes burning with exhaustion, as Senrid tended to his kingdom affairs, she fell into the old battle against the weakness, the futility of emotion.

She tried wearily to focus on the book she'd brought, which was the next on the shelves she'd been toiling through. And she wasn't comprehending it at all. She blinked at the page. No. Not one word. She'd been moving her gaze over it while feeling sorry for herself.

Aware of that, she sat up straight, and settled the book firmly on her lap. Because of that stupid emotion, she would read twice as long the next day, and give up her ride.

Stupid stupid stupid emotions—worthless, useless, weak emotions. From now on, anything she discovered herself looking forward to, she would cancel.

She firmly turned back to the beginning. This would be useful. This would train her stupid, weak, useless brain.

Rhythms in Soil Richness.

In the north meadow, shall we ever seed with corn, but in the south meadow, shall three-fold the rhythm be: after summer's heat shall be wheat, followed by a spring of sprouts, followed thence by a season of openness to birds of the air . . .

The second reading really did go easier. She was well into the third year—fifteen pages!—when Senrid returned from wherever he'd been.

"Keriam keeps telling me things my father said, and they sound good, but when I really think about what they mean, how to use them, I don't get it." He sighed and dropped cross-legged onto the other end of the window seat, where Liere sat with her books. "Like the difference between strength and power." He stopped there, aware of her distracted attention.

She was thinking, *More Marloven stuff.* She knew she should take an interest, but it was so hard to, because she knew she'd never need any of it. *Like old-fashioned harvests?* she taunted herself.

"Fenis Senelac is down in the riding ring," Senrid said. "It's a full moon night, and the heat has finally gone. Perfect for riding."

Liere clapped the thin book onto the fat lexicon of Ancient Sartoran, and leaped up happily.

Then she remembered her promise. She sat back down firmly, opened the ancient book, and said, "I can't go riding. I didn't complete my studying."

Senrid looked surprised. "Studying?"

Liere tapped the book. "My project."

"But you can read later. She's got a horse saddled."

Liere shook her head. "I didn't study earlier. I need the discipline."

Senrid sighed.

Liere forced herself to breathe, to calm herself. Rational discourse! "You've got discipline. I need to work on mine."

Senrid eyed Liere. She sat there in the window seat, her fingers gripping that old book from Bereth Ferian's library, her cuticles ragged. Senrid glanced down at the book. Ancient Sartoran. About farming, of all things.

"If I could go riding any time I wanted," he said, "I would."

Liere looked down, her mouth unhappy. Presented with the top of Liere's head, Senrid noticed that she'd taken a knife to her hair again; it was more ragged than ever. He knew better than to argue, though he thought it was crazy to force herself to read every book in that library, starting with the first shelf and moving through every single tome, just because that sounded orderly. Likewise forcing herself to learn Ancient Sartoran without knowing the modern language first.

When she got like that, he'd discovered, the only way to get her to act like a normal person was to ask her to go with him when he did fun things.

"How about if you lay that aside, and let's try tackling an easier lesson in Ancient Sartoran? It's more like code breaking, then, and less a toil of having to look up every second word," he said.

Liere set aside the dusty tomes, angry with herself for having revealed whatever it was that got Senrid to say that. She would triple the study time on the farming book the next day.

If only she had his sense of discipline, and his lack of stupid emotion. No, he had emotions. She'd seen him angry, ashamed, afraid. Hurt.

But he didn't let any of it out, it didn't get in the *way*. He got things *done*.

Atan anticipated her visit to Hibern's homeland with a pleasure that was the more intense for its being a secret. The more delving she'd done into her ancestors' private archives, the more often she'd discovered far-reaching state matters turning on personalities and private actions—abductions at one point numbering high on the list.

Tsauderei, in his efforts to educate Atan on Sartoran matters when Sartor and its archives were beyond reach, had initiated her into the histories written by scribes. She really liked scribe histories. Most seemed more even-handed than official court histories, and some scribal memoirs gave hints of the sort of thing she was doing, finding ways around the complication of protocol and tradition.

She was going to keep using her free hour for . . . freedom.

As she paced her study waiting for the bells that would herald Hibern's appearance, she wondered why it was that secret things were so much fun. And the idea that she would be the first Sartoran ruler to set foot in a kingdom depicted as full of villains made the fun that much more fun.

Hibern had promised her that Senrid wasn't a villain. At least, he was trying not to be one, though he'd been raised to be. All that made him even more interesting. Atan imagined someone even taller than Rel, more imposing, except blond, because the records indicated that the Marloven forebears were Venn, and everybody knew the Venn were mostly tall and light-haired and very good at war.

When she and Hibern reached Marloven Hess at last, Atan found herself looking down at a boy whose only resemblance to her inner image lay in the light hair. His short, light-boned form reminded her a lot of Hinder, except his quick, nervy movements were totally unlike Hin's casual drift, and there was a hint of more muscle in the bland white sleeves of his shirt and in the dark-covered legs above the riding boots.

Senrid stared up at a girl who was apparently even taller than Hibern, or maybe the effect was caused by the up-and-down effect of the purple silk edging to her robe, which extended all the way to the floor. Marloven formal House tunics always ended at the boot tops.

As Hibern performed the introductions, and Atan took in the little figure half-hiding behind Senrid, once again amazement flooded her. This frail little creature was the famous Sartora? The thin, unkempt child with the wide honey-colored gaze looked like she would have blown away at the first puff of wind, and yet she'd stood up to the evil Siamis!

Liere reddened. "Would you like a tour?"

"I would indeed, thank you," Atan said.

Liere, not Senrid, led the way.

Atan's third impression was that the place smelled awful: the warm, humid summer air brought the distinct tang of horse. Nobody here seemed to know a thing about air or light flow.

They walked past endless rooms of plain sand-colored stone. The monotony was broken along some halls by plaster reliefs in subtle shades of silver and gray depicting flying raptors and running horses. She counted one tapestry, and from the way it was wrinkled, it had apparently just been removed from storage and mounted on this bare wall at the top of a landing.

Senrid hung back during the tour. Before their arrival, remembering the discomfiture he'd experienced at the disgust with which CJ of the Mearsieans had described his home, he'd said to Liere, "Why don't you show her around? You'll know better than I what non-Marlovens will want to see."

So Liere did. She was nervous at first, then quietly indignant at the drift of Atan's thoughts. She knew she shouldn't be listening, but she could scarcely help it. They came here to learn the mind-shield, she told herself as they walked downstairs. This was why.

While Liere talked to Atan, Senrid spoke low-voiced to Hibern in their own language. "What happened to Jilo?"

"Tsauderei took him somewhere."

"And?"

"Don't know. Tsauderei's note to me that night only said that Jilo was with a mage who could help him. Maybe there's nothing more to tell. But I'll get Erai-Yanya to ask when she returns, if you need to know who, and what's going on."

Senrid scowled at the floor. "Is it you or me they don't trust?"

"They?"

"Tsauderei and whoever else he's drawn in." At Hibern's skeptical expression, Senrid muttered, "Tell me if I'm wrong, but don't these adult mages usually love nothing better than to lecture us about our ignorance?"

Hibern opened her hand. "I've been studying at the mage school in Bereth Ferian while Erai-Yanya is gone, and they haven't heard anything about Jilo. Arthur would hear if anyone was talking about a king our age that far advanced in dark magic. So maybe Tsauderei isn't talking to anyone."

Senrid said, "Where is your tutor? Seems she's been gone a long time."

"She was here, then went back to our sister world, Geth-deles."

"The ocean one? Why?"

"Norsunder is doing something suspicious there."

Senrid drew in a sharp breath. That fit the holes in the transfers of the head snakes in Jilo's book, he was thinking, but he didn't say anything.

When they reached the bottom of the stairs, Liere looked back inquiringly.

Senrid glanced at Atan. "State chambers, maybe?"

Liere led on. When they reached the throne room, Liere pointed inside the massive double doors. "This is where the Marloven jarls gather for Convocation at New Year's Week."

She observed Atan's gaze lifting to the banners on the walls, and the crossed swords below, with other artifacts of the Marloven past. She sensed Atan waiting, and added, "I don't know what those swords are for, or what those crown-like things are."

"Helms." Senrid stayed back in the shadows, watching. "Commanders' helms. Worn at specific battles."

"And those must be their swords?" Atan asked politely.

"Yes and no. Those are surrendered swords. From the defeated commander, some of them crossed by the triumphant commander's sword."

Atan wasn't interested in the swords, helms, or banners. She was more interested in Senrid. He didn't sound all that bloodthirsty, nor was his tone gloating or bragging.

Atan wondered what having these things on the walls here meant to Marlovens. Perhaps these disgusting objects were intended to scare the jarls into obedience. Either that or these objects were supposed to fire the Marlovens with the desire to go out, win battles, and have their own banners and steel stuck up on that stone wall. She hoped that their own homes weren't as ugly as this chamber.

"Very fine," she said in her first-circle voice.

"We're done here." Senrid ducked through the door, his boot heels ringing a quick tattoo on the stone. He was thoroughly unsettled by how much Atan's opinion mattered to him. Why should it? But it did. As if she were inspecting his entrails and finding them wanting, like a suspicious fish laid out at the marketplace. "Rest is the same," he said over his shoulder. "And you came for a purpose, not a hike through my castle."

The others followed, Hibern suspecting and Liere knowing that something had disturbed Senrid.

Liere was glad when they reached the study and Senrid said briskly, "You came here to learn mind-shields. You're better at teaching mind-shields than I am, Liere. Why don't I see about your favorite drink? Atan, do you like hot chocolate, too?"

"Certainly," Atan said in some surprise, and was more surprised when Senrid shot out the door. "What just happened?" Atan asked Hibern.

As they sat down in Senrid's study, Hibern turned a questioning look to Liere, who was not going to tell the Queen of Sartor that she was leaking thoughts.

Liere said, "Teaching you about the mind-shield will be very boring for Senrid to hear again, since he already knows it." She had been through this explanation enough times with the northern mage school, Arthur, Erai-Yanya, and anyone else who asked, that she could teach it fairly swiftly: building a wall in the mind, seeing the wall, concentrating on keeping thoughts behind the wall.

She paused to demonstrate each level, and then said, "That's it."

Atan gazed in surprise. "Really? That's all? I thought this would be a first lesson, that it would take months. Even years. And maybe hurt."

Liere's face turned a mottled red as she tried not to laugh. She said, "Next comes practice. That takes longer. Until it's habit."

"Ah. Of course." Atan nodded. "So tell me this, either of you. Those swords on the wall downstairs. Do those sustain some hidden idea, or a version of loyalty, or oaths, century after century? Hibern, you told me that written records don't often survive one change of king to the next."

Hibern said, "I think you could say that they're a symbol of pride, and power. Order. Much like the statuary in your city. The ones people talk about, I mean, not the ones they ignore."

"And yet those weapons aren't beautiful to look at." Atan raised a hand in the Sartoran gesture of apology. "I ask only to be taught. Do Marlovens look upon those swords as art, or are they symbols to remind them of the battles, the stories behind them?"

"The second," Hibern said. "Stories are important. And while Marlovens don't have written records, we do have ballads." She winced at that 'we' slipping out, because it always brought back her father's thick, angry voice. *Get out.*

"About smiting enemies?"

"About honor and privilege, including the honor, the privilege to go to battle, to die, for the—" *glory* "—preservation of the kingdom." She heard a memory echo of the Andahi Lament, and the back of her neck tightened.

"In Sartor we would call that duty, but no one sings about fighting to keep peace," Atan said, then added quickly, "At least now, they don't. We do have some fairly martial songs in the past." She sounded apologetic, like someone admitting to an error in taste.

Atan studied Liere. "And you, I think you're from Imar?"

Liere ducked her head, her smile vanishing.

Atan gestured apology once again, knowing she had erred, but not how. "I just wanted to ask, do you feel the same as the Marlovens? Are you going to live here?" She bent closer. "What brings you here?"

Liere said, "Senrid." She twisted her fingers together. "He's my first friend. My real one."

"What does that mean, 'real one'?" Atan asked.

In spite of the lessons, Liere was the only one whose mind-shield was in place. She tried not to listen, but the inexact nature of the Universal Language Spell distracted her; she could 'hear' whispers of meaning all around the translated words, and had to concentrate to shut it out. Senrid had told her she really needed to learn modern Sartoran first, the language people actually used. Discomfort tightened her middle, because she knew her wish to master Ancient Sartoran was in part a wish to truly fight ignorance and in part to merely appear less ignorant.

Perhaps that was really a wish to show off.

Unaware of how long she sat in reverie, she finally looked up to discover the older girls waiting. "Senrid never called me Sartora."

Atan stared in surprise. "You don't like that?"

"No. I do not," Liere said, her voice low and unsteady. "I am not Sartora. I am not a world rescuer. It was all an accident. At least, mostly—it was just that I was the only one who could use the dyr, which was a very common thing in the days of Ancient Sartor, so I'm told. And so many people helped me. And I don't live here. I visit Senrid, and he lives here, so here I am. I don't have a home anymore. I . . ." She heard her father's derisive voice about whiners, and how much people despised them, and closed her mouth.

Atan leaned forward. "Sar—ah, Liere, if you want a home, anyone would give you one. Don't you see what being Sartora means? You can have anything you want."

Liere eyed Atan. "No, not really. They call me a queen, but it's only in a symbolic way. I don't have a crown, or an army, or guards, or a treasury. And I don't want them! That beautiful palace in Bereth Ferian doesn't belong to me. It's a place where the mages put me. You might not understand, because you are a real queen. *You* can have anything you want."

Atan said, "I can't have my family back. I can't command Colend to return the Music Festival, which might sound silly to you. It did to me, at first, until I understood how ashamed all the adults are, the people born a century ago, who came back into the world to discover we're a hundred years behind everyone else. The world didn't stop to wait for Sartor . . . oh, never mind all that. I can work on those things, and I will. But you, you're completely free. You can go where you want."

"I can't have everything I want, either."

Atan smiled. "I think the world would give it to you if it could."

Liere bit her nail, then snatched her hand down as if she'd been slapped. She wriggled in her chair, head lowered. "Maybe they would. Now. Until Siamis comes back and I won't be able to do what I did before. How angry will they be that I can't be Sartora, the Girl Who Saved the World, again?"

Senrid had been listening from outside the door. He could hear how close to tears Liere was, even if the others couldn't. He could sense Atan's puzzlement, her striving to understand, and Hibern's uneasiness (because she'd forgotten her mind-shield yet again).

Time to intervene. "The only good thing about Ancient Sartoran Norsundrians is that they usually let a few centuries pass between their visits," he said as he entered. "Siamis is probably holed up tight, and won't pop up again until our great-grandchildren are old and gray. Hot chocolate coming right behind me."

Hibern and Atan stayed long enough to drink a cup. The conversation was resolutely superficial, and they took their leave shortly after.

As soon as they arrived back in Eidervaen, Atan said, "Did that go as badly as I thought?"

Hibern opened her hands. "I don't know Liere at all. But I've seen her get all tied in knots in that same way. It wasn't you. And I don't know why she does it."

Atan tugged gently on a silken tassel hanging from a hassock. "Art. Do Marlovens see art the way the rest of us do?"

Hibern snorted. "Does everyone else see art exactly the same way? No, don't answer, I know what you meant. I think you could say that the idea of art the way you have it here came late for us. Marlovens didn't have houses until they took over the Iascan castles. They didn't even know that the Iascans stripped everything out when they left. My ancestors lived with bare stone for ages and ages, but then they were very seldom inside. Still true. Ornaments tend to be badges of triumph. But art, oh, you could say it's in the songs, and in movement: the perfect gait of a horse, perfect form in shooting, the rhythms in the drums, the sparks shooting upward in the sword dance."

Atan's mouth rounded. "I see. Oh, that is so interesting! All right, last question, or rather, observation. Senrid is so short! He looks about nine, but he's too well-spoken for that."

"He's the same age as me." Hibern grinned. "Father quite tall, his mother small, so I'm told. But yes, Marlovens tend to be shorter. Erai-Yanya thinks it's due to the fact that the Marlovens' ancestors took to horses, and the shorter, lighter families thrived. They were just as fierce as the big Venn warriors."

The bell rang then, and Hibern took her leave.

Atan walked out into the hall, breathing deeply. Then she had to laugh at herself when she whiffed the faint, familiar scent of mildew, which had become so familiar she'd forgotten it. But she had noticed on her first tour of the castle. Despite the servants' constant, rigorous efforts to keep everything scrupulously clean, it seemed to be the inevitable consequence of centuries of little change.

If Senrid was ever to come to her palace, would he think it stank?

FOR a couple days, it took all Jilo's strength to walk out of Mondros's cottage.

He made it far enough to drop onto the late-summer grass and gaze down into Colend lying peacefully below. He watched cloud shadows ripple over the land, changing colors to blue tones, then the red-gold reappeared, except for the greens, which brightened with a buttery overlay. The long shadows slowly pulling in then moving eastward fascinated him.

The third day, the impulse to sit there forever and watch the sky and the land faded away. He was aware of a stronger pull, a fretful anxiety impelled by fear.

Mondros called him in to breakfast.

"I walked over the border, to assess the state of Wan-Edhe's wards. There was no time to ride to your capital. I wish there were, and of course I dare not transfer. But as little as I saw impressed me mightily," Mondros said when Jilo sat down. "You have improved things."

"Not much," Jilo mumbled. "Not nearly enough."

"Many senior students couldn't do as much as you have. In fact, I don't know anyone, old or young, who's mastered as much about dark magic wards as you have."

"Had to learn it."

"On the run, so to speak. I'll accept that, but if you really don't want to find yourself turning into a replica of Wan-Edhe, then you had better begin your studies in another direction."

"Which?" Jilo asked.

"Is it not obvious? The land. If you want to help the Chwahir, you will have to understand the relationship between land and magic. This corner of the continent has never been easy. Your Chwahir ancestors set out to enhance, to alter, to influence, to change. Well, all our ancestors did. Sartor as well."

"How do I fix that? Every book I spotted is for extending those spells. I know better than to release them all at once, even if I could."

"Smart boy." Mondros frowned at his pan of crushed olive. It had begun to steam, so he tumbled in the potatoes, garlic, and purple onion that he'd chopped.

The smell opened up a yawning cavern inside of Jilo. He had begun to think of cooking as magic. There were so many similarities.

Mondros shook the pan to even out the ingredients, then jerked a massive thumb over his shoulder at the opposite wall of the cottage, which was packed, floor to ceiling, with books. "You're going to have to begin studying light magic. And while you do that, you must begin the process of reversing that benighted sinkhole of evil in your castle in Narad. We will address that. Today, begin with the fundamentals. I set some books on the work table."

Jilo inhaled the delicious breakfast. With the return of energy came commensurate anxiety, proliferating questions. "Maybe I ought to start now."

Mondros could see the fret, and signs of resentment, in the narrow-eyed, speculative glances the boy sent his way. He decided to let Jilo guide the talk as he watched for manipulation, the smiler who tells you what you want to hear. He withheld judgment, aware that survival around Wan-Edhe would warp individuals as much as his magic warped the air.

The day passed in study.

As Mondros fried up the trout he'd caught for their supper, he observed Jilo still bent over the rudimentary magic book, the one given to ten-year-olds who thought they might want to become mages. The boy's lank black hair hung down unkempt, half-hiding his flat cheeks, and his shoulder blades poked the back of his shirt, which had lightened to a dull gray. Jilo didn't appear to notice, or maybe it had yet to occur to him he could wear whatever he wanted. That there were other possibilities besides the badly dyed, one-size-fits-all flatfoot-probationer uniform.

A week of hard study passed.

The day came at last when rain on the Colendi side, merely thunder and lightning with no moisture to the north for the parched Chwahir, caused Jilo to say, "I think I ought to go back."

"Very well," Mondros said. "I'm not stopping you."

Jilo's head lifted from its habitual droop. His pale brown eyes met Mondros's, then his gaze dropped again. "That's all?" he said to the scuffed chair leg, and Mondros made a mental note to do some sanding and varnishing. The summer weather, when he moved his furniture outside, was difficult on the wood.

Mondros said, "Did you expect something else?"

"Threats?" One side of Jilo's somber mouth curled up briefly, then he gave in to the resentment that had burned in him for years. "I know I ought not to expect a rescue, like Puddlenose got, time and again, which usually resulted in my being punished. Or Tereneth of Erdrael Danara's rescue."

"Who was a prisoner," Mondros said. "The first was a hostage. You are a Chwahir. Since all my efforts to curb Wan-Edhe's attempts to spread his evil influence had to be done from the outside, how was I to know that you were not in Narad because you wanted to replace Puddlenose as potential errand-boy to Wan-Edhe?"

Jilo could not suppress a recoil of angry revulsion. But he had to admit that from the outside, his compliance might have looked like choice, and not survival.

Mondros saw some of this. "There are two secret exits

in your fortress, one established by a Sonscarna mage-queen centuries ago. That one is magical, and I believe you now know of it."

Jilo shrugged jerkily, remembering what Clair had said. Senrid had used it.

"The other was through the dungeon, a very old tunnel. It's how Prince Kessler escaped, and how Puddlenose was able to get away. You should ask him about it." Mondros put his fists on his knees.

Jilo's chin came up. "He might still think I'm a villain. The Mearsiean girls called me a villain."

Mondros said provocatively, "You did some villainous things, if their stories are true."

"I did what I was told to do. You knew what would happen if I didn't follow orders."

"Always?" Mondros countered.

"Yes . . ." Jilo thought back, and a tide of heat burned up his neck and made his ears itch. "Not always." He scowled. "But that was my life. I didn't see anything else."

"You saw the life Puddlenose and the girls led. It was very different."

"They were Mearsieans."

"And you tried at least once to take it away."

"I wanted to have that life, and taking it away was how it was supposed to go," Jilo retorted.

Mondros gave an encouraging nod. "All right. I'll concede that you existed under a cloud of threat at least as palpable as that cloud under which you once lived. But from a distance, you were beginning to look like Wan-Edhe in training, until he put those spells on you."

"Well, I'm not Wan-Edhe. I don't want to be Wan-Edhe. I can't think of anyone I hate more than Wan-Edhe."

"Yes, everyone hated him. But who are you when you are not hating, Jilo? No, don't tell me. Show me. There are no wards keeping you from transferring."

Jilo transferred out a short time later, carrying a basket of Mondros's delicious food, and a carefully copied scroll of light magic fundamentals under his arm. It didn't occur to him to wonder until later, when he sat down to eat the first item in the basket, why Mondros had been watching over Chwahirsland, when he wasn't a Chwahir.

Late autumn, 4740, Sarendan

Peitar Selenna, king of Sarendan, had looked forward to Atan's next visit for weeks.

He knew that even if Atan did release the Child Spell and miraculously fall in love with him, that would mean two unhappy people, for there was no future for them unless one of them abdicated.

Yet when Atan appeared with tall, handsome Rel, whom Peitar immediately recognized from Lilah's and Atan's descriptions (and the praise didn't seem exaggerated), the pain was quite sharp.

It was a relief when Lilah leaped up, fired with inspiration. "Oh, Rel, would you come and drill our new Sharadan brigade like you did the Sartoran orphans in the forest?"

Peitar watched Rel covertly. There was no roll of the eyes under shuttered lids, no curl of lip, however brief. The only sign that Rel was not overjoyed to be thus summarily taken off was the quick, amused look he sent at Atan, and the swift, secret smile she returned.

But Atan said nothing. Rel smiled at Lilah's hopeful, expectant face, and said, "I'd be glad to." And he walked off with Lilah as if happy to toil in the bitter weather with a group of strangers.

"... and I told them you might come some day, because Atan did promise she would bring you," Lilah Selenna chattered on, proud and excited, as she and Rel walked down the steep hill into the eastern part of Miraleste, the capital of Sarendan.

Fire damage still existed here and there, and rubble-strewn empty lots where houses had once stood, but those were rare. Everything else looked newly constructed, or at least refurbished. Even in the bleak lighting under lowering gray clouds, the city was bright and clean.

"Won't your brigade see me as an interloper?" Rel asked.

"Oh, no, not at *all!* They've heard about what we Rescuers did in Sartor, and they all said, if you ever visit, would you come and show them what you showed the Sartoran

orphans, in case we have to defend ourselves against the
eleveners? I said you would," Lilah finished, her slanted
eyes earnest under puckered brows. "That you didn't think
the Sartorans better than us."

After that, what could Rel say?

The weather was as bitter as to be expected as the year
waned. Maybe none of her orphan brigade would show up.
He tucked his chin down into his fleece-lined coat.

". . . and so the guilds all contributed, and they rebuilt
the burned-out shop where we four hid while being the
Sharadan Brothers, and it's now our headquarters," Lilah
was saying proudly. "Sometimes Bren comes and does ex-
ercises with them, when he's in the city. Innon has, too."

Rel glanced down at Lilah's friendly face. She still
looked like a rust-haired, stocky boy. "I thought Innon was
noble-born. Doesn't Derek mind?"

"Derek likes Innon. He worked for the revolution."
Lilah rushed on, "And Derek knows all about you, and that
you aren't a noble, and he said he would like to meet you.
I wish he was here, but Peitar sent him on a mission. Derek
is Peitar's most trusted person. Besides me. And Tsauderei," Lilah finished as they turned down a narrow alley
with newly laid brickwork instead of cobblestones, the
buildings neat.

"All the locals, mostly our age, pitched in to rebuild.
Here we are," Lilah finished.

Rel's hopes sank when they passed through a narrow
gate into a newly flagged yard crammed with shivery, blue-
lipped youth.

They took one look at Rel's size, and Lilah's proud grin,
and sent up a cheer.

So Rel fell into his old routine, working them until they
were sweating. All the while he wondered what Atan,
Peitar, and Hibern were talking about during Atan's precious free hour that he was missing.

In the palace, Hibern began talking about an interesting
book she'd discovered in the northern mage school archive.
Peitar half-listened while he analyzed the physical sensation of sharp disappointment and regret.

How stupid it was to think that the Child Spell would
keep Atan—or her friend—from experiencing the emo-

tions of attraction. These things were not like following a recipe: the spell froze you at whatever age you were when you performed it, but it did not stop your mind from working. In that single quick gaze between Atan and Rel he sensed a natural turning to one another. They might never have kissed. Either or both might not even be consciously aware of their feelings. But they were there.

"Don't you think, Peitar?" Atan asked, and Peitar hastily recollected the thread of discourse, and joined in.

The hour passed far too swiftly, as it always did, from history to historical people to who wrote about famous people to ideas about justice. The discussion turned into friendly debate as they tried to hammer out exactly what 'justice' meant.

"That's one of the reasons why I am glad of my council, constraining as I find them," Atan said earnestly. "They still see justice clearer than I do. I listen, I feel for both sides, they decide, they explain why, later, and I say 'Oh-h-h-h, I did not see that.'"

"Perhaps you didn't interpret it that way," Hibern suggested. "One thing I've learned reading records, everyone sounds reasonable when they explain why they did something. Then you consider *what* they did, and you get the sick feeling." She made a fist and lightly struck her middle.

"And so it is, sitting in on justice." Peitar spoke in a low, ruminative voice, thin hands clasped, long dark lashes shuttering his eyes as he gazed sightlessly at his hands. "There are always two sides, sometimes three, which makes it even more difficult to find a compromise that fulfills the expectations of all parties. If the king has to make a judgment against one when there is no compromise, that party might go away feeling betrayed by what is supposed to be royal justice. The emotional price is one the king pays. It should be that way, or we risk becoming—"

The distant city bells rang.

Atan said, "Peitar?"

He looked up, and shook his head. "I lost the thread. I was blathering. It wasn't worth following."

"The emotional price," Hibern said, thinking of Senrid.

"You're in danger of becoming a tyrant?" Atan prompted teasingly, disturbed by his mood; she couldn't define it, but sensed somberness in the subtle tensing of his shoulders, his hands, his high, intelligent forehead. "But wouldn't a tyrant perpetrate injustice on whim?"

Peitar's hand lifted, palm out, and his smile twisted. "It matters not. I suspect I'm beginning to sound pompous."

Atan jumped up. "Not at all, but I can't stay to argue! We've already figured out that your bells ring noon very little before ours do." She held up two fingers as she turned to Hibern. "Will you be able to bring Rel back, if he wants to return to Sartor?"

"Glad to," Hibern replied.

Atan muttered a quick apology for transferring directly in company, and vanished in a puff of herb-scented air.

Lilah and Rel arrived a short time later. Peitar watched Rel look around, and his expression shutter as Lilah said in the tone of one who had been marshaling every persuasive argument she could, "So can you stay? I know Derek wants to meet you, and it's only two days until we expect him back. Maybe even tomorrow!"

Lilah turned expectantly to Peitar, who said obediently, "You are most welcome. We have plenty of room."

"There, you see?" Lilah exclaimed, bouncing on her toes, her short rust-colored hair flopping on her freckled forehead and over her ears. "You see? Peitar, you should have been there, they *loved* it. They were so *proud* of themselves. Rel, you *have* to show Derek those things you've learned, he's been trying, and trying, but he never had any military training . . ."

Rel looked slowly from one face to the other. He'd heard about Derek from Lilah, and Atan; on the surface, they scarcely seemed to describe the same person. But he knew that people were seldom all good or all bad, and that opinions were rarely uniform.

So. He was curious. He also wanted to keep his promise to Puddlenose and invite Peitar and Lilah into the alliance, since Atan kept forgetting. Most important, he'd already missed Atan's free hour; if he returned now, he would only have two more days of catching her at odd moments before Atan's noble watchdogs would expect him to be pushing along.

"If you truly don't mind," he said.

"Yah!" Lilah jumped around the room. "It will be such fun!"

Six weeks later

> *Rel: Will you be here to celebrate the anniversary of the Freeing of Sartor? If so, ask Lilah if she would like to come, since she was a Rescuer, too. I plan some special entertainments just for us. Atan.*

Rel looked up at Peitar, who had just received the note through his notecase. Atan knew that Rel didn't have a notecase, after having lost two on his travels, so she'd sent her note to Rel via Peitar.

His expression didn't change as Rel offered the note back to him. He glanced down at it and then handed it to his sister.

Lilah bounced up and down on her toes. "Oh, may I go?"

"Of course you may," Peitar said, and looked askance at his sister in her ragged old knee pants, scruffy haircut, and incongruously pretty blouse. "Lilah, may I in turn suggest you put on one of your better outfits? You'll be going as Sarendan's representative."

Lilah twitched a shoulder impatiently, but she was too happy at the prospect of seeing Sartor again to argue.

And so, the next day, Peitar gave them transfer tokens.

Peitar was surprised at the pulse of regret he felt when Rel vanished. Rel was smart, competent, easy-going, and utterly without pretense. Peitar had wondered how Derek would accept him, as he was wary around not only aristocrats and royalty, but anyone favored by them. But he'd been watching Derek when Rel said, "Don't expect me to know a lot about commanding, because I don't. All I've commanded have been fellow guards for small caravans when I earned my way through kingdoms. But I've done plenty of drills."

Derek said, "Someone called you Rel the Shepherd's son. Is that true?"

"Don't know." Rel shrugged his big shoulders. "My

guardian has never said. But my first job was tending the holding's sheep."

Derek's reserve had vanished in the genuine smile that Peitar knew meant acceptance, and the rest of Rel's visit had gone just as well.

As Peitar returned to his tasks, he found it hurt a little less that Atan would find Rel attractive. He felt it in a mild way himself.

Rel and Lilah transferred to the royal palace Destination in Sartor.

A page ran off to report. When they recovered, Lilah was instantly claimed by Hinder. They vanished down a corridor, high voices echoing back, as Rel was conducted by a self-conscious page to Atan's informal receiving room.

When Rel saw her formally dressed in complicated layers of green and gold over ivory, with cherry highlights, the differences in their rank struck him afresh.

She said, "The celebration was Hradzy's idea, actually, that we institute a new festival day, the Freeing of Sartor, and have our candle march. Even though New Year's Week is only a short time off, it still seems fitting."

Rel remembered meeting Hradzy Wendis during a previous visit. One of the youths born a hundred years ago, a skinny fellow with a charming smile, Hradzy reminded Rel a lot of Hannla. From a prestigious family, related to at least three duchas, the sort of fellow they'd want Atan to marry someday, he couldn't help thinking. If they didn't force her to marry some other kingdom's spare prince for treaty purposes.

Atan went on. "I put together this party beforehand, just for the Rescuers. I hired a group of singers to perform for us before they lead the singing on the parade. I don't know if it will take, but it's nice to be queen when you can try to get around something you know is unfair," she added under her breath, and Rel remembered hearing some gossip about how certain important nobles wanted the commoners among the Rescuers to be quietly yet tastefully closed out. "How was your stay in Sarendan?"

He'd been thinking about what he ought to tell her.

Atan hated military or war talk, and then there was that business about Derek.

Keep it short, he'd decided. "I ended up traveling around to give the orphan brigade some rudimentary training."

"Did Derek decide you were tainted by my friendship?"

"On the contrary. Invited me." Rel shrugged. "He was the first to admit he's a terrible military leader. I've had enough training to run beginners through the basics. Derek didn't even know that. His style of training was to tell them rousing stories, or make speeches to bind them together at heart, then loose them in a melee, that is, an attack in a crowd." Rel clapped his hands together, twined his fingers, and wiggled them. "No notion of discipline. I think in his mind, the idea of a chain of command was akin to the bad old king."

"Who very nearly had him executed," Atan said, as they paced down to the concert hall. "And Peitar along with. Go on."

"Not much more to say. I convinced Derek to see discipline as the people working together. A commander is there to call directions."

"And not act like a king," Atan said. "Does that actually work?"

Rel spread his hands. "So far."

"So this is a new army?"

"Don't know. Don't even know if their brigades will last out the winter. There was some muttering in some of the still-recovering trade towns about rowdy orphans playing with swords while others did the work to feed them. Criticism that Derek took hard, by the way, because it was from the workers and ordinary folk, not from the nobles."

Atan nodded slowly. "Good. Anything that gets Derek to see people as people, and not as bad-people-with-rank versus good-people-without-rank, will go toward proving Tsauderei's dire prediction wrong. I know he wants it to be."

Rel remembered the wild enthusiasm of the brigades when Derek spoke of raising their banner—defending the kingdom—heroism and fame and glory. He looked down at the trefoil patterns in the mosaic tiles, feeling as if he'd done something wrong, or that he was part of a huge something going wrong, and he had no idea how to fix it. Yet everyone around him believed they were in the right.

It was a relief to reach the concert hall where his Sartoran friends awaited his and Atan's arrival, everyone self-conscious in their best. Mendaen and Hannla closed in on either side of Rel, competing cheerily for news of his latest adventures.

Rel gave them a very truncated version as he looked about for the aristocrats among the Rescuers. None of them were present. And he saw Atan's true purpose: she had arranged this special party, and attended it herself, as a silent rebuke to her high council for planning a festival that only included the high-ranking Rescuers.

4741, New Year's Week, Marloven Hess to Bereth Ferian

On the other side of the continent, Senrid watched from his study window as Forthan commanded the third-year seniors in drilling the exhibitions intended as Second Night's entertainment for New Year's Week Convocation.

The exhibition far outstripped the lance demonstration the second-year seniors had been working on during mornings. This carefully choreographed fight on horseback, with real cavalry blades, was insanely dangerous, especially when they insisted on real strikes—'real' meaning sending sparks flying.

But Keriam officially did not take notice, and Senrid watched from a distance, knowing that these determined rehearsals in the face-cracking cold of nighttime were in part a kind of apology, and in part an attempt to shed the last of the shame of the academy troubles during spring.

It would be a relief to disperse those seniors at the end of New Year's Week for their two years of duty with the guards. Keriam had been very careful to split them all up, assigning the worst of the Regent's toadies' sons to the border garrisons, away from their special cronies. Those remaining in the capital, like Forthan, were mostly not troublemakers, save one whom Keriam wanted to keep under his eye.

Senrid nearly turned away, then spotted a lone figure climbing into the stone stands to watch the last of the rehearsal: the foreigner, known only as Shevraeth.

It had been impulse to accede to the surprising letter from that prince in Remalna. The Renselaeus family and Senrid were related way back in the family tree, but that shouldn't matter. Senrid was more nearly related to Leander Tlennen-Hess of Vasande Leror, and it would never have occurred to him to invite Leander to the academy.

Not that Leander would ever accept. He loved studying magic and history as much as he loathed anything military. If he hadn't ended up as king of that tiny polity that once had belonged to Marloven Hess, he would probably be in Bereth Ferian's mage school right now, or in Sartor's scribe school, studying magic at nights so that he could become a herald-archivist in the mage guild.

Shevraeth sat down there alone in the stands, papers and a book tucked under his arm, as he blew on his fingers.

The third year seniors might think Shevraeth was studying, but he was actually waiting for Forthan, as he was tutoring Forthan in secret. Usually early mornings before anyone was awake, except this week, when Forthan was overseeing the second-year seniors' exhibition.

Keriam had said to Senrid, *That is your future army commander. There isn't a better candidate in the entire country. Fix the problem now.*

Officially, Senrid wasn't supposed to know Forthan was illiterate, so he'd sent him to Shevraeth, who had no assignment, but could not go back to his home, where a bad king threatened his life. Turned out the foreigner was a good tutor. If only everything else were so easy to fix—

Senrid!

Senrid recoiled violently, then spun around purposelessly in a circle, his fingers whipping out the dagger he wore up his sleeve, as his brain recognized the cry as inward, coming from a distance impossible for the ear: Liere.

Senrid transferred to Bereth Ferian, and staggered against the Destination chamber wall, feeling like he'd fallen from a galloping horse. He heard Liere on the mental plane and ran toward her until he fetched up outside a room he recognized at a glance. Liere stood there, her stiff

arms held away from her sides, thin fingers spread like star-
fish.

"Senrid," she gasped on a high note. "It's gone."

Senrid glanced past her at the table. Siamis's sword was
no longer there. On the table lay a jumble of spell books
and other stuff as mages in gray and white robes walked
around the room, whispering spells.

Terror had widened the pupils in Liere's eyes, making
them look enormous in her blanched face.

There was more than met the eye, Senrid was absolutely
certain of it. Equally certain that somehow Siamis was
watching for reactions, he said carelessly, "Bet you he had
a transfer spell on it. He's probably a continent away. More.
Sitting in Norsunder Base, swigging bristic and laughing fit
to be sick."

Liere's wide, terrified gaze shifted to the table.

Senrid shut up. He stepped inside the room, and saw
that what he'd taken as a jumble of light magic stuff was
not: the spell books and the old scroll formed a careful
circle around a single object, a round gold coin. Senrid's
guts tightened as he took another step. Round coins were
a northern thing, and sure enough, this one had been hammered with a shape like a hawk's eye.

Senrid knew that shape, that coin. It sported the earliest
symbol of the Erama Krona, the Eyes of the Crown during
the earliest days of the Venn empire, before the Marlovens
left.

This hawk's eye had been adopted by Senrid's own ancestors.

A golden eye . . .

"Shit," Senrid said.

Two of the mages looked around in silent rebuke, and
a stern-faced old woman whom Senrid recognized as
Oalthoreh, the head of the Bereth Ferian mages, frowned
direfully and said, "What is he doing here?"

She talked past Senrid to Arthur, lurking in the doorway next to Liere.

"I called Senrid," Liere spoke up bravely, though her
voice quavered. She tapped her head. "This way."

Senrid schooled his expression, though deeply appreciating the effect Liere's gesture had on the mages, two of

whom stepped away. As if that would prevent Liere from reading their minds.

"I think it's an ancient Venn coin," Senrid said with what he hoped was a helpful air.

"We know that," Oalthoreh snapped.

Senrid resisted the impulse to bait her, which would be too much like the way Siamis (or his uncle, even worse) was baiting these mages by leaving that coin lying there. A coin that Senrid made a mental wager had lain outside of time since those early days, as it looked newly struck. The only people who might have personal hordes like that were Ancient Sartorans: Siamis. Or Detlev.

So what to do? Get Liere out of there. Senrid's first thought was to take her back with him to Marloven Hess, except it was New Year's Week. She'd been intimidated by the castle full of jarls and their attendants the year before. And then there was that kick in the gut he got when he first recognized the coin.

But. When he took in Liere's blanched face, he said, "Think, Liere. The sword is gone. Siamis isn't here. It's probably just a scare tactic."

Arthur watched in amazement as Liere's face colored up, and she seemed to breathe for the first time that day. "Oh. Oh," she said, her relief obvious. Though Arthur had been saying pretty much that same thing.

"Right. He's not here," she said quickly, her fingers twisting together. "So why is that coin there?"

"An insult, a challenge, another scare tactic. A different kind of being stupid," Senrid said, piling on the sarcasm, sure that Siamis was somewhere about listening. He itched to return to the room and try magic on that coin. But he had to leave it for the more experienced mages.

He tipped his head toward the door. Liere and Arthur followed him out, and they walked in silence until he felt certain there was no chance Siamis could hear them. "Look, it probably means Siamis is coming back, but as he hasn't actually done anything, and seems to want to scare everybody out of their pants with that damned coin, I think you should just go somewhere so you don't have to see it. Those Mearsiean girls seem to collect strays. I'll take you there, if you want to hunker down out of sight. I wanted to ask Clair if she's heard anything lately about Jilo. Or if you don't like going there without an invitation, how about Roth Drael, with Hibern?"

Liere brightened. "I remember that place. It's where we freed the dyr, isn't it? I loved it. Would Hibern mind?"

"I can take you, and we'll ask," Arthur offered.

They walked back toward the treasure room, encountering Oalthoreh and three of her mages coming down the hall, as a fresh group entered the chamber to investigate.

Arthur explained the plan. Neither he nor Senrid missed the obvious relief in Oalthoreh's face at the idea of getting Liere safely away, before she said, "We will continue to test for traps and wards."

As Arthur and Liere walked toward the residence wing, she to collect some things, Senrid took a quick step inside the treasure room to grab another look at that coin. Ancient Venn, definitely. Connection to his own family . . . maybe it was just borrowing trouble, because the first thing anyone does is see themselves connected to whatever is going on.

Yeah, Senrid thought. Like the old saying, he was probably putting one and one together to make eleven.

From Norsunder Base, the elite watched Senrid from the chamber they called the Window. Whenever someone successfully planted a spy-hole in a distant location, this was where they observed.

Siamis presided, urbane as a good host. It was fun seeing grim old Oalthoreh squawking orders like a hen, and the mages scurrying around muttering as they cast spells for traps and tracers.

The real fun for some occurred when the Marloven brat briefly showed up. He himself was disappointing. Looked barely old enough to cut his food by himself, and the only thing he said was so obvious it didn't need saying: "I think it's an ancient Venn coin."

Through the derisive crowing—"You think so?"—"The Marlovens have gone to seed if that's what's ruling them!"—"When Detlev finally gives us our Marloven party we'll clean them up in a day!"—Siamis said cheerfully, "You'll get your own hawkeye soon, Senrid."

The watchers fell silent, one or two telegraphing messages with looks. So, Siamis was poaching on territory Detlev had claimed for himself, was he?

Kessler stood at the back, observing them all. He never laughed. Never commented.

Chapter Twelve

*Various points around the world,
in reaction to bad news*

ONCE more, Hibern arrived in Choreid Dhelerei to be
told that Senrid would not be available for study.

The entire castle seemed gripped by tension, the
sentries—never lax—wary, with hands on the hilts of their
weapons. She knew better than to ask, and hoped the problem was merely more trouble with those teenage boys in
the academy.

She arrived in Sartor happily anticipating a free hour to
explore.

By now Hibern had ventured into several cities, and was
astonished by not just architectural differences, but ways
in which otherwise utterly different cities could be alike.
She suspected Atan would be appalled, for instance, to
have Eidervaen compared to Marloven Hess in that neither
capital city had scribble-scrabble words and drawings on
walls and fences, as Hibern had found in Miraleste, the
capital of Sarendan.

She'd asked Lilah, who explained proudly that Peitar

thought it was important for ordinary people to be able to make art and to express themselves. Lilah had added with a brief scowl, "It used to get you in trouble, under my uncle. My friend Bren was *really good* at drawings about how rotten things were then."

Hibern wondered if the so-civilized Colend would hand out death sentences if people marred their walls and fences with slogans and scrawls—except when invited.

She was ready to talk about that after another walk through Eidervaen, but when it was time to go to the royal palace, Atan met Hibern with a solemn face. "I have to give up my hour of frivolity," she said bitterly, then clapped her hands over her face, and dropped them in fists to her sides. "No, that's unfair. It's just that I insisted that I hear the high council's deliberations about what to do . . ."

Hibern was so surprised to be shut out by two study partners in a row that she didn't ask what they were deliberating about. "And so your new schedule doesn't even permit one hour a month?" she asked.

"So they say." Atan sighed. "And I have to accept it, or they'll shut me out of the real deliberations. When I dared to point out it was only one hour a month, they all looked at me like I'm a sulking brat, selfishly taking up time that ought to be put into finding ways to ward Norsunder."

A brat like Atan's wild little cousin? Hibern kept her opinion behind a blank expression. Clearly something else more urgent was wrong.

"We'll still communicate," Atan promised.

"Right," Hibern said, wondering what the etiquette was. She suspected that Erai-Yanya would say, "You leave the first letter to the Queen of Sartor."

She was ready to discuss it when she arrived back in Roth Drael, but fence scrawls and Atan's restrictive council went out of her head when she arrived to a waiting missive from Arthur relating the news:

Siamis took the sword.

"Horseapples!" Hibern exclaimed in Marloven, and threw herself down at her desk to start writing letters.

Siamis is back.

Word spread across the world faster than the sun's daily course, reaching everywhere but the most isolated corners. And Chwahirsland, as who talked to them?

Senrid, who might have, still wasn't used to thinking about communication going outward from him. His note-case sat forgotten on his desk as he conferred with Keriam, and with his army commanders via runner.

Most countries looked to their own defenses—magical wards and tracers, militias mobilized and armies drilled. Diplomats conferred earnestly, referring to defense treaties in hopes that the stronger would protect the weaker.

In Sarendan, Derek paced back and forth along the top rail of an old fence so the crowd of defenders in the city of Mira-leste could see him. His face lifted, his eyes wide so the sunlight struck glints of amber in them as he shouted, "It's just as we feared! But we shall fear no more! *Fear no more!*"

"Fear no more!" shouted the brigade.

"We shall not fear, we shall fight!"

"We shall fight!" the brigade echoed back.

Derek swung his sword, sunlight flashing along the steel as he walked. "We know that there's a vast army at Norsunder Base. But vast armies must move like anyone else, that much we won when Siamis was here before. The big rifts between Norsunder and us are gone."

A few shouted, "Gone," but the rest waited, or stirred, or whispered.

Instinctively aware that he'd lost the rhythm, Derek swung the sword higher. "They have to march. And where will they go, to get to the rest of us?"

Now they were paying attention again. "They either march to their west, which means carrying months of water through benighted land. Or they go north into Sartor, and risk magical traps. Or they try to come through us. We're the first line of defense! Sarendan!"

"Sarendan!"

"And it's not our king who can defend us, though he's a good king, the best who ever lived, my friend and brother. But his strength is wisdom and justice. He does not carry a sword. For that, he trusts me. And whom do I trust?"

A more confused response—"Us!" "The brigades!" "City guard?" And even, "King Peitar!"

Derek's voice lifted over the noise. "Do I trust the nobles?"

They knew that one. "No!"

"There aren't enough of them even if they were all united in wanting to protect us. Who has the numbers? *The people!* Who has the will to defend themselves? *The people.* Whom do I trust?"

This time he got the response he wanted, united in a heartfelt body of sound: "The people!"

"So let us train as one heart, one will, and one strong arm, to defend Sarendan!"

In Mearsies Heili, Clair and CJ stood on a balcony high on a spire in the palace on the mountain, looking out over a hushed world of white from an early snow.

"Why is it that everything turns beautiful under snow?" CJ asked, enormously pleased. She'd come from a part of Earth where there was no snow, and subsequently, could not get enough of it. As long as she didn't have to travel in it.

"No idea. But it does." Clair hated to ruin the quiet with anxious things, but even thinking that made her realize that the quiet was already ruined. And so she broached the subject that had made her brood for two days. "CJ, I got two letters, one from Puddlenose's friend Karhin in Colend, and another from Hibern. They both reported that Siamis's sword disappeared from Bereth Ferian."

CJ recoiled. "Does that mean Siamis is back? Where?"

"They don't know. Nobody saw it taken. All the wards were destroyed. They think it's some kind of warning."

CJ's shoulders hunched under her ears. "What are the grownups doing?"

"What they usually do, Hibern said, and I also heard

from the new addition to the alliance, Lilah of Sarendan. Plan defenses and drill armies and talk a lot."

"What are *we* going to do? We can't fight those spittoon-brains."

"No. At least Aunt Murial finished renewing the border protections, and this time she taught me as she went along. I know them, now. I have them all written down, and we'll at least have warning if anybody from Norsunder tries to invade. We might have time to get the word out to people to hide."

CJ didn't trust adults or their protections. If protections really worked, none of the villains would be able to attack, right? Wasn't that what 'protection' meant? "Did you hear from Atan about what Sartor's doing?"

"No."

"I knew it. She's too high and mighty for us—"

"CJ."

CJ sighed explosively. "Then why haven't we ever heard from her? Everybody else has written at least one letter to us all, to test the alliance net. Except Senrid, but I don't count him."

"Because she's terribly busy learning to be queen of the oldest country in the world? Because her high council won't let her? Because there's another alliance with Sartor as its center, like it's been in history for centuries? I don't know."

"Clair, Atan came and looked us over. She *did*. And didn't invite us back for a visit. I can see her not inviting me, because she might think I'm not a real princess. But she could have at least invited you."

Clair shrugged. "I don't care. I don't want to go to Sartor, particularly. More important is our alliance. If Atan is really a part of it, that's good for everybody, because Sartor always led the fight against Norsunder in history. But I think we need to work on spreading the alliance. Getting more people."

"Yes." CJ rubbed her hands, then stuck them in her armpits. "And that means finding more kids like us. But how?" She stared at the glimmering white forest far below, then glanced at her blotchy hands in vague surprise. "Hey, I'm cold!" Inside, she said, "Won't Puddlenose be showing up for New Year's Week? Maybe we can ask him if he's got any suggestions for new people, since he travels so much."

"Good idea."

Unaware of any events outside his dire quest, Jilo worked, and time slid past, unnoticed. He worked until colors leached out of the world, leaving it subtle shades of shadow-gray, and voices began to distort until he discovered he couldn't understand anything any guard said. Their voices buzzed like the drone of bees.

But he stayed until he had to write out every syllable, and then read out the spell with his finger on each letter, because he scarcely recognized the sense of the words.

It took the remainder of his dwindling strength to complete the last spell.

But complete it he did.

So when he collapsed, he woke where he had fallen, his head pounding, his mouth dry, but he was alive.

He woke up undisturbed because every guard, cook, and servant also woke up lying on the floor, blood crusted around their noses. They crawled off to recover, and then to assume duty as if nothing had happened. Nobody wanted to risk a flogging, or worse, if they complained.

Jilo staggered up to the desk, aware of the heaviness of the atmosphere. It scarcely felt different. But he'd made a start on breaking the life-draining magic.

At Norsunder Base, Dejain made her way to the Bereth Ferian window, as she had begun doing each day.

She thought it duty to visit when she was most likely to catch the Bereth Ferian mages in the process of searching for the magic that had permitted Siamis egress. The reward had been learning a great deal about their process.

Henerek and a couple of the other captains were there a lot, hugely entertained by the lighters' panic, the squawking, the horrified speculation after their discovery that the sword was missing.

In the days since Siamis had returned from Bereth Ferian, Dejain had noticed some patterns developing among those who habitually watched the lighters in their failed attempts to find the magic that had been slipped into their citadel—such as the spy window they visited each day.

The first thing she noticed was that Siamis was there less and less frequently, and he stayed a shorter time each visit. Second, Detlev never arrived at all.

Third, Kessler had stopped going.

Dejain peeked into the room and glanced at the magical window bespelled against the opposite wall. She recognized three of Oalthoreh's senior mages busy working methodically through magic books, page by page. Their talk centered mostly around some celebration being planned.

Dejain turned her attention to the watchers. Henerek was there, and several of the minor mages.

Dejain left, and went about her business.

One of the most disconcerting things about Kessler was that he didn't have easy patterns. But he did have to move about on his duties, and she knew the few places they would not be overheard either by physical or magical means.

She caught him later that day, as he was leaving the stable.

He paused, silent and still, a study in contrasts: black hair, pale face, flat blue stare; ignoring the general-issue uniform for a plain white shirt and black riding pants tucked into his riding boots. He wasn't all that much taller than she was, slim, and young, but her heart always beat harder when she was around him in a way that had nothing to do with attraction. It was fear. They had once worked together, then, convinced by a third mage that Kessler had betrayed her, she'd helped destroy his plans for ridding the world of kings born to privilege. He knew it, and knew why.

The thing she never mentioned, hoping he did not know, was that the blood-spell on the knife that had cut him, binding him to Norsunder, had been cast by her.

He made a movement to pass by.

She had to get his attention at once, or never. So she revealed the secret she'd been sitting on: "I know you're studying magic. You've been stealing my books, then putting them back. But I have tracers on them."

"What do you want?" he said, his angry light blue gaze direct.

She sure had his attention now.

Extortion would never work on him. "I thought you'd want to learn the ways of the enemy. But you don't watch at the Bereth Ferian window anymore."

His mouth tightened. "It's there to keep us busy."

"How do you come to that conclusion? It took months to build the location spell for it. And nearly that long to successfully place it."

"Yes, but who did the work? Not Siamis. He retrieved the sword, then afterward used the window exactly as long as it took to get Henerek and those other fools listening every day."

"We learn a lot."

The corner of Kessler's mouth curled. "You learn what Oalthoreh wants you to hear."

"So you think they know about the location spell."

"I think they did from the start."

Dejain had suspected that as well. So the question then was, "If you're right, why did Siamis bother at all?"

"To deflect us from what he's really doing," Kessler said, and made to push by.

"Which is what? I overheard him and Detlev talking. They're searching for something. All they said was 'it.' Do you think that refers to that dyr they looked so hard for when Siamis ran his enchantment?"

Kessler said impatiently, "They have to be looking for ways to create rifts. There is no way to bring over the armies stashed in Norsunder-Beyond until they can regain group access."

Dejain nodded slowly. In the meantime, the lighter mages kept finding ways to foul what were, for convenience, referred to as 'transfer tunnels,' though time and space were not so easily holed. People transferring even in small groups of ones or twos had been burning into nothingness if they followed one another too quickly. No one knew why only the ancient Destinations were the most stable, but even those couldn't be overused.

Kessler started away, saying over his shoulder, "And Siamis, maybe Detlev, too, they're not looking on this world."

She extended a hand to halt him, but didn't touch him. He had a nasty way of reacting with extreme prejudice if one crossed that invisible boundary. "Is that what the Geth project is? Looking for rift magic?"

Another expression of derision. "What else could it be?" He shoved past, turned, and said, "You should be watching closer to home. Henerek has been stalking your mages."

"They're not my mages," she said.

He lifted a shoulder, and was gone in a few quick steps.

Spring, 4741 AF (autumn in northern hemisphere)
Marloven Hess

The first warm night of spring, Senrid left all his windows open when he went to sleep.

He fell into a dream.

Through the door in the dream room he was working in walked a familiar figure, light from somewhere catching in his blond hair, outlining a shoulder, an arm, an empty right hand. The man halted before Senrid's desk in the dream room. He waved a negligent hand, and the jumbled elements of the dream whipped away quick as the wind.

"Senrid." Siamis's voice chided gently. "Are you really that unaware?"

Senrid bolted upright in bed, his heart drumming at a gallop. He flung aside the coverlet, wrestled into some clothes, took up his fighting dagger, then lit the entire upstairs and searched room by room.

By the time he'd done that, and had had time to slow his heartbeat, he remembered his wards and tracers. He returned to his study to check . . .

And found them broken.

So he widened the search. Morning light filled the windows, and the rooms, unnoticed; he missed his drill time on this determined hunt through every room in his castle, though he didn't know what he would do if he found Siamis waiting, sword in hand.

Finally he crossed to the garrison side, and climbed up to Keriam's office.

The grizzled commander sent away a runner and a couple of academy boys, still self-conscious in their new-made military tunic jackets and real blackweave belts. The boys saluted Senrid and clattered down the stone steps.

Keriam looked up from the neatly aligned stacks of papers on his desk, and said, "I was going to send a runner to you. Did you leave this for me?" He moved a stack of papers, revealing a golden coin.

Round, with the hawk's eye hammered into it.

Senrid's breath hissed in. "Where did you find that?"

"Oddest thing, it was on the floor."

"Where exactly?"

Keriam pointed to a spot between his desk and the rows of empty benches upon which during evening lessons sat the specially selected candidates for command class.

"Shit!" Senrid yelped, then smacked his hands over his eyes. He called up a string of complicated tracer spells, and sensed the magic flashing through the surroundings. In his mind's eye, the magic was like liquid lightning, splashing ineffectively from floor, ceiling, window frame, and walls, before vanishing.

Someone had tried to plant some kind of spell, but had been foiled by four-century-old magic. Senrid drew a deep breath, and let it out, glad of the mysterious Colendi mage only known as Emras, who had laid down the protections over the city and castle. History named her evil, but she had protected Marloven Hess.

Whoever in Norsunder had tried to break her wards had not succeeded.

When he opened his eyes, Keriam said, "What's the significance of this coin? It looks a little like one of ours."

"It's ancient Venn, I'm almost certain," Senrid said. "There was another like it left up north, after Emeth disappeared—"

"Emeth?" Keriam asked.

"Not a person. Name of Siamis's sword. Translates to 'truth.'"

"Odd name for a sword," Keriam said.

Senrid scarcely heard. Memory flung him back to the conversation he and Liere had had about that, when he first went to Bereth Ferian to visit her. He also remembered her

conviction that there was some symbolic meaning behind
the sword being there. Senrid hated symbolic meanings.
Lighter hyperbole about golden ages and peace forever sig-
nifying their own moral superiority were sickening enough,
but he'd take a year of that, non-stop, rather than symbolic
gestures from the likes of Siamis.

While Senrid stood there with distant gaze and his
mouth a tight white line, Keriam thought of the history of
the room he stood in, once known as the harskialdna tower,
used by the brothers of kings, by army commanders, and
during a brief period by mages. For the past few years it
had served as the academy office, as it looked right out over
the academy.

Keriam studied Senrid's grim expression. "Is this coin a
threat from Siamis?"

Senrid walked around the perimeter of the room. "Let's
call it a threat," Senrid said, jerking his chin up. "Siamis,
or someone, is either throwing down a war banner, or, more
like, giving us the back of the hand. The next one will probably be found on my throne." He remembered the dream
invasion. "Or maybe on my pillow."

Keriam swore under his breath. Then he said, "Right.
So we'll take it as a warning." And though he hated magic
with a passion motivated by fear, because it was nothing he
could fight, he was no coward. "Let's see what we can come
up with to be as disobliging as possible."

Senrid agreed, and walked out, resolving to be more
disciplined about his mental shield all the time, not just
when Liere was there—

Oh, shit. He stopped short. Two coins, one here, one in
Bereth Ferian. The sword might have been a warning, or
even bait. But two coins, one where Liere would see it, and
one here—Senrid was absolutely certain that Dena Yeresbeth lay behind all this mystery, which made Liere and him
specific targets.

That didn't mean there weren't other targets, too. He
spent the rest of the day making a transfer token, then protecting it with several different personal wards. The next
day, he chose his moment, when the lower school was playing a war game. This was the best time to catch one of the
radlavs—the boy group captains—without witnesses.

Senrid rode along the academy practice fields until he found Shevraeth, the foreigner. He stood alone on a small tree-lined ridge, watching the little boys under his charge playing capture-the-flags on the grassy meadow below. He looked bored. Why should that bother Senrid?

Because he looked like a bored courtier, Senrid thought as he looped the horse's rein over a branch so the animal could crop the spring grass. Senrid despised courtiers for their arrogance, their assumption of superiority in taste, brains, blood, whatever others held dear.

But he knew that Shevraeth had endured a tough year in the academy; in his first weeks, he'd had the snot beaten out of him. But he'd survived, and had not only found his place, but was doing well.

And Senrid was responsible for him.

So Senrid ran up to join him, and handed off the transfer token, which he'd attached to a gold chain from his mother's collection of fine jewelry. Satire? Intent to impress? Shevraeth took it with scarcely a glance as Senrid explained it, then added, "There's evidence that Siamis might return."

He meant to leave, but Shevraeth said, "And you expect to be his initial target?"

"It's not Siamis that worries me. At least, he's a big threat, bigger than I can handle. But there's a worse one."

"There is?" Shevraeth's head canted as he ran the golden chain through his fingers.

Senrid wondered how much the Remalnan boy knew, Remalna being about the size of an inkblot on the continental map. But small did not always mean backward. "Siamis was betrayed to Norsunder when he was a few years younger than us. Some records say it was by Norsundrians. Others—the ones I believe—say he was betrayed by his uncle, Detlev Reverael ne-Hindraeldrei. They called him a dyranarya."

Senrid stopped, struggling for words to define something he didn't understand himself.

"What is that?" Shevraeth looked puzzled.

"No one's sure. Except that they controlled people by thought, using these magical objects called dyra. Since Detlev was a dyranarya, it has to be something extra evil even by Norsunder standards."

Senrid suppressed the urge to go into detail about the mysterious Ancient Sartoran artifacts, and how Liere was able to handle a dyr because of her Dena Yeresbeth, and use it to destroy the Siamis enchantment. Either he took the time to explain all these terms—which he didn't even begin to understand himself—or he got to the point. "Here's what matters. Siamis and his uncle might come back. I tangled with Detlev once, and he promised me we would meet again. From all I can gather he keeps his word—when it suits his purpose."

Below, the small boys screeched and jumped and shouted, as the last struggle for the flags commenced. Around them the shadows had lengthened, leafing tree branches segmenting the field, light and shadow.

Shevraeth gazed between the screening trees at the little boys shrieking below as they pelted across the field with the enemy flag. His fingers opened, disclosing the medallion on his palm. "I take it I am to wear this?"

"Day and night."

"It seems unfair that the only living Ancient Sartorans would be those one would exert oneself never to meet." Shevraeth put the chain around his head and slipped the medallion inside his tunic. One responsibility covered.

"Oh, there's also Lilith the Guardian, but she's as dangerous, in her own way."

Shevraeth's brows lifted. There was the courtier again. "She's real? I mean, not in the historic sense, but lives?"

The courtier was habit, Senrid reminded himself. Not intent. "She, too, has recourse to someplace outside of time. Because she does live. I've seen her."

Shevraeth whistled, something he'd picked up from the Marloven boys. No courtier would whistle. "And you can read Ancient Sartoran?"

"Some. Barely. Liere and I have been trying to study it. But with all the success of a couple of puppies trying to learn the famed Colendi flower symbols, their ribbon symbols, their fans and the rest of it."

Shevraeth laughed, a sound scarcely louder than a sigh. "I wonder which one is the more obscure, Ancient Sartoran, about which my father had some pungent things to say, when he told my tutor to confine his exertions to modern history, or Colend's court customs."

"Maybe the Ancient Sartorans weren't trying to be obscure. I think they used metaphor for when ordinary vocabulary wasn't working. They seem to have been a lot closer to the non-human beings in this world. Until we humans almost managed to destroy ourselves along with everything else. Anyway, for non-human ideas, human language isn't enough, is it? I mean, how would you describe red to a blind man?"

Senrid couldn't tell from Shevraeth's polite, courtly expression if he believed any of it.

Memory seized Senrid. Gone was the playing field, the courtly boy, birds, trees, flowers. Again Senrid stood on a cliff beside Detlev in the frigid winter wind, the very first day of his reign, as Detlev forced him to watch Norsundrian warriors decimate Marloven Hess's South Army on the border below.

Senrid had been helpless to do anything. South Army as well as himself would be dead now, except that Senrid had been given a name half a year before, a continent away, by a mysterious and ghostly figure, who had said, *When you want my help, Senrid Indevan Montredaun-An, ask for it. Once, only, you may call upon me and I will aid you. Say 'Erdrael,' and I will come.*

Senrid did not believe in ghosts any more than he believed in mysterious offers, but in utter desperation that day on the cliff, he'd shouted the name. It had evoked a blast of magic that effectively blinded the Norsundrians, forcing them into retreat. The remnants of South Army were saved, as was Senrid, leaving him with the bitter conviction he had just served as a pawn in a game so vast, and so old, that he couldn't see but a sliver of it.

He snapped his gaze to Shevraeth's waiting face. "Fall into the hands of Siamis, or worse, Detlev. They'd probably be glad to discourse on the verities of their day, right before they rip your identity from out of your skull, and all without moving their hands. See that you keep that thing always by you. If I do have to transfer you away from here, likely there won't be time for warning."

And he left.

Chapter Thirteen

More consequences of bad news
Beginning at Sarendan

IN Miraleste's royal palace, Lilah Selenna flung open the new doors to one of the rooms burned by the revolutionaries, glad to escape the smell of paint into the balmy air of spring. She sprinted across the garden, and was about to hop the low stone fence and drop onto the path that would lead to the palace gates, when she caught sight of Derek Diamagan coming from the other direction.

"Derek!" she yelled, surprised. "I was just about to go to drill practice. Only . . . why are you here?"

"I've been thinking about something Rel said," Derek replied as he drew up next to her. "Here I am, going on about the uselessness of the aristos, which I still believe, but also about the uselessness of the army, because it was commanded by the former king."

Lilah made a sour face. "Ugh!"

Derek grinned as she hopped around in a circle, pretending to shiver and shudder at the thought of her deposed uncle. Peitar might have a lot of sympathy (misplaced, Derek believed) for his uncle, but Lilah unreservedly hated him. "Why would you ruin a perfect spring day thinking about *him?*" she demanded, fists on her hips.

"Not thinking about him." Derek perched on the low wall, fists propped on his knees. "I'm thinking about what Rel didn't say. Much as I hated the king's army, they did know what they were doing. They defeated us without half trying, which is how I nearly got Peitar and me executed." He jerked his thumb toward himself, then up toward the palace on the highest hill. "So I thought, now that they're not commanded by the former king, maybe it's time to go to Obrin and become cadets. Learn something. Want to go with me?"

Lilah's mouth rounded. "Me?"

"Sure."

"But I don't even like army stuff!"

"You've been practicing with the orphans." Derek shrugged, and his expression turned rueful. "Lilah, you know how much I've spoken out against the army. Perhaps not as much since your brother took over as king, but the little I've said hasn't been good. I still object quite strongly to nobles being trained there. They already have enough power. But since Peitar declared that anyone may train there, boy or girl, commoner or courtier, perhaps it's time for me to learn some of the basics. And if you're there to protect me, they won't heave my sorry carcass back over the fence."

"Well," Lilah exhaled on a breath of satisfaction. "If you put it like that. Why not? Let's go tell Peitar, and pack a knapsack. It'll take us a few days to get there . . ."

Roth Drael to Delfina Valley to Marloven Hess

Liere enjoyed her stay at Roth Drael so much that she might have felt guilty getting pleasure out of a dire situation had not Hibern made it plain how much she liked having company.

"I thought I'd get used to living alone," Hibern said one morning as they lay side by side on a beautiful old Bermundi rug, a bowl of warm muffins between them. They ate as they gazed straight up through the cracked roof of the white-stone domicile, where the first cold rain of the season ran along the ward that took the place of a roof. This magic was ancient. Hibern couldn't replicate it, though it was one of her many ongoing personal projects.

"It was fine the first month or so that Erai-Yanya was gone," Hibern continued. "Then it got lonely. Especially in winter. Well, you can tell by how many times I came north to visit Arthur. I didn't even mind twice weekly transferring to Oalthoreh and the school."

Liere wrinkled her nose, but didn't say anything. She felt so uncomfortable around those mage students and their teachers, though at least the teachers showed her respect. Maybe too much respect? It was the 'Sartora' thing all over again. Maybe they wouldn't even want her back, now that Siamis's sword was gone, and she hadn't somehow found and vanquished Siamis with some mysterious spell.

She wasn't the only one thinking along a similar path. Not that Hibern thought Liere a fraud. But after a few days around Liere's finger-twisted worries and awkwardnesses, Hibern formed the impression that Liere was more of an ordinary person who might have stumbled into the right circumstances at the right time, and now was paying the price of fame.

As the days turned into weeks, she kept her word and began teaching Liere modern Sartoran in the mornings and Marloven in the afternoons. Instead of complaining the way students usually did about language lessons, Liere soaked in everything Hibern said. Liere also remembered everything the first time she heard it. She asked interesting questions about the origins of words, or word patterns, that Hibern hadn't thought about.

She knew Liere couldn't be slow in mental capacity. Senrid did not include patience among his better qualities. It wasn't that he despised people whose minds didn't crash and carom headlong the way his did, but he tended to avoid spending time around people who couldn't, or wouldn't, keep pace. Liere, though significantly younger than Senrid, didn't seem to have any difficulty in that regard.

But it wasn't until the local morvende (who left Erai-Yanya and Hibern strictly alone) sent a pair of youths on those amazing creatures that took the form of white horses, with an invitation to 'Sartora,' that Hibern began to suspect that Liere was more of a puzzle than she appeared.

Especially when she turned up three weeks later, a garland made of flowers that Hibern had never seen bound around her brow, her escort singing songs in those distinctive braided triplets that never failed to send Hibern's heart racing.

Liere waved a farewell, wandered back in, smiled, and asked how Hibern was. She was speaking perfect Sartoran.

"I'm glad you're back," Hibern said. "I have a feeling that you're going to be needed." Hibern was sorry to see the old, anxious look tighten Liere's face. She said quickly, "Tsauderei wants to meet with Senrid. And I think you should be there."

Liere's eyes rounded. "Me? Why?"

"While you were gone, one of those old Venn coins showed up in Keriam's tower."

Liere blanched.

Hibern said quickly, "Nothing more happened. So far. But after I got the letter from our alliance net, I told Tsauderei, because Erai-Yanya would expect me to. If Senrid's temper goes runaway-horse, it might take both of us to rein him in."

But Senrid didn't argue—at least with others. He'd already been through all the arguments with himself.

Norsunder was coming.

Everyone knew that.

The specifics of why the coin was there didn't matter. The overall message was clear enough: he was one of the pieces on their game board, and swearing didn't fix the fact that he was vastly outmatched in magic, power, brains, military, and experience.

The one most surprised at Senrid agreeing to meet was Tsauderei. He would have liked very much to get a glimpse inside the mysterious Marloven Hess, but Senrid wouldn't go that far. Hibern had explained, "With the military, you try to pick the ground, and if you can't, you try to take the battle to the enemy. That goes for magic, too."

"So I'm the enemy," Tsauderei said, and though he laughed, Hibern sensed he was not pleased.

She said, "Everybody is a potential enemy to him. It's the only way he's managed to stay alive."

Tsauderei grunted. "And so he doesn't want me nosing around his wards. Very well. Bring him here. I will even pass you all through."

So the three transferred across the entire continent. Senrid sensed their being passed through two significant wards, which made him warier than normal as they recovered from the rough transfer outside Tsauderei's mountain cottage, under the deafening crash of a mountain thunderstorm.

Hibern hastily motioned them inside.

Liere, terrified by thunder, shot through first. She hated storms at any time, but had never been on a mountaintop so close to a storm. She stared out the window at the tumble of grayish green clouds that seemed so low she could touch them if she stretched out her hand. When lightning flared, she gasped and backed against the wall, which shivered as thunder exploded right overhead.

Senrid gave his host a grim, assessing look, then turned to sweep his gaze over the floor-to-ceiling bookcases surrounding him on three sides in the one-room cottage.

Tsauderei took a moment to observe the newcomers. He'd briefly met that poor little Liere, who looked as if she'd jump out of her skin if he coughed suddenly. Best to leave her alone for now.

Senrid had a strong look of his grandfather, his expression exactly as wary. When the thunder had rumbled away over the land below, Tsauderei said easily, "So someone planted a Venn coin inside your citadel? What's your defensive strategy?"

Senrid's eyelids flickered up, betraying how tightly he'd been braced for demands, lectures, admonishments. "Detlev once said I wasn't worth bothering with yet. When he decides I am, I want to be very hard to get." He looked down at his callused palms. Then up. "It might not be me they want at all, but the Marloven army. So our strategy has been twofold: to make sure they cannot surprise us on the border again, and to make it tough to take the royal city."

'Twofold.' This little speech sounded rehearsed. "We can discuss your border," Tsauderei said, "but first, permit me to point out that your strategy is shortsighted."

Tsauderei observed Senrid's defensive hostility easing

to interest, and said, "Feel free to disagree, but I think the most effective defensive strategy is to determine Norsunder's overall goal, and to deny it to them."

"I know that." Senrid's chin lifted, his expression thoughtful, then the wariness was back. "We know what they want: the world. And tactics will preferably include wholesale slaughter for sport."

"That would be the means, or a means, but I'm not so certain it's the end. Not for the ones who matter most, the Host of Lords. If that were all they wanted, they would have come out of their lair beyond time centuries ago."

Tsauderei paused as green-white lightning filled the room with actinic glare, and Liere covered her eyes, cringing against the battering noise of thunder. She loathed herself for her stupid fear, *wishing* she could be like Senrid, who loved thunderstorms. Or like Hibern, who didn't seem to care.

Tsauderei spoke again, lifting his voice against the steady roar of hail bouncing on the roof: "Is it possible that there are competing strategic aims? Take the invasion, conquering, and enchantment of Sartor, now rejoined the world. That appears to have been a random act, isolated because it devolved into an internal squabble between Norsunder's military commander and the mage Detlev."

Tsauderei had all Senrid's attention now.

Senrid said, "Invasions are never random. Take too much effort. Too much cost. There has to have been some plan. What makes you think there were conflicting strategies?"

Tsauderei said, "The enchantment came at the point the kingdom had been overrun and the Norsundrian force had slipped their leash and were settling in for slaughter for sport, as you say. When the enchantment cleared away, the entire population of Sartor was there, but the Norsundrians weren't. Where did they go?"

Senrid shrugged. "Probably just transferred back to the Beyond through a rift. Because Sartor came out of the enchantment right before the Siamis attack, and the closing of the rifts, right?"

"Except there was no evidence of a rift."

"It had been a hundred years, almost, right?" Senrid retorted.

"Not to the locals," Tsauderei responded. "Not to the locals. They're still mostly a hundred years back. Anyway, my point is that Norsunder seems to have competing commanders. So that would indicate competing goals."

Senrid drew in a long breath, his gaze distant. "Right. Yeah, right."

"So," Tsauderei went on, hiding how pleased he was not at having won his point, which was minor, but in having won Senrid's interest. "I'd hoped, when you found that coin, you'd also find a suitable threat, or warning, or something indicating Siamis's goal. Alas. We'll have to look at patterns of movement, but first, would you tell me about Norsunder's attack on your border, right before Siamis first appeared?"

"Hibern didn't tell you?" Senrid glanced her way.

"Hibern has been here fewer than five times, and has never stayed very long. She is not my student." Tsauderei's voice was sardonic.

Senrid flushed at the implied rebuke, as Tsauderei thought with mordant humor, yes, let us narrow the chasm between Us and You that you seem so determined to dig.

Senrid began to speak in a far less hostile tone. "I'd barely been king for a day. Detlev captured me and—" He decided not to mention Leander of Vasande Leror's annoying sister, who he'd beent traveling with at the time. She was immaterial to what had happened. "Detlev forced me to watch them march a couple of companies over my border. They'd been hidden from view by illusion. I know now that the idea was to shock me into thinking that they'd appeared suddenly. Well, it worked. Wasn't until later that I learned about the rifts. Norsunder sent 'em over from Sartor's southern rift. I found out that the king of Perideth let 'em march through his kingdom on the understanding they were coming to attack us." Senrid's voice was bitter.

"They were coming to take over your uncle's Marloven Hess," Tsauderei suggested, as lightning flared again, and the hail abruptly ended.

But it was farther away, and Liere let out a trickle of breath as Senrid looked down at his hands, the rope scars on his wrists whitish below the edges of his cuffs.

Senrid appeared to be struggling inwardly, then made a

sharp movement with one hand that again called his grandfather to Tsauderei's mind. "The southern companies were shorthanded because of, well, me. Trying to take my throne from the regent, my uncle. Half of them were first-year guards, right out of the academy, with no experience. What made it worse was, magic made the Norsundrians invisible to my army until they attacked. It was a slaughter. Detlev knew it was a slaughter. I think he was *enjoying* it. He forced me to watch . . ." Senrid struggled again. Then looked away. "The short version is, I'd been traveling with Puddlenose of the Mearsieans earlier in the summer. Came across some sort of, oh, magical artifact that thought it would be fun to take the form of a, call it a ghost."

Liere said softly, "Her name was Erdrael. Leander's sister called her an angel."

Senrid's voice was hard. "There is no such thing. It was some sort of magical artifact. It might even have been meant for Puddlenose." Though Senrid remembered Erdrael's words had been specifically for him. "Anyway, that sort of thing never happens twice."

Tsauderei leaned forward. "What exactly did Erdrael do, whatever she was?"

"Mirrored the invisibility illusion, but a lot stronger. It was so strong that Norsunder couldn't see any of my people, and Detlev was forced to withdraw."

Tsauderei let out a long sigh. "Whatever she, or it, was, no, we cannot expect to see that again. 'Erdrael.' I take it you never did figure out the mystery?"

Senrid's struggle this time was shorter. "No. I wasted a lot of time delving for mentions of 'Erdrael' before I discovered that the Sartoran language is full of them. Not surprising, considering there's a continent called Drael. I still have no idea what it means, other than the lighter syrup about blessings and sunlight and so forth."

"It's symbolic," Tsauderei said. "The root appears to be 'rael,' which we are still unable to translate, but the combination of the two syllables would appear to connote your metaphorical syrup."

Senrid grimaced slightly, then opened his hand in a gesture that could have been apology. Then he said, "It can't be too syrupy since the word, or the root, appears in the middle of Detlev's name. Hibern once told me that his family name is Hindraeldrei. Drael is the continent above us, so he lived there, is that it? 'Hin' means 'under,' doesn't it?"

Tsauderei said, "The scribes think the prefix indicates something subordinate, either a personal or familial rank. The 'dray-ee' at the end of the name meant 'oath-of-guardianship.' So, people of the area could say they were from 'ne' Hindrael, but a guardian was Hindraeldrei, or ne-Hindraeldrei."

Hibern spoke for the first time, lifting her voice above the distant thunder. "No maps of Ancient Sartor exist, so we don't know if Drael was even called that in the days before the Fall."

Senrid said, "Anyway, that was the military defense. Magical, we'd only had a single-point Emras Defense protecting the border. It was all I could manage to renew when I was ten."

"Many cannot complete one now," Tsauderei observed.

The implied compliment only made Senrid tighten up again. "Well, this past winter, I did it properly, around our entire border. A hundred anchor points. Took months. So at least I'll have warning if they break it, and I'll know where. But if they aren't conquering for the fun of it, I've got nothing more than you do."

"Ah, but I didn't say we had nothing. I told you we look at patterns of movement."

Senrid's eyes narrowed. "You mean, where someone like Detlev's been, since you can't catch him in the act?"

"We can't follow as closely as that, I regret to say."

Senrid understood then that they hadn't taken Jilo's book away from him. Maybe they didn't even know about it.

Tsauderei went on. "From what Erai-Yanya has managed to gather, Detlev has been seen more times in the past five years than in the past five hundred."

Liere hugged her elbows tight against her body; the low, uneven rumble of thunder sounded sinister.

"Then there's Siamis, whose appearance in the world is new. Why now, after all these centuries? Though it's possible he was around now and again before, there is no sign in any records, and the scribes have been searching patiently."

"So the Ancient Sartorans are out for a reason," Senrid said.

Tsauderei held up two gnarled fingers. "Two of the Ancient Sartorans. There are more, the ones who command them."

"The Host of Lords," Senrid said.

Liere thought that that would be the moment for the thunder to break right overhead, but in fact the rain was diminishing to drips at the corners of the eaves. Shafts of sunlight shot down into the valley, lighting up a lake hereto invisible behind the sheets of silvery gray.

Tsauderei continued. "There's some reason compelling enough to bring these two out of their citadel beyond time. Whether or not their appearance is on orders from the Host, Erai-Yanya believes their current goal is set in our sister world on the opposite side of the sun from us: the world called Geth."

Senrid lifted a shoulder. "Not our problem."

"It might become our problem," Tsauderei said. "But you're right. It isn't our problem at this moment. I asked Hibern to invite you so that we could exchange information, which we have now done."

Senrid eyed him. "That's it?"

"Since you Marlovens, for whatever reason, see fit not to establish diplomatic relations with anyone outside your borders, I hoped you would be willing to share any future discoveries. Insights. Threats." Tsauderei's sardonic smile was back.

"The jarls have never agreed to the Eidervaen Accord," Senrid said. "Yes, I know what it is." He'd learned of it only recently, but he wasn't going to admit that. He sensed he was being tested. "In that treaty, ambassadorial residences are deemed part of the country of origin. Our people can't get past the idea of inviting enemies right into your home to take notes on your defenses."

"And you don't think spies of these potential enemies wouldn't be doing that?"

"Of course," Senrid said, then admitted the truth. "I just learned about it. I don't know what to think. I'm still trying to learn how to rule what I have, before I figure out stuff we don't have. And I know I'm not strong enough to force it on the jarls at Convocation, especially since I don't see what we'd gain. We do have envoys going back and forth for specific purposes." Senrid walked to the window, then turned abruptly. "So what did you do to Jilo?"

"Took him straight to a friend of mine, who has in past years made it his mission to battle the former—I hope he stays former—King of the Chwahir. He was going to teach Jilo some magic specific to the Chwahir plight. I know nothing more than that. But when I do, I can see to it that Hibern learns the information, if you're not in the habit of communicating via notecase." The old mage dug in a pocket in his fine robe, and pulled out a golden case.

"I have one," Senrid said, thinking that Hibern hadn't told him about the kids' alliance net, either. Not that it was much use. His gaze met Hibern's black eyes, and her mouth curled sardonically. Oh, yes, she'd guessed what he was thinking.

Senrid fought the hot prickles of a blush. "I made my notecase myself. But I rarely use it," he admitted.

No surprise there, Tsauderei thought. Like his forebears. Ah, dark magic! So very predictable!

All Tsauderei said out loud was, "Fair enough."

Then Liere breathed, "This is. This is the place. Where you can fly?"

And Tsauderei watched Senrid turn from a tense bundle of distrust into a boy. "What?" His head turned sharply.

Liere didn't waste time on words. She shared memory images from a conversation about Tsauderei's Valley of Delfina.

Unaware of that fast mental communication, Tsauderei laughed. "Go ahead." He gave them the spell.

The door banged shut behind Senrid and Liere. She stumbled to the edge of the cliff, hands clutched together at her skinny chest as she jumped softly up and down, then her face lifted with joy as she floated gently above the new grass. But Senrid flung himself straight off the cliff, tumbling downward, then swooping up, turning end over end and whooping as he figured out how to control his body in flight.

Liere flailed after him, her shrill voice like a gull's cry.

"Go on," Tsauderei said to Hibern.

"I don't like heights," she admitted. "Just looking at them makes my stomach turn. A fast ride, I like, because a horse has at least one hoof on the ground."

Tsauderei laughed. "Then watch them, and rejoice. My guess is that neither of them remembers what fun really is."

When they left, Liere transferred with Senrid.

In his study, Senrid stood looking around, his expression absent. Mildly alarmed, Liere brushed the surface of his unshielded thoughts, to discover a confusion of delight and embarrassment.

"Senrid?"

"I hate being stupid." He turned his head, his face red to the ears. "I keep saying I'm not going to be like my uncle, but then I find out I am."

"No, you're not."

"In certain ways I have been. Stupid ways." He threw himself in his chair, giving a jaw-cracking yawn. In order to meet Hibern he'd had to rise earlier than usual. He looked around the sun-filled study, then let out his breath. "Have you ever had so much fun? Ever?"

"Flying!" She clasped her hands. "It was just like my dreams!"

"You fly in your dreams?"

"Oh, yes. I thought everybody did. Well, I know some do."

"I never have," Senrid said. "Though maybe I will after today." He paused to consider the thrill in flying so high the lake had looked like another sky below, then falling, no, stooping like a hawk, the air pressing his face so hard his cheeks rippled and he had to close his eyes to the merest slits, then arching his back and flinging his arms out a moment before he'd hit the water, and skimming above the surface so close that splashes stung his face, and he could see his own shadow within arm's reach. What was it about speed that was so exhilarating? He felt the same when galloping over the open plain. "We have to do that again."

"Tsauderei did say we can go back." Liere looked wistful. "Though I know you don't like to be away long. Because of your responsibilities."

"But that's just it. That's one way I'm like my uncle,

thinking I daren't be gone longer than an hour at most. Then when I do go, like transferring to Bereth Ferian to fetch you, I can't help worrying about what I'll find when I return. Well, we were gone half a watch, and here we are. I hear the boys in the academy. I can see the sentries strolling on the walls. Nothing's changed." He lifted a hand toward the open windows, and the spring air carrying in boys' voices shouting in cadence.

Liere sniffed the air, full of spring scents below the ubiquitous scent of horse. She almost didn't notice that horsey smell anymore.

"And another thing. That notecase," Senrid said as he rummaged through the neat piles on his desk. "I forget about it for months on end. Ah."

He opened it and grimaced when he discovered two notes inside.

"I'm going to have to put an alert spell on it," he muttered as he opened the first note. "Oh. I really am a horse-apple."

He held out the papers to Liere. One was written in the beautiful script of a scribe, from Karhin, another from Clair of the Mearsieans.

Inside Clair's note was another, short, written in Marloven, which Liere could read now.

> *Senrid: I am told you are still king. Maybe some day I will come back. But only if I know my father is dead. You and I never really understood one another, or even really liked one another. This makes your having watched out for me mean a lot more, and so I am writing to you what will probably be one last time, to thank you for that. I wish you well, and I hope when you remember me, you will imagine my happiness at having made a life I chose.*
>
> *Ndand*

Liere looked up. "This is your missing cousin!"

"Yes, and I really feel stupid now. Okay, let's see how bad this other one makes me feel."

Senrid read it, and threw it on the desk. "This is the kind

of thing I expected. Sort of. That an alliance would mean people might want my army coming in and strutting around and looking tough, or maybe even fighting. To clean up somebody else's mess. And then we go home again, and everybody hates the villainous Marlovens."

Liere said, "That does sound like your uncle."

"Except it's true. That is, in our history it happened over and over again. Both sides of our border."

"Did Karhin ask you for fighting?"

"No. She passed on word from Puddlenose, who says this prince our age wants help with training. Where is Erdrael Danara? Isn't it one of the little splotches west of the Land of the Chwahir? Hah. There's 'Erdrael' again."

Liere said, "Are you going to do it?"

"I think I need to know more, but listen. There's Forthan sitting over there in the guard, bored spitless because he has to do his two years patrolling the city. When he was the senior commander in the Academy, part of his duties was to organize the boys. I'll wager anything he could do that for someone else, what do you think? It might even be fun."

"I like him. He's so nice," Liere said.

Forthan's niceness was not the issue here, but Senrid let that pass. Liere was never going to take any interest in things military. "I was going to put him in charge of hand-picking some tightlipped friends to pretend to be Norsundrians and test the defenses of the city. Keriam and I talked about the coin and what it might mean."

Senrid snapped the back of his hand up toward the windows, and imaginary Norsundrian spies. "If Detlev decides he wants me, well, this city is where I live, and if it's the army they want, Choreid Dhelerei has the biggest garrison in Marloven Hess."

"Do you think they will attack?" Liere asked, shoulders hunching as she glanced at the windows.

"If they do want my army, it would be stupid to attack us in force, because all they get is corpses. But if they want to force us to fight for them, then they have to take the commanders, because they have to know that in this kingdom, you obey or you die. So they'll infiltrate, right? Execute snatch and grabs, then force the commanders to issue orders on behalf of Norsunder?"

Liere knew he was not expecting an answer.

He snapped his fingers. "This might even be better. Forthan knows the city. The Norsundrians won't. What if, at least at first, I ask that foreigner Shevraeth to lead the attacks? He doesn't know the city, so he'd be looking at it as a stranger. The city would love it," he added. "When there's an all-city war game, then I have to pay for the supplies, and the day's wages, which they almost always turn into a bonfire party at night."

Party? Liere mouthed the word. Every time she thought she understood the Marlovens better, something like this would make it clear she didn't. Maybe she never would.

Senrid's pen was already dashing fast, a little grin on his face. So she kept her thoughts to herself.

Chapter Fourteen

Colend

BECAUSE Colend was halfway around the world from Mearsies Heili, the three going on the alliance mission—CJ, Seshe, and Puddlenose—had tried to nap during the day, so they'd be awake and alert when transferring at midnight.

The sudden shift from rainy darkness to the clear mid-day skies of Colend made the town square of Wilderfeld, decorated with streamers, bunting, and silk flowers, look even brighter. Even if it was too early in spring for actual flowers.

But even with a dearth of flowers, little could spoil Flower Day.

Once they recovered from the transfer, the sound of singing drew their attention to a flower-decorated gazebo at the other end of the square. Three people stood there, wearing green and white, their heads crowned by garlands mostly made up of lilies, the Colendi flower.

Voices rose and fell. "What's that?" CJ asked, pointing. "Some kind of celebration?"

"A wedding, looks like," Puddlenose said.

CJ peered under her hand. "But there's three people.

And I know they don't have priests or rabbis or religious guys to do the vows here, that if you want somebody Up There listening . . ." CJ pointed heavenward. "You talk directly to 'em. Or you know they're already listening. Clair explained it, once, though I still don't get it."

'Religious guys.' Puddlenose shrugged, figuring this had to be another of CJ's incomprehensible Earth references. "Is there a problem?"

"Three? I guess weirdness like that is typical of Colend."

Seshe hesitated, not liking to contradict a friend, but Puddlenose grinned. "You don't think it happens right at home in Mearsies Heili?"

CJ made a gag face. "If by 'it' you mean sex, I know all about sex. I heard plenty of jokes on the playground, before I came to this world." She snorted, then said in a low voice, "If you mean marriage, I didn't think you could do that with three. On Earth, anyway. And thank goodness! On Earth, marriage really means fighting and arguing, and both take it out on the kids."

"I guess marriage is different on Earth than here," Puddlenose said, with a total lack of interest.

CJ scowled. Two people or ten, any thought of what she termed 'mush' made her squirm with disgust. But she had come all this way as an ambassador to the alliance, so she squashed down the desire to mutter about how three would only make the arguments louder. "Where's Thad's house?"

"Right across there." Puddlenose pointed to the rambling two-story house, with a sign hanging that read *Wilderfeld Scribes and Messengers.* Before they crossed the sward, Puddlenose held out a hand. "Look, CJ. Remember that we're here to make things easier for Senrid and Terry. I know you haven't been in Colend since you and Terry were snabbled as hostages by Wan-Edhe."

CJ scowled, loathing that memory: being captured along with a boy she'd called Terry—Prince Tereneth of Erdrael Danara. He'd barely survived a political coup before he was captured.

"I just want to say that if that should come up, Thad and Karhin—really, everyone in Colend—knows that their king is insane. Doesn't help to talk about it. Okay?"

"Clair already told me to be diplomatic," CJ said.

Puddlenose ducked his head. "Good enough, then." And led the rest of the way across the grass. He said as they stepped onto the porch, "Today being a festival, all the kids will have freedom from work. Thad said to come straight upstairs."

Before they'd gone two steps inside, a slim, graceful teenage girl met them, red braids swinging against her cream-colored scribe student over-robe, her grin wide and merry. "Puddlenose! You're here!"

"As promised, Karhin."

Before Puddlenose could introduce CJ, Karhin looked up at tall, calm Seshe, dressed in a fine linen long robe over trousers. Seshe was the Mearsiean girls' peacemaker, along to help in case she was needed. She'd loved beautiful Co-lend on her previous visit. As Seshe copied Karhin's peace gesture, Karhin said, "And you brought your princess!"

Seshe dropped her hands and reddened to the ears, which surprised Puddlenose and CJ both, but Puddlenose said quickly, "CJ's the princess." He jerked a thumb her way. "That's Seshe."

Karhin's lips parted, her wide blue eyes apologetic as she said contritely, "I beg pardon. I am so clumsy sometimes. Welcome, CJ, or should I say your highness?"

"Don't," CJ said. "We only do that junk when I'm throne-warming for Clair."

"Very well, then," Karhin said cheerily, smothering her intense curiosity as she gestured for the company to precede them.

Puddlenose bounded up the stairs three at a time. Karhin followed the two girls, observing how Seshe moved like one trained to courtly behavior, whereas CJ thumped up, bare feet twinkling beneath her plain green skirt. Karhin loved a mystery, and here was the oddest one, in a prince who called himself Puddlenose, and who seemed glad to surrender his rank to this girl in the black vest and green skirt, who didn't act, or dress, the least like a princess. And yet this other girl did.

CJ was determined to be a diplomat, but she couldn't help being on the watch for the slightest sign of snobbery or bullying. Her first glimpse of Thad was reassuring, as he was a beanpole of a boy, scrawny and knobby-kneed, with flyaway hair as bright a red as Falinneh's. He clapped his hands together in the peace, his grin merry.

So CJ's mood was high as Thad led the company into a pleasant room filled with comfortably shabby furnishings that had obviously seen plenty of use, the diamond-paned windows opened wide to let in the air wafting in over budding flower boxes.

The newcomers greeted Senrid, who sat cross-legged on the floor, and lanky Terry—King Tereneth of Erdrael Danara—lounging on the other side of a low table from Senrid. Terry was surreptitiously trying to get his bad leg comfortable, as he kept the hand with missing fingers curved protectively against his middle, mostly covered by his loose robe.

Terry wore his brown hair long, parted on one side to hide the awful puckered scar on his otherwise pleasant face. CJ, sitting next to him, glimpsed it and quickly looked toward the window, through which she could hear the melodic rise and fall of children's voices singing wedding songs. As long as CJ didn't have to see any mush, she could enjoy the music.

"Our mothers are down there, with Lisbet and Little Bee." Thad made a gesture toward the window as he named his younger stepsiblings. "And they think we're there, too. So we are free to talk."

"We even have some wedding cakes," Karhin said, triumphantly bearing in a plate of delicious-looking pastries: custard cakes glazed with lemon, puffy tartlets, and what looked like square oatmeal cookies with ground walnuts.

They sat in a circle with the plate in the center. CJ eyed her hosts, waiting for them to move first, Puddlenose having warned her that the Colendi tended to have elaborate customs, like not stepping on their shadows. At least the room was airy and bright, pretty framed mirrors on the walls opposite the open windows making sure there were no shadows.

Karhin gestured to the guests to help themselves, observing Seshe's neat manners, controlled to the fingertips as she took a single cake, contrasting with Puddlenose and CJ piling their plates. Senrid ignored the cakes, and Terry looked away, reluctant to risk making a mess, dealing one-handed with delicate pastry on fine dishes.

Senrid, impatient with politesse, said, "Terry, I understand you want military advice."

Terry sent a panicked look Puddlenose's way, and gestured with his whole hand. "It's . . . not military, in the sense of armies. It's our border guard." He sent another eloquent look Puddlenose's way.

Puddlenose said, "Terry's country had a lot of trouble not long ago."

A breathtakingly bland summary of several horrific years. "We were once three very tiny kingdoms," Terry said. "But the older generation, well, the short of it is that they all decided to grab each other's thrones. Assassinations. Fighting." No, he wasn't doing any better. Either you told it all, or nothing.

Terry shrugged sharply, pulling his marred hand in tighter, and Senrid grimaced, wondering how long he'd endured his injury before he could get to a healer. If he even got to a healer, who ought to be able to bind fingers back to a hand by magic. Assuming the wound was fresh. And the fingers were there.

"The Chwahir didn't make things any better," Puddlenose said grimly.

"Ugh!" CJ interjected, then remembered she was to be a diplomat, and she sat back, face red.

CJ's outburst enabled Terry—who was intimidated to be in Colend, whose customs and manners had been dinned into him as the model for nobility—to say more normally, "The border guards were either lazy, or leading the assassinations. You used to have to be born to the right families to belong. Most of them rode around in splendid uniforms, and that was about it. But there is so much rumor about the Chwahir and trouble there, and Norsunder, and everything else, I think I need somebody to come to the guard to tell them how to train. Oh. So many of them either died or ran off, that there weren't many left, and so I opened it to anyone. Birth rank doesn't matter."

Senrid's wariness thawed with every sentence. "So you really do want trainers, not mercenaries."

Terry looked hopeful. "Puddlenose says you described

a training school, people our age, who learn how to have discipline, right? Your people know what to do if there's an attack. They know how to use their weapons properly, and all that."

"'All that,' I can help you with. I even have someone in mind," Senrid said.

As the boys talked, Karhin noted how CJ met one's gaze straight on, whereas Seshe's gaze was a butterfly touch, brief then moving away lest it disturb or intrude. She sat so neatly, legs folded under her.

Karhin made a wager with herself that Seshe even crossed her feet, one big toe over the other, the way the Colendi nobles were taught from childhood. Why was CJ the replacement princess instead of Seshe? All Puddlenose had ever said was that his cousin, a girl queen, collected runaways and adopted them.

Puddlenose popped a last bite into his mouth, and licked his fingers. "So you'll do it, Senrid?"

"Forthan could use the experience." Senrid quoted Commander Keriam. "Yes."

The brother and sister put their palms together in the peace gesture, heads bowing in gratitude.

Karhin indicated the last of the cakes. "Let us celebrate harmonious agreement."

"You mean," CJ said as she lunged forward to grab the chocolate one she'd been eyeing, "the alliance really works!"

There was laughter as everyone agreed.

CJ went on. "So we need to get more kids in. And we need a name! Something that won't cause adults to snout in. Like our underground hideout, we never called a hideout. We called it the Junky, or Junkyard. What grownup would want to nose into a junkyard?"

Karhin said, "Maybe you should be in charge of the names?"

CJ wanted nothing better. "I already have a great idea. We'll call the group Fonebone."

"Fonebone?" the others repeated doubtfully, and CJ chortled, loving how the silly word sounded.

By now, CJ knew that saying *It comes from a magazine called MAD, back on Earth* would cause a zillion questions, beginning with *What is a magazine?* "In my birth language, I used words to make up an acronym, see? Fed-erated Organization to Negate Eleveners By Organizing New Enforcement-tactics." And at their bewildered looks, she waved her hands. "Never mind that. If nosy adults heard you talking about The Secret Organization, or the Sister-hood, or the Kids' Guild, would they ask?"

"Yes." Thad put his hands together in assent. "You must understand that our mothers, in accepting the guild license, made the scribes' vow never to become involved in politics."

"But *we* have not made these vows," Karhin explained. "And we see the alliance as something non-political, a net for the purpose of communication, and defense against Norsunder."

"So our new name is Fonebone," CJ stated, thinking privately that surely such a silly name was certain to keep bad luck away.

Chapter Fifteen

Marloven Hess

LIERE went to visit Senrid as summer ended in the south.

Under Hibern's tutoring, she had begun diligently studying the fundamentals of magic, but when she left Hibern, she couldn't resist setting aside the boring basics to delve into Senrid's magic books. He let her read anything she wanted, so, driven by her dread of Norsunder taking her by surprise, she skipped over years of stuff in search of transportation spells, and—the most frightening of all—rifts.

Of course she was not going to try them. The first time she opened one of the books, she tightened her hands into fists, just in case simply reading a spell made it somehow happen.

But she had to know.

And so, on a hot, humid day, with the sounds and scents of the world going about its business carried on the heavy air, she crouched in the window seat and read that anyone who studies the fundamentals of transfer magic, however the spells are formed ('dark' or 'light') learns early that with each successive person added to a transfer there is not just a corresponding reaction, but an exponential one.

All right. She understood that much.

More surprising was the observation that not all space between spaces was the same, no more than the density of objects (air, water, wood, soil, rock, ice, fire) was the same. Certain places had been fairly stable, if transfers were regulated, for centuries; some cities had grown up around such places.

The rest of the world could sustain the occasional transfer, though it was "more keenly felt" but became exponentially more volatile if more than one living being used the same space: they were more likely to come through nonliving. If at all.

That was scary.

> The shift of material objects in and out of the physical world, alive or inert, requires exactitude.

Senrid had underlined that. She wondered how old he had been when he'd studied this stuff.

> Using dark magic to force too much material or especially too many living beings too close together through even the most reliable Destinations can instigate an explosive friction that can destroy not only that which is transferred but anything within a considerable space around.

That was another one Senrid had underlined.

She closed the book, walked around aimlessly, then came back to it, feeling like she was picking at an invisible scab. But she had to know. Imagination was too frightening otherwise.

> After a double transfer, the Destination needs to be cleared of magic reaction before it's safe to use again. That's more expense. And the reaction for those transferred is unpleasantly strong.

Well, she'd felt the truth of that.

Reference to a name sent her to another book that covered the history of magic. Paging along, she discovered that as soon as mages had understood how transfer magic worked, dark mages had tried to create ways to transfer armies. They found ways to use magic to rip gaps between spaces, though the edges were very dangerous. These rifts caused other mages to develop wards against their formation. The larger a rift, the more involved the wards against them. In dark magic, those wards could be deadly.

She was working slowly down a page, her finger marking each word, when running footsteps, thumps, and boys' shouting erupted from Senrid's study down the hall.

She dropped her book and sped outside, to find a couple of guards and runners gathered at the door of Senrid's study. She was just in time to see a flurry of papers settling down as Senrid tapped out from his position flat on the floor, a big black-clad boy sitting astride him. Two others stood by, one of them hanging back, betraying uncertainty: Liere recognized Shevraeth, the Remalnan studying at the academy, whom she'd met the year previous. Liere had to look twice. Shevraeth had shot up to be quite tall, and he looked very much like the other Marlovens, except for the graceful way he used his hands.

His expression was a polite chagrin as everybody else in the room grinned in triumph. She knew what was going on. The 'Norsundrians' in the 'city attack' had won their way to the king!

Liere gasped. "I told you," she exclaimed, pointing at Senrid. "I told you!"

At the door, the runner laughed, waving in one of the guards, who from the resemblance was a brother or cousin.

Senrid sat up. Both he and his attacker had bloody noses.

"I told you so, I told you." Liere couldn't seem to stop herself.

Senrid grinned at the three attackers as he mopped his nose with his handkerchief. "Good job, you three."

He got up and started out, Liere following.

The guard, who last year had been an academy senior, closed in on Senrid's other side, saying defensively, "Not fair. No accident they broke through the first day Forthan is back. He knows the castle routine like no soul-sucking Norsundrian will. May as well waft 'em in by magic. We weren't slack."

Senrid sighed. "But that's the whole point. If Norsunder can cheat, they will. Still, report what happened to the guard captain. Tighter patrols are always a good idea."

The guard saluted, fist to chest, and loped off, leaving Senrid and Liere alone.

She followed him to his room. "Senrid, you aren't safe here. If they attack. I told you so."

"Don't you think I know that?" he retorted, carefully fingering his nose and wincing. "All right. I'm still a target, even inside the biggest guarded city on the continent. I think we're going to have to try Keriam's idea, a communication system, so we have a warning and can take action . . ."

Chwahirsland

Jilo never remembered walking outside the castle gates.

He barely recognized his lungs laboring and his blood whooshing in his ears past the weird buzzing sound in his head. The buzz gradually resolved back into voices, but they were still too distorted to understand.

The after-effects of two powerful spells counteracting one another had dropped enough people for the city-dwellers to have cautiously crept out to aid sentries they'd seen collapse on the outer wall.

Others had fallen in the street. Jilo, who still wore his shabby flatfoot-probationer uniform, was bundled by furtive hands into a way station, where he woke up the next morning. For a time all he could do was lie there and listen to his labored breathing. Gradually he managed to get enough breath into him to widen his awareness outside himself to others on the cots.

He overheard mumbled fragments of conversation: *What happened? We think Wan-Edhe might be back, but there have been no orders. Oh, right, I should get back to duty. We will all get back to duty.* (This last said in a raised voice, in case they were overheard.) *But first, the mess hall has food.*

Finally it was Jilo's empty belly, lying pinched and flat between his jutting hipbones, that got him to his feet and down an interminable hall of some twenty paces, to the nearest bench. A bowl of thin gruel, a crumbling of egg (one egg shared among four people), and some hot steeped tareweed woke him up enough to sort out a roomful of people unsure what had happened. But something had happened. Everybody was afraid of what it might mean.

Jilo crept back to the bunk, and fell into it.

When he woke next, it was easier to get to the mess hall, which was half full. The subsequent meal was heartier, and he was able to keep it down without any trouble.

The next day, he made it outside. His plan was to get out of the city, while that mighty spell slowly began to unravel the pocket Norsunder.

He only managed to reach the garrison at the east gate, but that was just as well, as thin, sleety rain fell. Even if he'd felt well, there would be no distance gained if he had to splash through puddles and mud.

By the following day, he felt strong enough to walk. He had his plan ready: he would be a probationary courier, which meant no one would ask for his twi, or rank, or army place. Couriers crossed the country bearing messages that they were not permitted to see, so no one would ask questions, at least not about his supposed messages, especially if he was regarded as probationary. Probationers never carried anything vital.

In this way, he figured, he'd be as good as invisible, and could learn more about the people. He didn't have the strength to go fast, but that was all right. He wasn't doing this to run a distance race. Sitting in mess halls listening was a better way to learn than running to see how far he could get.

Each day that Jilo got farther from the capital, he found himself a little stronger. He walked a little farther. When he stopped at night, he was able to study a little longer, and he remembered more of what he had learned. Meanwhile he gained the victory of being able to see a day begin, progress, and end. Counting them was still beyond him.

By the time he'd reached the outpost halfway between the garrison at Narad and the provincial one farther along the river, he had come to the conclusion that yes, he'd been suffering magical reaction, but it was not entirely due to the spells he hoped he'd completed. The entire city was ill from the effects of Wan-Edhe's magic.

If he really had managed to complete the spells Mondros had taught him, then he should come back to Narad and sense a change. What would that do to the people?

One day at a time.

He was still trying to accustom himself to how sharp sounds were when he joined the outpost mess. No one spoke, except about orders, of course. That regulation was fifty years old. He wanted to hear talk about orders, and gain a sense of who was issuing them. Who was going to try to fill the space left by Wan-Edhe? The clearer Jilo's head, the less he believed that he was going to succeed in his mad attempt to walk through the entire kingdom to learn what the people truly thought.

One day at a time!

He got up to get more to drink, and watched people's hands. Two might have been using that hand language. Maybe only one, and the other was absently tapping his fingers on the table. Jilo was distracted by those hands. Very small for a man.

Jilo got his drink and sat down again. He looked at the various backs and bent heads, all shades of black, from blue-black hair to reddish, and from new, well-woven and dyed uniforms to the dirty gray of a shabby, much-scrubbed tunic years old. The room was silent except for the little noises of eating, utensils ticking unmusically on clay dishes, a snort over here, a cough over there. Cloth shifting. From outside the window, the steady wash of the river.

Everyone appeared to be as isolated as he was. So why was the hand-tapper impatient?

Jilo decided to watch the fellow.

When the two benches filled, Hand Tapper rose to make space. Jilo also rose, and followed Hand Tapper through the low door, down the narrow corridor, which smelled of baked cabbage, to the outer door that looked over the river dock. A thin, bitter rain had begun to fall from under lowering clouds.

Jilo debated retreating to the barracks, as the air flowing off the river was cold and damp, when a small boat tied up at the dock, and Hand Tapper straightened up. A gangling boy waved a courier bag at the sentries at the dock, was passed, and ran up the stairs.

Hand Tapper greeted him with, "What happened? I wanted to get on the road before noon."

"Bridge is out again. We all had to take a watch binding the pontoon."

"Here's Narad." Hand Tapper dropped a slim packet into the newcomer's hand, and whirled around.

Jilo stepped aside, glanced up, and blinked. The fellow had female contours to his face, neck, and chin, though somewhat hidden by the graying hair, and blurred by the pouchy flesh on either side of his mouth.

The newcomer paused to shove the Narad communication into his bulging pouch, and Jilo wondered why Hand Tapper was handing it off one day's journey from Narad. Didn't these couriers cross the kingdom, collecting and dropping off communications?

He tried to formulate a question without actually asking, but before he could find words, the newcomer pushed past him and headed inside.

Jilo abandoned his questions. He had to be more observant, and patient.

By the time Jilo had crossed the country to Burda Garrison in the center of the kingdom, the impossible had altered to improbable, and from there to unlikely-but-possible.

He knew that some of what he heard was the result of his escape from the life-destroying magic in Narad. Everything was clearer, sharper, almost as dramatic a difference as when he first managed to dispel Wan-Edhe's brainfogging magic. Even with the centuries-old blight leaching life from sky and water and soil, the diffuse light carried subtle variations, the smells a complication of decay and growth, the wind whiffing of brine from the distant sea.

Then there were the sounds. At first he thought the sense of rhythm in the chopping of vegetables, the brush of a horse's hide, the creak of wheels on a cart nothing more than his own burgeoning awareness of the world, but slowly came the conviction that the fact that he heard these things at all, especially in a kingdom where any form of music, song, poetry, or dance had been outlawed on pain of death, was significant.

Then there were the . . . warriors? What ought he to call them?

The law had been strict for generations: females were not permitted in the army.

But Jilo was seeing them.

Girls, women, their hair clipped like men, their uniforms mostly shapeless, though as the distance from Narad increased, the less some of the older ones hid the shapes beneath the clothing. They were referred to as 'he' and they answered to male names.

But they weren't males, and he was fairly sure they weren't what the Chwahir called soft-shells, the women who for whatever reason wished to be transformed into men, and strove to earn enough credit to obtain the complicated, some said painful magic to make themselves into them. (Hard-shells, men who wished to become women, were put to death under Wan-Edhe's law.)

Soft-shells could never hold any position of command even after completion of the magic, they could only serve in menial tasks, but these women hadn't gone through any magic transformation. They used male names, and everybody used male pronouns when talking about them. Some of them were patrol leaders—many were couriers—stable masters. They just didn't go to Narad.

Wan-Edhe could not have known, or they'd all be dead.

Chapter Sixteen

WHEN Henerek found out that Kessler had been sifting through his carefully chosen and trained company there at Norsunder Base, recruiting his best for purposes of his own, he wasted little time in cursing. He put more time into trying to ambush Kessler, and a great deal of time concocting a parallel track to his plans.

Now everything was carefully prepared.

Unwitnessed meetings between Norsunder Base commanders were never easy to arrange. There must be a balance of power, or what appeared to be a balance of power, because few of these meetings ended up with agreement.

So first you have to catch the target's interest.

Henerek did that by intercepting Kessler at the stable, at a well-known corner inconvenient for fighting. Kessler never let anyone get within arm's reach, but all Henerek had to do was pass within sight, open his hand, and disclose a single twelve-sided onyx stone on his palm.

Kessler stilled.

Into the silence Henerek said, "Hill Five. Now."

Hill Five did not have a Destination, a window, or any other distinguishing feature besides being raised enough for commanders to view the war game field from the other side.

It was one place Norsunder Base's inhabitants could be reasonably assured of privacy. Henerek knew he had caught Kessler's attention, but that didn't mean Kessler would show up. Already there was a fifty-fifty chance he wouldn't, as most commanders who met there for private talks insisted on riding across the field side by side, the better to watch one another for treachery. Nevertheless, Henerek went through the motions: he saddled a horse, told the stable within hearing of several of the internal informers known as rats that he was scouting the field for an exercise, and set out.

When he spotted a lone horseback rider approaching the jumble of rocky hills from an oblique angle, the thrill of the chase burned through his nerves. Henerek urged his horse faster, as if he were worried that Kessler would get there first and arrange some sort of ambush.

Heh. If he was uncooperative, Kessler was going to be the one getting a surprise.

They approached the hill from opposite sides. Henerek tied up his horse and vaulted quickly from rock to rock to reach the wind-flattened top, which afforded a fine view of the rocky plain below. As he expected, there was Kessler, approaching from the other side, hands empty at his sides. His sword, if he had one, left with the horse.

Oh, stupid move.

Henerek resisted the impulse to touch the blood-magic-enchanted blade he carried safely in a sheath. He knew it was there. It hadn't gone anywhere. And best that Kessler thought it an ordinary blade of the sort he carried plenty of. Kessler himself was armed: steel-handled knife hilts winked in the gray light at both boot tops, at his belt, and there were probably more up his sleeves. A lot of good those would do him once the hidden attack team laid him out flat.

"The object-transport stone," Kessler said, coming forward to meet Henerek in the middle of the hilltop. Unimpeded, the wind cut like a steel blade and winter was still a month off. "Where did you get that?"

"One? I have four," Henerek said. He had no intention of revealing the whole of his plan, but he couldn't resist this little flourish. "I've had Pengris searching for a year. Or he's been gone a year. Who knows how long he spent ferreting in Norsunder-Beyond?"

Kessler was so surprised he actually looked surprised. Henerek took in a breath to suppress the laugh threatening to get past his ribs. Kessler said, "What did you promise to get a mage on your side?"

"Said I'd make him head mage when I take Everon."

"Where did you stash the body?"

"Where Siamis will never find him," Henerek retorted, gloating over the fact that Kessler would get the blame if he was found. Henerek didn't like that Kessler had guessed so quickly about Pengris's death. On the other hand, Kessler was fast with a knife. Maybe he expected that in everyone.

To get Kessler off the subject of the mage (and whatever the other mages were going to do if they found Pengris's corpse), "This is what's important. You're aware that over the past year, Siamis has been showing up once every three or four months to look at us."

"And he was here yesterday. Your point?"

"When he comes next, he'll find his precious army dispersed over two continents."

"What kind of transport will that stone bring out of the Beyond?"

"Ship. Four of 'em, actually. Four stones, four ships. Troop-transport ships are what I need to take my company to the east coast of Drael. When Siamis shows up next, I'll be securing a base of operations in Everon. Siamis can sulk, but I'm sure Detlev'll be pleased to see us get a jump on his plan."

Kessler said, "You don't know what his plan is. Nobody does."

"How many variations are there on invasion?" Henerek shrugged, anticipation making him want to protract the moment. Enjoy it the longer. "Those ships might've been transformed into these stones a thousand years ago or more.

Wonder what they'll think, coming back into the world again." He paused, but Kessler just stood there. To fill the silence, Henerek got back to the plan. "Bostian says that once I reach Everon, he'll launch his campaign against Sartor. It'll make the lighters panic like a hammer to an ant hill."

"So I'm here because?"

"I want you with me."

"Under your command." It wasn't a question.

Henerek shrugged again. "If you'd laid the plans, then I'd be under yours." A heartbeat, three, four. The only sound, the wind moaning around the rocks. Henerek lifted his voice. "Siamis can sulk if we've shipwrecked his campaign." *Shipwreck* was the attack phrase. "But he should have been here."

Kessler shrugged. "Not interested in 'should have.'" He made a half-turn, about to leave.

Henerek lifted his voice. "So you won't shipwreck my campaign, even if you won't join?"

Where was the ambush team? Henerek's nerves chilled colder than the wind as the impossible became probable. Angry, he pulled the bespelled knife, and threw it. All he needed was the tiniest nick for the blood-spell to take hold.

Kessler had not completed his turn; he sidestepped, and the knife clattered against a rock. Two, three steps, and Kessler slipped behind an enormous boulder and vanished from sight.

Henerek had placed his men carefully. He ran to the slab behind which the team leader was supposed to be waiting, and stared down at the slumped figure, blood already congealed in a black pool between two cracked rocks. When had Kessler done that? More important, how had he known?

The sound of horse hooves beating a rapid retreat made Henerek recoil wildly, but all he saw was the back of a dark head in the swirling dust kicked up by the wind.

Shipwreck. His hand tightened on the magical artifacts as he faced the fact that his month of careful planning had just been shipwrecked. No, it hadn't. He just had to act faster. The hunt was on!

He laughed, and rapidly assessed the shambles, deciding what to leave and what to keep. He wouldn't be able to wait for the horses being brought in.

He had better get what supplies there were, and march out that night.

At the same time in Sartor, directly to the north

Atan had begun to dread Restday ever since the council, singly and collectively, had convinced her that she was wrong to let the morvende take Julian to Shendoral, where she was happiest—but she not only was not getting any education, she also wasn't getting any older because of the way time worked there. The council had made it clear that Atan was the only person who could properly take little Julian in hand.

Atan had begun firmly but lovingly, as they suggested. Not every day, but once a week, that was her compromise.

She had chosen Restday, as it seemed to be Julian's favorite day, the one that saw her around the palace most often. Rather than ruin Restday supper with its wine and bread, candles and songs, she forced herself to go to Julian's room first thing in the morning.

She'd had the tailor make two outfits that would fit the child: a very plain tunic and riding trousers like any Sartoran child would wear, and the most beautiful dress Atan had ever seen. She would have loved it at Julian's age, living as she did in the hermit's cottage: it was a pale blue velvet, the color of the summer sky at dawn, embroidered with tiny birds and blossoms, with diamonds winking at each shoulder.

"Julian, will you choose one of these outfits today?"

"No." Julian scrambled into her oversized robe and long scarf, which at least the servants had been able to put through the cleaning frame while the child was asleep.

"Julian. Will you permit the maid to brush your hair?"

"No."

"How about if I brush it? I will be very gentle. You can stop me if anything hurts."

"No." Julian ran out the door.

That first time, Atan almost chased her, but stopped at the door. She could easily catch up. With all the walking about the palace that she did, and climbing of the dragon plateaus and other places she'd explored, she was strong, with plenty of stamina.

But when she caught up, what then? A screaming, kicking fight in the halls? At least she knew wherever Julian ran to when she disappeared like that, she always came back safe. People all over the city knew who she was, and shared food with her when she was hungry.

The next week, Atan nerved herself to the same conversation, to get the same result. At the end, she forced herself to say in her calmest, firmest, but most loving voice (knowing she was failing with every word, her throat was so tight with dread, and even anger), "Julian. I am going to ask you every week, until you decide it is time to be a person, and not a wild thing."

"I hate you!" And the sound of rapidly vanishing feet.

Atan looked at the rejected clothes, controlling the urge to toss them out the window.

She'd failed again.

She walked down to the steward's chambers, where she found tough old Gehlei, who had been in the queen's private guard in the old days. Gehlei had saved Atan's life, losing the use of one arm in the process.

Gehlei was now her steward. Gehlei had long wanted the position, but when young hadn't had the connections. Busy as she was, she always made time for Atan, not because Atan was Queen Yustnesveas the Fifth, but because they were both as close to family as either had left.

Neither counted Julian as family, not without the mental effort required by duty.

"She was yelling *I hate you*," Atan said.

No need to say whom she meant.

Gehlei shut the outer door. "She says that all the time," she said gruffly. "To the kitchen staff when they don't have her favorite orange-iced pastry at all hours. To the rest of us if we try to stop her. Nobody is going to touch her, and I think she knows that."

"Gehlei, this is a terrible idea, but the council says only I have the authority to do anything about her. I know Hin or Sin will take her back to the forest hideout, but we can't let her live in Shendoral all her life."

Gehlei wrinkled her nose at the thought of the weird

forest, where time seemed to stand still. Or even go backward. She tucked a strand of gray hair into her headdress, then said even more gruffly, "Send her to that baras."

"I don't like her."

"I know."

It felt so good to speak plainly, but that wouldn't solve the problem. "I don't trust her, either, even less than I trust Irza." Irza and her sister, the highest ranking of the Rescuers, had taken care of Julian during the days they'd hidden in the forest of Shendoral before the century of sleep was lifted.

As the baras tended to remind Atan, usually after a sickly sweet, "How is dear little Julian? My daughters miss her so very much, and would love nothing better than to have her live with them again." And she'd smile with her elder daughter's smug smirk. "My daughters often tell me little stories about how *good* the dear princess was when they had her under their care," she'd add, or something insinuating like it.

"Were the girls really good with Julian?" Gehlei asked, after scowling into the middle distance.

"As far as I could tell, but you know I joined the forest orphans so late."

Gehlei's mouth thinned. "Then let them have her."

"The baras is going to use Julian for political purposes, just as she was the one leading the campaign to shut out the commoners among the Rescuers. I really hate that. She doesn't care about Julian. How could she? She'd never even seen her until the enchantment broke, and has barely glimpsed her since."

Gehlei lifted a shoulder, as in the distance a bell rang the quarter- hour. "You have an entire council to deal with that. Do you want Julian civilized?"

"Yes. All right," Atan said, giving in. As she always did. "Next time the baras brings it up, I'll tell her to go ahead."

It happened a week later, after a temper tantrum down in the public areas, when one of the servants tried to get Julian to put on shoes before running into the rain. Atan thought later that this was a measure of how fast gossip traveled when the baras brought forth her invitation that very day.

And she watched, her spirits about as low as they'd ever been, as Julian looked back over her shoulder and said triumphantly, "Irza gives me what I want. I love Irza."

Gehlei was standing next to Atan as the baras's carriage rolled away. She smiled grimly.

Atan said, "I feel sick."

"Don't. The child knows the word love. An improvement."

Atan turned away, feeling even worse.

Two days later, she sat on her dais at the back of the public interview chamber, gazing through the colored glass in the windows at the great square as, on the other side of the room, district street and water guild representatives argued in bristlingly formal words, their voices heavy with innuendo. Each tried to imply that paying for the much-needed repair to a six-hundred-year-old fountain was the responsibility of the other.

Atan sat upright when she recognized a tall figure bearing some kind of burden.

The guild chiefs and the city officials paid no attention, of course. Knowing that they would be forced to rise if she rose, she got to her feet. The tedious argument ceased abruptly as everyone bowed.

Atan walked past, guessing how much resentment was constrained in those bent heads. A moment before the door shut behind her, she heard a low, angry, "*Now* see what you did!" from one of the district speakers.

"*I* did?" yelped a water guild representative.

The door snicked shut, and she hurried to meet Rel at the corridors' intersection, returned from his usual visit to Mendaen at the guard. His arms bore a mound of draggling fabric, a hank of tangled brown hair hanging down. Out of the middle of the swathe popped a red face as Julian declared indignantly, "I hate Irza!"

Rel set down the child, who scampered off as Irza herself appeared behind them.

Irza slowed, face red from running. Atan wondered if she'd chased Julian clear from Parleas Terrace to the palace as Irza performed a formal bow that was stiff with fury. "I relinquish her . . . to your care. Your majesty."

"Irza," Atan said. "What happened?"

Irza's face pinched up in an expression very like her mother's. "I do not know . . . what has happened to her since . . . our peaceful . . . days in the forest . . . but she has become ungovernable."

Atan didn't bother trying to deflect this blame. At the other end of the hall behind Irza, a white-haired boy appeared, waved, and retreated. Atan recognized Hinder, who should be underground in the morvende geliath for a family celebration.

Atan made herself speak formal words of thanks to Irza, though she knew it was a waste of time, that Irza and her mother were surely already spreading gossip blaming Atan for Julian's behavior. And Atan thought dismally that it was true. She was to blame as much as anyone.

As soon as Irza was put into a royal Landis carriage for the ride back (Atan knew that it would mollify Irza at least somewhat, being seen in a royal carriage) Atan and Rel began walking upstairs to Atan's private chamber.

"Found her running over the bridge, screeching. I called to her," Rel said. "Surprised when she came, but I think it was only because Irza was about to catch her."

Atan sighed. "I don't know what to do. The servants refuse to go near her."

Rel grinned. "Her hair smells like a bird nest. They can't trick her to step through a cleaning frame?"

"Not anymore. We used to. I don't know why she began putting up such a fuss. At least when the weather is warm she'll swim in the river with the other little ones, or when she goes back to Shendoral, she plays in the streams."

They reached her study, whose perimeter Hinder paced, his cobwebby hair drifting. "Atan," he said the moment she shut the door, "the elders sent me to warn you, and I wanted to tell you first: the Norsunder Base army is on the move."

"Where?"

"They were seen from the southeastern watch post, marching toward the coast."

"How many?"

"Hundreds. You have to remember we can only spy them out from a distance. But they were going toward the eastern coast."

Atan turned to Rel. "Then they must be taking ship. That makes it unlikely they're marching here, or against Sarendan."

At the first mention of Norsunder, Rel's smile had vanished. "I better get my gear," he said. "I promised Tahra I'd return to Everon at the first sign of Norsunder emerging from the Base."

Atan faced him. "How do you know that Everon is the goal?"

"I don't. But like you say, if they're taking ship, then they aren't marching here. King Berthold can decide whether or not to act on such scant information. I feel I ought to provide that information."

"The ambassador will be doing that," Atan said.

Rel smiled. "My three days here are up."

"I can give you a transfer token," Atan said as she reached for the bellpull. "It's time for me to summon the high council . . ." She stopped. "I will, of course. In a moment," she said, staring out the window at the courtyard below as she thought about Karhin's message a few weeks back, about the first alliance mission—Senrid of Marloven Hess sending someone to help train Terenth of Erdrael Danara's Mountain Guard—being a success.

Atan whirled to face Rel, and remembered the beautiful letter that she had received from the scribe named Karhin, who had said that Rel had personally recruited her. "But first I'm writing to the alliance, as I promised," and light filled her inner being at his sudden smile. "And then I'm writing to Hibern. For Sartor."

Senrid was sitting at breakfast, his knuckles throbbing from a good session on the mats, when a runner appeared, followed by Hibern.

"It's Atan," she said, and in Sartoran, "there's bad news on their south border. She wants to talk to you."

"Me?" Senrid said.

"I think she wants military advice, and she asked me to come to you directly, rather than going through Karhin Keperi."

"This is exactly what I didn't want happening," Senrid

muttered. But maybe it would only be another chance for
Forthan to gain some more experience training foreigners.
He'd certainly enjoyed going to Erdrael Danara.

Most important, Senrid had promised.

A short time later, he stood where he had never thought
to be: in Sartor's royal palace, parts of which were said to
be more than five thousand years old.

The longish walk from the Destination to the interview
chamber didn't surprise him, as he'd expected the mosaics,
the murals, the patterned marble in the worn floor and all
the fancy furniture. Unexpected was the way the low au-
tumnal light slanted in through filigree carvings, throwing
patterns on the marble, or reflecting again in long mirrors,
so that even though he knew he stood in a stone building,
the effect was of lightness and air and color.

Then they reached the interview chamber, and here was
Atan and a vaguely familiar tall boy who looked roughly
the age of the academy seniors. Was that the sense of fa-
miliarity? That he stood like someone trained? No. Senrid
had seen him. He just didn't remember where.

Atan noted that Senrid did not bother with formality
when visiting any more than he did in his own home: he
stood there in a white shirt, riding trousers, and boots, an
outfit that her first and second circles would consider positively undressed. At least he wasn't wearing any weapons.
Or, he didn't appear to be, she corrected herself as she took
in his wary, tight posture.

This conversation was going to be more difficult than
she'd thought. "Sartor's army was annihilated a hundred
years ago," she said, without any of the politenesses she
ordinarily began with. Her single visit to Marloven Hess
had made it clear that what worked as social easing in Sartor was pointless dither there. "The mages all think the
only way to deal with Norsunder is by magic."

Senrid backed up a step, his palms out. "Why do you
want me? I'm no expert in lighter magic. You've got your
entire Sartoran mage guild."

"But they didn't protect us a century ago. And," she said
quickly, seeing him stir, "I don't want anybody's army coming to our rescue, either. I have a very small palace guard,

and scant more at the border, the fewest permitted by some old treaty. And Rel here tells me that their military approach is a hundred years out of date. I don't even know what that means."

Senrid made a warding gesture.

Atan said, "Look, Senrid, we don't have any real defense. Oh, the council will shortly be telling me what to do. And I bow to their wisdom in so many ways. But this situation? I know they won't know any more than I do how we should proceed, and I can't help but hope that the kind of aid you gave to Erdrael Danara might do for us."

"They needed training." Senrid turned up his palms. "You're in need of action, right? You have to defend yourselves."

"How, without serving people up to the slaughter? At least tell me whom to ask? How about the person you sent to Erdrael Danara?"

"I sent someone his age." Senrid jerked a thumb at Rel, who stood silently by. "Ret Forthan will probably be a commander one day, but he'll tell you himself, he's not one now. All he did in Terry's land was give their newly reformed Mountain Guard some ideas about reorganizing, and improving their drills. He showed them some basic ones. Really basic. We Marlovens don't know anything about protecting mountainous land like Erdrael Danara." He made a motion up and down. "Plains horses don't like up and down."

He eyed Atan, who stared back, her desperation battering at Senrid's consciousness because of course she wasn't even thinking about mind-shields.

Then she said abruptly, "You're reading my mind. Aren't you?"

Senrid grimaced. "Yes and no. You're sending emotions at me like a charge of lancers, but I'm no good at sieving out sense from the emotions and jumble of memories, the way Liere has been doing from the time she was a baby. You need to practice your mind-shield."

Atan blushed to the ears, her lips compressed.

Senrid said quickly, "Here's the truth. We know war is coming, and we're not sure what will work to protect our kingdom, much less anyone else's."

"War," Atan said steadily, "is here."

Senrid struggled inwardly. He wasn't going to admit to anyone how exhilarated he'd felt after that little brush between Ndarga and his companies from West Army. It would be so easy to find another reason to do that again, especially when he thought he would win.

But that wasn't going to happen in Atan's kingdom. Atan didn't want him leading any battles, not that the Sartorans would follow him even if he did jump on a horse and start waving a sword and yelling orders. She wanted to make sense of something he'd spent his life trying to learn in order to survive.

Even if he didn't quite know what to do about it, yet.

His experiments with the city attack, and the secret communication network this past year, had taught him that much.

"Do you have a map?" he asked.

"This way."

Map-making had been one of the few activities Senrid's uncle had approved of while regent, so Senrid's first sight of the enormous table map of Sartor caused him to whistle in appreciation.

The map was actually a model, set on an enormous round table in the center of a round room, with a mirror set above it. Atan said, "My ancestors have had it remade over the centuries, as it needs constant repair as things change. Herald apprentices spend a year traveling the kingdom as part of their training. They bring back sketches, and the map is adjusted as rivers alter course, streams become rivers, towns add a building here, and take one apart there."

"And after wars," Senrid said.

"Yes. And after wars. You can see from the scars on this one how much was lost before the ninety-seven years of silence. But I cannot bring myself to order it destroyed. The scars here remind us of scars in the hearts of those who endured the attack and the enchantment."

She indicated the places where once had stood tiny porcelain villages and castles, the marred spots etched with stylized flowers. "There's building going on, of course. And a lot of trade coming over the border, which . . ." She paused, shook her head, then motioned for Senrid and Rel to join her at the south end. "Below here is Norsunder Base."

Senrid had been eyeing that gray expanse, with the ugly dark stone fortress made of unfired clay. "How accurate is that?"

"Symbolic only. Lilah told me it's completely wrong. She was a prisoner there before we lifted the spell. Uh, that's Lilah Selenna of Sarendan, whose brother Peitar is the new king. The newest members of the alliance."

Senrid shrugged Sarendan away as irrelevant. "I take it you don't have any inside information on numbers, defenses, that sort of thing?"

Atan's lips parted. "'Inside line of communication.' Is that what you mean? I was talking about that not three days ago in an interview. Quite an interesting fellow. Old. A prince of somewhere quite small, I forget."

Senrid had a feeling he knew. "Renselaeus?"

"I think that was it. I forget how we got onto it, but I asked him to define this phrase after he used it in conversation, and though he was very obliging, time was pressing, and I still don't quite understand what he was talking about, except that it sounded dauntingly military."

Senrid wavered, then thought, Why not? "Is he still here?"

"In Sartor? I believe so. He's one of the many who are trying to disentangle century-old trade agreements and funds. Nothing of that sort is done in a day." Atan frowned at the relief map, then said, "In fact, I ought to warn those visitors when I send word to the heralds to warn the city. Thank you. As for what the morvende told me . . ."

Little enough, Senrid soon discovered. He said, "Then here's what I think. Even if you had exact numbers. Capabilities. Intent. There's not a lot you can do in a military way if you don't have a military."

Atan nodded cautiously.

"So you have to use what you've got to make it as tough as possible for the enemy to invade. If you have wards, great. But we all know that lighter wards are mostly good for advanced warning. And it's not that much of an advance. There are very few light magic wards that can keep Norsunder out for very long. The only wards that seem to hold are those bound to magical artifacts of the sort we aren't able to make anymore."

He walked around the table to the southern border. "So, that aside. Is this city the heart of Sartor?"

"Yes."

"Then they will probably want to come up from the south, flank the city, and take it from both sides."

"I think that's what happened a century ago. They crossed the river at two places, east and west corners, and marched up the royal roads. They met my father's army here, and here, slaughtered them all, and then pushed on. It took them mere days." Atan had been an infant, but since she'd freed Sartor from its century of sleep, she had heard stories from elders for whom the grief was still raw.

"The map isn't telling me what kind of terrain, but if this river over here can be diverted to wash out this road, that ought to slow up a column of foot and horse. Water is also notorious for resisting magical manipulation, I'm sure you know . . ."

"I see," she said, her eyes widening. "Yes. I wonder if the magic council tried such things?"

"If they didn't, talk 'em into it. There is no easy save," Senrid said. "Eventually Norsunder'll get to your gates, then you better be ready with the close and personal defense. Though magical traps through the city will help. You know the terrain. They don't." He was silent, then said apologetically, "Though if this city has been squatting unchanged for centuries, they've got to have good maps."

"We can still try the traps," Atan said, her voice flat.

Senrid needed to get away from her whipsaw emotions. "The best person to help you would be Hibern. She and I have talked a lot about this plan for our own border. In my turn, I'd like to meet that prince from Renselaeus. You know where he might be staying?"

"I'm almost certain he's at the Carriage House."

"Carriage House?"

"It has a splendid name, but everyone has called it 'the Carriage House' for generations. Where visiting dignitaries stay if they don't have connections in the city."

"I'll show him." Rel spoke for the first time.

Atan threw him a look of relief. "Thanks, Rel."

Senrid had recovered the memory by now: this was the tall fellow dressed in a stolen Norsunder uniform who had pulled Senrid and that northern girl out of the prison cells at the Norsunder Base, at the beginning of Siamis's enchantment, and whisked them into a morvende tunnel.

Further, this had to be the same Rel that he'd heard about from the Mearsieans, both praise (Puddlenose) and insults (CJ).

A few steps into Sartor's chilly air, and Senrid wished he'd thought to bring a coat, but after matching a few of Rel's long steps, he decided he wasn't going to need one.

"From what I saw at the Norsunder Base that day, and from what Puddlenose has told me, you could take the field against Norsunder all by yourself," Senrid said as they crossed the square toward the bridge leading into the eastern part of the city.

"Puddlenose likes to joke," Rel said.

"So I take it Atan isn't going to be sending you off to the south, waving a sword and acting heroic?"

"The only time she's seen me waving a sword," Rel said in his deep, even voice, "she watched me get trounced by a fellow a head shorter than me."

"I should think most of the world is a head shorter than you," Senrid commented, wondering where CJ got the idea that this Rel was an arrogant blowhard. Of course, everybody had their bad days.

Senrid had been taking in his surroundings. He had to admit he was impressed, even if the first impression was a lot of clutter: statues, fountains, decorative carving that would be the first thing smashed in street fighting. But Sartor was too civilized for that, wasn't it?

Oh, yes. The war in which Atan had lost her entire family wasn't hazy generations ago, but relatively recently, for most of the people walking around before his eyes.

Rel had taken in the direction of his glance, and obligingly furnished names and dates and a brief story behind the local sights. Senrid grinned at the funny ones, and then they were there. The Carriage House was an imposing building on a corner where five streets met, its walls made of marble, with gargoyles and the like carved over all the tall windows.

Senrid was about to thank him when Rel said quickly, "I understand you know magic. Would you send me to that southern harbor so I can do some scouting?"

Senrid squinted up at Rel, a tall silhouette against the low northern sun resting on the city rooftops. "You don't think anyone is going to scout?"

"The mages might. I don't know. But they won't be looking for the same things I would."

Senrid could understand that. "Here's the problem. You say 'southern harbor,' which isn't a Destination. Unless you know there is one, and you can give me the pattern, I can't send you. Beyond my skills."

"No Destination that I know of."

"I think you'd need a mage like Tsauderei."

"Tsauderei," Rel repeated. "Great suggestion. Atan can send me to him. Thanks."

With a casual salute Rel left him, and walked off. Senrid watched for a few steps, wondering why CJ hated this Rel, who made no pompous speeches. He was going to do what needed doing. Anybody else would call that heroic behavior.

He shrugged it off and headed for the formidable building called the Carriage House.

He approached the front desk, whose carved wood depicted a sylvan scene. "I'm looking for the Prince of Renselaeus."

"He is dining in company," was the reply. Interesting, how this fellow's Sartoran was subtly different from Atan's. Regional difference or time difference? "But he has left instructions to pass on messages. Do you wish me to do so?"

Senrid hesitated, wondering if 'dining in company' meant no one was permitted access, or what the etiquette was. He found the whole question annoyingly pointless, but he didn't want to antagonize someone who found such stuff important.

So he said, "Senrid Montredaun-An would like to speak to him."

The smooth-faced man behind the counter mangled Senrid's name with a heavy enough accent to make Senrid want to grin.

A very short time later, he was back, leading a white-haired elderly man who leaned heavily on a cane. Senrid glanced at, then ignored, the fine velvet long coat over an old-fashioned tabard-vest, the loose long trousers and embroidered shoes, and met a pair of heavy-lidded dark eyes.

The old courtier greeted him in a smooth drawl, but the man had never heard of mind-shields, and Senrid braced against the sharp, anxious question.

"Your son is fine," Senrid said. "Right now he's sitting in my castle library, I'm sure, along with several others who stay at the academy year round." And left the question open: if you're so worried about your son, why haven't you brought him home?

"Please. Come this way," the old prince said, gesturing through a pair of tall doors carved to match the relief-work on the panels along the front desk.

Beyond these doors lay a hall, off which opened small, discreet anterooms, each with its tall window that overlooked the five-points intersection. Senrid could make out a couple of the palace spires above the inward-slanted rooftops across the way.

The chairs were big, comfortably cushioned. Senrid sat on the edge of one, glad it was low enough that his feet weren't off the floor, as the elderly prince took a moment to sink into the other.

During the walk, Senrid had been turning over what to say to Shevraeth's father while half-listening to Rel's explanation of the local sites.

Senrid had acceded to the prince's request to invite his son to the academy, but at first he hadn't liked Vidanric Renselaeus, Marquis of Shevraeth, known only as 'Shevraeth' in the academy. Then Liere had made the painful, but true, observation that jealousy lay behind most of Senrid's dislike.

Jealousy because Shevraeth had a living father.

True.

But Senrid had thought about it ever since, and knew that there was also Shevraeth's apparently effortless self-possession, a quality Senrid didn't have, knew he didn't have, and doubted he would ever have.

Well, he'd seen enough evidence that Shevraeth didn't have it all the time—that it wasn't effortless. More like habit, and when he was hurt, he broke like anyone else.

And so here Senrid was, facing Shevraeth's admired, wise, beloved father . . . who was alive. "The Sartoran Queen is going to be letting people know soon that Norsunder is on the march, down below the border," he said.

The prince sighed. "We have been dreading such news, but rumors have been flying too frequently and fast for it to come as surprise. As well I've finished my affairs here. Thank you for informing me."

The question he was too courtly, or too something, to ask, lay heavily in the air. Senrid said, "Your son's doing very well with us. As I think you know from his letters." Senrid made the gesture people recognized as tapping the lid of a notecase. He'd given Shevraeth one so he could communicate with his family.

The prince said, "Affording me the opportunity not only to thank you for this news, but also for providing us with the means for that communication."

The man was a courtier. Senrid should have known not to expect anything but empty flattery put in polite parlance. But in spite of the prince's dignified posture, trained into bone and muscle, Senrid sensed on the mental plane the weariness and anxiety the old man had no idea he was revealing. Remalna might be an inkblot of a kingdom, but it was home to this man and his family, and that home was being squeezed dry of its lifeblood by an evil king.

"So I came," Senrid said, "to tell you that, and also to make an offer. If you happen to know your exact Destination pattern, I can send you home by magic, before I return to my own home."

Surprise and gratitude lifted the weary lids. "Permit me to gather my belongings? It is little enough," the prince requested.

"Certainly. If you'll tell me your Destination pattern," Senrid said, "I can set up the spell. I'm not nearly as fast at sending another somewhere I've never been as my mage friends are."

"The Destination in my own palace, then." The Prince of Renseleaus described the pattern to Senrid, then excused himself with a polite word.

Alone, Senrid decided to test the spell first, though even

that much would hurt like a punch to the gut. But he'd feel better if he made a trial.

So he looked around. Someone had set an aromatic plant on a table in front of the window. Senrid pulled off a leaf, set it on the carpet, depicted the Destination, muttered the spell—and withdrew so fast he staggered backward, missed the chair, and fell on his butt. He sat there on the rug, shock ringing through him, then mentally worked backward. The leaf ought to have vanished with a little puff of air. But the stench of burning metal that had smacked him backward meant that a lethal magical trap awaited anyone who used that Destination.

A present for the prince from the evil king, maybe? Senrid waited impatiently until the prince returned, then told the prince in a few words what he'd found.

This time, the courtier mask didn't hold. The prince's face blanched, and he groped behind him, sitting down far quicker than he had before.

"Where else can I send you? That is safe?"

"Perhaps the harbor at Mardgar? I know that Destination. Used it often when I was younger. I can hire transportation to carry me north along the coast."

Another leaf, another test. Poof! They both watched the leaf vanish. The Mardgar Destination was safe.

Senrid transferred the old man. And as soon as he'd recovered, he transferred home. After that much transfer magic, he needed to sit and gather his wits again. As soon as he could move, he went straight to find Keriam.

If it was true that Siamis (or Detlev) wanted a ready-made army, then they'd destroy Senrid's wards and protections and come in intending to take and hold, not slaughter. If that was their initial tactic, Senrid and Keriam had decided the best defense was none—that is, there would be no army, and no academy, to find.

Time to step up the plans.

Chapter Seventeen

Chwahirsland

NO one but the Chwahir would understand resistance to tyranny expressed through nature, covertly and subtly shifted to make music or art.

Such as a dripping water trough.

Jilo entered a tiny village whose inhabitants made quilting for saddles and under chain mail. Everyone worked with the cotton grown on the north faces of the mountains, carefully tended; villagers carried pannikins of water to each plant during the long, dry days between rainstorms.

They lived in dilapidated, unpainted houses, with tiny blocked-in windows to conserve warmth. The way station for couriers was nothing more than a narrow bed of straw beside the stabling for two horses, meeting the minimum required by law. That was all the locals could scratch together.

Jilo had wanted to leave his horse and move on, but there was no fresh horse, the other having a strained hock. And so Jilo perforce must let his horse rest. He was impatient to get to Burda, to discover if there were women pretending to be men in the garrison there, if they had hand language, if they . . .

A woman offered him a bowl of stewed oats with shredded carrot to sweeten it, then withdrew in silence, and Jilo was left to eat where he might. He did not want to sit on that sagging bed made of sagging hemp rope under a thin, mildewing mattress of lumpy quilting, so he wandered around the village, the bowl tucked against him. At least it was warm. The days were definitely colder, the sun dropping lower in the north each day.

Jilo stopped out of the wind beside the last house, indistinguishable from the others but for the noise. He was barely conscious of it at first, though that was how it began with them all, and so he began actively to hunt.

He soon found the warped trough that carried water from the nearby hill to the village. Behind the house the trough dripped through cracks in the old wood. It looked old, broken-down, the big muddy-sided jars beneath the trough apparently abandoned.

Yet droplets from the cracked wood, on falling into the small hole in the enormous jug, plinked in soft melody.

Music. Forbidden on pain of death.

You couldn't hear it well unless you were close by. Jilo turned his head, and discovered open windows all along the back of the dilapidated house.

His shoulders tightened. He glanced behind him, catching no more than a flicker of movement. But retained in the inward eye, much like the distorted glow of lightning after the thunder has died away, remained a face, eyes like pits, mouth round in horror. It was too easy to imagine frightened villagers inside the houses, waiting for him to exclaim, to point, to kick aside the jar or say that he was going to report the trough for its noisy disrepair. But he backed away, and returned to the stable, where he finished the meal.

He returned the bowl. No one spoke. He didn't speak, and the villagers understood his complicity in his silence. His generous, unlooked-for, silence. And word swiftly and silently rang out behind him.

Unaware, he turned away from Burda, and headed toward the tiny town he'd only heard of, where his father's family had been born.

It didn't take long to reach. He'd been skirting the area all along.

As he closed the distance, he worked out a story in case anyone spoke to him. But they wouldn't. The law proscribed that, and everywhere he went, people existed in silent isolation, precisely as Wan-Edhe had wanted them.

But only on the surface.

In the old days, before the crown had assumed all land ownership, his family had worked in the guardhouse for the local *nanijo*, or warlord. That was a very long time ago, before family names were forbidden. Even so, Jilo remembered the few things he'd learned about the family Back Home. To the Shadowland Chwahir, Chwahirsland was always Back Home, even though the Shadow outpost was several centuries old.

Before Jilo's father vanished, he'd told detailed stories about his single visit to the castle where his ancestors had lived. Jilo recognized the castle the moment it came into view: the twin towers, one crumbling, both overlooking the river road. The confusion of houses built up against the walls, which were honeycombed with passages, the stone removed to reinforce flimsy walls of mud and old wood.

This castle, like pretty much all midlands buildings, showed the cost of many years of drought. The quarries, under Wan-Edhe's orders, supplied the border garrisons against an invasion that never came, and served the coast against his next planned war.

The buildings were as described, but as Jilo entered the castle courtyard, he ran into difficulties with the people. Jilo remembered his father's description of his Uncle Shiam: "He looks much like me, but taller, with a limp from the battle off Imar."

Jilo expected a hale man of thirty or forty, father-aged, but the guard commander was grizzled and stooped. The only thing Jilo recognized was the limp.

Had to be the same man. Jilo mentally added a generation of aging to those remembered features. Then there were the unknown young faces who had to be the cousins of whose existence his father, and therefore he, had been ignorant.

Nobody asked questions. They went about their business, scrupulously quiet, until the silence coagulated in a way that seemed to cut off all the air. The only signs of his connection to this world being glimpses of people with light brown eyes shaped like his, and his father's pendulous ears.

His attention went to those closest to his own age. The girl (cousin?) whisked herself out of sight, quite properly, whenever she saw Jilo walking about, but the livable portions of the castle were so small that the people were in fairly constant contact. Jilo found an old arrow slit while he was poking around, from which he could handily see an inner court between the stable and the garrison kitchen. There he saw the girl cousin in head-bent, earnest conference with a brother who had to be her twin. They were exactly the same size, their hair the same blue-black, somewhat like his own, only thicker. He hadn't known that girl and boy twins could be identical; it wasn't until the vagaries of wind brought their voices, which were so alike he could not tell them apart, that the obvious occurred to him: the supposed boy might actually be a girl.

Interest sharpened. He had to test his theory.

A rainstorm, thick with sleet, provided a convenient reason to postpone his having to carry his false messages onward. It was while he was trying to find another way into the stable, and lost himself in the broken honeycomb of small rooms long since ruined by law-enforced neglect as well as the weather, that he unexpectedly came face to face with the girl.

Girls were forbidden to speak first. He stepped aside (which was strictly against regulations, as it was for females to get out of males' way) and moved on, prompted by a pulse of guilt for spying. But when he reached the extremity of the ruin, which was little more than piles of broken stone rejected for reuse elsewhere, that it hit Jilo. She'd been stalking him.

And here it was again, so unexpected: danger.

For all the years he'd been Kwenz's student, he had lived with danger as his daily companion, far away when Wan-Edhe was distant, brought sharp and close with his proximity. Since Prince Kessler had taken Wan-Edhe away, the danger had been from his magic, and the possibilities that Jilo dreamed up: What if the army revolted? What if the people revolted? What if they caught him (whoever 'they' might be) and squashed him flat for his temerity in pretending to be a king?

He clutched at the ring on his finger, ready to transfer back to Narad, whose poisonous atmosphere was at least a familiar danger.

But while he stood there in the half-sheltered ruin listening to the hissing roar of sleet, and nothing happened, his heartbeat slowed, and his breathing eased from the rasp of fear.

Nothing was going to happen. Now. Wild thoughts of a knife in the darkness assailed him, to be dismissed. That was thinking like Wan-Edhe. It made no sense. Thinking himself threatened made no sense. He was only a courier. This was an unimportant flatfoot garrison. The girl was curious because . . .

Her curiosity sharpened his own. Wan-Edhe's conviction that females, generally born smaller than males, were therefore stupid and useless, had been proven abundantly wrong by the Mearsiean girls.

This girl, possibly a cousin, was curious, and that made her interesting. Jilo had to find out why she was curious.

The bell rang once, a sour iron clang. He made his way around to the mess hall.

Jilo's entrance shut everyone up, and they moved in strict rank order to the long benches. But Jilo kept the image in his mind's eye, the natural groupings that made it clear where the twia were, and further, that family members were bound into some of the twia, though that was also forbidden. Twia were supposed to become patrols or support staff if one member attained officer status, entirely military in purpose.

Jilo was about to enter when he heard a light footstep from behind: the girl cousin again, bearing a tray of food. She stepped against the wall, but did not lower her eyes. Jilo could see fear in the tautness of her high forehead. The tension of her shoulders was not due to the heavy tray she carried.

She licked her lips, and then spoke. "I am Aran." And waited for the axe to fall.

So simple and natural, those words, proscribed by law and regulation. Jilo, thrilled by her daring, said, "I am Jilo."

She gulped in air. The dishes rattled on the tray, and Jilo became aware of rustles and whispers around the corner. That had to be the rest of the females, waiting in line to bring the food.

So Jilo ducked into the mess hall, and awkwardly fumbled his way to the place where couriers always sat. Those seated there quietly made space.

And though everyone's attention appeared to be strictly on his plate as the women and girls served the food, Jilo was sensitive to the weight of their collective scrutiny. The tuneless, random clatter of eating implements on plates, the rustle of cloth, here and there a quick tread did not mask the sense of . . . of a rounded scrutiny, an instinctively arrived-at roundness divisible by eight. Though Wan-Edhe had denied Jilo a true twi of his own, he could see, he could feel, the rightness, the balance of the twia he saw before him.

After the meal, he was climbing up to the rooms over the stable, when he came up short in a low doorway, face to face with the commander himself.

"Has my granddaughter trespassed?" he asked.

Jilo fingered the onyx ring, ready to transfer out. "I think we're related."

The commander said gravely, "You're the son of my nephew Dzan."

He wasn't asking a question, and so Jilo said, "I'm Jilo."

"We know," the commander said even more gravely.

"You do?" Jilo asked. "Oh. Do I look like my father? All of you, that is, many of you, remind me of him."

There was a pause that grew almost to a silence, then the commander said gently, "We know who you are." He amended quickly, "That is, along the courier routes."

The words struck Jilo like a blow to the head, only from the inside. Of course the couriers would talk. Though not to him. They had their twia. They could not, dared not, read the dispatches they carried, customarily sealed with lethal spells against tampering, but just because they were expected to remain silent, that did not mean that every person was not using eyes and ears exactly as Jilo did.

"Why are you here?"

Jilo hunched defensively. "Trying to learn . . ." Words failed him. As always. He looked down, hating his inability to articulate his thoughts. But because Commander Shiam still waited, he said, "Everything."

And because that steady gaze reminded him of Mondros, up there in the distant mountains barely visible to the south, Jilo said, "To see what damage Wan-Edhe has done. If . . . if he doesn't come back. How to fix it."

The commander let out a slow breath. "We call him The Hate. That word cannot be magic-bound against mention."

Jilo still had not managed to ascertain whether or not Wan-Edhe actually had a spell to warn him whenever his name or title was spoken, the way many believed Norsunder was warded. He jerked his head in assent, accepting that a fuller conversation was impossible.

"If he is not dead, and some believe even then, he will return," the commander said.

Jilo shrugged again, more sharply. "I know. I think on that each day." More he dared not say.

He didn't need to. Jilo's demeanor, his lack of regulation reaction, the dropped tone of his voice when he said 'I think on that each day' implied to Shiam that there was more going on than met the eye. It implied that he was not Wan-Edhe's creature, that he was possibly, miraculously, taking steps against the evil tyranny that had begun to seem inescapable. Eternal.

So when Jilo asked the question he had not been capable of considering until he had been days away from Narad's poison—"Does my father still live?"—Shiam did not hide his surprise.

Jilo flushed guiltily, old habit, after using the forbidden words 'my father.' "Prince Kwenz warned me never to ask, for my loyalty might be questioned."

Shiam accepted that, and said in a voice of low regret, "We were told he died in a border dispute with the Danarans. He was in charge of the supplies."

We were told. Jilo inclined his head.

They parted then, Jilo to wander over and peer out at the dreary sleet, and occupy himself as he might until the next meal. A gradual awareness of a qualitative alteration in atmosphere resolved into a repeat of the sound patterns he'd noticed on his travels. Furtive, brief: tapped fingers here. The clatter of nut shells on a string, which he discovered suspended high up under a rafter above the scrawny cows. He was very certain he had not overlooked it on his first exploration through the barn.

A whistle, soft and low, that might have been mistaken for the wind moaning through the rocks, but it wasn't. It was too regular and too short for that.

As night fell, and the storm abated to drips and plops along the edges of eaves and overhangs, the shadows closed in, and once more Jilo found himself in the ruins.

This time Aran came toward him deliberately, barely discernable among the deepening shadows.

"Is there anything I can get for you?"

Jilo took another cautious step toward understanding. "Information only."

"As in?" Aran replied.

"Your twin."

Aran stiffened. "What about him?"

Jilo said, "Him?"

That was all. Aran stilled. Jilo could hear her breathing, then she sighed softly, and began to speak in what at first sounded like storytelling mode: "Long ago, it is told in great Chwahirsland, under the great king . . ."

That way every story, false or true, had always begun, fanciful stories being forbidden by Wan-Edhe as frivolous and time-wasting when drought conditions required a steady mind and constant labor. But then she said, "In faraway Shadowland, the law required every family to kill or shell a second girl—"

"That's not true," Jilo interrupted. "I was in the Shadowland. That law was here."

Aran said firmly, "In faraway Shadowland, the law required every family to kill or shell a second girl."

And Jilo had it: the storytelling mode hid a truth behind "in faraway Shadowland" the way his own folk had hidden it behind "long ago."

When he didn't interrupt again, she went on more softly, "There was a family who had two sons. The regional commander spread the word through the land that a third son would gain the family a better placement, and as they had no daughter, the birth of one would not cause lament."

Jilo was silent. He knew about Wan-Edhe's method of dealing with the encroachment of drought upon the resources of a hungry kingdom, where all must support the army above anyone else. Second daughters were a luxury Wan-Edhe decreed the kingdom could not afford.

". . . and so, to this family was born twin girls, named Aran and Kirog. But the decree raised consternation among them, and because twins are rare, word had spread all through the region, unto the ears of the regional commander himself. His merciful solution was to shell Kirog to Kinit—"

Jilo's nerves jolted. Until this moment he had not known that magic could force a person to change gender. He'd assumed the will of the changee must be obtained first.

"—and so the process was begun, but somewhat into it, Wan-Edhe assembled all mages for great purposes of his own, and so the process was incomplete. But Kinit was accepted by the family, and by his twi, and by the regional governor who assigned that twi unto the study and maintenance of horses."

A pause, which became a silence. Jilo stared at the silhouetted girl, his mind proliferating so many questions he had no idea where to begin. Or if he should.

The first being: what did that mean, 'the process was begun'?

Did it matter?

Until now he had not troubled himself thinking about what lay under anyone's clothes, so why should that become an item of interest now? Identity was a matter of mind, that much he had learned from observing those Mearsieans: Falinneh, a Xubarec, who shapechanged between genders as easily as people changed clothes; Dhana, whose natural form looked like a crack in water, but who had decided to experiment with human form, one closest to that of the girls she'd been watching from the water; and even Puddlenose, who had a habit of disguising himself as a girl when he was bent on escape. When he dressed as a girl, people believed he was one, tall and bony as he was.

Enough. The matter was plain: Aran's twin was, to the

family, to his twi, and to the world, Kinit the stableboy. No more, no less.

And so Jilo gave the prescribed reply, "Long ago, in great Chwahirsland, under a great king, life was truly great."

He expected her to leave him to himself. He would not have minded if she had, because he wanted to think through everything he'd heard.

But she said softly, "Come."

The note of her voice sent a frisson through his nerves, for so profound a change—a girl in effect giving him an order, though her tone was invitation—meant that he had been tested without his knowing, and something else was about to occur.

Then fingers bumped against his arm. He jerked it back, and took a couple of steps away.

Aran said, "I will leave you if you wish, but . . ."

It was that *but*, in the same invitational tone.

Every sense alert, he stepped forward once, twice. This time he reached, and when he encountered the girl's cold fingers, he stilled as her hand patted his arm lightly, then slid under his elbow. And tugged with gentle insistence.

He walked with her through the dripping ruin, into the barely warmer stable, and through that into the garrison mess. But that room, too, was empty, though light spilled, pale gold, down the staircase from above.

On they walked to the kitchen, and through that. Jilo followed in growing surprise as they entered the unlit larder; he fought a sneeze from the sharp scents of dried herbs. Dimly he made out a narrow entrance beyond the barrels of bitter beer.

Down they walked, not into the dankness of rot and moss, but into a malty-warm vapor of ancient brewing. He could see nothing, he could hear nothing, but he knew that the cellar was not empty.

Aran pulled the cellar door closed, and then one by one came the scritch of sparkstones, and light sprang into being: candles wavering here, throwing dramatic shadows up the plastered walls, and in the center a single glowglobe, its magic fading. More candles were lit, and set on a bare little table in the center. Above it someone had hung a cloth so old it was almost rotted, fragile beyond belief, age-spotted.

When Jilo made out the circular pattern on it, shock flared through all his nerves: it wasn't even the forbidden circle symbol of Chwahirsland. This was far older, long forbidden, the eight intertwined linden leaves, heart-shaped, the twi symbol that had become Chwahirsland's circle, which in turn Wan-Edhe had forbidden because it implied loyalty to one's group, and loyalty must only go to his person.

Jilo stared up at it, shocked by the trust implied in his seeing this sacred treasure as, in silence, someone ladled something whitish yellow and unfamiliar-looking into tiny bowls that were then passed from hand to hand, the fragrance rising from them delectable.

When a bowl reached him, he stared down at the tangle of nearly translucent vermiform shapes, then he gasped. Rice noodles! Kwenz had occasionally eaten them, in the Shadowland days: Jilo had sometimes slipped in and finished the old prince's bowl if he wandered off, forgetting the meal he'd been eating. They had been delicious.

And they were absolutely forbidden to the ordinary Chwahir, again, on pain of death—a death not only for the eater, but for his entire village. Rice, once the great Chwahir staple, now so precious, had been reserved for the upper echelons for at least four centuries, and in this century, reserved for Wan-Edhe and his elite guard only.

Yet here. In Jilo's hand. Was fragrant rice, beaten with milk into batter, laid out on wooden racks to dry, and then cut into noodles, an act that required secrecy from all involved.

The weight of the village's trust nearly overwhelmed him, the sharing hollowing him with emotions he had no experience with except that they hurt, and yet it was a sweet anguish.

Jilo didn't even know how to eat the noodles; he had no eating sticks, which of course had also been forbidden to the people. Spoons only. No one could assassinate with a spoon.

So he tipped his head back and let the warm noodles slide into his mouth. The pungent flavor was unidentifiable, but it tanged on his tongue, shading to sweet, with a lingering hint of sour. Two swallows, and the little portion was gone.

He opened his eyes and discovered the empty bowls being passed and stacked. He relinquished his.

When all bowls were stacked, the people stepped forward, not in their tidy regulation rows of rank, but forming a circle. What's more, hand moved to hand, linking at elbows, until they stood in two circles, one within the other: females within, males in the greater circle. Aran left Jilo with Kinit, the sister turned brother, whose firm arm interlocked with him on one side, and old commander Shiam on the other, his arm gnarled as the branch of an apple tree.

Jilo scarcely had time to take his place, with these people pressed up against him on either side—strictly forbidden—when the first sounds reached his ears: a soughing, that reminded him of the sea that he had sometimes visited from the Shadowland, half a morning's ride.

Hiss, rush. The people breathed in unison. In benison. Jilo's heart beat in rhythm, his breath sibilated, in, beat, beat, out, thrum, thrum. A little giddy, he let his eyelids fall, and faint as a distant bird's cry far over the water came a high-voiced "Ah-h-h-h."

Thrum, thrum, a low rumble, "Ho-o-o-o-h-h-h-m."

The two voices splashed through the rhythmic tide of hiss, hiss, hrum, thrum, gradually subsiding into harmonic resonance, and cold showered through Jilo's nerves when the truth struck him. They were humming.

Absolutely forbidden! On pain of death!

A new high voice: "Chika-chee, chika-chee, Tsa-tsa-tsa," the mating cry of the marsh river's bird.

New voices joined, "Hoo-wee, hoo-wit!"

"Caw, caw, caw!"

"Orble-roo, orble-roo!"

On Jilo's right, Commander Shiam uttered a subsonic rumble that Jilo felt more than heard, an abyssal fremitus resounding steadfast as mountains, "Hrummmm-hrumhrummm . . ."

Here the rhythmic popping noises, made by lips and tongue, the snap of beans and greens, there the chuckle of boiling liquid, sung on a note that blended into the chord that now sustained itself through at least six voices, three male and three female.

"Korroo, korroo," the cry of the rooster.

"Sssssa, ssssa," a winding snake.

Hrumm, thrummm, bound together by the low, eternal rhythm of the sea, the glorious music encompassed the comforting sounds of life and the shared cadences of work: the clop of horse hooves, the keen of the saw, the chink of stone, each voice adding to the rhythm until all found a place in the syntonic chord, a sound that reverberated through his bones, drenching his being with the blessedness of tears.

How Wan-Edhe would hate this flouting of his decrees, the evidence that there was more to life than fighting, and feeding warriors so they could fight! Jilo found himself sustained by the will of the people, unspoken evidence that the Chwahir did not exist to serve Wan-Edhe's will, though he had exerted his vast power to that end.

And they were trusting him enough to count him in the circle.

Trust. How simple a thing. How powerful, when one trusts eight, and each of the eight reaches out to another twi, which becomes sixty-four, and sixty-four becomes four thousand . . .

Jilo's fragile cage of bone and flesh could not contain the intensity of his joy and wonder—and of sorrow, for all they had lost.

Sobs welled up, shuddering against his ribs, and would have sent him running, but those arms held him tight, the sound swelling in glory and pain and brightness and darkness, drowning his own voice with the birth of a new emotion, as yet unrecognized. But it was there.

He got his ragged breath under control, though he couldn't see for the burn of unaccustomed tears, as around him and through his body flowed the Great Hum of the Chwahir, which had never gone silent at all. One by one the voices ceased, except for the rhythmic breathing, and the moment, precious as life, flowered into memory.

PART THREE
The Alliance Meets

Chapter One

Winter, 4742 AF
Unnamed bay east of Norsunder Base

THE alliance had a name, and a communications center, but as yet it had never met in a body.

It was going to take the advent of war to achieve that, as we shall see presently.

Right now, everyone was busy thinking of home defense, except for Rel, who sat alone on a wintry palisade overlooking the green-gray ocean, watching for Norsundrians.

On his fourteenth early-morning sweep of the horizon, Rel was surprised to discover his first sign of Norsundrians coming from the land, and not the sea.

He'd expected to see the transport ships arrive first, but wariness had forced him to survey in all directions as soon as he opened the flap of his tent.

So though he was surprised, he was not caught by surprise.

Obedient to his promise to Tsauderei, at the first sight of movement cresting the far ridge that stitched the gray, rocky landscape to the equally gray low sky, Rel crawled all the way out of the tent the old mage had given him, and said the words he'd been taught.

The tent's interior had been chilly but livable. The cold struck hard when the tent vanished. Rel hunched into Tsauderei's magnificent yeath-hair coat, yeath hair being extraordinarily hard to glean high in the mountains, the hair scraped off by the animals onto brambles and rough rocks each spring.

The world this far south had dwindled to infinite shades of gray, including the thick hat that Rel had pulled down to just above his eyelids, the heavy scarf he'd wound around his neck and lower face to cover his nose, the mittens, and four pairs of socks stuffed inside his forest mocs.

Forcing himself not to hurry, he crouched to keep from making a silhouette, and lowered himself with painstaking care from upended, treacherously slippery rock to rock. Tsauderei had said that the day the tent reappeared in his cottage, he would transfer Rel away at sundown. A transfer token would easily be traced if mages did a sweep. But if Rel had nothing magical about him, any mages would not find him.

"I watched that harbor for one miserable season sixty-five years ago," Tsauderei had said, "when we were still uncertain whether Norsunder was going to move against Sarendan the way it had against Sartor. The crevasse my predecessor watched from, and showed to me, is the equivalent of two stories up from the sand, which means you will be climbing down the cliff about three stories. You must not descend all the way to the sand, unless you wish to leave footprints. Or wade through the tide. Your limbs will freeze beyond the ability to heal."

Rel had spent lonely days watching the invisible progress of the northerly sun behind the clouds, and observing the milky rime slowly building along the coast and along the old stone jetty put in the natural harbor centuries ago, judging by the long greenish streamers surging in the surf.

To pass the time, Tsauderei had given him a court history of Sartor, which was exactly as boring as it sounded, but from which, the old mage said, "All Sartorans will quote, as they were all brought up on it." He also gave him a gossipy history of Eidervaen written by a retired house-

hold goods mover in the century before Sartor was bespelled, which recounted all the local legends that were most
definitely left out of court histories. Crammed with stories
about the insides of famed houses, this one entertained Rel
so much he could ignore the uncomfortably rocky ground,
the continual drum of the wind on the tent, and the pervasive chill.

Now those and the tent were gone. He crept down the
face of the cliff until he reached the crevasse, whose ancient bracken still held sturdily against wind, weather, and
time.

He crouched in the mossy slime, one hand alternating
with the other as he peered through his field glass. The free
hand, he pressed between his chest and thigh as he perched
in the tiny space with his knees up under his chin. His feet
had begun the inevitable pins-and-needles prickling by the
time the distant movement had resolved into a column snaking its way down the ridge on the extreme southwestern side.

He was still too high to overhear the Norsundrians
as they streamed down onto the sand at low tide and
marched toward the jetty. He caught the occasional word
on the brittle air, mostly curses, as the thickening overcast
began spitting slushy rain. Winter was nigh, and the desire
to get well out into the water before the first freeze of the
coming season was apparent in the way the marchers were
crowded up onto the rocks.

A perimeter team made a fast, thorough search along
the edge of the sand where it met the rock, and another
marched along the top of the ridge. Rel had done his best
to make certain he left no prints, never treading on any
moss, no matter how thin. Still he held his breath, ducking
down when the inner perimeter passed directly below.

The searchers moved on, clapping their arms to their
sides, rubbing mottled noses, stamping, and generally making it clear that the cold wind was fast getting even colder
as the short day drew swiftly toward its end.

When they rejoined the column picking its way like a
trail of lumbering ants along the rocky jetty, Rel relaxed
enough to lift his field glass to scan them. It was frustrating
to be so near, and yet not near enough to overhear anything. At least he could count up the force.

He had positioned himself in the crevasse so that he could see along the jetty. Thanks to Puddlenose's having introduced him to Captain Heraford, he'd spent a little time crewing on board the *Tsasilia*, which had taught him something about currents and tides.

On the far side of the bay, a lone figure peered down from the crevasse through which the Norsundrians had marched. He made a perfunctory visual sweep, but didn't see Rel. His attention was on Henerek as the husky man moved carefully from rock to rock along the jetty, to where the sea splashed up.

Rel also scrutinized that bundled-up figure, wondering if there was something familiar about the way the fellow moved, or if it was only his imagination.

The man paused on a huge stone jutting out over the seaweed trails in the water, and peered back toward the beach as though measuring something. Then he dug deep in the pocket of his bulky coat, cocked back his arm, and threw something as far as he could out into the choppy waters.

White water boiled up in an enormous splash, and in less than an eyeblink, an entire ship appeared, an old-fashioned thing with an up-curving prow of a kind Rel had never seen before. It rocked dangerously on the water, sending an enormous greenish-gray wave splashing up onto the rocks to drench the waiting warriors, who gave a huge outcry. Many fell painfully. Several were knocked from the rocks entirely.

On board the ship, the crew fell to the deck, then struggled to their knees, or grabbed for ropes. Rel knew enough about ships to see the immediate danger: if the crew did not get some sort of sail up, the ship would swamp on the beach.

The captain seemed to recover first, bawling something at the man on the rocks, who had staggered back, dripping wet.

Aboard the ship, the captain began kicking and striking his crew to get them moving. After they had accepted the mysterious Ramis's offer to send them beyond time, the captain had ordered his crew at the first sight of the great crack in the world to lay aloft on yards and mastheads. So when the magic released them, they were already in position. They scrambled into action, unreefing a sail that the crew below sheeted home. The ship came alive, shivering in the water as it moved against the inexorable tide toward the very tip of the jetty.

On the rocks, the man removed his sodden scarf, which he flung down. For a heartbeat his face was visible as he took in the ship from tumblehome to masts, and Rel's breath hissed in when he recognized that arrogant countenance, and the sandy hair: Henerek, the would-be Knight who had been dismissed for too many infractions to remember.

This had to be the Everon attack force that Kessler promised.

Henerek turned away and began clumsily hopping from rock to rock farther along the jetty. He had to be freezing. His waterlogged coat clung to his long body. He, too, had aged from a weedy teen to a man heavy with muscle along chest, shoulders, arms.

At the extreme tip of the jetty, as the ship beat out to take up station a short distance away, once again Henerek threw something. This time, he ducked down behind a rock when the expected wave surged over the jetty. The rest of the Norsundrians having stayed where they were, there was no other damage to those waiting. This ship recovered itself and got a sail up, as the first one lowered a longboat into the water.

Twice more this happened. As the light began to fade, the ships withdrew to a safe distance, sending longboats to the beach to fetch Henerek's waiting force and ferry them back.

They had begun lighting lanterns when abruptly Rel transferred, his cramped, shivering body falling to the thick red and gold rug in Tsauderei's cottage.

The old mage remembered the extreme cold. He had a warm change of clothing, hot food, and drink waiting. When Rel could get his jaw to work without chattering, he gave a concise report.

"Four ships," Tsauderei repeated. "From what you describe, they sound rather like vessels from the bad old days when the Venn ruled the seas. Records insist that Norsunder used to grab pirate ships wholesale, shoving them through powerful rifts, before the mages learned to close those rifts. Now, it seems, they are going to begin reappearing. This is grim tidings."

"So we should look for vast armies appearing on the coasts?" Rel asked.

"It is possible, and yet . . . only four to transport that force. I wonder if this is an experiment by someone higher up the command chain. Yet one would think they would be sparing. The magic that put those ships beyond time has been unreproduceable for centuries."

"Henerek might have stolen the means. He was a thief as well as a bully and a liar."

"Always possible. But even so, the higher-ups have a way of catching out unruly underlings and taking advantage of their resourcefulness." Tsauderei sat back. "Here. Eat the rest of that food. Get a good night of rest up in the loft, where it's warmest. I'll send you directly on to Everon in the morning. Tonight, I have some letters to write."

Everon

The next morning, Tsauderei transferred Rel to Everon as promised.

Once he recovered, he was brought by a footman into the royal presence. Though Everon was quite a ways north of the border mountains where Tsauderei's valley was located, to the sun's movement, it was perhaps an hour to the west. The royal family was at breakfast, their faces sharing similar expressions of concern when Rel was conducted in.

Rel made his bow, then once again issued a report, this time with precise numbers.

On the name 'Henerek,' the king reached for the hand bell to summon a page, as Glenn grinned fiercely down at his plate. "Please request the presence of Commander Dei," King Berthold said.

The king left his half-eaten breakfast. The queen went off in another direction, leaving Rel with the royal children.

Glenn threw down his napkin. "They *have* to let me ride with the Knights," he declared, and he, too, ran off.

Tahra scowled at her plate, then looked at Rel. "The alliance needs to know."

Rel said, "I don't have the means to communicate with them."

"My friend Piper is a scribe student, and she writes regularly to Karhin for me," Tahra said as she pushed a last bite of berry tart around on her plate. "Her Sartoran is better than mine." She tapped her fingers twice on the table, the side of her cup, then the table again before looking up. "Do you think the alliance can help us?"

"I'm not sure.," Rel admitted, and when Tahra's thin brows crimped anxiously, he said, "I think it's a good idea, but I don't know how it's supposed to work other than as a way to pass news."

Tahra's long face seemed to lengthen as she glared at her plate. "Glenn is wrong to think everything will be fixed by swinging swords. Norsunder must have millions of warriors, if they never die."

"They can die. Unless they're soul-bound. But then they lose their wills."

"So what happens when they are inside Norsunder? Are they statues?"

"Maybe it's like what happened to Sartor, you just . . . stop. Until you go again."

Tahra folded her arms across her front and ran her thin fingers up her arms, her stomach tight with disgust. "I thought it was horrible when my family was enchanted. But that sounds so much worse. How can anybody even fight them, if they have millions?"

"We don't know that they have millions, and anyway, they aren't in our world. They need rifts to bring them to the world from Norsunder-Beyond. Transfer magic is dangerous, so they can't even bring them in by twos and threes without a safe period in between."

"I know that much." Tahra's straight dark brows crimped, then she turned her head sharply as a page entered. "What is it?"

The page said to Rel, "The king requests your presence."

Rel was shown into the king's interview chamber, where the king himself was busy unrolling one map, the queen another.

They occupied themselves looking at the map of the Sartoran continent, tracing the natural harbor where Rel had spied the Norsundrians, and estimating how long it would take to sail northward. Rel listened, aware that none of them knew the winds and currents enough to be certain of anything.

But it gave them something to do until Roderic Dei arrived, looking as if he had hastened away from his breakfast. Once again Rel gave his report, after which the Commander said, "I'll talk to the fleet captains, but one thing for certain, we'll need to work on shore defenses."

"Yes!" The king slammed his hand down in a gesture of agreement. "That, we can do over winter." He looked up at Rel. "Thank you. I trust you will honor us with your skills?"

Rel had been about to ask to be sent back to Sartor. Except what could he do there? The high council scorned military action. He could march around holding a candle in parades, but they didn't want his help, or even his presence, in Sartoran affairs.

"If you can use me, I'm yours," Rel said.

Roderic Dei smiled, well pleased. Maybe he would gain Rel as a Knight after all. "Come along with me. We'll report your findings, and get you situated."

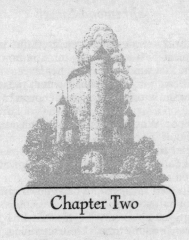

$$\boxed{\text{Chapter Two}}$$

Roth Drael

HIBERN woke up late, startled by the internal tick of
her notecase. She groped for it, wondering who would
send her a note by magic before dawn.

She snapped the glowglobe alight. The note was written
in a shaky hand, strong on the downstrokes:

> *Hibern: I am certain Erai-Yanya arranged an
> emergency signal with you. If your demonstration is
> prepared, now would be the time to use that signal.
> I've Atan and Veltos ready to meet tomorrow. Erai-
> Yanya's presence might make all the difference.*
>
> *Tsauderei*

Hibern scrabbled on desk for the token Erai-Yanya had
made. She picked it up, murmured the words she'd been
taught, and the thing snapped away from her fingers and
vanished.

She heard rustlings from the outer room, and sighed
inwardly. Liere, whom she had removed from Marloven

Hess at Senrid's request, had rendered the past few days tedious almost past bearing by her stream of questions about magic that was way beyond her level as a beginner.

For someone who claimed she wasn't the least bit special, she certainly seemed to expect special tutoring. Hibern pulled on a wrapper against the cool drafts moving along the floor. Why hadn't the senior mages put Liere in a magic school?

She found the girl hovering over the basket of food transferred daily from the Bereth Ferian palace's kitchen. Liere looked rumpled, as if she'd slept in her clothes and forgotten to step through the cleaning frame, her short, raggedly cut hair sticking out in all directions.

"Why are you up so early?" Hibern asked.

"I was awake a long time," Liere mumbled. "My mother was dreaming bad things about me again. I had to fix things inside her dream. So she knows I'm all right."

Hibern's skin chilled. "You can do that?"

Liere looked startled, as if she'd been caught committing a crime. Her cheeks mottled with color. "Siamis did that to me once, talked to me in my dreams, I mean. When I was with Senrid, running away from the eleveners. When I had the dyr. He tried to scare me into giving it up. I figured, if he can do it, I can. I was used to hearing my mother's dreams. Hadn't known that I might be able to talk to her in them and make it all right."

And that was probably why they didn't put Liere in a magic school. Hibern turned away, hiding her expression of revulsion as she concentrated on her mind-shield. Neither school would want a mind reader among them, much less someone who could wander into dreams and 'fix' them.

"Is the bread still warm?" Hibern asked. "Pass the elderberry jelly."

As the sun began sifting golden shafts between the eastern trees, they finished, worked together in dunking and drying the dishes, then Liere picked up her garden tools and went outside in the clear summer air while Hibern looked at her piles, trying to decide which project would be least annoying to be pulled out of when Erai-Yanya arrived.

A blast of warm, oddly scented air startled her. Erai-

Yanya appeared in the corner reserved for magical transfers. She staggered as if she'd run down a couple of steps, sneezed violently five or six times, then lifted a hand to her head. "I'll never get used to how different the air is. Emergency?" she said, rubbing her sun-browned face. She looked unfamiliar, wearing an odd, brightly colored outfit that seemed comprised of three layers of thin cloth.

"In a way. Tsauderei asked me to send for you."

"Do you know what it's about?"

"We've spent the past three weeks talking about almost nothing else."

"We?" Erai-Yanya asked, "You, Tsauderei—"

"And Senrid, and Peitar—"

"Peitar Selenna of Sarendan?" Erai-Yanya rubbed her eyes again. "Please don't tell me he's discovered the sport of kings, and is marching to war."

Hibern said, "Peitar's friend Derek has organized the orphans of Sarendan into defense. But that's made Peitar more determined than he was before to find some way to defend his kingdom without bloodshed."

"All right. *That* sounds like Peitar Selenna." Erai-Yanya sighed. "I'm glad people haven't changed out of all recognition while I've been gone. Tell me your part."

Hibern looked down at her hands, clean and warm right now, but the echo of bitter cold pulsed there as she considered how much to report. And how very important it all was to her—this first time she had been asked to act as a mage, instead of being exhorted to watch and learn as a student.

But what can seem vitally important for all kinds of reasons could sound really boring, especially when performing dangerous and yet tedious tasks again and again, as she and Senrid had endured the late-autumn winds and rain, toiling along Marloven Hess's southern border, where Norsunder had crossed a few years back.

"I worked with Senrid," she said. "Our strategy was that illusion works when it's unexpected. Especially if its traces are subsumed by stronger magic. So we created false roads on Marloven Hess's southern border."

Unlike in Sartor, there was no mysterious forest in Marloven Hess for Senrid to guide invaders to. His illusory

roads were meant to guide any attacking Norsundrians onto
ground that Forthan and Senrid had chosen, guarded by
wings of South Army.

That meant walking the entire area step by step, and
altering the landscape one boulder and weed at a time, in
order to fool the sweeping eye—taking care never to create
an image so out of place that it required a second look.

When they finished, Senrid gratefully went back to his
capital, but Hibern was not finished. Once Tsauderei chose
the likeliest locale, Hibern had transferred to Sartor, where
she spent four long, bitterly cold days in heavy snow grubbing along the southern border. She'd stooped and searched,
paused and whispered illusion spells over and over as she
broke seed husks in half, and placed moldering bits of brick
or wood to mark the place where each illusion would be
evoked.

She looked up into Erai-Yanya's waiting face, and it occurred to her for the first time to wonder how many hours,
days, months, even years of labor, performed with dread
and hope and maybe even glee, but mostly grimly endured
tedium, adults did that no one knew about, though it was
for the world's benefit.

She squared herself on her cushion, and summed up
those untold hours in the cold, her bleeding hands and unexpected bruises, with, "I took what I learned to Sartor,
where I transformed the road Tsauderei suggested, mask-
ing it and creating a new road to Shendoral. I'm to demonstrate for Atan and Chief Veltos. Tsauderei said you really
ought to be there."

Erai-Yanya smiled thinly, in complete understanding.
"So . . . you did all the work, but I'm to be there to give your
labors a semblance of legitimacy in the eyes of the Sartoran
mages?" She sneezed again, nodded, and said, "*Now*, I'll
look at my notecase."

She vanished into her own chamber, leaving Hibern to
appreciate how her tutor had understood not only everything she said, but everything unsaid.

When Erai-Yanya emerged again, she had brushed out
her hair and skewered it neatly on her head, and she wore
her usual warm, shapeless robe. She said briskly, "You will

not be surprised to learn that I've been invited to join you in your meeting with Tsauderei and Chief Veltos of the Sartoran mage guild on Sartor's border tomorrow."

Hibern flicked up her palm in assent.

"Currently under a blizzard, Tsauderei says. So tomorrow might turn into the day after." Erai-Yanya's thin smile faded, and she indicated the dramatic crack in the wall that served as a window. She gazed out at Liere in the abandoned kitchen garden, who crouched over the now-neat rows, straightened, then walked into the woods with something in her hands before returning. "What's she doing?"

"Carrying snails and caterpillars to the weedy area down by the stream."

"Snails." Erai-Yanya made a warding motion. "One of the many, many things I loathed about gardening was grubbing for snails, and picking caterpillars off the cabbages." She grimaced as an uncomfortable idea occurred. "I suppose she can hear snails' thoughts?"

"Thinking of all the snails you squished?" Hibern asked her tutor candidly. "I did. And I asked her. She said it's not hearing or seeing, but the closest she can come is perceiving tiny, dim lights in the realm of the mind. That's how she finds them so easily."

"Why is she doing it? More of the self-punishment that Arthur can't seem to talk her out of? She can't enjoy it."

"She says she likes doing it because she knows how," Hibern explained. "Tending their kitchen garden was hers and her sister's job where she lived before. But here, nobody criticizes her. I guess her father never noticed anything anyone did, except to criticize." Hibern grinned as she gathered up the breakfast eggshells. "She thought your abandoned garden was hundreds of years old."

"Just twenty." Erai-Yanya huffed out her breath. "Walk with me."

Hibern complied, glad she hadn't begun work.

"My mother gave me that garden to tend when I turned six or seven, saying I needed to understand the connection between human and soil, water, and air. How the Waste Spell we use every day, and the animal droppings we wand, are spread through soil, where they in turn enrich the plants. She also declared that I needed discipline. All I thought about when I flicked snails out of the garden or yanked weeds was how much I hated that chore."

Hibern was grateful for her own escape. She would have done the work if Erai-Yanya had demanded it as part of her magic-learning, but she knew she would have hated it.

They stepped onto the terrace, and turned toward the pathway that would lead to the garden some hundred paces away.

Erai-Yanya continued. "So when she managed to lose herself mysteriously in that struggle over the dyr in Everon, when I was sixteen, I abandoned the garden that day. And Evend, who you know took over tutoring me, didn't say a thing about it. That was one of the reasons I sent Arthur to him when it became apparent that Arthur needed to be around people."

She bunched her skirt in one hand, and Hibern followed, watching birds darting overhead as she crushed eggshells in her palms.

"Patterns," Erai-Yanya said. "My mother was fifty-five when she got me, after disappointment with the brother I've never met, who hated magic and ran off to sea. Her mother was even older when she was born. We who stay here share certain traits, you could say family traits, though not everyone in any family is exactly the same. My mother never knew how to play. She saw only wasted time. I think play has an important place. But she was an excellent mage."

Hibern sensed that the point was coming. Erai-Yanya stopped, and shut her eyes. Hibern wondered if she was having some kind of reaction to her cross-world hop, and then her neck prickled when it hit her: Erai-Yanya was concentrating on a mind-shield. Hastily Hibern reinforced her own, annoyed that she'd let it lapse yet again.

As Hibern began dropping eggshells around the plants, Erai-Yanya said, "My mother spent many years trying to winnow out the truth about the powerful, mysterious dyra of Ancient Sartor." She held up her thumb and forefinger as though holding one of the magical artifacts. "As did some of her foremothers. I inherited that task, and stubbornly stuck to it. And so I came to be recognized as the expert on dyra, though I know little enough." Her voice dropped low, the words coming in a rush. "And that shop-keeper's daughter out there in our garden, who never had a magic lesson in her life—she didn't even know how to *read*—took up the thing, and used it against Siamis as if she'd been trained all her life. Everything is changing into an unrecognizable world, that is going to belong to you young people. But." The sunburned little wrinkles around her eyes shifted as her brows rose. "Hibern. What are you doing with those eggshells?"

"Putting them around the vegetables. Liere says they discourage the snails."

"My mother had me put the coffee grindings on the soil. It sometimes worked, though not when rain was heavy, but I suspect nothing works then. Or are eggshells better?"

"We haven't been at it long."

"I see." Erai-Yanya blinked absently at the green shoots neatly growing sunward, then continued. "But. Back to the dyr. Since Sartor has returned, I've delved in their records, to find nothing. Admittedly the records are sparse, after so very many centuries. Even so, to find nothing whatsoever? Either dyra were so dangerous they were not written about, or they were so much a part of normal life that people didn't write about them any more than we write each day about the air we breathe. But this we know from the Siamis enchantment: those things are dangerous. And maybe poisonous."

She waited as Liere picked another plate of snails from the rows at the extreme edge of the garden, then vanished down the slope toward the stream.

"You know I study patterns. In magic. In families. In everything. Liere demonstrates patterns for . . . oh, maybe I'd better not say it. Most of what I know about her is sec-ondhand. From my son, from the mages up north." She looked troubled.

Hibern shivered. "You think something's wrong with Liere?"

"I think there's a reason she's so frail, so colorless . . ." Erai-Yanya shrugged. "I thought at first her family starved her, but in spite of the fact that everyone who hosts her provides excellent food, and comfort, she doesn't look a whit more healthy than she did when she was running over the world using the dyr to destroy Siamis's enchantment."

"You think the dyr poisoned her?"

"That's my guess. Pending more information. I think she needs to be observed more carefully..." Erai-Yanya looked like she was going to say more, but Liere had returned after depositing the last of her snails, and approached them, an inquiring look on her face.

Erai-Yanya smiled at Liere. "Hibern and I need to go south tomorrow. Something about strengthening Sartor's southern border ward. In the middle of a blizzard, as it happens. I suggest you rejoin my son in Bereth Ferian. You like midsummer up there, as I recollect."

Liere said, "Senrid thought I ought to hide here."

Erai-Yanya took in the neat rows in the garden before saying cordially, "I realize that to a certain extent Senrid's life depended on his being able to out-think his uncle, but it does not follow that all adults are as easily out-thought. Or to put it another way: stupid."

Liere flushed. "Senrid doesn't think all adults are stupid." At Erai-Yanya's wry eyebrow lift, Liere turned even redder. "Well, he knows when he's been stupid."

"I don't doubt it, and I have nothing else to say on the subject, having exchanged little converse with him. But I truly believe that Chief Oalthoreh and the entire northern mage school are all capable of keeping you safe."

Sartor

What Atan saw when Chief Veltos entered a room was iron discipline, focused austerity, and above all, authority.

What Veltos Jhaer saw in her own mirror was a middle-aged failure.

She yanked down her dark blue robe with its three hard-earned stars, and headed for the Destination, thinking grimly that when she was dead, she hoped it would be said about her that she never shirked her duty. But she suspected that her only claim to fame would be that she lost the mage war to Detlev of Norsunder, causing Sartor to vanish for nearly a century.

Her defensive strategy—the greatest share of her work time was given to this—was to reproduce that spell, only to be used to remove Sartor magically from Norsunder's grip. But such a defense could only work if it was an absolute surprise, which meant keeping it secret.

So far, she had not been able to reproduce Detlev's magic, or even to penetrate his intent. Meanwhile, she must wrest the time from her research to train a young, uneducated queen who knew just enough magic to ask dangerous questions. Veltos had to make certain that the girl didn't become willful, which would make her dangerous herself.

Veltos's head already ached after a restless night. Transfer magic turned her inside out, then thrust her back into the world. She pulled on her thick mittens, her head turtling into the scarf she'd wound around her neck and ears.

A thin silhouette in the bleak, low sunlight resolved into the gaunt form of Tsauderei, seated on a carved stone bench.

As Veltos stepped off the temporary Destination, she controlled the spurt of disappointment. She knew it was unworthy to have deliberately come early, a silent gesture of moral superiority. In her day, only kings and queens kept others waiting.

But here was the old mage. He had chosen the site, traced the Destination magic onto an old terrace, and provided everyone with a transfer token. That meant he had also swept the area for magical traps or tricks, but still she crossed the tile terrace, recognizing the interlocked garland pattern as one popular some nine centuries back, and reached to drop the token into Tsauderei's hand.

"Thank you for timeliness, Veltos," Tsauderei said.

"You will forgive my desire to be sure of her majesty's safety?"

"Contrary. I would expect you to do your duty as you perceive it," he said, and watched as she paced the terrace's perimeter, whispering her tracer spells.

She was aware of his scrutiny, aware of his smile, this elderly man who had been born a generation after her fiftieth birthday while she was senselessly prisoned outside of the world. Having ascertained that no evil spells lurked for the unwary, she looked around. The terrace was the only solid part of what had once been a sizable dwelling overlooking the Hvas River below, beyond which lay the uninhabited lands that eventually led to the Norsunder Base.

"Do you know whose baras-territory this was, and what happened to it?" Tsauderei asked. "The ruin being much older than last century's war."

"All I know is that it had to have been subordinate to Chandos." She was going to add that she had never studied wars, so she didn't know which had resulted in the destruction of what had probably been a beautiful dwelling. Her life had been dedicated to constructive matters. Civilization.

Until she led the mages to defeat, and the kingdom to ruin.

And so she bowed her head, prepared to let this upstart from Sarendan lecture her on her own history, but he said, "I wondered. Found it by accident, when the spell over Sartor began receding. Never mind. It's a perfect spot from which to observe the southeast end of your border—"

He abandoned the rest of his observation as the air flickered and Erai-Yanya appeared, managing to look scruffy to Veltos even in a heavy coat, scarf, hat, and mittens. She was followed by that Marloven girl whom Erai-Yanya had unaccountably selected out of all the possible mage students in the world.

The two looked bewildered, as to be expected; the time difference was not all that much in east-to-west measure, but to them it must look as if the sun had leaped far to the north, plunging them into cold.

Veltos put her hands together in the polite gesture of greeting, then walked away to the edge of the terrace not only to let them recover from the transfer, but to scold herself into composure. She gazed hard at the silvery ribbon of iced-over river below. Erai-Yanya might look like a northcoast beggar, but she was a Vithyavadnais—a formidable line of mages, many of whom had apparently been at least as idiosyncratic. That did not lessen their skill.

There was no excuse for the young queen to have turned to that Marloven girl for aid for this venture. Veltos could only see this unexplainable preference as a covert reminder of her own failure a century ago, and her current inability to secure Sartor against further enchantment.

Erai-Yanya and the Marloven girl began chatting with Tsauderei, their voices distinct, curiously brittle on the frozen air, then they all fell silent at the brief stir of air of a new arrival, and there was the young queen, who insisted on her parents' intimate, family-only heart-name, Atan.

"I hope you will pardon my tardiness," Atan said, and her polite smile widened. "Hibern! You're here!"

"Ready when you are," Hibern said.

"First." Tsauderei thumped his gloved hands on his bony knees, his breath clouding. "Erai-Yanya, is there anything to report from your time on Geth?"

"I could talk for half a day about how differently they do things, and about the difficulties of making oneself clear when the Language Spell turns out to be two centuries out of date. But I won't. We know that Norsunder has been poking around, and the Geth mages think it has something to do with transfer magic."

"They're looking for rift magic," Veltos exclaimed.

"Or ancient, hidden artifacts?" Atan asked, turning from one to another. "The way we've been searching?"

"Little success either will bring, I should think," Tsauderei commented. "My understanding is, that world was mostly settled by runaways from Sartorias-deles after the Fall, who then instituted extreme measures to control magic, so there would never be a repeat of the Fall. The only way they'd have powerful ancient artifacts would be if they brought them, and I defy Norsunder to find what Geth's mages have spent centuries making sure is well concealed."

Erai-Yanya said, "You know the problem with spying on Norsunder, how sparse information is, and that's usually distorted. But I'll give you details later, if you like. When we aren't freezing our noses and ears off." She turned to Tsauderei. "The last time I was here, someone was talking about instituting an Emras Defense, one that is perfectly balanced between light and dark."

Veltos bit her lip. With these two, she did not need to point out the long-standing debate between the Sartoran Council and the Bereth Ferian mages about who Emras's tutor really had been. Whether or not he was actually Detlev in some guise, or a Marloven dark mage, didn't really matter: the best Emras Defense that magic could manage now, with hundreds of anchor points, would only buy time. Magic could always be broken by stronger magic.

She said, "As for hidden artifacts, there is one we all know about, and you have charge of it. You even have someone who does know how to use it, though she is a child." Veltos would not willingly speak that highly inappropriate name 'Sartora,' and she kept forgetting the child's given name.

"I sent Liere away," Erai-Yanya said. "She doesn't understand the dyr any more than we do. Less."

"But she used it."

"For one spell," Erai-Yanya said. "To break an enchantment that built an illusory boundary around minds. The dyr is only useful for that same spell. Liere was relieved when she surrendered it to me, and she has never asked me to bring it out of hiding."

"If she does, don't," Tsauderei cut in. "The magic in the dyr augments these other spells in some way none of us understand. All we know is we cannot control it."

Veltos began a noiseless sigh, halting when the clouding of her breath betrayed her. "But from all reports she has no discipline, no course of study, and is most often to be found in Marloven Hess, of all the inappropriate places." She turned Hibern's way, palms together. "I speak only the truth as I see it."

Atan spoke quickly. "I only met Liere once. She didn't seem undisciplined to me. A little odd, and ignorant, but she was aware of that. She made mention of a lot of reading."

Hibern let out a slow breath of relief as Erai-Yanya said sardonically, "Do you want to lecture a child who can read your innermost thoughts on what you perceive to be her duty?"

Veltos recoiled, then shook her head.

"Exactly," Erai-Yanya said, more cordially. "The fact is, no one quite understands what goes on in her mind. In the meantime my son has done everything possible to make her welcome in Bereth Ferian. As for her friendship with Senrid of Marloven Hess, my understanding is that he was very close to a female younger cousin until she left to study music, and Liere is used to older brothers. She's a sister substitute, he's a brother. No doubt, like all youth, they will grow apart."

Veltos's brows contracted, her gaze downward lest the others somehow see the pain she couldn't quite control, or hear the whispers from her youth about the future King of Sartor, *Prince Connar Landis falls out of love as fast as he falls in it.*

He certainly hadn't fallen out of love with Diantas Dei. And Veltos had never lost her painful, hopeless love for him, even when he was a middle-aged king with thinning hair, a large family, and a war he did not know how to fight. Every time she looked into Atan's face, she had to stop herself from trying to find traces of her father there.

Veltos said to the countryside, "Children need to be learning discipline. They need good examples to emulate. Especially someone with her gifts. Liere's parents relinquished authority, then?"

"If you had met her father, you would understand why no one wished to send the child back to him. In any case, he did not really want her, for the same reason neither one of the schools has tried to take over her instruction." Erai-Yanya tapped her forehead. "Everyone agrees that, pending Lilith the Guardian coming forth from beyond time and directing us, Liere needs to learn to control her gifts before undertaking formal training. And none of us can teach her to do that."

Veltos bowed again.

"Then there's my own worry, one I expressed to Hibern today, after not having seen Liere for months. She looks ill, though she insists she's fine. Given no other discernable cause, I wonder if the dyr poisoned her somehow. Do you really want me bringing that thing out again? Especially if we're expecting a Norsunder attack? How long do you think that child would escape their hands this time? There is certainly no chance they would be surprised again."

Veltos sighed. "They'll probably be after her anyway."

"Bringing us to our meeting now," Tsauderei said. "And the sooner I get my old bones out of this cold, the better. Hibern, tell them your idea."

Hibern said, "It's not a great solution, but if nothing better comes along, well, you've got this weird forest here, that the record books say distorts time."

"Shendoral," Atan, Veltos, and Tsauderei said at the same time.

Erai-Yanya said suavely, "I believe that's the one in which inexplicable things happen if you're within its border."

Tsauderei said, "Correct. If you commit violence, that violence recoils upon you. It is quite real."

"Time is not trustworthy in Shendoral," Chief Veltos said. "Or direction. But what has this to do with this meeting?"

Tsauderei smiled Hibern's way, but smoothed his face as he said to Veltos, "It has to do with our proposed plan, which is to set up careful illusions that will lead Norsunder's warriors into Shendoral."

"Illusions?" Veltos exclaimed. "Those are so easy to dispel."

"Only if you know they're there," said Hibern.

Veltos frowned. "But surely Norsunder will send along mages to perform tracers."

"And they'll sense all these wards meant to deflect, or to swallow, their magic. Illusions are so easy, so deceptive if they're placed right. If they aren't expected, they can be quite effective." Tsauderei grinned. "Hibern, time to demonstrate."

Hibern walked with self-conscious care over the slippery ground toward the extreme edge of the ridge. She slipped off her mitten, pulled from her pocket the handful of carefully preserved seed-halves and rocks, held them on her open palm, and whispered the transport spell over and over as the objects vanished one by one to meet their other halves. As the others watched, the landscape below transformed itself in subtle ways. Illusion can be done by design, like drawing from memory, but it is most convincing when images are made of existing things combined so that the effect is not mirror image.

The mages looked down at new hills, ridges, and thick copses of trees that hid the road, creating a new road over flat areas.

Atan exclaimed, "Oh, Hibern, that's *wonderful!*"

"This is just the bit we can see from here. I don't know your countryside all that well, and I only had a few days. As you can see, my false road gently divides off from the real road by connecting to existing paths. So, the invading army will think they are on the road to Eidervaen, but if they follow the illusory road, they'll find themselves in Shendoral."

"Excellent job," Tsauderei said with a glance Veltos's way.

"The spells would have to be renewed frequently, as they wear off so fast," Veltos said doubtfully.

"Which is easy enough. Of course you marked your locations on a mage's map?" Erai-Yanya said briskly.

"Right here," Hibern said, withdrawing the scroll from inside her coat, with its carefully measured lines, its exact ratio of fingerbreadths to paces, and the magic symbols for her spells at the proper locations.

"You could put your students to that," Tsauderei said to Chief Veltos. "Do the same from the Luyos River. You can even get the magic to last longer by binding it to the moving water of the rivers without the least harm."

"What did you do, precisely?" Veltos asked, peering out over the countryside.

"Create what looks like impassable objects at road crossings, to direct them along the roads you wish. Mask landmarks," Hibern said. "And recreate illusions of famous landmarks where they ought to lie on their maps. Their maps are going to be wrong anyway, as so much repair has been going on." She was quoting Senrid directly.

"It's wonderful," Atan said firmly, and asserted herself again. "I intend to bring this idea before the high council, and then the circles. I trust you will support it, Chief Veltos."

Veltos looked at Atan's long face, but she wasn't seeing the teenage girl. She was thrown back in memory, hearing Connar's warm, husky voice as he bent over his daughter in her cradle, whispering, "I suppose we ought to name her Yustnesveas, which will satisfy several and insult none, but to me, she will be Atanrael . . . Atanael . . . Atanelen . . . what do you think, Dian?"

"Atan," said Diantas Dei, who had legally given up her family name to marry a king. "She is too small for more."

"Ah, love, as always you are right." And he'd straightened up to kiss her . . .

Veltos had to physically turn away from the memory. He was gone. Now a century in the past. And at least all those Deis were gone, too, except for that poor mad child Julian.

She bowed. "I shall, your majesty."

"Then we're done here," Tsauderei said. "Back to defrost my old bones at my fireside."

Atan watched as Chief Veltos and Erai-Yanya walked toward the edge of the cliff, speaking in low-voiced conversation.

Atan said equally low-voiced to Hibern, "This is the first time I've told them what I want to do, rather than them telling me what I ought to do. You did a brilliant job. Thank you!" Then she raised her voice. "Chief Veltos, Tsauderei. You're shivering. You have to be cold. Please return to warmth."

Hibern knew a hint when she heard it. "Erai-Yanya?"

Atan smiled at Hibern, and as the elders vanished, Atan transferred to Miraleste, capital of Sarendan.

Atan had been corresponding with Peitar and Lilah long enough to know not only the time difference, but Peitar's schedule. So much less ritual in Sarendan!

Peitar and Lilah sat at their midday meal, each with a book propped before them. Atan's heart gladdened at the genuine welcome in the two faces, so unlike: Peitar slender, his dark hair waving back from a high brow, Lilah short and square, freckled and slant-eyed, like so many people in both Sartor and Sarendan.

"Atan!" Lilah leaped up. "Want some lunch?"

"I've only a short time before I'm expected back. Am I keeping you?" She looked around, hoping Derek was not nearby. "If you're expecting anyone . . ."

"Aunt Tislah went home in a huff, as she always does after trying to matchmake for Peitar," Lilah said with a grin. "Bren is traveling with Innon, and Derek is at Obrin."

"Obrin? Is that not where the Sarendan army training takes place?" Atan said in surprise.

"Derek has become quite popular with the remnant of

my uncle's army, at least at Obrin." Peitar's smile faded into pensiveness.

Lilah put her spoon down. "I went with him to train the summer before last," she said proudly. "They didn't much like him, at first, on account of our civil war. But Derek said we should go to the back row, with all the age tens, and work our way up. That was kind of fun, especially when he made jokes, and told stories in the dorm at night. By the end of that summer, I made it to scout trainee, and Derek got promoted to leader of a foot patrol. Then we returned to Miraleste, and he taught the orphans things we learned. He went back last spring, but I didn't, because I was visiting up in the Valley."

Atan's attention was on Peitar. He listened to his sister with a thoughtful air. Atan knew how much Peitar cherished this friend of his, and how distrustful he was of war preparations, so when Lilah finished, and no one had anything to add about Derek, Atan used the rest of her time to describe how Chief Mage Veltos had reacted to Hibern's demonstration.

At the end, Lilah clapped her hands, and Peitar gave his rare, thoughtful smile. "If Chief Veltos was impressed, then I have more confidence about the illusions I placed around Diannah Wood. I could only get away for a day or two, and then there's the fact that Diannah Wood is not as strange, and as inhospitable to enemies, as Shendoral is reputed to be. But it's a great idea. And if Chief Veltos agreed, well, we can hope the illusions will at least discourage the enemy."

"I know Tsauderei will be giving you his impressions of Hibern's demonstration, but I wanted to tell you first," Atan said.

Actually, she wanted what she'd seen: the genuine glow of friendship in both their faces. They would have accepted Atan the Mage as happily as they accepted Atan, Queen of Sartor. Sometimes she needed that reminder.

Veltos arrived back in her quarters, her head pounding. She tried to walk off her irritation at having found that Marloven girl there, after all the work the high council had done getting rid of her. It was clear that the young queen was corresponding on her own, in spite of all the thought and care dedicated to surrounding her with the very best tutors the kingdom afforded.

Well, if her mages liked the illusionary diversion plan, at least they could dismantle everything the Marloven had done on the southern border, and make their own.

When Veltos had her temper under control, she summoned her mages to report. As she expected, they hailed the illusion plan with cautious enthusiasm, and added a lot of froth about how wonderful it was that their queen, young as she was, showed signs of becoming a fine Sartoran monarch. Veltos endured it in smiling silence.

Over the next few days, she took volunteer mage students to the border. As the young will when inspired, they set to the task with almost frightening alacrity.

And so she was able to return to her normal rounds of duty and study, keeping her thoughts to herself until her brother, a scribe, came to visit her, as he did every week or two. He felt for his older sister, who had lost more than people realized, during the war.

But even so, a short way into their discussion, he exclaimed, "Veltos, remember how much we hated being twitted by our elders? I don't agree that these young folks coming south from other lands have no manners or wits. They're simply different from our day."

Veltos said, "Come here to the window. Look down there. No, that way, at the end of the street. Do you see what's going on there?"

Her brother obliged her, his graying hair brushing his shoulders as he leaned in the thick stone window to peer out. "Someone seems to be getting rid of their furniture, as far as I can tell."

"No." Veltos gripped her elbows. "What you see is a man—a young man, though he's from our day—losing his home. Not just his home, which has been in his family for a very long time, he is losing everything."

"What happened?"

"What else? A hundred years ago, when the word went out that Norsunder had crossed the border in force, he sent his young wife with everything they had to her family somewhere up north, including the house-deed, which he'd made over in her name as a measure of safety. Then he did his duty as he saw it, joining the king to mount the defense. He being an artisan, not a warrior, he was wounded almost at once, and left for dead. He was still wounded when we came out of the spell. When he recovered, he wrote first thing to that family in the north, who, it turned out, no longer lived there. His wife had remarried, thinking him dead with the rest of us, and all his holdings had been passed down through her second family. With those holdings had been the deed to this house. They own it. He doesn't."

Her brother grimaced. He'd thought the busy scene at the end of the street was an everyday occurrence, the sort of thing you could see anywhere at any time. But now the steady stream of workers carrying furnishings out took on a new meaning. "That's horrible. There must be something that can be done."

"The family wishes to bring business, which this country sorely needs, and so two guilds backed the family. His guild offers him a room among the old folks, but as his wound prevents him from doing fine silverwork anymore . . ." She gave a sharp shrug. Her mouth twisted bitterly. "There are those who consider the family generous, as they have given the old furniture they least want to the man. It means nothing to them, of course. Even most of the family relics in the room of honor are also cast aside, except someone told me that they'll keep the most prestigious of them, because after all, where can the man put them in his single room? In so many ways, brother, that man represents Sartor."

Her brother patted her shoulder. "He is relatively young, and he has his training. He'll find a place in the world. As will Sartor."

"I told myself that," Veltos retorted, "until Tsauderei came to us with the news that we're facing another war."

Chapter Three

Marloven Hess

ONCE Hibern and Erai-Yanya had spent a day catching up on Hibern's studies, Hibern transferred to Marloven Hess to keep her promise about reporting on the success of the Sartor border illusions idea.

Senrid wasn't in his study, or in the public rooms. Hibern walked to Keriam's tower, and as always, the moment he saw her, he waved off the cluster of gray-coated boys with which he always seemed to be surrounded.

She asked, "Where's Senrid?"

Keriam pointed a sheaf of papers at the window.

Hibern had already glanced out Senrid's study windows at the bleak winter sky. From Keriam's tower she got a different angle over the plain roofs and dull light brown stone of the academy. This time she caught what she'd missed previously, the small figure sitting on the farthest roof out, his shapeless gray blending with the gray of the sky.

She turned back to Keriam, her question in her face.

"He's watching the lance practice," Keriam said.

"Lance practice? Way out beyond the corrals?"

"Unofficial," Keriam said.

"What does that mean?" Hibern asked, trying to hide her exasperation.

"It means that the boys are forbidden to do heavy weapons training unsupervised, but they are not fighting each other, they are rehearsing a demonstration. Working very hard at it," Keriam added in a reflective tone. "Let's just say they have something to prove, to themselves as well as to the rest of us. As for Senrid, I suspect he could use the diversion."

Sure enough, Hibern thought, the explanation didn't really explain anything other than that there had been trouble among the academy boys. No surprise there! But one thing she did understand: Senrid was fretting.

So she ran down the stairs, bent into the bitter wind, and made her way along the barren stone walls. The air smelled of snow. Senrid perched on the roofpole with his knees drawn up under his chin and his arms wrapped around his legs. He looked over, his face nearly invisible between his scarf and his knit hat, except for a plum-red nose and a pair of narrowed eyes. "Did they go for it?"

"Yes. But Atan and I agreed to leave you out of it. The Sartoran mages think it was my idea, and even then, Chief Veltos eyed me like I'd farted in their Star Chamber. Erai-Yanya reminded me about five times that she does belong to the last century."

"Which means she was probably around at the same time as my unlamented great-grandfather Senrid."

They considered the songs and stories about the bloody warfare during that reign, Marloven against Marloven, as the Hesean plains jarls and those of the northern reaches led by the Olavair family tried to conquer one another. That particular Senrid-Harvaldar had led a campaign of such destruction that the squabbling northerners had united long enough to fight him to a standstill, forcing him to a treaty.

Senrid went on, "You'd think she'd be able to figure out that I'm not him. I wasn't even named for him."

"I suspect to Sartor, there isn't any difference between the Senrid who reunited the old Marloven Hesea centuries ago and your great-grandfather. How much attention do you pay to Sartoran affairs?"

"I can name maybe ten of their rulers. Point taken. So Erai-Yanya is back?"

"Yes."

"It's about time! Did Tsauderei ask her how the dyr can be used to ward Norsunder?"

Was that the weight on Senrid's mind? "He didn't send for her until now because whatever she's doing on Gethdeles is more important than what's going on here."

"More important than a Norsunder invasion?"

Hibern said, "Yes. But rather than argue about which problem is worse, let me remind you of what Erai-Yanya said before: we don't know how to use the dyr, she can't find anything in the ancient archives on how to use it, and if we try, we're almost sure to draw the likes of Detlev or Siamis like arrows to the mark."

"They can probably smell it from beyond the world," Senrid agreed. "They sure were good at hunting Liere and me down. Shit. I knew it was too easy."

"As for working with the thing, part of the problem is the necessity for Dena Yeresbeth." Hibern touched her mittened fingers to her forehead. "Which you have. If you get an idea, go ahead and talk to her, but you're going to have to convince her that—"

"I would never think of using it for war," Senrid cut in impatiently.

"Convince her," Hibern said with deliberate emphasis, "that war isn't a game."

He eyed her, recognized the Marloven-to-Marloven irony, and said, "But it is a game. It's one we play to win until we're killed."

Hibern knew both the songs he was quoting from. She rubbed her hands together, then stuck them in her armpits as she stared out at the boys on horseback circling around one another, waving long sticks. It looked uncomfortable in the extreme. "Senrid, something's galling you under the saddle."

Senrid struck the roof flat-handed. "I want to know what they want."

They? The boys out there on horses? No. Norsunder. "You know what they want," she said.

"I *don't* know what they want. All Detlev's experiments with mind-magic at high levels, and maybe these weird enchantments that cut whole kingdoms off from the rest of the world, have to be a part of it."

"The scariest thing to me was hearing that he's been in the world more times recently than in the last five centuries," she said.

"Right." He sighed. "I've got my east, west, north, and south armies placed at what we think are best spots for invasion for each border. But where are Norsundrian invaders going to come from in order to get here? They don't sprout out of the ground. If they do manage to punch another big rift in the south, large enough to shove an army through, what's the use of attacking Marloven Hess in the middle of Halia and fighting us to a standstill, which is going to take out half the population?"

"Half?" she drawled, and he flashed a quick grin.

It was gone a heartbeat later. "And those left will be resisting covertly until the last one is dead. Unless the soul-suckers want us as a bloody training ground, it makes no *sense* to come after us, not unless they have armies and armies ready to take the entire continent. If they did, yeah, all my reading says we'd make a perfect foothold, they grab Halia, press east. If they've got enough of 'em."

"We know they've got armies and armies. We even know some of their names."

Senrid's lip curled. "I hope I never actually get to meet great-father Ivandred. He's bound to come thundering through here first in as a warm-up exercise."

Hibern watched as Senrid thumped his fist lightly on the roof tile. In certain moods he could be really annoying, the way he'd carom around a room, rapping lightly on things as he uttered a fast stream of talk. But seeing him so still, wrapped in a little ball like that, was unsettling.

He said, "I don't think they're going to attack us in force."

"You think it's going to be a mage war?"

Senrid turned to face her, his chin grinding on his knee. "I think it's going to be Siamis's plan again, enchanting everyone's brains out when they don't see him coming." He looked away. "Only worse. I remember that Siamis kept refining that enchantment as he went. At first it was a few people, then a village, then a town, and then he was able to enchant entire kingdoms through their loyalties, once he'd hunted down the right person. Yeah, Liere broke the enchantment, but he's had years to learn how to get around it."

Here it comes, she thought.

Senrid's voice flattened. "I think their being around so much, and experimenting with magic that messes with minds, has to do with this damned Dena Yeresbeth. That I probably inherited from my mother, she being a direct descendant of the Cassads."

Hibern knew all the stories about the Cassads, or Cassadas, who had ruled before the Marloven invasion, and some stories insisted they were related all the way back to the mysterious Adamas Dei of the Black Sword. The Cassads had been mages, and all the old stories and songs insisted that some of them heard thoughts and talked to ghosts.

She turned up her palm. "If anyone would inherit Dena Yeresbeth, it would be descendants from them. But why 'damned'?"

"Because I don't know how to control it. I don't know how to use it. What if that's what Detlev and Siamis want? What if Detlev gets to me, rips my brains out with Siamis's spell, and forces me to order my own army to cross the border in Norsunder's name?"

"Then you tell everybody if you don't sound like yourself . . ." Her mind raced ahead of her tongue. "Oh."

Every Marloven grew up knowing that you obeyed orders or you died.

Senrid said, "I thought about trying to change a thousand years or so of tradition, naming kings whose orders were flagrantly stupid, but Keriam pointed out to the seniors in command class that when everyone knows that the commander, whether king or riding captain, is responsible for the order, then people obey, knowing that even if they disagree, they're protected. It's those at the top who pay the price for stupidity. Eventually."

"And of course, if you issue a command to ignore you if you sound funny, then any troublemakers can claim you sounded funny if they don't like your orders."

"Right." He said in a low voice, "If Siamis gets to me, I think I'm going to order Keriam to pick up a crossbow and shoot me dead."

Hibern's insides cramped. She pressed her arms across her middle, and reached for logic. "But Senrid, people under Siamis's spell didn't have any volition, they just sort of existed. If you issue commands, you're going to have to sound like yourself, or nobody will believe you. You remember what people under the spell were like? Sleepwalkers."

"That was then. What if he's refined it, either he or his shit of an uncle?"

"Then you prepare a token, give it to some trusted people to drop a stone spell on you, with a transfer to Tsauderei's Valley of Delfina, where the wards are so ancient and so powerful that Norsunder never has broken them. Which is another reason I'm here. I think the alliance should pass the word to hide out there, if Siamis comes back looking for rulers to enchant. We all know people our age would be the easiest targets. If you end up there, Tsauderei will know what to do."

"That's not a bad idea." Senrid's expression eased. "Hibern, that's great. Have you written to Thad and Karhin to sound out the others?"

"Last night. But listen, Senrid. Here's what's important. If you're alive, there's a chance to fix things. If you're dead, you're dead. Would you do that to Marloven Hess, force Keriam to shoot you?"

"Would you be my heir?" His voice was thin, as if the words had been wrung from somewhere deep inside him.

Hiding the surge of nausea those words caused, she struck the air with the flat of her hand. He was unsettled now, but she knew instinctively that he would hate pity as well as sentiment. Much, much better to be brisk, treating the question as a joke. "I turned on you once, to prevent my becoming a gunvaer, remember?"

He grinned. "I thought you turned on me so you wouldn't have to marry *me*."

"You or anyone, I am not the kind of person to become a queen." Hibern managed to laugh, relieved to see him catching himself. It wouldn't do to let Senrid know how disturbing she found this conversation. "Look, nobody would accept me as Hibern-Gunvaer even if I wanted it. The Askans haven't put anyone in the field for generations, and you know how important that is to the jarls."

"I don't have anyone else."

"So, I'm very sorry, but you're just going to have to stay alive."

His gaze flicked back and forth between her eyes. She stared back, her eyes squinted against the cold. She knew her mind-shield was shut tight.

Senrid's quick grin was more pain than humor. "Right." He looked away. "I'm still making plans for possible invasion. Because Siamis took all that trouble to leave that coin here, so why not deny him what he wants most? If my wards vanish I've ordered the entire city guard to melt away— dress civ and become carters or blacksmiths or bricklayers. Same with the academy. And the army. Norsunder won't even get our horses."

"The horses will go into the Nelkereth Plains?"

"Yeah. Soon's we begin seeing grass, the stable girls have their orders to go to the plains and get lost. We're not waiting for word, we've decided the horses would like a summer out there even better than their usual winter."

"If you can get them there before the rains wipe out the trail, it'd take Norsunder Base's entire army just to find 'em and round 'em up."

"That's what Fenis Senelac promised. She's got relatives out there, in old Tlennen territory, and they know even the farther reaches. If my brains are enchanted out of my head, it'll take me time to round everybody up. Maybe by then someone will either shoot me or turn me into a statue."

"Go to Tsauderei's Valley before they can get you."

"Yes." He let his legs down, his heels knocking against the roof. "Is Liere all right?"

"Erai-Yanya sent her up north. Listen. Erai-Yanya thinks Liere might have been poisoned by the dyr. Carrying it so long."

"What?"

"You carried it," Hibern said, as he crouched down again, gazing intently into her face.

"Yes."

"Did it make you feel sick? Or anything?"

"Nothing like that. Well, except when we did the magic. Not sick. It . . ." Senrid shut his eyes, then said after a protracted pause, "It made me feel like my skull had vanished, and my thoughts spread out beyond the sky. Ech, how stupid that sounds in words. Why does Erai-Yanya think Liere is poisoned?"

"Haven't you asked yourself why she looks so . . ." Hibern put her thumb and forefinger together. "Frail, and like a sheet that has been washed too many times?"

"I think that's something she does to herself," Senrid muttered. "But maybe it could be due to the dyr. Except she looked like that when I met her, before we got the dyr. Of course she'd been on the run for months." He climbed quickly down to the wall, hopped to the ground, and walked away with his characteristic quick step.

Hibern sat there on the roof, considering how Senrid's dread kindled hers. It had been great, thinking about how Tsauderei and Erai-Yanya had looked at her with respect after her demonstration in Sartor, but the exhilaration dissipated like her breath in the cold air when she thought about what Senrid feared: a war they couldn't win.

But that didn't mean they couldn't try.

By now, calculating what time it was in various parts of the world took Hibern only a moment or two: it was early for the Mearsieans, but a promise was a promise.

She transferred to the white palace and was sent to the underground hideout, where she found them all at breakfast, including Clair.

The girls listened to the illusion idea, CJ and Clair thoroughly enthusiastic. Then, as usual, the rest of the girls turned the entire matter into a joke, offering silly suggestions like pie fights, or greased stairs, or short-sheeting beds. Hibern waited it out as long as she thought it polite, then said she had to contact the rest of the alliance.

"You mean Fonebone," CJ said. "I even made up names for every kingdom, really funny ones, that the villains would never understand. I've written about these to everybody, but nobody's written back. Maybe if you mention it?"

Hibern suppressed a sigh. Maybe being silly was the Mearsieans' way of dealing with fear. She said with what she hoped was a diplomatic tone, "I think that's your project.

Meanwhile, if Siamis comes after you, get yourselves to the Valley of Delfina however you can."

"Okay," CJ said, thumping a thin fist into her palm.

Norsunder Base

The Norsunder Base resounded with the sharp voices of those anticipating action. Gossip flew, and Lesca amused herself at her listening post, reporting to Dejain each night.

One day midway through winter, Kessler abruptly confronted Dejain. "Henerek is on his way to Everon," he said, answering one of the questions everyone had been asking.

She understood immediately that Kessler was following his own rule: even trade, one for one. She had not told anyone he was secretly learning magic. Rather than trying to extract a favor, or threatening to reveal some secret he'd winnowed out about her, like a normal person, he was offering a fact she might not know.

And she hadn't known that. Henerek and his followers had made a large noise about conducting a training mission in the mountains.

"On orders?" she asked, dread crowding her heart at the prospect of Kessler having learned enough magic to determine who had cast that blood-spell on him.

"Absent of," he said.

"Ah." She said, testing, "You could take this base. They'd all follow you."

"Why?" His expression didn't change, but he managed to convey contempt in the angle of a shoulder, the slight turn-away gesture of his right hand. "Why would I get them into shape just for Siamis to walk in and take over?"

When Kessler actually conducted a conversation, there was a reason. She ventured a guess. "You're leaving. To take Sartor in spite of Bostian?" She named one of the up-and-coming Norsundrian captains—this one obsessed with the desire to conquer Sartor, oldest kingdom in the world.

"He's an idiot," Kessler said. "Sartor is a bowl. Anyone who takes it can squat and say 'I hold ancient Sartor,' but what use is that? And while there aren't enough of 'em to

put up much of a fight, I don't ever want to find myself in
Shendoral again."

"He's asked me to ward Shendoral Forest," Dejain said,
and when Kessler lifted his shoulder slightly and began to
turn away, she said, "Chwahirsland?"

He flipped up the back of his hand. "It's a useless ruin.
And Efael will one day send Wan-Edhe back."

She hid a flinch at the casual mention of the youngest
and nastiest of the Norsunder's Host of Lords. She said,
"You want a beachhead. In the east? That would either be
Sarendan, or if you have ships, Khanerenth."

She had little interest in military planning, but she'd
perforce learned something about it during the time she'd
allied with Kessler. She knew he hated stupid questions. It
was the sure way to get nothing from him, so she considered swiftly.

Both Sarendan and Khanerenth would put up a strong
fight. He would like that, if he was to exert himself at all.
Sarendan would furnish better supplies once he won, but
there would be those mountains to get over before he could
advance into the eastern end of the Sartoran continent, the
prize being Colend, the richest country in the east—many
said in the entire continent. Khanerenth would give him
easier access to Colend, but scarcer supplies, and he would
have to get there in ships. "You don't have ships. Or do
you? Is that why we found Pengris's corpse at the foot of
the mages' hallway? He'd been gloating about some find
deep in Norsunder."

"Pengris winnowed out a stash of old transport-object
artifacts that Detlev had secreted centuries ago against just
this situation. Henerek killed Pengris for them. I just shifted
the body, because Henerek set up the murder to point to me."

"Did Henerek get all Pengris's stash?"

Kessler turned away without answering, which she took
as a no.

She called after him, "Sarendan or Khanerenth?"

He had nearly reached the end of the hall before he said,
"Either promises to be fun, but Sarendan is closer."

Chapter Four

Sarendan

ON a cloudless New Year's Firstday, the northern light shimmered on the ice like hammered silver as Peitar Selenna walked with his sister Lilah and Derek Diamagan into the throne room, which he seldom used, especially in frigid weather.

It was packed solid, which almost took the chill off. The marble columns were slick with moisture from so many breaths as he walked carefully up the shallow steps to the dais. Peitar no longer needed a crutch, or even a cane, but the echoes of old pain still twinged when he mounted steps, especially in the cold weather.

Lilah hopped up, grinning at her friends among the youngsters who'd started out calling themselves the Sharadan Brothers, in honor of Lilah's secret group during the war. The girls among the orphans left by the civil war had changed the name to Sharadan Brothers and Sisters—then Sharadan Sisters and Brothers—and now they were the Orphan Brigade.

Peitar's solemn expression lightened when he saw the eager faces, but then his humor vanished. Derek flashed a grin, and twiddled his fingers at his side, a semi-surreptitious wave, which sent a thrill through the mass of youngsters.

At the right, the King's Army not on duty roaming the borders stood in ranks, their captains at the front.

Peitar hated war. The prospect of it harrowed him to the edge of nausea. He hated the fact that he could do nothing to ward it, nor could he lead a defense.

"If there was anyone else," Derek had said the night before, as the three of them sat in the library, Lilah bouncing on her chair, "I'd happily relinquish command."

"Who else is there but you, Derek?" Lilah asked loyally.

Derek had spread his hands. "I've asked, and I've looked. I know I was no good leading the revolution, but I've learned so much at Obrin."

But had he learned enough? Peitar only knew that war was coming. If Norsunder Base was astir, the first two kingdoms likely to be overrun were Sartor and Sarendan.

So here he was. He stepped to the edge of the dais. His manner caused the front rows to fall silent. Gradually the rustles and whispers died away, and all faces lifted expectantly.

"As you have heard, Norsunder Base is on the march," Peitar said. "This is what Darian Irad, my uncle, had prepared for all his life, and his grandfather before him. But my uncle has gone to our sister-world to help there, and so the trouble has fallen to me, who has no knowledge of warfare."

He paused, and looked out over the straight ranks. "You are what remains of his army. Your commanders went into exile with my uncle, or died, as you all know. But this past year, Derek Diamagan, once considered your enemy, has gone among you to learn your skills."

A rustle from the brigade quickly died.

"I told you when I became king that I wanted no more division among the people of Sarendan, and Derek has done his best to bring everyone together again. The captains at Obrin have met with me, and we are agreed: to face this new threat, we need someone in command whom all will willingly follow. Someone whom you trust. Someone I trust."

Lilah and her friends held their breath.

"And so I come here before you to present Derek Diamagan, who is now Army Commander in Chief—"

His next words were lost in the spontaneous cheer that rose, first the high voices of the Brigade kids, who could not contain their joy. They were joined by the deeper voices of the army ranks.

Derek's grin flashed again, then he turned to Peitar and nodded, almost a bow. Everyone who knew him understood how important this moment was to him, how deeply he was aware of Peitar's trust, and how deep was his own trust in return. The cheering doubled in intensity and volume, going wild when Derek turned, eyes gleaming with tears as he raised his fist and shouted, "The king!"

"The king! The king!"

"Sarendan!"

"Sarendan!"

"Freedom forever!"

"Freedom forever!"

"Death to Norsunder!"

"DEATH TO NORSUNDER!"

Peitar's eyes closed. How many of them would be left alive when the coming war was over? The shouting voices brought back the shouting crowd of the revolution, and images of fire, the dead and dying, during those first terrible days of the revolution.

Derek glanced at Peitar's profile, saw the grief there, and raised his hand, tears drying on his lean, sunbrowned cheeks.

The noise died away. "I'll meet with all the captains for a strategy session. Orphan brigade captains, this means you, too. We won't leave you out."

A ragged treble cheer rose, and quickly died.

"We'll set up our defensive plan, and we'll spend the winter preparing, since spring is the most likely time for attack."

Another cheer rose.

When at last it ended, Peitar turned to go. Lilah lingered, looking between Derek, who was surrounded by army captains, and Peitar walking alone toward the back exit, then she ran after her brother. "What is it?" she cried. "I know a lot of people are complaining because our brigades are marching around drilling instead of doing spring planting, but you yourself said we have to defend Sarendan. And Derek is the best one to do it. So why are you upset?"

"I think . . ." Peitar studied his hands as if someone had written a message there. "Because I've seen the fervor of hatred of the former king and the army shift to hatred of Norsunder."

"And that's bad?" Lilah cried, hopping from toe to toe. "Why is that bad?"

"Because harnessing hatred is . . ." Peitar shook his head slowly. "Don't you see, Lilah? Because it's still hatred. It's such a powerful weapon, a poisonous one, and once loosed, can it ever be sheathed?"

Sartor

Anyone in Eidervaen could make the napurdiav—walk the palace's Purrad, the ancient labyrinth—except on Restday dawn, when it belonged exclusively to the royal family. That tradition had been ingrained for so many centuries that it carried the force of law.

On non-Restdays, Atan had gradually taken to appearing there before dawn, walking its four three-fold loops among the sheltering silver-leafed argan trees. She walked it in solitude with a candle in hand, but she was finding that frequency did not guarantee peace of mind. Maybe it was the impending war.

She meant to put war, and Julian, and her unspoken tension with the council out of her mind; she understood that she was not going to gain peace and insight if she brought her problems into the sacred space.

Or maybe it was memory. It had been Atan's idea to coax Julian to walk the Purrad with her, promising a reward if she completed it. What did she expect would happen? Atan resolutely forced herself to return to the starting point.

She was bitterly cold, yet tears burned her eyelids when she looked at the now-peaceful patterns of water-smoothed stones worked into the twelve points under the shelter of beautiful trees, and how Julian had run hither and yon screaming, kicking the stones, and yelling "Stupid! Stupid! Stupid!" when she discovered the 'reward' was to be a good feeling inside when the pattern was complete.

Atan stood, her breath shuddering against her ribs. She winked and blinked, trying to control the tears, but they came anyway, and so she gave up. It was already late. There would be no peace today.

She retreated indoors. She'd scarcely gone ten steps when the hiss of slippered feet heralded arrivals from a side hall, and there was Chief Veltos leading a young mage, maybe a few years older than Rel, his curly red hair a pleasant contrast to his blue robe. His greenish-blue eyes were wide as Chief Veltos bowed and said, "Your majesty. Nalar here witnessed a Norsundrian mage breaching the border." And to the mage, "Report."

Nalar bowed, speaking the entire time. "I was assigned to take the fourth-year students to the border to oversee the illusions leading to Shendoral. I left the students to form a suitably aged-looking stone sign naming the western reach of Shendoral as Leath Wood, and transferred to the border to oversee what we had done."

He paused to glance at the chief, who nodded for him to speak.

"We were told that on no account must we permit anyone to see us. So I hid when I perceived a rider approaching from the south, a woman, wearing a white coat. She rode a gray. Difficult to see against the snow. I hid and watched. She rode alongside the river, with something in her hand."

"Magic?" Atan asked.

"I report only what I saw, which was little enough. However, whatever it was glowed blue briefly at the anchor point for the border protection. She bent and laid something on a rock, then rode the other way, past the bridge, to the west. I moved parallel to observe. When she reached the next anchor point, she laid something down, and then retreated to the bridge and rode across."

"When was this?" Atan asked.

"Not an hour ago," Nalar replied. "I transferred straight to the chief."

Veltos added, "She has broken the border wards with

mirror spells. I myself just came from checking. Anyone can now come across between those two markers, without our knowing."

"It's got to be preparation for the invasion," Atan said, sick and cold inside.

"And she's riding ahead. She'll know at a glance what we've done. Whatever she's doing, she cannot discover the illusions," Chief Veltos exclaimed. "Or all our work comes to nothing."

Atan looked from one to the other. "What can we do?"

Chief Veltos said, "Nalar now knows where all our illusions are. I think he must transfer ahead of the woman and remove them all."

Nalar said apologetically, "We can always restore them as soon as she has passed. I know my students would—"

"No students," Chief Veltos said quickly. "This is a matter for mages. Your students may demonstrate what they've done. Then seniors only. If your majesty desires," she appended quickly, turning Atan's way.

Atan had been about to suggest she see for herself. But she knew what she was going to hear: her place was to hide, to stay away, with the useless youth. To agree to the command that Chief Veltos had just uttered, before her *If your majesty desires*.

So Atan did what was expected of her. But then she added, "I want to know what that woman is doing."

Chief Veltos bowed, not hiding her relief. "You shall know first thing."

Atan easily translated that to mean after the senior mages, the high council, and whomever else Chief Veltos deemed more important.

Off the continent of Drael

Eight and a half centuries ago, Tosta Orm, captain of the *Grebe's Claw* raider, which was one of the fleet of raiders attached to the warship *Gannet* of Lefsan House, had known that Rainorec, the doom of the Venn, was nigh.

Generations of the orderly Breseng kingship election

had been disrupted by murder, followed by whispers about the Dag Erkric, who was said to practice blood magic. When House Lefsan ordered their entire battlegroup across the Sea of Storms to attack the Venn colony for no discernable reason beyond House politics, Orm and eight other raider captains decided to flee.

It was breaking every oath they had made. It meant, if they ever returned, a painful death atop the Sinnaborc Tower, it meant iron-torc shame for the entire family, but what meaning had any of it, if those who ruled no longer honored their own oaths?

When the scar-faced pirate dag named Ramis, master of an ancient drakan-ship, offered to the nine a transfer token out of the world, they had accepted it. In trade they agreed to carry whomever needed carrying once they found themselves back in the world. Two days out of the Land of the Venn, they were on their way to fetch their marine fighters, the Drenga, who had been on a training mission related to the attack. A convenient storm began to rise, and the ships wore out to win sea room while their sea dags shifted to the command ship to confer with the *Gannet*'s dag, who was Erkric's chosen.

This was their moment, or never, in spite of the weather. Nine ships hauled their wind and slipped away, a full sea-voyage of supplies in their holds. Each raider captain used the magical device that Scarface Ramis had given them, touching the fire-eyed gem to his captain's torc. The device created a night-black chasm, ripped between sky and sea. All nine ships sailed willingly into that crack between sky and sea ...

... and Orm's ship emerged into bitter winter, nearly thrown by the frigid seas onto the shore.

Because he had ordered all *Grebe Claw*'s hands aloft before they had sailed into the chasm—expecting anything from ice-demons to firestorm—Orm was able to crack out an order that was instantly obeyed. Barely—barely—they skimmed the jagged rock teeth below the surf and beat out into the tiny bay.

But not before he witnessed, with his own eyes, this black-clad fellow with hair shorn like a thrall toss stones into the water in three different directions. These stones brought three more of his fleet out of the chasm, *Grebe's Eye*, *Grebe's Wing*, and *Grebe's Heart*. Orm's own heart mourned when he saw that his brother Luka, captain of *Grebe's Crest*, was among the five missing.

Who would be stupid enough to cause a sailing ship to emerge nearly on the shore, and on the last of the flood tide? Only the wind howling over the land out to sea, and his sailors' speed and strength, had kept them from beaching on this desolate coast, and all hands drowning.

Stupid as this fool perched on the rocks might be, Orm would keep faith with Scarface Ramis, who had kept his promise, unlike Orm's own people, for he had never seen this rocky coast before. Scarface Ramis's second promise was that they would be free to sail the seas once they completed their obligation.

And so Orm ordered the longboats down, and the three of his fleet who had sailed out of the chasm also lowered their boats. By the time the tide had turned to flow inward again, all those warriors perched upon the rocky jetty, and along the shore, had been brought aboard the ships.

It was then that the fool stamped into his cabin, and uttered a string of words. When Orm shook his head, the fool said distinctly, "Everon."

"Everon?" Orm repeated, wondering if this be name or verb.

Henerek had scowled at the pale-faced, flaxen-haired idiot before him, who didn't appear to understand a word of Sartoran, the most common language in the world, much less Norsundrian—an easy offshoot of Sartoran. Was this ship captain one of those idiot dawnsingers with their eternal, nauseating warbling, flitting around eating nuts and building treehouses?

Henerek glanced impatiently around the cabin, spotted rolled-up papers that had to be maps, and reached for them. "Everon," he stated louder, jabbing his thumb toward those maps.

The maps turned out to be charts, to Henerek a backward sort of map. He made no sense of the big one with the colored lines on it, but he recognized the shape of Drael's coastline above the long strait, and jabbed his finger on the place where Everon should be.

"Ev-er-on," he said distinctly. "Take us there."

Orm gazed at the chart, recognizing the coastline of Ymar. Why would this fellow wish to land above the better harbors at Jaro and Beilann? Though there were a few natural harbors, the coast rose steadily steeper, with treacherous currents around the many islands.

It did not matter. His pact with Scarface Ramis had been to serve as transport for whoever brought them back into the world. And so he would.

Three and a half months later, Orm's and Henerek's opinions of one another had not changed.

Orm took such a dislike to the arrogant young fool Henerek that he avoided direct contact, but he knew that a few of the young sailors had spent time with some of Henerek's younger warriors, trading words by sign, and when they'd found enough common words, they traded stories.

As for Henerek, he thought of ships as wagons on water, existing to ferry goods or transport warriors. He hated these Venn whose food stank of fish and vinegar, and their pale, arrogant gazes.

Three long months and more he had to endure the vile cold and wet of shipboard life, beginning with constant nausea as the ships tried to beat into howling east winds that sent them back again and again. Six weeks until they rounded the southeast corner of the continent, off Sarendan's mountainous coast. He'd expected them to pass that in a matter of days. Then they had to waste another three weeks in a desolate natural harbor while the Venn scavenged wood and rebuilt the masts destroyed in the worst of the storms.

At least the Venn captain obeyed his mandate to preserve the element of surprise by avoiding all other ships.

Or so Henerek assumed.

Orm paid no attention whatsoever to Henerek's orders, even after his youngest crew member, the boy in charge of flag signals, learned enough of the interloper's tongue to communicate. Long before he understood that Henerek wanted surprise, he'd said to his men at the whipstaff, "Keep every vessel that nicks the horizon hull down." And to the lookouts, "Mark any rigging. I want to know who's out there, or what's out there, but don't risk us being seen."

This order soon furnished the disturbing information that no rigging looked familiar: there were no signs of the distinctive Venn profile on the seas, nor the fore-and-aft rigging of the southern ships of their day.

Orm came to the conclusion that Scarface Ramis had caused them to sail beyond their own time long before the flag boy and Henerek's youngest scout found enough common words to trade personal information. They had gone nearly nine centuries beyond their time. Discovering what this new world might offer them must come after they ridded themselves of these warriors.

Orm counted the days.

Henerek counted the days.

The night before the fleet of four expected to make landfall in Everon's main harbor, the Venn flag boy and Henerek's scout sat on the taffrail eating hot, spicy buns and talking, hand motions taking the place of modifiers.

"Why you no survey first?" the Venn youth asked the scout.

"Commander was a boy in that harbor. Says he knows it. Says also, they notice a stranger nosing around." Seeing that most of his words confused the Venn, the scout put his hands up beside his face and spread his fingers. "Surprise!"

"Midday? Not so good. Dawn good," the Venn said, and motioned behind him. "Sun."

The scout shrugged. He didn't care about tides or any of the rest of that. What mattered to him was the fact that he wouldn't get to sneak in and scout out the harbor first, which was his job. But nobody crossed Henerek.

So the scout drilled with the others, each patrol having their own target. And once the harbor was secured, they'd march up the river to Ferdrian, the capital.

"If we're fast, and strike hard, four days will do it," Henerek predicted. "Six at the outside."

The next morning, half of the Norsundrians were puking again, as waves splashed along the heaving deck, and low clouds shot stinging arrows of sleet at sails, ship, sailors, and the massive kelp-veined breakers.

Two days later the storm died away, leaving fretful whitecaps on a running sea. The ships had worn well out into the ocean, making Henerek impatient. After so much toil, and waiting, his hand clenched with the mounting desire to strike his sword through King Berthold's heart.

Should he make the king kneel first? Roderic Dei was going to be kneeling before Henerek cut out his liver before the eyes of his daughters, but the one who was going to linger a very long time was that insufferable snot Valenn. Henerek was going to take out, as painfully as possible, every brooded-over insult and sneer upon the noble Lord Valenn's body . . .

Wind, weather, and tide finally appeared to be cooperating. Orm had been trained to rise well before dawn for the hour of meditation, a time to marshal the will and consider one's decisions, thus inspiring followers with surety and strength.

Orm had been reflecting through most of the night. When he was certain his fellow captains would be awake, he walked out onto his deck, noted everyone in place, discipline tight in spite of all the changes and those unspeakable Norsundrians snoring and farting in the hold, so sick they scarcely had the strength to mutter the Waste Spell.

He ran up the 'captains meet' flag himself, and bade the duty hands to let down his boat without making noise. And, as when they decided to leave the world (except then it had been all nine), he met his fellow captains in the waters between the ships, the boats bumping against one another, as they all knew how sound carried over the sea.

"Midday?" *Grebe's Heart*'s captain repeated, hoarse with his effort not to shout his disbelief. "He wants the midday tide, when he has the perfect tide at the perfect time, the sun directly behind him to confuse 'em?"

"Won't listen, won't risk the boats before there's light," Orm said. "Thinks his attack will come as a surprise."

Grebe's Wing's captain snorted, his blue gaze wide. "Surprise? There are only two places between those two rivers for an attack. His enemy must be asleep, not to expect them."

The others agreed, for they all had seen the chart. The southeast corner of Everon had flat beaches, but that meant a very long march all across the kingdom to the city now serving as the capital. The only other place was the estuary that opened into the natural harbor. Surely it was guarded. Everywhere else were tall, rocky cliffs, with jagged rocks below. A deadly coast.

They considered that, then they considered their passengers, as the water wash-washed against the hulls of their boats.

"Norsunder," said *Grebe's Eye*'s captain. "You hear they are evil," he began.

"Any worse than Erkric?" Orm retorted.

Grebe's Eye's captain raised his hands. "I know. I know. All mages seem bent on bringing Rainorec the sooner. My point is, evil they may be, but stupid?"

"Land warriors," said *Grebe's Wing*'s captain. "Arrogant as our Drenga."

"Who at least were Venn, by the Tree!" exclaimed *Grebe's Eye*'s captain, and the others agreed. "But we are oath-sworn to land them, stupid plan or not."

"And this is why I signaled you," Orm said. "I know you will not like this any better than I, but I'd rather lose timber than lives. I say, let them take our boats. We aren't trained in landing attack any more than they are."

"So you are certain there is no surprise, that the defenders are expecting them?"

"Even if they are not, we know how difficult it is to land a force and go straight into attack. We've watched our Drenga drill landings again and again, and even they can suffer accidents. I don't think these know what to do from sea to shore, however good their skills are once they stand on firm ground." Orm shook his head. "I don't foresee anything but trouble, and this is not our fight. Our oath to Scarface Ramis was to bring them to their destination, which we have now done. Let them take our boats. We will build new ones."

The other three agreed, one reluctantly, one angrily. But they agreed.

They were all there watching from the sides, rigging, and yards of their ships as Henerek and his force clambered down into the boats.

Henerek was furious, of course. He'd expected the Venn to row them neatly ashore, then conveniently vanish. But he'd seen them drilling on deck, and knew that a fight would seriously harm his own people. And even if he won, how was he going to force the Venn to get them safely ashore?

The Venn had expected rich amusement from the sight of the Norsundrians clambering down the steep tumble-homes and dropping into the boats tossing alongside. They weren't disappointed. A gratifying number of Norsundrians managed to drop between boat and ship, or overbalance if they made it to the boat, but none of them drowned. Silver drams exchanged hands as a result of wagers.

The Venn also expected some entertainment out of watching Henerek's force attempt the oars. A couple boats spun in circles, oars clattering and clashing amid hot curses, but shouted orders from neighboring boats made it clear that some'd had experience on the water.

Would that experience extend to beach landings, the worst sort of attack short of running uphill? Orm and his captains watched through their glasses, expecting to see a rain of arrows commence at that vulnerable moment when the boats hit the breakers.

And so it would have been, had not Lord Valenn commanded the harbor defense. Orm and his captains noted the uncharacteristic quiet of the ships bobbing in the harbor, yards crossed, no one in sight, the lack of the usual harbor business on quay and jetties. Even the harbormaster's tower flew no flag.

"Lying in wait," Orm said to his second in command.

They watched until their boats, inexpertly rowed by the Norsundrians, reached the breakers. Two boats turned sideways as oars flailed uselessly, and broached to, spilling out warriors. More wager tokens exchanged hands.

Orm cast one last look at those suspiciously empty ships, and smacked his glass closed. "I'd say they're waiting on a signal, and we are not part of this foolery." He motioned to the flag boy. "Signal 'make sail.'"

The Venn ships' yards bloomed, sails catching the wind, the distinctive prow, not seen on that coast for centuries, turning seaward.

Up behind cover, Lord Valenn watched through his glass. "There is no retreat," he murmured. "Unless there are more ships beyond the horizon."

"Oh, let us shoot," Harn said anxiously, taking no notice

of the ships. His attention was on Henerek's people forming into groups, weapons ready. "Look at that. There has to be a thousand of them."

"And they're scrambling about, soggy wet," someone else said. "We should attack now, while they're still fishing their fellows out of the water."

Valenn silenced his young knight-cadets with a stern look. "We are Knights. We take no action without honor. As soon as Henerek is on firm ground, we will proceed as planned."

'Honor.' It silenced discussion. If attacking an invading enemy while they were relatively weak was dishonorable in the eyes of their admired leader, well, nobody wanted to be the one to suggest otherwise.

Valenn returned his attention to his field glass, and ah, there he was, just as Rel had said. Henerek was instantly recognizable, though he had changed considerably from the weedy, pouting boy Valenn remembered, always shirking the more boring tasks, always looking for insult, and whining about privilege and rank without ever understanding the weight of duty commensurate with that privilege.

As soon as Henerek reached the shore, Valenn snapped his field glass to, handed it to his squire with a word of thanks, checked to see that his gloves were not awry, and glanced right and left at his flank captains to make certain they knew their orders. When he received short nods in return, he straightened up, walked around the wagon that had served as his cover, and started alone down the quay. His heart thundered, but he breathed deeply, aware of his sword loose in its scabbard.

Henerek marked him immediately, his sharp features aligning into a smirk. Around and behind him, he heard the rustle of cloth and the creak of blackweave straps as shields, slung over backs for the landing, were pulled around.

Surprise was gone. "Surprise," Henerek shouted anyway, a little too soon. His voice was weakened by the shore wind.

Valenn resisted the impulse to call "What?" just to disconcert Henerek. Weak his voice might have been on the wind, but Valenn had heard it, and he would stay strictly within the rules of war.

So he bided his time as he walked up to Henerek, who put out a hand, holding back his dripping force. So far, the rules had been obeyed.

"Henerek. Your quarrel was with me. I challenge you to single combat."

Henerek's smirk widened. "And here I thought you were strutting out to take us all." He glanced to the side, making a long face, and won some snickers from his force. "We were trembling in fear."

Valenn's heartbeat quickened as Henerek took one, then another sauntering step nearer. He seemed no worse for being soaked to the waist, in spite of the cold wind of early spring, and his boots making squelching noises at each step. Somewhere, someone had seen to it that he had developed enough discipline to put on muscle.

Valenn resisted the impulse to clear his throat, and spoke slowly, to keep his voice calm and measured. "If you win, then let battle be joined. If I win, you will return whence—"

Henerek began to shake water from a glove, and as Valenn's gaze flicked that way, Henerek used his other hand, driving a hidden short blade through Valenn's ribs and up in a vicious undercut.

Pain flowered through Valenn, followed by spreading numbness in knees, joints, lips.

"Surprise," Henerek said again, laughing as Valenn fell dead at his feet. "Damnation," he exclaimed, stepping over him. So much for the week of protracted play. Already the plan was going sideways—

Sitting there waiting for Norsunder to attack had been unnerving, but seeing their leader cut down without warning shot red rage through the defenders. The two flank captains were not quite a heartbeat apart in signaling their archers.

A familiar crackling sound followed by a very familiar hissing hum, and here was the steel-tipped rain. Shields whipped up and the hiss became a hammering thud as arrows hit them.

Henerek extended his hand, and the patrols took off to envelop the harbor—the fastest runners jerking in surprise then tumbling to the ground as ropes, hidden in the mud, winched taut.

Henerek's fury ignited. So maybe the Everoneth were not the hapless idiots he'd come to believe. That only made him angrier.

A couple quick steps and Aldi Nath, his senior captain, joined him. She was a square woman with a frizz of light hair, her face seamed by years of sun. "This isn't a day's defense. They've had all winter to dig in." She lifted her chin toward the apparent clutter of wagons, stacked barrels, and dilapidated barns.

Henerek glanced back. The Venn were gone. Half the boats were beached, half bobbing around in the waves. As he watched, shielded groups of Everoneth splashed into the surf and began chopping the centers out of the boats; as his rear guard ran to engage them they scattered, two-legged turtles under their shields.

Henerek's master charge was already disintegrating into fierce little battles everywhere.

Nath's light eyes narrowed.

All Henerek knew about her was that she'd been some kind of guard before she lost her fiery temper once too often, and ended up with a stone spell on her, in some Garden of Shame, until some other Norsundrian went harvesting. "If we take the harbormaster's tower, and set a defensive perimeter," she said, "we can regroup and relaunch."

Henerek gave a short nod. So the Everoneth wanted a fight. Well, he'd never really expected surrender. He'd give them a fight. "Do it."

Chapter Five

The Garden of the Twelve, Norsunder-Beyond

THE garden was beautiful: each blossom perfect, each blade of grass green, each shrub full of shiny new leaves. All frozen by enchantment at the point of death, Yeres had said with her slow smile, just showing the tips of her teeth, the first time she brought Siamis there as a child, before handing him off to her brother's untender lack of mercy.

At that time, he'd been a terrified boy of twelve. Now he found the lovely, dead garden a precious conceit, while still appreciating the implied threat.

Yeres could not get into his mind, though it seemed to amuse her to keep trying. Yeres and her brother Efael had been born on another world, plucked from there by Svirle, who found their inventive viciousness useful and their perversions entertaining. They did not have Dena Yeresbeth, which guaranteed that they would never be equal to the architects of Norsunder, though Yeres expended great effort with magical mind-tortures in an effort to gain similar skill.

Timelessness, Siamis had discovered, growing in fits and starts as four thousand years rolled away beyond Norsunder's gates, could hang curiously heavy in the borderland places where the body was not merely an illusion.

Yeres stepped close to him, tipping her chin back to look up into his face. Seemingly they stood alone in the Garden of the Twelve, but here, no sense could be trusted, even on the mental plane: the layers of lies and deception appeared to be endless, an eternal fall that never reached the ground of truth.

The implication, he knew, was that there was no truth to be found.

"So you'd left your sword behind as a threat? How charming," Yeres said as she traced a finger from the hilt of the now-recovered sword named Emeth to the top of Siamis's hand. He did not respond, but knew better than to move.

She was close enough for him to smell the floral scent that did not quite mask her brother's musk. Siamis's stomach clenched. The physical memories, usually quiescent, stirred briefly, but he was long practiced at shutting those away.

"Not a threat," he said, sidestepping her deliberate ambiguity by assuming the context was Bereth Ferian's mages. "Merely another move in the game."

The corners of her smile tightened. "Provocative."

"Entertaining," he said austerely, taking refuge in obliviousness. When he was twelve she had enjoyed watching Efael toy with him.

His first defense had been to take refuge in their expectations: if he bored them long enough, they punished him for it, but then they went away. "And your little game in Marloven Hess?" she asked.

"I thought that was obvious," he replied. "Detlev wants the Montredaun- An boy isolated and angry, ripe for recruitment when the time comes. That was a gambit to hasten things along." It had also been a gambit to test how closely he was observed.

The answer: right now, very closely indeed.

So, time to be both boring and cooperative. "Oalthoreh and her minions provided a protracted lesson in their current arsenal of wards," he said, and began reciting a catalogue of magical defenses observed through the Norsunder Base window until the Bereth Ferian mages made it a little

too obvious they knew they were being spied on. But they
had done what Siamis had expected of them until then:
kept watching eyes busy.

He could feel Yeres's disinterest in his catalogue, but it,
like their apparent isolation in the Garden, could be another deception. Her waylaying him could be mere cupidity
or whim, but it was more likely a deflection. And always a
test.

Still talking, he took an easy sidestep, and dropped onto
the stone bench, where he leaned back and propped one
foot on a decorative stone. He clasped his hands around his
knee as he kept up the catalogue.

Though he'd never had any interest in the twins' sexual
preferences beyond defensive tactics, he had learned that
Efael always took his targets off-world, the young ones terrified, the older ones full of fight, the only common pattern
being their unwillingness; Yeres had nauseated Siamis long
before he had the remotest interest in such things with lingering, lascivious descriptions of what a good lover her brother
was, and how that tenderness might be earned. Her tastes
were for young men, or boys just barely over the threshold,
the prettier the better. Above all, she liked the spice of seduc-
tion. Adoration was sweet for a time; the only mood she
seemed indifferent to was perfunctory acceptance.

When the tracing finger drew up his leg, he obliged by
setting his heel on the grass, his knees wide, as he embroidered the theme of the Bereth Ferian mages' ignorance. He
was the very picture of perfunctory acceptance.

When the toying finger lifted, he permitted no reaction,
not even an alteration in his breathing. ". . . and it suits us
to keep them on the hop."

"Us," she repeated. "You are such a very good boy, aren't
you? Running errands for your protector?"

"Detlev is not my protector," he said, permitting a hint
of his ready anger to heighten his tone.

Yeres smiled. "And yet here you are, his loyal minion.
How sweet is the family bond."

"I like his plans. So I'll obey his orders," he retorted.
"Until I don't."

That made her laugh, as she twined her fingers through
the lock of hair that had dropped on his forehead. In the

Garden, which was mostly her design, she had all the power. All he had were his wits.

She left his hair and the finger traced around his ear as she leaned close. "What does he really want in Geth? Humans have been there half as long as they have here. Not even half."

"Without nearly eradicating themselves as well as magic." He stated the obvious to be boring, to prod her toward her purpose. When her eyelids briefly shuttered, subtle as a butterfly's antennae, he ventured a verbal backstep. "Detlev insists that their transfer magic can be learned and brought here, the intention to force rifts."

"Why have we not heard about this?"

He lifted a shoulder. "Because he's still seeking the fundamentals. If he's right, this method is akin to intensifying the effect of light through refraction, the mirror behind the sconce. Can it be intensified enough to rip a hole in the between?"

Rifts. Even the Host of Lords could not move until the powerful spell that Evend of Bereth Ferian had sacrificed his life in making could be broken, permitting rifts once again between Sartorias-deles and Norsunder-Beyond.

She lifted her hand, and sighed. "You had better get to it, then, errand-boy. Your master is waiting."

He made the sign to transfer to Norsunder Base. As soon as the transfer magic dissipated he walked straight through a cleaning frame, and resisted the nearly overwhelming impulse to step through a second time, as if her touch, and that whiff of Efael, still lingered. But he knew it didn't; a second step-through would do nothing but raise interest, if he was being watched.

He intended to get a meal and listen to a status report at the same time, but the first two sentences spoken by the desk flunky in the command center caused him to abandon his meal untouched: in her last gesture of spite, Yeres had not kept him a few hours, she had kept him for nearly two years. In those two years, the Base had apparently disintegrated into quarreling factions, resulting in Henerek going off to invade Everon, Bostian busy planning to march on Sartor with all the warriors Henerek and Kessler didn't want—all stupid, short-sighted campaigns that made a hash of this crucial stage of Detlev's plans. And no sign of Detlev.

Siamis went to fetch the world transfer token from Detlev's warded room, where he stood, tossing the transfer token on his hand as he considered his next move.

Yeres's purpose had been to anger Detlev. And he would be angry. But she wanted the anger to fall squarely on Siamis.

Power, he had long ago decided, was a fluid concept. In the Garden of the Twelve, it meant privacy. Yeres spied as she willed, and expended much effort in breaking into minds, yet she herself was used by Svirle or Ilerian, whose thoughts, and intentions, were shared with no one.

If Yeres didn't know what Detlev was doing on Geth, then that meant Efael didn't know, either. Efael's most recent surge of malice was probably the result of his being warded from Detlev's project on Five, which meant that Yeres's random pulse of concupiscence was the first move in their latest lethal game.

Well, figuring out that game was for later. Right now? She had yanked Siamis's strings, so he'd better be dancing.

But before he could nerve himself for the bone-socket wrench of world transfer to Five, Detlev himself appeared in a whirl of singed metal smell.

Of course he'd have a window; impossible to know who else did. Siamis sustained the mental contact as Detlev reviewed the memory of the conversation with Yeres. He was clearly irritated at finding Norsunder Base nearly empty, the captains scattered pursuing their own plots.

Siamis was supposed to be holding the Base in readiness. Detlev said contemptuously, as avid eyes all around watched and eager ears listened, "You walked right into that, didn't you?"

Siamis retorted, "I was in Norsunder on your order."

"You may commence your dance." Detlev flicked his fingers. "But leave Marloven Hess to me."

Sixthmonth, 4742 AF
Sartor

What remained of the Sartoran Guard still patrolled the outskirts of the city, and the southern border, below which

Norsunder Base existed in constant threat. Mendaen of the Rescuers, now captain of a small company, was riding the familiar road between the capital and the border when a cloud of dust ahead signified someone galloping belly to the ground.

Mendaen urged his mount to the side, but placed his hand on the hilt of his sword. That hand fell away when he recognized one of his border scouts, a seventeen-year-old redhead, who pulled up, eyes round as robin's eggs.

"They're coming!" the scout gasped.

"Who—what, Norsunder?" Mendaen demanded.

"Yes. Riders and marchers both, in column!"

Mendaen muttered, "It has to be an advance force. Go—" No. He looked at the scout's sweaty horse, then said, "Ride back and tell the patrol to go to ground. Don't attack. Just watch. My horse is fresh—I'll get word to Eidervaen."

The scout wheeled about to obey.

Mendaen kneed his mount into a canter, then let her stretch her legs into a gallop as they rode hard for home. That was orders, any sighting was to be reported. He hated the thought of just standing by, but a hundred Royal Guards scattered from the border to the north of the city was not going to do much against an invading army except serve as target practice.

He didn't slow until he spotted Eidervaen's towers on the horizon. By now he was dodging traffic on the royal road, forcing him to ride up embankments and splash across summer-shallow streams, as the Guard no longer carried pennants that gave them the right-of-way.

Orders were specific: report first to the mages, not to the palace. That wouldn't keep him from yelling the news as he passed down the great parade ground before the palace, if he spotted anyone he knew, who might be able to get to Atan first. But all he saw was poor little Julian, still looking no older than six and filthy and bedraggled as ever, crouched down as she fed bits of something to a flock of birds. Probably her lunch.

Mendaen rode straight to the mage headquarters. He tossed the reins to a waiting apprentice, shouted, "Walk her," past the boy's inquiry after his business, and ran inside. "Where is the mage chief?"

A very short time later, there was Chief Mage Veltos. At least she listened as Mendaen delivered his one-sentence report. Then she turned her head and began handing out orders to the blue-robed mage students crowding around, beginning with, "You. Report at once to the queen."

Once all of the mage students had been sent with orders, Veltos shifted her attention back to Mendaen. "Thank you for being timely. You may go."

Mendaen was now free to spread the news, as the mages, who had been practicing emergency procedures daily, went in ordered haste about their arrangements.

Veltos stood in the headquarters and took a deep breath, mind racing with tasks to protect the city. Presently a young student pattered up in slippered feet, saying, "Chief Veltos! I was sent by Verias at the desk. The alarm protection on South Road, it—"

"Thank you," Veltos interrupted. "Return to your classroom." So, the magic alarm laid over the road was not faster than a human, probably because the magic required proximity, and that Guard's patrollers had seen the evidence of the approaching invaders some distance off. She must remember that.

A short time later, she, Atan, and certain senior mages stood on the cliff where, during winter, they had first planned this elaborate illusion. At the first sight of the long column riding up the road, she suppressed the urge to hide behind a boulder. The mages had already cast illusions before themselves—if the enemy should look up their way, they would only see a blurred reflection of the sky overhead. As long as no one moved, there would be no reason to look hard.

Atan stood by Veltos, her fingers gripped tightly as the black-clad enemies, each holding a spear, rode steadily toward the crucial point. None of them seemed to be looking at any of the illusory terrain.

Closer . . . closer . . .

Without any hesitation, they rode past the true turn in the road, and headed down the false curve. In complete silence, Atan and her mages watched until a forested hill intervened, hiding the enemy from view.

Atan said to Veltos, "I'm going. I have to see." And before the chief mage could voice the objection Atan saw in her face, she touched a transfer token she'd secreted in her pocket, whispered the transfer word, and felt herself jolted from the cliff to a hiding place she'd selected in spring without anyone knowing.

Veltos, furious at the useless risk their young queen was taking, had long since arranged for another vantage from which she could observe the road. Separated in heart as well as by distance, she and Atan watched from behind the safety of trees as, two by two, the invaders rode straight into the sun-dappled shadows of Shendoral Wood.

Marloven Hess

Senrid's two visits to Chwahirsland had been a dramatic lesson in the difference between light and dark magic. Light magic was useless for military purposes, no matter how many spells you layered. It would run off harmlessly, like an overfilled bucket. Dark magic was not much better, unless you interlocked dangerously volatile spells that required a terrible cost. Chwahirsland was living proof of that.

Senrid could consult Keriam on everything except magic. That, he alone was responsible for. So he'd decided not to rely solely on the illusions, which were too easy to get rid of once you knew they were there, but to create a spiderweb of tracers along the border. By the time any Norsundrian could dismantle his webwork of tracers, Senrid would know, and could get his secondary plan—equally laboriously put together with Keriam—into action.

He was so certain the threat would come in the middle of the night that he'd taken to sleeping in his clothes, with his notecase next to his dagger under the pillow.

But he was halfway through breakfast on a bright morning that promised a hot summer when the mental poke somewhere behind his eyeballs caused him to look around for a heartbeat. He dropped his bread onto his plate.

"The tracers," he said to the bread crumbs.

He thrust his hand into his shirt pocket, where he had stashed his fast-escape ensorcelled shank button, then he whispered the transfer spell that would pull him to whatever, or whoever, had tripped the tracer.

Shock washed through him with the impact of ice when he came out of the transfer reaction to find himself high on a cliff overlooking a winding river valley that he recognized instantly.

Standing at the extreme edge, looking down, was Detlev.

Senrid clutched his escape shank and said his transfer word. Horror suffused him when he found it blocked.

Detlev said, "Sentiment?" One hand, an empty hand, gestured toward the scene below.

"It is not!" Then the real meaning struck Senrid: Detlev knew very well that sentiment was no part of why Senrid had chosen this cliff to anchor his tracer web. He'd chosen it as a reminder of the humiliating defeat he had suffered while watching his own people being slaughtered by Norsunder.

There'd be no Erdrael now.

Detlev watched the slow river winding down the middle of the valley below, a random updraft stirring the light brown hair on his brow.

Senrid stood poised to run, knowing he probably didn't have a chance. He'd run anyway if he saw even a sliver of opportunity.

Detlev said to the view, "Incompetent in two forms of magic, are you? Now that, I am afraid, can only be attributed to sentiment."

His left hand came into view, also empty, but Detlev didn't need to carry weapons. One thing all the records agreed on, he could kill with a thought.

Detlev glanced upward, then to either side, as if listening to something or someone Senrid could neither see nor hear. His impassive expression altered to faint disgust, as if he regarded shoddy workmanship, then he met Senrid's gaze, the morning sun striking a cold pinpoint of light in the center of his hazel-framed pupils as he said, "It seems there is another demand for my attention. When I do find the time to undertake your education, you will not see me coming."

He vanished. Leaving Senrid to discover that the entire

webwork of wards and tracers he and Hibern had labored over so painfully had been swept into nonexistence, like a stick through a spiderweb.

Senrid gave himself a few moments to breathe as his heart thudded in his ears. He dared not transfer with his carefully prepared token, lest Detlev had altered it somehow. He flung it away with all his strength, then stood there with his breath shuddering, his knees watery, as the shank spun end over end until it vanished below.

He braced—and spoke the old transfer spell.

Magic flung him inside out, then restored him in his study. Alive. Unharmed. He forced watery limbs into motion, and presently dashed through Keriam's office door, panting for breath.

Keriam glanced at Senrid's pale face, his pupils huge and black, and his pen dropped. He had never seen Senrid that afraid, even in the darkest days under the threat of his uncle.

"Detlev." Senrid whispered the name, as if the man could hear across time and space. "He was there. My protections . . ." He snapped his hand flat, as though smashing something away. "Give the signal," he croaked. "It's begun."

Keriam strode to the door, beckoned to the runner waiting outside, and said, "Sound the retreat."

Senrid heard the rap of departing footsteps, and within a very short time the tower overhead rang *tang-tang, tang-tang*, the signal for which everyone had been practicing all summer.

Senrid ran to Keriam's tower window, which looked out over the academy. For a heartbeat or two, nothing could be seen. Then as the garrison bell picked up the rhythm, *tang-tang*, and then the south tower, followed by the city bell, Senrid saw orderly lines of boys running low to the ground below a wall. One by one the boys vaulted the wall into the corral, then completely vanished from sight.

Elsewhere, a couple of blond heads bobbed, then vanished abruptly, as if yanked. Senrid imagined lines of boys running low along the fences and vanishing into the practice grounds beyond the stables, and from there following the lines of creeks into wilder country, where he knew that the senior boys in charge of each group had stashed supplies.

All over the castle, the garrison guards had gone into alert mode. Runners would be departing through the gates to warn the army garrisons to vanish. Everything happening just as he'd planned.

It was a relief to see those empty stone corridors, but fear still churned inside him, twisted into worry—what if he was wrong, and Detlev wasn't launching an army over the border? There had been that moment of distraction before he uttered that last threat.

Senrid scowled down at the empty academy. Why else would Detlev come to Marloven Hess? Unless the target was not the kingdom, but Senrid himself. *You will not see me coming.*

"Senrid," Keriam said, more loudly.

Senrid realized the commander had said his name a couple of times. He looked up, as Keriam said gently, "They're gone. Now it's your turn."

At the same time
Sarendan

The galloper dashed into Peitar Selenna's private family chamber in his palace in Miraleste. The teenage scout, mud-splashed to the waist, nose and ears raw with cold, had ridden through a wild hailstorm to bring the news.

"They're coming," he declared, eyes wide with excitement. Then bowed belatedly, falling against a curve-legged table in his weariness.

Peitar's heart constricted, more at the excitement in the boy's face than at news too long dreaded to be a surprise.

Derek got to his feet. "I'd better join my defenders."

"Wait. Wait," Lilah exclaimed.

"I don't think you ought to ride at night. Especially in this weather." Peitar indicated the rain beating against the windowpanes, as he signed to a waiting servant to take the shivering galloper somewhere and get something hot into him.

"Storm's nearly blown." Derek flashed his careless grin. He was excited, too. "You know I'm used to riding in bad weather." He turned to Lilah. "Norsunder won't wait."

Lilah swallowed, then said stubbornly, "I have to pack."

"Pack?" Peitar and Derek said together.

She forced a nod. "I promised the orphan brigade. I would fight with them."

"Most of the younger orphans are staying right here in the city," Derek said, with a glance at Peitar's distraught expression.

Derek felt the same way about sending children into battle. He eyed Lilah, a sturdy figure for a child, but in no way ready for what lay ahead. "You haven't been drilling but during summer," he began.

It was the wrong tack. "Same with many prentices," she retorted, bravely meeting that assessing gaze. At least Derek wasn't angry. She had seen him angry, the day he started the revolution, and she dreaded his anger. "They had to divide between work and drill. I *promised*." Her voice rose anxiously as she turned in desperation from one to the other, afraid of a worse thing than bad language and glares: that they were going to laugh at her. Dismiss her promises with a sickening, *But you're just too young.* "I promised."

Derek heard Peitar stirring, but half-raised a hand. "All right, then. If you can beat me in a sword fight, you can go with me."

"Beat you?"

"If you can beat me, then you can beat a Norsundrian," Derek said reasonably. "But if you can't, then all you'll do is serve as target practice, which will make everybody who didn't defend you feel terrible. Want that?"

"No," she said grittily. "All right. Let's go. Right now."

They trooped off to the salle, where Derek chose one of the side rooms, away from the city guard's own drill space. Lilah looked doubtfully at the weapons—real ones, not wood—and said, "How many tries do I get?"

"As many as you like," Derek said.

She picked up a sword, braced, and held it up. And attacked.

He struck the blade out of her hand.

She ran to get it, saying over her shoulder, "I wasn't ready."

"That's all right," Derek said. "Go ahead, strike when you are."

Peitar began to breathe again as three times, Lilah launched herself grimly at Derek, who blocked her moves, then struck the sword out of her hand.

After the third, she sighed, wringing her numb fingers. Her throat tightened with defeat. "If you see any of my friends, tell them I tried."

"None of them will be there," Derek said soberly. "We put all the orphan brigade through a similar test."

Lilah turned away, aware of a sickening sense of relief. It felt like betrayal, somehow.

Derek set out a short time later, his galloper having been fed and issued new, warm clothing and a fresh mount. His news had been lamentably brief, not much more than that a sizable force had been spotted in one of the older mountain passes. Peitar and Derek had hired shepherds to watch all the passes, against this very situation.

As Derek climbed onto his horse, he thought grimly that already they were at a disadvantage. Shepherds were not militarily trained: they didn't even think of counting heads, noting weapons, and so forth. He was going to have to fix that if they survived this attack, he promised himself. He saluted the two anxious faces up in the library window and rode off.

As soon as Derek was out of sight, Peitar withdrew to let Tsauderei know.

Derek's mood rose as he and his scout rode through the city gates. All right, they were through waiting, at least. It was finally time for action, a realization that filled him with fierce joy. This was so much better than the revolution: a clear enemy, and training behind his army.

He and the scout verbally sifted the few words of the brief report for any stray details. So far, at least, everything was going exactly according to plan. He'd put their very best people in the south, camping in Diannah Wood. From there it would be relatively easy to reach any of the southwest passes, as they all debouched roughly in the same area, feeding the rivers that spilled into Tseos Lake below Miraleste.

Derek left the exhausted galloper at the first changing

post, then set out alone on a fresh horse under a clear sky. The moon crested the mountains, not full, but casting enough light over a road Derek knew well.

He slept in snatches in the saddle, pausing long enough to get bread and cheese at the posts he'd established along the road in order to change horses.

At noon the third day, he rode into his camp, where he found everyone honing weapons, their voices sharp with excitement. They sent up a cheer when they saw him. "Come," he said to the three captains. "Let's look at the map one more time."

They had worked up contingencies for all the passes, but now that they knew which one would bring them face to face with the enemy, it was reassuring to go over everything again. He felt it, and he could see it in the captains, the old, grizzled one—a stonemason who had fought for Khanerenth in his youth—his son, and the upright captain with the neatly tied-back dark hair, who had been a patrol leader under the old king.

Derek no longer resented the remnants of the king's army. War was really happening, soon. Now that it was close, doubt twisted his guts. He looked at that patrol captain, remembered the inefficient scout report, and once again wished he had the equivalent of the old king's army, with its training and discipline—but without the arrogant nobles.

It was then that they heard noise outside the tent, high voices protesting and low voices arguing. He burst out to discover three boys struggling in the arms of older fellows.

"I promised Ma he wouldn't be here," declared the tallest, a rust-thatched young silversmith, his voice breaking as he fought to contain his eleven-year-old brother, nicknamed Ruddy.

Derek signed for the boys to be let go, then frowned at them. "I told you all to stay in Miraleste. You'll be needed as scouts and errand runners."

"Not if you fight 'em off here," Ruddy said fiercely.

"Lilah said she's coming," a twiggy blond, son of a seal-maker, spoke up.

"She's in Miraleste," Derek said. "She'll be a runner for the king."

A brief silence, then Ruddy burst out, "But she and the

real Sharadan Brothers, they were in the revolution. They were *heroes* in the revolution."

"But they didn't fight," Derek said, at the same time as Ruddy's older brother said, "They got information, and thieved from collaborators. Anyways, that was us against us. Not us against Norsunder."

The third boy, the lanky son of a joiner, muttered, "So Lilah is a princess. Of course they'd keep *her* safe. Bren is somewhere fighting, I bet anything."

Derek heard the scorn in the word 'princess,' knowing that the boy was reflecting his own contempt for royalty, nobles, and their attitudes. But now was not the time to be divisive. "Bren is also going to scout, but in his town. Listen, since you sneaked here uncaught, that means you're good at sneaking. We were just saying that we need more scouts up above the pass, to signal us when Norsunder is spotted. The most important post, right now, is that. Go up the trail and report to Granny Innah, who has a magic ring. You say the word 'Sarendan' and touch the stone, and the captain here will know that Norsunder is sighted, so we move into position."

The older captain held up his hand, displaying the ring twin to the one the scout had.

"Now that we know which pass is the one, Granny Innah will probably want you on different cliffs, to make sure we see every possible trail, in order to get the earliest sighting," Derek said. "Get some trail supplies, because she won't have enough for you, and run!"

The three brightened at having real orders, important orders. Within a short time the boys had journey-bread and vanished up a back trail.

The silversmith said to Derek, "Thanks. My brother thinks it's a game. He doesn't remember seein' our dad lying dead in the street, trampled by the mob during the revolution. Wasn't even the king's men that did for him." A brief flick at the dark-haired captain. "All he remembers is, Dad was a hero. But Ma remembers, and she made me promise."

Derek said, "I know. She made me promise, too." Their red-haired mother had been one of his fiercest supporters before the revolution. Until the viciousness of the city battles turned her against both sides, after half of Miraleste went up in smoke.

With the boys safely out of sight, Derek gave the order to break camp and move to the mouth of the pass, which squeezed down to a funnel. They would hide on either side of the tumbling stream, and attack the Norsundrians coming down the last of the rocky, narrow path in ones and twos.

As they streamed along the dappled glades of Diannah Wood past spring goldenrod dancing like candle flames, high in the eastern peaks, Tsauderei cursed under his breath as he put together a few necessities. He did not look forward to several transfers in a row, as he sought the best vantage from which to observe the invaders.

In the pass, Prince Kessler Sonscarna led at the front, walking with the Venn renegade he'd winnowed out of Norsunder itself.

Kessler had occasionally heard reference to the Venn as legendary warriors, but he'd always assumed that was hyperbole. After all, how good was 'legendary?' That meant 'formerly good,' right? From what he could discover, the Venn were now locked inside their borders, which did not signify formidable warriors to him.

But after he'd seen those strange ships appear in the ocean, he wondered about those old Venn. Their language wasn't included in the Universal Language Spell. Mindful of the ship tokens he'd wrested from Pengris, he'd sought out a renegade Venn to teach him some of their language.

The man was a snake, but willing enough to brag about the customs of his homeland, and to teach Kessler the rudiments of Venn, in order to get out of scut work. Kessler had always had a facility for languages, so they were arguing in basic terms the advantages and disadvantages of attacking in column (disadvantage, flank exposed to archers) versus attacking in line (easier to break) when the scouts sent the signal back: *Enemy in sight.*

Up on the trail above, the orphan brigade boys, having eaten all their bread early on, were looking forward to a camp meal as they toiled the last paces to the summit—until Ruddy, in the lead, halted the other two. "Something's not right," he whispered.

The brilliant day abruptly turned sinister for small, twiggy Sig. Lanky Faen scoffed, "What?"

Ruddy muffled his mouth, then glanced at the rocky outcropping that screened them from the cliff. "S'posed to be Granny Innah. There's two voices. Men."

Everyone knew Ruddy had the quickest ears of their group. In silence, the three crept to the nearest mossy rock, and peered beyond. There, they gazed in shock at the blood-covered remains of Granny Innah, and the two gray-clad strangers who stood at the edge, looking down, their backs to the boys.

Ruddy counted three swords. One fellow had a long-sword strapped across his back, and a rapier at his hip. They also had bows, arrows, and several daggers. Those were the weapons in view.

So when Faen predictably whispered, "Let's fight 'em," Ruddy put his lips to Faen's ear. "With what?"

All they had were their daggers. Each of the three took another long peek at the pair chatting as though no old woman sprawled in death five paces away. When Ruddy saw a fly wandering over the sightless eyes of a woman who had often made him berry tarts, anger burned inside him.

He motioned Sig and Faen back, well behind the rock, and said, "We'll push 'em off."

"How?" Sig looked frightened. "Have you ever pushed someone? You go forward, too. We'll fall off as well!" He hated heights.

"Not if we use Granny's stick. Sig, you're going to fling dirt straight into the eyes of the left one. I'll get the right. Just like Derek said, working together. And you, Faen, be-ing biggest, you take Granny's walking stick and shove the nearest one off. Sig and I will do for the other one."

Sig didn't want to 'do' anything. The sight of popular Granny Innah all bloody and dead made him sick. His fin-gers shook as he bent to pick up two handfuls of dust. He didn't feel real, except yes it was real, and he wanted to pee, he wanted to run and run. But if he left Ruddy and Faen, after all the promises they'd made each other, he would be as good as dead.

As good as dead.

Derek had said, "You're only as good as your team, when you are small."

The urge to pee was fear, that much Sig recognized. He whispered the Waste Spell, then poised himself to run. When Ruddy nodded, they bolted head down as hard as they could go. The Norsundrians heard the footsteps and turned, hands going to weapons. Ruddy got his man square in the eyes with dust. Sig's splattered across his man's arm, but it didn't matter, because Faen shrieked as he rammed Granny's walking stick directly into the man's chest, and the man toppled over the edge, arms windmilling as he fell.

The second man flung himself away from the cliff edge, swinging his sword in furious arcs as Sig and Ruddy scrambled back. Screaming incoherently, Faen darted in with the stick, which the sword struck with a crack. The stick ripped out of Faen's hands. The man stamped, sword flailing around him as he cursed violently. Ignoring his throbbing hands, Faen scrambled for the stick, and remembered one of the drills. This time, he whirled the stick high so the sword would come at it, then he shot it between the man's legs.

The enemy tripped, falling to one knee.

That was when Ruddy hit him in the face with a huge rock. Swearing in a guttural howl, the man groped for his sword, but Sig picked it up with both hands, and, whimpering, his fingers slippery with sweat, he stabbed it into the man's stomach, then let go, retching at the horror of how that had felt.

He didn't have the strength to do more than break the man's skin, and the sword fell. Faen caught it and stabbed again and again, but the man still wriggled. Ruddy hit him again with a bigger rock, and this time he lay still, stunned. Faen and Ruddy each tugged an arm, getting him to the edge. Faen keened and Ruddy's breathing harshened as they sat down, planted their feet against the Norsundrian's back, then kicked him over the edge.

Sig had moved away, coughing as he tried to control his sobs.

Ruddy straightened, triumph spiraling with fear inside him, making him dizzy. They'd done it! Working together, they'd done it!

But then Faen said in a voice of horror, "Look."

Ruddy joined him at the edge. Sig followed on his hands and knees, peering down, past the two bodies sprawled on the rocks below, at the moving heads in a narrow crevasse, like ants in column.

"The signal," Ruddy said. "We have to let Derek know!"

They sprang to Granny Innah, and stared down at her hand. Sig's stomach lurched again when he saw that the Norsundrians had cut off her finger. The ring was gone. Probably now lying on the rocks below.

The boys looked at each other. "Can we yell?" Sig asked.

"If anyone hears us, it will be them." Faen pointed at the advancing enemy below.

"Then we have to run," Ruddy said, and the boys got their trembling limbs into motion, and bolted back down the trail.

Derek's force moved in a mass.

A scout at the front heard the rhythmic noise of tramping feet above the rush of the tumbling stream. He held up a hand, and when no one paid him any heed, he pushed through the crowd whose voices drowned his own, and ran straight to Derek. "I think Norsunder's already here."

Derek flung his head back to search the cliffs framing the sky, but he saw nothing. Where was Granny Innah?

"Shit." He whirled around.

His sudden movement caused those around him to stop talking, and as reaction ringed outward, he jabbed a hand toward the steep crags above the bottleneck.

Then he pointed violently, deploying his people. They flung themselves behind what cover they could as the first gray-clad enemies emerged.

The air hummed with arrows, causing birds to flap skyward, scolding. Shields came up with a clatter, and the arrows drummed against them like the roar of hail on rooftops. "They're fast," Derek said.

"They expected us," the grizzled stonemason replied, his accent strong.

Derek swallowed. Surprise was definitely gone. He thrust his fist upward, launching the two main forces. The third and fourth scrambled behind rocks and scrubby bushes to provide covering arrows.

Only the covering arrows were mostly bouncing uselessly off the crags, or, even worse, falling among the struggling lines of their own people. Derek hopped on his toes, desperate to see, and the last order he was able to give was the signal to cease the arrows.

After that he couldn't see. Things moved too fast. Everywhere he looked, his people, people he knew, recoiled, screamed, bled, fell, to be lost from view in the mass pushing inexorably forward to help, to see. They crushed together, so that some couldn't raise their weapons; the front fought the more desperately. One, two—five of the gray-clad ones fell. They could be killed!

Then a miracle happened. A horn brayed, and the Norsundrians turned smartly and began retreating back up the rocky slope, the last of them fighting a rear guard action.

Derek shouted, tears of angry joy in his eyes. They were in retreat! It was working!

Far above, Tsauderei watched from a rocky escarpment, his heart grieving as the gray mass spread into the colorful one, causing a crimson froth. Then, with no warning, they reversed. What was this? Tsauderei could see how many Norsundrians still waited in the pass. Was it possible the commander was a coward? He expected moral cowardice from anyone who would cleave to Norsunder, but weren't those who did the fighting bloodthirsty killers?

Something was amiss. He glanced upward, gauging the tumbling clouds with decades of experience. Then he leaned dangerously out as Derek's people gave chase. "Good, hit them hard from the rear," he muttered.

Tsauderei, like Derek, had no military experience, and so they were both stunned when the Norsundrians stopped at the top of the slope spilling out of the bottleneck. Then, in one of those timeless moments, as emotions spiral out end over end, Derek gazed up into the face of the commander, who stood a little apart from his forces, dressed unlike them entirely in black. Derek had expected some monster of a man, grizzled and scarred, but the slim fellow with the short, curly dark hair was his age.

And he knew that face.

His heart gave a sharp rap against his ribs, then thundered with horror. Kessler Sonscarna's face had featured in nightmares ever since Derek's escape from the assassin-training compound.

Kessler Sonscarna's hand went up, tightened into a fist.

His Norsundrians turned, and with withering effectiveness, demonstrated the first truth of mountain warfare, that he who has the higher ground has the advantage.

Tsauderei saw it before Derek did: Derek's people had chased the enemy straight uphill into a trap. It was going to be a slaughter. Sorrow and anger drummed his heart as he looked upward again, this time with intent.

Though light mages very seldom interfere with weather patterns, Tsauderei knew the mountains, the air currents, the patterns of rainfall. A late spring storm was already forming. He drew the currents together with such speed that the resulting thunderstorm shocked both sides below. In moments nobody on either side could see much beyond their own weapon, as hail pelted them, the rocks, and the tumbling stream with the merciless dispassion of nature.

"Retreat." Derek's numb lips could barely move, and as his captain stared uncomprehendingly into his face from two handsbreadths away, Derek made the motion for retreat.

There was no argument: the stonemason bent to pick up the lifeless body of his son, and leaned into the icy shower to stumble down the slope.

Chapter Six

At the same time
Sartor and Sarendan

"BUT I warded that damned wood," Dejain protested, as she and Siamis stared down a grassy slope bright with wildflowers toward the dark line of Shendoral Forest. "I traveled up here in winter. I would swear that no one saw me."

"Then you would be swearing to little purpose," Siamis said, and indicated the evidence of muddy footprints in the road below.

Dejain stared from those to the weathered sign that indicated travelers were about to enter Leath. Then she turned back to Siamis, whose light gaze had narrowed, reminding her unpleasantly of his far more dangerous uncle.

"Second question," Siamis said, evenly enough. "Where is Kessler Sonscarna? I cannot believe he was a part of this idiocy." A sharp lift of the hand, indicating all of Sartor, not just Bostian's invasion army now wandering around in the weird forest beyond.

"He is," Dejain said, with a spike of malicious pleasure. "He decided to take Sarendan."

"Yes." Siamis's gaze went distant. "He's holed up in a cave outwaiting a storm. Go fetch him." The gentle voice gentled further. "Now."

"When I do?" Her nevers chilled in spite of the mellow sun of early summer.

"Bring him to Eidervaen."

She vanished, and he signaled to the horsemen waiting at a prudent distance. When they drew near, he motioned for a horse, saying, "I will have to ride in there myself, it seems. Meet me in the city."

And he rode toward the forest alone.

Part of its strangeness was the suddenness of its border, as if an invisible ring had been laid down by some monumental hand. Most forests began with clumps of trees, or with shrubbery that thickens along the road until greenery surrounds the traveler. Sometimes there was a dramatic difference in vegetation between one slope and another, largely having to do with the angle of the sun as well as soil, but here, the road led into a sudden stand of trees that dimmed the light to greenish shadow, broken by slanting shafts of gold.

He entered Shendoral.

Late spring blossoms dotted the glades, a reassuringly normal sight. Siamis found it peculiar, how navigating here was not unlike navigation in Norsunder; it brought to mind the dire consequences of any kind of violence. Humans had not imposed this rule onto Shendoral. He did not know who had. Perhaps the indigenous species, who existed outside of time and space, as did Norsunder; only here, the animals as well as humans were forced to live in peace.

Did this cause surviving predator species to turn to nuts and fruit for sustenance, and had that spread outward, as had the dawnsingers' and morvende embargoes on killing any living creature for food?

He gave himself a moment to appreciate the long view that such changes required, and then it was time for business. He focused on Bostian, the brash young commander who was too eager to make a name for himself by conquering Sartor, and so had ridden past elementary illusions, straight into Shendoral forest and its formidable magic.

This humiliation was going to be salutary.

Siamis found him around the next bend, as he expected, though anywhere else they might have been as much as a week apart in distance. Bostian, a big, burly fellow a year or so older than Siamis, looked almost comically dismayed, a reaction that intensified after Siamis told him where he was, and how long it had been.

"But I've only been in here a day!" Bostian protested. "Look at our stores. We've camped once."

"Yet it has been eight weeks since you crossed the border," Siamis said, his sense of humor tickled at the sight of rows of tough warriors walking their horses, treading carefully lest they step on some small creature unawares, and fall down dead. Shendoral was exact: a life for a life. "We can continue this unedifying exchange outside the forest border, if you wish, lest another couple of months pass while you argue. You can follow me out."

Bostian's interest was entirely confined to the cut and the thrust. As Bostian and his company fell in behind, Siamis focused on the border of the forest—and there it was.

Once they were well away from Shendoral's imperceptible grip, Siamis said to Bostian, "I'm going ahead into Eidervaen, to see if I can rescue this fool escapade of yours from disaster before Detlev gets here."

He watched Bostian's rugged, tanned face blanch, then added, "When you arrive, you will become an occupation force. Everything will be peaceful and orderly as you take charge of the city."

Siamis did not need mind-touch to sense Bostian's anger, frustration, and above all disappointment. He laughed as he left them there, and left to conquer Eidervaen alone.

"They're out of Shendoral," the young Sartoran mage student reported, her eyes huge. "And Olvath, who was on watch duty at the forest road, says she's certain it was Siamis who brought them out." She looked around at Atan, Chief Veltos, and four of the high council.

"Siamis," Atan breathed. "Then he's here. In Sartor?"

Veltos whirled. "Call the high council to Star Chamber. Stay, the entire first circle—" She broke off, and made a profound bow to Atan.

It was sincere, but it was too late.

Everyone knew that only the monarch could summon the first circle of nobles. Atan forced her palms together, opening them outward in the gesture of royal order, an empty gesture as the order had already been given. By someone else. She watched them watch her confirm the order, confirming the fiction that she was the queen, then she said, "I will withdraw while they assemble."

Everyone bowed deeply, and Atan saw in those lowered heads the silent acknowledgement of who really ruled Sartor. It was not Atan.

She went straight to her private chamber, where she looked for her notecase to report the sighting. It was not in its place. She frowned, her hand reaching to summon the duty page, but she hesitated. The pages, the cleaning servants, even Gehlei would not touch it without leave.

Atan wandered about the room, looking from round tabletop to lyre-legged chair to window sill where lay two private histories written by ancestors when they were her age. She remembered laying the books down. She remembered laying her notecase in its place on the table.

Who could have taken it?

She shook her head. Siamis on the way . . . This was not the time to bother with inquiries about absent-minded servants. She should be warning people, like the rest of the alliance. Beginning with Sarendan over the mountains. Since Chief Veltos was summoning the council (Atan sustained a flash of anger, and then determinedly dismissed it), Atan had time. She had the will. And she had the means.

So she transferred to Miraleste in Sarendan. While she was standing on the Destination tiles, she remembered hearing the quick patter of feet down the hall outside her rooms. Julian? Would Julian have taken it? Impossible. Julian wouldn't touch anything that she thought connected in any way with lessons or princesses or queens. With responsibility, Tsauderei had said, when last they talked about her.

". . . there?"

Atan blinked, to discover herself peering into a pair of familiar tip-tilted eyes widened with anxiousness. "Lilah?"

Lilah cast a sigh of relief. "I thought you were Siamised!" Lilah exclaimed. "Did you know a bunch of eleven-ers attacked us?"

"Siamis himself," Atan said, "is in Sartor."

Lilah gasped, then took Atan's hand. "Come on."

They found Peitar in the residence wing, where Atan stopped short, blinking when she saw Peitar wielding a paintbrush, busy sloshing black paint over a plaster wall. In the ochre light of late afternoon, the streaks in the paint looked oily.

He turned around, and waved the brush in greeting. At the look on her face, he grinned, and Lilah said, "I've been bothering him to redo the throne room all in black marble. You know, veined with gold. It got kind of ruined in the revolution . . ."

"And I'm doing this to demonstrate what an entirely black room might look like," Peitar said.

Atan nodded, thinking that of course he wouldn't order servants to paint it, when he knew very well that it was going to have to be unpainted.

Almost as if he read her mind, he said in a lower voice, "I pick up the brush every time I need to keep myself busy—"

A bustle at the door interrupted him. Lilah flitted to peer out, then turned back, paling beneath her freckles. "Derek is back," she said.

Peitar flung the brush into the bucket, where it sent out a glurpy tide of black onto the floor unperceived. "Success? Success?" He could not bear to say the opposite.

The sharp stink of sweat nearly knocked Atan back, as a cluster of filthy, mud- and blood-splattered men entered Peitar's interview chamber, exhausted after their battle and a three-day headlong gallop.

They collapsed onto the satin-upholstered chairs unin-vited, unheeding; so dazed were they that Derek's gaze crossed Atan's and, other than the faintest check, passed on with no reaction.

Lilah gripped Derek's arm. "Atan says Siamis is in Sartor!"

"Peitar," Derek said. "Kessler Sonscarna is the one leading the invasion."

Lilah gazed from one to the other. "Kessler? He's scarier

than Siamis," she exclaimed with heartfelt horror. "He chased us in Sartor—" Lilah was about to remind them of those frightening days before Atan ended the enchantment over Sartor, but she saw that nobody was listening to her.

She sighed as Derek said hoarsely, "We would all have died. If it hadn't been for a fierce storm. We ran. We ran and left our dead there." Derek's face puckered. Tears dripped down his face. He thumbed them impatiently away, and his head dropped back tiredly. "I think half are gone. Maybe more. I must go back." His voice roughened. "And Disappear the dead. Do it right."

Peitar said, "The rangers in Diannah Wood will have done that by now, if Norsunder's warriors are no longer there."

"They have to be right behind us," Derek said. "At most a day away, if they were slowed up through the wood. We had our guides, who probably fouled the trails for them."

"Then we have at least one night to prepare," Peitar said. "Captain Leonos will raise the city guard, all watches. Including your defenders." His voice changed to concern. "Derek, you need to get some rest."

"I can't sleep," Derek returned flatly.

Peitar said, "At least eat, then. Mirah-Steward will have seen you enter, and unless I miss my guess, hot food will be along any moment. Surely you will not insult her by turning it down."

"I can't," Derek began—as the door opened, and an impressive row of servants entered, bearing silver trays that trailed enticing smells.

Peitar's gaze shifted as if he sought answers to unspoken questions, then his expression warmed briefly when he caught sight of Atan. "I beg your pardon. What news did you bring?"

Atan told him in a few short words as servants passed round plates, utensils, and food. Atan refused a plate. "I have to get back," she said. "Can you report for me to the rest of the alliance? And don't forget . . ."

"I know. If I lose the kingdom, I retreat to Delfina Valley," Peitar said with a crooked smile. "So I don't lose myself, and the kingdom with it, to Siamis's spell."

Atan walked to the door, then cast a thoughtful look

back. Derek yawned between bites, his red-rimmed eyes marked with exhaustion. He seemed too tired to pursue his grudge, which made her own resentment dissolve. They were just two more weary humans, dealing with a new crisis. Why did it have to take a war to get them there?

She slipped into the hall and transferred home, where she plumped down at her desk until the swirl of tiny dots evaporated from her vision. She counted the pangs in her head until they were faint, then stirred her limbs. A last throb, and she could move.

She opened her door. Where was the duty page? A few steps, and she knew by some subtle sense that something was not right. Yet there was no noise, no clamor, no smell of fire. Through the open windows drifted birdsong.

It was the quiet, the empty hall. Halls were never empty. The duty page was missing. No one was in sight.

The back of Atan's neck gripped. She whirled around and ran back to her room, then opened the old servants' door, which led to a narrow stairway, the glowglobes dim. She picked up her skirts and skimmed down the stairs to the stewards' quarters.

Then she froze in the doorway when she saw Gehlei pass through in the direction of the kitchen without looking right or left. Atan took a few steps in her wake, and glimpsed the senior staff moving about, no one speaking. As if asleep.

As if enchanted.

Horror wrung through her. What now? "The council," she whispered. Back she ran, using servants' byways to get to the Star Chamber. She paused outside the door to listen, and heard an unfamiliar man's voice. A tenor voice, like a singer's, pleasantly rising and falling—

A hard tug on her skirt jolted her. She looked down into Julian's face. "Go away," Julian said, clutching her dirty robe to her. "We don't want you."

"We?" Atan repeated, struck in the heart.

"My friends," Julian said, as her quick fingers lifted the latch to the great door and she darted inside.

Atan heard the laughing male voice say, "Ah, here is our little friend back again."

She knew who had to be in there, and the fact that no one reacted, no one even responded, meant she was too late. They were enchanted, and because everyone who really ruled the kingdom was inside that room, it meant that everyone in Sartor had fallen under the soft, dream-like spell along with the council.

Siamis had enchanted Sartor once again.

Atan choked back a sob and mumbled the transfer spell. When the black dots—bigger this time—faded away, she remembered Julian's angry voice, the push of her little hands. The sickening realization that Julian had not fallen under the spell because she had no loyalty whatsoever to anyone.

Atan covered her face with her hands as sobs wracked her.

"Go ahead. Cry it out." Tsauderei patted his guest chair invitingly. "Then tell me what happened."

Dejain had had magical access to Kessler, back in the days when she was working with him on his mad plot to eradicate bad kings from the world. Since then, she had been very careful not to remind him that she had this access, particularly since she'd found evidence that he was studying magic. Somehow. Without anyone else catching him at it, much less teaching him.

But now there was this direct order from Siamis, who was far too dangerous to cross. She saw no way around transferring directly to Kessler—with a fifty-step margin of safety—if she was to stay out of whatever trouble was brewing, and pretend to be an obedient minion, until she found someone strong enough to take Siamis down.

She transferred. It wasn't a long distance, but the pain was sharp enough. She found herself in a cave behind a waterfall. When she could trust her body to move, she stepped cautiously into the gloom, toward voices. Kessler's face, lit by the ruddy leap of a fire, tightened to anger when he saw her. She held her breath, ready to transfer out if he made a move toward his weapons.

But he jerked his chin in dismissal. His captains withdrew, weapons clanking and boots squelching, into what appeared to be a honeycomb of caves.

She did not make the mistake of assuming she was safe. But she pretended she was, as she looked around and tasted the air, registering the loud roar as a violent rainfall. Then made a discovery. She said to Kessler, "It's not a waterfall, it's a storm. It has magic in it."

"I thought lighters did not do that to weather."

"Someone did." She took a step toward the fire, hating the chill air. "Siamis has summoned you."

"Where?"

"Eidervaen. He should have it pacified by now." She added acidly, "Or so he appeared to think would be the case." And when he made no move, she said, "The palace in Eidervaen."

He said, "Do you know the Destination pattern?"

"Yes." So he was going to cooperate.

"Take me there."

This was going to hurt more. But she could not show weakness.

They transferred, both appearing in the cool blue and white vaulting of Sartor's Destination chamber. The clawing nausea of a double transfer faded enough that she could stalk on watery legs around a corner, then sink against a wall, shivering and shaking. As soon as she could bear it, she used the transfer token in her pocket and returned to Norsunder Base, to recover in peace.

Kessler had already forgotten her. He glanced bemusedly up at the golden sun above the middle panel, the dragons rising on the attack, and a derisive smile twisted his lips. Would they ever want to actually see any of those things? He didn't think so.

He left and began to search for Siamis. People moved sedately, paying him no heed. So the enchantment had happened again. He turned a corner, figuring he'd look for the most important rooms, but when he reached a marble-banistered stair, he was almost knocked over by a small figure hurtling down.

He backed up a step, a hand half raised, then lowered it when he gazed down into a vaguely familiar small face.

"I know you," the child said. She barely came up to his middle. Her brown hair was tangled, full of leaves. She clutched some kind of grimy garment to her, looped and wound around her and dragging behind in a filthy train. "I do! You're the one who almost broke my fingers."

Kessler laughed. "But I didn't." Now he remembered: when he and Dejain were tasked to halt that Landis girl from breaking Sartor's century-long enchantment that was, apparently, already weakening. No doubt the lighters had made a hero of her anyway.

The child went on. "They were talking about you. They thought I didn't listen, but I did, when I was riding on your horse."

Kessler was going to move away, but the girl darted in front of him, her round, droopy eyes intent. "I'm Julian. They want to make me one of Them, and then I'll be dead. You're the prince who ran away so you wouldn't have to be a prince."

He laughed again. "So I am."

"You can do anything you want," she accused.

"I will be able to, soon," he said, entertained enough to lean his wrist on the bannister's marble-carved acanthus leaves, smoothed by generations of touch.

"Can I go with you? Show me how to get what I want. All They do is try to make me do what They want. I hate that. I don't want to be Them. I don't want to be dead," she said, a memory flash of her mother's slapping hands, her low voice when she pinched Julian, whispering in her ear, always that phrase, *You would like to be a princess, wouldn't you?*

Kessler stared down at the child whose eyes were shaped like his own, one of those random features that appeared from time to time in descendants of the Landis family. He liked teaching. He'd always wanted to find young people similar to himself after he'd escaped Wan-Edhe, ambitious.

But there were standards. He said, "You don't even have the self-discipline to clean yourself up. Why should I teach you anything?"

Julian opened her mouth to yell, but he turned away, his indifference plain. So she said speculatively, "If I do that? Will you?"

"Maybe," he said. "But you'd better be fast. I'll be out of here soon. If you're not here waiting before I leave, then you'll have to find your way same as I did."

He walked off, forgetting Julian within a few steps. His search was systematic; he was beginning the second floor when he spotted Siamis exiting a room in the midst of a lot of sleepwalkers. Hatred spiked for Detlev's strutting pet.

Kessler paused to enjoy the spike, to speculate on the success of an attack right now. But Siamis was carrying that sword of his, and a marble hallway was a stupid place for swordplay. Kessler would wait until he found the right ground. "How long before that brat with the dyr thing shows up to blast this spell of yours?"

"Soon, I hope." Siamis smiled. "This spell of mine is only meant to hold them until Detlev finds what he's looking for on Geth."

"Which is?" Kessler asked.

"Rifts," Siamis said equably enough. "They transfer in tunnels, which apparently can be broadened to rifts. As yet I don't know the details. I was kept elsewhere for an appreciable time." He made a large gesture, and then added, "Some don't appear to understand the difference between enterprise and stupidity. I'm surprised to discover you among their number."

Kessler shrugged. "Why not? If nothing else, mounting an invasion gives us seasoning."

"Leave the seasoning to me. As for the idiot who started this stampede. Henerek, as you probably are aware, decided to smite his childhood rivals, and is in Everon botching the job. Detlev wants you to go clean that up."

He walked past, leaving Kessler standing there.

So Kessler transferred back to his cave, where he summoned his captains. "We're done here." Before they could express their disappointment, in which he had no interest, he said, "Though I think, since we're going in that direction anyway, we'll stop in Miraleste first. Resupply. Then we're going to double it across Sarendan, and take ship at the nearest port."

"What's the target?"

"Everon," Kessler said, and smiled.

Julian ran upstairs as fast as she could, giggling with triumph and anticipation. So there! She should have thrown that notecase thing of Atan's down a well long ago. Now everything was going to be fun, if that runaway prince could really teach a person to get everything she wanted.

Julian burst into her bedchamber and looked at the trunk full of clothes that she had refused to touch. She flung her wrap on the floor and took out the first thing on top. It was riding clothes, a top and trousers, not a horrible princess outfit.

Only how were you supposed to pull it on, from the bottom or the top? In the forest, before anyone talked about princesses, all she had was somebody's robe. That had been so easy!

She tried to stick her feet through the top, but the head part wouldn't go past her upper legs. So she kicked it off, laid it on the floor, opened the hem, and crawled into it, feeling the way into the arm holes and head hole. When that was on, she jammed her feet into the trousers and yanked them up. She was about to run through the door, but caught sight of her hair in the mirror, and grimaced. A hairbrush lay on the table below the mirror, never before used.

She had seen people brush their hair. She tried the brush, but it stuck right away, and stung her scalp. Gritting her teeth, she dragged the brush through as much of her hair as she could reach, at least in front. It still looked horrible. So she dug through the drawers in the table until she found winter things—gloves and caps. She shoved all her hair up into a cap, and flung the hairbrush at the mirror as hard as she could. She smiled when the glass cracked like a big spider web.

Then she ran downstairs, where she found the tall friendly one with the sword talking to two more of the ones in uniforms. But the runaway prince with the black curly hair wasn't in sight. "Where is he? He said he'd wait. I went as fast as I could! But he's gone."

The friendly one said, "I fear we all get less attention than we feel we deserve. Except when we don't want it."

Julian ignored his smile. "He didn't wait!" she yelled.

"Who didn't wait?"

"That man. The one who ran away from being a prince. Who can do anything he wants."

"He's gone, I'm afraid. On my orders."

"So he doesn't do what he wants?"

"He would like to. But he must do what I tell him."

"Why?"

"Come along, and we'll talk about it," said the yellow-haired man.

"You won't try to make me a princess?" Julian said suspiciously.

The man sat down on the broad marble steps. "Why wouldn't you want to be a princess?"

"I hate it," Julian said. In memory, there was her mother, with her jewels, and her mad face, pinching Julian hard and hissing, *Don't you want to be a princess?* before telling her to smile at the baby princess, take a flower to the queen, be the first to say this thing, or that thing, to be pretty—*pinch*—smile—*pinch*—be pretty and smile—*tweak*—wear her pretty clothes and smile. "I *hate* it," Julian burst out again.

"Well, then, let's see if we can find a use for you," the man said. "Where nobody will expect you to be a princess."

"Promise?" Julian demanded.

"I promise," he said, laughing. When he got up and walked away, she followed along behind.

Chapter Seven

Chwahirsland

THE alliance began to gather at last.

In Chwahirsland, without any idea of what was going on beyond its borders, Jilo turned a cup around in his hand, then finally said, "What's a neckin?"

Granduncle Shiam glanced up in mild surprise.

Jilo twisted uneasily in his chair, distracted by the patiently painted dots indicating patterns of raspberry clusters alternated with grape around the rim of his cup. "I know it's old army slang for 'a lot,' but why wouldn't someone just say 'a lot,' in talking about a wager? Don't they usually mention an amount for the stake?"

"Because they were really wagering a trip to the wall," the commander said.

"I heard that before." Jilo looked puzzled. "'A trip to the wall' usually meant an execution. They were wagering on deaths?"

"No. Sex." Shiam remembered that Jilo had no close family to explain sex, and of course he hadn't had a twi to exchange information with, much less indulge with in practice sex play. If he was even of age enough for that.

But Jilo had been running around a garrison all his life. "It's sex? Against a wall?"

"Sex in the army was forbidden. 'Neckin' was originally slang for the number of floggings you would get for capital crimes, such as having relationships. The Hate wanted all loyalty strictly to on him. But people, being people..." The commander waited for Jilo to ask the questions that would indicate he was ready for the answers. "There was a certain amount of humor in choosing slang for a long punishment resulting from a brief act," he finally said.

Jilo shrugged off the unpleasant subject. Sex as mechanics was familiar. You didn't do stable duty without knowing the rudiments, and the language of it was everyday around rec time back in the Shadowland. The feelings that led to it? Those were as distant as the winter stars.

So he lifted the cup to study the painting around his rim. He wondered if the cup was old, from before the edict against painting things had been issued. Yet another forbidden thing that made life better, if you chose to have it.

Jilo looked up at his granduncle. This was his third visit to his relatives since winter. After lifting the killing wards around the castle Destination, he'd placed tracers on it so if anyone arrived he would know.

His granduncle noticed his interest. "Grandfather Nissler made those cups. He was a potter, before the edicts." Uncle Shiam furrowed his brow.

"Maybe that ought to go on our list? Releasing the edicts binding the potters to the army for ten years."

Jilo had agreed that they ought to release Wan-Edhe's terrible edicts a bit at a time. Food first: this spring, the secondary army fields had been opened under the strict control of local commanders, who measured off spaces for each village and town, a certain amount of ground per household. There had been no riots, though trouble had been threatened over hoarded seed, until Jilo let it be known that seed was coming from overseas. He did not say that he'd used some of Wan-Edhe's terrifyingly immense hoard of gold to buy it—Senrid had set it up through the king of Erdrael Danara, who turned out to be a friend of his.

"Slow," Uncle Shiam said. "Very slow. If people are busy, they will not revolt. If you give them too many choices after no choice at all . . ." He shook his head. "We do not know how to negotiate choices anymore. I've seen death struggles over the possession of extra boot ties, and that in an army where any action whatsoever outside of orders gets you a bloody back."

Jilo swallowed. "Maybe over winter, then—"

His cousin came in carrying a tray of corn cakes, but just as Jilo reached for one, a tracer warning poked him inside his head.

Someone had actually used the Destination he had so carefully de-trapped?

Unless it was . . . "I have to go," he said.

His family reflected surprise, but no one asked. And he wasn't sure what to say. If there were normal patterns of conversation for such moments, he had yet to learn them, a thought that made him feel sorrowful.

"Take a corn cake with you, Cousin Jilo," Aran said practically.

Jilo thanked her, and did. The cake was still hot when the transfer magic left him standing in the castle, making him reflect on how heat transferred as well as bones and skin and clothes.

It had cooled by the time he recovered from the transfer; it had also left a pink spot on his hand, which throbbed faintly. He didn't mind that. It was somewhat better than the way he used to feel when he returned to this castle. There were actual air currents along the lower floors now, and sometimes he heard voices. The time binding was still there, but it had begun to lessen the farther you got from the third floor, and people were showing tiny signs of possible recovery, in very small ways. Like, someone had dared to ask him a question, "Would you like a meal?"

He walked through the Destination chamber door, which he had removed half the wards from. He stopped short when he recognized Senrid of the Marlovens.

Senrid had been looking around the library, but turned at his step. "Haven't you been keeping up with that book of yours?" he asked without preamble.

"It's locked up. While I go places," Jilo said. Then he caught up mentally. "Something happened?"

"Detlev and Siamis are back. Siamis, I heard about. I know Detlev's back. Saw him myself, three days ago."

"At the head of an army?" Jilo braced for worse news.

"No. But he destroyed all my border wards. Everything. Then smoked." Senrid swiped his hand through the air, as if pushing something away. His lip curled. "If he does come back, he's going to have to look hard to find our army." His smile vanished. "Hibern says that Norsunder did launch armies against Sarendan, Sartor, and Everon. And I'd love to know where Detlev smoked to. Can we look in that book?"

Jilo was already moving into the next room. "Wan-Edhe will be back," Jilo said in a weird, flat voice.

The way he said it made Senrid's nerves jump. He knew why. Substitute 'My uncle will be back,' and there was Senrid's own fear. That was the real horror of Norsunder. Well, one of them. People you saw dragged off, who should be dead and gone, weren't.

"Then you make sure your army isn't there for him to command, at least, as much as you can. But Jilo," Senrid said sharply, and the other boy turned his way, the glassy expression in his eyes turning to worry. At least he was listening. "Siamis doesn't seem to bother with armies. According to Hibern, who got it from Tsauderei, he entered Eidervaen's royal palace, and exited half a glass after, leaving the entire kingdom sleepwalking. It's just like before."

"What do we do?"

"My suggestion is, get yourself out of reach of Siamis, or whoever they might send here, and join us in our alliance fallback." Senrid described the Delfina Valley Destination.

"Me?" was all Jilo could think to say, then reddened at what he knew sounded like witlessness.

"You. Or, better, take this transfer token." Senrid dropped a cheap brass ring of the sort found at festivals onto Jilo's palm. Jilo could feel the tingle of magic on it. "Get yourself to Delfina Valley, where Tsauderei is hiding out. Used to be some kind of lighter mage hideout. Norsunder can't get past the protective wards."

"Are the Mearsieans going to be there? You know they won't want me in their alliance."

"Mearsieans?" Senrid exclaimed, in disbelief. "You mean Clair and the rest of those girls?"

Jilo ducked his head in a nod.

Senrid stared at the kid who had taken over a vast kingdom with a formidable reputation, who had been wrestling single-handed with magic far beyond Senrid's skills. Was Jilo really worried about some bratty girls who couldn't manage a sword between them? "If they don't, then they are an almighty pack of lighter hypocrites. But Clair was the one who brought you to me for help." Or had she thought Senrid would have Jilo put up against a wall? His gut curled at the bitter thought.

"It's not Clair I'm thinking about."

Senrid laughed. "CJ, then? She was the one who said we should recruit. I'm recruiting you. She can like it or shut up."

Senrid flicked the subject of CJ aside impatiently. He wanted, needed, to see that book. "Jilo, listen. If Siamis gets you, then that means he's got your entire kingdom. Whatever you've set up to get around Wan-Edhe, Siamis can make you put it all back again. He can make you do anything, and you'll do it." Senrid's features lengthened with horror. "Nobody can tell me if you feel yourself doing what he wants, or if your mind just goes somewhere else. Either way . . ." He snapped his fingers. "So much for all your plans."

Jilo blinked. "Yes. Right. My Uncle Shiam and I . . . there's an order I can give. It will go through all the captains. The army will go into the fields, because it's our first year of allowing general planting—"

Jilo abruptly stopped babbling, and muttered spells. His 'locked up,' Senrid saw, was in the magical sense. The book appeared in a tiny flash of light and puff of air that smelled of singed paper.

Jilo flipped it open, and stared.

"What does it say?" Senrid demanded impatiently.

"There is nothing for Wan-Edhe," Jilo muttered. "He must still be in Norsunder-Beyond."

"What about the head snakes?" Senrid rapped his knuckles lightly on the table as he fought the nearly overmastering desire to grab the book and transfer out.

"Detlev's last mention was Norsunder Base. That was right after Marloven Hess, three days ago." Jilo glanced up briefly. "Siamis has been moving around a lot. A *lot*. Sartor, Imar, a bunch of places I've never heard of—"

"Like?"

Jilo rattled off names, during which Senrid said, "Got to be a scouting run," but then a pattern emerged, just as Jilo said, "Mearsies Heili?" He looked up in surprise. "Why would he go there?"

"Bereth Ferian, Roth Drael, Mearsies Heili."

"All in the same day?"

"Yes." Jilo glanced up in question. "He must have the world's worst headache."

"He's hunting Liere," Senrid whispered, raised his hands, and vanished.

Jilo started. Senrid's abrupt disappearance was somehow more unsettling than his news, which Jilo had been dreading since the day he'd first walked into this castle and made his first spell.

He scrabbled among the papers for a pen, dipped it, scrawled the pre-arranged message to Uncle Shiam, then whispered a transfer spell over it. The paper vanished in a tiny puff of air.

He was about to send the book back to its hiding place, but Senrid's words caused him to hesitate. He wasn't used to using it to track other people's enemies, none of whom had shown any interest in Chwahirsland. However, what if someone else tried to take it?

If he hid it . . .

He placed the book between the two light magic guides given him by Mondros, closed them into a travel bag, and looked around. Enemies—Wan-Edhe—might come. He could do nothing beyond the wards he'd already laid to trap him. Anywhere Jilo went beyond his border seemed to be among enemies. But he had learned there were degrees of enmity.

And maybe things could change.

Like this alliance?

He looked down at the transfer token Senrid had given him. He had to find out.

Sarendan

Derek Diamagan had taken the poorest house on the east side of Miraleste as a sort of temporary home. He traveled too much for the idea of 'home' to be much more than a place to store the things he didn't want to take on the road. He'd chosen that sorry little house to demonstrate his contempt for the perquisites of being friends with royalty.

He sometimes bunked at the city guard barracks because it was convenient, but Lilah and Peitar could never get him to stay in the palace except during the worst of winter weather, and then he always stayed with the servants.

Derek's house was meant to be ordinary, but people had gradually, always while he was away, taken to improving it for him. As gifts. So each trip he'd returned to find new articles of furniture, each plain but well-made. Dishes. Curtains. Upholstery on the chairs, then embroidery on the upholstery. Good traveling boots, sized to his footprint in the mud when he left. Then he returned to a lack of mud, the street having been paved with good stone.

Once the house was painted inside and out, and re-roofed, the adjoining houses were cleared out and the former owners resettled in good locations. He had to admit it was convenient, because he always had people waiting to talk to him, and they could wait in those houses. He could feed and house the more skittish orphans because he had a fully equipped kitchen and willing hands and donated food as well as those extra rooms.

He protested that it was too grand, but his protests were mild because he could see the pride in the artisans' faces.

Guilt underlay the fury that oppressed him as he walked down the hill away from the palace in the streaming rain, though every bone and muscle in his body ached, and the little casket in his hand weighed as heavily as the guilt and grief, fury and remorse. He longed to shout, "Nobody told me!"

There had been no lessons on fighting in mountains. But the knowledge hadn't been kept from him, because no one in his army had experienced anything like that Norsundrian attack, and as for mountains, they had always been regarded as the kingdom's protection. Battles happened on flat fields, or alongside rivers, or along streets.

He walked faster, thinking furiously. Kessler Sonscarna and his Norsunder force were coming. Maybe not that night. The weather was too bad for that: horses would mire on the road, and he'd already sent people to hack the bridges apart, once the support magic was broken. The Norsundrians would have to ford the high waters, and get shot at from the banks.

But they'd still come. There was little that could divert Kessler, Derek had learned once, a lesson that had nearly cost his and his brother's lives. But he'd learned this much, so he could learn more. If a runaway prince could learn to command like that, Derek could learn faster. And better. Commoners had self-discipline that no noble ever had.

Next time it would be Derek winning.

Anticipation brought him smiling grimly to his street, where he found the rain-washed square full of people waiting. At the front stood familiar faces, clearly hoping for word of their loved ones. Or for personal condolences, for those whose bad news had run ahead.

All right. This was his duty as a commander.

He set the casket on his desk and turned to the first anxiously waiting face, laboring to find words that would hurt less.

There were none.

The man looked into his face, then backed up a step, saying, "No! No! He's just seventeen—"

It was near morning when the last of them departed. Stupid with exhaustion, Derek forced himself into his bedroom, where he discovered a new rug, woven in bright colors. He shut his eyes, which brought the dizziness, and he swayed, then jerked upright.

He would not look at that waiting bed. He picked up the casket again. Inside rattled the coins that had been turned into transfer tokens. Tsauderei had begun making them directly after that battle. Before Derek left the palace,

Peitar had made him promise that all the brigade children under thirteen were to be transferred to the Valley.

This promise made sense in all directions. Those loyal children were Derek's future officers. When they all got training along with their strength, it would be them winning against the likes of Prince Kessler Sonscarna.

But that was for the future. He had to deal with them right now. Once Derek got the children to the Valley, Tsauderei would be able to keep them locked down.

A muffled laugh, and the sound of a rock skipping over the stones, brought him to his window. The orphans were already gathering, in spite of the rain that was now tapering off. They were going to be angry with him; they would probably consider it a broken promise when he took them out of harm's way, because he'd so easily promised them all an important role in defending the country.

He knew that no one could reason with youngsters who thought danger would be like the hero songs and tales, or the plays on stage, in which there might be an exciting fight, but only the villain would fall to the boards, and there would be no blood.

Until a week ago, Derek had led them in believing it.

To get away from that thought, he marched outside, oblivious to the rain. Ruddy whistled, and the orphans scrambled into their rows. Derek counted, then counted again. Not including Lilah and her three friends (one of whom was outside the country altogether), ten were missing.

"I have special orders for you," he said. "We have to be fast, which means travel by magic."

The questions burst out. He gave evasive answers as he passed along the rows, handing each kid the thin copper coin called a flim, which had been bespelled into a magic transfer token for one journey. Peitar had reasoned that the flims could then be tendered to pay for room and board.

"Now here's what you do," Derek began, and told them the sign and word that would carry them all directly to the Valley, then he made them count between transfers, giving them a graphic description of what could happen if they all tried to transfer to the same Destination at the same time, even in the Valley. Though Peitar had told him that a mass transfer using light magic wouldn't work, Derek didn't trust magic any more than he trusted kings.

He waited until they had all popped out of existence, one by one in orderly fashion, then followed last.

He found what he expected, a milling group of youths all yelling over one another to be heard. Faen and another boy were already shoving at one another.

"Quiet!" he shouted.

They subsided, and cast quick looks around. They found themselves on a broad cliff, with a cottage built in the middle, surrounded by grass. Tsauderei opened the door and shuffled out, old-fashioned robes swaying in the pearly morning light. There was no storm here.

"What's our special orders?" a girl shouted, her expression a mix of hope and, for the first time, wariness. Derek hated seeing that wariness. He hesitated, too tired to think of special orders that would satisfy his followers.

"Would you like to fly while you wait?" Tsauderei asked.

The children whirled around.

"Fly?" half a dozen voices responded in disbelief.

"I am a mage. I made a spell the lets you fly all over this valley, and the mountains nearby." Tsauderei let that sink in, then said, "Here are the rules. You can fly anywhere you want, but don't disturb the villagers on the lower ledge that way." He pointed down at the circle of houses on the westward slope of the mountain. "Or any other houses. You also stay away from the flowers on the other side of the lake, unless you want to sleep forever."

"Listen to what he says," Derek ordered, but he hadn't needed to.

The orphans were too intimidated to argue. A mage! He could turn them into toadstools, and looked like he might if they sneezed wrong.

The old mage taught them the spell, and as kids launched into the air like so many ungainly birds, Derek looked around for somewhere to sit until Tsauderei could send him back to Miraleste.

"Come along. I've some extra Sartoran steep already made," Tsauderei said, and Derek started. He'd nearly fallen asleep on his feet.

He was going to argue, but couldn't find the words.

It was easier to walk those few steps inside, where vague curiosity flared briefly. He'd never seen the inside of the mage's cottage. It was as plain as any laborer's hut, a single room, with a sleeping loft above the fireplace. Only the books on all the walls but the front, which was all window, differentiated it from a commoner's house. Derek looked around with reluctant approval. He'd assumed mages would whistle up palaces for themselves, and invisible servants to provide for every need.

At a gesture from the mage, Derek sank into an upholstered chair. Tsauderei pressed a cup into his hands. Derek drank deeply, leaning his head back on the chair to appreciate the warmth going down. Maybe now he could think again. Special orders . . . something that would keep that loyalty, so very important . . . loyalty . . . He closed his eyes . . .

And fell asleep. Tsauderei glanced at him askance, then sighed, shaking his head. He didn't particularly want Derek Diamagan in his cottage, and was overdue somewhere else, but from the looks of the boy, he wasn't going to waken any time soon.

He finished his own steep, set down his cup, cast a quilt over Derek, then braced for the long shift north.

Mearsies Heili and Vasande Leror

Senrid stepped off the Destination on the terrace before the white palace in Mearsies Heili's tiny capital. He gazed up at the spires of the palace, which owed nothing to symmetry, yet did not look like a random collection of towers. What kind of design was that? It would be impossible to defend in a war. You'd think. Yet it was still standing after unknown centuries.

Not ten steps into the nacreous light of the hall, he shut his eyes hard. Something was trying to make him dizzy. He listened on the mental plane, then recoiled, slamming his mind-shield tight against a subtle shimmer of dark magic, a thin sheen like oil spilled upon a lake.

Siamis has been here. Senrid controlled the urge to flee, and ventured farther, keeping his footfalls quiet. All senses alert, he crossed the broad, empty hall to the open doors of the throne room. He'd never seen anyone in that room until now.

Surprised, he gazed at Clair, a small white-haired figure sitting on the carved throne. He had never seen her in her throne room in all his visits.

Did he look as ridiculous perched on his own throne? Probably worse.

He approached. She could have been a square-faced kid statue, her waving white hair falling in ordered locks down to her lap where her hands rested loose, palms upturned. It was so uncharacteristic that his skin crawled: it was too easy to imagine her body hollowed out, brains, wit, and heart removed, leaving this empty shell.

But her color was a normal, healthy light brown with rose beneath, and her rumpled blue tunic stirred slightly with her breathing.

He remembered encountering people under the grip of the Siamis enchantment. They could answer specific questions. But then they would report the conversation, as ordered.

So he wasn't going to mention Liere directly. "Where are the girls?"

"I don't know," Clair stated.

Senrid looked around, and wondered if they'd escaped the spell. Otherwise, wouldn't they be sitting here with Clair, like a row of live dolls? 'Did you send them somewhere?' No, that question might put Siamis on their trail—if he hadn't already asked it. He eyed Clair, then bent closer, perceiving the glint of metal above the first button of her tunic, nestled below her collarbones.

He reached, then pulled his hands back. Those medallions were loaded with magic, and if someone tried to take them from the girls, they'd get a spark of fire on their fingers.

"Will you give me your medallion?" he asked. "I want to look at it."

Clair sat still for a breath or two, as if her thoughts came from very far away, then her hands moved to her throat, and she lifted the chain over her head and dropped the thing onto Senrid's palm with a soft *ching*.

"Thank you. I'll be right back," he said.

He walked out of the throne room to the hall, where he fingered the medallion, then shrugged. Why not try? He whispered the transport spell, picturing the girls' underground hideout, and moments later staggered a few steps forward on the brightly colored wool rug in the main chamber. The stuffy air smelled stale, laden with traces of a long-ago meal.

"Anyone here?" he called.

The quick patter of bare feet on the smooth dirt tunnel heralded one of Clair's friends. Her brows lifted, then snapped together. "What are you doing here?"

"Looking for Liere, so I can get her to safety before Siamis nabs her," Senrid said, and remembered that this particular girl, though she looked ordinary enough—thin, with short hair a soft tint midway between brown and blond, and a light scattering of freckles across her high-bridged nose— was not actually human. He remembered her name then: Dhana.

"Not here," Dhana said with an air of triumph. "None of 'em are."

"They escaped Siamis's spell, then?"

Dhana's changeable expression hardened. "Clair made them promise. If Siamis showed up, and he did. Walked right into the interview room. She couldn't get away. Me and Ben are watching over things. Ben stays in animal shape, and Siamis's magic can't do anything to me," Dhana said. She grinned. "So I got to see Andrea chase the eleveners out of the forest."

"Who?"

"Andrea. The forest ghost," Dhana stated.

Senrid couldn't help the derisive expression the word 'ghost' sparked, but Dhana just laughed. "Go ahead. Call me a liar. I was just talking to her this morning."

"Talking. To a ghost," Senrid said.

Dhana shrugged. "She usually only talks to Seshe. When she appears, which isn't often. Maybe they get foggier over the centuries."

Senrid was thinking that it couldn't be a ghost. Magical anomaly, maybe. But he wasn't going to argue.

Dhana had been eyeing him, trying to figure out what Clair would want. Well, she knew what Clair would want. She knew as soon as Senrid appeared. The problem was, in this instance, what Clair would want might not be what CJ wanted.

But she decided to do it anyway. "They're at Kitty and Leander's. Something about the spell Hibern was going to teach Leander, to break Siamis's enchantment."

Senrid stared, astounded, forced himself not to blurt questions, and said, "Thanks. Here's Clair's medallion." He dropped the thing onto her palm and braced himself for another transfer, to a long-familiar Destination.

When he came out of it, he found himself sitting on the gravel outside a familiar small, square castle, the size of an outpost.

This was the royal castle of Vasande Leror, an inkblot of land adjacent to the northeast corner of Marloven Hess, above the Nelkereth plains. Vasande Leror had once belonged to Marloven Hess. Its king, Leander Tlennen-Hess, was even related to Senrid way, way back in their family trees. And they both had endured similar problems in coming to their crowns.

Senrid got to his feet, shrugging away the ache in his joints from so much magic transfer. It would be harder to shake away the reaction of irritation he'd felt at Dhana's news.

It was strong enough to make him angry, so he took the time to sort it out.

One. There was no reason Hibern ought to have come to Senrid first, if there really was an antidote to Siamis's enchantment. He could easily imagine her saying, "Yes, I could give it to you, and what would you do with it? You'll sit around and watch your academy play games, whereas Leander will go out and use it."

Two. Leander was really good at magic and history, which was why Senrid had made sure that he was invited into the alliance. But Senrid hadn't invited him himself because—

Three. Leander's stepsister, Kyale. She'd once helped Senrid, grudgingly, when he finally defeated his uncle. But she was the most self-involved, annoying person Senrid had ever met.

No help for it. He brushed off the last of the dust, noting that if Leander still had guards, they weren't very competent, and walked in through the barren stone entrance, then turned in the direction of the kitchens, where most often Leander was to be found if he wasn't in his study.

And there was Kyale's high voice echoing down the hall. Considered as a voice, it could have been pleasant, but her constant, simmering anger (akin to his own, he was very well aware) made it shrill. At least he didn't sound self-righteous.

He hoped.

"Leander, really, a king ought to at least receive royalty in a drawing room. Let's get them to move upstairs. It's such a pretty room, and it's silly, sitting there with nobody in it, and here we all are, crammed into that smelly old kitchen."

"The Mearsieans like to gather in their own kitchen, Kitty," Leander said patiently. "And CJ never acts like a princess."

"Well, maybe she should."

"I don't see the purpose in getting the kitchen help to haul all that food and those dishes upstairs, and then haul it all back again, when they've got things to do to get ready for the festival."

"There isn't going to be any festival if Siamis comes!"

This was obviously a private conversation, but Senrid decided it was time to interrupt. "Are the Mearsieans here?" he asked, rounding the corner.

The two turned, Leander as tall as Puddlenose, dark-haired, with bright green eyes that he'd inherited from the ancestor he and Senrid shared. He dressed like a forest ranger, in a rough old long tunic over loose trousers. Kyale was tiny, with silvery hair and light gray eyes, wearing a gown of lace and fragile tissue over satin, festooned with ribbons and bows.

Leander smiled with genuine welcome, and Kyale scowled. "Yes, they are," Leander said. "In the kitchen."

There was no irony in his voice, sparking amazement and admiration in Senrid. Though Leander regarded himself as Kyale's brother, he wasn't. The only relation between them was the disastrous marriage Kyale's mother had tricked Leander's aged father into making before she arranged his murder so she could reign as queen.

But none of that was Kyale's fault. In fact, Senrid's private suspicion was that Kyale might even have been stolen from somewhere else, a conveniently acquired daughter for the ambitious queen.

He showed no sign of these reflections as he followed the two into the servants' mess area beyond the kitchen, Kyale sighing dramatically.

Leander held open the door, whispering, "Maybe you can convince them to get themselves to the Delfina Valley." He sent a glance at the Mearsiean girls, who had crowded around the plain table that Leander and his servants customarily sat at.

Seven faces turned his way. Senrid searched among them, his disappointment so sharp he couldn't keep it from his voice as he said to Leander, "Liere isn't here? Is she safe, at least?"

CJ hopped up, a short figure in her habitual white shirt, long black vest, and green skirt, bare feet planted wide. "Who cares about Sartora?" she demanded, the black line of her brow furrowed over angry blue eyes. "I mean, I care!" She exclaimed, hands going out. "I do! We all do! But she can take care of herself, can't she, with all those mind powers?" CJ's fingers whirled little circles on either side of her head. "Clair got Siamised, because of her. And I want to go back to make sure she's safe." She shifted her glare to Leander. "And to unspell her, if it really works."

"You can't," Senrid said. "Unless you want to walk right into whatever trap Siamis laid. In which case, you'll deserve what you get for willful stupidity."

CJ kicked an imaginary object, then said in a less belligerent tone, "We have to do *something*. We can't just leave her there."

"That's why we have to wait for Hibern," Leander said.

Senrid said, "What's going on?"

Kyale, obviously tired of not being the center of attention, spoke up in a self-important tone, "There's been a horrid war in Bereth Ferian."

Leander said quickly, "Mage struggles. Not armies."

"Should we try to help?" Senrid offered, thinking of Liere in the middle of it, probably believing it her duty, and Arthur struggling to cope, knowing it was his. Though he was merely a mage student.

"I suspect they wouldn't take your offer." Leander's smile turned wry, and when Senrid had to laugh, acknowledging the truth of it, Leander added, "They wouldn't take me, either, I'm sure. Having been largely self-taught."

CJ's fierce blue gaze shifted from one boy to the other, and she said, "You mean they don't want kids. Think we're stupid and useless."

Senrid tried for fairness. "I think it's natural to look to the strongest and most experienced."

CJ crossed her arms with a thump against her scrawny chest. "Did you get that from your stenchiferous Uncle Bully?"

Senrid flushed. "When people—not only Marlovens—can't defend themselves, they look to someone stronger. It's human nature. Not Marloven nature. Or Sartoran nature. Or whatever else you want to call it. A boy to his older brother, the older brother to his father, his father to the jarl, the jarl to the king. Whatever regional authorities are called. And kings turn to their armies, or to their law."

CJ glowered. "I remember your laws," she fired back. "The first time I ever heard of you was when Leander came here to warn us that you were going to come into our country, and drag Falinneh back to yours for execution. Because why? Because she helped some people, and what did Leander say your fine and superior law was? 'You don't cross Marloven kings and live.'"

Senrid flushed to the ears. "Leander didn't know shit about our laws," he retorted, then reined his temper hard, and forced himself to really look at her pale face, at the betraying signs of anger and fear. This was stubborn loyalty he was seeing, not Kyale's equally stubborn wish to be the center of attention. CJ was clearly one spell away from transferring back to rescue Clair any way she could.

Leander walked between them, holding out a tray of

fresh cinnamon buns that he must have fetched that moment from the kitchen behind them. "Take one," he invited. "Both of you. And please, don't pull me into your argument." To CJ, "When I told you that, I was ignorant about Marloven Hess. Which has its problems. Did, and does. But, well, I learned that that was never law. More like tradition. *Old* tradition. No longer in force."

Senrid added, "How many times have you crossed me? Enjoying every moment. It seems to me you're still alive."

"Okay. Yeah." CJ grinned, but she still radiated tension. "True! On both counts."

Before anyone else could put in unwanted opinions, a faint sense of magic alerted Senrid.

Leander glanced toward the door. So he'd felt it as well. But whatever tracer had alerted him didn't disturb him unduly, so Senrid relaxed.

Then Hibern walked in, tall and gaunt as always, her long black hair flagging against her blue robe. Her black eyes were marked underneath, indicating too little sleep.

She glanced from CJ squared off to Senrid's tight shoulders and curled lip, and said quickly, "I'm sorry I haven't answered any of your notes. We've been working so hard, and transferring back and forth between Murial's and the northern mage school until Siamis's mages attacked, and I left my notecase . . . well," she stuttered to a stop, seeing impatience in Senrid and subtle signs of tension in the others.

She let out a short breath. They clearly didn't care about the months of study, trial, and error, error, error. She forced herself to skip to what they would care about. "Erai-Yanya," she stated, "has figured out an antidote to Siamis's enchantment."

And everyone started talking at once.

Hibern waited until they stopped exclaiming and shouting questions, then added, "And we just discovered that it works. I was there with Erai-Yanya. We freed Oalthoreh from the enchantment. We left her freeing all the other mages up north. Murial—"

"You mean Clair's Aunt Murial?" CJ interrupted.

"Yes. I think you know that she and Erai-Yanya studied together as students, right? She's been helping all along.

Right at this moment, she's still trying to break the magical traps around that palace, and said that you girls should stay away. Erai-Yanya says someone Siamis would never lay magical traps for must go break the enchantment over Clair."

Leander said, "That would be me. Want to come?" He glanced at Senrid, a friendly grin. "Like old times."

Kyale scowled resentfully, as Senrid grinned back. Whenever they could, that first year or so after they both came to their thrones, they'd tried setting magic traps for the other, and breaking them. Win or lose, they'd go back and study. But since those days that now seemed a lifetime ago, they'd had less time for that kind of fun.

Hibern added, "And she also warned that if you break Siamis's spell, he's probably going to be able to trace the magic. And come after you."

Leander said, "I counted on that. Everything is ready here. As soon as we do this, we all have our transfer tokens to get to the Valley of Delfina. Though I doubt he'll bother with Vasande Leror. We're too small."

"And I've given certain orders in Marloven Hess as well. He wants my army? He won't find it," Senrid said. And in a lower voice, "All that's left is the city guard, but they won't take Choreid Dhelerei easily. And Detlev can't get in at all. What about Liere?"

Hibern said, "She and Arthur were swept off by the northern mages to someplace Norsunder can't possibly find them. Without the dyr, Liere can't break that enchantment, though she feels really bad about that."

Senrid said, "This new antidote doesn't need the dyr?" He knew that Liere had to be writhing with guilt and anxiety over not being able to rescue the world, but if there was a new way around that nasty object . . .

"No." Hibern made a negating motion. "We know that Siamis and his evil uncle want the dyr back, very badly. All the mages agree that this magical attack up north was a ruse to flush out Liere and the dyr, so they could grab them both. As I told Leander, the antidote is not easy. First, you have to get the attention of the enchanted person through using a personal object of theirs . . ."

Two conversations were going on, CJ and the Mearsieans dividing off to plan their raid to reclaim Clair, and Hibern instructing Leander and Senrid in the new spell.

Kyale looked from one to the other, and sighed. "I may as well go pet my cats," she said loudly.

Everyone stopped talking. "Let's go," Leander said.

For CJ, the rescue of Clair, her most important priority, was almost an anticlimax. First of all, none of the girls could go near the white palace because of magical traps.

They found Murial alone at the top of what had once been the town square, and now was a broad street leading away from the palace terrace and Destination down the eastern slope into the town, the townspeople keeping a prudent distance. Dhana sat on the terrace steps near the Destination, swinging Clair's medallion on its chain.

When all had arrived one by one, then recovered from the transfer, Leander said, "First I need a personal object of Clair's."

Dhana silently held out the medallion, then joined the anxiously awaiting girls as he and Senrid proceeded cautiously into the silent palace made of strange white almost-stone that somehow always got remembered as marble.

Clair was a still, small figure on the throne, exactly where Senrid had left her. Leander swung the medallion with intent. When Clair's hazel gaze lost its blind affect and her eyes began following the medallion, Leander said the spell.

Sensitive to magic, Leander and Senrid stepped back a pace as a not-quite-blow, not-quite-wind radiated outward. For an instant the air scintillated, then the spell was gone, and Clair stirred, blinked, and said, "How did you two get here?"

Senrid turned to Leander. "Want to explain?"

A short time later the three walked out, and Clair was surrounded by shrieking, jumping girls. Leander and Senrid approached Murial.

"Good," the woman said. "This is our second success. I'll take care to spread it. Now, get out of here. I'm certain Siamis layered traps within that enchantment, which will alert him. I'll prepare some nice surprises if he or anyone from Norsunder does show up."

Murial stepped up to the crowd of girls, who fell silent. She and Clair hugged, then she said to them all, "I want you all to go somewhere safe. Don't tell me where, in case. But I believe I am much safer than you, as I am not Siamis's target. *But listen to me first.*"

Everyone fell silent, Senrid wary.

Murial said, "Keep the antidote spell to yourselves for the moment. It's still new, and while we now know it works, we don't know if, or how, Siamis will retaliate. And we certainly don't want all your friends haring off to try the spell without any plan or protection. It's terrible that people are enchanted, but at least they are in no pain. Correct?"

Clair said, "True. It's like being asleep, kind of."

Murial gave a tiny nod. "So waiting until the senior mages decide how best to deploy it is the best course right now. Will you do that?"

They agreed.

"Then go somewhere safe," Murial said gently.

Senrid longed to check on Marloven Hess, but remembered what Clair looked like sitting on that throne, her expression utterly empty. Asleep or not, he loathed the idea of it happening to him—and of being unable to resist anything Siamis might tell him to do while he was 'asleep.'

He yanked out the token he'd readied the day the bells rang in Marloven Hess, and transferred to Delfina Valley.

Clair met Leander's gaze, and she saw agreement there. She said to Murial, "I'll fetch my notecase. Will you write to me if anything happens?"

Murial said, "You may be sure I will."

$$\boxed{\text{Chapter Eight}}$$

Sharmadi (Seventhmonth), 4742 AF
Sarendan and Delfina Valley

IT was late at night when Peitar Selenna heard footsteps outside his study.

He noted them, hoping Lilah was not awake so late, but this new line of inquiry into the nature of Dena Yeresbeth was so intriguing!

He put his finger on the moldering page he'd been translating mentally from Sartoran. He'd stumbled across the ancient book, which had been completely mis-shelved among books for beginner mages trying to learn the quake easement magic. Its extreme age had caught his attention, an anomaly.

Tiredness vanished as he reread a passage in growing wonder. It really seemed that the translator, twelve centuries ago, had misinterpreted the Ancient Sartoran. Unless the meaning of the word had shifted . . .

"The first," came a pleasant voice. "But the misinterpretation goes back much farther than twelve centuries."

Peitar looked up, startled, at an unfamiliar fellow maybe a year or so younger than he was, wind-tousled wheat-colored hair glinting in the candle light, his white linen shirt dappled with raindrops. "Who—"

"I just arrived from Sartor," the newcomer said with a smile. "Why candles? Where are your glowglobes? Surely they provide better light to read by."

"I made a promise," Peitar said, "not to work long past midnight. So I made time candles. What's your source for the mistranslated word for ancient magic, and how did you find it?" He sat back, pleased at the prospect of discussing magic, his mind open with questions. "Did Tsauderei send you?"

"No," said Siamis, and closed the trap.

He glanced through Peitar's books, then gently shut them all, as Peitar gazed beyond the walls into timelessness. "It's almost a shame you won't remember your discovery," Siamis said, listening on the mental plane as the enchantment ringed outward. Asleep or awake, all those within the border who shared the same loyalty for which Peitar served as symbol slid into that same timelessness.

"Almost," Siamis said, and made that one book vanish. Then Siamis caught Peitar's gaze and issued the instructions that Peitar was to follow.

Derek woke to the rumble of distant thunder. He blinked, his eyes burning. He sat up, rubbing the crust from his eyelids and working his dry mouth. The sound of voices emerged from the fading thunder: Tsauderei's gravely old man's voice, and the nasal honk of a teenage boy.

Derek turned his head, finding a broad window overlooking a sky full of tumbling clouds, gold-lit at one end, purple at the other. A flicker of lightning briefly outlined the clouds as they sailed away.

He sat up, his head pounding. He had slid to the floor, tangling himself up in a quilt.

He flung away the covering and looked around. At the other end of the cottage, the old mage sat with a hunch-shouldered, black-haired young teen whose pasty face was completely unfamiliar. The kid wore shapeless garments of rusty black.

They each looked Derek's way, then Tsauderei said something in another language, his tone kindly.

The teen ducked his head, mumbled an answer, then

sloped out the door. He reappeared in the window a moment later, shuffling toward the edge of the cliff the cottage sat on. As Derek watched, he made an ungainly, tentative hop, then came down slowly. He hopped higher, arms wiggling, and floated down. Then he sprang upward, limbs flapping like an ungainly crow as he shot out over the cliff into air. Derek heard a faint, strangled yell through the thick window glass.

Tsauderei approached, leaning heavily on a cane. The old mage's face looked more furrowed than Derek remembered it.

"Who's that?" Derek asked. Even his voice felt crusty.

"His name is Jilo."

"Why is he dressed like that? Someone's livery?" Derek didn't hide the contempt in his voice for whoever would put his servants in such willfully ugly garb.

"Jilo is a Chwahir. They all dress like that."

"Chwahir," Derek repeated. That explained the sickly, pale skin. He'd never seen any Chwahir, but he'd heard jokes about moon- and platter-faces.

"He is, I hope and trust, the first of several refugees from the various kingdoms Norsunder is currently attacking."

"Someone else besides us?" Derek asked.

"Everon," Tsauderei stated, "is at present getting the worst of it."

Worse than the other day? The tide of memory flooded unmercifully, prompting a deep desire for vengeance. "I've got to get back." Derek struggled to his feet, head swimming. He leaned against a bookcase. "I promised Peitar I'd get those youngsters out."

Tsauderei sank into the empty wing-backed chair, and let out a long sigh. "Derek, I have bad news for you."

"Worse than the battle I lost? Another battle," Derek said wryly, lunging toward the door in reflex.

"To a degree it's worse than that." Derek jolted to a stop when Tsauderei waggled a hand back and forth. "After you fell asleep, I had to go to aid my fellow mages in Bereth Ferian. But while I was there, expecting magical attack from Siamis, he was here. In Sarendan. He put Peitar under enchantment, which extends to the entire kingdom."

Lightning shot through Derek's nerves. "I've got to do something!"

"You can stay here. Until the situation is clearer."

"I failed. Again," Derek muttered, his gaze going sightlessly from object to object.

Tsauderei waited for comprehension; Derek glanced up. "But I can't stay here. There are those children still in Sarendan. Including Lilah, Bren, and Innon. I promised Peitar I'd get them to safety here."

"I'm aware."

"The flims you put the magic on are still sitting in my house."

"Most likely."

"So give me the magic to go back and rescue them."

"No. Not yet. Not until I know the nature of the magic on Peitar, and . . ." Tsauderei paused, and decided against explaining how the few mages who as yet knew about Erai-Yanya's antidote were waiting to discover if it held. ". . . and what Norsunder would do."

And Derek didn't care about magic. "You can't keep me here," he stated.

"I can't stop you from walking out," Tsauderei retorted. "It'll take you, oh, maybe six weeks to clamber the mountains to the border. Longer, in the storms I predict as a result of my interference the other day."

Derek remembered the sudden storm, which sparked an older memory: the sudden storm the dawn he and Peitar were marched out to face execution. "That was you?"

Tsauderei brought his chin down, his white beard rippling on his chest. "The local weather will be disturbed for a time, but this is the mountains. Such storms are frequent. It will do little harm. Except maybe to lone travelers scrambling over the cliff faces. I trust any such will be Norsundrian stragglers."

Derek drew in a shaky breath. "Where is that little girl who ended Siamis's enchantment before?"

"She's expected here any time, as it transpires. We will discuss that when she does arrive."

Derek let his breath go. "All right." A plan of action, of sorts. He could live with that. "What can I do?" He added, "Don't tell me I'm useless because I don't know magic."

"There is a very important service you could provide, actually. Those children you brought, added to others who are gathering here, will need organization. This Valley has served as a refuge before, from time to time, and I believe we can accommodate them, but when they tire of swimming in the lake and flying, they will probably get restless. I would not like to see them disturbing the villagers unduly."

Derek gave a short nod. He had a lot to learn before he'd become a good commander. But he did know how to organize a rabble.

"All right," he said. "Where are they? Who claims authority here? Some damned noble, no doubt?"

"'Damned' is not for me to decide," Tsauderei said wryly. "But you may look to me for whatever authority exists. Now, sit down. There's fresh bread on the table over there, and some good goat cheese. If you like Sartoran steep, you may fill the kettle from the pump in that corner. The dried leaves are in that lacquered canister with the flowers painted on it, that Lilah's mother made for me when she was about ten."

Derek was surprised enough to obey without question.

Tsauderei nodded, and smiled benignly. "You can eat, and listen, while I claim the privilege of the old and regale you with the Valley's history so you will understand how things are done here. We need to go far, far back in history, when magic was much stronger in the world. This valley was a home for aging mages, or those who needed to retreat from the world, as well as for the small population of people whose descendants' houses you can see on the other plateaus. . . ."

Everon

Princess Tahra Delieth of Everon sat up in bed. There was nothing to get up *for*, but too much to get away *from*.

She swung her feet out of bed, pressing them to the floor at exactly the same moment, all ten toes. Then she got up and walked to her dresser, five steps each side. Even stayed clear. Odd was brown, and brown meant a bad day.

Tahra knew that counting steps and touching her things in the right order didn't make any difference outside her room. Her father had told her. Her mother had told her. Uncle Roderic had told her. Rel had told her. Mearsieanne had told her. Even Glenn had bored on at length.

That was fine. Nothing she did or didn't do in the right way, the right order, affected other things, except she knew if she didn't do them right, she had a bad day. If she did them right, she might have a good day. Might was better than nothing. Clear was better than mud brown.

But all the days had been bad, ever since this war happened. Going on three weeks, now, she and Glenn had to stay in the palace all day, and their parents were always in conference. Always with long faces. Every couple of days there seemed to be new skirmishes somewhere, which meant somebody new was dead.

Here it was, Restday again, the third since the Norsundrians had invaded, killing Valenn and taking over the harbor.

Today was to be the memorial for the latest dead.

Tahra stepped through her cleaning frame, one two, and decided that yesterday's trousers and shirt would do. No one would notice if she put on a proper mourning robe over them. She lifted the white one from the trunk, shook it out twice, then pulled it on, both arms at the same time. Sash, over, over, under, through. The ends . . . yes, they hung together. Clear, so far. Everything in order.

Relieved, she put on stockings and shoes, then brushed her hair, twenty strokes left, twenty right.

When she stepped out, she found her mother having just left her suite, her shining dark hair with white starliss braided into it. "Darling," Mersedes Carinna exclaimed, eyeing her daughter. "I was about to send Jenel to you."

"I'm ready. And my hair is neat. See?" Tahra turned, so her mother could see her ordered hair. Tahra had cut hers to shoulder length, like Glenn's, so she wouldn't have to sit there and endure someone's fingers in it. Just the thought made her skin crawl.

Mersedes Carinna saw Tahra's long face turn obdurate. Her heart already ached at the loss of Alstha, her husband's new sweeting; life was so fragile, she believed that joy should be embraced fiercely wherever it came. Her arms ached to hold her daughter within their circle, but Tahra had pushed her away long ago.

She forced herself to smile, and to say, "You look quite proper. Come, let us not keep Uncle Roderic waiting."

Tahra's maid Jenel was standing by with an understanding smile, holding the dethorned white roses that Tahra would carry. She quietly surrendered them into Tahra's keeping without permitting their fingers to touch, which Tahra was grateful for.

They waited until the king's door opened and he joined them, sorrow carving lines into his face as he reached down to kiss Mama.

Tahra stiffened when it was her turn, and grimaced at the warm, moist pressure of his lips on her cheek, the brush of his beard against her neck.

As the king saluted Glenn, Tahra hastily wiped her cheek against her shoulder, then walked beside her brother behind their royal parents, leading the procession into the court.

There, people waited for them. Tahra looked into each face; last was Uncle Roderic, his head down, only his graying beard visible. It wasn't until she was within ten paces that she discovered it wasn't Uncle Roderic at all, but some gray-bearded man wearing the white robes of the Knights of Dei with the commander's gold trefoil embroidered on the shoulder.

Her parents had been watching. The king flashed a bitter smile at his wife, a shared moment of anticipatory triumph.

Henerek, watching through field glasses from a rooftop in the city, saw that brief grin, cursed, and lifted his hand in a fist, signaling his galloper waiting at the end of Woolens Row: whatever caused that smile, there was a good chance his surprise attack wasn't.

And that meant the Knights—or someone—weren't all ranged down below, but were about to attack his hostage towns.

"Go, go, go," he yelled.

Below, the stately procession followed the four biers along the tree-lined path leading from the palace to the

Knights' square. The citizens of Ferdrian tossed showers of
white petals, gathered in the dew before sunup.

The royal family and the supposed Knights were barely
visible in the soft, fragrant snow of petals, tranquil and
melancholy for the space of twenty steps.

Zing! Then the first arrow hissed through the air.
Shields whipped up, as citizens screamed in terror and outrage. Henerek's assassination team began to converge, to
find themselves in turn shot at from behind chimney pots
and attic windows that looked down on either side of the
royal parade: while they had crept over roofs into position,
watching the palace, young Knight candidates had gained
their rooftop vantages through the houses, and one by one
shot half of Henerek's assassins, Roderic Dei's daughter
Carinna leading the team.

A day's fast ride away, Rel sat behind a honeysuckle shrub,
watching bees bumble between blossoms as the summer sun
rose, baking the back of his head. Down beyond the slope,
along a sluggish river, lay the two towns that the Norsundrians had taken when they were driven from the harbor.

Behind Rel, Roderic Dei sat in the lee of a squat juniper,
talking quietly to his new captain, another of his weedy
teenage daughters serving as squire. She looked as upset as
all of them had to feel, not to be present as the rest of Everon sang the memorial farewell to the gallant Captain
Alstha and three other Knights. Rel's mind wandered to
Atan, far to the south. He hoped Sartor was all right. But
he could do little there—the royal council had made it clear
that the mages were in charge.

The commander raised a hand, halting the conversation. Everyone stilled as he flicked open his notecase, read,
then beckoned to Rel, who was the duty runner for the day.

Rel hunched over, hoping his head and shoulders were
not visible above the curling tendrils at the top of the honeysuckle.

The commander said grimly, "It's as the king expected.
Henerek has not sufficient a sense of honor to grant us this
Restday memorial. Our decoys are busy chasing his assas-
sins over the rooftops right now."

"Ah," said Rel. Not only did that give the Everoneth leave

to attack in turn, by their own code, it probably strengthened their resolve to rescue the hapless citizens whose lives the Norsundrians had threatened.

"Also, Henerek is apparently leading the would-be assassins, which means he's not here," Roderic said. "And so, let us put the secondary plan in motion."

Rel nodded his assent, backed away, and returned to his position, which was in line of sight of two watchers. He held up his hand, then pumped it twice, once to each side.

A count of fifty as the signal spread to the other side of the river, and then it was time to move.

Rel hated covert movement. He was not made for skulking. His neck and spine ached by the time he had duck-waddled, hunched over, from bush to bush along a gentle inward slope carved by a chuckling spring that emptied into the river; his shield and sword seemed to grow extra corners just to gouge him in unexpected places. Sweat soaked his clothes and ran down the back of his neck by the time he'd reached the candle-bloom chestnuts along the base of the hill.

They'd nearly reached the village when the first signs of the enemy appeared: archers on the rooftops. A hail of arrows slowed the Everoneth slightly, but everyone had shields up.

Then the first wave of attackers boiled out from between sleepy-seeming cottages, two forces going for the Knights forward of Rel's position. Rel ripped free his sword, whirling it in tight circles to either side as he charged.

A furious battle compounded of dust, sweat, the fierce glint of sun off steel, and he was through the line of Norsundrians, but glimpsed more beyond the houses. Where were the villagers who were supposed to rise against the enemy? A sense of foreboding grew as he loped down a narrow alley between cottages, and he peered cautiously over a projecting porch rail.

The village square was crowded, the villagers gathered in a tight group, ringed by Norsundrians. Swords and knives held at the throats of all the children. Along the perimeter, hidden Norsundrians attacked the occasional Knights who burst through singly or in pairs. Rel dropped back, then retreated at top speed, his breath burning his throat. He caught sight of Roderic and the main body descending in columns fifty paces away.

Rel caught up before Roderic reached his first cottage. In a few gasped words, he repeated what he'd seen.

Roderic's face blanched nearly as gray as his beard. Then he jerked his mailed fist at the signaler. "Sound the retreat."

Nauseated from thirst and heat, Rel fought his way past the laughing, hooting enemy, and at a gesture from his patrol leader, helped to pick up a fallen comrade to carry up the hill.

Stalemate—again. And again, new dead to mourn.

At that same moment, in Sarendan's capital, Miraleste, Kessler marshaled his company.

They'd enjoyed a couple days of rest and relaxation in the enchanted city, while Kessler amused himself with locating Peitar Selenna's annoying sister, one of the brats who had caused him so much trouble in the Sartoran enchantment fiasco a couple years back.

He tested the limits of Siamis's spell to see how it was put together by asking questions, and repeating demands, over and over. Before he left, he laid a blood-enchantment over a blade. All it needed was contact with Derek Diamagan's blood to work. He pressed the enchanted blade into Lilah Selenna's hand, and ordered her to stab Derek Diamagan on sight.

Laughing at the brat's slack face, he summoned his company and said, "To the coast. Double-time. We're off to Everon to have some fun."

Chapter Nine

Othdi (Eighthmonth), 4742 AF
Delfina Valley

"YOU'LL stay here," Tsauderei said, as he and Jilo flew past the main plateau of the Delfina Valley. Jilo glanced down at steep roofs made of slate. Otherwise the houses reminded him of those in Mearsies Heili, with colors on the shutters, the doors, and the plastered walls.

Jilo had assumed the old mage couldn't fly, he was so stiff-jointed, but flying clearly made movement easy for him. It was odd, how his body felt bird-light, but his hair and clothes did not float upward, the way they did in water. He wondered how the flying spell was bound, and who had done it.

Tsauderei led Jilo to the largest house in the Valley. It had been built on a plateau of its own, in the midst of a wildly overgrown garden. "This belongs to Peitar and Lilah Selenna," Tsauderei said, his voice low with regret. "It once belonged to their mother. They won't mind its being used."

When they landed, Tsauderei winced as the magic dissipated, the ground again pulling at his joints the moment his feet touched down. He lifted the latch and led the way into a slate-floored foyer, past a beautiful salon done in white and black. "Run upstairs, and pick out a bed," Tsauderei said. "Go ahead. I'll wait, in case you have questions."

Jilo walked from room to room and back again, up the steep stairs and down, just looking at all the colors, and how each fitted well with the next. He found a trunk filled with art supplies next to a bed, the edges of the paper curled from age. He knew an abandoned trunk when he saw it and dared to claim it for his own.

Also in the trunk, he found folded clothing: tunics of various sizes, riding trousers, socks, various types of shoes. All in summer-light fabrics, even colors.

Elsewhere in the room was another bed, another trunk. There were two gabled windows, and between them a desk. On the corner opposite the window, there stood a wooden frame that looked like a window frame with no window. When he approached it, he felt magic. A cleaning frame! For two people? In Chwahirsland, the only ones left were in barracks, for officers.

He ran downstairs. "I found a chamber," he said. "Is there someone living here who does drawing?"

"Bren." There was the regret again. "He won't mind sharing. Whatever art gear he left wasn't what he wanted to take back into Sarendan. In fact, I encourage you to investigate the clothes in the trunk, which are donations from a couple generations of family and guests. Unless you're fond of yours."

"No," Jilo said. "But may I use the cleaning frame?"

"As often as you wish. You might consider resuming your studies. If you do, I recommend visiting Atan, who lives in the hermit's cottage, on the platform at the western end of the Valley."

"Atan?"

"She's your age. An accomplished mage student."

Jilo nodded, but he couldn't get his thoughts past that cleaning frame for a single bedroom. Why wouldn't Wan-Edhe permit people to have cleaning frames? Because he despised the people. Because the onerous task of scrubbing laundry and trying to dry it in the harsh weather kept people busy who might otherwise be fomenting revolt, of course.

Jilo was going to change that first thing when he returned.

"As for meals, I have an arrangement with a colleague at a very popular inn in Colend. We will not burden the locals with feeding the refugees."

Tsauderei had explained on Jilo's first night that under ordinary circumstances the Valley was nearly impossible to get to. Transfers were strictly warded. Access to the Valley was by flying, and the prospective visitor appeared in Tsauderei's scry stone. He could block the magic with a word, and deny their entry.

But for the current refugees, he had created special transfer tokens like the one that had brought Jilo directly to his cottage. Jilo found this demonstration of the power of waxer magic so intriguing he was almost tempted to talk to a stranger, this Atan.

That night and the next, Jilo only saw Tsauderei at meal times. Otherwise he was alone. He dared the trunk, choosing one of those soft shirts, dyed a bright yellow, with blue embroidery in fanciful blossoms down the front. It felt good next to his skin, and he liked the cheerful color, but years of habit were difficult to break, and he didn't want anyone actually seeing him.

Yet when the sun was out, he couldn't bear to be inside. Sometimes he left through the window, because he could. He still didn't like the idea of putting himself into the deep waters of the lake. He had only swum in small ponds during the Shadowland days. He watched from above as other kids swam, always staying away from the far end, where some kind of noxious flowers grew.

And the food! Goat cheese was familiar, but the flavor, so delicate and delicious, wasn't. Jilo knew that this was because the goats ate sweet grass and clover, far better than the bitter, drought-tough weeds eaten by Chwahir goats.

All the food was delicious.

But by the end of that second night the questions began to proliferate, bringing back the old worries: was Chwahirsland safer with him home, or away? If he returned, what could he actually do, if Wan-Edhe was sent back from Norsunder?

He checked the book convulsively. That raised more

worries: what if someone found the book? Tsauderei had said that the Valley was laced with very deep protections, ancient ones impossible now to reproduce—like the flying spell. No one could do any sort of magic without Tsauderei knowing. Creating a tiny pocket beyond space and time was (this surprised Jilo to discover) considered a major piece of magical working, and Tsauderei would know immediately. Did that mean he'd know what was in the book? Or demand to know?

The last worry was what would happen when the Mearsieans showed up and found him (ostensibly) part of their alliance. Or maybe they'd think him only a refugee, as Tsauderei did. In all his talk, the old mage never mentioned the alliance, whereas he was clear about this valley having served as a refuge from Norsunder many times in the past.

The third morning, Jilo woke to the sound of high girlish voices elsewhere in the house. He decided he'd better get it over with, dressed, and went downstairs, to discover the Mearsieans newly arrived.

"Jilo! You here?" Falinneh exclaimed, echoed by others.

Falinneh pointed and laughed, almost doubled over, at the idea of Jilo in normal clothes. She didn't intend to be mean, but he just looked so . . . so odd!

Several laughed, surprised to see a Chwahir in anything but rusty black, except for Seshe, the tall quiet girl, who studied Jilo's mottled face and said, "I think it looks nice."

"Yes!" CJ said, bright blue eyes going from Jilo to the tall girl and back. "That is a pretty shirt. Where did you get it?"

Now they all stared at Jilo. He cringed inside, waiting for the punch line of the joke. Or was she accusing him of theft? Of course they were making fun of him. They always had. He'd never understood those girls and their fast games and slang.

CJ tried again. She said to Jilo, "Did that grunge-bearded geez of a king splat back on the throne?"

Jilo stared back, and by the time he understood she meant Wan-Edhe, CJ thought he was ignoring her, and turned away to join the other girls crowding protectively around Clair, all talking at once, as they left the house and took off like a flock of starlings to experiment with flying over the lake.

Jilo fled back to his room, ripped off the green silky shirt, put it through the cleaning frame, then put it at the very bottom of the trunk.

When he was back in his old clothes, he took off again, his intention to avoid any encounters at all by exploring the limits of the flying area.

On his return mid-afternoon, he angled down to the open bedroom window, where he surprised Senrid and a tall, thin, dark-haired boy startlingly symmetrical of feature. No, not just symmetrical, it was the way he was put together. Was this what people called 'handsome'? Jilo discovered an urge to draw him in order to figure out what compelled the eye.

Senrid whirled around, one hand going to the other sleeve, then dropping when he recognized Jilo. "Tsauderei told us to bunk in here with you. They expect to fill up the other rooms. This is Leander."

"Jilo."

"Well met," Leander said pleasantly.

Jilo didn't know what he was supposed to say to that, so he mumbled something and retreated to his side of the room. He'd learned from Senrid that Vasande Leror was a tiny kingdom next to Marloven Hess, and that its king was a boy named Leander. These two who were historically supposed to be enemies worked together to sling a canvas hammock between candle sconces on adjoining walls. It took the effort of both boys to get the thing stable, after which began a friendly argument about who was to get the second bed, and who the hammock.

Senrid said, "Look, the way we've got this thing hung, whoever is in it is going to have their knees up by their ears. Since you're taller than I am by at least a hand, that means you'll hang lower, right? I don't want your butt directly over my head. If you fart, I'll have to kill you."

"So you put your head at that end of the bed," Leander pointed out. "And we'll cinch this hammock up tighter." He moved to the sconces and efficiently retied the hammock at both ends.

Then Senrid leaped up and landed in the hammock, which swung dangerously. The way he grinned, it was clear he liked it, and Leander gave up, throwing his travel pack on the bed.

The two born princes acted more like the lowest recruits as they took turns swinging in the hammock and trying to launch themselves from it to the open window. Jilo watched, fascinated; they laughed as one or the other got tangled in the hammock, or knocked into the windowsill or wall.

When Leander got himself successfully out the window, he let out a whoop of triumph, then circled back and peered inside, arms swinging as he tried to stabilize himself mid-air. "I'll never use a door again," he predicted. "While I'm here. I should probably make sure Kitty is all right, and then how about some exploring? I want to get used to this."

"Your sister will be happy as a bird as long as I'm not around," Senrid predicted, to which Leander flashed a wry smile. "I'll catch up." And to Jilo, as Leander skimmed away over the treetops, arms waving awkwardly, "Where is it?"

"Where is what?"

Senrid said impatiently, "You've got two magic study books there on the table. That means you've got the enemy-tracking book hidden somewhere. Mattress? Another room? Come on, that's what I would have done."

Jilo grimaced and pulled the book from under the mattress.

"I want to see where the head snakes are."

Jilo opened the book. "Wan-Edhe, no sign. Siamis is in Roth Drael. Roth Drael?"

Senrid's stomach hurt. "Where Erai-Yanya and Hibern live. He's probably trying to track them down, if he found out they're the ones who discovered the antidote to his enchantment."

"Detlev, still nothing," Jilo said.

"I wonder if our guess is right," Senrid mused.

"Going out of the world?"

"Hibern told us that Erai-Yanya thinks he's gone back to Geth-deles. You know, our sister world, the one we never see in the sky because it's always on the other side of the sun. Though I'm told *they* call *us* Darkside."

"Hope he stays there," Jilo said.

"No." Senrid struck the air as if pushing something away from him. "Don't you see? If he's there, and not here handing out commands right and left, then it has to mean he's on the hunt for some kind of magical weapon he can come back and hammer us with."

Jilo considered, then said, "If he is, what can we do about it?"

"Probably nothing." Senrid scowled. "But I have to know."

Jilo was more concerned about the book, and how Senrid had hustled his friend out the window so he could ask about it. Hoping this would prevent trouble, instead of starting it, he said, "Well, you know where I keep it. Look at it any time you like. Just don't let anyone see it."

"I can't read your language. And it's probably as well," Senrid said so quickly that Jilo eyed him uncertainly. "Can I tell Leander?"

Jilo grimaced. "I don't know him."

"I do. You can trust him." Senrid's smile was not particularly humorous. "He's far more trustworthy than I am, but the Mearsieans will tell you that's not saying much. Though they like him."

"I wouldn't ask the Mearsieans anything," Jilo retorted, mentally excepting Clair. And maybe the tall one, Seshe. Maybe. If only he'd had a real twi! How did anyone figure these things out about people? "All right. But only him."

"One more," Senrid said. "Only one. Hibern. When she gets here. She's very good with secrets."

Jilo thought he may as well give in now. "Done. That's it."

"Come on. Show us around."

In the Valley, Atan and Derek existed as polar opposites.

Derek's Sarendan orphans had been taken in by Valley families on the central plateau. Derek drilled them each morning, his determination no more ferocious than theirs.

Derek's anger at his failure had gradually metamorphosed into anger at his lack of training. There were times when he held imaginary conversations with King Darian, whom he had helped to oust, as he lay restlessly in bed through long nights. "I understand now why you wanted the army alert and ready," he once admitted. "You were right. You were right."

At the extreme western end of the Valley, almost not in the Valley at all, lay a single cottage tucked up on a cliff

amid thick forest. In centuries past, this was where mages
who required solitary tranquility had been housed, leaving
a formidable magic library almost as good as Tsauderei's.

Atan had spent her childhood secluded in that house,
and here she was again, only without Gehlei, the faithful
steward who moved about in an enchanted dream-state in
Eidervaen.

Atan wept a great deal those first few days, missing Gehlei
and worrying about everyone else; she wept about the hard
irony of her ending up back here in this cottage that never
quite stopped smelling of mold no matter how vigorously
she scrubbed every surface. And she did scrub, but restoring clean and shining order did not take away the truth: she
had lost Sartor as assuredly as her father had. At least no
one had died on a battlefield. The Siamis enchantment had
been broken once before, and by a ten-year-old. That meant
it could be broken again. Just not by her.

Tsauderei came to visit her those first couple of mornings. He told her about the shy Chwahir boy who had apparently assumed an infamous throne. But this Jilo did not
appear, and Atan was too dispirited to seek him out. What
had she to offer him, save lessons in how to lose a throne?

When Tsauderei came the third morning, he said, "Sinking into self-pity isn't going to do you or anyone else any
good. Use those skills of yours. Find Jilo, because he really
needs help."

She grimaced. "I keep trying to overcome—to plan—
but it's impossible."

Tsauderei lifted his hand, gnarled as an apple tree.
"Choose a happy memory. Sometimes mine are my best
companions. Think of your Sartor in celebration, after the
enchantment broke. Imagine how it will be when everyone
is free, and you've helped to make it that way."

She admitted, "I've tried to walk the Purrad in my mind,
and I remember every step and turn, but it hurts. I don't
feel I deserve its peace."

"Tchah!" Tsauderei's expression was so explosive his
long, snowy mustache fluttered. "That is exactly why those
things were built. You dishonor their purpose, child, with
this mood."

He left, and she promptly sat down to make a napurdiav in memory.

He was right. If she approached it the way she ought, walking it mentally did lift her spirits. As soon as she was done, she left the cottage, flying by habit toward the village plateau. But when she recognized Derek Diamagan down there, leading children in some kind of exercise with sticks, she couldn't bear to risk his sneers about royal blood and failure, and she retreated again.

She tried again on another day, flying well away from the main plateau. When she caught sight of a group of girls flying over the lake, she slowed and hovered. The one who drew the attention by cartwheeling in a gleefully awkward, limb-flapping manner was a redhead in bright, mismatched clothing. Prominent in the admiring circle were a girl with pure white hair and a smaller one with long black hair.

Sharp disappointment caused Atan to recoil when she recognized the Mearsieans, the Rel-haters. And no word or sign of Rel for months.

Atan retreated to her cottage once again, too angry to attempt a false napurdiav. So she pulled out a book at random to study.

Her solitary struggle was summarily broken early one morning a few days later, when Tsauderei reappeared, this time towing a figure burrowed in a heavy coat still sparking with melting snow.

"Hibern!" Atan exclaimed.

Hibern smiled, making a mental note to remember what she could say and what she couldn't say. That morning, Erai-Yanya had told her, *Now that the antidote is out there, Tsauderei will do much better at herding the cats, that is, dealing with the senior mages, than I ever could. I am going back to Geth-deles. My quest is even more urgent than it was before, and I believe that Roth Drael isn't safe—Siamis might show up looking for the dyr. Tsauderei invites you to join him in the Valley. But remember, no mention of the antidote until he has the senior mages ready to deploy it.*

Forestalling possible questions from Atan, Hibern looked around with an air of interest. "So this is your famous cottage? I would never have left, if I had a library like that."

"Come, get rid of that coat," Atan said. "Where did you come from? Have you eaten?"

"I was up north. Oh, it's a long story. One thing I can say is, I found Arthur and Liere, and gave them transfer tokens. They should be along soon."

Tsauderei said, "Show her around, Atan. There are some friends who have been waiting to meet you, but dislike imposing."

Atan studied the old mage, who smiled back, the diamond in his ear winking in the light of the fire on the hearth. "What does that mean, they think I'm a snob? Too good for everyone else, is that it?"

Tsauderei did not deny it. "Prove them wrong."

Chastened, Atan frowned down at her hands. 'Friends.' Such an easy word to say, but what did it really mean? She knew that her prejudice against the Mearsiean girls was wrong. Rel had said himself that they were his friends. He hadn't explained how he could be friends with that loud-mouthed princess who complained about him behind his back, but Atan struggled to dismiss her own prejudice. They were allies against the evil of Norsunder. They had to work together.

"Very well, then." She forced a smile. "The one bad thing about this cottage, buried in the woods as it is, it never gets any sunlight." She indicated the leaping fire. "So getting outside will be good, especially if the weather is fine."

"It is right now," Tsauderei said. "Which probably won't be true by afternoon. So. I have to see about making arrangements for the kitchen at Selenna House, now that we're gathering quite a crowd there. And troll for news," he added.

Atan remembered the Sartoran mage council, yet again caught in a web of magic, and the familiar sick sense of humiliation and defeat tightened around her heart. She caught a sympathetic glance from Hibern. That much, at least, Atan could share. "Do you truly want to hear it?" she asked.

They'd reached the ledge, and as Hibern made the sign for flying, she wrinkled her upper lip. "Please tell me everything. Then I don't have to think about how much I really, really hate heights. Especially with nothing below my feet but air."

Atan unburdened herself as they floated above cliff and crevasse. Hibern listened in sympathy, severely tempted to reveal that the Siamis enchantment could be broken, but she had to keep her promise not to talk about it. *It won't be long*, Erai-Yanya had promised.

Presently they approached the village on the main plateau. Atan would have veered away, but Hibern caught sight of familiar figures. "Hold, isn't that Senrid?"

They were unnoticed by the orphan brigade, who formed up into their lines, as they did every morning at dawn.

The girls watched from above as Senrid sauntered up. "Is this open to anyone?" he asked. He missed his morning exercise.

"Sure," Sig said, remembering how Derek always welcomed new people. He added, "Your accent is funny."

Ruddy put in, "You must be one of the foreigners that old geez said might come."

"Yep," Senrid said.

Someone else shouted, "Derek is coming!"

The lines instantly straightened, and the orphans began doing the warm-up arm swings that they always began with. Senrid took up a place in the back row.

Red-haired Falinneh of the Mearsieans emerged early from Selenna House, seeking breakfast. She always flew over the big plateau if she saw people. When she spotted those uniform lines, most of them boys, drilling in unison, the urge to have some fun with them was irresistible.

She landed in the front, and promptly began copying the drill with loud groans, groaning, making popping noises as if her joints creaked, and falling down.

The rest of the Mearsieans streamed after her.

Derek had pulled a small boy out to demonstrate a better grip on his sticks, and hadn't noticed the addition. When he looked up, irritation flared through him at this garishly dressed urchin making fun of his war refugees. He started toward her, hot words forming, when the rest of the Mearsieans landed.

He glanced their way, then his head snapped back when he recognized CJ.

From the air, Atan and Hibern watched as Derek Diamagan made a profound bow to CJ.

The orphans, knowing how Derek felt about bowing, gaped.

CJ flushed, at first suspecting she was being ridiculed. She gazed warily at Derek, her chin lifted. Then her lips parted. "Don't . . . I know you?" she asked.

"There is no reason you should remember me," Derek said earnestly. "But I will never forget you, the person who saved my brother and me."

CJ blanched as pale as the shirt collar above her black vest.

Derek turned to his orphans. "Some of you had parents who did not believe young people could be useful. To them I always said, 'black wool and ambition.' It was this girl who proved that people your age have smart minds, and brave hearts." And to CJ, "I see that you still wear the vest made from the wool of a black sheep. I never understood what you meant when you said that you were that kind of person, but when I spoke of a uniform for my orphan brigade, here, I thought it should include such a garment, as it symbolized those stout of heart."

CJ scowled at her bare toes, red to the ears, and when Ruddy said, "Tell us what happened!" she muttered, "I hate even thinking about that mess with Kessler."

"I'm starved," one of the other Mearsieans said loudly, sending a worried glance at CJ, who stalked away, then looked back with the oddest expression, a mixture of regret, embarrassment, and concern.

"Is your brother all right?" CJ asked Derek.

Derek said, "He's up north in western Khanerenth, trading for horses. He'll regret not having been here to meet you."

Senrid could see how every word made CJ flinch. Mentally resolving he would get that story out of someone, he drew Derek's attention by saying, "I don't understand using two sticks." He pointed at the pair resting on the grass beside each orphan. "One would be a practice sword, but two?"

Derek smiled. "Welcome! I didn't see you there in the back. No, we do not use swords. The weapons are these sticks. Any sticks. The art of the two sticks comes from Khanerenth. Like many things in that kingdom, it is said to have originated as a form of marine warfare, on ships."

"Oh?" Senrid said innocently, knowing very well that his own ancestor, Inda-Harskialdna—known elsewhere in the world as Elgar the Fox—had spread double-stick fighting to mariners, more than eight centuries previous.

CJ didn't trust Senrid's earnest, inquiring air as far as she could throw him, but she recognized his distraction of Derek away from an embarrassing moment, and flashed him a grim smile of gratitude as she took off.

Derek bent to pick up a pair of double-sticks. "I brought a simplified form here before the new king came to the throne, as commoners were forbidden to possess steel. But any hand can pick up a stick from field or road."

Derek paused, and motioned a pair of his orphans forward to demonstrate. Senrid stood with his hands behind his back, and what he hoped was an interested look on his face. He knew the basics, but until his uncle was deposed, the only hard training he'd had was in archery and hand-to-hand knife fighting. He could tell that Derek had gotten decent training somewhere, though he wasn't very practiced.

Atan offered space in the cottage loft for Hibern, which she instantly accepted. She could hardly wait to get at that library. By afternoon, when thunder heralded a brief storm, she and Atan sat on either side of the leaping fire, absorbed in study.

Or Hibern set out to study. She discovered that the library was mostly handmade copies of Sartoran histories and magic books that she was already familiar with, and a few personal records by unknown mages, obscure and difficult to read. She earmarked the oldest ones for priority reading, but sat back, reflecting on what she'd seen so far.

The alliance was gathering for the first time. But instead of cleaving together in order to combine knowledge and strength, they seemed to be separating out into disparate groups. They had little in common but a shared hatred of

Norsunder, she was thinking. And hatred was never a good way to bind people together.

Part of being a mage was trying to negotiate between people. As Hibern stared down at her cup of wild berry juice, she wondered where to begin.

Why not with what she knew? She turned her gaze up to Atan. "Shall we start our studies again? Only not just us. Senrid, you've met. Tsauderei tells me that Jilo is interested, and in desperate need of light magic guidance. I think that kind of help is exactly what the alliance is for. Also, I think you'll like Leander Tlennen-Hess. He loves history, especially how language forms and changes. And he knows as much magic as either of us."

"Study," Atan said, "is exactly what I need. Shall we go find them?"

At first Atan was distracted by the chiseled beauty of the green-eyed, dark-haired Leander Tlennen-Hess. His manner reminded her of Arthur: scholarly, a little absent about his environment. He has no idea how beautiful he is, she thought, and turned to the sallow, awkward Jilo so Leander wouldn't think she was staring.

Though Jilo didn't talk, he soaked in every word of that first discussion.

The day after that, Hibern brought Clair, who was quiet, polite, and burning with interest.

The study group was a success beyond Hibern's hopes. After a shy first day, except for silent, listening Jilo, they began talking so fast their words tumbled over one another as they flung history and magic record citations at one another to bolster their admitted lack of experience. Hibern rejoiced when she saw Atan leaning forward, elbows on knees, arguing with Senrid.

Senrid enjoyed it, too. He considered giving mornings to the study group, but Tsauderei's library seemed to be mainly composed of musty old tomes. Senrid's primary motivation was to research Erdrael, but he hated the thought of anyone discovering what he was doing and asking nosy questions.

Since it sounded like the mages were planning to dispense the antidote to the Siamis spell soon, he would take a short leave from magic studies.

Over the next few mornings, he flew down early to drill with the orphans. By now he was convinced that Derek's double-stick form was a variant of the ancient Marloven plains's snap-staff fighting, an artifact of Inda-Harskialdna's seafaring days. He kept that to himself, and continued to stay in back so he could observe better. But he couldn't hide how well he moved, after all his years of drill in close-in fighting with knives.

Derek, experienced enough now to spot military training, was as interested in Senrid as the latter was in Derek. At the end of the week, on a warmer-than-usual morning, Derek dismissed the brigade early. They promptly stampeded to swim in the lake.

Senrid was going to go with them. Like most Marlovens, any swimming he got was in rivers or ponds at the height of summer, and that rarely. The lake was almost as good as flying.

But when Derek said, "I have some questions," Senrid's interest sharpened.

"So do I," he said. Swimming could wait.

They flew up to sit on the emerald grasses beside one of the two waterfalls filling the lake, under the shade of resiny-smelling, soughing pine.

Derek said, "Ask away!" He proved to be very ready to talk about Kessler Sonscarna's assassination training camp. Senrid learned that Derek had not been abducted, like Puddlenose and Rel—he'd actually been recruited. "I was seventeen, and I thought it was a perfect plan," Derek admitted, the residue of his fanatical fervor bombarding Senrid on the mental plane. "Promotion through pure merit, not birth! The world would be far better, would it not?" he asked mockingly, and then laughed somewhat bitterly.

The problem came when Derek had found himself being promoted rapidly (he had to be a natural leader, Senrid thought, remembering Keriam's lessons on the subject), and of course his popularity was his downfall.

Derek bitterly and lengthily described being set up for betrayal by Kessler's trusted lieutenant, the near execution, and then CJ's intervention.

"Wait. CJ was there? In a military camp?"

Derek nodded. "All of them. Except the white-haired one, who later broke Dejain's magic. Kessler made no distinction between boys and girls, and the younger the better. Fewer bad habits to be trained out of, so he said. He favored the Mearsieans because the King of the Chwahir hated them. There was even a rumor that Kessler wanted to make CJ his heir. But Kessler's second in command, a nasty piece of work who'd called himself Alsais, took against anyone Kessler favored. When she was supposed to prove herself by assassinating the white-haired girl, the Mearsieans disrupted the deployment by interfering with Dejain's magical business—and then Dejain turned on Kessler. That boy they call Puddlenose went for Alsais," he finished up. "Near as I can tell, he got him, too."

Senrid whistled. No wonder easy-going Puddlenose had never talked about that experience.

Part of Derek's gift for leading was understanding that you give before you demand. Senrid saw this, appreciated it, and let himself talk more than he might have when Derek began his own questions. Especially when Derek didn't react with disgust or distrust at the word 'Marloven.'

"That is exactly what Sarendan needs," Derek exclaimed after Senrid described the academy. "Under the old king, they only studied for a season, then they spent the summer playing games."

"Wargames have purpose," Senrid said.

Derek waved a hand. "The way you describe, yes. Without a horde of servants to do all the actual work."

Senrid grinned. "We train people to be self-sufficient because there were never servants on the battlefield. At least, in our ballads, nobody holds up his hand and declares, 'Wait,' to his enemy. 'I need to send someone to fetch my second-best hat.'"

Derek slapped his knee and laughed. "Oh, yes, this is exactly what we need here in Sarendan. I trust we can come to some arrangement, as soon as we rid ourselves of these soul-suckers."

Senrid thought to himself that Retren Forthan would probably love to come work with Derek, and adapt some basic training for Sarendan's infant army to use—Senrid assumed he was talking to a fellow monarch, though Derek thought he was talking to a Marloven academy trainee.

As he flew away, Senrid reflected back, puzzled. He knew there'd been a revolution in Sarendan. Only if Derek was the new king, then who was the anchor for Siamis's enchantment?

Chapter Ten

Off the coast of Drael

WHEN Christoph was a youth in a very small part of Flanders, before the turn of the eighteenth century, he'd learned a motto: *carpe diem*, or 'seize the day.'

A brush with death resulting in a trip through the worldgate had strengthened this attitude. There were mysteries unexplained at work in a universe that he could not understand. So why try? His next brush with death might hurl him into yet another world, or it might smite his body into the four elements and his soul into the ethereal, a prospect that seemed almost as mysterious.

Life therefore was for having as much fun as one could, and on this world, he'd found the next thing to a brother in Puddlenose of the Mearsieans, whom he'd met on his travels. They began traveling together, sharing similar tastes in food, tastes in jokes, tastes for comfortable surroundings with people who knew how to laugh. They talked about everything except serious things. Sometimes they talked around serious things, though never for long. He was fine with that.

They were fresh from one of their favorite midsummer

festivals, having discovered the Mearsiean privateer *Tzasilia* in Breis's harbor, off The Fangs at the northeast corner of the long Sartoran continent.

Captain Heraford had promptly hauled Puddlenose along on errands as a convenient message runner, telling Christoph to report on board. Having tossed his knapsack onto a hammock, Christoph was up on deck enjoying the brisk breeze in the sunshine, and regaling his friends among the crew with their recent adventures. ". . . and if the prentices win the games, see, then they get to command their masters. I assure you, there is no finer sight than a parcel of windbag city aldermen having to hop to the meeting hall on one foot, hooting like owls—"

Heads turned, gazes shifting beyond Christoph, who abandoned his tale to see what caught their attention. On the quay adjacent to their pier someone was shoving through the crowd of lounging mariners, passengers, workers, pie-sellers, pickpockets, and patrollers, judging by the way people staggered, jumped, and dropped things; in the wake of the force burrowing its way faint shouts of protest rose.

The crowd boiled, parted, and . . . it was Puddlenose shoving everyone aside, and running at top speed. Puddlenose bounded up the ramp, skirting a line of dock workers bearing the last of the supplies to stow in the hold.

Puddlenose rarely moved faster than a slope-shouldered amble, except when confronted with three circumstances. One was war, and the second and third were persons who happened to be related, though they would kill one another if they could: Wan-Edhe of the Chwahir, and Kessler Sonscarna, his grandson, or grandnephew, or whatever-he-was.

"Uh-oh," Christoph said under his breath.

Puddlenose spotted Christoph's sturdy form and sun-bleached hair.

He galloped straight to him, then leaned over, hands on his knees as he fought for breath. "Kessler." He expelled the word like a curse. "Sure it was him. Description matches, black short hair, pale eyes, black clothes. Wiry build. On some kind of ship with a weird bow. Leading a fleet of five. Weird tree on the foremast sails." He flung a hand upright, hooking the fingers like a dragon prow.

"Everyone's talking about it. Passed outside two days ago, heading north. Should have reached The Fangs by now."

Christoph said, "Wasn't that the same kind of ship that everyone said brought Henerek and the eleveners to attack Everon?"

Puddlenose didn't wait for an answer. "We've got to warn Everon."

Captain Heraford, a weathered man, spare of form, had been right behind Puddlenose. He looked from one boy to the other. "Clair gave you one of those notecases. Now would be the time to use it."

"Lost it." Puddlenose grimaced. "And you know Rel. Travels light."

The captain gave a short nod. "Take the boat," he said. "We'll meet up later."

Off the coast of Everon

"What do you fight for?"

Kessler leaned against the taffrail next to Luka Orm, the captain of the *Grebe's Crest*, his fingers in reach of one of his knives.

It had been a fast, smooth journey, and he liked the taciturn Venn, even if he didn't understand all that about Venn Doom and damnation. But if this man thought for a heartbeat that Kessler must sustain interrogation before he and his command would be put ashore, he'd kill the man right now, heave him over the side, and take the ships. It wouldn't be easy, but he had no doubt he could do it.

"What do you fight for?" Orm said again, his eyes a paler shade of blue than Kessler's own. Strange, how little they had in common, and yet there was that, and the familiar smell of fish in vinegar, a staple in coastal Chwahirsland. He hadn't eaten it since he'd run from Wan-Edhe, but he remembered the shore villagers who had sheltered him and fed him before he'd managed to escape . . .

A fine splash of spray brought his thoughts back.

"You do not answer. It is orders, then?" Orm persisted. "You do not think beyond orders?"

"They don't think beyond." Kessler tipped his chin toward the foredeck, where his warriors drilled by turn. One command—no more than a raised fist—and they'd turn on the Venn sailors.

"This is why they chose Norsunder to cleave to, because they do not think?"

"Norsunder chose us," Kessler retorted. But that veered too near the personal, so he said, "Many of them like to fight. Most of them like to kill. At least half were adjudged criminals before some court or other, given stone spells and planted in a Court of Shame."

"A what?"

"Ah, that's right, you come from the old Venn," Kessler said with a sardonic twist to his mouth. "You either killed your criminals, or put iron torcs around their necks and made them into thralls. Well, you will discover as you travel about in this enlightened time—" His teeth showed on the word 'enlightened.' "You will discover that in the interim, many kingdoms conceived a way to deal with violent criminals tried and convicted: put a stone spell on them that would last for a century and set them in a Garden of Shame, as a reminder to the rest of the populace. These Gardens of Shame have gone out of fashion in most places. You can still find them here and there. Norsunder mages recruited by releasing the stone spell and then using an enchanted knife to cut the recruits. Bind them by their own blood." *Like me.* "Such retain free will, but no free rein. Then there are the soul-bound, who are essentially dead, but their bodies kept alive by magic. I don't have any of the soul-bound to show you as example. They're obedient, but profoundly stupid."

Orm listened to the half-understood words, appalled. This was the result of oath-breaking. He must serve such a person.

To ward the question he could see in Orm's expression, Kessler said, "I'd like to take a look at your maps—your charts—again."

Brine dripped off the creaking ropes into Kessler's face, stinging his eyes as they made their way down to the captain's cabin. Orm spread out the chart that displayed the right-hand side of the continent of Drael. Kessler took a moment to appreciate the complication of navigational lines that the Venn had apparently used by magic, and overlaid on these, in different colors, beautiful lines showing the track of the sun in different seasons. It was by these that this captain now navigated, bringing them in sight of The Fangs, off Chwahirsland.

Orm ventured a remark. "Our Drenga would land with the sun behind them. If your enemy is surprised, he cannot count you."

Kessler gave a short nod. Surprise was unlikely. But he would never waste an advantage. "I always fight with the sun behind me if I can. How long before we reach Everon's harbor?"

Luka Orm glanced up at the bulkheads as if he could see the sky and smell the air. "With this wind, some days. Unless it changes to aid us." Then he proceeded to what was most important to him. "We are agreed, then. We have kept our bargain. You will tell your commanders this? We land you at the time and place you wish, and go our way."

Kessler's mouth tightened on the word 'commanders' but he said, "You get us there. Then, as far as I'm concerned, you are on your own."

Captain Heraford's 'boat' was a tender, built for speed.

While Christoph had no liking for Prince Glenn of Everon, he understood the need to warn the king, and he was not about to let Puddlenose sail alone. It took at least two to handle the tender. They traded off sailing and sleeping, scudding before the friendly summer winds sweeping down the strait out of the west.

It was this same wind that caused the Venn ships to tack and tack again, fighting their way northwest toward Drael.

The boys caught up by the second day, and trailed the fleet with reefed sail until well into the night. Dousing their lanterns, they sped silently by as far away as they could while still being able to watch through their field glasses. As it was, all they could see were tiny figures moving about on the deck, and blocking the golden pinpoints of light in the scuttles belowdecks. There seemed to be a lot of people on board.

They'd nearly given up when a sail being changed briefly silhouetted a slight masculine figure who otherwise would have been completely invisible in the gloom. He stood on the captain's deck, at the rail—

Christoph gasped. "He's watching us!"

Puddlenose shrugged. "So? He can't see us any better than we can see him."

"It's Kessler. I'll never forget that silhouette, standing at the top of the dungeon entrance."

"Yeah, but would he recognize us, on this tiny thing? Out of all the people he threw in his dungeon?"

They each tried to convince the other as well as themselves that Kessler couldn't see them, but both were relieved when the ship sank beyond the horizon, leaving them alone under the peaceful summer sky.

The wafting night breezes strengthened into the winds of oncoming weather by morning, bringing up gray, heaving seas with frothy whitecaps. Rejoicing—those big three-masters would lug with the wind directly on their forward beam—the boys felt the tender come alive, surging and plunging into the waves as the taut sail vibrated overhead.

They reached the Everoneth harbor late that night, which looked ruined through the glass. So they bypassed it in favor of one of the smaller coves farther north. They drew into the shallow waters, bowsed the tender up tight, and dragged sea wrack onto the narrow stern in hopes it would remain invisible from the sea.

Then they waded ashore, and grimly toiled up the vertical palisades. As they climbed, they tried to figure out where to go first: up the river to the capital, or the short way to the harbor? But what if the Norsundrians held it?

They were still arguing when they topped the palisade at last, as early dawn light spilled like milk along the horizon behind them. Around a grove of cedar rode a patrol of Knights. The boys dove behind a tangle of flowering vines at the sound of horse hooves, but the sight of the patrol brought them out again, waving and yelling.

After a short exchange, the patrol leader sent Puddlenose with a fast escort toward the capital, and took Christoph up behind her to report to her captain at the harbor.

Puddlenose and his escort reached Ferdrian as the sun set. By then he was nearly fainting with hunger, not having eaten since a scanty meal of stale bread the day before.

The Knights took him straight to King Berthold, who glanced at Puddlenose, red-eyed and fighting yawns. "Whatever it is can wait. You need food and rest."

"No it can't," Puddlenose said, propping his shoulders against a wall in spite of the scandalized glances of the more correct of the two ever-present bodyguards. "Kessler is coming."

"Who?"

Puddlenose groped for words, not knowing where to start.

The king turned to his steward. "Get something hot into him."

Puddlenose was too weary to protest.

By the time he'd wolfed down a substantial meal, he was nearly falling asleep at the table. He sat back, gazing heavy-eyed at the pattern of twined leaves and flowers carved under the ceiling, until familiar voices roused him. He sat upright as the king walked into the dining room, with Christoph and Rel in tow, both mud-splashed to the eyebrows, Rel having been posted to the retaken harbor as a courier, and subsequently tasked to bring Christoph.

The king said, "Now, let us begin again. Who is coming?"

"Kessler Sonscarna," Rel and Puddlenose said at the same time.

Rel added, with a hand turned toward Puddlenose then toward Christoph, "At least, they're pretty sure."

"I saw him," Puddlenose stated. "We both did." A thumb at Christoph, who nodded, his mouth full of pastry. "Yes, it was dark, and the ships were far apart. But I know it was him. I will never forget that silhouette."

Rel agreed with a "Yes," on an outgoing breath.

King Berthold gazed from one to the next. He could not recollect ever seeing Puddlenose serious. "Who is this man? Sonscarna, the 'ssler,' it all sounds Chwahir."

"He is. He wanted to take over the world," Puddlenose said.

King Berthold burst out laughing, but when he saw no corresponding smile in his guests, he looked askance. "You cannot mean to tell me he had a chance."

"He's crazy, but his plan might have worked. For a time." Puddlenose was taken by a sudden yawn. "Rel, explain." He blinked watery eyes.

"Kessler's plan was not to invade with armies. He trained assassins to take out kings—"

King Berthold interrupted, his expression genial. "Who would he put in these dead kings' place? Himself, of course. From where did he plan to rule this empire, or would he hop about as the sun moves?" The king leaned against the table, his silken tabard gleaming in the rich candlelight.

Puddlenose thoughtfully moved a plate of butter away from a careless fold of that silk.

Rel said, "No, he planned to place people on thrones who had demonstrated merit. By his standard."

"Since I never heard about it, I take it he failed." King Berthold laughed indulgently. "Then he couldn't have been very smart, eh? Or let us say, not very experienced? How old is this prodigy?"

Rel said reluctantly, "Not much older than I am."

And watched the king smile and shake his head. "So this formidable world-conqueror is coming by ship as well? Do you think he'll attack the harbor, or will his highly trained teams land along the coast and scramble up the palisades like spiders?"

The king got his expected chuckles from his attendants, and not all of those were obsequious, but when he saw the stolidity in the three faces before him, especially Puddlenose, who was always first with a joke, he relented.

"You came at great cost to warn me, and I will not forget that. Boys, get some rest. You earned it. Rel, return to the harbor in the morning. It's late, and isn't that thunder in the distance? Yes, morning will do. Tell Captain Berneth to send scouts within line of sight along the coast in both directions, equipped with those magic rings. And tell him what you know about this Kessler Sonscarna, so that he may provide a suitable welcome. Will that do?"

Perforce the boys agreed.

The king then turned to one of the equerries behind

him. "I want you to apprise Commander Dei, and tell him to be prepared for Henerek to be attacking the harbor from landward, in support of the newcomer. That is probably our biggest worry."

Rel couldn't sleep.

He tried. Ordinarily he slept through thunderstorms with no problem. But every flash jolted him from sinking below the surface of constant thought into the dream world of deep sleep. And each jolt was welcome, because he knew that what lay in wait in those depths were not dreams but nightmares forming around memories of the days cooped in an underground cell with Puddlenose and Christoph, waiting for death as they listened to the cadences and clashings of steel as Kessler trained his assassins.

When the storm lifted, leaving the air outside his windows a musical concert of drips, Rel got up and dressed. Being a scout and courier for the Knights, he had access to horses whenever he wanted; rather than rouse up sleepy stable hands, he chose one he was familiar with, strong enough to easily bear his size for a long ride. He saddled up and set out under the full moon high in the sky.

He chased the storm eastward, gradually catching up until the starry sky gave way to a thick layer of clouds that made it seem he would forever ride in semi-darkness.

He was tired enough to be unaware of the time after he'd changed his third horse. It wasn't until he crested a hill and saw the bright glow in the east that he thought gratefully, sunrise at last.

But wait. As the horse slowed, ears alert, head tossing, Rel caught up mentally. Sunrise was long past, he just hadn't noticed the gradual lightening under the gray overcast.

So what was that glow above the harbor?

He clucked at the horse, urgency burning the lassitude from his tired body. The horse pranced nervously, ears twitching, nostrils spread. She snorted explosively. Rel couldn't see anything wrong. He snapped his legs to her sides, and she plunged forward, her gait jerky, ears flattening. When they rounded a curve, Rel stared down into the valley emptying into the river above the harbor, and made out a massive column of brown smoke pushing up against the undersides of the clouds. Flame glowed the entire length of the harbor.

Smoke. That was what the horse smelled, the scent still too far away for Rel to catch, as the wind was at his back.

The horse turned in a circle, fretting; Rel was trying to decide what to do when a couple of horsemen bore down from either direction. He wheeled his mare and kicked her sides, but she was too tired to outrun pursuit, and Rel was surrounded.

One Norsundrian caught the bridle, and the other leveled a crossbow at Rel, who sat back, hands raised, his heartbeat thundering.

"You're wanted," one said in Sartoran, rather than the Fer Sartoran dialect spoken in Everon. That meant they knew he was not a local.

Rel sighed. He hadn't so much as looked right or left in the past few hours. Of course he had been spotted. The worrisome aspect was the possibility he was recognized.

A short ride later, they crested the last hill before the harbor, from which he could see most of the surrounding countryside. They reached a makeshift camp, no more than a fire and bedrolls piled beside a string of horses being saddled. A force of maybe forty sat on rocks or the ground, eating from shallow travel pans as a faint whiff of wild onion carried on the air.

The biggest two of Rel's captors closed in on either side, and all three horses walked a little ways beyond the camp to where a familiar slim, taut figure stood. Sick with helpless fury, Rel recognized Kessler Sonscarna, who stood at the edge of the cliff, sweeping the land with a glass.

At the sound of hoof beats thudding in the turf he turned, and when he recognized Rel, he said, "Ah." He made a quick gesture with two fingers, and Rel's captors turned away, leaving Rel still mounted on his horse, his sword untouched in the saddle sheath.

"You joined the Knights?" Kessler asked, looking interested, the faint orange glow from the distant fires sidelighting the planed bones of his face, the heavy-lidded eyes that were shaped so unsettlingly like Atan's.

"I'm serving as a scout," Rel said.

"And so you rode to the capital to report my landing to Berthold? No, that couldn't have been you on the little boat. Never mind. Whatever orders you bear are immaterial. They're all dead." Kessler jerked his thumb over his shoulder at the harbor.

Rel's throat closed, rendering him unable to speak.

Kessler's lips curved in a humorless smile. "Henerek has run out of time. So they sent me."

Rel fought against shock. "He's no longer in command?"

"He has other things to occupy him right now. Like a broken knee, a fractured jaw, and a set of cracked ribs. He objected to my taking over the command, so I gave him something else to think about."

Rel remembered Henerek: big, husky, brutal. He stared down at Kessler, short, slight, but made of solid muscle.

Kessler's soft, slightly husky voice changed to that reasonable tone he'd always used at his maddest. "The fastest way to clean up his failure is to burn my way to the capital. Put anyone who gets in my way to the sword."

Rel's fury congealed to dread. He knew Kessler would do it without any hesitation.

Kessler ran a hand through his short, curly hair. "Slaughtering civs is boring. There's no sport in it. But some of them think otherwise." He tipped his head toward the camp a few paces away, where Norsundrians went about finishing their morning meal as if nothing had happened.

No, that wasn't quite right. Rel heard the sharpness of tone, the cracking laughter of after-action triumph. Anticipation.

Kessler took a step nearer, and lifted his hand back toward the road. "Run." He swatted the shivering mare's hindquarters.

The horse leaped into a gallop, nearly unseating Rel. As he clutched at the reins, he heard raucous laughter rising behind him.

Rel's dread sharpened to terror, no longer for himself, but for the unheeding people along the east-west road. Kessler never made idle threats, or exaggerated. When he said he was going to burn his way to the capital, he was going to do just that.

Rel didn't waste time trying to figure out why Kessler

would tell him, much less save his life. It had to be some kind of game, or contest, or challenge he was playing with the Norsundrians who commanded him—Rel knew that Kessler had not gone to Norsunder willingly.

None of that mattered. What did was getting the word out, as fast as possible.

The royal roads were straighter than the old, civilian roads that wound around hills alongside meandering streams, and circumvented ancient borders. The royal roads tended to avoid villages and towns, whose traffic would slow up couriers.

So Rel turned off the royal road and watched ceaselessly for the first sign of civilization. When he spotted farmland, he left the road and kept his tired horse at her best speed until he came across a small hamlet alongside a river. He dismounted and banged on every door, and when disgruntled people came out with questions and demands, he pointed to the smoke cloud in the east, and said, "They're coming. *Now*."

In a short time he'd borrowed a fresh horse from someone with animals to spare, who offered to keep the mare from the royal stable with her.

An old baker pointed out the road—not much more than a wheel-rutted path—to the next town, and Rel took off at a gallop, leaving people scurrying to pack what they could, gather their livestock, and head deeper into the hills. He forgot them within moments, goaded by the ghost of Kessler's voiceless laughter.

He crossed three streams, then rode down into a river valley as a rainstorm passed overhead. He forded the slow-moving waters and surged up the riverbank toward the cluster of buildings on the other side.

His new mount, a young stallion, splashed dramatically through puddles into the square, tail high even after that long run.

Rel gathered what strength he had left and bellowed, "Fire!"

A couple of apprentices busy carrying display tables outside paused to laugh. Everyone else, shopkeepers, customers, strollers, stopped what they were doing, with various expressions, hope for entertainment foremost.

Rel tightened his middle and lifted his hoarse voice. "Norsunder has burned the harbor, and they are going to fire their way to the capital. That means you are next. If you don't believe me, climb on the roof of the highest house, and look toward the sea."

His horse circled, head tossing and ears twitching.

Faces changed as the two teenage upholstery prentices dropped their samples onto the display tables and raced one another up either side of the carved supports holding up their awning.

Gathering villagers watched the boys clamber over the gabled windows upstairs, then one boosted the other to the roof, the first reaching to pull his friend up behind him. A clattering of loose tiles, and the two reached the ridgepole.

"He's right!" One boy yelled, his voice cracking. "Smoke all across the sky!"

Voices rose, a couple of worried shouts. Rel cut across them all. "I'm riding to the capital. Send someone to warn your neighboring villages!" He pointed south and north, then nudged the stallion, and rode on.

Chapter Eleven

Delfina Valley

TSAUDEREI would later reflect that it was inevitable that the secret of the antidote to Siamis's spell would get out—and it was probably as equally inevitable that it would be Derek who spread it.

After a week of drill with the orphans, followed by chat with Derek over breakfast, Senrid discovered he was wrong in his assumption that Derek was a king when Derek, fretting over how the days were dragging by and nothing was being done to rescue Sarendan from the enchantment, confided to Senrid the promise he'd made to Peitar.

Thunder rumbled over the distant peaks as Derek and Senrid floated high over the lake, which rippled below, a deep, stormy gray-blue. "Peitar is my oldest friend, better than a mere king," Derek said suddenly, startling Senrid. "He'd put the orphans' lives above his own, if he knew what was going on. I've got to find a way back down the mountain so I can rescue them before the mages get around to breaking the spell on Peitar."

Senrid hesitated, aware that he had the wherewithal to

help Derek do both. He wanted to help Derek, who was the kind of person he admired most—fearless, loyal without being sickening about it, always looking to improve, because it was the only way to fight Norsunder.

"Wouldn't Tsauderei be the one to talk to about that?" Senrid asked, hedging.

"Did." Derek shrugged, then stretched his arms over his head and swooped downward, his long, tangled brown hair flagging in the wind. "He's a mage," Derek said over his shoulder as Senrid dove after him. "They jaw on about how they study for years, but all they seem to talk about is caution, watchfulness, and doing nothing."

Senrid wished that Detlev would do nothing, remembering that *You will not see me coming.* Disgust made him fly faster. He hated whining, including in his own thoughts. "Tsauderei has tough wards," he shouted against the wind. "Nobody is going to get in or out without him knowing, unless he's away."

"He goes out a couple times a week," Derek said, swooping close enough for Senrid to see the honest frustration narrowing his brown eyes. "All I need to do is get to Miraleste, grab the youngsters most important to Peitar, and bring them back. I even have a casket of transfer tokens to get them back here. One for each."

Senrid struggled, reminded himself that he had made a promise, and said, "I'll talk to Hibern and Leander."

Derek heard that as agreement.

Senrid saw his chance when everyone broke for lunch before the big tag game the Mearsieans had organized for the afternoon. The study group—Atan, Hibern, Jilo, Leander, Senrid, and sometimes Clair—were picnicking on the roof of Selenna House, because eating on a rooftop was more fun than eating in Atan's gloomy cottage, especially in the bright sunshine and cool breeze, with interesting cloud towers piling up in the west.

Senrid gathered Hibern and Leander with a glance, and flew down to the boys' room in Selenna house. They streamed through the open window. Leander dropped onto his bed, Hibern sat on the edge of Jilo's, and Senrid shot into the hammock as he explained his conversation with Derek.

At the end, Leander said, "I don't get what you're asking."

"It's simple enough. Derek wants to transfer down into Sarendan to break the enchantment over some kids he's sort of guardian for. It would be so easy to help him. Transfer tokens, to and from, he knows the specific locations so we can use that as Destination, in and out."

"How many?" Leander asked doubtfully.

Hibern shook her head. "Didn't we agree—"

"Less than a dozen." A shadow appeared at the window a moment before Derek did.

The three started, Senrid annoyed at his own lack of awareness. But if anyone had the right to nose into this conversation, Derek did.

Then Derek said, "I knew it. I *knew* you had the means to break that damned enchantment. This is why I hate mages, doing absolutely nothing for selfish reasons."

Hibern said, "It's not selfish to wait to see if Norsunder retaliates against *entire kingdoms* after the enchantment is lifted. The antidote is new, so new we don't know if there is other magic we have to watch for."

"I'm not suggesting you mess with entire kingdoms," Derek shot back. "I'm talking about fewer than a dozen boys and girls. None of whom Norsunder has ever heard of."

Senrid looked at Leander, who was smart, dedicated, but a lighter through and through. Leander was clearly hesitating.

Hibern said slowly, "I'd like to rescue a dozen people of any age. But . . ."

"There's no but about it," Derek said. "I can't believe Norsunder mages would put a lot of extra spells on the children of boot-makers and fisherfolk." He added quickly, "I understand old—that is, Tsauderei has a lot of other concerns. He's worried about kings and kingdoms. Rightly so. I'm just talking about a dozen youngsters I was responsible for—and who were lost when I came up here and fell asleep. Sometimes I want to cut my own throat because of my stupidity," he added ferociously.

Senrid certainly understood that, and the other two saw in Derek's face that if he wasn't going to act on his own yet, he was close to it.

Hibern sighed. "Give me one day. Will you? I want to talk out magical problems that I might not see."

"Not Tsauderei," Derek said. "You know he'll nail you down for your own good."

"I was thinking of someone else," Hibern said, and because Derek was still there, blocking the window, she slid off the bed and opened the door.

She left Selenna House, shot into the air, and bypassed a swarm gathering for the tag game to head for Atan's cottage. She found Atan there alone, not interested in tag. Atan had three books spread before her, but she set the one she was reading aside when Hibern entered.

Hibern sat down and, having ordered her thoughts during her flight, began to explain.

Hibern's nightmares usually fell into two categories. There were the nightmares about her home, and then there were the ones where she would be stuck in mud, or weighed down some way, and somehow the more she labored, the less success she had. The harder she strove to explain, the more angry Atan looked, until Hibern—aware that she had repeated herself at least twice—said helplessly, "I guess I'm not explaining well."

Atan had been struggling to keep her temper in check. But at this invitation, she burst out, "Oh, you've explained quite well! You know, all of you know, how to lift that enchantment, and you kept silent?"

Hibern stared in shock. "But we promised."

"Didn't you think *I* could keep a promise?" Atan shot back.

"Of course," Hibern said. "That was never a question. But I don't think anyone believed it would help you to know you had the antidote, but couldn't use it. Sartor would be the first place Norsunder would lay lethal spells, surely you see that? I think everyone assumed it would be better if you didn't know, until it could actually be used."

"How is that better?" Atan cried.

Hibern was so shocked she stared back, hot tears blurring her eyes. She dashed them impatiently away with her sleeve, her throat tight. As she groped for words, Erai-Yanya's calm, practical voice whispered in memory, and she said slowly, "Maybe it's a fault in those of us who become mages. Erai-Yanya says we tend toward a type, the sort of person who prefers book things. Certainly every senior mage I know is single, if not an outright hermit. In fact, Erai-Yanya told me once that your Sartoran school had a reputation for selecting out mage students who showed an interest in political questions and moving them over to the scribes before they started using their magic to meddle in questions of state. You're thinking in terms of state, now."

"And you will no doubt tell me why that's bad?" Atan asked, eyes narrowing.

"It's not bad, it's . . . well, how much do you think your royal council would welcome a mage who was really interested in how kings get and keep their power?" Hibern asked.

It was a wild guess, barely connected, but she saw in how Atan's eyes widened that her stray thought had a powerful effect. "I think that's a fear every government has about mages," Atan said, in a subdued voice.

"So you can see that there are different ways of seeing the world, and trying to serve the world. Right now Erai-Yanya—well, no, she's at Geth-deles, but these others, they're seeing the possible *magical* threats. They can't think about political things. The Siamis enchantment is cruel, but it's not life-threatening, and no one is actually in pain, at least that's what Clair said."

"She knows?" Atan asked.

"Yes—she was the second one we freed, the first being Oalthoreh, who we knew would willingly sacrifice her life in case there were hidden lethal spells."

Atan's mouth thinned. "So the Mearsieans know about this spell, too?"

"Yes, but Murial made them promise not to speak of it, the same promise I had to make. And Leander, who I taught it to, in case something happened to me."

Atan's expression didn't ease, which worried Hibern a little. Atan was thinking that those irritating Mearsieans, out there laughing and playing tag, didn't think about the rest of the world, so long as *they* were all right.

But she didn't say it. There was no use in speaking resentful thoughts, as satisfying as it might feel. "All right, I get it. So Senrid wants to help Derek rescue a dozen children from the enchantment, to make things easier on Peitar. I think I can see it. I absolutely believe that Peitar would be grieved at any of his young friends being imprisoned by that magic a heartbeat longer than necessary. When is this going to happen?"

"Right away."

Atan said, "Why don't you bring the two boys. I want to hear what they have to say."

Relieved to escape, Hibern went to fetch Senrid and Leander, who were hovering on the edge of the tag game.

She passed Jilo, who was making his way to Atan's cottage in search of a book that Arthur had loaned him, that he'd left somewhere. As he went through the stacks, Atan slipped out and awaited the others in midair above her cottage, thinking how wonderful it was to be able to hold conferences in places where one could see in all directions, even beneath.

When Hibern returned with the two boys, Atan raked them all with those gooseberry Landis eyes and said abruptly, "Derek ought to have brought this up to Tsauderei, who is the person most concerned. In fact, I suspect he has, and was turned down."

Hibern said in surprise, "You think so? But why would Derek then turn to Senrid? Derek hates kings."

"For a while there I thought Derek was a king," Senrid said flippantly.

He expected them to laugh at him, but instead Atan's expression shuttered, and Hibern pursed her lips. He gave a mental shrug and went on. "Derek doesn't know who I am, only where I come from. He wants to keep his promise to his king friend, and grab those orphans of his. I don't see anything wrong with that, if we do it the same way we rescued Clair, checking for magical traps first."

Hibern took her bottom lip between her teeth, needing time to work out in her own mind whether or not teaching Senrid the antidote spell and standing by while he transferred with Derek into Sarendan would be considered a trespass against Erai-Yanya's and Murial's implied trust. Because on the positive side, it seemed a right action for the alliance.

She could see impatience in Senrid's face. He flung his hands wide. "It's not like it'll be a secret, now that Derek knows about it! We'll go, find the brats, and get out."

His expression changed as Leander, who faced the direction of Tsauderei's cottage on the other side of the Valley, pointed. "Is that . . ."

Two small figures emerged from Tsauderei's. As the group watched, the figures bobbed up and down, testing the flying spell. Then the taller one launched wildly into the air, arms and legs gyrating as he tried to figure out balance. The smaller figure was slower, limbs stiff.

From above the lake the tag game ended in a flock of girls zooming toward the newcomers, who resolved into Arthur, tousled and ink-splotched, and Liere, skinny as ever, her hair hacked off so unevenly above her ears that she was nearly bald on one side. Atan and her companions shot across the airy expanse to join them.

Senrid grimaced when he saw Liere. "Somebody's been calling her Sartora," he said under his breath.

A group of the orphan brigade followed. They'd been with the Mearsieans, trying to learn the rules of the complicated tag game the girls had invented. One urchin said in disbelief, "That's Sartora? Really? Somebody must have tortured her!"

CJ's fluting voice carried over all, calling happily, "Hi, Sartora! Does this mean we can go home now?"

Uh-oh. CJ had managed to say the worst thing possible, though it was clear that nobody knew that but Senrid.

Liere's first reaction to the warm, beautiful Valley and the prospect of flying had been thrill. But CJ's question struck hard, with all its expectation that Sartora had of course Saved The World once again.

"No," Liere said, hating her weakness.

CJ halted in the air, black hair flagging in the wind, her wide eyes as blue as the sky overhead. "Didn't you get rid of Siamis? Isn't that what you've been doing?"

"I've been hiding," Liere said, as all the kids pressed around her.

Senrid tried twice to get past them, then gave up as whispers and explanations rang outward.

CJ goggled, her amazement plain to those watching. Her sharp sense of disappointment, no, of betrayal, smote Liere mercilessly on the mental plane.

"Hiding? But . . . why? You saved the world before! Everyone's talking about Bereth Ferian, and Sartora, and—" CJ heard her own voice rising, and halted. Liere had once been a hero, the first world-renowned girl hero, but now she wasn't. It seemed disloyal to crab about it, but why hide when you've got all those mysterious mind powers?

Liere was going to explain about how she couldn't break the enchantment without the dyr, and she certainly couldn't flash from kingdom to kingdom without that strange being made of light, whom she had no idea how to summon, but at the looks on all those faces, her throat closed and she couldn't get past, "The mages thought I should hide . . ." She hated her bleating voice, and she stopped.

Aware of everyone staring, CJ forced herself to speak cheerfully. "We're going to play a big game of spy-versus-spy. Remember, we played it in Bereth Ferian, only this is going to be even better, because we're in the air!"

As if that served as a signal, everyone began clamoring around Liere, begging her to be on their side. Liere dreaded the inevitable discovery that she was terrible at games, and turned to find Senrid in the crowd, in time to catch sight of him and Leander flying off, talking earnestly.

Liere turned away, sick at heart at the intensity of CJ's sense of betrayal, which the girl had no notion Liere sensed. Liere loathed herself for a coward and a weakling, and she deserved all the disappointment and contempt she was going to get.

"Very well," she said, reaching out to the nearest hand. "Tell me the rules."

At last Senrid had a project, and it had nothing to do with Erdrael or ghosts. His restlessness eased as he threw himself into the tedium of creating transfer tokens, once they elicited exact descriptions from Derek for the location of the first rescue.

Leander had decided to go along with it because he knew Senrid, and suspected that if Senrid didn't have this rescue to work on, he might hare off and do something reckless and dangerous, if only to himself.

So they worked hard through the night, making transfer tokens for four. Leander was going along with Derek and

Senrid to demonstrate the antidote spell one more time. They left Jilo sitting alone in their room with the door blocked and the window shut and curtains closed, watching his book. It was Senrid's idea to lay tracer spells on the brass rings they were using as transfer tokens: if Jilo's book said that Siamis or Detlev had transferred into Sarendan, he'd use his ring to send a burst of illusory color to the rings worn by Leander and Senrid. They would all three transfer instantly out.

Their target lived in a village called Riverside, in the principality of Selenna. Derek had described a wooden bridge to use as a Destination, a bridge he knew well, as it had been a meeting place during the bad days before the revolution. They transferred, all three gasping as lowland summer's intensity enveloped them. Heat shimmered off the newly paved stones of the road on either side of the bridge, and broke sunlight into brilliant shards in the river running below the bridge.

"This way," Derek said, looking at the ground. He'd borrowed a battered hat from someone in the Valley, which he'd pulled low over his forehead. He wore a plain-spun thigh-length tunic-shirt, sashed with rope, and his usual saddle-worn riding trousers. Being a brown-haired, sun-browned young man, he looked anonymous enough with his face hidden.

Leander and Senrid took the lead as they tramped down the bridge into a village that seemed to be undergoing vast renovation. Cottages made of stone had been, or were being, freshly thatched, some subsequent to additions. Vegetable plots were framed by flower borders, and everywhere wild olive trees grew.

As in Mearsies Heili, people drifted through their days in eerie silence. The boys overheard no conversation, saw no innovation and no tempers good or bad.

All eyes would watch for whatever Siamis had commanded them, through the enchantment, to watch for.

Derek shuffled along behind the two boys as they crossed the square and then proceeded down a narrow lane bordered with berry shrubs.

"On the right," Derek whispered.

They stopped at a house indistinguishable from the others.

The kitchen door stood open. Inside, a woman kneaded bread with slow, absent movements. Leander and Senrid moved past her, blocking Derek from her view. Senrid held his breath as her absent gaze passed indifferently over him.

This enchantment might not look cruel, but he found it obscene, how effectively it wiped out all traces of individual thought and will.

The little hall opened into three small rooms, one of which contained a gangling boy with a rust-colored thatch of short hair. Derek's sudden smile made it clear they'd found Bren. Drawings and paintings covered all the walls, mostly village scenes of people working, dancing, eating. Celebrating. Bren sat on the bed, his hands loose. Drawing on paper, it seemed, did not come under the mandate of the enchantment, though it hurt Derek not to see Bren with chalk in hand, sketching his commentary on life at wall, eave, fence, door.

Leander had to look away from the drawings. The contrast between the papers full of joy, anger, interest, laughter, passion and this blank-faced boy clawed at his heart.

He glanced at Senrid, who leaned his shoulders against the door, blocking it. Derek took up a stance at the window to watch for danger from that angle. He kept his face averted; he couldn't bear to see Bren's slack expression stripped of all personality. It was too much like he was dead.

Leander whispered to Senrid, "You want to try?"

Senrid murmured, "I'll watch. One more time. Next one, I'll do."

Leander cast his eyes over the drawing table angled to catch the window's light, and found what he was looking for, a much-used nub of a drawing chalk.

He picked it up and held it out to Bren, saying in a low voice, "See it, Bren? This is your chalk. Take your chalk and draw a picture. Can you see it? Pick it up."

Bren's breathing changed. Then he stirred, as if some semblance of thought winked into life down deep under the smothering layers of magic.

"Do you know what that is?" Leander persisted.

Bren stirred again, his fingers flexing.

"Does this chalk belong to anyone?" Leander asked.

Bren's lips twitched. His hand made a vague grasping motion.

Now, Leander thought, and leaned close to whisper the spell.

Magic shimmered in the room, a quick, vague flash not unlike the reflection of light on water, and Derek instinctively turned around before Leander could finish the spell.

Bren blinked, his gaze widened, his face suffused with red, and he sucked in his breath and shouted a word.

"Get him out of here," Senrid ordered Leander sharply, and to Derek, "That was magic. Go!"

Leander finished the spell. Bren started, gasping and looking around wildly. "What did I do? What did I do?"

"This will get you to the Valley," Leander said, pressing a token into Bren's hand.

Bren jerked his head in a nod and they vanished, followed by Derek. With them safely gone, Senrid was about to use his token when he perceived the dark flicker in air that meant an incoming transfer. He looked at the ring. No Siamis. He could get away from anyone else. Why not see the result?

He flung himself into a corner and threw up an illusion a heartbeat before two Norsundrians appeared, the wind caused by all the transfers sending loose papers flying around.

The Norsundrians briefly scanned the room, their gazes moving past Senrid's corner, which he knew would appear vaguely shadowy as long as he didn't move. One stuck his head out the door; from his vantage, Senrid could make out the woman who kneaded bread.

"Gone. We'd better report," one said to the other.

They transferred away, and Senrid did as well.

In the Valley, the orphan brigade was delighted to welcome Bren. He was delighted to see them, and to return to Selenna House, but as soon as he understood that he'd been enchanted, he looked around anxiously at the unfamiliar faces, and his joy diminished.

"Where's Lilah? Where's Peitar?" When he saw Derek looking to one side, Bren's shoulders slumped. "You got me first."

Derek beckoned, and they flew away in low-voiced conversation.

Tsauderei returned from Mondros's plateau on Chwahirsland's border to find Arthur deep in one of his books, as usual. But he wasn't alone. Hibern was there, waiting.

Hibern cast a glance at Arthur, who was obviously lost to the world. So she lowered her voice and gave Tsauderei a succinct report about the breaking of the antidote spell secret, and the first rescue.

"I should have foreseen it," Tsauderei said when she was done. "Derek, obsessed with his version of making things right, and dismissing the necessity for keeping silent about that antidote spell. And Senrid plunging right in." He sank into his chair, his brow furrowed. Finally he looked up. "I didn't want to warn Derek that if Siamis gets hold of him, he could easily layer an enchantment over him."

"Why not? Surely that would give him pause."

"I'm beginning to wonder if that spell of Siamis's can be altered to take advantage of people's natures. You may have noticed that Siamis did not bother to order Peitar to form up an army. But Derek? What if Siamis could order Derek to lead all Sarendan against Colend? Even if he listened to my conjecture, for we have more truce than trust, I don't think he'd believe me. He's more likely to scoff about the weakness of magic, and declare he could outthink a mere Norsundrian, but might there be a spark of, oh, let us call it ambivalence? It's been plain to me for several years that Derek is happiest when leading a crusade, and of late he's fallen in love with military might."

"Oh," Hibern said, her stomach lurching. "Should I tell Senrid? He and Derek have become such friends."

Tsauderei let out a deep sigh, his gnarled fingers absently tracing the line of his mustache. He said at length, "Your friend Senrid hasn't spoken ten words to me since his arrival, so I cannot answer that."

Hibern got up from her chair. "I think I know what to do."

"I wish I did," Tsauderei said, but after she'd left.

Chapter Twelve

LIERE liked flying with Hibern and Senrid.

It was quiet. Peaceful. She could enjoy the wind through the pines, the way their branches were in constant rippling movement, like an emerald-green sea. She loved the glinting stripes of muted color in the tumbled rocks, some as big as houses. She loved the towering mountains in the distance, crowned by never-melting snows reflecting the colors of dawn and sunset, for she came out at both times just to watch the change of the sky and the way the land woke up and then shrouded itself at the end of the long summer's day.

She liked the fact that Hibern and Senrid remembered mind-shields, so she was alone with her own thoughts without having to concentrate on shutting others out.

By gritting through morning flights on her own, Hibern had conquered her fear of heights—at least while flying—and had come to love soaring around the lake at the prettiest time of day.

The morning after the rescue of Bren, Senrid told Liere the details, since everybody was now talking about how the enchantment could be broken. Liere had already heard about the rescue the night before, as the orphan brigade made much of Bren. They seemed to admire him almost as much as they admired Derek.

"We decided to wait a day, then go back for the next one," Senrid finished.

"There are more?" Hibern asked.

"Ten."

"Can it be done without Derek along?"

Senrid's sharp "Why?" caught Liere's attention as Senrid shot a considering glance Hibern's way. Then he said, "You're thinking there might be people on the watch for him. Derek being some kind of commander. Though, hoo, he's kind of like one of our academy first-year seniors, from what I can see. You know, pretty fast, really enthusiastic, but he thinks he knows more than he does. Of course, so do I, but—"

Hibern sighed. "I know, I know, I've heard you before about how Commander Keriam says the worst of ignorance is not knowing how ignorant you are. I have no interest in your war blabber. None."

Senrid assumed an air of injured dignity. "I wasn't going to quote Keriam." He dropped the manner. "I was going to say that Derek does know the risks, but as it's only himself—"

"But it isn't." Hibern flew backward, her long black hair snaking around her sides as she held out her arms to balance herself. To Liere, she looked like an eagle, with her fingers outspread and her sleeves snapping, and her blue robe flagging like tail feathers.

Liere said into the silence, "You said Derek is some kind of commander. If people are loyal to him . . ."

"I hadn't thought of that," Senrid admitted. "But Sarendan is already enchanted. Do you think nailing a second leader intensifies the enchantment? Damn, that's vicious."

"When it comes to evil," Hibern stated, "don't underestimate Siamis."

Senrid waved that off, then flipped around to fly face up, eyes closed against the sun. "I'm going to remind Derek of that. I'll wager Tsauderei would agree. Maybe it's time to talk to him. I know he knows what we've been doing—"

"Yes," Hibern said cordially.

Senrid flashed a quick grin. "Well, and he hasn't hauled

us in to shake fingers in our faces. Maybe Derek will agree that Leander and I ought to go alone." He opened his eyes. "In fact, I could go myself, after I see one more use of that spell. It'll give me something to do."

Hibern said, "But that goes for you, too. About enchanting leaders."

"Except that I've dispersed the army and academy," Senrid said. "And if I show up acting the least bit weird, Keriam has a token that will drop a stone spell on me. I'll be fine," he added with a hint of impatience, resenting the implication that he hadn't thought ahead.

Hibern said, "Senrid. If you get captured, and Siamis muscles you back to Marloven Hess and enchants you, then *they'll be enchanted too*. Keriam won't be *able* to drop that stone spell on you."

"Then I won't get caught," Senrid retorted. And looked askance. "I wonder if Dena Yeresbeth interferes with the enchantment. Anyway, I have a transfer token. The first I see of any Norsundrian, I rabbit."

Liere's heart squeezed. 'Something to do.' She'd wondered how soon Senrid was going to get bored playing those chase-and-tag games he was so good at. Her joy in playing had vanished that first day when she saw the others' surprise, or scarcely hid disappointment, at how bad she was at it.

She knew why Senrid was the best. No mystery there. After watching the academy boys play similar games ever since he was five, and reading everything he could about strategy and tactics because his kingdom—his life—depended on his knowing, he couldn't help but be better than a bunch of boys and girls who mostly just flew around hooting insults, or yelling orders at each other that no one paid any attention to.

Liere hadn't expected so much competition in games that everyone declared to be fun. She hated competition, especially when unspoken anger and spite and hatred streamed on the mental plane after certain people. It took so much concentration to shut it out, and she knew she shouldn't care, that caring was more evidence of her stupid emotions, which meant she deserved to feel rotten.

"Yep. I'm going to talk to them both." Senrid left.

Hibern was alone with Liere. Something that happened

rarely. So she said, "I know you don't like to talk about Dena Yeresbeth, but Atan keeps asking questions. I was wondering if you might answer them yourself."

The Queen of Sartor? Liere felt so shy around her. Somehow Atan's friendliness made it worse. But Liere said, "If you want," because her reaction was a stupid emotion, and she deserved to feel worse for not having controlled it.

When Liere and Hibern reached Atan's cottage, they found her deep in magical studies with Jilo, Clair listening closely.

Jilo flushed and fell silent at the entrance of the newcomers, but Atan said in a coaxing voice, "Go on, if you would. How exactly did you release the time bindings?"

"They aren't completely broken," Jilo mumbled, acutely self-conscious. "I don't know how to do that. Maybe no one can, outside of Wan-Edhe, because there are layers and layers. But I got it started by weakening the spells that used the life forces of the castle guards . . ."

Liere shuddered at this blithe mention of life forces being sucked out of living beings. No wonder Senrid was so impressed with awkward, limb-tangled Jilo—she could not imagine herself fighting single-handedly against such violently lethal magic.

Not long after, as the others went out to watch a thunderstorm, Liere sank down with her back to the windows. She was startled when Atan emerged out of the gloom. "Now that everyone is busy, may I trouble you with a question?"

"Of course," Liere said, biting back the 'your majesty.' Atan had made it plain that she wanted to be called Atan— that titles and honorifics hurt her especially now, when she had lost her kingdom—and she had never said 'Sartora' once. Which was more than Liere got from some of the others, who thought 'Sartora' was a wonderful honor, and that she should love it.

Atan said, "Someone said you can hear people thinking from far away."

"Only if I know them." Liere caught herself picking at her cuticles, and sat on her hands. "And if they don't have mind-shields."

"Oh yes! I forgot about that," Atan returned, looking away. "I apologize if any of my thoughts have been intrusive."

"I try to shut everybody out," Liere said. "But sometimes I get tired . . . well, anyway, I haven't heard yours."

Atan looked back, her expression somber. "Not that I have any real secrets, except feeling sorry for myself about Sartor. I wouldn't want you to have to hear that. I do worry about everyone in Sartor. But I'm also worried about a friend, one you know, who helped me when I broke the century-long enchantment over Sartor, which was so very much worse than this one Siamis has spread everywhere. You met Rel, right?"

"Oh, yes. I traveled with him once. He's a really, really good traveler," Liere said, smiling as she remembered tall, sturdy Rel. He'd reminded her so much of the brother she liked—the one her father had prenticed out to a baker, so she seldom saw him.

"He is. I just want to know if he's all right. Do you think you could find him?"

"I can listen for him, but I did teach him the mind-shield," Liere said. "However, if it isn't habit . . ." She didn't bother explaining, but shut her eyes.

Distance on the mental plane was deceptive, not always measurable in days of travel. There were times when she could hear Senrid, or her family, like they were in the next room, and other times they were more distant than dreams.

She reached a thread, a tendril, toward Rel—and gasped.

"What is it?"

"He's . . . he's . . ." Liere felt him sway as he climbed out of the saddle, felt her dry tongue cleaving to the top of her mouth, felt her eyes burn. She saw the glow of fire like a false dawn in memory, heard the casual voice, low, flat, a little husky, *They're all dead.*

She jerked her thoughts free, then curled up into a tight ball as she fought the resultant vertigo, until she'd sorted her own thoughts from his.

Then she opened her eyes and stared at Atan, her face blanched, eyes huge. "He's in the middle of a war."

A short time later, she, Hibern, and Liere sat in Tsauderei's cottage, as Liere related what she'd seen when touching the surface of Rel's thoughts.

As soon as she finished, Atan said, "What can we do?"

Tsauderei said, "What do you want to do?" And when she didn't answer, he added, "You knew about this attack on Everon weeks ago. Is it suddenly real because someone you know is in the midst of the slaughter?"

Atan's temper flared, and then she remembered her heated accusations against Hibern about keeping the enchantment antidote secret and her brow creased. She saw at once that this was somewhat akin. "Yes. No. It's not more real. War is real, and horrible wherever it is. But when a friend is in the middle, it becomes more immediate. Urgent. Is it because I know I can't stop a war, but maybe I can stop him from being killed in it? I apologize if that's wrong."

"It's not wrong, it's human. So you would have me transfer in, and take Rel away?"

"Yes," Atan stated.

Hibern listened with a growing sense of loss, wondering why the Everoneth princess and prince hadn't contacted anyone. The alliance was definitely falling apart.

Tsauderei said, "But from what Liere tells us, Rel is spreading the word about the imminent attack. He might be the only one carrying that news, if those he was reporting to are all dead. Do you really want me to take him away?"

"No. Yes. Why isn't anyone *doing anything?*" Atan asked angrily.

Tsauderei sighed. "Why do you think I've been traveling so much? Which is not particularly good for old bones. King Berthold immediately attempted to invoke his treaties with his neighbors. The elderly queen of Wnelder Vee, to his north, who was in her nineties when she assumed the throne on the death of her son a couple years ago, fell into a stroke when she heard about the Norsunder attack. She was insensible, and though the healers did their best, she died a week ago. The new king is a boy about your age." He nodded at Liere. "Who is apparently being fought over by various guild factions in Wnelder Vee. Which is largely rural, with no militia, much less an army. As for Imar . . ." He sighed again. "Prince Conrad and Princess Karia—I should say, the new king and queen—officially expressed concern, but. You know the political situation there."

"I remember," Atan said. "The nobles of Imar are like pocket kings in their own land. The monarchy is very weak."

"It doesn't help that King Conrad and Queen Karia, with no real authority, are mostly concerned with social life. Neither of them has the will or the ability to honor the treaty, and the last I heard, the most powerful nobles are all digging in to defend their family holdings if Norsunder comes over the border."

"So Everon is left to itself."

"There is nothing we mages can do. We're forbidden by centuries of treaties to interfere in non-magical affairs. And there isn't much we can do about war anyway."

Liere heard Atan's thought as clear as if spoken: *I am not willing to do nothing.*

Hibern said to Atan when they left the mage's cottage, "There's still the alliance. Not that it seems to have helped so far. But I do know this. Princess Tahra has a notecase."

Everon

Mersedes Carinna was increasingly uneasy, but other than the obvious, could not define the cause. She had no success in getting Berthold to listen, and couldn't blame him for kissing her and saying, "It's just the war. Strikes us all differently."

Six couriers arrived, claiming that half the countryside was on fire. Berthold said after the first three, "You know how wild rumor spreads. I will not have people harming themselves through panic. If Roderic hasn't sent anyone from the western border, or Berneth from the harbor, then there is no real news. Just countryside gossip."

Mersedes Carinna tried to believe it until the fourth report, then she took her husband by the shoulders. "Are you certain this is mere gossip? Or is that what you want to believe, so strongly you are trying to make it true through will?"

Berthold covered her hands with his own. She saw in the quick flicker of his eyelids, the jut of his beard, that her guess was right, and she intuited with a thrill of sorrow that he couldn't let himself believe it, because he did not know what to do other than what he had already done.

And so she kissed him, then said, "I hope it's true." She kissed him again, harder, because he was a man underneath the trappings of kingship, a man enduring as much fear as his subjects. More, because they looked to him for a way out. And he had no one to look to.

She ran her hands up his sides to cup his face. "I'll feel better when we hear from Roderic." A third kiss.

A clatter of footsteps announced another arrival; the king's head turned slightly, and she excused herself and sped to her own rooms.

When she came out, she had changed into a riding outfit of dark blue velvet, and had bound up her hair under her coronet. She headed toward the stable, where she nearly collided with Rel.

"The harbor is on fire," he began, and coughed.

"You're the sixth person to come in with that news," she said.

"Why isn't anyone doing anything?" Rel was too exhausted to be diplomatic.

"Because we thought it was rumor. Until now. I was about to ride out to find Roderic myself, but I think that shall have to wait. Rel, if you will help me, it's time to rouse the city. I'll wrangle with the nobles, who'll be watching one another, and talking absurdities about standing and fighting, as if—like my darling son thinks—war with Norsunder will be the same as the Knights' martial displays, only better. Because it's an enemy you can really hate."

Rel was hesitant to agree, but she saw in his lowered gaze what he thought to hide, and she went on, "If you'll begin with the merchants and the older sections. Tell them to take refuge in the hills. It is where we traditionally went, back in the bad old days when the Venn raided up and down this coast. They couldn't kill people they couldn't find. Remind people of that, but if they argue, move on."

Rel held the back of a chair. "Understood."

"I see how tired you are, and if we survive this, you shall be awarded a medal you will probably be embarrassed by, and a grant of land that you won't use."

Her smile trembled, and sorrow constricted her heart at

the thought of what the destruction of Ferdrian would do to Berthold. If it came to that. She would rather be the foolish queen who sent the populace of the capital scrambling for the hills than a queen reigning over ghosts. "I'll send another equerry to Roderic, in case your Kessler ordered someone to cut off any communication between us and the Knights flanking Henerek's last position."

She compressed her lips, longing to go kiss her darling, difficult children, but she knew that Tahra would push her away, then feel guilty, and Glenn would fret about his duty as a warrior prince, arguing and sulking, because those emotions were easier to bear than helpless anxiety. "Before you go, please help Puddlenose get my children out of the country. I think they'll listen to you boys quicker than they will to me. If Puddlenose still has the boat he told us about, it would be perfect. You know the path to take, the Knights' trail through the northern forest. Norsunder will probably avoid that, in the unlikelihood they even know about it. Difficult to maneuver in."

"Done," he said.

Mersedes pressed his hands, then dashed away.

Rel forced himself down the hall to the heirs' wing.

He found all four youths together, the boys clustered around Tahra. They all turned, their expressions so individual: Glenn sulky, Tahra stolid-faced, Puddlenose lazily smiling except for his watchful eyes, Christoph clearly wishing himself elsewhere.

"You look like you fought a war all by yourself," Christoph said, running a hand through his short blond curls so they stuck up all over his head. His expression was the habitual mild one, but Rel recognized in that swift gesture the frustration he sought to hide.

Tahra scowled at the ground, unsettled because the world was breaking into angles and uneven numbers, all murky, muddy shades. That morning she'd received a note from the scribe student Piper that their mutual courier friend, who had been translating Tahra's notes into good Sartoran before sending them on to Thad, was dead, killed at the harbor. No one knew when it had happened, but Tahra could assume that any notes she'd written had not been sent on.

Not three glasses after, her notecase, silent for so many

weeks, had 'tapped' again. Before Rel could answer Christoph, she said, "I just got a note from Hibern, who was requested by the Queen of Sartor to ask if you are all right." She nodded at Rel, eyes wide with curiosity.

"Atan?" Rel stopped short. "Is she all right?"

"She and many others of the alliance are in the Valley of Delfina," Tahra said. She was embarrassed to admit that she hadn't written directly to any of them because she didn't want them to see her mistakes in Sartoran.

"Cowards," Glenn sneered. "Hiding. They don't have anyone locking *them* in the nursery wing."

It didn't take more than a breath to figure out the truth: Glenn wanted any excuse to go riding off to war, which he believed would be won by the daunting presence of that golden circlet on his brow, and the king had tasked Puddlenose to use his ingenuity to keep the prince in the palace, out from under everyone's feet.

No wonder the queen wasn't there herself. Glenn would spend the entire war arguing with his mother while Ferdrian was attacked from all sides.

Tahra gave a short nod. "Maybe someone ought to send an official letter to that snot Conrad, that the Queen of Sartor is thinking of us, at least."

"What?" Rel asked, remembering the difficult prince from Imar. "What's he done now?"

"Nothing," Tahra and Glenn said together, Tahra adding, "They're supposed to come to our aid. But haven't. I think it's because he's so high and mighty."

"I hate that soul-sucker," Glenn snarled.

While Rel tried to find a way to shift the subject, Tahra said indignantly, "He thinks we Delieths are upstarts, because our dynasty is only four centuries old, and we were originally a fisher fleet."

"As if Winstanhaeme is as old as Landis," Glenn said, kicking the rungs of Tahra's chair.

"Stop that," she said irritably. "They aren't. Their throne has changed hands more often than ours, and the Haeme family was from Sartor, yes, but only through a cousin who had nothing to do with . . ."

As she went on detailing the minutiae of family history

that no one else cared about, Rel decided this was his chance.

"As it happens," he said as soon as Tahra stopped to draw breath, "I know that the Queen of Sartor would personally invite you to her. . ." He glanced at Glenn. "To her strategic retreat. Her *royal* retreat." And because he suspected the underlying cause of Tahra's lack of communication, "If you'll permit me to function as your secretary, I'll write to her and I can assure you of a royal invitation to join her."

He saw the effect of these words on the siblings. He knew that most royal children, at least in the south, were taught 'pure' Sartoran. But lessons in a language they didn't use daily didn't make them fluent. Tahra had asked him countless questions ever since she found out he spoke the language.

"You can send it in my notecase," Tahra said. "If you know the sigil to send a letter to the Queen of Sartor."

"I do," Rel said. "And if you'll teach me your sigil, so she can write back, I'll send a note right now."

Rel took up a pen, and sat down at a little distance. Puddlenose, judging correctly that Rel did not want anyone overseeing his words, said to Glenn, "So what would you do to lead the defense?"

Glenn had taken a few steps toward Rel. He turned back. "I wish Uncle Roderic would ask that, instead of you. If they listened to *me*, we would have been rid of Henerek weeks ago. All it takes is a charge with lances . . ."

A short time later, Rel handed Tahra her notecase, shoved the token that had been wrapped with Atan's answer deep into a pocket, and said, "It's even better than I thought. You can write to Prince Conrad that you're invited to visit the Queen of Sartor in the Valley of Delfina. She is in company with several other young rulers. Such as the King of Marloven Hess."

Glenn's head came up at that. "*He's* there?"

"Discussing strategy," Rel said, figuring it had to be true from what little he knew of Senrid. "The Queen of Sartor's issued you an immediate invitation. They'll send transfer tokens to your notecase, Tahra, once they make them." He took a chance. "But you'd better leave the palace now, because the tokens might not get here before the imminent attack."

Glenn said warily, "But my parents? My father might still permit me to ride in command of a company."

"Before I came to this suite I encountered your mother. There are no companies in need of leaders at present, and I believe she would appreciate your making diplomatic connections." With every word Rel felt he was treading closer to becoming the kind of liar he despised. Back to the truth—though the truth they most wanted to hear. "In the Valley are two kings, a queen, and a couple of princesses. All your age. In the alliance. Discussing countermeasures against Norsunder."

Glenn grinned. "*Finally* someone will listen to me! Let's go."

Tahra looked puzzled. "Mother? Wants us to go?"

"You know they will be pleased to hear you taking diplomatic initiative," Puddlenose said, hands out wide. "And you also know they aren't going to let either of you pick up swords. So why not do what you can? Impress them with your resourcefulness?"

"If we leave now, we can reach the coast by nightfall," Christoph put in. "Where we have hidden a fast sailcraft. Why not grab a suitable outfit or two? But no more than you can carry. We'll go by a secret path, because Norsunder would like nothing better than to capture the two of you."

Secret path and the risk of capture? Glenn's expression changed from stubborn to enthusiastic, and the royal pair departed.

Puddlenose turned to Rel. "Captain Heraford said he'd be following us from a circumspect distance. If those tokens take a while to make, we can return the boat to him. It'll be tight, with five of us." He grimaced.

"I'll sleep on deck," Christoph said hastily.

"Just four of you." Rel quickly outlined what Mersedes Carinna had requested of him. Then, "So I'd better get to it. Tell Tahra and Glenn I have courier duty. To the merchants," he added, thinking of Glenn.

Rel ran out, breathing a sigh of relief. He spotted a half-eaten meal sitting in the outer chamber, and paused long enough to pick up a chicken pie, a peach, and a hunk of cheese. He devoured the food as he ran.

He wondered if he should begin with the royal palace, but discovered the queen was ahead of him there. The Sandrial family and all their subordinates, who had been stewards for the Delieths as long as Delieths had been in the royal palace, were buzzing about like bees in a hive, packing for evacuation.

When he reached the high street, the alarm bells in the palace began to ring. People emerged from houses and shops, making his task easier at first: they spotted his mud-splashed white tabard, and crowded around.

Rel repeated over and over, "The queen orders . . ." which they responded to with endless questions.

He answered as patiently as he could, but by the time darkness closed in, he saw that he'd not even completed one street.

He pushed on until he stumbled over the low threshold of an empty house. He sat down with his back to the wall to rest . . . and woke up with an aching head, a fiery thirst, and a driving urgency to carry out his orders.

Rel worked his way from house to house, and street to street, repeating the same words until they leeched of meaning in his head. The responses fell into patterns: pleading, angry, bewildered. Some were shouted in his face, as if asking more forcefully would bring a different answer.

And some he couldn't answer, like "Why didn't the king deal with them earlier?" and "I thought the Knights were invincible!"

When he got to the narrower streets, many people had already heard gossip and had evacuated. He found a woman hastily washing dishes, as if leaving a clean house would somehow guarantee order when she returned. Halfway down the otherwise empty street, he found a family setting up defenses, determined to protect their shop and home. As he moved on, he had to help carry bushel baskets of belongings, tie down furniture jumbled onto carts, and lift squalling children after harassed elders.

"I've lived here girl to widow," an old woman declared,

her voice wavering. "And my grandmothers before me. No one crosses this threshold without my permission!"

Rel tried to argue, but the woman shook her head. "Where would I go? How would I travel? I can barely walk to market each day."

"If you come with me to Prince Solenn Road going east, someone will help you," Rel said. "I'll find you someone with an extra corner in their wagon or cart if you'll come now." But she shook her head and shut the door in his face.

He'd been at it a couple days by the time he began finding more empty side streets. Through the middle of the city the royal road leading north toward the mountain filled with streams of people bearing baskets and parcels, and the occasional wagon loaded with the elderly and young, furniture, and baskets of food. Most of those were pulled by family cows, or goats, for all horses had long since been commandeered; many carts were pulled by the families who owned them.

Rel forced himself to the last street at the extreme west end of the city. Darkness had fallen once again, broken by no lights anywhere. He walked into the open door of a cottage, and sank down into a chair by the cold hearth. He leaned on the table next to the chair, which cradled his aching body, the cushions shaped by a generation of some unknown family.

He only meant to rest his eyes a moment . . .

Chapter Thirteen

Delfina Valley and Everon

FLYING was the most wonderful sensation in the world, but Liere discovered that she missed smells. If the wind shifted one way, she could catch a pine scent, and the other way, snow. But it wasn't anything like walking on a road and sniffing fresh bread baking, or wildflowers, or the fragrance of soil and grass just after a rain. Still, she thought as she followed the swarm swooping, diving, chasing, and laughing, she wanted to remember every sensation concerned with flying, because Atan had said this was the only place in the entire world that had this magic. There were, she said, flying people in another range of very high mountains, but you had to be born one.

Liere flew with the chase games to be part of the group, but she never tried to catch anyone, and never tried to be the target. It was more fun to watch the ones who were the most graceful.

She was watching when Tsauderei came out of his cottage and took to the air. He was another who became graceful in flight. Liere watched him go to Derek, which surprised her, because usually the two avoided one another. She realized then that she might be snooping instead of watching, and so she flew in another direction.

Tsauderei was not aware of her scrutiny. He had considered everything going on, and decided it was time to try talking to Derek. Derek, Senrid, and Leander had been leaving more frequently.

To Tsauderei's surprise, Derek came willingly, and he wondered if this apparent cooperation was due to Derek having his own set of demands.

As soon as they stepped inside the cottage, weight mercilessly pulled Tsauderei's bones. He winced as he sat. Joint pain made him more irascible than he'd intended to be as he eyed Derek standing there, arms crossed, head at a wary angle, then said bluntly, "You know Peitar would hate your risking yourself, so we'll take that as a given. But what you might not know is that both Leander and Senrid are kings, which is something Siamis could use against their kingdoms if they get caught."

Derek's eyes widened. "Impossible."

Tsauderei snorted, his mustache fluttering. "Go right ahead and ask."

"Both of them?"

"Right next to each other. Of course Leander's Vasande Leror has, as far as I know, one tiny town, and the rest of it isn't any bigger than one of the middling counties here in western Sarendan. But Marloven Hess . . . you may have heard of it."

Derek frowned. "Kessler talked about a regent who . . ." He stopped. "Senrid's the crown prince?"

"He's been king for a couple years now."

Derek shook his head. "He doesn't talk or act like any king. Why, when he joined my orphans at morning drill, he went to the back. No prince or king would do that."

"Ask him. Or don't. I don't care. My point remains, if you keep pestering them to go with you into Sarendan, you're risking more than you think. And that goes double for snatching Lilah, if she's being held at the palace, which has to be laced with magical traps. Wait until I can go."

"Why can't you go now?" Derek tipped his head the other way.

"Because we need to free more mages, so that we can

break the Siamis enchantment at the same time, all over
the world. Then it won't matter if breaking it brings Siamis
at the run."

Derek left, brooding. He wasted a breath or two thinking that Tsauderei had to be lying, but why would he? He
floated in the sky, watching from a distance as the others
played, Senrid faster than anyone except Bren, and better
at directing others. Maybe Senrid was like CJ, with no pre-
tenses. Even though he'd been born a prince. As Derek
watched Senrid, the thought occurred that if Senrid was
really a king, then he could not just talk to whoever was in
charge of the Marloven academy, he could make them accept Derek there, so he could learn all they had to teach.

He decided to put it to Senrid after they'd rescued the rest
of the kids. But, mindful of Tsauderei's threat, he waited
until nighttime, when the boys showed up to plan the next
foray.

"You two are kings," he said. "Maybe you should stay
here."

Senrid rolled his eyes, looking pained. "Someone got
gabby, huh? Look, I've already had this argument. I carry
a transfer token with me. If I catch a whiff of Norsunder
around, I'll be out of there faster than a heartbeat."

"Most of us are rulers of some sort," Leander said ami-
cably. "That's what our alliance is." He held up his hand.
"But Senrid and I are both trained in magic. We'll get out
if we have to."

Derek grinned. *I tried, Tsauderei.* "Then let's get back
to planning . . ."

They decided to rescue the remainder of the Derek's orphan brigade in one day. Mindful of the kingship argument, Leander and Senrid recruited Hibern and Arthur to
help. This meant talking Jilo into letting Arthur in on the
secret of the book. He gave in reluctantly.

At the other end of the Valley, Atan received a slightly
peculiar note from Tahra, stating that they were now sailing aboard a little boat called a tender, and that as soon as
they sank the land below the horizon, she and her brother
Glenn would use the transfer tokens.

Afternoon had shifted the shadows from west to east

when two figures were spotted on the grassy Destination outside of Tsauderei's cottage. Atan and the study group went to welcome them.

They found a pair of dark-haired, sallow-complexioned young teens recovering from the transfer. Atan led in speaking words of welcome, then they went around the circle introducing themselves.

Tahra stared from one to the next through droopy gooseberry eyes, marking a connection to the Landis family in her background, then said flatly, "I promised Puddlenose I would tell you that he will come after he sails the tender back to the ship it belongs to."

Glenn waited for her to finish, then stated, "Now that my sister is safe, I'll wait here until Rel sends for me. I told my father I'll lead any company whose commander has fallen."

Silence fell, some exchanging looks, then Arthur said easily, "Why don't we show you where you can stay for now?"

And so the Delieths joined the group.

On the surface, that week was uneventful, at first even cordial. Glenn stopped talking wildly about war and duty after a short, pungently expressed set of questions from Senrid about numbers, terrain, and tactical observations, none of which Glenn could answer. After Senrid, with trenchant cheer, admitted that he wouldn't know what to do himself, Glenn stopped talking about commanding wars and contented himself with counting up how many had titles, and ignoring anyone who didn't.

The first evidence of strain occurred when Kitty offered to introduce the Everoneth siblings to the famous Sartora; on hearing herself addressed that way, Liere sidled off as quickly as she could, but not before she heard CJ say, "Sartora was great at world-rescuing one time. But I guess even she can't do it again, in spite of all those mind powers."

It was no more than the truth, but CJ's sharp disappointment acted like a whip to the spirit.

The second bad moment occurred a couple mornings into the newcomers' stay, when Glenn discovered the orphan drill. If Senrid had gotten there first, things might have gone differently; as it was, Glenn landed, surveyed the plainly dressed, barefoot orphans, then marched with princely assurance to the front.

Faen, one of the orphans' leaders, gathered a couple of the bigger boys with a glance, and all three summarily muscled Glenn to the back row with unnecessary vigor. "Beginners start here," Faen said.

"But I'm Prince Glenn Delieth of Everon," Glenn said in a reasonable tone. "Should we not go in order of rank?"

"Well, *I'm* Lord High Emperor of the Brick-Layers, so *I* go first," Faen retorted, to gusts of laughter from the orphans.

"And I'm King of the Silversmith Prentices, so I'm next," Ruddy added, prompting more laughter.

Derek stood to the side, arms crossed, and smiled to see the arrogant young prince get the trimming he deserved.

When Glenn saw Derek's smirk, and realized that he was not going to interfere, he flew away in disgust, and never came back.

Hibern's morning flights had changed.

Senrid now attended the orphan drill every morning, rather than flying with her and Atan, but Liere had taken his place. Liere was now living in the hermit's cottage with Hibern and Atan.

One morning the three flew out at dawn to watch the sun rise over Sartor far beyond the mountains.

"You're both unhappy," Atan observed after a very long silence. She did not want to point out that they looked as unhappy as she felt during this protracted waiting.

Hibern said, "I think it's this waiting. Though I know it's necessary, it isn't good for us. The alliance, I mean. There are some of us who are used to acting on their own, and, well, I'm afraid the alliance is in trouble."

Liere said solemnly, "CJ is angry with me. But I can hear her trying so hard not to be. It's that she wants so strongly for me to be a hero. But I'm not. I try to stay out of her way. I'm sorry if my being here makes the trouble."

"It doesn't," Hibern said quickly. "And CJ isn't the only problem in their group."

All three girls glanced across the valley to Selenna

house, where some of the Mearsieans sat on the roof eating breakfast. Sitting with them, her silken skirts spread around her, was Leander's stepsister Kyale, her silvery hair a shining fall down her back. Kyale, who veered between wanting to be called *Princess* Kyale and Kitty, reminded Liere of spun glass—beautiful to look at, but fragile, and sharp-edged.

Atan contemplated Kyale's penchant for sticking to CJ's side, trying hard to create an inner circle exclusively made up of princesses. CJ seemed typically oblivious, trying a little too hard to organize group games whether others wanted to play or not.

Hibern said, "At least Jilo seems to like studying light magic with Arthur. And I was glad to see Clair joining them."

"Who wants to wager," Atan said with a smile, "they're over there right now, half the breakfast things set out."

"Water filled, but the fire forgotten," Hibern suggested.

"Bread sliced, but nobody remembered to make the toast."

Liere chuckled soundlessly. "Yesterday I saw Arthur with the jam pot beside his dish, and a knife, and no bread. Then he got up and went off with Jilo to study something horrible called mirror wards, thinking breakfast was over."

"His theoretical breakfast *was* over," Atan commented.

"What are mirror wards, anyway?" Liere added, with a thoughtful glance.

Atan grimaced. "I don't understand them at all, except that this is very, very dangerous magic."

Hibern said, "Imagine a mirror behind a candle sconce. You've seen that, right?" At Liere's cautious nod, "Well, the magic reflects the image, doubling the power. Especially if you are strong enough to make interlocking mirror wards, in effect breaking the connection between real and unreal, just as the flame in the candle is real, but the one in the mirror isn't. And yet it reflects light."

"This," Atan said, "is how dark magic distorts time and place. And if you also draw on life itself, you are on the way to creating Norsunder."

"I'm sorry I asked," Liere whispered, and dove down in an effect to let the wind scour away the horror.

But it went right along with her, so she willed it away, and as she, Atan, and Hibern finished their circuit all around the valley, Liere turned her attention to her surroundings in order to impress all the details she could into her mind: the little goats hopping along steep slopes, juts of striated rock glistening in the sun, wildflowers of colors she had no names for. She wanted *these* memories to show up in dreams, after she had to leave. And nothing about mirror wards.

They finished, as usual, at Tsauderei's hut. Hibern caught sight of Seshe's long light hair through the window, and thought that a good sign, as she was hungry. Though she had no objection to fixing breakfast, she wasn't very good at figuring out how to estimate, much less cook, food for more than herself and Erai-Yanya.

She opened the door first, then recoiled when she smelled smoke. Alarm flashed through her, just as Liere darted past her, yelling happily, "Rel, you came!"

Atan was right on her heels.

Except for Seshe, quietly toasting bread at the fireplace, Tsauderei was alone with Rel, who looked unfamiliar in his white tabard edged with midnight blue and gold, the formal wear of the Knights of Dei. Rel wore no device on his chest, as he was not sworn a Knight, but somehow the tabard made his chest look broader, and emphasized his height.

Atan stared. He was thinner, the hard bones of his face pronounced. It struck her that she now knew what he would look like as a man, and as warmth pulsed in her middle, she thought in alarm, not now, not now, I am not ready for that.

"Rel, what happened?" Hibern asked, with the freedom of easy acquaintanceship. "I smell smoke."

"Ferdrian is burning." Rel indicated Tsauderei's cleaning frame. "I stepped through that first thing, but before I could, I guess I still stank up this cottage. I've been wearing these clothes for . . ." He thumbed his eyelids in a gesture of tiredness. "Ten days? Two weeks? I've lost count." He looked around, as Tsauderei made a casual gesture and the side windows to his great bay opened, flashing briefly with magic.

"I've been asking Tsauderei what I should say to Glenn and Tahra," Rel began, but not two heartbeats later the door slammed open, and Glenn flew in.

"I saw you arrive," he said, his eyes wild. "I saw you

from the other ledge." He pointed at Rel. "Why did it take you so long to come get me? Where are my parents?"

"I don't know," Rel said, and after a hesitation, "Ferdrian is on fire. I had to leave."

Glenn's face reddened as his angry gaze swept over the faces, then he whipped around and zoomed out again, flitting past the window in the direction of Selenna House.

Hibern made a gesture as if to follow, feeling some sense of responsibility, but Tsauderei said, "Let him be. If he or his sister want help dealing with the news, or lack of it, they'll let us know." He turned his head. "Rel? Tell us what happened."

By now several others, seeing Glenn's wild arrival and departure, had come to see what was going on, including Kyale, whose secret, unexpressed desire was to be accepted into Atan's select group, so that one day she might be invited to Sartor's court. She had a happy vision of stunning the Sartorans with her most beautiful gown—then, afterward, she could come home, and everyone would be impressed when they heard where she'd been, and they would finally give her the due respect of her rank! Only every time she flew out to that secluded cottage, they were talking about such boring magic or history stuff.

She saw Atan's attention on Rel, so she added her voice to those pestering him, "What happened in Everon? Tell us!"

"It fell to Norsunder." He looked around for a subject change. "Is that the house where everybody is staying?"

Hibern leaned out the door, peering toward Selenna House. "Speaking of Everon. Where are Glenn and Tahra? I thought they were coming right back?"

Arthur scratched his head with the inky quill clutched in his fingers, leaving spots of dried ink in his tousled yellow hair, and said vaguely, "I saw Glenn, I think. I was reading this, and didn't really notice." He brandished the scroll he'd been carrying. "Where's Leander? I thought he was right behind me."

Jilo spoke up from behind him, "No. He and Senrid were talking to Glenn when I left."

Jilo had finessed that a little.

At Selenna House, Glenn had burst in on the boys while

Senrid was dressing for the morning drill, and Leander was assembling his study materials.

"Rel is back," Glenn said, his sallow face blanched to the color of paper. "Ferdrian is on fire. He didn't see my parents. Uncle Roderic. Anyone. I have to go back. Will one of you send me?"

Jilo sidled a glance at Glenn's angry face, faded straight out the open window, and headed for Tsauderei's house.

Senrid and Leander met each other's gazes. Leander said slowly, "He should. Be able to go home."

Senrid knew that Leander was loading the words with meaning, but what meaning? He leaned against the wall, his eyes closed, and reached mentally.

He recoiled at the intensity of Leander's memories from the time Senrid's uncle invaded Vasande Leror. Senrid gritted his teeth, hating his own memories of that shameful episode. Through came Leander's thought: *It was important to be there. Though I could do nothing.*

That, too, hit Senrid hard, in an unprotected place: that inward conviction he'd fought against ever since he was five, that he ought to have been there when his father was killed.

"Let's go," he said, more in reaction to his own memories—the instinct to get away—but once he said it, Glenn's whole demeanor made so dramatic a change that Senrid listened to his thoughts instead of warding them. He heard below the anger and frustration a gnawing anxiety.

"Let me get Tahra," Glenn said, and arrowed out the window.

Leander felt obliged to say, "Tsauderei won't like it," and when Senrid shrugged sharply, "nor will the others. If we find something bad, they'll say our taking them was cruel."

"Let 'em. Glenn wants to be there. He yaps a lot about princely rights, but this is one I agree with."

"And I don't disagree." Leander sighed. "Transfers?"

Senrid picked up the tokens waiting for the orphan rescue the next day. "We'll use these. We can get Arthur and Hibern to help us make new ones tonight."

Tahra and Glenn dashed in, Tahra tousled and heavy-eyed from being wakened. Her mouth was pressed in a thin line.

"Where do we go? Give us a Destination," Senrid said.

Tahra did, with her usual meticulousness. Senrid and Leander altered the transfer spells, changing Destinations. Then Senrid handed the tokens to the siblings. "Don't lose these. There are two transfers on each, there and back here again. Let Glenn and me go first. We'll wait while the Destination clears."

When they arrived in the Ferdrian royal palace's Destination, smoke and heat nearly knocked each pair down. Everywhere flames roared and snapped, withering the textiles that the Sandrials had not been able to remove. They raced down a hallway, dodging small fires and bending low, to fetch up short at the first blood-splattered, hacked body sprawled in death.

Tahra choked. Glenn gripped her hand and tugged her onward before Leander could get the words past his tongue, "We should go back."

Glenn put on a desperate burst of speed. In his father's chambers they found three dead guards, all known to the siblings; one was a cousin. He ran out again, batting furiously at the drifting smoke. Eyes burning, the others followed until he stopped again on the terrace above the square, giving an inarticulate cry.

The king lay below the first step, surrounded by the remainder of his personal guard. All dead, King Berthold with a sword loose in his hand.

Glenn jolted forward as if yanked by invisible strings. His chest heaved on a sob, then he dropped to his knees, and reached a tentative, shaky hand to straighten his father's tabard.

Tahra threw herself down on his other side, heedless of the darkened pool of gore. She kicked the sword angrily. It clattered away, fetching up horribly against a lifeless Knight. Glenn shot her a venomous look, retrieved the sword, and gently laid it by his father's side.

Tahra pulled her father's hands together, then tried to order his hair, but it was filled with spiky black blood from a killing blow to the head. So she smoothed the jagged wrinkles in his clothes, though her joints had turned to water, and the world had broken into rust-colored elevens and sevens.

While Glenn and Tahra laid out their father, Leander and Senrid watched the perimeter, Leander troubled, and Senrid stone-faced.

"Shall we Disappear them?" Senrid asked when the siblings had done what they could.

Glenn's lips moved, but he couldn't speak.

Leander and Senrid stepped carefully to each of the fallen. They left the king for last. Glenn's face was a rictus. He'd given up the fight against weeping, as tears of rage dripped onto his father's chest. The king's body, his kingly garb so lovingly woven and embroidered, and the steel he had borne when he was killed, broke down to their components and vanished into Everon's soil.

Tahra said, "We have to—"

A noise behind caused Senrid to grasp the hilts of his forearm knives, and Leander to grip his transfer token. But they stilled when a bloody figure staggered through the door. "Gone." It was a young Knight-cadet. She stared at the ground, her lips working. "He's gone? I came to . . ."

Glenn closed the distance between them. "Where's the queen, Perles?"

"They say she fell. In the attack on Roderic. Someone else said that they were taken prisoner. She and Commander Roderic." Perles raised her unwounded arm, making a vague gesture at the fire. "Somewhere."

Sickened, Leander said, "Let us go. Perles, is that your name? Do you want to transfer with us?"

Perles backed away, raising her hands. "No. No. Take the princess and prince away. Keep them safe. We fight to the last." She turned away, and was lost in the smoky entrance.

Senrid said, "We can do nothing more here."

Glenn managed a short nod.

One by one, the four transferred out, Senrid going last.

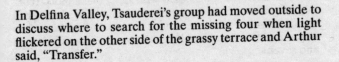

In Delfina Valley, Tsauderei's group had moved outside to discuss where to search for the missing four when light flickered on the other side of the grassy terrace and Arthur said, "Transfer."

One by one, the four appeared, staggered, then took in the circle of faces.

Tahra leaped into the air and flew away. Kyale and one of the Mearsieans peeled off to chase after her, ready to coo and pet as needed. Glenn looked indecisive, then stuck his jaw out and crossed his arms, glowering in spite of the tear tracks still wet on his face.

As the crowd lit on the grassy path beside the cottage, forming a half-circle, Atan said, "Where did you go?"

"Everon," Glenn said in a flat, belligerent voice. "We had a right."

"And so we took them," Senrid said, indicating Leander and himself.

Hibern had heard that tone in his voice before, and seen that nasty grin with too many teeth and no humor. Senrid, for whatever reason, was spoiling for a fight.

Hibern had little expectation that anyone would listen to her, but she raised her voice. "I think we should give Glenn and Tahra the choice whether they want to talk about what happened, or to be private."

"I agree," Atan and Derek said at exactly the same time. Then cast a startled glance at the other.

People took to the air, with many questioning, doubtful glances cast back. Glenn flew off alone. Senrid sensed he was at the end of his self-control, and didn't know whether to go with him or stay. It seemed cowardly to leave him, but he loathed the thought of sticking around unwanted.

He was distracted by Jilo's appearance. Jilo sidled up, glanced furtively around, then muttered, "The book says that Detlev's in Everon."

Chapter Fourteen

Everon to Norsunder Base

DETLEV peered down at the smoking ruins of Ferdrian from the hilltop where Kessler had pitched camp while he waited for the worst of the fires to burn out.

He snapped the glass to. "Where is Roderic Dei?"

Kessler remembered a report in the constant stream, something about Henerek's men hoarding prisoners to play with, but at that time he'd been commanding the last, fierce battle at the Ferdrian palace. "Henerek has him."

Detlev cut in. "You didn't think to ask Henerek where before you rendered him speechless?"

"Nobody gave me orders concerning prisoners." Kessler knew how weak that sounded, though it was the truth.

Detlev said derisively, "That's because those orders came from Yeres. You did know that Henerek is her current toy." His tone implied that it was obvious—and in retrospect, it *was* obvious. Henerek never would have gained this much command without backing from higher up.

Detlev didn't wait for the answer that Kessler couldn't give. "Go back to Base. I'll deal with the detritus."

It had not occurred to Kessler until that moment that he had been set up.

He transferred, and while still recovering, left the Destination at Norsunder Base, and walked the short distance to the command center. The prickling hairs on the back of his neck and the faint but distinct metallic not-quite-scent, not-quite-taste warned of a window opened from Norsunder.

He walked into the command center, and there was tall, dark-haired and sharp-faced Yeres, dressed in crimson, lounging in a doorway from the Beyond—wasting enormous power—in the middle of the room. Because of the way windows were made, no matter where people walked in the room, they saw the same angle, which meant she wanted an audience.

A lot of people had crowded into the command center, clearly expecting entertainment. Siamis did not number among them.

Yeres ran her fingers through a long lock of her glossy dark hair, then said, "Efael is not happy with you at all, Kessler."

Silence.

Yeres spoke slowly, as if to one of the soul-bound. "Everon was Henerek's reward."

Kessler said, "He was losing. I was told to go clean it up."

"Your orders, I believe, were to clean. It. Up. Not destroy everything and everyone in sight. I'm sure it was fun, but Henerek was to capture Roderic Dei for Efael, and to lure Berthold Delieth and his wife from their citadel, so that Detlev could use them. He also wanted whatever artifact they had in that palace that prevented our getting mages in there. Did you find the artifact before you torched the place?"

Siamis had never mentioned any of this. Kessler had been framed, and he knew how much his admission was going to cost, but said it anyway: "What artifact?"

Yeres looked around in mocking disbelief, then put fingers to her forehead. "'What artifact?'" She got the expected laughter from the avid audience, then said, "Did you ask Henerek for his orders? No. Though he can barely speak, he has given me to understand that you did not."

The room had gone silent.

She continued in a sweet, mock-sorrowful tone. "Now, Kessler, everybody likes their fun, and a short temper can be useful, except when you manage to destroy not one." She raised a forefinger, in case there was dispute about the number. "Not two." Up came another finger, the back of her hand aimed at Kessler in deliberate insult, causing snickers around the perimeter. "But three, count them, three people's plans. Detlev's, Efael's, and *mine*. Henerek says he had Roderic Dei, but your followers squabbled with Henerek's leadership—yes, dismal, but at least he understood orders—and the old man hobbled away in the midst of the tiff."

She *tsk*ed, causing another wave of snickers.

She went on in that chiding, slow voice, as though he were a lackwit with no will. "We do not like waste, so you will be given a task that might be easier for you to compass. You are to take that token there on the map desk, and remove yourself to Geth. It seems our two favorite busy bees are not cooperating in establishing their little hive, and Siamis wants a drone to set up and maintain the guard station, which will free him up for important tasks. *Now*."

Kessler took up the token; the moment he touched it, the room vanished, and he found himself enclosed in a bubble somewhere in the weird area on the outer perimeter of the Beyond.

He and Yeres were alone.

She smiled. "If everyone despises you, they do not notice you."

Kessler said nothing.

She said, "Siamis scorns you, and Detlev ignores you. Can't you see what a useful weapon you can be? Go to Geth. We cannot get into the city Isul Demarzal."

Kessler had no interest in Geth-deles, much less any of its islands, but he had to maintain a semblance of obedience because of that damned blood-spell Dejain had inflicted on him. Until he got rid of it, he was Norsunder's minion.

So, "What is Isul Demarzal?"

Yeres smirked, always glad to demonstrate the ignorance of a captive audience. "Isul Demarzal," she stated, "is the oldest city on Geth-deles. All their mages and magic are centered there. You hold Isul Demarzal, and you hold the world. Surely that makes sense to your military mind?"

Kessler stood impassively.

She sighed, cast her eyes skyward, then said, "Siamis managed to lure its leader out, and used that enchantment of his to make them permit him access. He's now inside. He says he's working to break the wards keeping us out, but no one believes that. It's unlikely that you're warded from getting inside, since no one on Geth-deles knows your name, or even that you exist. Siamis wants you to run his guardhouse, but Efael thinks what that really means is, he wants you running backup."

"In?" Kessler asked.

"Efael thinks that this is the battleground Siamis has chosen to fight dear Detlev. You handle the bloodletting, he the magic."

Kessler shrugged, and Yeres sighed. "My very dear boy," she said, though they looked exactly the same age. "It is the first time any of us have breached that city. I want in. Efael wants in. Svir wants in. You achieve that, and you can have anything you want."

She snapped her fingers, and the transfer token hurled him out of the world.

Delfina Valley

At Tsauderei's cottage, Senrid stared at the old mage, then exclaimed, "But this is the right time to go to Miraleste for the last rescue, while Detlev's in Everon!" Then he stopped, appalled. How could he be so stupid?

Tsauderei's brows shot upward. "He most definitely is not in Everon. But he was. How did you know that?" He regarded Senrid steadily, as Senrid rapidly formed and discarded lies.

After a silence that felt like two days to Senrid, Leander, and Jilo, the old mage sat back, saying with dry humor, "Well, it takes no intelligence to understand that you youngsters have your own methods of communication. Or you would not have seen fit to take the two Delieths to

Everon in the middle of battle. However, no harm came of it, and you did get them back safely. So least said, soonest mended."

He paused as lightning crackled outside the cottage, and a sudden downpour nearly drowned the thunder. He spoke more seriously now. "I know you think that because you've been successful so far, by rights you should be able to get Lilah out of Miraleste. Have you considered that she's the lure to a trap?"

Senrid said, "Of course we have. This is why we saved her for last. We've run ten other rescues, the last two in Miraleste, and nothing's happened. We're really fast by now."

"Miraleste," Tsauderei said, "but not the palace. Correct?"

Derek put his hands on his knees. "I promised Peitar."

He didn't say it aggressively, or angrily, just with that utter conviction that made him so appealing a leader. Tsauderei could see in subtle movements, the lift of chins, the inadvertent smiles, the way the youngsters all faced him, that the kids responded to Derek exactly the way Peitar did: with their trust.

So he came at his objection in another way. "As I said, I appreciate that you youngsters have your own communications—yes, Derek, at my age, I regard you as one of 'em—and I commend you all for keeping within safe margins. If a little closer than your adult guardians, whoever they may be, might have liked. You've seen I've been away on my own concerns. Oalthoreh and I have been rescuing mages from Sartor, one by one. However, when Murial tried to rescue Chief Veltos, she nearly walked into a trap. Actually, she would have, if Veltos had been in another chamber. But the one she sits in happens to have some very old magic left in it, with a protection afforded by an artifact of the kind we cannot reproduce today. It exhibited a warning that only a mage would perceive, before she set foot in what seemed to be an unwarded room. We thought we'd removed all the Norsundrian wards. And there are a lot of them."

He saw the sobering reaction in Senrid and Leander, who understood magic. Derek looked like he was patiently waiting for Tsauderei to finish speaking.

So he tried again. "Lilah will be free very soon, as well

as Peitar. Soon—at most, three days. The antidote spell is being taught to all mages who are deft with ward and tracer magic, while other mages do their best to spot and ward hidden magical traps that might bring Siamis back to this world. None of us want *that*, right?"

He looked at each young face, seeing ambivalence in Senrid, but resistance in Derek's tight forehead, the lift to his chin. Bren and Innon both turned pleading eyes to Derek, and Tsauderei knew, with a sinking heart, that they were going to act with or without his leave.

So he said more crisply than he'd intended, "I can't go with you. There is a heavy ward set against me, a mirror ward with a lethal trap built in, so any magical attempt to remove it if I choose the wrong side of the mirror will rebound onto me. As well as alert Norsunder before I can remove it. I've been waiting for one of the stronger mages to have the time to deal with it in tandem with me, but it will take us considerable time to test and remove the traps. We've chosen to work on the universal deployment of the antidote to Siamis's enchantment first."

Derek still sat there, arms crossed, blank of face. Senrid grimaced at the mention of mirror wards, but he said nothing.

Tsauderei gave up. Short of dropping Derek with a stone spell, which would guarantee his followers going wild with what they'd consider a betrayal, there was no stopping him from doing whatever he was going to do.

And then he had it, the motivation underlying everything. The mage rescue could be a matter of hours away, but Derek would contrive to get there first. It mattered to him to be the one to free his particular charges from the enchantment, and he considered Lilah one of his charges.

Tsauderei sighed. "If you're determined to proceed, I suggest you take not one, but three of you to scan for further wards. Each with transfer tokens gripped in your fingers."

He nodded at Hibern, then turned to Jilo and Senrid. "You two are probably familiar with every likely form of dark magic that might be laid down. If you find anything suspicious, promise me you'll transfer immediately."

They promised.

Tsauderei's attention shifted to Jilo, who was more

hunched than ever, as if he was a breath away from running out the door. Because he'd been coerced into this reckless plan of theirs? No, he'd entered calmly enough. That tight-shouldered hunch had happened . . . ah. Directly after Senrid uttered his remark about Detlev.

He was going to need to probe that.

But not now. "However, I got sidetracked. Permit me to finish what I was saying about Detlev. I just received a communication, sent between worlds by Erai-Yanya, that Detlev has been seen on Geth-deles a lot in the past few years, ever since Evend destroyed Norsunder's rift magic."

Tsauderei jabbed a finger at them. "Think about that. A man born four thousand years ago, whose appearances in the world are usually once a century, has been spending appreciable time there. If he finds a kind of rift magic that will get around Evend's binding spell, you know he's going to bring it back here."

He stopped there, afraid he'd said too much. But no one seemed to be making the leap to the weaknesses in Evend's binding.

Jilo's eyelids flickered, then he rubbed stiffened fingers down his trouser legs.

Not the rift, Tsauderei intuited. But definitely something, and Jilo was the key. Probably some dire scrying object created by Wan-Edhe, though what it might be, Tsauderei could not imagine. It would have to be extraordinarily powerful (and dangerous) to track the movements of someone like Detlev, and Jilo clearly was wary of sharing it with Mondros, or Tsauderei would have heard about it by now.

"All right, I think that answers your questions," Tsauderei said.

That broke the meeting up, Senrid streaming out with Jilo and Leander, talking in low voices. Hibern followed, and Atan headed after her until she caught Tsauderei's gaze.

She waited behind until everyone else was gone. Tsauderei's expression was grim, which made Atan press her arms tightly against her ribs. Whatever he was about to say was bad news.

Then a horrible idea hit her. "Julian," she gasped. "They found her . . ." The word *dead* could not get past her lips.

"Not that," Tsauderei said quickly, and smoothed his mustache, one of his rare unsettled gestures. "I debated within myself, then decided you would want to know. Siamis seems to have taken her to Geth."

Atan turned away, disheartened and sick with failure. Her one living relative, this small cousin, and Atan hadn't even been able to get the child to acknowledge her as anything but a possible enemy.

She flew through the rain back to her cottage, where she found Hibern setting slices of bright orange cheese on hunks of bread, which were laid out on a pan ready to be set over the fire in the fireplace.

Hibern glanced at Jilo and Arthur sitting at the table at the other end of the room, muttering over 'wards' and 'chained spells,' then back to her work in such a way that Atan suspected something was wrong.

In fact she was certain of it. She hadn't seen the usual group playing around in the rain. "What is it?" she demanded.

The two boys looked up, then down again as Hibern said, "You really want to hear it?"

"Maybe I'd better hear it," Atan said.

"Well, I guess CJ told Rel—"

"Stop." Atan shut her eyes as she flung up a hand. "Stop right there. I changed my mind. I *don't* need to hear it. Here, give me that knife. Let me do something useful. At least I can toast bread."

Hibern set down the hunk of cheese, handed over the knife, and pretended not to hear Atan as she muttered, "I hate that girl."

"Bring Lilah right to us, promise?" Bren said, hopping up and down on his toes.

Innon stood next to him, his pale blond hair hanging in his eyes, wet from the lake. Swimming in a thunderstorm was a double pleasure. "She'll want to see us first thing. Especially since Peitar is still in the enchantment."

"I promise," Derek said, holding up both hands. "We'll come straight to you two first. Even before Tsauderei, though if he turns me into a tree stump, be sure to explain to Lilah."

The boys laughed, then took off, arguing happily over what to do first while they were waiting.

That left the four standing in a circle—Hibern, Senrid, and Leander alert and ready, Jilo tense. This would be the first time Jilo wouldn't be monitoring his book during the rescue, but Detlev and Siamis were not even in the world, so it was easier to agree to Tsauderei's stipulation that Jilo aid Senrid in sniffing out dark magic traps at the palace.

As always, Derek had to keep his face well hidden. He'd stuffed his shaggy brown hair up into a winter cap, and pulled the front down to his eyebrows. He wrapped a scarf around his lower face, leaving a thin slit to peer through. He'd look suspicious to anyone not under enchantment, but to the enchanted, he would be unrecognizable.

He'd told the boys the best place to transfer would be the fish market along the docks below the lake. If there were any Norsundrians left in the city, they surely wouldn't patrol there during summer. Bren, with an artist's eye, gave them an exact description of a locale that they could use as a Destination.

Nobody was in sight, except boats bobbing gently on the water as a hot summer wind kicked up. When they recovered from the transfer they found themselves baking in the summer sun, the odor of fish strong. They forced themselves to move at a slow, steady pace.

The only conversation was from Derek, who muttered as they turned up toward the royal palace on a road bare of people, "I will never eat a boiled potato again without remembering this day." He touched his head in its wrappings.

Hibern grimaced with sympathy. She usually wore her hair loose, except in summer. High in the mountains, she hadn't bothered with a braid, but now she wished she had. To avoid the glare of the sun she watched her sandaled feet treading stones placed by unknown hands unknown years before.

Leander, Senrid, and Derek found the quiet eerie. That much reminded Jilo of Chwahirsland, though nothing else about the city did. He stared in astonishment at new buildings jostling old smoke-damaged ruins, everything dappled with painted and chalked slogans and drawings. Some were actually well done, though most were messy scrawls.

The people themselves were also unlike Chwahir. They didn't dart furtive looks around them, or converse in hand signals. They looked like a city of sleepwalkers. He wondered if Wan-Edhe would demand that spell from Siamis, then he remembered that it was predicated on a sense of loyalty to a leader. Wan-Edhe would never lay that enchantment over himself. The thought made Jilo shake with silent laughter.

When they reached the palace gate, Senrid and Jilo both searched for tracers. Nothing happened.

"This way." Derek motioned toward a narrow path between a couple of buildings made of light stone, with fine slate roofs. This was not the main part of the palace, which was built of marble.

He led them along servants' paths. Senrid fingered the silk scarf that he'd been given for the purpose: as soon as they saw Lilah, Senrid, being the fastest, was to bind the scarf around her lower face before Derek came into the room. That way she wouldn't be able to perform any tracer spells that she might have been commanded to use while under the enchantment.

Derek silently pointed to a discreet entrance in what was obviously a wing of the royal residence. No guards in sight. Senrid held out his hands as a signal to tread warily. It stood to reason, you hedged your royal prisoners with either human guards or magical ones.

He and Jilo moved to the front, testing for wards and tracers.

Jilo halted them before the door to the room Derek indicated. He'd already found a bad trap. He whispered another spell, and Hibern saw with her magical sense a flash of green around the door. Senrid reached for the latch, but Jilo shook his head, and Senrid pointed to the latch.

"Nothing here," Senrid mouthed.

Jilo shook his head. He knew he might be slowing them up, but dealing with Wan-Edhe's complexity of deadly wards had taught him about chained spells. He crouched down, holding his hand flat above the floor near the bottom of the door. And once more he whispered. Once more there was a subtle flash of green.

Senrid whistled soundlessly.

"Clear?" Senrid breathed.

"I think so. But . . ." Jilo flicked his fingers outward. Maybe that was the way this particular spell dispersed. It was a nasty one. He had the sense there had been a secondary spell, though there was no trace now.

That was enough for Senrid. "Let's be quick."

Derek gave Jilo a grateful clap on the shoulder, which startled Jilo into jumping backward, nearly colliding with the inlaid buffet outside the door. Senrid and Hibern both caught his arms. He blushed as he righted himself.

Senrid led the way in. Hibern took up a station inside the door, to listen for footsteps or sense magic.

She gazed across the room at Lilah, a sturdy girl of twelve or so sitting decorously at her window. "She's wearing the same clothes she had on that night. When I returned after my defeat at the pass," Derek whispered.

Lilah's head turned. Her eyes were wide and glassy as a doll's. Hibern's heart galloped at the girl's tense stillness. She found it impossible to believe that she'd sat like that for all these weeks, and wondered how time distorted under Siamis's enchantment.

Derek peered in the open doorway, then stepped into the enormous salon with its fine old desk and the comfortable circle of low chairs with embroidered cushions that had somehow survived the revolution. Everything was the way it was supposed to be, except that was not Lilah behind that flat stare.

Hibern shut the door and set her back to it.

Lilah didn't move even when Senrid whipped the scarf around her face, firmly covering her mouth. She just stared.

The boys began picking up objects in the room and holding them before her eyes, but she never gave them a glance. It was as if they were invisible. Lilah's blank gaze was turned toward Derek.

He met that flat gaze and ripped off the mask. It was time to end this nightmare, and get out. He knelt before her chair so she'd see him well enough to focus for Leander's spell.

Lilah brought her hand up in a fast, deadly arc. Senrid was the first to react to the glint of steel, smacking Derek out of the way, the green-glowing tip of the knife cutting the air a fingernail's breadth from Derek's throat. Leander, Jilo, and Hibern all lunged toward them, then stilled as Derek fell back on his butt.

"Lilah?" Derek exclaimed. "It's Derek."

"Somebody took extra time inside the enchantment," Senrid muttered. "Gave her this blood-spelled knife, and commanded her to use it on you."

"Blood-spell?" Derek asked.

"All it has to do is nick you. The magic gets into your blood, and Norsunder can get at you," Senrid said. "Control you." He grabbed Lilah's wrist from behind, and twisted until she dropped the knife onto the floor. "The spell is very hard to make."

"And very hard to break," came a new voice from behind them.

While everyone's attention was on Lilah, the door had opened noiselessly. Hibern felt a strong arm bend her right arm up behind her and a hand clap over her mouth.

Senrid, Derek, Jilo, and Leander whirled around.

"Siamis," Senrid whispered sickly.

Derek's first reaction was disgust at yet another failure of magic, but maybe this was better: hand to hand.

Hibern stomped as hard as she could on the man's instep, but she could feel her sandal sliding over his boot, and Siamis's soft laugh stirred the top of her hair. Then his grip tightened, bending her arm up behind her to an excruciating degree. She groped with her free hand, trying to get her elbow up to dig into his ribcage.

A Norsundrian warrior stepped up to her side, crossbow pointed directly at her ribs, and she subsided, her heart crowding her throat.

Derek rose slowly to his feet, readying for an instant of inattention on Siamis's part. Come on, Hibern—someone—distract him, he was thinking.

Jilo nudged Leander, glancing toward Lilah, who twitched, blinking. Leander softly whispered the antidote spell as Senrid kept one hand on Lilah's wrist, his other gripping the transport tokens so tightly his knuckles crepitated.

Siamis said to Derek, "Well, king-breaker. What's it to be? Her life or yours?"

'King-breaker'? Rage ignited in Derek. He snatched Lilah's knife from where it had fallen and flung it straight at Siamis's head.

But Siamis was faster. In three moves he thrust Hibern stumbling, swept the crossbow from his guard to whack the knife spinning—

"*Now*," Senrid yelled, his voice cracking.

Siamis shot the bolt as everyone said their transfer words—

Senrid landed hard, rolled, then sprang up, ignoring the transfer nausea as he stared witlessly at Derek, who lay lifeless on the grass outside Tsauderei's cottage, the bolt sticking up from his heart.

Lilah staggered, then flung herself down beside him, crying, "Derek? Derek?" And then, holding tightly to his lifeless hand, she let out a long, desolate howl that soon brought everyone running.

Tsauderei came out, leaning heavily on a stick, and gazed down at Derek's lifeless form. The old mage looked even older, face furrowed with grief and regret. It was Senrid who laid hands to the bolt sticking up so horribly from Derek's chest; everyone flinched as if it were pulled from their own bodies as Senrid drew it out then snapped it angrily over the cliff.

"We have to take him to Selenna house," Lilah wailed.

"We have to get Peitar first, we have to," Bren shouted.

"Yes," Faen cried. "You get the king. We orphans will guard Derek's . . ." He choked on a sob.

Tsauderei put up a hand for silence. "All of you know that Derek Diamagan would prefer being Disappeared in the open air," he said. "And Peitar will prefer knowing everything was done properly, beginning with a cessation of this quarrel over Derek's lifeless body. Lilah, you, Bren, Innon, Ruddy, Sig, the five of you may take him to the village. The rest of you, get yourselves cleaned up, and find candles. There are plenty in the storage cupboard at Selenna House; you needn't raid the villagers for all theirs."

Nobody argued with that.

Someone in the village brought out an artisan's table as a bier, over which the grandmother in the house where Derek had been staying produced an heirloom quilt to

cover the table. The five kids—all five still weeping—laid
him on that as gently as if he could feel their tenderness,
and many hands came forward to straighten his clothes and
limbs, and order the long, tangled hair that he had rarely
bothered combing in life.

Lilah collapsed by the bier, weeping wildly; Bren keened
on the other side, next to Innon, who stood, head bent,
tears dripping down his face. Most of the brigade wept with
them until the first paroxysm was over, and then, in ones
and twos, they all repaired to bathe, and dress in whatever
they thought was their best.

Senrid remained behind with Tsauderei to give a report.
At the end, he said flatly, "King-breaker?"

Tsauderei gave his head a shake. "You know how Norsundrians look for the worst in people, and then use it to
divide others. Let it go. It's immaterial now."

Senrid turned his palm up in assent, but those words—
king-breaker—continued to fret him, because once again he
sensed knowledge shared by others that they weren't going
to tell him. He wasn't sure if this was because he was a Marloven, and therefore not to be trusted, or because Tsauderei
and Derek had been antagonistic, but as he turned away he
promised himself he would find out.

Ordinarily it was left for the next of kin to do the Disappearance spell, and failing that, the highest-ranking person
there. Given the preponderance of those with royal claims,
and the fact that Derek's brother was in another country
altogether, Tsauderei snuffed the possibility of argument
by declaring that he would do the spell himself, as eldest.
No one objected to that.

So at sunset he stood at the head of the bier, holding a
tall candle in both hands, though one of his knees shot
pains up his legs to pool at the base of his spine. But he was
determined to see this memorial through with utmost respect. He was grateful that he would never have to hold the
conversation with Peitar that he had been rehearsing in his
head for a couple of years now—well knowing that it would
be useless. Peitar would never have believed ill of Derek.
And the worst of it was, Tsauderei was fairly certain that
Derek would never have intended ill.

King-breaker. How unsettling, this oblique corroboration from a source such as Siamis. Why would the Norsundrian have said that?

What did he hear inside Derek's head?

Tsauderei shifted position minutely, as yet another child stepped forward, clutching a candle in tight, sweaty fingers, to speak a long, disjointed, sob-punctuated memory.

The sun sank beyond the snowcaps in the west overlooking slumbering Sartor, and still they came forward to speak their memories.

The Mearsieans stood in a tight group, eventually their surreptitious nudgings of CJ becoming more obvious, until finally she stepped forward and said in an uneven voice, "I didn't know Derek's name when we all got taken prisoner by that evil skunk Kessler. But I met him when he refused to fight in Kessler's disgusting army, and I . . ."

That wasn't coming out right. She looked back at Clair, who stepped to her side. "CJ saved Derek's and his brother Bernal's lives," she said in a firm voice. "Without knowing who they were. Derek told us that moment was important to him. That showing mercy to a person not because of who they are, simply because they are another person, was important. We don't . . . we didn't know Derek. But we'll always remember that about him."

She and CJ stepped back together, holding hands tightly, as a brief rustle of approving whispers went around the watchers.

Atan, standing at the back with Rel, murmured for his ears only, "That was actually civilized."

Rel shifted, his breathing changing. "You've seen the worst of CJ. You haven't seen the best."

"Is there a best?"

"Yes. You just heard about one incident."

Atan struggled to control the corrosive sense of dislike. It helped no one, it never did anyone any good. "I'd like to hear more," she said. "Not just for me. But because, especially at times like today, there needs to be more best in the world. Peitar is going to be so hurt."

Rel's chin came down. "Yes. He and Derek should have been brothers. Did you know?"

"Peitar and Lilah both told me something about Peitar's

mother having loved Derek and Bernal's father, but she was a princess and he was a stablemaster. How sad that is, when stupid rules . . ." She sensed herself nearing uncomfortable thoughts, *personal* thoughts, and said instead, "I hate the idea that Peitar will come out of that enchantment to this news. I wonder if he would like to walk the labyrinth." Then she thought back, and it occurred to her that Peitar had never actually been to Sartor. "I should invite him. When the troubles are over. Don't you think he would love it? He knows so much about history."

Rel said, "From what I saw, I think he would like that very much."

And as the painful memorial went on, Atan called the royal Purrad to mind and set Peitar there, imagining his reaction to the wind chimes, the sough of leaves and branches, the scents, the sound of footfalls on pebbles, the unfolding of quiet beauty all around. Some of the pain banding her heart loosened.

Hibern observed Atan and Rel whispering, then raised her head to take in the alliance all gathered. And no one arguing. She looked down, grief and guilt intensified by a new thought, that it took tragedy to unite them. Her gaze lit on Derek's still profile, and the unsettling way the flickering candlelight made it seem as if he breathed. It took leaders to draw people together for good purposes, she was thinking.

She glanced inadvertently at Senrid, who stood in the second row on the other side of the bier, between Jilo and Leander.

Senrid was unaware of her glance, unaware of anything. He was shut tightly inward, lest Liere hear his thoughts.

Memory and custom both threw him off balance. The sight of Tsauderei standing in a robe of sky blue, embroidered down the front in gold with the ancient symbols of the Twelve Blessed Things, was so unlike Marloven custom, and yet Senrid was thrown back in memory to when he stood at his father's bier, a shivering five-year-old, surrounded by black-clad people tall as the castle towers, the bier framed by leaping torchlight.

In Marloven Hess, a king's memorial was held at midnight, with everyone singing the Hymn to the Fallen. This ancient hymn was accorded all kings, commanders, and jarls, but also every warrior who fell in battle, no matter what his background or degree.

Senrid remembered the deep male voices singing the hymn, and in his own mind, he sang it over again for Derek Diamagan. He shut out the kids' halting, rambling memories, which had no place in Marloven custom: the stories and anecdotes were reserved for the banquet following the burning of the person's private effects by the family.

I know why you did that, Siamis, Senrid thought, icecold conviction flowing along his nerves. *You didn't want Derek to make Sarendan ready to fight you off. You're the real king-breaker. At least, that's what you intend. But I'm going to make sure you don't get your chance.*

I'm going to kill you myself.

Nobody saw that Liere had already slipped away.

PART FOUR
The Alliance Acts

Chapter One

GETH-DELES is an azure gem in the night skies of the fifth and third worlds from Erhal, the sun.

Scattered across that blue expanse, a necklace of islands rises on the sea, vanishing in a horizon where the sun burns itself out among the monumental clouds.

The islands offer a marvelous variety, dark forests and grassy plains quilted with ordered avenues of crops, and evenings alive with multicolored fireflies. White-glare sunlight splashes in shards off the endless sea by day, and silver nights glow on cascades down low mountains, flowing into calm shores along the smooth sweep of the sea.

Humans—mostly Ancient Sartorans, fleeing the cataclysm known as the Fall—are latecomers to this much-populated world, calling it the World of Floating Islands.

Many of these islands, it transpires, truly do float, bolstered beneath by an endless tangle of growth that supports soil and rock, hill and tumbling water, but the rest are true islands, connected to vast elongated continental shelves in constant motion. The undersea beings cared nothing for constant quakes; it was the mysterious former surface-dwellers who bound the floating islands, tamed the quakes to gentle rocking, and left here and there monuments whose design united forests, sea, sunset, and air into a conspiracy of beauty.

On the largest island of a complicated archipelago sits the largest and oldest city in the world, Isul Demarzal. Here, walled within the city walls, is Charlotte's Palace, a ramble of a low building, patchworked with gardens, housing all the human world's archives and a library, a center of magic and learning, until recently well-protected against Norsunder.

Down the centuries there was little contact between the two worlds revolving opposite one another, until relatively recently, as Sartorias-deles recovered enough magic for world transfers. Geth's mages, descendants of Sartor but now with their own customs and disciplines of study, fashioned their own methods of transfer.

It was this magic that Norsunder was after.

Liere didn't know that.

She didn't know anything about Geth-deles, except that Siamis was there, and, as frequently happened when shocked or grieved, she heard her father's bitter, scornful voice ranting in memory that she was selfish, stupid, clumsy, and that whatever happened was surely her fault.

So it was time to stop being weak. It was time to be like Senrid, and do something about it. When the memorial was over, and Tsauderei returned to his cottage, she overheard him reading just-arrived messages to Atan and Hibern: Siamis was already back in Geth.

Clarity soothed Liere's jangling nerves. Erai-Yanya, who was Keeper of the Dyr, was on Geth-deles. Siamis was on Geth-deles. Liere knew how to break Siamis's spell by using the dyr. Therefore she ought to stop being weak and selfish, hiding in the Valley while the world's mages struggled to vanquish Siamis's spell, go to Geth-deles, get Erai-Yanya to pull the dyr out of its magical hiding place, give it to her, and then . . .

Well, then she would either win or die.

She considered telling Senrid, but sensed the darkness of his mood. Besides, he'd find all kinds of reasons for her to stay, and really, what they amounted to was that she was weak. And useless. Just as her father said.

But she'd prove them all wrong. Yes. That was the way to think.

She knew that Hibern and Arthur both had the world transfer spell in their books. All she needed was a Destination. She understood that much. So, while the others talked, or consoled the grief-stricken Sarendans, she slipped into Tsauderei's cottage and went through Arthur's books until she found what she sought: the world transfer spell. And in another book, a description of the Gate of Isul Demarzal.

Everything was happening at Isul Demarzal, so that was the place to go.

She fixed the Destination firmly in mind, spoke the spell, and magic seized her.

Atan went to sleep feeling tense and headachy from hiding her reaction to Derek's death. Which had been . . . no reaction. To be truthful, even a little relief, but acknowledging that increased that sick inner sense because she knew that was wrong. So she'd made herself attend the memorial, staring dry-eyed down at Derek's still profile while surrounded by the genuine grief of people she liked, and while she hid her own lack of emotion, she hoped some of their grief would enter her heart and clean out the residual anger.

Hibern spent a sleepless night, her mind insisting on seeing that horrible scene over and over again, beginning with Lilah's crazy-eyed swipe with the knife, and her own futile, stupid leaping forward. And then those hands grabbing her from behind.

She knew that Siamis, and not she, was to blame for Derek's death, but the overwhelming grief and anger sparked a deep conviction of guilt. When a bleak dawn at last lightened the cottage, it was a relief to get up.

She and Atan bundled into their coats. The flying magic kept them from getting drenched and frozen, but the chill gripped them the moment their feet touched the ground, and they hurried into Tsauderei's cottage.

The old mage and Arthur were not alone. The study group stood around feeling, and looking, awkward, and Senrid was there, grim-faced, as Lilah tearfully argued with Tsauderei, "Oh *please*. Just Peitar. Why would it hurt to rescue just one person? Why do you have to wait?"

Tsauderei said, "It's best for the kingdom, for the world, because there is a larger plan."

"But it's horrible!" Lilah sobbed. "That Kessler, he tied me in a chair for *days*, and there was never any dark so I could sleep—"

Tsauderei said, "Lilah, Kessler's Norsundrians were only in Miraleste a day at most before they set sail."

"And you've got no rope burns," Senrid pointed out, indicating Lilah's freckled wrists; the movement slid his shirt cuff back slightly, revealing the white scars of his own rope burns. "What you're remembering is distortion because of the enchantment."

Lilah turned on him. "But don't you *see*?" Another sob shook her. "Don't you see, it *felt* like days and days, so what are they doing to my brother? Right now? It could feel like years and years of telling him over and over to do horrid things."

Tsauderei said, "I'm sorry, Lilah. If it helps at least a little, neither Kessler nor Siamis is in Sarendan. So it is doubtful that Peitar is being told anything."

Lilah's chest heaved and her breath shuddered as tears bounced down her face. "You should have gotten him out first."

She didn't sound angry, she sounded broken, and no one had the heart to say that her rescue was at Derek's insistence.

Atan and Hibern both backed to the door. Arthur followed them, his customary vague expression brow-furrowed with question. "Did either of you move my books?" he whispered.

"Didn't touch them," Jilo said, at his shoulder. "Wouldn't."

"Me either," Clair said softly.

"Nor I, without permission," Atan said.

Hibern said, "Is something missing?"

"No, but my new study book, the one I copied all Erai-Yanya's notes about Geth into, it was moved, and so was my spell book."

Lilah headed for the door, beyond which they stood. She gave another heart-wrenching sob, freckled fingers covering her face. The study group moved aside. Lilah's desolation was reflected in their averted gazes, Arthur absently wiping his inky fingers on the sides of his already-ink-stained trousers. The girls exited, and Arthur withdrew to his pile of books.

Atan and Hibern hunched into their coats, the bitter wind fitting the bleak mood. "I think this might be a day to spend by the fireside reading," Atan said.

As they lifted into the air, a short blond figure chased after them through the sheeting of rain, and Senrid caught up, his yellow hair blowing straight back off his tense forehead. "Have you seen Liere?"

Atan and Hibern looked at one another. "Isn't she with the other girls?" Hibern asked. "She didn't come back with us last night."

"She wasn't at Tsauderei's, either," Senrid said. "If you see her, pass the word that the Mearsiean girls want to have breakfast with her, will you?" He left abruptly.

Hibern and Atan retreated to the hermit's cottage, closing the door hastily to keep the warmth inside. As Atan sliced the last of the previous day's bread, she said slowly, "That does seem a bit odd. That no one can find Liere. But if Senrid, who seems to have appointed himself Liere's big brother, is not worried, then—well, good."

Hibern looked up from glancing at and neatly stacking all the books on the table. "Senrid loathes fuss. Don't assume anything from his demeanor. I think I'm going to take a quiet look around after I finish my toast. I just won't say anything to anyone."

"I'll join you," said Atan, bringing the toasting fork to the fire. "Four eyes being better than two."

As Hibern sliced cheese to bring to the toast now that the underside was done, she thought back through the previous evening, and then exclaimed, "Atan, I haven't seen Liere since the memorial."

Atan looked up from the golden cheese just beginning to bubble. "Nor have I, now that I think about it."

Hibern went on, remembering what Arthur had said, and hating the possible conclusion. "Further, I think Senrid knows that. In fact, I think he knows where she went, but he's being extra careful to make sure."

Atan looked startled. "Where? Back to Bereth Ferian?" She set the fork down, and the two poked the hot bread to their plates.

Hibern reluctantly spoke the words, as if saying them aloud would make it true. "Geth-deles."

"What?" Atan's expression of surprise turned to skepticism. "Liere? That poor little thing is frightened by her own shadow. And she knows no magic."

"She can be very determined, when it comes to what she thinks of as her duty."

Atan drew in a breath. "But still, she doesn't know any magic."

"Yes and no," Hibern said. "She has a perfect memory. I guess because of that Dena Yeresbeth. She successfully used a very complicated spell to bring the dyr out from timelessness, where it had been hidden behind years of protective wards. And she did it by herself. Without knowing how to read. When she was ten."

Atan hastily swallowed the bite she'd just taken. "Would she do something crazy like transfer to Geth? Why?"

A tight voice spoke from behind: "If she thought it was her duty."

Hibern and Atan whipped around to find Senrid standing in the open door. He added, "When I first met her, she thought it was her duty to climb on the back of a horse made out of lightning and go around the world flashing that dyr while half Norsunder was howling after her blood. And yesterday, I'm very sure she managed to convince herself that Derek's death was her fault, and therefore it was her duty to go after Siamis herself because she'd failed the entire world."

The sharp precision of Senrid's consonants revealed how angry he was.

Senrid pointed at the door. "You left it open." He shut it. "Arthur just told me that Tsauderei reported a transfer out of the Valley. He thinks it was one of us on another errand."

"We've got to tell him what happened," Atan exclaimed.

Senrid's teeth showed as he lifted a piece of cheese-topped bread from the plate. "After I'm gone."

"But—"

Senrid cut in. "You know—" He paused, jerking around when the door he'd shut behind him banged open. But when he saw that it was only CJ, not Tsauderei, he continued on, "You know what we'll hear, a lot of horseshit about how children can't do anything, and—"

"And planning, and waiting, and let the adults think it through," CJ said, coming around the side of the battered old couch. "While they take another million years to get around to doing anything. We think Sartora's gone to Geth to chase Siamis. And we're going to help!"

"What can *you* possibly do?" Senrid poked his half-eaten bread at her.

"What we did in Bereth Ferian when Siamis attacked with that enchantment the first time. It was your plan," CJ retorted, crossing her arms, as the Mearsiean girls crowded in behind her, Clair looking troubled. "We can search, or lure Siamis out, or—"

"My stupid plan that nearly got us all killed?" Senrid shot back. "You still don't see that, do you? The only reason why Siamis didn't kill the lot of us was because Oalthoreh and the northern lighters were also decoying him, so Evend could walk into that rift and die closing it."

"But we aren't dead," CJ said, spreading her hands. "Sartora's *alone*. We need to find her. And *help* her. The more we have to search, the better, right? And then we can also break Siamis's spell, if he's spreading it around there."

"Stay here," Senrid said. "There's nothing you can do—"

"Who," she said loudly, "was just blabbing about children can't do anything?"

"You're useless," Senrid said. "Except in making things worse."

"Oh, yeah, Mr. Too-big-for-your-britches? I've been in as many adventures as you have. More! And I never tried to—"

Senrid's temper ignited. "If you try to fling my uncle's penchant for executions in my teeth—"

"You'll do what, execute me?" CJ cut in, and waved a hand. "Save it for Siamis. In fact, if you want to execute him, I'll hold the arrows. I already hated him before he did that to Derek, and now I hate him even more."

She and Senrid glared at each other, both fighting guilt

and regret. CJ harbored a secret terror that she might be responsible for Sartora going off like that to another world. She wasn't quite sure why or how. It was just those nasty looks Atan had been shooting at her.

Senrid endured the goad of guilt because he'd known very well that Derek's insistence on rescuing Lilah had been needless, but he'd agreed mostly out of restlessness and boredom. Because the other rescues had been easy— though Tsauderei had warned them more than once that there were probably extra traps waiting.

Clair nodded at Hibern. "Right before the memorial yesterday, Liere was asking me about signs, and how to pronounce certain words, but I thought she was just asking to know. Not that she was going to do anything."

"We've waited around long enough." Senrid pulled a piece of paper out of his pocket. "Arthur taught me the world transfer spell."

By then all the alliance had arrived, and everyone looked at Atan.

She looked back, knowing what they expected—caution, threats to tell Tsauderei, her tutor and first guardian. But all she could think was, *Julian.*

If Liere had gone after Siamis, who had taken Julian . . .

She said to Senrid, "When do we start?"

Senrid gazed back, surprised.

Hibern looked from one to the other, knowing she was missing something, but more important than that, it looked as if a whole lot of people were about to go haring off separately to Geth.

She braced herself, remembering what Erai-Yanya had said about the future, and her place in it. And she raised her voice. "I won't go straight to Tsauderei if you all promise to just find Liere, and bring her back. No chasing after Siamis or trying to end his spells. Geth-deles is not our world. We know nobody there, or how they do things."

CJ looked belligerent, but when Senrid stated, "I agree completely. I don't know why Liere suddenly thinks she has to go rescue Geth-deles, but she can explain it all to us once we get her back."

"Yes," Clair said. "That's the best plan."

CJ sighed. "I'd love to boot the stinkard Siamis right out of the world."

"As long as he gets booted," Senrid said. "Who cares who does it?"

At the back of the crowd, Bren whispered to Lilah, "Sooner they get rid of Siamis, sooner we can free Peitar."

"Then let's go with them," Lilah whispered fiercely. "I *can't* stay here. Everything is memories. Let's go, too. And I am going to pretend that Peitar is with us."

Innon said soberly, "We all will."

Bren jerked his head in a nod, rubbing his red, swollen eyes. "Yes. We'll talk to him like he's with us. And we'll even say what he says back. And then when we get back and he's free, we'll tell him all about the good things he said and did."

As several voiced agreement, Hibern looked at the faces that had been so grief-stricken, now firm with resolve. She knew they were going to go anyway, so the best thing would be to keep everyone together. And maybe two world transfers in a day would land everybody in bed for a week, so they wouldn't try any more stupid ideas.

She raised her voice. "I'll agree, and not tell Tsauderei, if you also agree to take notecases, in case the magic somehow separates us. So get whatever you want to take. We'll find Sartora. And everyone transfers straight back. Agreed?"

Everybody spoke or signaled their agreement. Then the door banged open, and people streamed out.

Hibern said to Senrid, "I mean it about the notecases."

His lip curled, but he patted the pocket in his black uniform trousers. "I've got mine here."

Hibern knew she was right, that she'd caught him before he was about to hare off alone after Liere. "I still think we ought to tell Tsauderei that we're going."

"Why?" Senrid retorted. "We let Tsauderei dictate the plan for rescuing Lilah, and look where that got us."

Hibern flashed back, "That is not true, or fair. He didn't want anyone to go. He wanted us to wait. But when he saw that Derek meant to go anyway, he added those extra cautions."

Senrid jerked a shoulder up. "Then tell me how having

Jilo staying here, watching in the book for Siamis transferring and alerting us, was wrong?"

"Book?" Glenn asked.

Senrid's face blanched, and Hibern suspected he hadn't slept at all, or he would never have made a slip like that.

She turned to Glenn. "Magic book." And saw Glenn's complete lack of interest—he was only interested in swords and battles.

Senrid crossed his arms, a sure sign that whatever he was going to say next, Hibern would hate. He shifted to Marloven. "If you're about to yap out that we should tell Tsauderei now, then you can save your breath. How long before he and a posse of mages hunt Jilo down and wrest that book away from him because 'no powerful artifact should be left in the hands of a child?' Don't try to tell me they didn't do that after Liere took the dyr around when Siamis first showed up. They couldn't wait to separate her from the damned thing."

Hibern stood on the low table, and faced everyone. "For the last time. The plan is, we go, we find Liere, we come back immediately."

Leander said, "What Destination?"

Arthur spoke up from the back. "The city everyone is worried about is called Isul Demarzal, but Norsunder is there now, Tsauderei said, so I wouldn't use anything in that city. When Erai-Yanya first traveled there, she used a white sand beach as her Destination. There's one near Isul Demarzal, an unlikely place to find Norsundrians."

"Don't we need tokens?" Atan called over heads, as Rel silently joined her. "This is a world transfer."

"But this spell works differently from ours," Arthur said. "It's kind of like a tunnel, or lights strung along the way. It's . . . different. Everyone who's going, form small circles."

He might have said more, but Senrid had already memorized the spell. He vanished.

CJ had been watching. The Mearsieans grabbed hands, and Clair, who had been practicing silently, did the spell.

Aided by Hibern and Arthur, the others popped into transfer.

Tsauderei was sitting in his cottage, staring in dismay at the note he'd just received from Erai-Yanya, who had transferred all the way from Geth just to send it.

He was pondering what—if anything—to say to that half-grown, half-trained, thoroughly wild bunch of puppies currently eating breakfast in houses around the valley when a tracer alerted him to sudden cluster of transfers.

Instantly suspicious, he hobbled to his door, launched into the air, and scowled at the revealing emptiness all around. He reached the deserted hermit's cottage to discover that even Atan was gone. He cursed himself, suspecting what had happened: he should never have told Atan about Julian being taken to Geth.

He slammed out. As soon as he reached his desk he ignored the rain soaking beard and clothes, pulled out paper, and began writing letters.

Chapter Two

Geth-deles, Isul Demarzal

JULIAN walked down the street.

She liked Geth. It was warm, and the air smelled like gardens and fruits. She liked looking at the houses, so different from what she was used to. She liked the shiny wood that they were made of, and she liked those roofs that sloped at a gentle curve upward to a flat top. Like houses with hats. So much prettier than the slanted roofs in Eidervaen, with gargoyles and things carved around the eaves. And much too high. None of these were high buildings.

Siamis told her they couldn't build high because of all the ground shaking, and the roofs could be flat because it never snowed here. The big thing they called Charlotte's Palace was only one story. She liked that, but she didn't like how you had to walk and walk and walk to get anywhere inside. It was more fun to walk outside, and see how many kinds of wood and how many kinds of houses there were.

But if she tried to go out the Charlotte's Palace Gate and the runaway prince wasn't there, the mean-faces in black or gray slapped her back inside. If he was there, they didn't slap her, but she still couldn't go out.

"Why?" she asked, the first time she saw the runaway prince again.

"Because Siamis wants you here, for now."

She scowled, then said, "You didn't come back for me."

"I did. You weren't there before I had to leave."

Julian eyed him. "He said he gave you orders."

"That's true."

"So he gave you orders to guard this gate?"

"No. This gate is the result of his orders," Kessler said. "Because he lied." Then he rode out to inspect the perimeter teams, leaving Julian standing there.

So she couldn't explore outside the gate. She was stuck with the dream people inside the gates.

At first she'd liked how quiet the Geth people were. How nobody cared when she traded those stupid clothes from the trunk in her room for a long silken thing of crimson and gold with speckled green flowery things, so long she could wrap it around herself and still have long streamers, the way many did here. Nobody noticed when she took a robe thing of bright blue out of someone's house, when it rained and the air turned a little bit cold at night. Nobody noticed if she walked in and took food right off people's plates.

It was just like in Eidervaen, when Siamis had talked those sharp-voiced, frowny grownups like Chief Veltos into smiling and quiet.

She heard noise. Galloping horses. She sighed. That meant more of the mean ones in gray or black. At least they no longer slapped her every time they saw her, like they'd done at first back in Eidervaen, before Siamis told them not to.

She missed those days, when he talked to her a lot. Only he'd asked such boring questions. Not about swings, and living in the forest with Irza and Hinder, but about Atan, and Chief Veltos. After Julian said how much she hated them all for trying to make her into a princess, the way Mother used to, he didn't ask any more. He let her do whatever she liked. He was wonderful!

But he was the only wonderful one. All his followers were worse than Atan, and worse even than Gehlei or the baras Irza was growing up to be, or Chief Veltos, always telling her to brush her hair, and learn letters, and wear stupid princess clothes. The followers didn't do any of those things, but they uttered ugly words when they saw her, and sometimes they would spit right in front of her, or where she'd been. If she didn't want to step in the spit, she had to move away. One time she stepped in it without knowing, until her foot got slippery, so she dropped the clothes right there, wiped her foot on them, and ran off in her skin to get new ones. She heard a woman in gray laughing the ear-hurting kind of laugh as Julian went away, and a man mocking the one who spat, saying, "That puts you in your place."

She hopped to the side of the road so she wouldn't get spat upon, and watched as a bunch of them galloped by. What was that in the front of the middle one? A girl!

Julian stared with interest, getting a good look at a skinny girl with short hair flopping around her face. She had a red mark on one cheek and on her jaw, and a big scratch on her arm.

Julian waited until the last gallopers passed, then she ran after them to see who this visitor was. Another girl would be very nice, if she wasn't bossy. She didn't wear princess clothes, so maybe she wouldn't be bossy.

Julian made it to the big space at the front of Charlotte's Palace. It was so very pretty, made with shiny wood that was mostly a pale gold, that Siamis said came out of the sea.

The horse riders stopped, and one of them pushed the girl off the horse so she landed on her hands and knees.

They laughed as they dismounted, and one (it was the same one whose spit Julian had stepped in) yanked the girl up by her hair, and when she gasped, led the laughter.

Inside they went, past all the lights that hung down with the pretty globes of glass around them, to keep fires from streaming, Siamis had said. When the ground shivered, the lights swayed and swayed, making shadows dance in rhythm.

They passed the first big book room where a lot of the people who lived here went about putting all the books and scrolls back on the shelves after those crabby people in gray had thrown them. Julian had watched them one morning in one of the many other book rooms, moving from shelf to shelf, taking things down, looking, then throwing the books on the floor.

Julian had tried to help by grabbing some books to

throw, but they'd screamed at her to go away. Julian hated books, so she didn't understand why they would want to look at them before throwing them. You'd think they'd just throw them if they hated learning, too.

They passed the hall where another three of the crabby gray ones did magical spells and passes. The air glittered here and there, but nothing else happened, and they looked crabbier than ever. Good. Julian didn't like any of them.

Finally they came to the room with the pictures painted on the ceiling, of winged horses and people, and clouds upon clouds, building toward strange stars, as if the ceiling were higher than the sky. Julian liked to lie on the floor and look at this room when no one else was in it.

But right now Siamis was in it, talking to two crabby grays.

He looked up, and smiled as Spit Mouth shoved the girl into the room, followed by the rest of his riders. Julian crept along the perimeter of the room so she could see, as Siamis said, "Liere Fer Eider! I wondered who might be venturesome enough to perform a world transfer directly outside the city gates. This is a surprise. What brought you here?"

The girl's voice quavered. "I came to get rid of you."

That made the followers laugh so hard that Julian hated them all the more.

The girl jerked her chin up. "I did it before."

Siamis smiled his nice smile. "Yes, you did," he said in his nice voice. "And I trust you brought the dyr? No, I can see from the lamentable state of your dress that you were thoroughly searched, and you neglected to bring the most important element of my defeat. Well, we shall have plenty of time to talk about its whereabouts. But not right now. Put her in . . . where? The biggest building I have ever had the misfortune to get lost in, yet no convenient lock-up. One of the cold-cellars will do."

He pointed to a couple of the followers in black, but the girl shrugged them off, pointed to the shiny sword leaning against the table, and said, "Why did you leave the sword named Truth in Bereth Ferian?"

Siamis stopped what he was doing and got very still. The girl also was very still. Julian struggled to understand the silence, then Siamis said in his nicest voice, "It was a gift, Liere."

The girl stiffened as if he'd poked her.

"It was a gift," Siamis said gently, almost sadly.

"And the coins were a gift too?" Her voice shook.

"No, those were in the nature of a warning, exactly as you surmised. Take her away." He flicked his fingers and turned back to the grays.

Each of the followers in black grabbed one of the skinny girl's arms, and they marched off, the girl's feet barely touching the ground.

Julian trotted along behind.

Siamis watched her go, until interrupted by the ambitious young mage who had carefully pointed out all Dejain's shortcomings in order to be assigned to this job. "That urchin will be pestering your prisoner," he said sourly.

"I want her to," Siamis retorted. "Though Julian is as ignorant as a garden slug, she's not stupid. As you ventured to take an interest, and you've been singularly useless in locating anything related to the Geth transfer magic, you will station yourself somewhere nearby, where the urchin cannot see you, but you can hear them both, and you will write down every word they say."

The pair of guards shoved Liere into a cellar room from which everything had been carried out. Here, in the dark, she took stock of her injuries. One elbow throbbed, she had a cut on the side of her face, and her shins were scraped. Everywhere else ached from the gravel she'd fallen on when they knocked her down. She could ignore all that.

What she could not ignore was her self-hatred, her disgust at her own stupidity. She had heard Senrid say so many times that you scout first, and figure out what to do afterward.

But no, she'd blundered straight into the enemy. Of course they'd be guarding the gate of the city they'd already conquered. She deserved exactly what had happened.

For a time she sat there bound so tightly in self-loathing that she wished Siamis would come in and strike her head off with that sword. A *gift!* Somehow that was the worst threat Siamis ever could have uttered, all the worse because she didn't understand at all what made him say that. It could only be for some unexplainable, horrific reason.

Then she thought guiltily how angry Senrid would be if she admitted to wanting Siamis to strike off her head. She could just hear him saying that was the coward's way out, that it wasn't her fault evil people did evil things. Her job— she could hear him, could see him pacing around his study, rapping his knuckles on the sills of the four tall windows, and then the desk, and then the carved map case—her job would be to *resist* evil.

Well. There was one thing she was good at, thanks to her mean brother, and that was, if they sent a bunch of bullies in to rant and rave and threaten, she could lock herself inside her head and she wouldn't hear a thing. Until she came out. But she wouldn't think about that unless she had to.

"Girl?"

That voice belonged to a child.

"Yes?"

"I saw you. Do you want me to ask Siamis to let you out of the cellar?"

"Siamis told them to put me here."

"Did you do something bad? My mother used to put me in the closet when she said I was bad."

At first, Liere thought that the little girl's voice might be some kind of Norsunder trick. But she could hear the emotions under the surface thoughts on the other side of the door. This little girl's memories were sharp and clear, so clear they hurt. Liere saw her mother, a pretty woman with a mean mouth who talked in a hissing whisper. She had jewels set in her fingernails that sparkled when she slapped and pinched . . . Julian. The little girl's name was Julian.

Liere whispered, "I did nothing bad. Siamis will try to make me tell him where—" She halted before mentioning the dyr. She didn't know if Siamis had a daughter. He wasn't old enough for that, surely; maybe this little girl was a spy, or why else would she be permitted to run around? She certainly wasn't dream-walking under the enchantment.

Or, somebody from Norsunder might be listening. Senrid had told Liere once how his uncle used to put prisoners together so they would talk, and reveal things that they wouldn't when interrogated.

Liere said in a firmer voice, "I don't know anything."

"Me either! Learning is stupid and boring," Julian said.

Liere had to laugh, though she wasn't sure why. That sounded more like an ordinary child, not some kind of mysterious Norsunder child spy, if they even had such a thing. "What's your name?" Liere asked, so Julian wouldn't know her thoughts had been listened to.

"Julian. What's yours?"

"Liere."

"If you come down, and look under the door, maybe I could see you."

Liere crouched down, put her throbbing cheek on the cool tile floor of the cellar, and peered under the door. She saw a mat of messy brown hair, and part of one eye. Small, dirty fingers wriggled under the door insistently, and the girl's thoughts came clearly. Liere briefly touched the reaching fingers, and was surprised by the flow of good feeling caused by so simple a touch.

"Would you like me to get you a piece of bread from the kitchen?" Julian asked.

Liere's stomach lurched. Until then she hadn't thought about food. Her last meal had been at noon the previous day, before the terrible news about Derek.

Hunger woke, simple and insistent. Liere remembered what Senrid had once said about being a prisoner in Norsunder Base: your job was to survive, and then to escape. In order to escape, she needed all her strength.

"Yes," she said firmly.

"I'm hungry, too," Julian announced. "I'll come back after I get something to eat. I don't think they should put people in the dark who didn't do anything bad. Is it dark in there?"

"Yes."

"I'll tell Siamis." And the feet pattered away.

Geth-deles, on a small island south of Isul Demarzal

And so the alliance took action for the first time, transferring to Geth-deles in order to find Liere. That was the stated goal, the group goal, but as usual, certain individuals had private goals.

Those left behind knew that this was more reaction than action. Tsauderei sent an emergency token to Erai-Yanya, to report that he'd lost them all.

The ground coalesced under Senrid's feet.

Or that's what it felt like. He sensed an intense flash of magic fleeing outward into the air, and wondered who might have tracers in the area.

It wasn't dark magic, so he looked around, finding himself on the beach of a small, crowded inlet. None of the others from Sartorias-deles were with him, but with no definite Destination, he'd expected the magic to scatter them. Just as well. He'd be faster alone.

He fought mild vertigo, but the transfer hadn't wrenched muscles and bones as did long transfers at home. It felt more like he'd been falling down a long, long tunnel, streaming past barely perceived sparks of light, like the ones on the mental plane when he concentrated with Dena Yeresbeth. The falling wasn't the same as diving out of the sky toward the lake as fast as he could go, as he and Puddlenose and Leander had tried in the Valley of Delfina, where his ears whistled, his eyes hurt if he opened them too wide, and the wind battered his face. There was no wind, but he'd felt that sense of sliding down and down and down.

He looked at his boots, half-sunk in white sand. That partly explained the sense of unsteady ground.

He lifted his gaze again, and this time took in more detail: the sand beside a pier, at the seaward end of which clustered long, low, narrow boats. They floated on water of a startling blue even more dense than the blue of Delfina Lake.

The air was also bluish, colors subtly different than what he was used to. The pier joined a sandstone quay surrounded by low houses made of some kind of polished material that resembled wood, except the ruddy brown color was unlike any wood he'd ever seen, more like melted chocolate with streaks of berry juice stirred in.

Lusty male singing soared over the everyday noises of chatter, hammers, and footsteps on the wooden pier. The singing poured through the open doors of a tavern next to the pier. So much for this being a children's world, Senrid thought, as he took in flirting couples, and big dock workers hauling goods back and forth along the pier.

Though youth there was aplenty, he was glad to see, because that meant he didn't stand out. Much. The boys all seemed to be wearing colorful nightdresses. No, they wore light robes, some over the sort of loose trousers he'd seen in pictures of his ancestors, only those had been gathered at the ankle and stuffed into boot tops. Some were bare-legged somewhat like that morvende boy Senrid had seen at Atan's, but the weave and colors were different: the garments had loose sleeves, and were tied with sashes or scarves, and people wore headbands of bright colors. At least nobody seemed interested in him, but he yanked his shirt from his waistband and let it hang over the belt on his riding trousers.

The Universal Language Spell worked better than he'd hoped. Someone had clearly been adapting it. The language itself was pleasant to the ear, with trills and bits that sounded like coughs at the back of the throat. Like the 'ch' in Chwahir. And it was all the same language, not the cacophony of tongues he'd heard in Jaro Harbor during the first Siamis attack.

He saw a row of boys sitting on a rail eating grilled fish on a stick. It smelled of pungent spices; he walked up to the boy on the end. "Have you seen a girl wearing clothes kind of like mine, but gray on top and green trousers? Bare feet, short hair?"

The boy waved a hand in a circle, which Senrid took to mean 'no.'

"I mean, in the last day."

Another negative.

"Where is the magic city, Issal, Isool . . . ?" he asked, to test the Language Spell as well as to orient himself.

The boy turned his head, his dark brows rising as he looked Senrid up and down. "You are a curious one! From a far island, is it? If you mean Isul Demarzal, you'll be going north." He waved his hand at the sea.

"Where's your boat?" someone on the end asked.

Senrid waved vaguely in the direction of the water, and

went on to ask people who seemed to live or work there. He'd thought to pick up Liere's trail first thing, but to his dismay, his description of Liere only caused incurious stares and negation.

So he ventured father along the shore, and still nothing.

That meant she'd done the worst possible thing: transferred herself directly to where the enemy was, instead of scouting. He let out his breath as he turned in a circle.

What now? Find out more. Like, north as in walking, or north as in another island? Instinct prompted him to look around more slowly, breathing in the familiar scents of garlic, smoked fish, hemp, and unfamiliar spicy scents.

He turned again, his attention drawn to the pier, and the boats bobbing alongside. He liked boats, liked the pleasant sound of laughter floating over the water, and the rise and fall of a lone voice in song from somewhere beyond the end of the pier. A kid's voice.

He turned his steps that way, and stepped up onto the warped boards, more poured chocolate, unlike the grainy oak or pine that came from carefully coppiced wood at home.

Each boat had at least one person in it, working away with ropes or barrels or nets. When he reached the end of the pier, he spotted the longest vessel. The singer was a girl about Senrid's age, as she sanded the rail forward.

Senrid caught the gaze of a comfortably plump, grandmotherly woman who met his gaze steadily, her expression benevolent. She sat in a kind of hammock chair, slung on the roof of what was probably the living quarters, rising waist-height from the smooth deck. Now here was someone who had surely sat right there for a while. Without much hope, he asked about Liere.

"No, she was not here," the woman answered, her gaze steady and her tone final.

"Can I get a ride to the magic city, ah, Isul Demarzal?"

"You've a few days' sailing ahead of you."

Senrid stared at her. He'd expected to be a short walk away. How had he managed to transfer a few *days* off? Clearly a lot of island beaches had white sand. No wonder no one had seen Liere! "How do I get there?"

She chuckled. "If you step aboard, nothing easier. This vessel is sailed by those your age."

That was far too easy. He backed away, scanning the
boat, which was long and narrow, with a tall mast slightly
forward of the middle, and a shorter one behind the roof
on which the old woman sat. At the bow, three girls and a
boy worked at something. They as well as the singer paid
no heed to the old woman or Senrid.

It was too convenient. Nothing was more unthreatening
than an old woman, except maybe an infant. Senrid knew
he'd spoken first because of this assumption; he never
would have addressed a brawny man sharpening a sword.
Old women didn't raise suspicion.

That in itself spiked his suspicion. So, either he could
stand there and dither, or do something. He looked around
once more for any obvious threat as he braced his feet on
the pier, and then he lifted the habitual mind-shield and
focused on the old woman, making an effort to skim the
surface of her thoughts.

It was like falling out of the sky into a new world, one
that expanded beyond the horizons, flickering with un-
countable memories filled with poignant joy, with sharp
sorrow, with the calm, infinite waters of peace. A soft inward voice said: *You do need training, do you not, dear boy?*

Senrid would have resented anyone calling him 'dear,'
except he could sense that she meant it. Further, that
everyone present in that inlet and beyond was dear to her.

And he'd heard that inward voice before—in Liere's
shared memories.

"Lilith the Guardian," he breathed. Because life had
made him wary, "You just happened to be here?" He spoke
in Sartoran.

"No," she answered in the same tongue, but her accent
carried an unfamiliar lilt. "Let us say that your arrival by
the spell given to Erai-Yanya alerted a number of people,
after your young friend Liere's unfortunate arrival before
the gates of the city. I was fastest, and I thought you might
find this conversation easier if I let you find me, rather than
my approaching you."

Senrid's nerves flared at that mention of Liere. But first
things first. "And them?" Senrid jutted his chin at the kids
working in the bow.

"They are what they seem: a group of your peers. They're on what is called on Sartorias-deles 'the Wander.'"

Senrid shrugged. There had been a time when he'd traveled with Puddlenose and Christoph on the Wander—and not by choice. It was during that journey that he'd encountered the weird whatever-it-was called Erdrael.

He eyed Lilith warily as she indicated the working teenagers at the front of the boat. They seemed completely unaware of her, or Senrid. Lilith said, "The lightest of illusions keeps attention away. You may converse safely." She smiled at the space between them. He stood on the pier, well out of physical reach, though if she were even half as powerful as legend had it, she could probably smite him with a word. A thought.

So she was permitting him to feel in control of the situation, though he wasn't. He wasn't sure how he liked that. "You said Liere's 'unfortunate arrival.'"

The furrows in Lilith's ruddy face deepened to concern. "She transferred directly to the gates of Isul Demarzal. She was immediately seized and taken into the city as a prisoner."

"Shit," he exclaimed in Marloven. "Send me there right now."

"So that you may be taken as prisoner as well?"

"Better two of us than her alone."

Lilith shook her head. "But Siamis would not put the two of you together. From what I have gathered, Detlev has marked you for his future project. Siamis would have to send you along. Do you want that?"

"No." The word was a voiceless exhalation. He didn't even try to hide his horror.

"Then you should gather your friends and go back to your world," she said. "There is nothing you can do here."

"No." Senrid said it sharply. "First, I don't know where they are. We didn't transfer together, and I don't see them. Second, I'm not in command."

"They are scattered between three islands," Lilith said. "You don't know the nature of the magic here. Suffice it to say that world transfer requires magework at this end to complete the, oh, we'll call it a tunnel, to save half a day's digression into magic as used here."

"Scattered on purpose, I take it?"

"Yes. In hopes they will think better of their decision and return home."

Senrid decided against arguing about this piece of high-handed interference. He didn't know the people or the situation here. He was clear on one thing: Lilith was sitting on the top of a boat instead of doing something.

But the answer was obvious. Whatever magic had been laid over that city surely had wards against her magical signature as well as against those of Tsauderei and the rest of them. That was the tough part of being a famous mage: other mages knew your work, and could exert their own powers to keep you from interfering with theirs.

"None of us can act," Lilith said, paralleling his thoughts. "Not only has Siamis effectively and specifically warded all the senior mages of both worlds, but he set the enchanted mages to watch for any appearance of their colleagues, using a lethal mirror ward—yes, I can see you know what that is. It was carefully thought out, and it took appreciable time to lay."

And you walked right into it, Liere. Senrid's stomach roiled.

Lilith went on. "There is even a theory that Siamis's enchantment over Sartorias-deles was, at least in part, practice for this very situation. Isul Demarzal is the oldest city in this world, the seat of magic learning."

"I won't let her sit there alone," Senrid stated. "Tell me what I can do, or I'll try to figure it out for myself."

"If you wish to help your friend, you should go home and let those best trained free her."

"No," Senrid said again, more forcefully. "Because you just told me they can't do anything. I'll bet you anything there are no mirror wards, or any wards, against *me*. I could get in and out, probably better than any senior mage they're on the watch for. And I won't use magic. And before you start telling me there are people better trained in sneaking than I am, they don't know Liere like I do."

Lilith was quiet.

Senrid grinned. "I also know the antidote to Siamis's enchantment. You need someone Norsunder doesn't expect to get inside that city. Right? Let me do it. I'm going to try anyway, unless you drop a stone spell on me, but you lighters don't do that, right?" He knew he was goading her, but he was far too angry, and too upset, to stop himself.

Lilith gazed back at him. "We are at an impasse," she said finally. "We do need someone inside who can break Siamis's enchantment—"

Senrid cut her off. "I'll look for whoever the leader is that the spell is anchored on, but I'm going after Liere. I won't let her sit there and rot." *While you lighters run around trying to be fair and nice and moral,* he didn't say.

"Go, then," she said.

Senrid was so surprised, he exclaimed, "What?"

Lilith said distinctly, "Go with my good will. I will speak to the local mages. Perhaps the sharron can find a way to get you inside." She swallowed the 'r,' and emphasized the last syllable, speaking the 'o' a little through her nose.

"'Sharron?'"

"Think of them as the long-separated cousins of the Sartoran dawnsingers, the forest dwellers. The children who sail this boat will tell you all about them. Before you go, you need to know that the First Witch was not just enchanted by Siamis in order to bind the city, we have been able to detect from a distance that she has also been warded. If you walk up to her and try magic on her, you'll kill her as well as yourself," Lilith said. "No magic can be leveled at the city wards until the wards on her are lifted." Her tone, even, reasonable, was more effective than sarcasm: *Did you really think it would be that easy?* "We know that Siamis has used a mirror ward. Do you know how to break it?"

"No," Senrid said. That level of dark magic had a habit of burning up the mages who attempted it. But Jilo had been studying wards. He would definitely know where to begin. If he found Jilo, they could do this in tandem. "First Witch?" he said.

"The woman you could say is in charge. It is a respected title here. No one can aspire to it until he or she has lived and practiced magic for fifty years. The current one is a woman, who resembles me in many ways. She has a distinctive white streak of hair right here." Lilith touched the top of her head. "The rest of her hair being dark."

Senrid said, "I'll find her. After I find Liere."

"There are two more aspects to consider. First, Siamis has set Kessler Sonscarna to guard the city."

Senrid grimaced at the name. "He doesn't know me."

"You don't actually know that," Lilith countered. "Though you have not met him, that doesn't mean he hasn't observed you. Second, we are fairly certain that Detlev is warded as well. So he might conceivably be stirred to investigate, which is another reason why the local mages feel the pressure of time. No one wants to be caught in a possible magic battle between Detlev and Siamis."

Senrid's nerves prickled. "Where's Detlev?"

"At present he is said to be somewhere in the estuary between two hill ranges, called the Marshes. There is magic centered there, akin to what is found in Shendoral and a few other places on our own world, but much wilder. Time and space are problematical."

The prickles turned to that nasty neck-gripping sensation. A sudden spurt of laughter from the tavern overlooking the water startled Senrid. "I want to kill Siamis," he burst out, then braced for the lighter lecture on morals.

Lilith said, "Is that a declaration or a request for permission?"

Senrid flushed, suspecting that his outburst just made him sound like a scrub on the swagger. Here was someone who had lived four thousand years ago. Even though she had escaped the pressure of time, she had seen the real Ancient Sartor. "So you really were there, in what they call the Fall?"

"I was." Her intent gaze softened to sadness. "My view was limited to the struggle I lost, so I cannot answer most questions."

"Maybe you can answer this. In the histories Hibern has given me, written by lighters—that is—"

"I understand your context. What is your question?"

Senrid considered that, and decided against arguing that she didn't know what he meant, but maybe she did. Maybe she could even get it from his memories. He made an effort to shrug that off, and said, "So they warn us that the native beings who have always lived on Sartorias-deles will kill off humans if they transgress enough. Is that just lighter hortatory, *Be good, or else*? I mean, wasn't the Fall about as big a transgression as you can get short of destroying everything?"

"There are two things that took the worst destruction, magic and human lives," she said. "The world was largely unharmed. Not to say that mages don't fear the indigenous life ridding the world of the human stain once and for all. Much has been said over the centuries about that, and no one knows the answer for certain, but this is my own guess: that though human greed and anger and intent to destroy were very much a part of the Fall, it was not caused by humans."

"It wasn't?" Senrid looked askance.

"Humans joined in, as you very well know. But they didn't start it. There is someone, or something, else, from outside our world, something that consumes life in order to, ah, to metamorphose, I guess the word would be. My circle believed that to be the catalyst, if not the cause, of that war, and we think it still dwells at the heart of Norsunder, wearing human guise. If it is there, surely it is waiting to make another attempt. If we are right, humanity's survival is not part of its plan."

Senrid flexed his fingers, feeling out-maneuvered and out-weaponed.

But that could wait. He needed to focus on the present problem: Liere was a prisoner, and he had to try to free her. He would always have to try, until he couldn't anymore because someone had stopped him dead.

Before Lilith could burble about children being unprepared for danger, he said recklessly, "My second question is this. Who, or rather what, is Erdrael?"

Her expression shuttered. Water slapped the sides of the boat, and from a distance came the sound of voices as the kids reworming the foresail rigging passed materials back and forth, and, farther in the distance, the singers in the tavern wailed another ballad.

Then Lilith said, "It was a common enough name in my day. What is the context of your question?" She smiled. "Besides provocation?"

He looked at the sparkling water, reminding himself that she had the kind of Dena Yeresbeth that Detlev did.

Being a lighter, she was unlikely to kill at a thought, but she had the same sort of ability. And she was definitely hearing his thoughts. That meant his mind-shield wasn't all that great when he was talking. He'd have to remember that.

But she'd riposted his question with her own, and he really wanted to know the answer. So he said, "Never mind the circumstances. Someone once transferred me to another continent, where I met up with a couple of Mearsiean boys. While we traveled in search of transportation out of there, a . . . thing appeared. Looked like a bad illusion, as it was partly transparent. But it spoke. To us. Me." And—there was the memory of that freckle-faced girl.

Senrid hated remembering the end of that episode six months later, with Detlev on the cliff on that first bloody day of Senrid's reign. That sense of helplessness still haunted him, the despair that forced him to surrender and yell for Erdrael, though he'd had no hope of succor. The memory was as vivid as the day it happened, so he let it come, and sensed Lilith's awareness.

He opened his eyes. "That was Erdrael."

"The magical illusion called 'Erdrael,'" Lilith said, "was fashioned to resemble my daughter, Erdrael, who was killed early in the Fall."

"Your daughter," he repeated, his stomach churning.

"Yes. Age was no defense against Norsunder then, any more than now."

Senrid ignored the implied warning. "So someone was using me to get to you, all this time later?" He knew he was right about being used as a piece in a game, if nothing else.

"I will have to think about what it means," Lilith said. She indicated the kids at the bow. "They'll be finished soon, and wish to set sail. If you're determined to go forward, you should probably go talk to them."

Senrid turned away reluctantly, and approached the teens at the front of the boat. "Where are you going, and can I get a ride?" he asked.

The Universal Language Spell worked oddly, with curious lags, or mental image overlays on some words, making it hard to concentrate. It felt a bit like he was trying to hear a conversation in a noisy room.

But the boat's owner, a weather-browned girl his own

age and height, said they were willing to take passengers as long as the passengers were willing to work. Senrid said he had some experience with boats, and he was invited to find a hammock in the crew quarters under their feet.

When he turned toward the hatch leading below the weather deck, he was not surprised to discover that Lilith was gone.

Chapter Three

At an enclave, on an island east of Isul Demarzal

TO Erai-Yanya and the Geth mages, Lilith related the conversation with Senrid, leaving out only the exchange about Erdrael. That, she had not known about, and she would have to contemplate it—when she had the leisure for it.

"And so Senrid is on his way now," she finished. "I suspect if I were to confront the rest of the children from Sartorias-deles, I will hear similar arguments."

"I can yank Hibern out, at least," Erai-Yanya stated.

"Do what you think is best, but I hope you will not do that to Senrid Montredaun-An," Lilith said. "I believe anyone who does will make an enemy of him. That means nothing to you, of course," she said, indicating the five Geth mages. "But it would be a very bad thing for your sister world."

The mages sat in a circle on a shaded terrace in a fragrant garden, regarding her in silence, their expressions ranging from distrust and disgust to worry.

"Senrid," Lilith said, "is going to try to rescue his friend, no matter what anyone says. So you senior mages have three choices. You can use force to take him back to safety.

Relative safety. You can leave him alone, which will probably end with his being captured by Norsunder. Or you can lay parallel plans, that is, let him—and those who will follow him, as I suspect most of those youngsters will choose—to provide exactly the distraction we need," Lilith said.

"This goes against instinct," murmured one of the mages. "We do not know these Darksider youths."

The others regarded him with varying expressions.

"They should be taken away for their safety," another, older mage stated. "And returned to Darkside of the Sun."

"If you summarily send them back to Sartorias-deles, you will deeply wound their trust, which is already tentative. Perhaps irreparably," Lilith said. "They are not only testing themselves, they are, in a sense, testing us, the elders, who have not kept them safe in spite of all our efforts."

Erai-Yanya had been nodding slowly. She remembered the trouble that she, Murial, and Gwasan used to get into in their mage student days. "So we have to work around them as well as with them, and keep them as safe as we can, without their knowing?"

"That I believe is the wisest course of action." Lilith indicated the map of Isul Demarzal's island that rested on the table between them. "We are in a situation where the unexpected, which can only be used once, might act in our favor. Here is my suggestion. The young people must be permitted to enter the city, but with a safeguard. Don't tell them it's a safeguard, of course. Convince them that they need illusory disguises, and ask the sharron to weave in certain magical precautions."

Expressions lightened around the circle as they began to plan.

Various locations on and around the main island

Kyale wrote:

> *CJ? What happened? We landed on a beach with*
> *a village around it. Their houses are really ugly, and*

the girls are all wearing nightgowns, but they are very nice. Their food is delicious. If they'd told us that it was made from nuts and ground-up ocean plants, I would have refused to eat it, but I didn't know until after we ate.

We can kind of understand the people, but when we said that we came to rescue them from Siamis, they said Who?

Leander told me Hibern says to go to the east of some big city called Issill Something.

Where are you?

CJ to Kyale:

We're heading toward some mountains. It looks like forest ahead.

We also landed on a beach, but not near any people. It took a while to find some. Clair got a note from Hibern. We're supposed to meet in the forest east of that city. Boneribs has some kind of plan. I don't see why we can't make our own plans, but everybody seems to want to meet up.

CJ hesitated, then crossed out the last few words, put a period after 'plan,' and sent the note. She'd been sitting on a rock while the others took a break from the hot walk in the sultry air by playing around in a stream. But then Clair beckoned, and everyone joined her.

"Weather here might be different, but at home that flat sheet of puff clouds looks like rain. Shall we try to get there?" She pointed down the slope to where a small village lay on either side of a tumbling waterfall.

Nobody argued. They slipped and slid down a narrow goat path, until they reached the first houses, which looked like others they'd seen: low buildings made out of smooth chocolaty-looking wood that reminded CJ of manzanita. The language the people spoke sounded to her kind of like French—or at least the kind of French they spoke in cartoons, as she had never heard a real French person before she left Earth—and kind of like Hebrew.

As Falinneh and Irenne ran ahead to talk to the locals about staying, CJ walked slowly, brooding about the news Clair had passed on: according to Hibern, Liere was Siamis's prisoner.

When the rain came, they were cozily gathered on a broad porch. The etiquette was, if you didn't have any money, or whatever they used for money, then you had to work to get a meal. That meant not only helping to prepare the food, but entertainment afterward.

Ordinarily CJ loved an excuse to show off some of their favorite songs and plays. Two girls snickered, blonde and red heads together as they shucked beans and pulled silk off corn for the kitchen people. They alternately rehearsed one of Irenne's many plays, and laughed with anticipation over how thrilled their audience would be.

Dhana had gone off dancing in the rain.

CJ fidgeted, knowing that she was going to get stuck with dishwashing. Not that that mattered. If she got everyone to help, it would go faster, because she really wanted to reach that forest before anyone else.

She moved restlessly, hating how everybody had given her the stink-eye, especially that snobby Atan, before they all magicked away. Like Sartora going off to defeat Siamis was a bad thing. Like it was her fault.

CJ wished she had her magic boot, made in the days when Jilo was the worst villain they'd ever faced. Her boot was great for knocking villains off balance with a magic-propelled whoosh of wind. How things had changed! And not in a good way, except that ol' Jilo was no longer on the villains' list.

But his place had been taken by far worse villains, ones you couldn't boot into a mud puddle and expect to slink off to the Shadowland while you laughed loudly. Sartora, with all her mind powers, was the best one to boot Siamis out, right?

CJ resisted the impulse to kick the railing. She was afraid that weird wood might crack, and everybody would give her the stink-eye again. Even if those snobs . . .

She grimaced fiercely, knowing it was no use calling Atan a snob. The Queen of Sartor seemed to like Clair okay, so it couldn't be that she looked down on the Mearsieans in their little country with no court or army. It was that Rel business. Atan really seemed to like the hulking galoot, and CJ knew she couldn't accuse Rel of buttering Atan up because she had a title, because Rel didn't butter anybody up. He didn't even seem to know how to crack a smile.

And *I don't hate him. I don't,* she thought firmly. She wanted to get to the forest first, before anyone else, so she could be seen giving him a big fat welcome, and also she wanted to be in on any plans to rescue Sartora, just in case they did think she was to blame.

Only why did people have to be so weird?

Isul Demarzal

Liere's determination to survive received aid from two unexpected directions.

The first occurred a day later, after Julian threaded through a gaggle of Norsundrians to tug on Siamis's arm. When she got his attention (causing every one of the scouts and flunkeys waiting to deliver reports to wish to be the one he would order to knock the vile brat out of the room) she said, "There's a girl in the cellar."

"Yes." Siamis chuckled.

"Can I talk to her?" Julian thought she was being sly, because she already *had* talked to her. Three times.

"She's all yours."

"Mine?" Julian exclaimed. "Mine? Really?"

"Promise," he said, mock-solemn.

"But she doesn't have anything to eat!"

"Why not?" Siamis asked.

"I can't open the door, and the bread wouldn't fit under it."

Siamis laughed. "We'll see about that."

He summoned the mage, who duly furnished his account of Julian and Liere's conversations (the last two solely on the subject of food), and asked with genial sarcasm, "Don't you think the quality of words might improve if someone troubled to open that cellar door and put in something to eat?"

The mage, who loathed this duty, said, "You gave no orders."

"I am giving some now, and so plainly that I believe even you can take my meaning: see to it that Liere Fer Eider has a jug of clean water, and some food."

Liere had been walking back and forth in her cell, after exploring its dimensions. Remembering what Senrid had said about keeping your strength up for escape, she'd even tried running around the perimeter, but she was so hungry and thirsty it had made her feel dizzy. So she sat down again.

A short time later Liere's door opened, and an armed guard set down a jug of cold water, and a plate of stale bread, the end of a cheese, and the crumbled remains of a vegetable pie. Then the door closed, leaving Liere in darkness.

She slurped down the water, relief pouring through her veins. Then she tore into the vegetable pie.

Strengthened by her meal, Liere listened for Julian's voice on the mental plane. She was with Siamis! "I saw them give her food, but they wouldn't let me go in to talk to her. Why does she have to stay in the cellar? Why can't she come out and talk to me?"

Siamis said, "Detlev wants her for his pet experiment. I might just have to comply, if I lose my gamble. Until then, talk to her through the door all you like, Julian. Ask her about the dyr. It's a magic thing."

"I hate magic things," Julian retorted, thinking of Atan and *lessons*.

"Ask her anyway." Siamis laughed. "Run along."

Liere withdrew her mental tendril and sat back to think. So Siamis wanted them talking about the dyr. No surprise there.

Even if she knew where it was kept she wouldn't talk about it, but there was something she *could* do: figure out why Julian hated Atan, and find out if it had something to do with her terrible memories of being shut in a dark closet by that whispering woman with the jeweled fingernails.

Senrid got himself acquainted with his new travel mates, did what he was told, and, when he could finally get a corner alone, he dug the notecase out of his pocket, pulled out the last note he'd received, and turned it over. He used the pen from the ship's log near the tiller and wrote a quick note. Wondering if the magic would work on this world, he put the note in the notecase and tapped out Hibern's sigil.

The paper vanished.

He went below to climb into his hammock, and dropped immediately into sleep.

Over the next few days, Senrid heard a great deal about Geth and its many islands from his shipmates. The captain whom he'd taken to be an agemate turned out to have done the Child Spell decades ago. You could tell if you got close enough to see the lines in her face that she wasn't fourteen or fifteen. But she sort of acted like it . . . and sort of not. He found the idea somewhat repellent, but then he did not want to spend the rest of his life looking as if he were fifteen.

Senrid could feel the impulses to break the spell holding his physical growth back, but stronger was the conviction that he ought to keep hiding in plain sight to the likes of Detlev, to whom the passing of years had to be meaningless.

Ten days after his conversation with Lilith he was obligingly set down at a point that afforded the shortest path to the forestland directly south of the city. He wasn't there half a morning before he found Jilo sitting dismally at a crossroads, puzzled by which way to turn.

Astounded that Jilo couldn't gauge the geography that seemed so obvious, Senrid pointed him northwards, saying, "The forest seems to lie that way." And, as Jilo had expected the moment they saw one another, "What does the book say?"

"It doesn't say anything, because Wan-Edhe never came here to ward any Destinations."

"Well, chances are pretty good we wouldn't have any

idea where any of them would be if it did, since we haven't a map. Right. May as well hide it away again."

Jilo promptly stashed the book inside his tunic, where it pressed comfortingly flat against his stomach. They walked together, as Senrid told Jilo about parts of his interview with Lilith the Guardian. It never occurred to Jilo not to try breaking Norsunder's wards over this Isul place. His life had defined itself since the disappearance of the Shadowland in trying to break Wan-Edhe's formidable wards. So they spent time talking about what Jilo had learned about lethal wards.

After a day, Jilo and Senrid were found by two of the sharron Lilith had spoken of: dark-haired people, one young and one old, in green and brown clothing. They were very shy, scarcely speaking or meeting anyone's eyes. Not that Senrid or Jilo had much energy for talking, for it took all their concentration to follow their swift, sure-footed guides up razor-edged cliffs and down narrow trails shadowed by gnarled trees of types they did not recognize, or kind of recognized.

When it seemed they couldn't walk another step, they emerged abruptly in a central clearing where they discovered half of the alliance already there, some doing various chores under Rel's direction as they set about cooking fresh-caught trout on sticks. Others made biscuits with the meal that the sharron had given them before departing into the woods.

"Senrid," Hibern said with relief. "Here you are! Everyone is full of questions."

"So the mages haven't broken the mirror-ward over that city yet?" Senrid asked, his appetite waking up with a cavernous gape as the aroma of herb-rubbed fish wafted his way.

"No. Everybody has ideas about rescuing Liere. We wanted to hear what you were told."

Dappled light played over Arthur as he wandered from below the low, spreading branches of a cousin to the chestnut, a book that he'd either found or brought with him tucked under his arm, and a quill pen sticking out from his ear. "All we've seen are the sharron who brought us. They gave us a bag of some kind of meal, and said somebody would come to lead us to the city."

"They don't talk much," Hibern added.

"We noticed," Senrid said, looking around appreciatively. It wouldn't be accident that they'd been ushered to this deserted area, probably unknown to Norsunder's scouts.

Jilo faded to the perimeter as Senrid said, "Here's what I learned."

The alliance gathered over the space of a few days, and fell into a companionable rhythm, with Rel as leader. They had a goal and an interesting new environment, and for some, the onslaught of emotions over Derek's death gained distance.

Not all gained the relative comfort of distance.

Rel was good at camp life. He liked spending the day scouting fallen timber for firewood, and teaching people how to fish and to toast wild tubers that they found growing.

Camp food got even better when Leander arrived. Having spent a lot of his early childhood as a forest-dwelling outlaw with a price on his head, Leander knew how to find and cook tasty greens and wild onions and herbs. He even discovered varieties of sweet berries that they could eat for dessert.

Rel welcomed the work, but in spite of keeping himself busy all day, as soon as he fell asleep his dreams filled with flames and people screaming. It didn't help that those first few days, he could still smell the lingering traces of smoke if he coughed.

He was not ready for the arrival of the Mearsieans, especially when CJ marched up scowling, having discovered that not only were they last to arrive, but someone had gone ahead and made Rel the boss of the camp. He overheard her remark to the air that it seemed all you had to do was be a hulking boy and everybody fell all over trying to put you in charge.

Hibern also heard that, and to forestall anything else from CJ, climbed up on a rock and called out, "Listen! Now that everyone is here, and we know that Liere is a prisoner, we need to figure out what's next, unless anyone wants to return to Sartorias-deles?"

She had hoped that most would raise their hands, the Mearsieans first.

No one did.

She went on firmly, "Rel is in charge of the camp, so listen for your jobs, and everything will be faster."

Rel sighed as he glanced across the fire into CJ's bright, derisive blue gaze. He wished even more strongly that he could have had one night of real sleep before facing CJ's temper.

Atan had been watching. Her own temper simmered.

Hibern took in Atan's anger, Rel's stolid expression, and CJ's lifted chin, and her heart sank. No matter how far you traveled, even to another world, you brought your trouble with you.

She climbed down, wishing she had kept her mouth shut. Rel sighed, and stepped up beside the rock.

With that many people crowding around, there was the inevitable tangle, exacerbated by Kyale, who loathed dirt, eating off sharpened sticks, and sitting outside, and by Glenn, whose grief found expression in a series of small irritations, beginning with the lack of proper protocol and ending with his sister's weird, irritating counting of steps and fussing with twigs and rocks so that they were square or parallel.

Rel attempted to avoid the Mearsieans in hopes they'd go off and play. But no, Clair kept them waiting for jobs.

Rel thought up some easy ones to get rid of them, but halfway through, Kitty pushed through, shrilling indignantly, "There are bugs over there! I can't sleep anywhere with bugs!"

"You can have my spot," CJ said in her most goading voice not two paces from Rel. "Unless King Rel gets mad, because whatever King Rel wants is so important."

Rel wasn't aware of the red flash of irritation until it happened. He reached with his fingers, gave CJ's shoulder a flick as he said, "Just clear out." He meant to add something about how they'd just arrived, and they could wait until the morrow to work, but the second his fingers collided with her skinny little body he knew he'd regret it, that he'd broken his own code.

CJ had recoiled to avoid his touch, but when two of his fingers collided with her shoulder she was so furious that she sucked in a breath and shrilled, *"He hit me!"*

On the other side of the fire, Lilah whirled around, her eyes rounding with honest horror.

Rel gritted his teeth. It had been a gesture of irritation, but he may as well have socked her.

"Sorry," he said, knowing that that sounded as if he really had hit her. But anything he said would make the situation worse.

Clair said, "Come on, CJ. The sooner we pitch in, the sooner we eat."

"Did you see that? He hit me!" CJ felt the falsity of every word, like biting into an apple that looked fresh but was rotten. But she couldn't seem to help herself, as a lifetime of pent-up anger forced her to the summit of self-righteousness.

"Well!" Kyale's voice rose as she eagerly climbed that summit beside her. She gloried in all the shocked eyes.

CJ's mind flooded with angry joy, but her triumph—*see? He really is a bully*—died when she caught the contempt in Atan's face before she walked to the other side of the camp, where she sat with Tahra and Arthur, her rigid back squarely toward the Mearsieans.

And here was the most tenderhearted of the Mearsiean girls, her big blue eyes almost tearful as she whispered, "Did he hurt you? I never thought Rel would ever . . ."

CJ sat down next to Clair, her gaze on her lap, her stomach boiling with a sick sense of wrong. She knew what getting hit was like. The actual touch had been barely a flick, but she'd sensed the irritation Rel had tried to hide.

She knew she was being unfair. That she had lied. Somehow that made her even angrier. It was all Rel's fault or she wouldn't have had this problem at all! But . . . that stomach-churning sense that she'd lied, that her sense of moral superiority was completely fake, kept her silent, furious with rage.

She stayed where she was when someone called for music; she forced laughter when Falinneh and Irenne acted out the play they'd worked out over the past few days; she clapped hard when Tahra recited a long, boring poem about some old war in the flattest voice ever; she watched without enjoyment as Dhana rose and danced light-footed around the fire, the flickering light playing over her soaring form as she leaped and twirled.

Finally, *finally* it was all over, and CJ was the first to leave, staking out the soft grass under a broad tree. Gradually the other girls appeared, except for Clair, who remained at the fireside, a small figure staring down into the flames.

Clair became aware of a quiet conversation on the other side of the fire; she lifted her eyes, but her vision dazzled, and all she could see were silhouettes.

". . . know what to do," Atan was saying. "It's like in the forest group in Sartor, one ill-tempered person can break the group into little groups. Kyale likes to see things stirred, and Lilah is upset, which means all her friends are upset. I wish we could send them both away and let them figure it out, except I feel so for Rel, after what happened in Everon."

Ill-tempered, Clair was thinking. It hurt the more because right now, it seemed true, if you didn't really know CJ, the most loyal friend ever.

Puddlenose sauntered up to the campfire, the firelight under-lighting his square face. "Put CJ in charge."

He wandered away.

Atan sighed sharply, but Clair understood. "I think he's right," she said, though she hadn't been invited into the conversation. But they were talking about her friend.

Atan sighed again, as if she were trying hard to get rid of her own bad temper. She said, "How is that going to help? Unless she's figured out how to defeat Siamis, rescue Liere, and send Detlev back to Norsunder forever."

Clair sat back, trying to fit words to the emotions she was feeling, then was surprised when Hibern, filled with a kind of cautious hope, said slowly, "There's this ballad where I come from. It's meant to be funny, but it kind of fits. Tomorrow, put CJ in charge of all the camp jobs. Everything that Rel's been doing, or asking people to do."

Atan repeated doubtfully, "Everything?"

Clair said, "I think that will do it."

But she felt like a traitor as she retreated through the quiet, leaf-scented air to the grassy area where the other girls lay. Insects sang and chirruped in the distance as she curled up by CJ and Sherry.

Sherry was already asleep. Clair could see starlight reflecting in CJ's eyes as she stared upward. So Clair rolled over and stared up at the stars through the leaves. She thought she recognized some of the twinkling patterns, though they looked sideways to what she was used to. She still felt a sense of shock at the idea of two moons, but there they both were, on opposite sides of the sky, one small and one big, though only half lit.

Clair whispered, "Are you all right, CJ?"

"I'm fine," CJ muttered. "I just want to find Liere, and go back home."

"We could talk to Hibern. Maybe she'd send us back. I'm sure not all of us are needed."

"No, we better stay. They think everything is my fault," CJ whispered bitterly. "I have to help rescue Liere. In fact, I have to be the one to find her, or I'm a gigantic villain, worse than Detlev, Siamis, Kessler, and all the rest of them combined."

If she brought up Rel, Clair vowed to tell her. But CJ didn't, and Clair stayed silent, hoping that CJ's bad mood would break before morning.

CJ was too angry with everyone, but herself most of all, to speak Rel's name.

Clair's warm hand stole over CJ's. She gave her fingers a gentle squeeze, then Clair sighed and turned over, leaving CJ staring upward.

In the morning, the noise of those early to rise got everyone else stirring, yawning and stretching, talking and laughing as they brushed grass off their clothes. They wandered to the center of the camp, where Atan was sitting on a log. When the Mearsieans approached, she said in a clear voice, "Since you object to whatever Rel does, you can run the camp, CJ."

Atan pointed to an axe by her feet. "You'd better start

by fetching the firewood, since we've already burned all the gleanings. There is a fallen log over that way."

CJ looked at the circle of faces, some hard, a few friendly, but nobody said anything until Clair came up beside her. "Want help?"

CJ lifted her chin. "No." She meant to say that anything that galoot can do, she could do better, but the words stuck in her throat.

She grabbed the axe and marched off, glad to get away.

The fallen log lay some hundred paces off. CJ walked around it, trying to decide where to begin. As she did, she argued mentally with friends and enemies, vilifying Atan and Rel and justifying herself, but every word seemed to escape into the air.

Meanwhile, here was this gigantic log.

She hefted the axe, and hit one of the dried branches, which splintered into a thousand bits, splinters hitting her hands and face. Ugh!

She marched to the big end of the log, and swung the axe as hard as she could.

The blade bounced off the log, twisting so hard her fingers stung painfully. She wiped her hands on her grimy skirt, and tried again. This time the blade landed awry and bounced away without leaving a dent. She tried again, and got the blade to stick, but when she tried to pull it out, she had to tug hard.

Three more hits, and she'd made three little gashes that weren't even close together. Her palms were fairly tough from a lot of tree climbing, but even so they were beginning to sting with promised blisters if she kept it up.

But she had to, right? Because . . . *Because it's my fault.*

Smack! A chip flew off, nearly clipping her ear. The axe fell to the grass.

Footsteps whished through the grass, and there was Rel, looming like a mountain. CJ hunched up, braced for war.

Rel sat on the log.

He said, "They think you've got a grudge against me."

"I don't," she shot back.

"Yes," he said. "It's something besides that. I know our

first meeting was bad, but you had worse experience with Jilo."

CJ jerked her shoulders in a shrug.

"I think you're envious," Rel said.

"I am not!"

His eyes crinkled briefly, but he didn't laugh. "You're not envious of me. That is, I know you don't want to be me."

"Ugh," she said, crossing her arms.

This time he did laugh, a brief, voiceless huff. "I don't think you want to take away my friends. Or my life. It's what you think I can do, isn't it?"

"How do you mean?" she asked warily.

"You seem to think I should be smiting Norsundrians, but you don't see that I'm not that far ahead of you, except for size and a few years. Or maybe it's the size and the years that's the problem? Someone once said to me that when things like size, and age, and strength are a problem, then maybe they were used against a person, instead of to protect them."

CJ fumed. She suspected that 'someone once said' was really 'when we were talking about you,' but far worse than that was remembering her life on Earth. Oh, yes. Size and strength were *definitely* used against you *there*.

Envy.

She squirmed, hating the word, an old and familiar enemy.

Maybe he was right. To lie to herself was to lie to the world, that's what Clair had said once. She'd seen how envy came out of anger.

CJ sidled a look at Rel, who sat there as patient as a mountain. Waiting. So she looked within herself, past the ugly memories, and forced herself to endure the nastiness.

Anger was like that. She'd think she'd gotten rid of it, but there it was again. It was worse than the time she'd fallen on the sandy blacktop at school and scraped both her knees, then had to run to the restroom and endure the torture of wiping the sand and blood out of the scrapes. Every time she thought she got it all, and she could dare to go back to her classroom (because if the teacher saw she'd get into trouble for running, which was against the rules, and then she'd get into worse trouble at home for being in trouble at school), she'd look down, and there was more blood. And she'd have to use that rough paper towel again, which hurt worse than fire.

"But everybody thinks you're perfect," she said bitterly. "And you are." *And I am so, so not.*

"No, I'm not. I'm good at some things, and bad at others, just like anyone else. I can't learn magic. The strange words don't stick in my head. I can't draw. I could never build a loyal group like you have with the other girls. I don't seem to be able to settle in one place. And as far as size and strength are concerned, they don't guarantee wins. Every time I tangled with Kessler, I lost. I'm only alive because he decided not to kill me. But he could have."

At the mention of Kessler's name, all CJ's anger whipped away like smoke before the wind. "I hate thinking about him," she said fiercely, not wanting to be reminded of the terror of those days.

"But you'll have to. We all do. Senrid said that he's in charge of guarding yon city. If we want to rescue Liere, we're going to have to get past him." He picked up the axe. "That's for tomorrow. Today, this is the sort of thing I'm good at. I'm glad to do what I'm good at. Same as anyone else."

CJ watched him heft the axe and chop the wood in exactly the right place. He'd split off the rotten bits of the branch she'd first attacked, creating a good pile of firewood, before she said, "They want to make me do all the chores."

"Oh, I think if you help me, nobody'll say a word. They're all hungry, and want a hot breakfast more than anything else. And Leander found some wild olives so we can crisp the potatoes."

CJ swallowed. "Let's get to it. Maybe it'll be faster if you chop and I stack."

They did, working in silence. She was relieved at first, but as the stack of firewood grew, so did the thing inside her, until it felt like a stone the size of a bowling ball.

When Rel said presently, "That should be enough," CJ sucked in a deep breath and muttered, "I'm sorry."

Rel took in the tight fists and the black hair swinging, hiding CJ's averted face, and did not make the mistake of taking that surly mutter as insincere. He had a pretty good idea how much that apology cost her, and how humiliated she'd feel if he gave in to the laughter fluttering behind his ribs. Or made a speech.

So he grunted, "We're square."

And saw her skinny shoulders drop away from her ears.

Another silent fifty paces and they entered the camp together, each carrying a stack of firewood. Nobody said anything. Atan watched narrowly at first, but when she saw Rel's brief smile, and heard CJ talking as if nothing had happened, she decided to act as if nothing had happened.

Everybody else fell into their usual patterns, except for Kyale, who found time to whisper to CJ, "I hope you told him off. Those boys are so bossy, but Senrid is the worst of all."

CJ sighed, relieved to have it over. Except it wasn't over, not with Kyale saying things like that, and the looks she got from Atan and others. They thought she was a villain. And, even worse, that tiny voice way, way inside: *I was acting like one.*

To Kyale she said tiredly, "We gotta think about how to get into that city now."

Kyale wandered off, disappointed, and Clair stepped up beside CJ, her smile pensive. "Are you all right?"

CJ side-eyed her. "Why didn't you tell me I was being a bat-head?"

"Because that would have made you madder," Clair answered.

CJ scowled, knowing it was true. "I hate anger. Getting angry makes me angry!" And when Clair snickered, she muttered, "I don't know how to get rid of it."

Clair watched CJ sigh, her bad mood obviously gone as quickly as thunderstorms pass.

If you figure it out, CJ, she thought, *you could fix the world.*

The group was finishing up clearing their campsite when a sweet, heart-catching cascade of pure, clear notes echoed through the forest.

"Oh," Kyale breathed, sitting down abruptly on the log she'd disdained as filthy the day before. The air scintillated with color, something that usually annoyed her, but this time it and the sounds matched so perfectly that she clasped her hands and stared.

"What is that sound?" Hibern asked.

"Some kind of bird?" Arthur asked, for once not absent.

"I've never heard one like that," Leander said, as he peered under his hand through the bluish-white light shafts in the wooded shadows. "I think it's coming this way."

"Hide," Senrid said.

"I don't think that could come from any Norsundrian," Lilah said. "It's sounds so pretty!"

Atan murmured, "I'll bet that's what people were saying about Siamis right before he took their wits away."

The Mearsieans bolted up trees with the ease of long practice.

The melodic cascade intensified, and CJ hummed a counterpoint below it; that meant she was memorizing that melody, possibly for making a song later. Clair's eyelids prickled, though she couldn't have said why. And over on the rock, Kyale noticed that, as usual, nobody else saw the colors like gleaming ribbons in the air. And she blinked them away as a couple of pale-haired figures walked into the clearing.

Everybody took in the two boys, the taller sturdy one with a round, genial face, dressed in a shapeless long shirt belted by a bit of rope. He carried a pitchfork in one hand, and something greenish poked out of the other sleeve.

The second boy was smaller, his perfectly oval face lifted. The filtered bluish light fell softly on his high, intelligent brow, his definite jawline beginning to emerge from baby-round cheeks. He, unlike the older boy, stood still and alert.

"Hiya Darksiders," the big one called.

"Darksiders?" Kyale popped up, fists on hips. "Do you think we are dark magic villains?"

"No, no!" The taller boy patted the air. "Darkside of the Sun is our name for your world. On account of we can't ever see it."

Kyale crossed her arms. "I assure you, we have just as much sunlight as you do."

"I know! And I understand a very fine place it is. But it's an old name, see? So here's me, to lead a lot of Dar—foreigners to the cave under the city, and all I find is trampled grass. Do I smell?"

He lifted his arm, sniffing at his armpit, then made a show of gagging as he reeled, arms flapping.

Puddlenose almost broke his sinuses holding in a laugh, but when he saw Christoph's red face, it escaped, and he dropped down out of the tree, figuring any kid with a sense of humor would never join Norsunder.

"Who are you? I'm Puddlenose," he said.

"Bena Dak." The newcomer hefted his pitchfork. "But you can call me Dak. That's my brother, Cath."

The green thing in his sleeve moved, slithering out. A snake!

"Hoo," Puddlenose said. "Did you know you had a snake in your shirt?"

"I do?" Dak pretended to be shocked, then laughed. "This is Alivier. She travels with us."

By then, the others were approaching. "What is that?" Dhana asked Cath, pointing to the flute-like object in his hand.

"We call them silverflutes," Cath said. His childish treble was precise. He held out the silverflute on his palms, so those interested could see the pearlescent wood that wasn't quite white, nor silver, though it gleamed at a distance.

"You must've been playing since before you learned to walk, to be that good," Kyale said enviously. She'd tried to learn a couple of instruments, but could never stick with practice long enough to get past the boring basics.

"A year," Cath said.

That left his audience silent as he slid the silverflute into a kind of sheath hanging from his neatly tied sash.

Dak said with his friendly smile, "The sharron sent me, on account of, I know some o' them, and I got to be friends with some mages." The Mearsieans liked his accent, which CJ thought of as sort of French.

"The sharron are in a pucker over these stone-backs. We call the enemy that on account of those gray jackets they wear—"

"We call them Norsundrians," Kyale offered importantly.

Dak grinned. "Well, the sooner we hoof 'em out, the better, is what I'm saying."

"Then lead the way," Hibern said. "We can talk as we walk."

Chapter Four

Isul Demarzal

TALL trees towered overhead, long-lobed leaves of every shade of green, blurring in great swoops back and forth. Julian was dreaming about the swing again.

Liere liked this dream, or this part of Julian's dreams. All the rest of Julian's dreams were different kinds of horrible. There were the ones where all the furniture was distorted and giant and the walls red, as if seen from the floor. Those were the ones with the whispering woman in them, jewels in her headdress and at her neck and on her fingernails glittering like tiny needles and knives. Those dreams always carried remembered pain.

The forest dreams had unknown children singing or playing games. Sometimes those began as swing dreams, but below those were sharper memories: being interrupted by tall, pretty Irza, who came to take Julian away from Atan, whispering things:

"Atan will make you do your duty."

"I will always give you whatever you want."

"You're our baby, our dolly, our perfect girl."

Liere could hear Irza's thoughts across the distance,

brought close and painful. In Irza's memories she didn't think Julian was perfect, she thought she was a spoiled brat, and yet she gave her whatever she asked for, smiling, smiling, smiling.

Atan didn't hurt Liere with distortion because the Atan she saw and heard in Julian's dreams and memories was the Atan whose actual thoughts whispered across the distances.

Liere knew what was dream and what was memory. If someone appeared in her dreams, and she stepped through the mirror into their dreams, she had found that she could think away specific ugly symbols, like red walls, and sometimes the feelings that came with them, and then walk through into a better memory. She had done that for her mother many times.

When Irza turned Julian's dreams sour, Liere thought the dream-Irza away and brought dream-Atan back, and when she did, she brought some of Atan's own memories of the forest glade into Julian's dreams: Her joy in pushing Julian on the swing. Julian's toes twinkling among forest grasses. Julian laughing, her flower garland shedding blossoms on the breeze. Julian warm and happy and clean.

As the days drifted by, Liere, so used to separating out dreams from memories, and memories from thoughts, caught flickers that surprised her. She woke up one day comprehending that Atan was here. On Geth. In Atan's dreams, she searched and searched for Julian, worried and scared.

Liere ventured further and discovered that not only was Atan on Geth, so were many from the alliance. Including Senrid.

Liere promptly shut her mind-shield tight. She was good at dream-walking, but she knew that Siamis was far better, and better yet was the sinister Detlev, whom she had never met, but whose presence sometimes passed through the mental realm like the shadow of a predator bird blocking the sun.

They were here. Because Liere had been stupid and managed to get herself caught. But still, joy closed tight as a flower seed in her heart. She was not alone, and she knew that Senrid would look for her.

Meanwhile, Julian was not conscious of Liere in her

dreams. She only knew she was happier. One day she felt so restless she got tired of crouching on the floor to talk, so she ran outside to look at the people and the streets.

She wanted to talk to the runaway prince again.

Outside the city

Cath's oddness partly explained itself when Senrid felt a brief, subtle sense of widened perception or echo on the mental plane. He knew that sense. He'd first experienced it with Liere. When he looked around sharply, he met the boy's steady gaze.

I was asked to listen for the enemy. Cath's mental voice was as clear and precise as his spoken voice—unlike Senrid's hard-to-control mental contacts.

Senrid said out loud, "We're not enemies. But I'd do it, too, if I had as good a control as you have." Unspoken was the term 'Dena Yeresbeth,' which Cath caught.

Cath's thought came: *I don't know what Dena Yeresbeth is. 'Marsh mad' is what we call it.*

With that came an almost dizzying sense of weird space, full of rich scents, an echo of which Senrid had already experienced.

That was the difference, Senrid perceived. With Cath, it was like their minds met somewhere, and with Liere, it was not a place, but more like in his head.

Yes, Cath thought. *I heard that girl. Dak did, too. But we daren't listen long for her. The enemy can hear in the Marsh.*

Dak thumped his pitchfork on the ground. "I was told you want to go in, searchin' for where the stone-backs keep First Witch, which we can't do, because we're warded. But they didn't ward you, because they don't know about you bein' here."

"That's right," Senrid said.

"We'll find her," Hibern promised. "If you can tell us where to go."

"But we don't rightly know that," Dak admitted. "They coulda put her anywhere."

"Then we'll be faster and more efficient if we divide up and hunt through the city," Leander said reasonably.

"Yeah, and we can't run, or change our expressions," CJ said. "We have to act zombified. That's what people look like under Siamis's evil spell."

Dak thumped his pitchfork in agreement on each point, then said, "The Witches said, you need disguises."

Puddlenose walked backward. "I dunno." He scratched his head. "Nobody loves disguises more than I do. An adventure isn't a good one unless I get to wear a false beard, or a fancy dress. But don't you think Kessler would recognize some of us even in disguises?"

"In a city?" Leander asked. "He can't be everywhere at once."

"These would be illusion," Dak said, as Cath lifted his head to watch a flock of long-tailed birds erupt from a flowering vine that had overtaken an old fence.

"I don't want to go looking for some old woman," Glenn muttered. "I thought we were here to kill Siamis. That's what *I* want to do."

Atan said to Dak, "Illusory disguises would keep us from being recognized by any Norsundrian who has seen us on our world, but what about Norsunder's wards?"

"That's been thought of," Dak said, thumping his pitchfork again. "Talk as we walk. They told me to get you to the tunnel by sundown tomorrow."

They camped, and the next morning, Dak led them behind a waterfall in a rocky, rough portion of hill, but instead of the trail skirting the hill, it opened into a tunnel hidden by the falling water. Some found it fun to slip and slide over the green, mossy rock, others picked their way carefully.

Down and down they hiked, until the sound of the waterfall was replaced by the susurrus of a rushing underground stream.

Dak was explaining the general layout of the city as they walked. "Over our heads right now is Weavers' Row. Then comes the park, see the tree roots way up there? Then over here begins what they call Charlotte's Palace. We don't know what part Charlotte actually lived in, it's been rebuilt and added onto so many times, but it's the biggest building

I've ever seen. Some say in the entire world! Now, down this here tunnel, and then we're—ak!" Dak stopped short, dropped his pitchfork onto a flat rock, and put his hands on his hips. "There you are, Cath. Good. Right in time."

Cath had brought an older boy, skinny, as brown as the off-world visitors, with jug-handle ears and a big grin.

"Ol' Bones!" Dak exclaimed with pleasure. "Explain to 'em about vagabond magic."

Old Bones faced the allies. "My magic is something new to Geth. It's pretty much illusory, and Les is only teaching it to a few of us. It isn't like regular magic. It fades away on its own, except at sunset and sunrise, and when other kinds of magic are done. They can't put the magic tracers on it, any more than you can shape a statue out of ocean water, no matter how much you use." He turned to the others, without explaining who Les was. "So I can give you any kinda fake face and form you want. 'Long as you don't touch anybody, you'll fool 'em."

The rescuers considered thoughtfully, then CJ said, "I want to try being an old bat. With a warty chin! No eleven-ener will pay any attention to an old bat hobbling around."

"Me, too! Me, too!" Kyale shrilled. "Warts on my chin *and* my nose!"

"I want to be an old geez," Bren declared. "Beard down to here." He indicated his knees as he hunched over and shuffled in a circle.

"Pirate captain!"

"And I'd like to be a raptor," Senrid said. "But we're supposed to be keeping attention away from ourselves. Pirates and a whole lot of warty old people aren't going to go unnoticed."

Dak thumped his pitchfork on the boulder. "Whatever you choose, make it quick, as the day is getting late."

"Line up," Old Bones said.

Isul Demarzal

In Charlotte's Palace, Liere and Julian crouched at the doorway.

"Siamis said it is a joke, see?" Julian explained. "He says they named the sword Truth in the old days, but there isn't any truth."

"I know. He said the same thing to me once."

Julian shrugged, uninterested in the subject of truth. "At least he got a sword as a present. In the bad days, *Mother* only let me have *jewels* and *princess dresses*." The emphasized words came out in a tone of sullen resentment, underscored by the memory of terror, which Liere had seen in Julian's dreams.

"I think there's truth," Liere said.

"What is it, then?"

"Well, I think truth is . . . when you make a promise, you keep it. And if you know you can't keep it, you don't make the promise. Truth has a lot of things in it, but one of them is trust. Like, I trust my friend . . . Devon," Liere avoided mentioning Senrid, in case that lurking listener might somehow know that Senrid was somewhere in this world.

Liere had seen him twice in her dreams, once alone, sitting on a boat, looking down at the sea, and another time with Atan and Leander, eating smoked fish off sticks.

"If Devon doesn't know a thing, she says so. If she sees a thing, she tells me what she sees, not what she thinks I want to see. And if she can't keep a promise, she won't make one. Devon speaks truth."

Julian was running her fingers along the underside of the door, back and forth. "Irza didn't keep her promise. She said if I liked her best she would give me whatever I wanted."

"Did she?"

"When we lived in the forest. Those were the good days. But when we had to come into Eidervaen, then she didn't."

Liere thought that over. "Did Atan make promises?"

"She said I didn't have to be a princess."

"Did you believe her?"

"No. Irza said Atan wouldn't give me what I wanted. And she didn't! She tried to give me what *she* wanted. Clothes, and lessons, and stupid things that make princesses. Just like Mother."

Liere thought back through all the dreams. Atan had come all the way to another world to get her cousin free.

Liere knew better than to say that; Senrid had said once that the nastiest weapons were the ones you can't fight, and to Liere that meant the way her father always used to finish a scold by adding another scold for not being grateful. "But wouldn't lessons let you be what you wanted?"

For a time all Liere could hear was Julian's breathing. She didn't want to break the mental wall, lest Siamis pounce, but she was tempted. Then Julian said resentfully, "I said I don't want to be a princess. It *hurts*." And there again, sharp as a knife, were the memories of pinching and slapping, enforced by the whispering voice, *If you want to be a princess, you have to smile, and be sweet.*

"So you don't have princess lessons," Liere said calmly. "There are lots of kinds of lessons. You go to the stable for lessons if you want to be a . . . a horse rider. You go to the kitchen to learn how to cook tasty things. There are lessons to be an artist, or make music. Did Atan mean to offer you those?"

Julian said, "I don't know."

She got up and ran away. She hated those old memories. She ran as hard as she could down one long corridor and up another, until the memories turned into questions.

She stopped at the kitchen to get a cake, then took her cake back to the place where Siamis usually could be found. When she saw him, she said, "The runaway prince told me you broke your promise."

Siamis smiled. "I may have."

"Why?"

"Here's a lesson," he said, and Julian looked wary. Lessons again! But he went on, "When you are in power, you can keep promises when it suits you. And ignore them when it suits you."

"What if people don't keep promises to you?"

"Then I destroy them." He laid his hand on the hilt of the sword named Truth, only there wasn't any truth, so maybe he was lying. Then he made that motion with his fingers that meant he wanted her to go away.

Atan doesn't lie, Julian thought as he turned his attention to one of the crabby grays waiting impatiently. In memories and in dreams, Atan just got sad if people broke promises.

Julian wandered off, and watched the cooks make rows and rows of pies. They had power, too, she thought. Everybody needed food. They kept the promise of being cooks by making pies every day. So that was one true thing and it had nothing to do with being a princess.

She pondered asking them for lessons, and wondered what Liere would say about that.

From hidden vantages all around the city, mages from both worlds watched through the illusory magic set up to protect the young allies as they covered the last distance alongside a vast underground pool.

"Here's the stair," Dak said, his voice echoing in the stone cavern. "This stairway will put you in the center of Charlotte's Palace, in the servants' wing. This used to be the laundry, centuries ago, before the mages invented cleaning frames. Me and my brother will wait for you here. Cath is listening for the mages." He tapped the side of his head, then perched on a rock nearby, his pitchfork laid across his lap.

The young allies looked at one another in their illusory disguises, then down at themselves. Hibern saw from Senrid's narrowed eyes, Arthur's thoughtful expression, and Atan's careful testing of the illusion that she was not the only one who felt extra magic worked into the illusion, though it was impossible to categorize. She suspected there was some kind of protection woven into the mysterious 'vagabond magic.'

Hibern walked up the first few steps of the mossy stairway, wondering if Erai-Yanya was somehow connected to the mages behind the extra protection. "We're a decoy," she whispered to Senrid, who was right on her heels. "I feel something under these illusions."

"I don't care." He shrugged. "As long as it doesn't interfere with me finding Liere and yanking her out of here."

Hibern knew Senrid would have walked in without illusion, protection, or anything. She'd chosen the most nondescript form she could think of, which wasn't much different from her real form, except that she looked older, and Old Bones had given her the illusion of a common Geth robe-gown, loose from the shoulders, with a long contrasting swath of fabric draped crosswise around and over one shoulder so the ends hung behind. She'd chosen muted colors.

She looked past Senrid down at the waiting faces on the steps behind her, many unrecognizable in their disguises. Even distorted by illusion, faces betrayed tension and uncertainty.

So maybe it was time to repeat what they already knew, because knowing was a kind of protection against the unknown. "Remember, as well as looking for Liere, we're looking for the First Witch: old, dark hair, white stripe. Fetch Senrid and Jilo so they can break any dark magic wards on her. As soon as she's found, retreat. We'll gather here."

Atan added, "You know what the enchanted look like. Don't stare. Walk slowly. Ignore any Norsundrians as if they aren't there."

"Whether we find her or not, return by sundown," Leander added from the middle of the crowd. He'd chosen a male version of Hibern's nondescript person, complete to robe-gown.

"That's right," Dak called from the other end of the cavern. "The illusions will fade by then. If no one discovers you, we can camp here tonight and try again tomorrow."

A murmur of agreement rose, then by ones and twos they mounted the stairs, counting to fifty between each so no crowd would be seen emerging into what they'd been told was a forgotten stairway at the back end of the palace.

Atan had asked only for an illusory Geth outfit. When she looked down, her hermit's tunic over riding trousers had scarcely altered, the hem of her tunic extending past her knees, her old hermit cottage riding trousers billowing around her ankles in the same dull dun color.

The station she'd volunteered for was the front side of the palace, which Dak had said was a lot of right turns from where they'd emerge. Though she intended to do her part in the search for this mysterious First Witch—and for Liere—she meant to find Julian first. No one else would be looking for her.

She found herself in a narrow hallway. The ground shivered slightly as she walked. Alarm burned through her, and faded: another quake. The tenth one since their arrival. The building creaked warningly around her, but she reminded herself that it had survived this long. It was not likely to fall around her ears now, and all the quakes had been small, no more than the swaying of a small boat on a pond. Surely that had to mean that quakes here were like the ones on Sartorias-deles, lessened by ancient magecraft. But at home, they were made much smaller, so no one felt them.

She emerged from a hall across from an open door, through which she glimpsed neat stacks of various sizes of brooms and mops. The hall stretched in both directions, meeting what looked like other halls. Right turns.

She struck out, meeting another intersection, then another, always turning to the right; she noticed that these were not squared-off turns, which meant she was bending gradually in a long arc.

After the seventh right turn the hall widened abruptly, the floor of reddish tiles becoming a mosaic pattern of twined geometric shapes making forms around fish and blooms and birds.

She peered inside the countless rooms for a blank-faced middle-aged woman with a streak of white in her dark hair. She saw people of every age, some going about simple tasks in a rote manner that made her skin crawl, others sitting quietly, the way people had in Sartor.

None of them fitted First Witch's description, and she wondered if Norsunder had put an illusion over First Witch. She wasn't sure she'd be able to pick out an illusion seen across a room.

She pushed on, until the inner blow of extremely powerful dark magic caused her to stumble, staring around the silent hall.

All over the palace, everyone looked up and around uneasily. The Norsunder mages stopped their search through the libraries, and exchanged glances: someone was in trouble, judging by the power of that impact. They returned to work with a sedulous air. Nobody wanted to become a target.

At the key intersections in the city, and at the gates, the

Norsundrian patrollers who had begun another boring day
of useless duty among the mindless sheep straightened up,
alerted by that sense of teeth-gritting, metallic danger,
smelling of burnt steel.

Inside the Palace, Siamis stilled, then dropped the map
he'd been rolling. It fell to the table, half on, half off, then
slipped to the floor, bringing with it a whispering cascade
of papers.

But the cascade went unnoticed. He was already out of
the room.

Julian looked up as footsteps approached. She scrambled to her feet and backed away when Siamis reached for
the cellar door.

A few moments later, Liere saw the door swing open for
the first time in days. She blinked in the bright light as Siamis took hold of her shoulder, drew her out, and said,
"Detlev is getting impatient. He's trying to break my wards.
I knew you would come in useful."

"Where is she going?" Julian asked, dismayed.

Siamis glanced absently down at her. "Let's see if our
young friend here can distract him."

He did not say for what: Liere staggered as the hard
fingers let her go, and transfer magic seized her, and flung
her back into the world again. She staggered and looked
around in fear, finding herself in another bare stone room
lit by a single slit near the ceiling.

A door opened. Blue-white light slanted in, bringing in
a heavy scent of mimosa.

Liere wanted to run, but where could she run to? She got
her trembling legs moving, and ventured out.

Unkind laughter met her. She looked across a low room
full of low curved chairs like half-circles in which various
people sat. Her attention passed over them, then snagged
on the derisive gaze of a brown-haired man.

She knew from Senrid's memories that this was Detlev.

"So this is the famous world-rescuer, Sartora, Queen of
Bereth Ferian!" he said, and the people laughed.

Every word stung. She dropped her head forward, shutting her eyes, her mind-shield tight.

"Where is the dyr?" came the amused voice.

She braced for the careless roughness of Siamis's searchers, but no one touched her. She looked up, instinctively putting out the tiniest tendril of mind quest . . . and he was waiting.

Lilith had exhorted her to practice her mind-shield. Liere had exhorted others to practice theirs, and she had what she thought was a good shield against the battering of others' thoughts, but now she learned how very, very inexperienced she really was.

Detlev was there in the surface of her mind. Terror struck through her, knife-sharp in agonized expectation of him tromping through all the corners of her mind, opening and slamming doors into memories. She cowered into as small a ball as she could as his mental voice shouted endlessly, *Where is the dyr? Where is the dyr?* while ignoring her mental voice whimpering *I don't know, I don't know.*

Finally he gave up in disgust. His presence was gone. She snapped her mind-shield around herself so hard she scarcely heard as Detlev turned to the avid watchers. "Meet the mighty mage who defeated my nephew. Are you impressed yet?"

Raucous laughter battered Liere. She collapsed onto the floor, arms wrapped tightly around her knees, her mind shrinking into inward focus. She knew she was isolated, totally without defenses or the possibility of aid.

"Who is going to save the world-saver?" came the scornful voice, followed by excoriating laughter.

But when Detlev shifted to describing in remorseless detail how cowardly, self-centered, and hypocritical her so-called allies were, and how none of them would stir to save her, she thought: *Not Senrid.*

She clung to that thought with all her strength. She knew what Senrid's faults were. He'd told her himself. She'd seen them, but among them cowardice, self-centeredness, and hypocrisy did not number. She knew he would be there if he could—that wherever she was, he'd try to find her.

Then there was Arthur, with his endless patience. And Rel, and Hibern, and even CJ, who believed that 'Sartora' could do miracles—that girls could do miracles. Though CJ had a temper, and struggled with it, she was so fiercely loyal, Liere knew that CJ would come running if she thought another girl was in danger.

Liere hugged those thoughts tightly, deep inside her shell. She even felt a pulse of pity for Detlev, whom everyone hated, even Siamis. He was alone, in the world of the heart.

I am not alone.

She did not know how long she could endure, but right now, that thought sustained her.

Abruptly Detlev's mental voice vanished.

Liere kept her head down, but peeked to the side; she half expected the light to be gone, for it felt like she'd been under bombardment for a hundred years. But the square of sunlight on the floor had scarcely shifted.

"She's useless. This," Detlev said contemptuously, "is nothing more than a diversion."

A rough hand seized Liere's arm and drew her to her feet. Pins and needles made standing difficult, and she was dizzy.

"Let us make a little journey," Detlev said.

Chapter Five

AFTER that soundless impact that reverberated through
teeth and bones, Atan paused, her back flat to a wall,
as she listened for alarm, shouts, footsteps, any sign that
one of the rescuers had been discovered.

Nothing.

The pulse of strong magic was not followed by another.
She had to go on.

The rooms she passed now had double doors. They appeared to be libraries. Most were empty. Down one more
hall of library rooms she trod until she was startled to hear
voices.

They weren't supposed to talk! But as she neared a
doorway, she discovered that these voices did not belong to
people her age. These were adults, their tones irritated.

"What that spell means is trouble," somebody was saying in Sartoran, "but not for us if we can find that damned
book."

Atan put her head down, and peeked out of the sides
of her eyes as she walked slowly past the door. Her heart
thundered, but the glances cast her way were distracted,

uninterested. Several of the adults in there wore the gray uniform tunics of Norsunder, two wore gray mage robes, and one stood out, a small blond woman in a velvet gown.

Atan had seen her before, on a tower, using magic to fight against Atan when she freed Sartor: that was Dejain, the chief mage of Norsunder Base.

Atan began to suspect that the Norsundrians were also pressed for time, though she had no idea why. She wondered if she ought to try to find out as she turned toward a hall from which enticing smells emanated.

Kitchens! Julian used to raid food from the kitchens, rather than be seen in the dining room, where she might be expected to sit at table and use utensils. Atan was wondering how big the kitchens would be for so large a place when a small figure hurled into her, and she stared down at Julian in wit-flown shock.

Julian was equally startled. "Atan?" She said fiercely, "Go away!"

Julian scampered off. Atan set out after her, but between one turn and another Julian darted into a room or hall and vanished. Atan grimly kept looking until she knew she was lost.

Her eyes stung, sorrow seizing her chest so hard she couldn't breathe. But others were counting on her. She had lost Julian, so it was time to keep her promise and search for the First Witch.

Her eyes were so blinded by tears that she didn't see Julian peering from behind a tapestry until Atan had passed safely by. Everything hurt, especially inside her. She couldn't stop thinking about the sad, afraid face Liere had made before Siamis pushed her into that magic. If he saw Atan, he would do that to her, too!

Julian wasn't mad at Atan any more. Atan never caused bad dreams. She was nice in the dreams. She did keep her promises, even if they were boring ones. She wasn't like Irza, or Mother. And Siamis was just like Mother and Irza, smiling and soft when other people were around, but doing mean things to people, and never keeping promises.

Atan had to go away and be safe!

Julian found who she was looking for: there was the run-away prince at the gate, with a whole lot of warriors ready with bows and arrows and swords and things. But they didn't move, much less spit, so she ran past the rows.

Kessler glanced down at the crimson-faced child who dashed up, trailing her grimy rags. "You said you keep promises," she gasped out, breathing hard.

"If I make them." He glanced down at those eyes shaped so much like his.

Julian looked around, shoving sweaty, matted hair off her cheek, then said in a low voice, "Atan is here."

"Atan?" Sharp interest caused him to wave off the runners waiting for orders. He knelt down. "Atan? On this world? Where?"

"In there." Julian waved impatiently at the palace. "I don't want Siamis to put her in magic, like he did to Liere. She was scared! It was mean. Will you make sure Siamis doesn't do that to Atan?"

Kessler said, "I will take care of Atan. But you must do something for me."

Julian gazed at him in surprise, not unpleased. Nobody asked her to do things, unless it was stupid stuff like putting on princess clothes. "What?"

"Go find Dejain. She's the yellow-haired one, usually in a pink or rose gown. Tell her I want to talk to her, and if she will not come to me, I will come to her. Have you got that right? Repeat it."

Julian repeated it exactly as he'd said.

Kessler gave a brief nod. "Quick."

The child scampered off, bare feet twinkling among the dusty rags. Kessler watched her go, suspecting that if Atan Landis was here, there were surely others from Sartorias-deles. It was actually a clever move on the part of the lighter mages, sacrificing brats who Siamis would never think would turn up, so hadn't warded.

Kessler beckoned to two of his scouts. "You know where they stashed the First Witch."

"Yes."

"Watch without being seen. If anyone suspicious goes near her, you follow them until you find out where they're coming from. Then report back to me." And to the second, "There's at least one Sartoran youth running around. Find out where they're hiding."

One of the most valued of all the architectural professions on Geth was that of the joiner. The best of them did quite well, and were always in demand. Their guild subsequently had a prominent place in the city, as in all cities on Geth; and, as it happened, the First Witch had a brother who was the head of a successful shop.

In a back room, sitting in a rocking chair that moved gently back and forth as if she would go on rocking until the end of time, sat a woman of about sixty-five, with dark hair bound up, not hiding the white streak.

Leander was the one to find her.

When he saw that white stripe, he backed up slowly, then forced himself to compose his face. His body. To walk slowly out into the square with its fountain, across which Norsunder patrols rode frequently.

Leander fell in behind a couple of people carrying empty baskets. Did they think those baskets were filled? The evidence of the enchantment gave him the creeps, but he kept his pace slow, his attention unfocused as he traversed the square in the direction he'd last seen Senrid.

He caught sight of Senrid's middle-aged man guise at the end of a long street. Of course he was moving away, but Leander forced himself to walk slowly, though he increased each step a bit more until finally Senrid turned his head, then moved to one of the benches, and sat down.

When Leander caught up, he explained about the woman in the rocker.

"Just sitting there?"

"Yes."

"Wards or tracers or traps?"

"None that I could discern."

Senrid uttered a soft laugh, then shut his eyes. Leander knew that expression: Senrid was doing his mind thing. Presently he opened his eyes. "Cath knows. I hope that means Lilith is out there listening, and will do whatever it is they planned to do."

"Let's round up the others," Leander suggested.

"Start that. I'll go see if I can sense a trap. If you see Jilo, tell him where I am."

"Right."

Senrid and Leander forced themselves to rise with dreamy slowness, and to shuffle off in opposite directions.

Leander spotted Jilo (in old man form, but as unlike Wan-Edhe as imagination could make him) two streets away, slogging grimly through a row of upholstery and finishing shops. He drifted up, and said low-voiced, "I found her. Senrid's on his way. I'll go warn the others to retreat. Here's the directions to the joiner's shop."

He described the route twice, then Jilo set out at an awkward lope under the low eaves for the joiner's. Senrid spotted him from the other end of a long palm-lined path, and forced himself to move slowly to join him, without looking right or left.

When they reached the shop, they slipped inside—without noticing Kessler's scout watching from the midst of a flowery pocket garden, or the Norsundrian patroller who noted a pair of old men shuffling into the joiner's shop that he knew was supposed to remain empty.

Both patroller and scout went off to report, as inside the shop, Senrid and Jilo separated and began feeling out dark magic wards, tracers, and traps.

Jilo was halfway around the perimeter of the room when Senrid spoke.

"I've found at least two, maybe three traps around her chair," Senrid said to Jilo. "So far. I think we'd better work on these first."

A short time later, "Mirror ward," Jilo sang out.

"You handle that," Senrid said, and began crawling around the room to finish looking for other tracers and traps.

Julian found Dejain, and delivered her message.

The mage stared down at the filthy urchin, fighting the urge to run, to transfer away. The moment she'd dreaded was here.

Her fingers twitched toward the secret pocket in which she'd put the transfer token she'd prepared against disaster, then her hand dropped. She did not want Kessler coming after her. He was unnervingly single-minded when he went on the hunt, and it would only make him angrier. If she pretended cooperation, she might be able to deflect him.

"Show me where he is," she demanded of Julian. To

Dejain's annoyance, the child trotted at her heels. "Go on back," Dejain said. "Scat."

"No," Julian said.

"Go pester Siamis."

"I don't like Siamis anymore," Julian retorted.

Dejain uttered a harsh laugh. "No one likes Siamis."

She turned her back and walked faster, forcing the child to pound grimly behind, dragging her load of cloth.

Dejain spotted Kessler standing at his post by the gate, and slowed as she considered her options. She halted in the lee of a flowering jessamine tree and watched as one, then another scout rode up to report.

Dejain hurried her pace, but didn't make it in time to hear either scout make their reports; Kessler saw her, dismissed both his scouts, then gestured to Dejain. "Come with me."

He didn't wait for her corroboration, but scooped up Julian, tucked her under his arm, and took off with rapid step. Dejain lifted her skirts to keep pace, while she reviewed her exit strategies.

Kessler didn't stop until he reached the side entrance to the palace. He set Julian down before the stairway opposite the broom closet. "My spy tells me that you'll find your cousin down that way. Run along. I'll be right behind you." He gave the little girl a push. After one disconcerted look behind her, tear tracks marring her grimy face, Julian ran.

Kessler faced Dejain. "Remove the blood spell."

She stared at him.

He said distinctly, "You enchanted the blade I ordered for someone else. I've known ever since it struck me and threw me straight into Norsunder. Did you really think I did not know?"

Her hand slid toward the secret pocket sewn into the seam of her gown, but Kessler gripped her painfully by the elbow. "Now."

They both knew Detlev and Siamis were involved in a magical struggle. Judging by the impact of powerful magic, it was happening now. Kessler had no more interest in helping the two Ancient Sartorans than Dejain—less, as she still claimed a place at Norsunder Base—and at this moment, they were both unwatched.

She knew Kessler carried at least one hidden weapon. He could kill her in a heartbeat and no one would know. Or care.

She had dreaded this moment so long that it was almost a relief. Without denying or uttering the myriad falsities she'd concocted as excuses, she whispered the long sequence of spells, memorized long ago.

Kessler let her go the moment he was free of Norsunder's hold.

Dejain plunged her hand into her pocket. She had nowhere to go, nothing to be, except chief mage at Norsunder Base. There, precarious as it was, she had power. Anywhere else, she'd have to fight for it, and be on the watch for the greater powers who could be endlessly vindictive. The mere thought made her feel old.

Lesca would make her comfortable until Dejain saw who won. She used her cross-world transfer.

THE guards at the gate stood around speculating about why their commander had taken off with the brat and the pretty mage.

"Look," one muttered, causing all heads to turn.

Beyond the open gate, the air shimmered. The smell of mimosa and wild thyme gusted outward in a ring, heat buffeting watching faces, and then a host appeared directly outside the gate. Armed. On horseback. At the center rode Detlev, next to a skinny girl clutching the mane of her horse.

Every mage in the city felt that mass transfer as an inward blow, sharper than the first.

The guards withdrew to either side as Detlev and his force rode slowly in, Liere in the middle, looking blanch-faced and incongruous holding on desperately to the mane of a horse whose reins were held by another rider.

They rode up the street toward the palace.

"What was *that*?" Jilo asked.

Senrid shrugged, and was about to say *Let's get back to work*, when they heard the sound of many footsteps on the pale stone tiles outside the door.

"Who are you?" Armed warriors blocked the door, though as yet they hadn't drawn their weapons. They'd reported the sighting and had been duly ordered to bring in the old men who had entered the shop, but they weren't worried about a fight from a couple of geezers.

Senrid and Jilo avoided looking at each other, knowing that the illusion did not hide their expressions, only distorted their features.

Senrid waggled his hand surreptitiously to Jilo, and rose to his feet as slowly as he could, blocking Jilo from sight as the latter got back to work on breaking the chain of spells.

Hoping he sounded like the enchanted, Senrid said in a monotone, while staring a little above the head of the patrol leader, "I am here to check my sister. I always come to check my sister upon this day."

The patrol leader looked at the others, who looked back. "Nobody's supposed to be here," he said, and when Senrid just stood there, "You can come along and tell Siamis that," he said.

Senrid's thought careened wildly. What to say when he was supposed to be enchanted out of his wits? Of course.

"I am here to check on my sister. I always come to check on my sister this day."

"Yes. Come along." The patrol leader motioned impatiently. Then winced, and cast a troubled look at the window.

Senrid felt the teeth-scraping, burning metal sense of great power building. Behind him, he heard Jilo hiss in his breath.

"Come along!" The Norsundrian's voice sharpened. He took a step toward Senrid, hand going to the hilt of his sword.

Senrid's right hand drifted to his other wrist, though he knew that taking on a patrol with a knife was not going to keep them off longer than a moment or two.

Greenish-white light flashed from horizon to horizon.

Senrid winced; Jilo said, "The ward on the city gates. It's gone." He began whispering, and magical light glittered greenish, smelling of solder.

The patrol leader had interrupted himself to look out

into the street. He turned to one of his followers and said, "Find out what that was."

Behind Senrid, Jilo muttered, "First one on her gone." It seemed forever, but was only a moment or two before Jilo said, with satisfaction, "Two, and three."

Senrid was uttering the first phrases of the antidote to Siamis's spell when he remembered he was supposed to catch the victim's attention with a personal object. He cast a despairing look about, glanced at the Norsundrians, and performed the enchantment spell anyway, in the time it took for the patrol leader to draw his sword and advance three steps.

"Lilith," the First Witch murmured on an outgoing breath, gazing into space.

Senrid knew immediately what that meant: Lilith the Guardian had been listening on the mental realm. Oh, yes, the mages were outside the city with their own plans.

But that was pretty much what Lilith had said. At least she played fair. *I did my part, Lilith. Over to you. Now I'm going to find Liere.*

Senrid looked up at the patrol leader, who was motioning impatiently to what he obviously thought were slow old people. The First Witch blinked rapidly, touched Senrid and Jilo to protect them, and spoke several words.

Light slammed into the Norsundrians, freezing them between one step and another.

"That will not last long," she said. "I seem to have little strength. But it ought to be enough to get us past them." She tried to rise, then sank back. "Oh." Her voice was soft, breathless. "*Very* little strength. Will one of you give me an arm?"

Jilo stepped back, expecting Senrid to take care of that, but Senrid was gone, his footsteps rapidly diminishing. So Jilo awkwardly took hold of the old woman's thin arm. She rose with a grunt, and slowly they walked out, Jilo stumbling a little before he found the right pace to match hers.

"There's a shorter way to the palace, up this path," she murmured, pointing to an archway connecting two buildings with what looked like palm-frond roofs. Past Weaver's Row and the Pearl Garden . . . "Let us hurry," she added breathlessly, leaning on Jilo as she increased her pace.

Siamis strolled out the main door to the palace, backed by a company of armed guards, who spread out along the perimeter of the main plaza. They blocked off access from the various tree- and shrub-lined pathways opening onto the plaza, as a small number of vague-faced denizens drifted along oblivious as they went about some habitual task.

The warriors formed up, shield to shield, swords out, as Detlev and his force came riding up the main street from the gate barely visible in the distance.

Siamis gripped his sword by its sheath and sauntered to the center of the plaza.

Detlev reined in, halting his company.

"You're here again," Siamis said as he stepped up to Liere's horse, his back to Detlev.

"I appreciated the diversion," Detlev said, looking down at the top of Siamis's fair hair, his faint smile acerbic. "You knew she was completely ignorant?"

"I thought," Siamis said, "if she did know where the dyr is hidden, you would be the one to discover it, surely." Siamis's lips parted in a smile up at Liere.

Detlev turned his head. His eyes narrowed, and the ring of Siamis's guards surrounding his company stirred. Their patrol leader staggered, then righted himself, saying hoarsely, "Fall back."

Swords rang as they were sheathed again, and shields lowered. The Norsundrians Siamis had ordered to surround Detlev's force now began to line up behind Detlev's warriors—it was clear that Detlev had superseded whatever command they had been given by a mental order to the patrol leader.

As if nothing had happened, Siamis smiled up at Liere, closed his hands around her arms, and lifted her down, keeping his grip on one arm, his other hand still holding the sword.

At that moment Jilo and the First Witch appeared from a side street, as the handful of Isul Demarzal denizens began stirring and looking around with returning awareness. Some sat down abruptly, putting heads in hands, others glanced around bewildered and fearful.

The First Witch tightened her grip on Jilo and raised her
voice. "You had better go now. You are not wanted here,"
she declared. "Your spells are broken. And my allies are
coming."

Detlev's head turned sharply. He didn't answer, but
raised his hand, and those who knew magic sensed the in-
gathering of power.

The First Witch struck first, but she was too far away,
and too weak, to drop a stone spell around him the way she
had around the patrol in the joiner's house.

But her attempt diverted Detlev for a crucial moment.
He turned to look for her as the air flickered blue-white
and a host of people in layers of bright, filmy fabric appeared.

"Ah," the First Witch said. "I knew the Ones would
come."

In the square, a white-haired man wove a spell that
raised a wall of virulently glowing green around the Norsundrian warriors. Detlev muttered a spell and struck it
down, but the mages united in raising a larger, thicker magical ward.

"Ones?" Jilo asked.

"Help me sit down, young man, will you?" the First
Witch asked, pointing to a pretty little bench carved of the
shiny wood that looked to Sartorias-deles people like
poured chocolate.

In the plaza Detlev raised his hands, which began to
glow, but the mages worked together to dissipate the spell
he was forming, as the First Witch said, "The Ones is what
we call our roaming mages. For a time they give up name,
family, home, to wander and do good in the world. They
are called simply Ones while they serve."

Detlev turned their way. Jilo hunched down, terrified,
as the First Witch called in her cracked, tremulous voice,
"You know you do not have the secret of our tunnel transfer. You have only an echo, and we shall break that. I say
to you, unwanted enemy, that you had better use it now to
remove yourself and these." A gnarled hand dismissively
waved at the armed force. "You can fall upon us, and many
will die, but we'll—"

Jilo could see that Detlev wasn't listening. His head

turned, his eyes searching, and Jilo realized that Siamis had abandoned Detlev. Detlev was alone, facing seven powerful mages, who began to chant in unison. Once again the air shimmered, and the chant became a harsh hum; Jilo started, though the hum was as different from the Great Hum as a scream from a song. But both were products of voice.

The shimmer coalesced into fog, swallowing Detlev and his force, then vanished, blasting the area with a rush of hot air.

At once the newly disenchanted Isul Demarzal people began clamoring for explanations, as more people poured out of the palace, looking about wildly.

Jilo said, "Norsunder was hunting for rift magic, right? But you do it differently here?"

The First Witch looked into his earnest face. "Yes. We call it a chain. For transfer between worlds, the number doesn't matter. Our method is different—it takes several of us to safely chain a transfer."

"So it's not a real tunnel?"

"No, but the word is a way for our minds to grasp how we manipulate space between destinations." By now a couple of younger Geth mages had spotted them, and came hurrying toward their leader. The First Witch rose to greet them, but smiled back at Jilo. "Norsunder will find no co-operation from us now. And that one, he knows it. Thank you for your aid. Go in peace."

Jilo backed away, and anyone who cared to saw a slightly blurry old man loping through the gathering crowds. Inside the palace, it was left turn, left turn, left turns all the way until he reached the stairs.

Glenn was the first one to find his way back to the underground cavern by the dark lake. He'd never had any intention of looking for some old woman. He'd gone straight to spy on Siamis, hoping to be able to kill him for unleashing Henerek on his home, but the fire for vengeance in imagination was doused by the cold splash of reality: Siamis was a fit-looking young man carrying a saber with the absent comfort of one well used to his weapon, and surrounded by guards.

So Glenn had retreated, joined by his sister. She'd lost count of the rooms, which disturbed her so much she intended to start over. But Hibern found her first, and said that Leander had spread the word to retreat.

They descended to the cavern to find the Mearsieans trickling in, having received the news that the First Witch had been found. The ever-growing group of young allies milled around, exchanging stories and speculations about what was going on, as Cath sat silently in their midst, eyes closed.

Then Cath gasped, opened his eyes, and got to his feet as Julian appeared on the stairs. She began to hop from step to step, but tripped as a swathe of her filthy clothes caught underfoot. She pitched out over the stones, but before anyone could do more than exclaim, Rel took two fast steps and caught her midair.

He set her down, and she ran straight to Atan, saying over and over, "I hate him, I hate him, I hate him. I want to go home."

Atan waited, arms kept stiff at her sides until the solid little body collided with her, and then—tentatively, gently— she put her arms around the little girl, who sobbed herself into hiccoughs.

So intent were they all on this reunion that they didn't see Kessler until he appeared at the top of the stairs.

Rel started forward protectively, but Kessler raised a hand as he leaped down, four stairs at time. "Siamis is on the way. I suggest you get out."

Some looked around uncertainly, and Dak turned to his brother, who nodded.

"But we're missing three of our people," Hibern said.

"Two," Atan corrected, pointing to Jilo in old man illusion at the top of the stairs. When he saw Kessler he backed up, looking around wildly.

Kessler glanced up, and said with complete indifference, "Siamis is right behind you."

Jilo looked back and forth in a way that Kessler found comical and Atan heartbreaking, then he hustled down the stairs, nearly tripping in his haste. He slunk past Kessler, as, at the other end of the cavern, Dak was silently motioning the allies toward the far tunnel. Hibern lingered, hesitant to leave until she saw Senrid safely among them.

Rel pushed past her to confront Kessler. "What are you doing?"

Kessler's sword scraped free of its sheath. "Waiting for him." His smile made Hibern's nerves chill. "I'm going to cut out his heart with the sword named Truth."

Hibern said to Rel in an urgent undervoice that hissed in echoes, "Senrid's missing. And we never did find Liere, so he has to be looking for her."

Cath's young voice echoed from the other end of the tunnel, "Siamis has the girl. The boy is following them."

Rel said, "Let's get out of sight, at least." He indicated the archway.

Hibern followed, glancing back every few steps in hopes of seeing Senrid and Liere.

On her last glance, she saw what she feared most: Siamis appeared at the top of the stairs, gripping Liere with one arm.

He smiled down at Kessler, let Liere free, and drew his sword from its sheath.

Senrid catapulted himself through the entrance at the top of the stairs, then stilled in astonishment at the sight of Siamis, fair hair gleaming in the light slanting down from the stairway, facing a shorter, slight, black-haired fellow in black Norsundrian uniform.

Liere cowered nearby, her drawn, anxious expression lightening to joy when she saw Senrid. He jumped down the stairs, reached her, and their hands met and gripped tight, Liere reassured by Senrid's solid, callus-palmed grip, and he unsettled by how thin her fingers were.

She turned her huge eyes to him, and her thought came, clear as speech: *Siamis said it again, he left the sword as a gift. What can that mean, a gift?*

Senrid grimaced, watching as Siamis and Kessler sized each other up, swordpoints making tiny testing motions. Siamis was taller, wearing a loose, light, open-collared tunic shirt sashed around his hips. He wore forest mocs rather than riding boots, and moved with ease over the smooth stone. Kessler, shorter, reminded Senrid of something with antennae, the way he'd go still, then move so fast he was a blur. Both held their weapons well.

Liere tugged his hand: *Senrid?*

He dragged his gaze away. He hated trying to form words with Dena Yeresbeth—it was too clumsy, with memories and emotions and images leaking into his thoughts, making it difficult to concentrate. But he tried: *Whatever he meant doesn't matter. Because you didn't take it.*

Her response was swift: *But it scares me, Senrid, what he said. I keep thinking, he was twelve when Norsunder took him. I was twelve when I did the Child Spell.*

Senrid's return thought was swift and sarcastic: *He's not twelve now.* Then he got her meaning: *You think he's threatening to make you into a copy of him?*

Clang! The first move in the swordfight was almost too fast to follow. A flurry of exchanges, and the two stepped back, Siamis smiling. Kessler's expression remained blank.

Senrid thought: *What are Detlev and Siamis really after? Did you learn anything while they had you?*

Liere's mental response rocked him back with emotion-charged memory: *They wanted the dyr. Thought I had it.*

Kessler feinted, jabbed, fast as lightning. Siamis side-stepped lightly, just enough for the point to pass uselessly by his ear, and whipped his blade inside Kessler's guard—to find only air.

Senrid's mind ran with images, memories, connections as Kessler and Siamis circled one another on the ancient stone, worn smooth by millennia of flowing water.

The gift. The threat . . . Detlev's *You're not worth my time yet.* "They want us to grow up," Senrid murmured, as maintaining a conversation by Dena Yeresbeth took too much effort.

"Is that it?" Liere whispered, her gaze unwavering. "And then make us into Norsundrians? I never want to grow up, ever."

Senrid watched another flurry of attacks, feints, ripostes from Siamis and Kessler as he struggled against the conflict inside him. There were times when the Child Spell felt like a pair of boots that were too tight, only it was his spirit so confined. One day, he knew, he was going to get rid of the Child Spell.

But if Detlev and Siamis wanted him to do it now, for whatever reason, well, that was easy.

"So we won't," Senrid said, and because he could feel her longing for safety, he cast a fast scan behind them. "Rel's over there," he whispered as Siamis extended his blade in a deceptively leisurely strike, which Kessler evaded with minimal movement. "Let's go."

Liere gave a shaky sigh of relief, and tugged on his hand. Senrid followed, but walking backward. He did not want to miss what so far promised to be the duel of a lifetime. Senrid wasn't all that experienced in training, but he'd watched the academy boys train, and he could see that both Siamis and Kessler were in a class beyond the best the Marlovens had to offer as they circled, upper bodies motionless except for the subtle movements of eye and wrist as they exchanged blows, almost like a conversation.

He let Liere's hand go so he could watch.

Liere ran on a few steps, until she passed the water-carved archway. The illusion made Rel look weird, but she knew he was Rel from the mental plane. She stopped beside him, and shivered, every bruise aching, as she stared at the back of Senrid's head, knowing that Senrid would always stop to watch the duels. *But he will stay a child with me*, she thought. *He won't take the sword gift any more than I will.*

Senrid was not aware that he'd stopped.

Siamis sidestepped an attack, smiled past Kessler, his light gaze reaching across the cavern to meet Senrid's. He deliberately flashed the sword up in a mocking salute, and then returned to the attack.

Kessler's teeth showed at that salute. He had learned three things so far. One, that they were nearly matched in speed and strength. Two, Siamis's training was probably better, or Siamis could read his mind in spite of his mind-shield, because he always knew where Kessler was going to attack.

Third: he was not going to win this match.

But he could try. He flung himself into a risky attack

high, low, high, double-bind. The blades rang, bringing a laugh of sheer pleasure from Siamis.

And then came a firm female voice: "The Witches are roused. You know what comes next."

Both swords lifted as the duelists glanced at the new arrival at the top of the stairs. Siamis recognized Lilith the Guardian, as she began whispering a spell. "Late," he said. "Again."

Then he made a motion, a token gleamed briefly, and he vanished: by accident or by intent he was gone before his sword, which stood in midair for the single beat of a heart, as if in mockery. Or challenge. Then it, too, was gone.

Kessler lifted his head, his expression disturbingly flat of affect. "Was that for you or for me?"

"I will have to consider," Lilith replied, looking down sadly. Kessler made a sign, murmured, and also vanished.

"Kessler knows magic?" Rel asked, from the cavern archway, where he, too, had been determined to watch that sword duel. "That's bad news. Terrible," he added under his breath.

"It seems he does," Lilith said. "But I believe he's just broken his enforced allegiance to Norsunder. He trusts no one, and with a background like his, who could blame him?"

"I could," CJ whispered from beside Clair.

Rel agreed, but he said nothing as Lilith descended the rest of the stairs. They all began to move, as if released from some kind of spell. Norsunder was truly gone—it began to sink in.

Liere's control gave way at last, and a deep sob shook her as she ran back and cast herself on the Guardian's comfortable bosom. For a time Lilith stood looking down at the tousled head, the unkempt hair hacked so badly, and her smile was tender.

Liere raised teary eyes. "I can't be Sartora. Why can't you stay and teach me?"

"You know my limitations," Lilith said softly. "And there is a world full of wise people who can teach you many things, even if they don't have your talent. But you have to listen to them."

Liere straightened up, aware of the sound of many footsteps as everybody reappeared from the far tunnel and crowded around. She wiped her eyes on her sleeve, and said, "Siamis didn't kill me. I thought he would."

Lilith looked at the space where Siamis had been. "Perhaps he had a trade in mind? Or he didn't want Detlev to keep you? I don't know. He is not your friend, but I wonder if he might be the enemy of your enemy."

Senrid snorted, then cut a fast glance at Liere, whose fingers clutched her elbows in the old worried manner. Moderating his voice, he said, "So why can't we use the dyr against them? It has to be powerful if they want it so badly."

Lilith had been staring at the air where that sword had been, her expression difficult to define, though it wasn't triumphant. Senrid remembered that *Late. Again.* He wondered what history lay behind it—then he remembered that Siamis had once been on the lighter side in the Fall, before he was taken as a child of twelve. Senrid wondered if Siamis was blaming Lilith for not saving him. Then he remembered what she'd said about her daughter, and winced.

Hibern and Rel stepped up to either side of Senrid and Liere as Lilith said, "Ordinarily I am a firm believer in sharing knowledge, and I know how annoying it is to hear 'I can't tell you.' But in this case, really. Believe me. The less you know about those objects, the better for everyone." She raised her hand, palm out. "Yes, I am aware that to some, my words would act only as a goad. But there are so many better uses of your time, and pursuing the dyra will only bring further trouble."

By then all the others had joined them, Dak and Cath standing a little way away.

"Ah," Lilith said, and turned to Glenn and Tahra. "I wanted to tell you two that the news is perhaps not as dire as you feared. Your mother was taken prisoner. I am sorry to report that we know nothing more than that, but there is one good thing that is definite: your Uncle Roderic escaped from the Norsundrians. He is in Ferdrian now, with what remains of the Knights, busy restoring the city. They need you both."

Liere was saying to Arthur, "Senrid will have to straighten out the mess in his kingdom. Maybe it'll be done by New Year's, when I always visit." She sighed. "I have so much to learn."

Arthur smiled. "One thing about Bereth Ferian. Throw a pen and the ink will splash ten teachers."

Liere smiled at the mild joke, thinking of her quiet room, hot chocolate, books to read, and a walk among the beeches. She no longer wanted to join the Mearsieans, who couldn't seem to see Liere instead of Sartora, but that was all right. They wouldn't have come all this way to help if they didn't think Sartora was their friend, even if she wasn't a very good heroine.

They are all friends, Liere thought. *The alliance is real.*

Lilith turned her head to survey the gathering and lifted her voice. "All together, I see. Good. The Witches are ready to unite in sending you all home." She looked from one to another. "Siamis's enchantment is gone from Sartorias-deles, and I believe it will be impossible to use it again without its being removed instantly. The antidote is being spread to mages of both worlds."

"Hurray!" the Mearsieans shrieked. "We won! Siamis lost twice, ha ha!"

A noisy cheer went up.

No, we didn't, Senrid thought, remembering that mocking salute with the sword named Truth. *That wasn't a battle, it was a scouting foray.*

He didn't say it out loud, but it was heard by all those listening on the mental plane.

Chapter Seven

Sartorias-deles

THE young allies found themselves transferred back to Delfina Valley, from which they all returned to their own homes.

Prince Glenn and Princess Tahra of Everon arrived to a devastated kingdom with only a few months in which to prepare for the winter ahead. The queen was still missing. Roderic Dei had survived his capture, and returned to hold the kingdom for the underage prince and princess. Most of the royal palace had been burned as well as looted, but the Sandrials had been cleaning what they could, and hauling back the things they'd saved. Everyone, from the two royal children to the servants, crowded into a single wing for winter.

Sarendan emerged from the enchantment to be plunged into grief for the loss of the gallant Derek Diamagan. Peitar Selenna, who shared similar personality traits with his exiled uncle as well as physical resemblance, threw himself into mastering magic with all the singlemindedness with which his uncle had once thrown himself into building military might—all to withstand the threat of Norsunder. Peitar understood that though Siamis and Detlev's race to find and control the Geth-deles transfer magic had failed, it was only a temporary setback.

Sartor emerged from the enchantment to discover that the erstwhile commander Bostian had been unable to keep his bored battalion from beginning to sack the city around their oblivious eyes. The guilds were quite angry with the mages for having failed, again, to stop the magic attack—and for having so diminished the Royal Guard that it could not stand against Bostian's invaders.

But at least the invaders themselves were gone: about the time the alliance first transferred to Geth, Siamis had had to drop his search for the source of Geth-deles's transfer magic to return to Eidervaen, which he wanted intact once he was successful.

Since Bostian had proved to have so little control over his command, Siamis confronted him, acidly pointing out that they were completely exposed to a flank attack from, for example, the Marlovens from the other side of the mouth of the Sartoran Sea. They were ordered to plan and drill a defense at the same harbor from which Henerek's army had departed. They marched south and east, and duly planned their defense.

On a wild summer night, they discovered that they *were* being invaded, and a sharp, nasty fight ensued until combatants discovered that they were nominally on the same side. This was Kessler's and Henerek's combined forces, back on the ships they had commandeered, assuming that Sarendan had been raised against them.

By the time the miscommunication was straightened out, orders came down to retreat to Norsunder Base.

Marloven Hess, which had not been invaded, merely had to resume normal life. The horses had enjoyed a splendid summer on the plains their ancestors had come from; the academy had only lost a couple of weeks, which customarily ended with a weeklong wargame in the plains. They had withdrawn deep into the plains, where their instructors taught them to forage, and conducted a protracted game. They returned, sunbrowned and lean, to find that the king was back.

When their families showed up to fetch them, Senrid had to endure questions, silent queries, and a certain amount of oblique chaffing for his having disrupted the entire kingdom for . . . nothing.

He endured it grimly, reflecting that at least he still held his throne.

The least disturbed was Chwahirsland, still in the grip of the glacially disintegrating time binding that Wan-Edhe had laid over Narad, the capital city. To that city, Jilo might never have been gone. To the rest of the kingdom, the season of planting resulted in a slightly more endurable winter than usual, though much bitterness arose in certain army factions at their having had to lower themselves to labors outside of the endless drill they were used to.

Jilo departed Tsauderei's sunlit, beautiful Valley, and transferred back into the toxic grip of that magic, where he got to work.

Hibern: I promised myself I would inform you when Stefan was cured. Your father succeeded in removing the spells that your meddling made worse. Stefan is himself again, and though your father still refuses to acknowledge you, I asked your brother if he wished to see you home again. I know not what your father said to Stefan during their many wearying magical sessions, but Stefan's bitterness and resentment mirrors your father's.

Some day it might be different. I find my own anger abated, especially after many conversations with my own relations. I trust you are learning useful skills, but then you were always an excellent student. I wish you success in your endeavors, my daughter.

Tdor Askan

Peitar:

Lilah will surely tell you how much we talked about your visiting Sartor. I still cannot believe that you have yet to visit Eidervaen. Rel says that when he visits next, he hopes by then Sarendan will be settled, and you and Lilah will come, even if you can be away only for a few days.

I say 'by then' partly because I know how much is left to be done after recent events, and that includes a time for grief and memorial. I have made a vow to light a candle each year for Derek, whose gallantry will never be forgotten by any who knew and loved him.

But the other reason is because when I arrived back in Eidervaen, it was to discover that the royal Purrad, our labyrinth, which we often talked about showing you, had been destroyed by the parting Norsundrians in a final act of petty malice.

I say 'petty' because if the intent was to frighten us, it had the opposite effect. Everybody in the Eidervaen palace, from the smallest curtain runner to Chief Veltos, remembers exactly how it lay, and we have all made a vow to work together until every pebble, every plant, every chime, is replaced exactly the way it was. Their destruction will be erased as if it never happened.

Atan

Atan sent the note and set the new notecase down as Julian entered, almost unrecognizable with her hair cut short to get rid of the impossible mats. Julian wore a neat child's tunic and comfortable riding trousers. Though they were made of unadorned cloth, they fit. What's more, Julian took them off at night, and even put them through the cleaning frame herself. She had decided that baths were the most wonderful thing ever invented, sometimes taking two in a day—one for serious and one for fun.

"What would you like to do?" Atan asked, with a pulse of guilt. But nobody would stop her if she abandoned the tight schedule the high council had bound her to. They were too busy dealing with angry guild leaders and envoys from other parts of the kingdom that the Norsundrians had marched through, taking what they wanted.

"Visit Hannla," Julian said. "She lets me push the broom, and gives me pastry if I do a good job."

"Very well. Maybe she'll let me push the broom, too, and we both can earn a pastry." Atan half-held her hand out, ready to drop it at the first sign of a scowl.

But Julian took that hand, letting out a sigh of contentment as they walked together downstairs.

Marloven Hess

Senrid's foot tapped in counterpoint to the enthusiastic thundering of hand drums played by Retren Forthan's old academy friends, gathered from all corners of Marloven Hess for Forthan's wedding to Fenis Senelac.

Fenis was a young bride now, a tall figure in her wedding robe of crimson, edged with shiny black cord and embroidered along hem and cuffs with blue and gold and green figures. It had been made by a many-greats-grandmother and worn by every Senelac bride since.

Senrid watched as she led the singing. Anyone seeing them would take her for Senrid's elder, though they had been born around the same time.

Senrid had survived. The army was back, the garrison as well. On the surface, everything looked normal—he had received a note from Liere, saying that she was now a student at Bereth Ferian's mage school.

Everything looked normal, and yet he knew it wasn't. He forced an attitude of good cheer as he watched Retren Forthan get to his feet, flushed with wine and with the genial, bawdy jokes of his friends. Forthan held his sword high over his head, hilt in one hand, tip balanced on his left fingers, as he began the wedding sword dance.

One by one the other young men joined as Fenis's friends took over the drumming. Men dancing, women watching, and soon they would turn about, making ribald comments—Senrid understood the words, but as yet the meaning was beyond him.

That was fine. He had enough to do, and to think about. Like that last salute of Siamis's. *Gift.* He kept coming back to that. He and Liere were the only ones with Dena Yeresbeth, which was more of a burden than anything else.

Siamis's threat about gifts, his salute with the sword, had been aimed specifically at the two of them. Surely being singled out for oblique threat had to do with Dena Yeresbeth. So maybe, once Liere was used to her new school, they should try to seek out some kind of training—

His notecase ticked in his tunic pocket.

He'd gotten pretty good at remembering to check it. Satisfied that nobody was interested in the short figure sitting midway between the old folks and the children trying to gobble all the wedding tarts, he palmed the case from his pocket and unrolled the piece of paper.

Chwahirsland

Senrid:

You were correct in what you said about laws that people can point at, that my granting things will look like favoritism and whim if some get what they want and others don't.

But we also know that Wan-Edhe could be sent back at any time. I had my first meeting with the army leaders. Uncle Shiam and his third cousins were there with me, as we talked about the future of our kingdom.

We are agreed that Wan-Edhe will come when he or Norsunder wants, not when we are ready. But until then we shall live as if he will not.

Tsauderei knows about the book, and Mondros wrote to ask where it is. I told him it's stored beyond reach. Now that the secret is no longer a secret, there's no use in trying to discover who blabbed, because after all, it will be the first thing Wan-Edhe demands when he returns.

It reports that Siamis and Detlev are back at Norsunder Base. None of my tracers have alerted me to the presence of Kessler Sonscarna, but the book says he's been here. Twice. I wish I knew what that means.

Jilo

Prelude

North of Sartor

AND so the young allies survived their first action. I
have endeavored in this, the first record of their alliance, to introduce them before I must introduce their ad-
versaries, as yet unmet.

The last summer storm had washed the sky clear overhead,
and left the newly turning leaves bright as jewels. Rel was
descending the last of the mountain trail north of Sartor's
border when he heard voices echoing through the trees, and
a rising shout, "Help!"

Rel slung his pack onto a boulder and unloosed his
sword as he splashed through the undergrowth to a clearing. The thud of retreating steps reached him, and a faint,
floating laugh on the wind—the laugh of a teenage boy,
from the sound—as he stumbled to a stop. There in the
middle of the rain-soggy glade lay a boy, bright blotches of
color marring the snow all around him.

Rel's gaze snapped to the crimson first, but as that was
surrounded by bright splashes of blue and yellow, the fear
that the boy's blood had been spilled vanished. It was paint.

The boy struggled to rise, and Rel hastened to help him up. He was thin and gangling, in age anywhere from thirteen to eighteen. A pair of wide-set, mild brown eyes gazed out of a thin face half covered by a cloud of curly brown hair, now matted with mud.

"Thank you," the boy said breathlessly. "I don't know what they would have done if you hadn't come along." He looked around, blinking mud off his eyelashes before he wiped a grimy sleeve over his face. "At the very least, they would have smashed all my paints."

Rel looked around. Besides the paints, brushes and other artistic items lay scattered in the snow. "I'll help you." He sheathed his sword and began collecting scattered bits.

"Oh, look at that," the boy mourned. "Demolished my primaries, and it takes so very long to make the blue . . ." He wiped his face again, smearing the mud even worse, then stared in dismay at the splintered remains of little ceramic pots, the colors already soaking into the ground, impossible to retrieve.

Rel said, "There are a few unspilled. See? Three right here."

"Maybe a few more," the boy said with a hopeful air. "They flung them at the trees." He indicated a venerable oak, whose bark had been liberally lightened with a splash of yellow.

In a short time they'd gathered everything they could, and restored it to the boy's travel knapsack, which was full of papers.

"At least they didn't get to your work," Rel said when he discovered the knapsack on the far side of a mossy boulder, where it had obviously been thrown.

"That was probably next." The boy sounded resigned as he dropped the last of the salvaged art materials into the knapsack, then looked up at Rel.

Faint smears of paint streaked his face under the mud. Or maybe those were bruises. "Thank you again. Who are you?"

"Name's Rel. You?"

"Adam." His Sartoran was so good that Rel couldn't quite tell the origin of his accent, except that Adam didn't sound like the Sartorans. Nobody outside of those born in

Sartor did, their accent being separated from the rest of the world's use of the language by a hundred years. "Are you going north toward the port city, by any chance?"

"Going through there, yes," Rel said. And, as was considered polite on the Wander, "Want company?"

Adam's relief was unmistakable.

Rel glanced behind them, then said, "Weren't you heading south toward Sartor?"

"I was," Adam admitted. "Someone warned me about brigands, but I didn't believe it. Someone else warned me that the Sartorans probably won't want itinerant art students. Maybe that warning is as good as the first. I can always go back some other time," he said. "That is, if the brigands don't do me in first."

"Have a weapon?" Rel asked as he started back along the path to retrieve his pack. "Any training?"

Adam held his muddy hands away from his sides, his grin rueful.

"I'll walk with you to the next town. You can report what happened."

Adam shrugged into his knapsack, then fell in step beside Rel. "Will it do any good?" he asked.

"Probably not, if you mean, will they go searching. I've been in this area before when brigands attacked, and they didn't do anything then. But there's always hope that the next report will convince someone they've had enough."

"If that's so, I guess I've a duty to be the next."

Adam talked cheerfully as they proceeded up the road, readily answering Rel's questions, not that he asked many. The etiquette of the Wander, Puddlenose had told Rel when they met on Rel's first journey, was not to delve into people's backgrounds unless they offered the information. But a few questions were considered permissible—What's your name? Where do you come from? Have any skills? If the answers were vague, then you dropped the questions, but if detail was offered, you could ask more.

Adam didn't seem interested in origins or whereabouts, anyway. He was far more enthusiastic about his artwork, something he clearly loved talking about.

By the time they glimpsed a market town beyond the last hill, Rel had learned that there were thirty basic sketch techniques, the benefits and drawbacks of dry watercolor versus wet on wet, and the difficulties of making color. "I shall have to start again," Adam finished ruefully. "Remaking my primaries." Then he ran off to a rocky bluff to catch sight of some winter bird, whose plumage he compared to the same sort of bird, but with slightly different plumage, as found farther north.

They stopped once when Adam spotted what he thought an artistically twisted tree, sat on a rock, and pulled out a rumpled sheet of sketch paper.

Rel watched him sketch, impressed. Adam had the shape of the entire tree suggested with no more than three quick, assured lines, then used the pencil to demonstrate a great many of those thirty techniques as he roughed in a bit of the corrugated bark, the gnarled shape, the shadows, the piny spines, the cones, and how the shadow lay on the piled-up leaves left from the recent storm.

Adam had an astonishing eye for detail, so when they reached the town and found the local magistrate, Rel expected such an exact description of the brigands that the miscreants could easily be identified.

What the magistrate got was a confused blur of contradictory facts, all of those hazy. Her exasperation manifested itself in gusty sighs as Adam dithered. "No . . . the leader was not as tall as Rel. Or maybe he was, but he was bent, some. And I was on the ground, so my perspective was distorted. How many? Well, that I'm not certain of. It felt like a gang, but there couldn't have been more than four or five. Three, at the very least."

The magistrate put down her pen. "That will do."

Adam said anxiously, "Is that enough? I am so sorry I don't seem to remember more. But I was so frightened, and then my face was in the mud . . ."

"No, no. It happens. The most assured witness can't always recollect the details, especially when you are taken by surprise," she said, and as Adam walked out, the woman caught Rel by the arm. "Look, you. I don't want to cast aspersions on our duchas, but as Sartor has not kept the old treaty, he's saying if he has to mount and pay for patrollers, then he ought to have a king's treasury, if you catch my meaning."

"I do," Rel said.

The magistrate nicked her chin in Adam's direction. "Your friend there clearly couldn't defend himself against a kitten. You had better see him to wherever he's going."

"I will," Rel said, and had a happy thought. Atan and Hibern were both determined to keep the alliance communicating, which meant a visit to Thad and Karhin Keperi in Colend. Hibern seemed to think that putting someone besides a bunch of busy young rulers in charge of communication was better than leaving everything haphazard.

Rel had agreed; any excuse to visit the Keperis was fine by him. He could see Adam fitting right in with Thad and Karhin. And everybody agreed, the alliance needed more members, if they really wanted it to be effective against Norsunder.

"Would you like to see some of Colend?" Rel asked. "I've friends there."

Adam hefted his knapsack. "I would like to meet them," he said.

Sherwood Smith
Inda

"A powerful beginning to a very promising series by a writer who is making her bid to be a major fantasist. By the time I finished, I was so captured by this book that it lingered for days afterward. I had lived inside these characters, inside this world, and I was unwilling to let go of it. That, I think, is the mark of a major work of fiction...you owe it to yourself to read *Inda*." —Orson Scott Card

INDA
978-0-7564-0422-2

THE FOX
978-0-7564-0483-3

KING'S SHIELD
978-0-7564-0500-7

TREASON'S SHORE
978-0-7564-0634-9

To Order Call: 1-800-788-6262
www.dawbooks.com

MICHELLE WEST
The House War

"Fans will be delighted with this return to the vivid and detailed universe of the *Sacred Hunt* and the *Sun Sword* series.... In a richly woven world, West pulls no punches as she hooks readers in with her bold and descriptive narrative."
—Quill & Quire

Bradley P. Beaulieu

The Song of the Shattered Sands

"Fantasy and horror, catacombs and sarcophagi, resurrections and revelations: the book has them all, and Beaulieu wraps it up in a package that's as graceful and contemplative as it is action-packed and pulse-pounding." —NPR

TWELVE KINGS IN SHARAKHAI
978-0-7564-0973-9
WITH BLOOD UPON THE SAND
978-0-7564-0975-3
A VEIL OF SPEARS
978-0-7564-1636-2
BENEATH THE TWISTED TREES
978-0-7564-1460-3
WHEN JACKALS STORM THE WALLS
978-0-7564-1462-7

"Çeda and Emre share a relationship seldom explored in fantasy, one that will be tried to the utmost as similar ideals provoke them to explore different paths. Wise readers will hop on this train now, as the journey promises to be breathtaking." —Robin Hobb

"*The Song of the Shattered Sands* series is both gripping and engrossing." —*Kirkus*

DAW 202